HERITAGE OF LOSS

ARDEN EMIL

Tears of the Aashahl vol. 1

Contents

HERITAGE OF LOSS

Prologue

The sun's last gleaming pillars burst through the sable veil of smoke;
like columns of some great building whose ceiling was of mist and
cloud. Within one of these radiant beams Kaileth slumped over the
front of his horse's saddle, cradling the small bundle in his lap. A long
thin shadow from the arrow shaft that was lodged in his left shoulder
ran over the etched steel of his pauldron and down onto the rings of
his maille shirt.

He stopped his horse upon the crest of a ridge and turned his face
toward the setting of the sun. The landscape that surrounded him resembled a grand painting of dynamic colors, both beautiful and sad.
The warm sunlight felt comforting as the touch of a longed-for friend,
driving the chill from his tears.

Turning his gaze from the warmth of the sun, he looked upon the
sight that caused his grief. In the distance lay a great city, lit now by
the fires that burned within it. Her once golden stone walls were now
black from the scorching of fires, and red from the spilling of blood.
The sounds of battle had changed from foe against foe to the sharp
ringing death cries of women and children. The roar of the conquer-
ing enemy echoed through the streets, filling the air about the lofty
towers. Kaileth slowly turned from this terrible sight and continued
to ride away from the city. As he turned, he shifted the cloth-wrapped
bundle he held close in his arms.

The sharp pain from the arrowhead within his shoulder twisted his
face in agony as he moved. With his free arm he reached back to try to
snap the shaft off. As the tips of his fingers were about to touch the arrow shaft, the bundle he still held moved and made a small noise. With
a gentle hand, he pulled aside the bloodstained cloth to disclose the
infant. The child's clothing was spattered with more blood, thankfully
not the babe's, but that of his slain kin. The child's peaceful dark eyes

peered through the locks of his jet-black hair and met Kaileth's. The innocence and calm that seemed to emanate from the child allowed the horror of the day's events to drift away for a moment. He allowed a hint of a smile to cross his face, and at that, the babe seemed to take pleasure. A somber hush fell over them both, and Kaileth urged the horse forward.

Soon the horse brought them over the crest of the ridge to meet a large war hound. Kaileth again took some relief from the hound's calm, signaling that way a head was clear for many skain before them all. He looked back one last time toward the burning city.

I wonder how many escaped...

His horse continued down the ridge, and they all plunged into the shadows. The sounds of the fallen city faded. The pain from his wounds seemed to amplify in the quiet, and he again slumped over the front of his saddle, letting his mount carry him toward the rolling ebb of night.

All that night and the next day he rode, keeping an eastern route toward the Vagath'Oth Mountains. The sound of the horse's hooves mirrored the beat of Kaileth's heart, both slow and steady. Every time he closed his eyes, images of the burning city slashed his mind anew. These thoughts hurt as much as the still untended wounds of his body did. He wiped the sweat away from his fevered brow with a shaking hand. The distant mountains formed a looming purple curtain before them.

We had better find friends in those mountains, not all the Andohrase could be slain...

They did not stop that night, nor the next. The countryside was empty of both beast and man, bare in the invading armies' wake. Great plumes of smoke drifted skyward from the many burning farms and towns, leaving a thick foul haze in the air. Numbness eventually blurred with his pain, distorting any sense of time. He tried to stay focused on the task at hand, escaping the reach of the attacking army. Escape into the mountains.

"They will send skirmishers soon, we can't stop, not yet...But where is the army from Akaroche? Where are our allies?"

The sun sank, the light failed, and still Kaileth and the babe continued into the haze. Time passed in a miasma of confusing thoughts, aching memories and painful bouts of somber clarity.

It was twilight now on the second day from the city, or was it the third day? He was not sure how many days it had been. Kaileth could tell his fevered daze had almost run its full course. Death would not long remain a stranger. Foreseeing his demise, he had secured the sleeping babe to the rigging of his war saddle. His hope of getting the child to safety was slipping, if not altogether lost. It would seem that they too would perish, along with their city.

"Shayar, have mercy on your lost son, guide us to shelter. Paldrii, stay your hand yet a while more." It seemed to take all his strength just to utter this simple prayer, but it gave him a feeling of peace.

They went on a little further until, sapped of all strength, Kaileth slipped from his saddle and fell to the ground. His mount continued a bit longer, dragging him by the sabaton-clad foot still lodged in the stirrup. The war hound cut off the horse's path of travel, halting the horse and freeing him. The hound paced nervously, whimpering as Kaileth faded from consciousness. He fought to keep his wits, focusing on the pain of his wounds. He took a deep breath and the sharp burst of pain from the arrow cleared his sight for a few moments.

A rush of sudden wind drew his weaving mind to the horse's saddle. A great falcon stood tall, perched upon the now grazing horse. The great bird seemed to be focused on the child, though whether it was watching over the child or considering it as a potential meal was unclear in the darkness.

"Mirris?" Kaileth half croaked, half whispered.

The falcon shifted its keen eyes from the sleeping child to the far eastern horizon. Kaileth followed Mirris' gaze. Was it a light? Or just a trick of his failing sight. Kaileth tried to rise once more. Yet he could no longer force his body to his will, and he collapsed into oblivion.

***

Epri and her father Rahmith had been slowly making their way north from the city of Syrah. They had been traveling as part of the army of Mantorah for some months now, in an attempt to aid Anoth in the north and lift the siege of Ell'Anoth, its capital. Another army had taken to ship and together the two hosts of Mantorah planned to join their northern allies and crush the army of the Subjugate. Epri took pride in her father's role as a master armorer for the Paladin of Syrah, as her father's father had been also. After the first large battle just north of Ectin Fords, Epri had helped him repair several hundred breastplates that had been damaged by the Dao'Tai's war hammers.

He had devised a new method of fluting that made the armor much more resistant to the hammers and in the next battle it proved to be the difference between life and death for many of the Mantorahn soldiers.

When the war started, Epri had just celebrated her eighteenth birthday and was still unmarried, unlike most of her friends. While they were saying goodbye to their husbands, she was urging her father to let her come with him to help the war effort. She had always been more interested in reading and helping her father than in boys and suitors anyway.

The campaign had seemed doomed from the beginning. The numbers and size of their foe were too great, and they wielded a dark power, the Ikthii. Despite this, the Mantorahns had won the first several battles and even found large numbers of their northern allies still able to fight.

Not even a halfmoon ago, Epri had been dancing to good music and high spirits with many of the girls of the baggage train. Charming Andohrase archers, brave Dashran axmen and the indomitable Mantorahns all gathered round with numbers of the Freeholdn and even some of Thenill's army. The northern Freeholdn and Andohrase soldiers paid her special attention as her warm umber skin, bright yellow-green eyes and small lithe frame were an unusual and enchanting female form.

It had been just like the fablettes Epri loved to read; the band of exotic heroes joined together to crush their evil enemy. She could still see each of their bright cheerful faces in the firelight. Many her own age, strong and brave men from all the corners of the High Sun Realms eager for expectant victory.

But it would not be. Despite the valor of the Mantorah army and their unlooked-for allies, they were slaughtered almost to the last man while passing near the Fell Track Forest. With the army destroyed, invading soldiers scouring the countryside, and the total defeat of Anoth, Mantorah and their northern allies seemed to lie in ruins with the rest of the realms. Rahmith had deemed it safest to take refuge in Allinth, his mother's village of nativity. Epri had never been to Allinth, but she knew it was a village high in the Vagath'Oth Mountains, on the border between lands that were ruled by Anoth, Vagath, and Andohra. Few knew where it was, and even fewer ever bothered to go there.

They had escaped the destruction of the army by luck and the valiant efforts of the Andohrase, fighting hard to screen the baggage train. Fleeing fast out of the chaos, Rahmith had driven the teams hard to get clear of the terrifying onslaught. With the hopes of remaining unseen by hostile eyes, they had been making their way through the dense Fell Track Forest for several days, but now the trees surrounding them slowly began to thin. Epri was grateful for the change of scenery. The forest felt uneasy, and each shadowy tree seemed to menace their passage. She felt even more on edge now as the wide expanse that surrounded them offered no concealment from the bands of Subjugate skirmishers that surely were still roaming the land. It was pleasant though, with grass half as high as the wagon's wheels growing thick about them and the air smelled sweet.

It had been eight days since they fled the slaughter fields where the army fell. They had come to the border of the forest and the plains that gently roll on into the Vagath'Oth Mountains in the east. These high plains, hills, and plateaus were collectively called the Vagath'Oth, and they surrounded the Vagath'Oth Mountains themselves. The realm of Vagath once ruled the entire length of the mountain range, but some hundred sulsta—nearly four hundred years ago or more—Andohra and Dashra rebelled. The war left Vagath a small realm, but the mountains kept the name.

The wagon was moving slowly now as her father looked about to gain a lay of the land.

"Best I can figure, we are due south of Ell'Anoth, well behind the main enemy lines to the south, and hopefully plenty far south of their lines to the north. Tomorrow we should come to a brook that will lead up straight through the Vagath'Oth plain and into the mountains." Rahmith gestured easterly with his crop as he spoke.

"This way at least we will only be in the open for two, maybe three days as we cross the southern road."

"Then, we will stop here for the night?" asked Epri. "I think the horses are done for the day."

"The horses are spent, or are you tired of the creaking wagon?" Epri smiled.

"I am a book left open, nonetheless, the day has failed us."

"That it has. We will make camp, and tonight I think we will even venture a small fire," he whispered as though it were a secret. "Could be the last we dare try for a while."

Epri felt cheerful for the first time in a long time at the thought of a fire. The memory of the last camp with the army quickly sobered her. All those men, some her age and younger even. Their eyes bright in the firelight, they all were dead now. All of them. Her mind drifted back to the first camp with the army and the first few battles.

The army of Mantorah traveled fast and fought hard. They had hoped to cut through the southern battle lines and meet up with the armies of Anoth, Andohra, Dashra, and Taivadees near Vertain in the north. Epri had watched that first large battle from a hilltop. She wished she hadn't. That was when she saw firsthand what the soldiers whispered about, a carrion reaper. It is a creature both evil and powerful. They were lucky only Dao'Tai fell upon the army near the forest.

I still can't believe we escaped. I can't believe this is all really happening. Mistress Everkind, tip Brek's coin in our favor. Her prayer was met with a warm breeze, and she took it as a good sign, carrying her dark thoughts away.

Rahmith halted the wagon and they both got down from their seats. Epri drew a few paces away, letting her hands brush the tops of the tall cool grass as she walked. She took a long slow breath. It was so still now, so calm. The war seemed impossibly far away. Epri closed her eyes and tried to remember her home near the river. The cool water washing over her dark skin, smooth stones under her feet. Her bed and room where her mother used to read to her. It seemed like a dream now, far away, and unreachable.

Rahmith went about gathering wood and within a few minutes, Epri was warming herself by a small fire. It wasn't really that cold, but the soft glow and warmth was soothing. She watched the firelight dance on the smooth surface of her many anklets and bangles. Letting her mind drift back to the day her mother had given them to her. It was the way of her village, of most of the river villages south of Syrah to mark a girl's shift into womanhood with rings of jewelry and the family's tattoos. Epri had only been big enough to wear the anklets and bangles for the last year as she was much smaller framed than her mother.

She found herself tracing the lines of her tattoos along her wrists and up across her shoulders. She used to do the same thing to her mother's tattoos and wondered when she could have her own. The simple copper-colored lines and shapes formed complex organic patterns along the dark warmth of her brown skin of her slender limbs, weaving around to travel either side of her spine.

"They will hurt," her mother had said, "but our pains can teach us if we let them. They mark us in life and sharpen us as stones to iron." Epri could still hear her mother's voice, calm and melodic, not the small high tones of her own. Epri wished she could have been more like her mother, strong and unshakable.

Why did you take her? Epri wiped the sudden moisture from her eyes. She was not normally so prone to sad reflections. But everything over the last few weeks had just been too much. Her nerves were frayed to the breaking point. It seemed that each moment threatened to send her into a melancholy stupor of regrets and despair.

She took in a long deliberate breath. Staying busy made it easier, so she began to prepare their evening meal from what they had in their wagon. Epri had gathered porrets, cabbage, and several small wild onions the day prior, and she now prepared and placed them all in an iron pot along with a few spices. She then set the pot to boil by the fire.

Rahmith was nodding off just as the stew started to simmer. Seeing him fast asleep, she could not help but laugh softly to herself as she recalled the numerous times during the day, he had mentioned how much he looked forward to eating something hot that night.

Epri stood up and stretched, looking to the bright stars. As she stood there looking up, a large shadow darted across the stars of Ean Oich' catching her eye. She saw it again and this time she was able to follow it with her young, keen eyes. It looked to be a great bird circling over their camp. The dim light of the fire glinted off it as it turned overhead. Fearing it to be a scout from the enemy, Epri quietly woke her father and pointed to the sky.

"There is something flying over us, it is making circles like it is watching," she whispered. Rahmith took a few moments before he spoke, allowing the sleep to leave his mind.

"There, there it is again Da, look!" She spoke louder this time, unable to keep the worry from her voice.

"Yes, I think I saw it, but I am sure it is just an owl or some bird of the night Epri." Epri knew he was trying to comfort her, but it was not helping. They both knew his eyes weren't as good as they used to be. They continued to watch the sky, but it did not make another pass by them.

"You see, just an owl interested in our little fire," said Rahmith more convincingly this time. After several more minutes, Rahmith and Epri gave up the watch and shifted their attention to the now ready stew.

Epri took two wooden bowls from the wagon and filled them both with the contents of the iron pot. She felt calmer now thinking of the warm meal before her, the pleasant smell filling the air. Epri took a bowl and started over to hand it to her father, who was sitting against the wagon's wheel.

"I was thinking, when we get the—" Epri stopped short when she saw a short figure, just taller than the wagon's wheels, standing outside of the firelight behind Rahmith. He noticed her sudden change of expression and turned to see what caused her alarm. Without a second thought, Epri threw the bowl in her hand at the figure and drew her short dagger from her belt. The bowl found its mark, striking the creature in the chest. The sound of wood hitting steel rang out and the bowl glanced off its target. Rahmith was now at his daughter's side, ax in hand. The creature slowly advanced into the light, and Epri knew what it was, a battle falcon. Only the army of Anoth used this bird in war. This one's now stew-covered armor was also battered and bloody, bearing the marks of war that scarred most of the land around them. Epri felt terrible about her assault and hastily sheathed her dagger. Battle falcons were said to have been a gift to the royal Anoth line from Aseairpeth herself. She slowly walked up to the falcon and knelt a few feet in front of it.

"Be careful," Rahmith said.

"I will be, but I think it has been watching us for a while. If it wanted to hurt us it could have already." The bird walked up to where she knelt and allowed Epri to clean the stew and blood from the armor with the hem of her dress. Even kneeling the bird was near a head taller than her.

"Da, look at this," she said, pointing to the crest upon the armor. He approached and examined the symbols upon the steel scales. It was an intricate symbol within a white ellipse, marked with a blood red sigil.

"That is the mark of the royal family's guard," he paused and thought on this. "She would only leave her master if sent away, or to seek help."

"She? Is it a she?" Epri asked in surprise. She took a closer look at the fine features of the face and the shape of the bird's eye. This falcon did look feminine to her.

"The males are sent to the main army of Anoth, but the females are used in the royal guard. Their protection instincts are greater," Rahmith explained. Epri thought on this as she observed the falcon. She could not help but feel like the bird understood what they were saying and was waiting for them to talk to it.

"So, this falcon would only be here if it were sent, what if her master was dead?" Epri asked.

"If her master lives yes, but if her master is dead, she would return to the palace to guard the royal family. At least if what the guards back at Syrah say is true. If they are all dead though, I'm not sure then."

"And they are supposed to be very smart?"

"Yes, very. Some say they can even speak if they choose to." When her father said this, the falcon raised a feathered eyebrow and cocked her head. Much as any person might do if their intelligence became the topic of discussion.

"Very well then, why are you here Miss...Battle Falcon? Where is your master?" Epri asked the bird. The falcon made what could only be described as an expression of relief and she started to walk away from the wagon, checking over her shoulder to see if Epri was following. Epri looked to her father, who gave a nod of approval, and she then followed the falcon.

The bird continued to walk from the wagon for a short distance before taking to the air. Epri ran to keep up, but the bird circled often to make sure she was still following. This continued for the better part of an hour, and Epri was having a challenging time following the falcon in the dark. She finally lost sight of the bird and so she stopped.

Within a few minutes, she could hear the familiar sound of her father's wagon wheels approaching. Rahmith brought the wagon close to where Epri stood. The lantern's light from the wagon revealed the falcon to be standing quite close to Epri, waiting for the girl.

The falcon gestured toward the wagon seat with her head. Epri obeyed and climbed onto the wagon next to Rahmith. Once again, the bird took off, and they followed. The sliver of moon had failed them by now, and it was all Epri could do to keep the falcon in sight. Fortunately, it was not long after Rahmith had arrived with the wagon that Epri saw the bird land ahead of them.

As the wagon drew near, the light from the lanterns revealed the falcon along with a horse and several large shapes upon the ground. One of the shapes looked to be a fallen rider. The other shape shifted suddenly in the shadows as the wagon approached and began to growl. Rahmith let the wagon continue just far enough to illuminate the growling creature. Epri could now see that it was a war hound growling at them. A huge war hound. Epri had heard more than one tale of the ferocity of war hounds, and she had no desire to experience such a thing herself.

Minutes passed as Epri and Rahmith sat frozen by the hound, not daring to move for fear of provoking the large animal. Rahmith struggled to keep his frightened horses steady. The hound made no motion toward them, nor did it retreat. After what felt like ages to Epri, the falcon appeared from the darkness and walked up alongside the hound. It seemed to be considering the wagon and the two people upon it for a moment. Then the great bird leaned to the hound as though it was whispering something to it. Immediately, the hound ceased growling and retreated into the shadows.

With the terrifying hound out of view, Epri hopped to the ground and steadied the still startled horses. Only the falcon was now between her and the lone horse and fallen rider. Epri could feel her heart pounding as she cautiously began to walk toward them.

"Be careful daughter," Rahmith called after her. She waved back to him as she advanced. She was standing where the hound had been and could clearly see that there was a fallen man near the horse.

"Da, bring the light quick!" she cried. Rahmith did so, and the glow of the lantern drove more of the darkness away. The soft orange light fell upon the sturdy angles of the man's face. Epri found his age hard to guess. He was clad in intricately woven black and crimson maille over which hung a cracked and dented placard.

Expertly crafted pauldrons and interlocking plates covered his shoulders and ran the length of his spine. A long, elegant blade hung at his side in a leather sheath. The light of the lantern shown on the man's helm and shield where they hung, strapped to the saddle. Arrow shaft and weapon slash marred the smooth white surface of his elliptical shield, completely obscuring the heraldry that had been painted there. His skin was a smooth dark tan. His hair was black, shoulder length, and was partially pulled tight in a complex braid, complementing the intricacy of his armor-clad figure. Epri could only imagine how long braids like that would take to put into her own hair. His armor and weapons looked very alien in the darkness and Epri was not sure what army he was from. The flittering light from the lantern played across the motionless features of his face. He did not look like any of the young men and warriors from the host Epri and her father had been traveling with. Though this could be a trick of the poor light.

"Is he, is he dead then?" She asked, noting the substantial amounts of blood caked into his fine armor.

Rahmith checked the man again holding the back of his hand close to the man's mouth.

"He is still alive, barely, but we had better get him into the wagon and clear out of here before the sun comes up. I don't think we want whoever did this to him to find us." Epri agreed and Rahmith hurried to bring the wagon closer to the man as the falcon stayed nearby, watching closely.

With the wagon now at the injured man's side, Epri and Rahmith carefully picked him up and set him inside. They took great care not to upset the arrow lodged in his shoulder. Even so, they struggled with his weight, nearly dropping him more than once.

"Stay with him. I'll go and get his horse and we will be off," Rahmith said.

"Alright, but hurry. He needs more help than we can give, I think," said Epri, furrowing her brows in worry.

Rahmith had only been outside the wagon for a moment when Epri heard him calling to her. She quickly left the wagon. Her father was standing with the wounded man's horse. Before Epri could ask what was wrong, she was interrupted by the sound of an infant fussing. She walked closer to the horse, and there she saw upon the animal's war saddle a large bundle of cloth surrounded by leather straps. Epri stood upon the tips of her toes until she could just peer into the bundle. There, spattered in dry blood, was a babe. Shock almost caused her to lose her balance and she took a few stumbling steps backwards.

"Da, there is a baby on the saddle!" she exclaimed.

"I thought that was what I heard, but I do not trust my ears as I once did." Rahmith said.

A bit calmer now, Epri returned to the saddle and carefully took the child from the makeshift cradle. The infant was a dark-haired boy. Dried blood covered the babe's face and his remarkably well-made clothes. The child looked weak and as near to death as the man that now lay in the back of the wagon.

"Alright, let's get moving. This baby needs something to eat," Epri said firmly.

"Right enough. He looks big enough to stomach a bit of that broth that we so hastily left at the camp," Rahmith suggested as he looked at the child. Epri hoped he was right. They were many days from Allinth and the possibility of finding someone to suckle the child.

"Things being as they are, I think we should make a go at it through the night. Try to make up some distance before the sun rises."

Epri dreaded the thought of a night spent in the wagon trying to tend both wounded soldier and starving babe, but she knew the sooner they crossed the plains the safer they would be.

"You are right, just don't get lost in the darkness and drive us into a swamp," she teased, trying not to let the situation dredge up her anxiety again. Rahmith gave her a smile and a reassuring squeeze on her arm.

"We'll get there."

The child was weak, it looked like it had been some time since he had eaten anything. The baby was not truly an infant, and in the lantern, light looked to be nearly a year old, if not older. He had a few teeth, and so Epri went about feeding the babe the mashed vegetables and broth from the stew she had made. The child appeared to have no issues with this meal and ate his fill. Epri cleaned the child as best as she could and then placed him in a bundle of blankets and cloth toward the front of the wagon. With a full belly the child was soon asleep.

She yawned and rubbed her eyes. It was late, and she still had another to tend to. Epri was not usually one for the tending of wounds. The first time she had faced a maimed soldier she had fainted. However, over the course of the bloody campaign, she had faced her fear and could dress a wound well enough.

Epri moved to the back of the wagon. The wagon was large, so large that eight drafts worked to pull it, with another eight following for relief. On the inside it had cloth partitions that more or less formed three rooms. At the front was Rahmith's space and where a large part of the food was stored. In the middle was where Epri slept and kept her things along with the rest of their provisions. From the rear axles back was where the armor and tools were kept. This was also where the soldier was. Despite Epri and Rahmith's best efforts, it was all they could do to lift him in the wagon. Moving him further would have only worsened his wounds.

Epri parted the curtain and stepped into the back of the wagon. She hung the lantern from a hook in the wagon's ceiling of wood and surveyed the man. Now seeing him in the light, Epri thought she knew the arms and armor of the man to be the raiment of the high guard of the royal family of Anoth. That also meant that he was not human, but one of the warriors from the Alliix Isles, the Allitorii. That would explain his deep-olive tan skin. Epri remembered reading about them and their connection to Anoth, but what she knew of their physical nature was based only on rumor. They never left the capital city of Ell'Anoth as they were the sworn protectors of the city and royal family. She had heard that they did not age, were inhumanly fast, and that they healed at a remarkable rate, making them difficult to kill. She hoped that was true.

Epri took off her bangles and arm bands preparing for the grizzly task at hand. She coiled her long black braids into a tight bun and fixed it in place with a long pin.

"Dannitar, guide me."

Epri knelt and slowly began to remove the tattered cloak and placard. The rings of the warrior's armor were covered with blood and earth. Epri did not know where to start. The arrow was the only clear source of the bleeding, but there was much more blood than one arrow wound would produce. She lifted a few plates of the pauldron and could see that the arrow had pierced the man's shoulder all the way and was partially through the front of the maille shirt.

She knew that it would be best to push it out, but the matter of the armor would make it tricky. The rivets of the rings were popped, but the shirt of maille was of a weave she had never seen. It looked almost like two shirts of maille woven into each other with smaller rings passing through larger ones to the point that a needle would hardly have passed through the gaps. The bow that launched this arrow must have been unbelievably stout. Epri tried to push the arrow through, but the rings held fast. She checked to see if her actions caused much pain, however the soldier made no signs that he felt a thing.

Epri thought on this as the wagon bounced along. The jostling caused a set of armor nippers to slip from its place and fall close to her feet. She picked it up and began to cut the rings from around the arrowhead. It took all her strength to cut one of the rings, and as the ring gave way so did the nippers, breaking at the hinge and pinching her finger.

"Drestd!" She swore using a word she had heard several of the soldiers say. She felt her face flush as she shook her injured hand before instinctively sucking on her finger for an instant.

"Da, do we have another set of nippers?"

"No, I only had time to grab the one set. Why?" Rahmith replied.

"Just wondering." She would let him know they were broken later. At present, she still had the problem of removing the arrow. Then suddenly she had an idea. She looked through one of the many toolboxes and took from it a large hammer. She first broke off the fletching. Then, careful to time it with the bumps of the wagon, she struck the arrow shaft with the hammer, driving the head through the hole in the armor. The arrow slid a bit further through the man's shoulder, and this time he did stir and groan.

"Sorry. But it has to come out."

Epri set her teeth and continued to drive the arrow through the wound till she was able to pull it free.

With bloody hands she held the barbed-arrow and hammer and stood triumphantly looking at her work. It took a few moments before she noticed the man at her feet staring up at her in total bewilderment. With a shriek, she tumbled back into the curtain, pulling it down on top of her.

"Epri, what was that?" Rahmith called over the noise of the wagon.

"Nothing" She replied hastily fighting the cloth divider from on top of her.

Epri sat up as quickly as she could and looked to the wounded man from the jumbled mess, she now sat in.

"Are you going to finish me off with that?" The man's voice was just above a whisper. Without realizing it, Epri was still holding the bloody hammer in her hand. She blushed and dropped it. His eyes stole her breath away. They danced in the lantern light with a brilliant emerald green made more extraordinary by the contrast of his dark-olive skin. She lowered her gaze for a moment to her ankle bracelets as she often did when her nerves overtook her.

"No, I am quite done with it now." As soon as she said this, she regretted the word choice. She continued to get up to kneel by the soldier.

"The arrow was stuck in your armor, so I used a hammer to pound it out. You sure are made of tough stuff."

He almost smiled and Epri was struck by how charming he looked despite his current state. Even under the blood and grime of battle his strong jaw and noble angular features were distinctively handsome. His straight nose, pleasant curving lips, and high cheek bones each look like an artisan took most of a lifetime to place and shape them all. Epri wondered if all Allitorii looked thus. Presently she realized she had been staring as he spoke again.

"I fear the arrow was the least of my wounds," he said as he clutched his side in pain.

"Well then let's off with that armor and I will see what I can do. I am Epri, by-the-way, from Syrah. Well, near Syrah."

"A pleasure to meet you, Miss Epri of Syrah. I am Kaileth of—"

The wagon shifted as he moved to undo a buckle. The motion jarred Kaileth hard, he winced and slumped over, unconscious. Epri hurried to help, turning him over. She continued to undo buckles and straps until the armor was free and ready to be removed. To say it was difficult to remove the shirt of maille from the unconscious Kaileth would have been a gross understatement. By the time Epri had Kaileth stripped down to his under clothes she was sweating and a bit out of breath. The plates, hauberk, and gambeson were all soaked and caked with blood and hard to manipulate.

With his chest and back now exposed to the light, Epri could see the source of all the blood. On his right side, a large gash sat open to his ribs, oozing blood. It looked like he had been cracked open. Epri felt dizzy and suddenly a little panicked. She was no healer, and this wound looked lethal. She sat with her face close to the back of the wagon for a few minutes. She had not realized how much the wagon now smelled of blood. She shut her eyes and thought of more pleasant things before returning to the gore within the wagon.

Dannitar, help me.

Epri continued to pray as she began to bind the wound with strips of the torn curtain and what little healing herbs they had in the wagon. She carefully used the last of their sulf-char and hoped it would be enough. The bleeding in his side stopped, and she looked to the arrow wound next, soon seeing in part why it had been so difficult to remove. The wound had already begun to close and heal around the shaft. Epri cleaned and dressed this wound and a few other cuts and gashes on Kaileth's long lean-muscled arms and legs.

She could not help but marvel at how hardy the warrior was to have taken so many wounds and yet still live. With all the bleeding stopped, Epri slumped into the jumble of supplies and cloth and looked upon the warrior. He seemed to be resting well. Epri took a deep breath, as she often did to recenter after an arduous task, and wiped her hands and face clean with what was left of the curtain. All at once exhaustion set upon her, making it hard to keep her eyes open.

"Will he live daughter?" Rahmith called from the front. She looked down at the blood and grime on her short green dress. It had been her favorite for warm summer nights.

"I think he will. He will..." Epri mumbled as sleep took her.

***

The cool mountain air filled the wagon and slowly drew Epri from her dreams of far-off lands and forgotten magics. The events of the night past were hazy and dream-like themselves, and the grumbling stomach reminded her that she never did eat anything last night.

"Fair highsun, Miss Epri," Kaileth's voice was a bit stronger now as he sat with the child in his arms.

Epri was shocked. He looked so much better that she would have sworn it was a different man if she had not studied his face so closely the night before.

"It is highsun already?" she asked, trying to mask her wonder at this stranger's turn for the better.

"Some time past actually, your father only stopped long enough to change horses and then he went on. I think we are already high in the Vagath'Oth now. It seemed best to let you rest, Miss Epri, as you must have worked hard and long to put me into one piece again."

"You are...*were* near death. Your wounds were terrible. What happened to you?"

"I was in Ell'Anoth when it fell. I only managed to get this child out by the grace of Shayar and a hard fight." He took a long painful breath and continued. "We were set for a long siege, but we were betrayed..." his words trailed off and he turned and gazed out the back of the wagon.

Epri worried that she had spoken amiss and quickly began to think of something to say to change the subject. She was spared from this by the child's sudden wailing. Kaileth made what attempts he could in his current state to calm the child, but his efforts were in vain.

"May I?" asked Epri, reaching out to take the babe. Kaileth nodded his head, and she gently took the child and slowly rocked it in her arms. She noticed Kaileth studying her more closely now, and she kept her head down as she fought to not blush.

Within a few moments she had calmed the baby, and she smiled as she looked up at Kaileth. "Is this your child?"

Kaileth started and looked away quickly as she caught him staring. "No miss, it is not. Though his life is mine to protect."

Epri knew then that this child had to be someone of importance for an Allitorii to be charged as his guardian. She wanted to ask more but felt that there would be time for that later. She did not want to seem bothersome.

"We are heading to Allinth, it is a small village high in the mountains. We should be safely out of the war's way up there."

She hoped the news comforted him, but he said nothing in reply, only looked back to Epri and smiled. It was a cheerful smile, but Epri thought it veiled deep sorrow and loss. When Epri met his gaze, she felt as though she was peering into another age, it was the same as she felt when reading her books. Kaileth did not look away, and it seemed that he was looking right through to who she was, not just at her appearance. Epri felt her face flush, but she held his gaze in return. His eyes were too bright, as though they were actually a lite from within by a green fire. He took her in with them, following the lines in her small, delicately pleasant smiling face. Her narrow high cheeks and fast curving jawline drew his eyes to the gentle bow of her lips and thence to the soft curves of her neck and shoulders. Subtle elegant lines of coppery-gold tattoos pulled his gaze further down to what to Kaileth seemed a truly enchanting feminine form. Returning to her warm sunflower-eyes he spoke.

"I can take him now Miss Epri, you have a calming soul it would seem." Epri handed the child back to him and sat back for a moment.

"Thank you, sire, I'm happy to help where I can." She was not sure what it was, but Kaileth made her feel safe and on edge all at the same time.

"I'll just be a moment to check on my da." With this Epri gave a low nod and went up to the front of the wagon to check on her father and calm herself. Rahmith looked exhausted from the hurried journey.

He was getting close to sixty now, and his hands were calloused and strong from years of work. He still stood tall and could outwork most new hands even if his sight and hearing were not what they once were. He kept his hair cut short and his gray frosted beard braided, yet for all his strength his face was kind. His broad square cheeks and brow held the lines of years of warm smiles and hearty laughter.

Epri smiled as she looked on him, if it were not for the movements of the wagon jarring him awake from time to time, he would have fallen asleep and tumbled off the wagon seat.

"How are they?" he asked wearily.

"The child is weak. He definitely needs lots of care and food. I just don't know enough about babies to really say, though. The soldier is from Ell'Anoth. He was wounded nigh until death last night, yet now he seems to be mending." Epri waited to see if her father would surmise the nature of the warrior as she had, so she said no more. Rahmith sat quietly for a considerable time before speaking.

"His armor, it looked black and red last night."

"Yes, it is." Epri could practically see the thoughts turning in his mind.

"And you say he heals fast."

"Yes. Faster than any normal man would, Da."

"Well. Then I would guess he is one of the high guards. They are from over the sea, and do not age or heal as most do."

"What of the child then? Is he one of them too?"

"No, I doubt that my girl. I would guess that the child is the kin of someone of importance in Ell'Anoth. No matter. They both were brought into our path, and it is right to see to their care for a time. Who knows what the Patient Father has woven for us all."

The wagon creaked on for days. The plains and hills turned into steep ridges, plateaus, and groves of trees. They ate meals swiftly, changed the draft team often, and spoke little. Kaileth and the child slept most of the time, yet Epri would catch him watching over her now and again. He would give her a little smile, then close his eyes and drift back to sleep. Both he and the child were still weak though. Kaileth might not be dying anymore, but he certainly was not healed yet. Epri worked to see that Kaileth, Rahmith, and the babe were all tended to as best as their current circumstances allowed.

One more day saw them pass into the Vagath'Oth Mountains. A thick forest of pine and fir rose up around them, and the road became steep and narrow. The air grew thinner, and the sun was filtered by the thick canopy of evergreen boughs and leaves.

They were still days yet from Allinth as they drew near to the mountain crossway. The crossway was the only major joining of roads in the mountain. This was the last place where they stood any real chance of meeting anyone else on the road.

That morning the air was crisp and cool. Epri noticed that different birds sung here. After a breakfast of cold root cake and water she sat down in the back of the wagon with Kaileth. Several moments passed in silence.

"Sire, the falcon and hound, do they have names?" Epri had never had anything but horses and mules to tend to and she marveled at these two creatures that had been following closely behind the wagon on their journey.

"The falcon is Mirris, she and I have been in service to the royal family our entire lives." Kaileth spoke with an air of solemnity. "We were part of the personal guard. A falcon and warrior paired to guard the future of the kingdom."

"And the hound?"

"The hound belonged to the child's older brother. It was a gift from their mother. His name is Riidak."

The wagon suddenly jolted to a stop.

"I'd better see why we stopped," Epri said as she quickly made her way to the front of the wagon. She stepped out onto the wagon seat just in time to be snatched by a pair of stout armored hands. She spun and saw Rahmith already being held by several large soldiers. They wore the heraldry of a local noble. It had been rumored that the nobles had not been defeated, but that they had joined the invading enemy. The men laughed darkly as they took Epri from the wagon. The maille mittens bit into Epri's slim arm and she squirmed to get free.

"Let me go! Let me—" another hand clapped over her mouth, ending Epri's protests.

Suddenly a warm liquid splashed over Epri's arm, and she was free. The hand that had held her fell to the ground, cut free of the man it belonged to. She turned and saw four more dead soldiers with Kaileth standing above, the sword in one hand, the other holding his wounded side together as he fought back the troop of soldiers.

Epri ran back to the wagon and found her dagger. As she rushed back to the front Kaileth was already a good bow's shot up the road with the hound and falcon fighting several soldiers. Rahmith was free too and had started up the road after Kaileth with his ax in hand. Epri stood for an instant trying to decide if she should follow with the wagon, hide, or help fight. She had been caught in skirmishes before, but those times she was told what to do and it was usually to hide in the wagon.

Thinking that a swift escape would be best Epri started to get back onto the wagon seat when again she was grabbed by a soldier who had been hiding nearby. She stabbed at his hands and face with her dagger. He screamed in pain and struck Epri so hard that she lost her senses and tumbled from the wagon steps.

She felt like she was floating for a time. Then it seemed she was small again, on her mother's lap. She could smell the river and the lavender drying near the fire. Epri took a long deep breath of home. *"Will we be safe? Will it be alright? Will we make it?"*

Her mother smiled. *"So many questions small one. Yes, we will be safe, you will be alright, and we will make it together."*

The dream faded, Epri took a sudden sharp breath. Her head was aching. She opened her eyes and saw Kaileth sitting across from her. They were back in the wagon. He smiled when he noticed her coming to, though Epri could see that he was bleeding badly again from his side and a few new cuts. There had been near a dozen soldiers at the crossways. Her brow furrowed in concern over his new wounds and thoughts of soldiers in pursuit. Reading her expression Kaileth shook his head.

"They are all dead, Miss Epri. I could not allow them to report our movements."

She was sure her wonder must have shown on her face. "But how? Your wounds—they were so many."

"I had help from your father, and Mirris and Riidak. You yourself left no small impression on the soldier who was fool enough to grab you."

Epri grimaced. "I don't know what we would have done were you not here, sire."

"You saved me, how could I not return the favor?"

Epri was mortified to find herself coming to tears. Everything was so terrible, so much death and loss. She was worn out and tired of being brave. She soon could not stop their flow and wrapped her arms around her legs to cry softly to herself.

Suddenly, Kaileth was there wrapping a comforting arm around her shoulders.

"You will be alright Miss Epri." He paused and with a gentle hand raised her face, looked deep into her eyes, and smiled softly, "*We* will be alright." Kaileth's voice was gentle and warm.

Forgetting his wounds Epri leaned into his side, causing him to groan in pain.

"Ooh, I'm so sorry! I forgot—that is, I didn't mean to."

Kaileth laughed softly and smiled ruefully.

"Do not worry Miss Epri, I should have known better. After all, you stabbed the last man to put an arm around you."

Epri laughed out loud at what Kaileth said, at herself, at everything. It all seemed too absurd, terrible, and amazing at the same time, but she didn't care. She leaned back against the wagon and sighed.

"I guess we will be alright. Somehow, I believe you, sire."

"Kail, you can call me Kail, miss."

"As you say, Kail, we will make it." Epri closed her burning eyes and smiled. She was not certain about many things anymore, but Kaileth sounded certain, he seemed to still have hope. She could see it in the ocean of his green eyes, she could hear it in his voice, and feel it in his smile. Hope, a thing she had lost some time ago. He made her want to hope again. Emotional and physical exhaustion took hold and Epri drifted into a sleep of pleasant dreams.

A few more days passed without further incident. The child proved to be resilient and cheerful, satisfied by the care Epri was able to give. The road kept steadily heading up and deeper into the mountains. Kaileth unfortunately suffered a setback from the battle and was in and out of a fevered sleep most of the journey. Yet, under Epri's care he managed to recover again.

Soon the road became narrow and hard to find. Eventually, there was no true road, only a winding level path that most would have missed were they not looking for it. On the evening of the fifth day since the crossways, just before the sun was lost on the horizon, the wagon approached the wooden gates of Allinth. The gates were closed, and it took some time for Rahmith to get the attention of the old watchman in the guardhouse. They spoke for a long time.

Epri was in the back of the wagon watching over Kaileth. She held his hand in hers for most of the evening as he slept. She could feel his heartbeat, slow and strong, like his breathing. She was spent from the journey and had nodded off waiting for the gate to be opened. Epri and Kaileth woke as the wagon lurched forward and they passed the gatehouse entering the village.

"Kail, we made it!"

"And together it would seem," he gave her hand a tender squeeze and smiled at her. She didn't realize she was still holding it. She smiled back but did not let go. The babe stirred and started to softly coo.

"Yes, together."

1

Allinth

Of the Aashahl there are many orders and kindreds. Mastery of the elements and diverse facets of Miljah are given unto them according to their nature and ordinations.
But of these, Anthos sits as justiciar.
Essays of the Divine

Morning's first light cut through the cloudy blanket that had covered the little village during the night's reign over the land. Kaileth looked down from the rocky ledge he sat upon watching the sun creep into view. The chilly air bit at his face in contrast to the surge of warmth from the sunlight. Below him the village Allinth was in a steep valley, deep within the Vagath'Oth Mountains. It looked as if the houses and shops had fallen from the sky and settled as they landed in comfortable repose. The last grip of winter's chill still clung to the steep angles of the mountain's shadowy crags of stone and the corners of rooftops. Small trails of smoke drifted gently toward heaven from the stone chimneys atop the blue-slate roofs of the village. He closed his eyes and listened as the inhabitants of this tranquil place began to stir from their rest. They were following the work habits of countless generations before them— herdsmen leaving to tend to their flocks, shopkeepers opening their doors to customers. A clamor at the gate and watchtowers signaled the changing of the town watch. Ever since the rest of the lands fell to the Dao'Tai Subjugate, a close guard had been kept over the secluded village.

No great trade or mighty craft employed the people of this village, nor did any grand lord or lady take great heed of them. The people of Allinth lived simply and looked after one another in peace. They had little to do with the rest of the realms and this afforded them relative immunity from the wars, and politics of those who ruled. After the Subjugate War most of the High Sun Realms were no more, or so reduced that they carefully kept to their own affairs hoping the Subjugate would leave them in peace. For Allinth this meant no troop levies, no tax men. No contact at all. This also meant that wild animals and dangerous creatures were more plentiful in the forests and mountains, serving further to shield the little village from the surrounding world.

Kaileth stood and slowly started his climb down. Polished smooth from a thousand similar climbs, the cold stones were so familiar it was an easy climb even in the darkest of mornings. He moved steadily onto a well-worn path back down into the valley and the place he called home. The cheerful morning light sparkled on the dew-dampened roof slates, and a gentle breeze nudged at the sable and scarlet sign that hung over the door of the shop as he approached. The intricate carving of the wooden sign was extraordinary, unusually so for a shopkeeper's sign. Epri had insisted the sign be a work of art. She had worked on it tirelessly, carving the wood with great skill. Kaileth had set the silver inlaid lettering indicating that this was a blacksmith's place of business. Rahmith had said it was some of the finest work he had seen anywhere. Kaileth opened the door and stepped into the shop.

The warm light from the forge and cool light from two windows mixed and gently lit the interior of the workshop with one window facing the coming and the other facing the going of the sun. A variety of tools and projects littered the countertop that ran around the wall from the southern corner to the east. At the north corner, a few stair steps led to a low doorway that connected the shop to the larger house.

In the west corner, beside a forge and bellows, Kaileth set to work over the roaring fire, hammering metal bars into a large iron chain.

With hammer in hand, he skillfully turned the raw steel into link after link of a great chain. As his muscles strained and the hammer fell, the sparks and heat from the near molten steel brightened the room and showered his leather apron with smoldering slag. He stepped back from the radiant fire for a moment to wipe the sweat from his face.

After a moment's rest, the sounds of someone stirring in the room on the other side of the door caused him to set aside his hammer and workpiece. With his usual long, graceful stride, the one most of the townspeople of Allinth were surprised to see from a blacksmith, he left the forge, hung up his leather apron, then walked over and opened the door. He had to stoop to avoid hitting his head on the low entryway as he stepped through, entering a room filled with brilliant morning light pouring through a large window. Unlike the shop windows, which were narrow and open to the elements, this window was large and had real glass in it, something that had not been easy to acquire, nor was it an inexpensive item. Epri had never lived in a house with real glass windows. Kaileth could recall the look of surprise and excitement the morning she first saw the panes of glass. It was worth all the effort.

Quickly distracting himself from thoughts of Epri, Kaileth moved to the stone countertop that ran around most of the room, leaving his gloves on it. He briefly washed his hands and face in a small metal basin, then retrieved a blue tablecloth and spread it on the table in front of the window. The small wooden table was awash in the sun's rays, with four chairs around it. Next, Kaileth placed a plate, cup, and fork in proper position upon the table. From a small stone box in a corner of the room he took out three large pieces of a translucent orange fruit, putting one in his pocket and setting two on the plate upon the table.

The table sat in the center of the kitchen. On one side of the kitchen was the small cast iron stove. It sat upon four elegantly crafted metal legs. A brightly polished copper kettle upon the stove-top gave off gentle ribbons of aromatic steam. Kaileth filled a mug with the contents of the kettle as he placed a skillet next to the kettle. Soon a robust sizzling sound and a rich savory smell signaled that breakfast was about done.

Across from the table and stove were two doors, one of which swung open as a tall young man entered the room. He wore simple workman's clothing and had a leather apron in his hands. His dark-honey colored hair was pulled back to reveal a youthful, strong face with a straight nose and deep-set round dark eyes. The hint of a beard shaded his sturdy jawline and encircled the guilty smirk that currently played upon his lips. He was well-muscled and broad-shouldered as one would expect for a blacksmith's apprentice. The young man's smirk gave way to a nervous smile, and he spoke with an apologetic tone.

"I'm sorry I overslept again Kail. I was troubled last night by those nightmares again and—"

"Do not worry over the matter," Kaileth said as he took the skillet and scooped some of its contents onto the plate on the table.

"I have only the single chain to complete this morning. Today you have other things to be attending to. After all, today is your birthday."

Kaileth grinned at the young man as he saw the surprise on his face. He knew he had never really done much for birthdays before, a small gift and a special meal perhaps, but never a day free of work to be done. Kaileth had no idea what day Ralenn's actual birthday was. Epri had insisted that a day be set so they picked the day that they all had first come to Allinth.

"Today is your Imer'Antras, the day you have your rite, your trial, and earn your place as a warrior." Kaileth continued. He sipped a little from his mug and cleared his throat.

"On the Isle, we had many rites and orders of passage, as you know. You have become your own man, and next is the warrior. I will never forget my rite and the lessons I learned from it. Perhaps I will share that with you later. Today is your day, this morning is your dawn." Kaileth did not speak much about his past, but he wished Ralenn to know that this was more than just a birthday celebration.

Kaileth gestured for Ralenn to have a seat. He wished for the thousandth time Epri was with him, especially today to see the man Ralenn was becoming, she would have been proud.

"So would have the Alev—"

"What'd you say Kail?"

Kaileth didn't realize he had been thinking out loud. A smile streaked across his face, "Nothing, I simply wish Epri was here with you today, that is all."

A long moment of silence passed between them.

"I wish the same thing, every day." Ralenn slumped down into the chair, looking out the window at the mountains.

"I know you do, but today we must focus on happy things and your rite. You will need your full mental and physical strength today." Kaileth tried to sound cheerful, he *was* excited about today. He knew Ralenn would accomplish amazing things through his Imer'Antras. He knew Ralenn was ready to face this challenge.

Kaileth took a carved stone pitcher of violus nectar from a cupboard and set it down on the table. Then he sat down and looked at Ralenn. Ralenn smiled at him, and Kaileth's heart swelled with the love and pride that he imagined true fathers must feel for their children. He held back a chuckle at the irony of this given his own kin's methods of parenting.

"So, what does this rite, the Imer'Antras consist of? What do I have to do?" Ralenn asked a little nervously. "I well remember the rite of manhood, the Imer'Dhla."

Kaileth smiled. He had sent Ralenn to spend twelve days in the woods by himself with only a knife and a cloak. That was four years ago now, but it seemed like yesterday.

"The Imer'Antras demands that you hunt your hunter. That you face a foe in single combat, in your enemy's territory, and slay it. For myself, this meant sailing to another isle to face a yartoth." As Kaileth said this, he picked up the pitcher and filled a deep, thick-sided cup with the golden bubbling nectar of the violus flowers.

"As for you, you must hunt the grand frost lion. This will be your Imer'Antras. This will be your rite." Ralenn took several measured breaths. Kaileth smiled and silently watched the young man.

The silence continued, finally Ralenn nodded in understanding, but inwardly concealed his shock as he considered what Kaileth had said. He turned his gaze out the window toward the snowy slopes of the peaks of Vagath'Oth. The grand frost lion. Frost lions were rare and usually stayed away from people, but the grand lion was different. It did not fear man and would kill rather than flee. The grand frost lion was said to be larger than a normal lion, and yet the creature left no track on snow or earth. Frost lions were not necessarily arcane creatures, but they were dangerous when cornered, even more so when they did not fear man as did the grand lion.

Ralenn started to eat while he pondered all he could remember about hunting predators and where he should look for the grand frost lion. He was not sure if the grellit was better than usual, or if his anxiety made it taste better. *Kaileth's been getting better at cooking.*

The grand frost lion had killed several men over the years— older men, veterans from the wars, hunters. Ralenn was feeling extremely nervous the more he thought about it, though it gave him strength to know that Kaileth felt he was ready.

Ralenn had received countless days of training in the art of sword, spear, and bow from Kaileth. When they were not working the forge, they were hunting or practicing some new technique of war. Though Kaileth would never admit it, it was clear from what he taught that he was once a great warrior. Ralenn also knew he was no simple man. He showed no age, and his dark hair and bright green eyes showed no signs of time's alteration. As early as Ralenn could recall, Kaileth had spent time teaching him. Epri would even join in the practice demonstrating no small amount of skill with her spear.

Kaileth was again at the cupboards taking dried meat, fruit, and bread from different jars. He then turned with an expression of excitement that Ralenn had not seen since they had lost Epri.

"Do not be troubled, I would not send you to your death. Eat and calm yourself. I will prepare what you will need and set you for success. You are ready, Ralenn. Do not doubt that." With that, Kaileth left the room through the door closest to the window.

Ralenn sat in silence now, having lost interest in his food. His mind working over what Kaileth had said. Kaileth had spoken from time-to-time about rites of passage and the ways of the people of Alliix. He had even spoken about Ralenn going through this one, once. Ralenn just never thought it would be such an immense task, and so suddenly. He had never hunted anything like a frost lion.

Would my bow even do more than just irritate one?

Ralenn recalled that Lanos told him that frost lions had scales under their fur that were hard to cut through. He said that only a lucky hit or an avertyyn blade would work. Of course, no one believed most of what Lanos says. Avertyyn probably was not even real, just a legend, like so many things the townsfolk spoke of.

Ralenn sipped the nectar from the cup and the cool drink calmed his churning stomach for a time. He was sure Kaileth would not ask him to do something he could not do, but this seemed daunting, particularly for a common shop hand like himself, trained or not. Ralenn knew that true confidence usually came from real experience and this challenge would certainly be an *experience*.

Ralenn had finished off the last of the fruit and the grellit and was nibbling a biscuit when Kaileth returned carrying a variety of equipment.

"Good, you are finished," said Kaileth. "Clean up breakfast, and then take a look at what I have for you. I will prepare Riidak and Mirris."

"So, they will be coming with me?" at this Ralenn smiled broadly.

"Yes, they will make sure you survive, and I am not sure I could keep Riidak from following you, anyway." Kaileth set down the items and again left the room.

Ralenn washed off the dishes in a basin before walking over to the assortment Kaileth left on the counter and floor. A large cloak woven from thin iridescent strands of dark green and blue was the first item to attract his attention. Intricate bronze clasps shaped to look like shells and inlayed with azure stones served as the closure of the cloak. A belt of thick, peculiar leather with a silver shield-shaped buckle was next. Under the belt was a pair of snowshoes unlike any that Ralenn had ever seen. Crafted from strands of crystalline wire with small silver chains to secure them, it looked as though they had been grown or spun by some great spider, rather than made by the hands of men.

The last two items were not as remarkable as the rest but looked more practical to Ralenn. The first was a pair of black leather pants, strong and durable yet as soft as silk. The last was a pair of dark leather boots. They were sturdy and intricately made from the same strange leather as the pants and belt were, only thicker. Laces of sable cord and three crimson enameled buckles closed the knee-high boots.

Kaileth reentered holding a backpack and a shirt of the same strange leather, which he handed to Ralenn.

"Dress yourself in the leathers and meet me in the workshop."

Ralenn nodded and Kaileth went back into the room from which he had retrieved the cloak and other items. Ralenn quickly dressed and found that his new clothing and footwear fit him very well, though it had some room to grow. Once dressed, he left his room and entered the warm workshop, pausing to look around at the familiar tools and benches. Ralenn had the strangest feeling that he would never look upon this place with the same sense of home as he did now.

Kaileth entered the shop with a tightly wrapped bundle and placed it, some dried meat, and fruit into the pack on the floor. He then helped Ralenn don the cloak, belt and finally the pack. The pack was heavy but manageable. Kaileth looked over Ralenn's attire, checking that all was in place.

"There, those fit well, though you have some filling out yet." Kaileth said smiling.

He then stooped and with surprising ease removed a large stone from the floor near the forge. Ralenn looked into the wide dark hole that was now exposed to see the hilt of several swords, spears, three large shields, as well as two bows and a few quivers of arrows. He saw something else at the bottom, but Kaileth obscured his view before he could tell what it was. Kaileth took out a bow, sword and dagger then handed them to Ralenn and put the stone back over the hole. Taking the sword and attaching it to Ralenn's belt, Kaileth broke the silence.

"This blade was the sword of an Allitorii warrior. It has served in battle for many generations; it was built for the Great War with Achylle. This is a war bow from Akaroche. Yes, it is a real place, and once boasted the grandest army of the north." Kaileth paused for a moment as he took out the next item. He spoke with solemn reverence. "And this dagger is—this dagger is from your parents. Your father carried it on his rite, and he gave it to your mother who gave it to me. It was her will that you have it when you made the passage from man to warrior."

It was a long knife, closer to a seax than a true dagger, sheathed in a wood and leather scabbard. The steel danced in an intricate pattern against the red wood handle. Though it had an ancient look about it, the blade was sharp and ready for use.

Ralenn next examined the bow with wonder. The bow was dark red, almost black, and the fronts of the limbs were inlaid with shimmering vines of icy blue weaving back and forth. The bow was light as a wisp of cloud, and the string looked to be woven from long white hair. Ralenn was puzzling over the bow string when Kaileth seemed to read his thoughts.

"It is hair freely given by an epi'tharo. No creature of foul heart can pull this bow. No matter their strength."

Ralenn marveled the more, and with Kaileth watching he plied his hand to the string and pulled. The bow bent without much effort, it felt like pulling a child's bow.

"It feels too easy to pull to be lethal, Kail."

"That is the power of the arcane in the bow. A child could draw it, and yet with the right arrow it can fire through a stone wall." He reverently slung the bow over his shoulder and drew the sword. The blade caught the morning's light upon its surface and refracted it about the shop walls.

Ralenn had never seen its equal. The blade looked like a shard of black ice, straight and keen as a razor. Almost a tilldra long with a leather-covered handle of burgundy, it was inlaid with silver and just large enough for both of Ralenn's stout hands. The hilt looked like two forward sweeping silver wings. Ralenn sheathed the sword and again looked at the dagger.

Kaileth had never spoken much about Ralenn's family. Over the years Ralenn came to think it was because Kaileth blamed himself for their deaths. When plied for answers, he would say little more than, *"All shall be made known when you are ready."* When Kaileth said that Ralenn knew not to pry any further. While Ralenn was musing over his new weapons, Kaileth donned a fur coat.

"See that no one disarms you of these weapons. Their worth is far beyond the value intrinsic to their form and function." Kaileth spoke with a grim tone. Ralenn nodded fervently in understanding, still in awe of the weapons now in his possession. These were weapons and equipment far beyond anything Kaileth had provided for all the practice sessions over the years. Ralenn could hardly believe that all this time Kaileth had a cache like this. Weapons that up until this point

Ralenn would have thought only existed in stories or the keeps of mighty lords.

Ralenn looked up from his weapons and tried to ask calmly, "Kaileth, who was the last to kill a frost lion?" Kaileth smiled and said with an assuring tone, "The last that I saw fall was by my hand, and your father for another."

Kaileth held out a large gray cloak of simple linen to Ralenn, who took it and covered his raiment with it. While Ralenn adjusted his gear and clothing, Kaileth quickly finished dousing the forge fire and preparing the shop to be left unattended. With the fire put out, Kaileth opened the door and stepped partially out into the street.

"We have a few more things to gather, Ralenn. Come we must be off." Kaileth motioned for Ralenn to follow him outside. Ralenn stepped past Kaileth through the doorway and out into the street. He looked back into the smithy for a moment as Kaileth stepped out next to him.

Brek slip the coin in my favor, let me come back alive...

A strange and uneasy feeling washed over Ralenn as his eyes passed over the tools and benches of the familiar smithy. He and Kaileth had gone into the mountains many times before, but it never felt like this.

...Patient Father, still my mind, Shayar steel my will, he prayed, hoping the churning feeling in his stomach was only simple apprehension and nothing more. But what if it was more?

Kaileth noticed Ralenn staring back into the shop. He pulled the thick wood door shut and took a few steps past Ralenn and stood there facing the morning sun.

They both were still for a time in the chill morning air. The thick forest that surrounded the village looked like a great sea of deep green, complete with an occasional wave of motion as the wind stirred the trees. The snow-covered peaks of the mountains rose high into the air above the forest and village. Their height made them appear to be holding up the sky itself.

Though Kaileth stood close, staring at the trees at his side, Ralenn felt a thousand skain away. The building uncertainty formed a tangible force within his chest. Pounding with each breath.

How am I to face a frost lion alone? I've never even tracked one. It might take weeks just to find, only for it to tear me into little pieces. I'd never see Kail again. I'd might never see Lirah again...Frothvar master of the high forest, protect and guide this one.

"Ralenn, call Riidak and let us be off," Kaileth said abruptly, bringing Ralenn's thoughts back to the moment at hand. Ralenn called Riidak's name and soon he could be heard running toward them from around the side of the shop. Still panting, he came trotting up to Ralenn and Kaileth.

Riidak was a dog, but to call him that would be unjust. He was as large as the giant tigers that were said to dwell in the far south, standing as high as Kaileth's waist. He looked like a huge hound covered in tan and red-striped fur. His bright eyes smiled, and his cropped tail flicked back and forth in anticipation of the journey. This morning his large and powerful form was clad in silver-scaled battle armor, armor that Ralenn had never seen on him before. The scales of steel covered his shoulders, chest and back. It was all secured by several leather straps. Thanks to his new armor, Riidak looked even more impressive than his enormous size usually made him appear. Nevertheless, after the events that had already transpired so early in the day, Ralenn found the new armor of his four-legged friend none too surprising. Though he determined to press Kaileth for answers once he returned. Clearly there was much that Kaileth had never mentioned about his past.

Ralenn patted the armored side of Riidak as he came up close to him. He had many fond memories of playing and hunting with the great hound. Epri used to tease and threaten to feed Ralenn to Riidak when, as a boy, he would misbehave. At times, Riidak had even allowed him to ride him as a horse when Ralenn was a small child. The hound was very protective of Ralenn, even more so now that it was just Kaileth and he in the house.

With Riidak following behind, they sped off at a fast pace down the short-cobbled path that led from the shop door into the street. There were many familiar people going place-to-place in the streets of Allinth. Brightly dressed merchants, farmers from the valleys, wives of the herdsmen milling about the shops, and a few of the town guards on their way home from the night watch.

Of these people, many gave Kaileth and Ralenn kind greeting as they passed, and more than a few looked long as they walked by. Two large, armed men with a companion such as Riidak was not something often seen. Though many looked and spoke to one another in hushed tones, none dared ask to what errand the men and hound were about. Even those who knew Kaileth and Ralenn well only greeted them, asking nothing of where they were off to that morning.

Keeping at a steady pace, they soon left the main village road and started up the sloping path that led into the mountains and forests that fenced the village upon all sides. The birds in the trees brought the air to life with their song as they followed the road uphill for roughly a half-skain.

Out of the village, they passed the large, stone greenhouses that grew fruit and vegetables all year round. They had been built long ago, some said they were made by winged spirits of the forest that had once lived in the Vagath'Oth Mountains, centuries before men came into that part of the world. Whoever had built them, they were of wonderful use to the village now, providing food all year round. Warm, moist air flowed from carved fissures in the earth and heated the low stone buildings. Even in the bitterest of winters, they were warm within.

Soon after passing the greenhouses, they turned and followed a diverging path to the right. This path was smaller and less traveled, the brush and trees now growing much closer together. A unique and harmonic bird call sounded from further down the path, and Kaileth made an answering call of equal singularity.

Soon after his call ceased, a bird of enormous size came swooping down from the cloudless sky and lit on Riidak's shoulders. This was Mirris, she was a rare breed of falcon, known as hyphron. She was one of the few battle falcons who yet lived. She stood a full tilldra tall from talons to the feathery crest of her head. The white feathers of her wings were lined down the middle with gold and trimmed in brilliant indigo, as was the leading edge of her wings. Her back and cowl were a radiant blue beneath which her ashen chest was speckled with gold feathers that glinted in the sun. She wore a scale armor vest, like Riidak's, only finer. Above her beak of gold, her eyes were the color of an autumn sunset. She and Riidak made for an inspiring sight together, both now armored and battle ready.

"Glad you are both coming with me," Ralenn said to his animal companions. Mirris and Riidak had proved a good defense against most foes in past excursions. Ralenn deemed even the grand lion would be hard-pressed to face both the falcon and hound.

The morning was nearly spent when the path began to climb a steep hill. Once atop the hill the path widened, and to the west they could now see a large domed building of golden stones. Two tall spires of white and green marble flanked a high wooden door set in the middle of the eastern face of the building. A stone wall surrounded the grounds and the many buildings within. Near the center was a temple of Anthos devoted to the Patient Father and his wisdom, with two large statues of the Aashahl flanking the gate. They approached and entered the open gate. Kaileth stopped in a narrow path that wound its way through the well-groomed gardens the priests kept in the yard before the temple. He turned to Mirris and gave her a nod, she seemed to understand his mind and she leaped from Riidak's shoulders and flew away into the southeastern sky. Kaileth then turned to Ralenn.

"Please, wait here with Riidak. I have business with Gaileng, I won't be long."

"May I follow to talk with Lirah?" Ralenn asked. He enjoyed visiting his close friend and hoped seeing her would help calm his nerves.

He also wanted to show her the arms and garb that Kaileth had given him to use. She had spent much time reading the lore held in the temple's library and would perhaps know more of the items.

"There will be time for that later, for now think only of the task soon at hand." With that said, Kaileth quickly walked down the path and into the doors of the temple.

The grounds were unusually empty, though Ralenn could hear a few acolytes near the barracks sparring with staves. He strode over and sat upon a large black rock next to the path. He tried to think of all he knew of swordplay, hunting and of the legends of the grand lion. His review was disturbed, however, by a familiar giggle from the brush behind him. He stood and whirled around to meet Lirah as she came out from behind the row of short wild rose bushes.

Ralenn had known Lirah his entire life. Kaileth told him that she had come to Allinth in the arms of Gaileng only a week after Kaileth and Ralenn had. She was much shorter than he was, and even a little shorter than the other girls their age in the village. He knew some of the town girls said she was a little too muscled and lean to be very pretty, but Ralenn thought it suited her. The curves of her shoulders balanced out her small waste and stout legs.

She had a round pixie-like face with large wide-set hazel eyes, a small slightly upturned nose and heart shaped lips. Her eyes were sparkling with her cheerful demeanor, and a smile could almost always be seen upon her freckle dusted, sun-kissed face. Lirah's chestnut hair would hang past her waist when let down, but now it was done up into an intricate braid. She was wearing a quilted white and gray frock that was common among the acolytes and a flowing silken skirt that ended at her knees to reveal gray tights tucked into her low, fur-trimmed boots.

Lirah placed her hands on her slight hips in an authoritative fashion and said in an imitation of Kaileth's voice, "There will be time later for that, for now think only of the task soon at hand."

Ralenn smiled and Lirah giggled again, her full lips smiling even wider.

"What does he have you doing this time? You looked much too serious sitting there on that rock."

"I'm not sure that he wants me talking about it," Ralenn replied carefully, avoiding her gaze.

"Oh, please Ralenn, what could you be doing that needs to be a secret? Is it some sort of secret man thing?" Ralenn glanced at her in surprise and then looked away again, realizing he had given himself away.

Lirah used her soft, innocent voice as she came closer to Ralenn, the one she always used to try and get what she wanted from him. It usually worked. "Please tell me Ralenn—please?" She playfully skipped even closer as she spoke, trying to look Ralenn in the eye. Ralenn leaned over, resting his arms on his knees, and avoiding Lirah's inquisitive gaze.

When she teased him like this he felt as if a bird were fluttering around in his chest. No one else could make him feel like that, and he was not sure what it was. Ralenn did know that he cared for her very much, she was by far his best friend.

"I won't tell anyone, I promise. Brek curse me should I break it." She was now stooped in front of him holding her face in her hands and trying to catch his eyes. She continued this 'till at last Ralenn spoke.

"Alright, alright," he gave up. "All I can tell you for now is that Kaileth is sending me to hunt something, and yes, it is a secret man thing. He called it an Imer'Antras. He said we can talk after I get back." Lirah looked into his eyes for a few moments more, as if searching his mind.

"All you *can* tell me Ralenn, or all you *will* tell me?" Lirah now stood and turned with a snap toward the temple. She took a few steps toward the temple then turned her head back to Ralenn to see if he would tell her more or stay her.

Of late, Ralenn often found words hard to find when around Lirah, especially when she acted as she was now. He wanted to tell her, but Kaileth was clear, he did not want Ralenn telling anyone where he was going. Maybe the secrecy was part of the rite, Ralenn was not sure. All he knew was that he could not tell her, it would not do any good to explain. But he also did not want her to leave angry with him. Presently she must have seen the struggle on his face, and she relented a little. Her posture softening a bit.

"All right, I can see that is all I will get out of you for now. I need to go then; I am supposed to be back at the temple meditating." With that, she started to walk toward the temple but stopped mid-stride and turned to Ralenn with a worried look on her face. Ralenn was caught by surprise, she was not one to worry.

"Ralenn, you will be careful, won't you?" her voice had a timid, almost frightened tone, which echoed the worry on her face.

Ralenn was stunned at Lirah's sudden change of mood. "Of course, I will be Lirah. Why, what's wrong?" She stood still for a moment, swallowing hard before she exhaled.

"I have a bad feeling. Something is off, I just know it. The last time I felt like this was when Pyldin and Epri died." She took a sharp breath and then continued, "You remember, right? This is worse though, bigger. Do you know what Imer'Antras means Ralenn? It's Allitor for 'path snatched from death,' or 'out of death reborn'...That cloak doesn't hide your sword that well. Whatever you're about -- Please, come back to me."

Ralenn started to say he would be fine, but she turned and hurried into the temple, hugging her waist as if it hurt. Ralenn looked to Ri-idak who was wagging his short tail and staring at the temple. They both stood quietly for a few moments while Ralenn recalled the event Lirah spoke of

It had been nearly three years now. Pyldin had been about their same age, the son of the water mill keeper in the lower valley. Pyldin and Ralenn would often meet and sneak up to the temple to see Lirah.

They would find her at class in the gardens and toss pebbles to gain her attention. The three of them would then steal away and spend the day exploring, hunting, and dreaming of all they might do someday far from Allinth and its simple ways. Pyldin wanted to go south to Syrah, or maybe even Mantorah.

Then the day came when Ralenn arrived at the usual place in the forest by the temple, but Pyldin was not there. Lirah came running from the temple and told Ralenn she had a terrible feeling that Pyldin was in trouble. Ralenn and Lirah waited most of the day for him to meet them, but he never came. By the time they returned to the village a search party had been sent out. Ralenn and Lirah were placed under Gaileng's care as Kaileth and Epri joined the search. They were out deep into the night searching when a ravaging storm blew up. It was no normal storm, but a gryphon gale, a great storm that the creatures used to cover their migrations. The village was in chaos as the storm hit. With each bolt of lightning, shapes of huge flying creatures could be seen in the violent storm clouds. Trees fell, roofs were lost, and torrents of rain crashed down as though the great sea itself were upon the mountainside.

Most of the search party returned late that night, without Kaileth. They were speaking of wolf-like creatures moving in the wood. Epri was lost in the storm, as were several others. Kaileth was out all night looking for her and her father Rahmith, but by morning the damage was done. Rahmith and two others had been slain by the wolf creatures. Epri's cloak and spear were found bloody and discarded near a cliff's edge, though her body was never found. As for Pyldin, his father found his body the next day. He had drowned in the stream that fed his father's mill long before the storm struck. No one ever found out why he was playing in the stream, he was not one who enjoyed swimming. Lirah had taken his loss awfully hard, she blamed herself for not doing more. For a long time, Lirah held herself responsible for the entire night and all who were lost. Kaileth was never the same after Epri disappeared either. The lighthearted, cheerful side of him was lost in the storm with her. The pain was still so fresh Ralenn wondered if he, if any of them, would ever be whole again.

Ralenn pondered on what it might mean that Lirah felt the same as she had that night, before he came to any conclusions, Kaileth appeared from the temple with a water skin and a black quiver of arrows. He handed them to Ralenn.

"That took longer than I had anticipated, Gaileng was in a conversational mood, but now let us depart. I will point you in the direction you must go. We will part further up the road. When you complete your task, I will be waiting for you at home."

Ralenn wanted to tell Kaileth what Lirah had said but did not want him to know that he had told her anything.

"Kaileth, why can't you come with me? I am not sure I can do this alone."

Kaileth smiled and placed a reassuring hand upon his shoulder. "You will do fine. Do not let doubt enter your mind. I have taught you what you need to know, and you have more strength in you than you realize. It is in your being. It is in your blood, Ralenn. Your father and mother will look over you more this day than any of the days past. They will guard you, as will Riidak and Mirris, they will not let too much harm come to you. They will protect you in my stead, but you must do this. You must master your fear and your will. This mastery is what makes a true warrior."

Not too much harm? Ralenn thought to himself, not feeling comforted. He only hoped that Kaileth was right, that he could do it. As the three of them followed the road over past the temple and then over another hill, Mirris swooped down and landed upon Riidak's shoulders. Ralenn turned to look back toward the temple. The white tips of the marble spires and upper rooms could barely be seen as they cleared the treetops. Ralenn took a deep breath and slowly let it out, then turned and faced the road before him.

Did Lirah say come back to her?

***

Lirah peered from her window in the temple, watching as Ralenn, Kaileth, and Riidak followed the road up the hill. When they reached the crest of the hill, she saw one of them—Ralenn she hoped, stop and look toward the temple. After a short pause, all three passed over the hilltop and out of sight. Lirah pulled the window shut and paced her room, wringing her hands and breathing fast. She had to do something, she was sure Ralenn's life was going to be in peril. Her thoughts turned to Epri and Pyldin and her heart squeezed.

"This is the same—exactly the same feeling, only worse," she said aloud to herself. "This is the same, and I didn't do anything last time. I did nothing. Not this time, though. Leshay'ar and Paldrii will have to wait a little longer."

Lirah made up her mind. She took up her short, curved bow and white quiver of arrows, donned a long gray cloak, and slung a large leather pouch over her shoulder. A strange sense of urgency was upon her as she left her room. As soft as a breeze, she slipped through the temple corridors until the main door was in her sight. She moved to the door's latch and started to turn it, being as silent as she could, for she did not want to have to lie to one of the priests about where she was going. The door latch clicked, and she started to open it as a gentle hand landed upon her shoulder. The touch startled her, but she was relieved to turn and see the smiling face of Gaileng. He was the closest thing to a father that Lirah had ever known, and she now realized in this moment she wanted to say goodbye to him. She also knew he would not stop her; he knew her too well to try that. Often it seemed he knew her mind before she truly did.

"Where are we off to Miss Lirah? To the town perhaps, but with a bow and pack?" His voice was warm and kind. Lirah's face flushed, and she stumbled to find words.

"Do not fret, you are to follow him, it is right," Gaileng smiled peacefully and opened the door the rest of the way. Lirah looked up at him with a perplexed look upon her face.

"Gaileng, but how did you know I was going to follow Ralenn?"

"After all the years I've spent in the service of Anthos, do you not think that it has blessed me in some ways?"

Lirah grinned, "No, I didn't mean…"

Gaileng continued, "And after all the years I have known you, do you not think that I can tell what you are about to do? You feel that danger awaits Ralenn, don't you?"

She could feel the blood rushing to the soft curves of her cheeks at the thought of Ralenn coming to harm.

"Well, yes, I do. I can't say what will happen, but it is like when—"

"The night of the gale, and you do not want that to happen to Ralenn. Lirah, you have learned all that we can teach you here, or rather all we are able to help you learn. Thus, it is good that you should follow him, that you may gain experience from what life presents you." Lirah sensed a finality in his voice that concerned her.

"Gaileng, it sounds like you are saying goodbye. I will come back. This is my home." She tried not to sound fretful, but she was not sure what to make of the things Gaileng was saying to her.

"The same feeling that tells you Ralenn may come to harm tells me that it will not be the same here for you should you come back. But know this, whatever happens is the will of Anthos and the Aashahl, and thus it will be for the betterment of those who have hope and struggle for the cause of good, and for those we love."

Lirah's mind was now a tumult of thoughts and emotion. She felt pulled after Ralenn, yet terrified to leave. She could not keep herself from embracing Gaileng and burying her face into the warmth of his simple robes.

"Gaileng, all will be well though, right? When I get back it will be well?"

Gaileng took Lirah by her shoulders and looked at her lovingly. "Yes, it will be as it should. All will be as it should. Now go, follow after him. And if you do nothing else, see that he keeps hope always."

"I will Gaileng, but I will only be a while, a day at the most." Her usual smile returned now, and Lirah turned to walk down the path from the temple.

Gaileng did not speak but only raised his hand in farewell. There were times where he could make so much sense, but at the same time she had no idea what he was talking about. This was one of them. What did hope have to do with a hunting trip? Surely her feelings were just worry that he might get hurt or lost up there, or maybe it was something more? She wasn't sure, and her thoughts kept spinning with possibilities.

Lirah's feet soon found the road. Though Ralenn had a good head start, she knew some shortcuts, and she could move swiftly. She looked about for the traces of the way that he had gone and soon found them. They were heading up into the climbs of the Arah peaks and Ever-Spring Glade. Lirah wanted to run after them, but she stopped to look once more at the temple. She then hurried up the mountain, her chest still tight with worry for her friend.

2

Heights of Vagath'Oth

T o one it is given to be the muse of the great powers of Miljah. To be threshed upon the floors of destiny. For another, it is given choice. To choose a course of fates or a life of stillness. For they that be fated or they that have chosen it is the same. Seek the will of the Aashahl. Delve their labyrinthine hearts and forge a road through their favor and will.
Essays of the Divine

Ralenn had been climbing up the glittering slopes of the mountainside for most of the afternoon. The air was cold and clear, vapor from Ralenn's and Riidak's breath rose into the pale blue sky like thin smoke, but Ralenn's peculiar garb was surprisingly warm despite its lightweight and soft texture. Their progress up the icy slopes was easier than it should have been, thanks to the snowshoes that Kaileth gave him. The crystal snowshoes seemed to float over the frozen surface rather than press into it, letting him walk at an almost normal pace.

Ralenn stopped to look back over the way he had come. He had never been this far up the mountain, and the spectacular view helped distract from his anxiety. He peered back down the mountainside to see the trail they were leaving, a shadow from Mirris flying overhead crossed the slope below. As his eyes searched the snowy slope, he found no traces of his passing flying companion and only a few foot-prints from Riidak.

Must be these shoes...

Ralenn considered his comrade. "Well, Riidak, as far as the snow is concerned you are the only one walking up here." Ralenn smiled and patted the large hound kindly before continuing along their way.

After several more hours of climbing, Ralenn looked up and could see the forked peaks of Arah. Earlier that day Kaileth had told him that he should reach a grassy plain at the base of the peaks, and when he did, he was to remove the gray outer cloak. Ralenn had heard of this place as a child, Ever-Spring Glade. It was said that it grew green all year no matter the season. Kaileth said there would be caves near the glade, and they would be a good place to start the hunt.

Ralenn held a steady course up the slope until he came to an icy plain. Riidak was a few yards ahead of him, sniffing at the frozen earth and snow as they progressed. Meanwhile, Mirris circled overhead, keeping a wary eye out. Nothing but frozen earth and ice lay upon the level ground here. The whole plain must be a marsh in Erah'Nor, the hottest days of the year.

At the far side of the plain lay the final ascension to what must be the place Kaileth told him of. On the eastern side of the plain grew a line of low, snow-frosted trees upon whose branches hung long blue needles. It looked to be a good place to find snow leapers. Ralenn hoped to use the leapers as bait for the lion. He called Mirris and Ri-idak to him, they quickly came near and awaited instruction. Ralenn took a few moments to recall the proper phrases in the ancient tongue Kaileth had taught him from his youth. It was a language that both Mirris and Riidak could understand without misinterpretation.

"Riidak, duïu el raspall i treure tot el que trobahr. Mirris, cercle de la plana. Llavors matahr la primera leaper."

Mirris and Riidak acknowledged their orders with soft nods and quickly went to execute them. Ralenn lay in wait at the edge of the plain, holding a black arrow knocked upon the string of his new bow.

The arrows from the temple were not like any Ralenn had ever seen. They were made of a completely black metal, the same color as his new sword. It had to be avertyyn. The fletching's were dark red and carefully bound and glued into place.

I'll have to be sure to get these arrows back.

A few moments of silence followed, and Ralenn was beginning to wonder if he had given his instructions properly. The stillness of the air was shattered by the deep thundering bark of Riidak, followed by a howl that was as melodic as any instrument Ralenn had ever heard. Ralenn knelt, ready to fire, watching the snowy row of trees for movement.

Aseairpeth, grant us meat, he prayed, hoping the Lady on High would bless their hunt and her child Mirris. Aseairpeth was the aashahl of birds of prey, the hunt, and the air. Known as the Swift Sister in some realms, her love of the chase made her a common ally for the hunters high in the mountains.

Riidak continued to sound his charge, and snow began to shake from the brush and the low branches of the trees, announcing the first leaper was about to break cover. It was a large one, as big as a herdsman's dog, and resembled a great rabbit. Its long tail whipped back and forth, helping it to make sharp turns. Soon three more leapers had entered the plain, followed closely behind by Riidak. The scene looked like a strange dance upon the frozen earth. Riidak kept the leapers dogging about in the center of the icy flat, turning them repeatedly so they could not leave the clear field.

Ralenn was waiting for Mirris to strike when one of the snow leapers made a run for the thicket. He pulled back the arrow and was about to fire when the cry of Mirris stayed his hand. She came diving through the clouds as a dart cast by a heavenly hand and struck the running snow leaper with her talons, driving the animal's head into the ice with such force that it crushed the leaper's skull. Riidak stopped his harassment of the others and trotted off the ice. The remaining three leapers froze and sat looking at Mirris atop the slain fourth. This was the moment Ralenn was waiting for. Snow leapers would almost always stop running and hold still in the presence of a bird of prey. Ralenn thought they did this in the hopes that their white fur would camouflage them from the gaze of the predator. Regardless the reason, it made them easier to hunt.

Aiming for the snow leaper at the back, he sent an arrow from the string. Despite a mild crosswind and the distance of the shot, the arrow flew straight and found its mark in the leaper's neck. No sooner had the first leaper fallen than the second arrow was on its way to the leaper next in line. Mirris took to the sky and the fourth leaper ran for the tree line.

Ralenn rose to his feet, clambered over the rocky edge of the plain, and walked over to the snow leapers. Steam was rising from the wounds in the animals' throats, and he was pleased that he had made the shots so accurately, though he figured that his new bow could take most of the credit. All the arrows had passed clean through the animals and were lodged deep into the opposite mountainside. Ralenn pulled the first arrow from the frozen ground. To his relief it was undamaged. Only the nock and fletching were visible on the second arrow. He pulled hard and found the arrow had hit a large stone and cut right through it. He pulled again with both hands then a sound from behind startled him, stones and snow shifting.

Ralenn snapped around but saw nothing. He searched the brim of the plain, waiting and listening for another sound. After several minutes of total silence, all he could hear was the slow steady breathing of Riidak standing close to him. Riidak had looked for the sound as well but did not seem alarmed. Again, Ralenn checked all about the area, but still nothing could be seen or heard.

I swear I heard something...

He looked to Riidak who still seemed calm and undisturbed. Deciding he must be safe enough, Ralenn shrugged and went back to recovering his arrows. Again, he pulled on the stuck arrow, and slowly it came free from the stone and frozen ground. To Ralenn's amazement it was still sharp and straight. He stood dumbfounded for a moment wondering at the arrow.

"I'd better make sure I don't lose any of these, who knows where Gaileng had to go to find them?"

Ralenn left a trail of cherry red streaked across the pale snow and ice as he dragged the dead leapers near the base of the upward sloping hillside. After cleaning and dressing the game, Ralenn planned to set Riidak to guard two of the leapers while he and Mirris would continue with the third up the final slope. Not knowing how long it would take to find the lion, it would be prudent to have the extra meat. Ralenn sat down and cleaned his knife. He looked to the sun.

Far past highsun already? I might be up here for a while.

As Ralenn sat and gathered his thoughts, he realized that he was starving. It had been a long day already, and the climb up had not been effortless. Before setting out on the final climb, Ralenn thought it would calm his returning anxiety and his griping stomach if he ate something. He sat with his back to the slope and his face toward the warmth of the lowering sun and opened the pack Kaileth had given him. Inside he found dried fruit and meat, half a loaf of bread, and a vial of a metallic peach-colored fluid that Ralenn did not recognize. At the bottom was the wrapped bundle Kaileth had placed in first. While nibbling on a piece of dried fruit, he unwrapped the heavy bundle to find it was a shirt of fine maille and light aketon, the likes of which Ralenn had never seen nor heard.

"No wonder this was so heavy," he said in surprise.

"Would have been nice to know I had armor with me." He chuckled at such a typical Kaileth action. Stash potentially lifesaving armor in the pack with not a word, just the assumption that it will be found and used.

Ralenn unfolded the shirt to find a very tight pattern woven of crimson, sable, and silver rings. The base color was raven black, and it had a twelve-point star of glittering scarlet set in the chest. Within the star was a silver ellipse with an intricate symbol worked also in silver.

He pulled on the dark red aketon, then the maille, and found both to be less encumbering than he thought they would be. The sleeves ended just over the elbow of his stout arms, and the hem came to a curving point just below his knees. Ralenn replaced his belt, wrapped the third leaper in the gray over-cloak, and tied it onto his pack. After telling Riidak to guard the leapers and howl if he saw anything, Ralenn then started up the slope toward the forked peaks above him, following the shadow cast by Mirris above.

The higher Ralenn climbed, the warmer the air became, and after about an hour the snow underfoot gave way to lush green grass and wildflowers of all conceivable colors. With the absence of snow, it became necessary to remove the snowshoes. Ralenn sat upon the now grassy hillside and started to take the snowshoes from his feet. As he did, he could not help but look about him, wondering what powers of Dannitar or Frothvar could alter the climate like this. With the snowshoes tied to his pack, Ralenn stood and continued up the mountainside until at last he reached the top where the upward slope crested and sharply turned into a gentle sweeping meadow.

The meadow was even more out of place than the grass and flowers of the slope below. It was covered with a form of vegetation that was foreign to Ralenn. It flowed with the breeze as a field of wheat, with white stalks over waist high and violet plumes atop each stalk. Ralenn paused and looked across the plain for a moment. He then called Mirris to his side, and the two of them moved to the edge of the field and halted, considering the way before them. The setting sun gently kissed the purple tips of the field, causing it to look like a pool of lavender light, set in a ring of large white violus trees cradled high in the crystalline peaks of the Vagath'Oth Mountains.

At the base of a cliff, on the side of the meadow farthest from the two hunters, the gaping mouth of three caves could be seen, almost daring them to approach. Near the largest cave lay an old mostly eaten wool-ox along with other evidence of a large predator near a boulder.

Not a boulder...a foot! Ralenn nearly exclaimed.

He noticed massive stone feet jutting out between the caverns. Ralenn looked up and realized that the cliff face had been carved into the form of a cloaked woman some hundred rods tall. She wore a bodice of oak and violus leaves, in one hand she held a strange, curved dagger and in the other a many-petaled flower.

Dannitar.

Ralenn recognized the aashahl from the stories Lirah and Epri would share of the mistress of the green wood. She was the ally of all who love the earth and serve the balance of nature. The Mistress of Mercy and renewal Lirah would say, was kindhearted and quick to sorrow for the suffering in the mortal realms. Epri had said she was known as Lady Evernew and her people had held a festival in her name each Arah'Ashli as the land warmed and flowers blossomed.

Ralenn had never seen anything so large made by man. Her beatific features smiled down upon the glade, her arms spread wide cut back into the stone. The statue straddled the largest of the caverns, with a smaller one on each side of her legs. Ralenn stood, staring at the statue and the largest cavern's mouth and spoke softly.

"I suppose this is it, Mirris. That has to be where it lives." As he spoke, he recalled that last summer three men had come up the mountain to Ever-Spring Glade to harvest violus nectar and search for treasures in the caverns. None of them had ever returned. A knot was twisting in his stomach and grew more acute as he took off his pack and water skin and set them next to the snowshoes near the edge of the glade. He could not help but wonder if he should call Riidak up to them, but the light was fading and if he was to face the lion today, it would need to be now. If the lion came for him in the darkness he would have no chance.

He took the dead leaper and motioned for Mirris to follow him. Stealthily, he made his way to the tree line, moving swiftly from tree to tree, circling around the perimeter of the field until he was within a spear throw from the cave. Frost lions were known to hibernate most of the year, only emerging from their lairs to feed for a month or so during Erah'Juil, the end of summer. This made them viciously dangerous, as they would be starving for fresh meat so early in the season.

Ralenn stopped and turned to ask Mirris to circle above the clearing with the leaper, then drop it in front of the cave. Mirris gave a nod in the affirmative, took the game in her talons, and flew to her task. He watched his feathered companion clear the treetops and then looked back to the cave. Carefully, Ralenn crouched down and started to move a few yards closer to the cave where he stopped and knelt close to one of the trees. The hem of his cloak caught his eye, it had changed colors. The dark blue-green hue it had been once was now almost the same color as his woodland surroundings. Ralenn paused a moment to marvel at his cloak's newly discovered property, but before he recomposed himself a voice, warm as a summer breeze, inviting him to linger, sounded within his mind.

"Hmm, long has it been since someone of your quality has entered here."

Ralenn quickly placed arrow to string and looked all around him for the source of the voice.

"Where are you? Who are you?" Ralenn yelled. "Show yourself!"

"There is no need for alarm, young one. I am near, but I am disappointed that you do not recognize the voice of the one you think to be hunting."

Ralenn frantically looked over the grassy clearing and woods for the source of the voice. Nothing.

"The last to venture here were lowly peasants, weak of will, looking to make a profit from those trees you now hide amongst. However, you do not know who you really are, nor the full reason that Kaileth hides you in the village below, do you?"

*How does he know Kaileth...*Ralenn thought, his eyes still searching for a body to put to the sibilant speaker within his mind.

"How do I know him? He is the reason that my shoulder aches every winter. But he didn't tell you that, did he?"

"Tell me what?" Ralenn yelled out to nothing. He was growing both frightened and angry at the same time, his eyes still searching for the source of the voice. The sound seemed to be coming from inside his head, and everywhere all at once. The voice went on, ignoring Ralenn's responses all together.

"He didn't tell you of how I came upon him whilst he was hunting? He would have been my supper had it not been for his foul Akar spear."

While the voice within his mind was saying this, Ralenn watched Mirris let her burden fall in front of the cave. He focused on the cave entrance; his hand held the bow ready for a quick shot. Ralenn crouched at an angle that gave an unobstructed view of the cave and was easily within range of his bow. He could now feel that whatever or whoever was speaking was in that cave.

"Ah, planning a little ambush are we Ralenn? It won't work, not with your thoughts open to be read as the pages of a book."

The creature talking within his mind had a mocking tone in its voice that sparked Ralenn's temper. He was quickly distracted from his anger by motion from the cave's entrance. The white paw of a great lion had just stepped into the fading light, followed by a gold-streaked mane with a human-looking face at the center.

Ralenn was aghast, his hands frozen in shock. This was not a frost lion, but an ice sphinx, a terribly powerful creature of legend. This was the sort of monster that only the greatest warriors from fablette stories fought. Ralenn tried to steel himself as he watched the creature exit the cave. The body of the ice sphinx was pure white, a soft light radiating from within the thick fur. Its huge, dead-looking eyes were disproportionately large when compared to the rest of its face. They looked like two great pooling orbs of nightmare and seemed to lure the surrounding light into their woeful abyss. The air around the creature shivered with an angry-looking energy, sending occasional smoky wisps flying.

The creature grabbed the leaper with a chest-sized paw and tore into it. The ice sphinx's mouth opened far too wide for a normal animal, revealing three rows of long teeth set within. The teeth looked like jagged icicles, but they cut into the body of the leaper like razors.

With blood dripping down the front of its mane, the sphinx turned its gaze and looked directly at Ralenn, giving him a gory grizzled smile.

"I must thank you for whetting my palate with this morsel," it murmured in Ralenn's mind.

The sight of the beast's terrifying maw shook Ralenn from his initial awe and horror. As the beast again invaded his thoughts, Ralenn drew the string of his bow back to respond. However, to his horror as soon as he thought about his aim at the creature he was seized by a crippling pain.

The shot went amiss as Ralenn dropped his bow and fell writhing to the ground. He had felt nothing like this before, this terrible surging agony. It was as much a pain of the mind as it was a physical affliction, a stabbing into his very being. A flood of horror, fear and despair filled his mind, nightmarish images of Pyldin floating dead in the stream, Epri lost in the storm, then of a burning city. People were being slaughtered and driven out, the city's defenders fighting desperately to save their homes. As the pain still surged within him, the scenes of terror settled on a group of warriors fighting to defend a palace. Ralenn saw one of them fighting faster and harder than the rest, it looked like Kaileth. He stood all clad in armor similar to what Ralenn now wore with the addition of some plate. Kaileth fought alongside several others who were of like garb and stature. One-by-one they fell to their attackers, until at last there was only the one who looked like Kaileth. No, it *was* Kail, Ralenn had no doubt. He stood alone before the foe. Ralenn could now see that the attackers wore the armor of Subjugate soldiers, the Dao'Tai. In a mass, they charged Kaileth, and he fell to their onslaught.

Ralenn tried to scream, the image burning in his mind, but the visions continued. The city's streets and buildings flashed by till a woman and young man came to view. Riidak stood close by the young man. To Ralenn, they seemed more familiar than many people of the village he called home. She was richly dressed, and a true picture of graceful beauty. The young man was armored and looked more than a little like Ralenn did now. Ralenn knew he should recognize them, but he could not recall where he had seen their faces before this vision. Before he could puzzle it out, the pain grew more tangible, and he saw the attackers of the city cut their way through the door to the room these two not-strangers were in. Riidak was struck senseless by the shattering door.

He watched the young man fight with skill to defend the woman. Yet he was vastly outnumbered and fell to his foe, he and the woman were struck down by the swords of the dark-armored men. They did not hesitate, nor did they show mercy, and both the woman and young man fell, surrounded by a pool of their own blood. Ralenn could not help but cry out, part due to his pains, but part was due to a feeling of crushing loss at the sight of their savage deaths.

Ralenn cried out in anguish, "Why do you show me this?"

A new, horrid sound of crunching bones and gurgling entered Ralenn's mind, and he realized it was the sphinx laughing.

"*Do you not recognize your own family, your mother and brother? The one who gave you your pitiful life and the one who died trying to protect it?*" A chilling mirth could still be heard in the beast's voice.

"*Kaileth failed to protect them, and he has now completed his blunder by sending you to me. You are as lost as your own petty realm. Surely, she will reward me for killing you. If not her then our master surely will...*"

Ralenn snapped back, "You think I was sent to hunt you? I am no Ale's son. Kaileth thought you were a frost lion, that is how impressive you were!" Ralenn attempted to get to his feet, but a sudden sharp surge of crushing pain brought him down again.

"*A frost lion? The fool saw what I told his mind to see, and you shall enter the afterlife in ignorance it would seem.*"

The throbbing vision moved on to a scene of Allinth burning. All the family shops and homes Ralenn knew were set afire, doors and windows dashed to pieces, friends, and familiar people he had known from his youth were lying slain in the street. Amid the muddy roads he saw Kaileth lying motionless, pierced by many arrows. He tried desperately to push the visions of this massacre out of his mind. He had to open his eyes. He tried to find a thought, any hope to grasp to expel the power of the sphinx. It came to him like air to a drowning man: Lirah, her smile, her laughter, a lifetime of good memories and carefree hours in the forest and streets of Allinth. Ralenn focused on Lirah and forced all his mental power to open his waking eyes as though it might be the last time, he could ever see her.

As his eyes slowly opened, he saw Mirris get struck aside by the sphinx as it strode toward him. Ralenn again struggled to move, to do something, but no matter how hard he tried, he could not force the sphinx fully out of his mind. The sphinx came closer and soon it was under the canopy of the trees. Despair from the creature tried to fill Ralenn again, but then something wavered in the creatures hold over him, its thoughts turned elsewhere for an instant.

The animal paused its forward motion and said, *"Hmm, what do we have here...Ah yes, a girl. She thinks she is coming to save you."* A sadistic grin spread over its face. *"Her soul burns bright, poor fool. So many guests in one day! But what should I do with her?"*

"You won't touch her!" Ralenn cried. He could feel himself regaining some of his faculties as he yelled.

With more effort than he had ever summoned before, Ralenn slowly rose to his knees, despite the invisible weight that still felt like it was trying to crush him. The clear ringing of Riidak's howl now sounded, echoing off the mountainside above the sphinx's cave. Ralenn focused his thoughts into a single purpose, *Lirah. I must kill this thing and keep her safe...* He thought about Kaileth next. Kail would not die in the streets, no matter what price had to be paid. The more Ralenn focused on his loved ones, the less of a presence the sphinx held within his mind.

Ralenn drew his sword and leaned upon it to steady himself as he strove to rise fully. He slowly managed to get to his feet and stood on shaking legs, sweat dripping from his face, wrung from him by the pain. He held his black sword in a white-knuckled grip and looked to find his foe.

"I...will...kill...you," he said, soft and slow. Ralenn could feel the presence of the sphinx being pushed from his mind. Shockingly, Ralenn found that when he focused outward, he could feel and hear the sphinx's thoughts, not just the things it whispered in his mind. By what force this was possible Ralenn was not sure, nor did he have time to wonder over it, for the sphinx was now awfully close to him. The two faced one another, squaring off, an eager rage was on the sphinx's face, while Ralenn felt only determination.

The sphinx's long sharp claws slowly extended from its paws and into the grass of the glade.

Shayar curse me for not bringing a spear!

Ralenn took a defensive stance and readied himself and sword for the imminent attack.

"You think a mortal foundling like you could kill me?"

The sphinx paced back and forth several times, then suddenly lunged toward Ralenn, who quickly dove aside and slashed with his sword as the beast flew past. A spray of cobalt ooze was let loose as the tip of his blade just clipped the belly of the sphinx. The sphinx let out a stone-cracking scream that made Ralenn drop to his knees and cover his ears by reflex.

"Fang of the Cursed!" The sphinx shrieked in Ralenn's head and turned sharply, striking Ralenn's chest with a buckler-sized, claw-studded paw.

He was sent flying into the air from the blow, sailing into a tree with terrific force, knocking the wind out of him. The wounded beast now charged Ralenn, who watched it approach in a frozen moment of terror. As time seemed to slow, Ralenn felt a warmth flow into him from the earth under him, giving him strength. Forcing his lungs to work at the last instant, Ralenn managed to gain a breath and roll aside so that the sphinx's blow missed him and struck the tree, lodging all its claws deep into the bark.

Seeing this as his opportunity, and before the creature could free its paw, Ralenn swung his sword with all his strength, cleaving the ice sphinx's paw clean off. The rest of the animal crashed into the tree with startling force and fell to the ground nearly on top of Ralenn. Scrabbling to his feet, Ralenn plunged his blade into the sphinx's side, jets of smoke darted from the edges of the wound as though the blade burned its way in as much as cut.

While the sword yet stood in the wound, one of the hind legs of the creature reached forward and up under Ralenn's maille to sink its black claws into his thigh. The wounded sphinx then pulled its leg back and dragged Ralenn down to the ground, causing him to cry out in pain as the huge claws dug into his leg.

Then several things happened all at once. The ice sphinx turned its head and smiled savagely at Ralenn. Again, a warmth flowed into Ralenn from the ground, and he realized his grip on his sword had tightened greatly. Then suddenly the creature's massive muscles strained and flung Ralenn by his mangled leg across the glade into another tree. The impact was so brutal that Ralenn was left senseless in a heap on the ground, struggling to breathe. Fortunately, his grip on the sword held firm just long enough as the sphinx tossed him to draw the sable blade from chest to tail, spilling the contents of the beast's torso onto the grassy floor of the clearing. A fading scream rang out in Ralenn's foggy mind as the ice sphinx perished. Slumped against the tree's mighty trunk, he watched the life leave the body of the sphinx in a few last twitching spasms of motion. Still holding his sword, Ralenn half smiled, then winced with pain.

"Looks like I killed you after all..." His words trailed off in a cloud of dizziness. After a brief respite, Ralenn tried to stand, but his damaged leg gave way and he fell to the ground.

He did not try to stand again, but instead stayed on the ground and focused on breathing. Ralenn started to feel a warm pool form under him and knew it was his own blood. Reaching down he could feel five claws buried in the large muscles of his thigh, the warmth of his blood pouring out around the wounds. How they tore free of the sphinx he knew not. Tenderly Ralenn examined his wounds, three of the claws had pulled the aketon into the wound with them; the other two had missed all his armor and were lodged deeply in his leg, leaving it shredded from the throw.

Seeing the damage with his eyes he was now sure he would bleed to death. With significant effort, he managed to sit up again against the tree. His fingers started to feel very cold. He raised his right hand to look it over, it was very pale and felt distant as he peered at it. He assumed the rest of his skin looked just as pale. His mind felt sluggish and tired, and it was a struggle to stay awake.

I am dying…I am going to die right here. He realized the thought of death did not bother him as much as the prospect of failing Kaileth.

*Lirah, you will never see her again if you die up here…*This thought was clear, but it did not feel like his own. It was right though.

You must stop the bleeding. Now. Again, the thought didn't seem to come from him, but he listened to it. His hands started moving, taking his belt, and putting it around his leg above his wounds. More warmth flowed into him, and he pulled on the belt, tightening it as much as he could. Using his sheathed dagger as a windlass, Ralenn used what strength he had left to tighten it further. The sudden rush of pain sharpened his senses for a few moments.

Mirris, I have to get to her.

Using his sword as a crutch, he pulled himself up onto his knees, nearly slipping in his own blood. He managed to grab a low branch and finished his struggle to stand. He felt sick to his stomach and dizzy, the world around him felt like it was spinning.

I've got to find Mirris…Have to…

He took a small step forward, steadying himself with his sword. Then another. Each step caused cutting pain from the belt around his leg then a deep, consuming agony from the claw wounds. The pain helped keep his mind clear though, and he struggled on. After staggering a score of steps looking for the great bird, he saw her, head bobbing as she walked toward him. Ralenn could feel the life draining out of his wounds as he stooped to send Mirris for help. Only then did he realize that the sun had set, and the only light in the glade was a pale glow given off by the violet plumes of the grass.

Ralenn's focus waned into a daze— he slowed, staring at the glowing vegetation. He was becoming very dizzy, and after a few more feeble steps he slowly fell onto his knees, then his side, and then rolled onto his back. Mirris watched silently for a moment before taking to the air. Ralenn lay amidst the glowing grass, gazing up through the trees into the stars above.

Remembering through the haze the blow he had taken to his chest, he put his free hand to it. He could feel his chest slowly moving with his now shallow breathing, but as his hand searched for a wound, he found only a claw, torn from the sphinx's paw. There was no blood, no wound. *Well made...this armor is well made*, he thought distractedly. He closed his eyes and focused on breathing.

Get up! This is not your time. Get up! The woman's voice was commanding, yet Ralenn thought he heard a hint of loving concern as well. He opened his eyes and looked toward the voice. He thought he could see a woman standing near the edge of the glade.

"Must be...seeing wrong..."

Ralenn let his hand drop from his chest, and as it fell it struck one of the claws stuck in his leg. The sudden sharp and shooting pain brought back some of his senses. He looked around again but saw no one.

"It...is not my...time," his words sounded weak, but they summoned his drive to live. Once again, he struggled to roll over and got onto his hands and knees, feeling faint and distant from his body, almost dream-like. He slowly crawled toward the edge of the thicket to call Riidak to him. Nearing the rim, he saw a cloaked figure climb over the lip into the glade. Through the dreamy fog that clouded his mind she looked like the woman from the vision of the ice sphinx.

"Mother?" he whispered. Ralenn rose and stood. As the figure rushed toward him, his vision blurred, his legs gave way, and he fell into unconsciousness.

Ralenn opened his eyes to find he was standing in halls of gray-white stone. His wounds were gone, and he felt warm and safe.

I must be dead, he thought. Strange, that he could feel so peaceful at the notion.

In the mysterious hall, great flowing drapes of black and blue slowly danced upon a gentle breeze. Ralenn could hear the softest of singing coming from a room at the far end of the hall, and he began to walk toward it. As he walked, the hall stretched on before him with door after door and great tall windows. The first set of windows were dark save for an occasional burst of blinding lightning. Through the next set of windows, he could see a green rolling countryside with many white towers rising high into the cloudless sky. He kept slowly walking down the hall passing the doors and windows. Each window showed a different view: a desert, a dark forest, an island, a burning mountain. He stopped as he stood in front of a set of windows that viewed a dark blue place with long gently waving grass. A large fish moved through the grass, and he realized he was looking into the depths of a sea. He walked closer to the window and put a hand to the glass. It felt cold and damp. He gazed into the endless dark blue water and wondered at the magic at work in this place. Something darted through the underwater vegetation and for an instant Ralenn thought he could see the face of a woman looking at him from the darkness, large golden eyes taking him in. He blinked again and it was gone.

He left this window after a few more moments and continued toward the sound of the singing. He peered through the windows by this door, but warm red curtains blocked his view. He went to the door and listened. It was a woman who sang within. Ralenn thought he recognized the voice as though from a long past dream. He started to turn the latch of the door to enter the room when a crack of thunder sounded, and all became dark and cold. Ralenn could smell rain as he heard a woman speak.

"Oh no, you don't. You can't die, I won't let you."

Confused at the words, Ralenn's mind fell back into thoughtless black.

Ralenn slowly awoke to the light of a small fire. The grass around him was wet from an apparent passing rainstorm, but the sky was now clear again. His back was up against a tree and the familiar face of Li-rah gazed at him from across the fire.

"It is about time you showed some sign of life. I was trying to pick a spot to burn your remains." A weary, anxious smile flitted on her lips for a moment.

"You know, you're not the easiest person to follow. You barely left a track. How do you expect me to look out for you if I can't find you?" The smile slowly grew upon her face as she spoke swiftly, something she did when she was worried.

"I thought you said you were going to be careful! What part of charging up a mountain to fight a frost lion is careful? Did you even have a plan or anything beyond, 'almost get eaten on a secret man quest'? And alone! You came up here alone, with no one even knowing where you were going. How would we have found you? What were you thinking Ralenn? Well? Are you going to say anything for yourself?"

Ralenn blinked at the torrent of words. Working through them in his still-dazed mind he smiled and sat up a bit to say, "Thank you, Li-rah."

"For what?" She asked suspiciously.

"For following me up here. Most people wouldn't, you know."

Raising an eyebrow, she put her hand on her hip and said, "Do I seem like 'most people' to you?"

He thought on the question. She was not. In fact, part of the reason she and Ralenn spent so much time together was because the other vil-lagers their age did not seem to approve of her. She was too wild and spent too much time doing things that they did not deem as fit for a young woman. Hunting, exploring— the village girls especially would say she was too independent and headstrong for them. She had a quick and curious mind and wondered about things that the self-proclaimed 'simple folk' thought should be left alone. Lirah never met the village's expectations, and Ralenn preferred her that way.

Lirah tapped her foot impatiently. "Well?"

Ralenn hadn't realized she expected an actual answer. "Oh, no, not at all! That's not what I meant. Ah, that is...you see...what I was trying to say was that I think you—"

Lirah's merry laughter saved him from his befuddled speech. "Don't worry, I'm not upset. I think I know what you meant."

"Well that makes one of us," Ralenn said as he looked down at the claw in his shirt of maille and tugged at it.

"How does your leg feel?" she asked. "That was one nasty wound. I hope you got whatever did that to you."

He now remembered the fight with the sphinx. And the pain. He reached down to his leg, but to his surprise there was no trace of the wound to be felt. He looked to Lirah awe written on his face.

"You don't think that all I do in that temple is pray, do you? I happen to be a proficient healer," she said with a small amount of smugness. "Also, this place seems to be connected to...something. It has a healing power to it as well."

"I would say that's an understatement," Ralenn said quietly, remembering the warmth flow into him during the fight while he absentmindedly tried to pull the claw from his maille shirt.

She slid up next to him and held out a handful of large bloody hollow claws. They appeared to have been the outermost layers of the sphinx's claws, grown to pull off in the wound to hold it open, making it bleed all the worse. What Ralenn had taken to be the claws themselves lodged in his leg had been these insidious things.

"You may want to keep these, after all, they almost took your life. Your aketon saved your main blood way. I was so close to being too late."

"Maybe I can make a necklace or something," Ralenn smiled as he jerked the true claw from his armor and took the others claw shells from Lirah. He looked at the claws and pondered on what had transpired.

"Ralenn," she interrupted his reverie. "Where did you get your weapons and things? Not even a durnori can afford armor like that, it looks like something the ruler of Mantorah might have."

"Kaileth gave it to me. I don't know where he got these clothes, but he did say the sword was from Alliix and that the bow was..." Ralenn trailed off, noticing the bow was not nearby. He immediately started scanning the area around him for it.

"This bow?" asked Lirah, pointing to his bow and arrows next to her healer's pouch and Ralenn's pack.

He nodded in relief and continued, "Yes, that bow is from Akaroche, wherever that is, and the knife was from my parents."

"Kaileth and your parents must have been part of some important kindred then, an old one like Dashra, or Andohra. Maybe Anoth?" she asked amazed.

"I'm not sure if they were, Kaileth has mentioned nothing of it..." Ralenn's mind was drawn back to the vision of the city and the woman, but he didn't tell Lirah what he'd seen.

"Speaking of your mother," she said carefully. "Why did you call me 'Mother' when you first saw me?"

"I said that?" Ralenn could feel his face flush a little. Memories recalled through the haze of his exhaustion were returning.

"Yes, and then you fell down into the grass and almost died on me. I was scared that I had lost you, Ralenn. And when it started to rain, I think Paldrii had you for a while." She gently placed a hand upon Ralenn's and looked earnestly into his eyes.

"What did that to you Ralenn? What is that thing you killed? I didn't get very close, it is a nasty mess."

"An ice- a big frost lion, I guess."

"Did Kaileth really send you after something that deadly?" Lirah didn't sound convinced.

"Well yes, I was supposed to hunt down a big frost lion." Ralenn was starting to drift off again.

Lirah scowled a little "With frost lions I am not sure size makes any difference, they are deadly."

Lirah picked up the sword and looked at it in the fire light. "This is avertyyn, I am certain. So are the arrows. This sword is worth more than all Allinth, maybe half of all that Andohra used to be even. Maybe Kail—" she stopped short.

"Maybe he what, Lirah?" Ralenn could feel himself drifting off again. But this time it was a warm feeling, not the cold emptiness from earlier.

"Maybe he was an Allitorii, one of the royal guards? How else would he have this sword, or that armor you're wearing? You know, it is not like he looks any older as the years pass, people notice."

She curled to look down at the intricate work on the sword. When she turned her head back to her patient his head was starting to droop, and his eyes were falling shut.

"Well, I guess I'll see you in the morning then, sleepyhead," Lirah said softly. She stood up and watched over Ralenn a moment longer. It felt good that he was safe now. When she had found him so gravely injured, she had panicked. Ralenn was her best friend, and one of the few people in her life that she could be herself around. Gaileng was the same, though she knew he wished she would be more studious and reverent at times.

After the war, many people— many families found their way to Allinth. Most had originally come from there, or had family still living there, but not Lirah or Ralenn. They were orphans of the war. Reminders of the war even. She had always felt a connection to Ralenn. Maybe it was the fact that they both lost their entire family in the war, maybe it was something else, she wasn't sure. Lirah smiled as she thought over happy memories with her friend, days spent exploring the forest and the ruined towers near Thort, fishing in the streams and getting into trouble in town. He had always been there with her.

He was peacefully sleeping now, so Lirah decided to stretch her legs and slowly walked from the trees out into the softly glowing grass. The violet light gently floated up to meet the shimmering stars and she could now see the outline of a massive statue carved into the cliff face.

Dannitar. She smiled to herself, recognizing the aashahl, and gave a prayer of thanks for the aid she surely gained from the Merciful Sister.

The air smelled sweet from the passing rain and a refreshing breeze moved the grass back and forth. Lirah could still see the now distant storm, bolts of lightning illuminated the far-off Akarr river valley and the east, where the Dao'Tai had come from.

I wonder what it would have been like...I wonder who I would have been if the war never came. Lirah looked back at Ralenn and smiled warmly. She turned her back on the storm in the east and slowly walked back to the fire. Ralenn was still sleeping with Riidak at his side. Mirris gave Lirah a look, and she was sure the falcon was guessing her thoughts.

"You worry about him too?"

The bird bobbed her head and flew up into a nearby tree. Riidak had curled up close to Ralenn as he slept. The great hound had watched her healing efforts with the saddest eyes Lirah had ever seen in an animal. He and Mirris were both the most extraordinary companions a person could have. Far too smart to be dismissed as simple animals.

Suddenly all exertion of the day caught up to Lirah, she was exhausted. She curled up next to the fire in her cloak and watched over Ralenn until sleep at last overcame her.

***

Ralenn felt hands on his shoulders as he was shaken back to alertness. Lirah's face was right in front of his.

"Wake up, wake up! Smoke! Billowing black smoke, look!" She frantically pulled him to his feet and directed his gaze to columns of thick black smoke ascending skyward from the valley below them.

He still felt groggy and a little dizzy from yesterday's ordeal and a sudden aching hunger sent bile coughing into his throat, but his legs were firm under him. The images the sphinx had put in Ralenn's head came flooding back. He had thought they were false visions to frighten him, but the thought of Kaileth's body in the street spurred him to action through the devastating hunger pains.

"It could be coming from the village, we have to get back, quickly!" He croaked, his throat stinging from the bile.

Lirah was ready. She had put her cloak on and had her bow and quiver in hand. Ralenn called Riidak to him and slung the two dead leapers and Lirah's bag on him. He told Mirris to fly ahead and bring word of all that moved. The bird nodded and took off. Lirah halted Ralenn with a hand on his shoulder, then handed a vial to him. He recognized it as the one from his pack.

"I know this potion, it was wise of Kaileth to give it to you," she said. "It will clear your head. You healed fast enough thanks to the powers of this place but we don't have time to eat." Ralenn quaffed the cool liquid, and it seemed to help immediately. He put on his pack, water skin, and quiver and then took up his bow.

The warm rays of the new morning embraced them as the three companions started through the grass toward the smoke and the unknown.

3

Bells in the Mist

*T*o know the Tears is to know sorrow. To seek the Tears is to walk the paths of loss and despair. For such is the litany of the fallen stars. And they shall know pain and joy in ample measures.
Essays of the Divine

Kaileth...

He woke suddenly, taking in a sharp breath as he sat up in bed.

Kaileth...

The woman's voice lingered in his mind. Where was it coming from? The sound seemed to echo like in a cave. Now fully awake, he searched his room. Dim light drifted through the window from the star-filled sky. Looking around the room it was clear that two people had once used it. The large bed, two sets of shelves, one with large, darker clothing folded upon it and another with smaller, brighter clothing folded on it. Leaning against these shelves was a long, elegant spear. Kaileth looked over all these things but saw no one who could have spoken his name. The room was still and silent.

Another waking dream. He shook his head to clear his thoughts and let out a long sigh of exasperation. He had been having more of them as of late. Dreams of the war, the slaughter in Ell'Anoth, and of Epri. Sometimes he would wake to see her in the room, only to wake again and find it all a dream. His heart could not help but feel that she was still alive, somewhere, calling to him through the ether, but his head knew she had been lost to the storm. Kaileth got out of bed and walked to the shelves that had been Epri's. The necklace he had given her on their day of union caught the gleaming starlight and scattered it over the shelf top, revealing a jeweled case, a brush, hair pins, and a small hand mirror. Kaileth picked up the mirror and thoughtfully examined it.

After Epri was lost he spent every moment he could for the next three years searching for her. Many of Ralenn's fondly remembered hunting trips were in fact searches for Epri. Other times Kaileth would leave Ralenn with Lanos, the captain of the town watch and a good friend of Kaileth's. He would then travel as far as Thenill or Syrah searching for word of the gryphon gale or any bodies that washed up in the rivers. Finally, about a year ago Kaileth found cause to stop his search during his farthest travel from Allinth, far to the south on the Aril River. There he met a trinket trader who had Epri's union necklace. When asked where he got it from the trader confessed, he took it from a body in the river, a woman's body. Kaileth took the necklace and came home. After that Kaileth searched no longer, yet the dreams of Epri grew more frequent.

How am I to forget? How am I to move on? He looked at himself in the mirror. The cold blue light cast grim shadows upon his face, and Kaileth thought he looked tired and worn thin. He was about to put the mirror down when he saw a flash in the mirror, a face. Epri's face. Kaileth dropped the mirror and stumbled backwards into a cloak stand, knocking it over as he tripped and fell. His heart was pounding, his mind spinning, and his eyes were locked on the mirror that had landed softly in a shirt on the floor. He was awake, he was certain, wide awake, this was no dream and there was no doubt of what he saw.

"Why?" he exclaimed in anguish. "Why do you haunt me? Why do you torture my dreams? What is it you would have me do?" Kaileth closed his eyes and a few tears quietly fell. His chest ached with a hollow pain.

"By Shayar and aashahl surround, what must I do to find peace for us both?"

Kaileth sat on the floor for a long time, trapped in his thoughts, regrets, and sorrow. He could hear a distant storm on the mountainside. A dark part of himself wondered if all the torment was his due for pairing with one not of his own kindred. He watched the mirror, hoping to see her face again, dreading to see her face again.

Just a waking dream, that is all, nothing more. You know better than this. She is gone and your heartache only makes things worse. Makes you see things you want to that aren't real.

It couldn't be real. It certainly felt real. He watched the polished bronze surface of the mirror and let his thoughts run wild. All sense of time melting into the churn of his heartache.

It had been hours before daybreak when he first woke, but now the cock's crow told that the sun was soon to rise. Kaileth's attention was shifted from the coming dawn by a soft noise from the shelves. A small carving of a tok rune rolled from Epri's shelves, fell onto the floor, and came to a stop at Kaileth's feet. Ralenn had carved it for Epri when he was small. It was the rune for love and unity.

Ralenn? Thoughts of how Ralenn was faring consumed him. Thoughts of what his future should have been. The fanfare and celebrations for his coming of age. His father and mother smiling at their son, at both of their sons. That's what should have been. Would it be right for him to continue as a simple son of Allinth, or was it time to seek his heritage and birthright? Problematic questions for a sleepless night. How often had Kaileth found himself here, sorting these thoughts out? Twice a halfmoon? More? It was becoming more frequent, and Kaileth could not help but wonder if he would go fully mad.

Shayar, ground my thoughts, give me clarity to see the reality around me, he prayed, as so often he did when faced with Epri's hauntings.

The mistress of his people, Shayar, did not seem to be of much aid at such a great distance from her dominion on the Isles of the Seas. Yet he prayed nonetheless hoping the blood tie of his kindred to Shayar would help his prayers reach her ears. He prayed that the continued haunting had some purpose, and that the purpose was the cause of Shayar's apathy. A small part of him, a part he tried to ignore and bury, always reminded him that he should have gone home with the others.

As far as Kaileth knew all the surviving Allitorii had returned to their homeland far across the seas. With Anoth gone and Ell'Anoth sacked, their oath to the city was fulfilled in a way. Perhaps it would have been better to have gone with them, taken Ralenn from the western realms into the Isles of the East. There at least he would have been raised as a prince of Anoth should have been.

No use in second guessing now, he thought, forcing himself to stop thinking about it.

By now Kaileth knew there was no chance of sleep again. To ease his mind and pass the hours he dressed and made his way to the smithy. Soon the comforting glow of the forge filled the shop and helped settle his nerves.

Rahmith had owned the house and shop, and it was Rahmith who had taught Kaileth how to work the forge and steel. He was no master smith as Rahmith had been, but he had no equal in Allinth or the surrounds. Kaileth let his mind wander as his hands fell to a task familiar to them. The hammer struck the glowing steel, and the sound of it rang clear in the early morning air. His thoughts turned back to the hope that he had in Ralenn for a better future, but the Subjugate's hold on the land was strong.

The Dao'Tai invasion had taken place over five sulsta, before Ralenn was born. Alliances crumbled, allies betrayed allies, and no one stood long against her armies. Many kindreds and realms had surrendered to become vassals of the new Dao'Tai Subjugate. After more than five years of fighting the armies of the Freeholdn, Taivadees, Andohra and Dashra all were but destroyed, leaving the larger realms of Anoth, Akaroche, and Mantorah as the only real opposition. It was about this time when Ralenn had been born. The eastern line failed, and soon after all word from Akaroche had ceased. Anoth was beaten back to their capital of Ell'Anoth, Lea'Angleneth was surrounded, and Mantorah was trapped in the south by a host of the Aya Dao'Tai's best soldiers. Then the siege began.

Kaileth could still remember clearly all that had happened that day, still not far enough in the past for time to soften the sting. He could yet feel the despair as the walls of his city were scorched with the destroyer's flames. As he drifted in memory, the light of sparks and flames shot through the windows and out into the street with each rhythmic hammer blow. The sun slowly made its return for a new day, and Kaileth breathed easier as the work soothed him.

"I'd better get this chain finished today or the wool-ox won't be spinning any mill." He said aloud and smiled a little as his hammer fell.

Once again, the village of Allinth awoke. The fitful night storm had left wisps of fog low in the dells, filling the valley in ghostly mists. Shopkeepers opened their doors, and customers entered the market square. It was time for the town gates to be reopened, letting farmers and traders into the village. Lanos smiled at the familiar sight from his small guard tower near the village gates.

***

Lanos had been a guard of the gates for his entire adult life. More than twenty years and near fifteen of that as watch master. His father had been a gatekeeper before him, and his father's father before him, back to Allinth's founding. A fact their family took considerable pride in. The still night had passed his guard in peace, as most nights did so high on the mountain's slopes. The men below were now unlocking the gates as he awaited the next watch to relieve him.

Lanos was casually looking out of his watchtower when something caught his attention coming up the mist shrouded road. He called to his fellow watchman and the two stepped to arrow slits in the wall and peered out onto the road. There, coming up the damp road, was a young girl. As she made her way toward them, she called out.

"The gates," but as she yelled, she fell to the ground, clutching her side as if she was in terrible pain.

"Yes, the gates, hurry! Aashahl surround! Quick open them!" commanded Lanos. He rushed down from the guardhouse that overlooked the wall and hurried over to the gate. The men strained and pulled the large wooden gate open. They ran to meet the girl, who had gotten back up and was slowly drawing closer to the gate.

She was dressed in a stained and torn linen smock, once white in color. She was limping as she staggered along, and streams of tears could be seen running through the soot and blood that caked her small face. With the gate now open the watchmen, Lanos in the lead, rushed out to her. He caught her in his arms as she collapsed. The young girl spoke in a wisp of a voice.

"The gate..." she said, struggling to speak. Lanos could now see she had a great wound in her side. Two of the watchmen ran to get aid for the dying girl, who again spoke to Lanos. "No...the gate...you have to..." She gasped, trying to continue.

The girl reminded Lanos of his own daughter. He tried to sound calm and kind as he held her. "Yes, the gate, it is open, and you are safe now. We have healers." He turned his head to the gathering crowd.

"Hurry please! We need a priest or healer! Send a runner to the monastery quick!" He tried not to show panic on his weathered face as the lifeblood poured from the girl's side, pooling around them both. He looked frantically about the crowd for someone, anyone, who could help him, but he found no one. They all just stood watching, stunned. Those who had seen war knew there was nothing to be done, and those who did not know war were shocked beyond response. Once again, the young girl tried to speak.

"No, close it..." she coughed, sending more blood to run from the corners of her pale lips. "Close the gate, please! They are..." she gasped again.

"They are what?" Lanos asked, trying to keep her eyes locked with his.

"They...they..." Her eyes rolled back, and he felt her go limp in his arms.

"Who?" he asked. The question fell on deaf ears, she lay motionless in his arms. An eerie quiet fell over all in the crowd, as they all looked with sadness at the young girl. Lanos could still feel her blood, warm and thick, running over his arms and onto the cold muddy road.

A sharp whistling sound suddenly broke the reverent silence. Lanos looked to the woods around the road from whence the sound came. The mist was still very thick, casting an unsettling gloom under the boughs of the evergreens. He saw nothing, but his gaze quickly shifted to a man who fell amongst the crowd, a thick arrow lodged in his chest. Then the screams started.

"Run! Back to the gates!" Lanos shouted as he dropped the girl and jumped to his feet. The panic-stricken crowd was already running as another flight of arrows felled a half dozen or so men and women before they reached the gates. As Lanos ran, he felt his scale armor turn an arrow strike between his shoulders. He stumbled, almost fell, but regained his stride and made the gate. Lanos and the other watchmen rushed the remaining people back into the town and started to close the gates. Bursting from the brush and greenery of the woods about the road came running the unknown foe, bellowing as they charged.

Lanos and the other guards desperately pushed the heavy gate closed. The oak and iron slowly began to swing shut as spears, arrows, and deadly projectiles of all sorts came hurling at them through the gap until at last the gate shut. Catching his breath, Lanos put his back to the gate. "Sound the alarm and get archers atop the wall—" his words were halted by a spearhead and six inches of shaft that burst through his left shoulder. He tried to cry out but found no breath to do so. Behind him he could hear blades on wood as another spear, then a halberd burst through the gates.

"Gamdle!" he managed to call out to the man nearest the gates, an archer. Gamdle ran to Lanos even as the first attacker made it over the walls. With a fast stroke he cut the spear shaft and he and Lanos ran for the watchtower. Blood seeped from around the spear shaft onto the scales of Lanos' armor. Gamdle and the others looked on Lanos in terror. Seeing the panic in their eyes, Lanos drew himself up, ignoring the pain as he pulled his short sword free of its scabbard.

The men around him, some old, and some far too young set their jaws and seemed to be waiting for more. Lanos swallowed hard and looked them each in the eye. Each of them had loved ones to protect. Each had everything to fight for, and Lanos knew that most of them were about to fall to protect it.

"It be our homes, it be our families behind us lads. This be our Allinth. Come, let us hold the gates a while longer yet." He sounded far calmer and sure of himself than he felt, but the men around him nodded and gripped their weapons a little tighter knowing that he was leading them. Knowing that they were indeed fighting for their families and homes.

Lanos, and the others ran out onto the ramparts over the gate. Lanos slew two attackers who had made it onto the walls while Gamdle and the archers sent fletched death into the foe at the gate. With the walls secure for a moment, Lanos gathered the rest of the watchmen and prepared for the inevitable breach of the gates. Lanos could feel his strength leaving with each drop of blood from his wounds. He strapped a shield onto his wounded side. The town bells rang out, sounding the alarm. That was good, maybe there would be time for some of the townspeople to escape or prepare. Taking a spear from the weapon rack, Lanos left the guard tower and entered the street. He took his place with his men in the shield wall just as the splintered gates crumbled.

"Felairtarh, pass us by!"

***

Kaileth halted the work of his hammer. He was right, it was screaming he heard a moment ago. He set down his hammer and tongs and stepped a short distance away from the forge to listen again. The clear ringing of the town bells was now easy to hear over the purr of the forge fire. Kaileth walked across the shop to the door that led to the living quarters and locked it with the turn of a heavy key. With a deep breath, he then went over to a wall whereon finished work pieces hung. Among these were several spears. Kaileth took one of these spears and two good javelins and hurried to the door. As he opened it the morning mist swirled about him, still dense in the early morning. The bells clanged out one last note of alarm. Sounds of muffled battle drifted in the mist from the lower town. The clamor of the bells stopped. He turned and looked once more into his shop, then he stepped through the door and out into the mists.

4

Acquainted with Death

To some the whims of the Divine are ever callous and fickle. Wisdom is it, to see the guiding path cut through the tenderness of our entrapping childlike dreams. Comfort is rife with peril, in suffering we might yet be saved.
Essays of the Divine

The crunch of snow underfoot filled the crisp mountain air as Ralenn ran. They were making good time down the slopes. He stopped for a moment and looked over his shoulder to let Lirah and Riidak catch up to him. Earlier that morning, Ralenn took his crystalline snowshoes from his pack and gave them to Lirah to use on the ice plain. Despite the recent injury to his leg and the exhaustion of the day prior, he could run much faster than Lirah and even Riidak with his load. It must have been some effect of the potion Kaileth had sent with him, as Lirah was usually the faster.

Ralenn looked ahead again and down the mountain. The pillars of rising smoke in front of him were much closer now, but they were dissipating, and Ralenn's worry over what they were going to find grew every time he had to stop. Lirah came close now, followed by Riidak, both panting like Ralenn had when he first stopped. But now his voice was calm and steady.

"Mirris should have been back by now." He said, searching the bright open sky for any sign of her. "I think the road is only a bit more than a half a skain off."

The snow and ice of the upper slopes had changed to soft grass and dark earth. Lirah sat down and started taking the snowshoes off.

"I have never run this far, this fast, in my life," she was still breathing hard as she spoke. The air was thin and even though Ralenn had recovered his breath, his pulse was still pounding in his ears.

"Neither have I, I've only ever been this high in the mountains a few times. Makes it hard to run. Kail said you could get sick from the air up here." Ralenn lowered his head and let the rest of his words trail off. Kaileth could be in trouble at this moment, the village could be too. He had the worst feeling that something was wrong. Kaileth was in trouble, he was sure of it.

We must hurry! His thoughts were a desperate cry compelling him to move.

"Are you feeling alright?" Lirah asked.

"Yes, I mean I don't feel sick. And my leg feels strong. I'm just worried."

"I'm worried too, but I'm sure it's just a fire or a farmer burning a field, right?"

Ralenn smiled at her optimism, though the tremble in her voice was from more than just exertion, she didn't believe it was a farmer.

"What the sphinx showed me up there...I think we need to hurry."

Lirah shot to her feet, sending the snowshoes flying off her lap and down the hill. Ralenn took a few steps back out of reflex as she charged up to him.

"The *what* showed you? You said it was a frost lion! What kind of madness came over you, Ralenn? You were hunting an ice sphinx?! By yourself?! That's as daft as squaring off with a thryst! How stupid are you?" She shoved him, hard enough Ralenn nearly fell as she continued her tirade.

"Why would you...No wonder you were so...If it weren't for that potion you'd be...I didn't even think they were real!" The anger in her voice ebbed as Ralenn came close and took her shoulders with his hands. She stopped and looked him in the eyes.

"They are real, that much is sure, but it's alright. The Aashahl were watching. I am here, and healed thanks to you. And it is very dead." He gave her a reassuring smile as he spoke.

"Well, I can see that, you twit, but what if I hadn't followed?" She glared, pointing an accusatory finger. "You would be...I mean..." she sighed in frustration. "It is just that, besides Gaileng, you are the only family I really have, and it was terrible," her voice hitched, "seeing you hurt like that."

With that she shrugged out of his hold and turned to start down the hill toward the thickening forest below, calling back to a perplexed Ralenn, "Come on, we need to get home."

"If it makes any difference, I *was* trying to find a frost lion, not a sphinx!" he called after her.

Lirah turned and shot him a disapproving glance as she walked.

"Alright, I'm coming. Let's go Riidak." Ralenn gathered up the snowshoes and tied them to the hound's pack. He lovingly patted Riidak's shoulder and they both followed Lirah into the trees below.

There was no sign of life as they entered the forest. No bird calls, no rabbits or squirrels running for cover, nothing moved. Ralenn had caught up to Lirah when the three of them finally reached the trail that would lead them back to the temple grounds. The billowing smoke was now only a few wisps issuing from the Allinth valley, but there was still quite a bit of smoke lingering in the trees around them and in the dell where the temple grounds sat. Smoke, and a smell that Ralenn couldn't place hung in the air. A sickening sweet, burnt smell that seemed to stick to the back of their pallets. Lirah coughed hard.

"What is that? Gah, it's awful!"

"I'm not sure. It smells a little like when we burned that errvt nest near the granary," he said.

"I guess it does, but worse," she responded.

They were on the narrow roadway now, and the unsettling air was still present. Ralenn stopped again and looked around the group. He looked skyward, hoping to spot Mirris circling down. Nothing.

Where are you Mirris? Aseairpeth please show mercy, he thought.

"We should stay off the road I think, stick to the woods till Mirris gets back. We don't know what we are heading into," he said.

"Why, did you hear something?" Lirah sounded nervous.

"No, but something is wrong, unsettled. I'm just not sure what it is. But if that smoke is from a battle, or a raid, we don't want to be caught flat-footed on the open road."

"Right, but it could just be a bad fire, maybe even a bit of a forest fire." She tried to sound confident, but when she looked at Ralenn he could see the pleading in her large soft eyes.

Ralenn's stomach twisted at her anguish, and he found himself nodding. "It could be. Let's hurry and see." He didn't sound as convincing as he intended.

Sticking to the shadows of the trees, the companions moved quickly down the side of the road toward Allinth. The eerie stillness grew thicker in the air, as if even the trees were not at ease. Ralenn swallowed hard and wet his lips, trying to pinpoint the source of the uneasiness.

"What is it?" Lirah whispered and he realized he had stopped walking.

"I'm not sure." Ralenn closed his eyes and tried to focus on what he was feeling. It felt like trying to remember a dream. There was something there, at the edge of his awareness, and it felt wrong. Lirah was fidgeting nervously next to him, eyes darting from tree to tree and shadow to shadow, searching for whatever had set Ralenn on edge.

"Do you feel that?" Ralenn asked, half to himself, half to Lirah. They both stood quietly for a few moments.

"Something is wrong. The forest...It feels like it wants to hide. What is it Ralenn?" He could hear the edge of panic in her voice.

"I don't know. Maybe nothing. But something feels...off. Like you said. The forest is too quiet."

As they continued, she could not shake the feelings from their earlier pause. It was as though for a moment the tree's feelings were her own. Lirah was used to feeling a connection to the things around her when she focused on it, but it had never felt so uneasy and unsettling. She was now forced to bend her will to breathing. Breathing and not tripping as she ran.

The trio continued to move as fast as the terrain would allow. She tried hard *not* to think where Mirris was, or how the forest around her felt. Near a halfsun passed, and they were getting close to the temple of Anthos that she had left in such a hurry the day before. A wispy haze clung in the lower boughs and spaces between the trees before her. Lirah found her thoughts starting to blur with fearful anticipation the closer she moved to the monastery, her *home*. Ralenn slowed down with her, and they cautiously approached the slow rise in the terrain that signaled the path to the temple. The forest was thick here with greenery, towering pines, karran trees, aspens, and scrub oak. The path was steadily growing wider, and the dense undergrowth soon forced them all onto the trail. With Ralenn in the lead, they moved to the top of the hill until the temple could be seen. The temple grounds sat in a deep dell closely bordered by the dense forest and high mountain slopes. Lirah's breath caught in her throat as pure horror struck her like an icy blast.

Aashahl's tears...No! Anthos please let my eyes be false, let this be a dream...

She blinked hard, rubbing tears from her eyes with her clenched fists. Ralenn stood motionless, shocked by what he saw as well. Lirah forced her eyes back open and made herself look. The outer walls of the temple had been breached in several places. Near the wrecked and smoking gates Lirah could see two acolytes, Bruist and Fodir, both blood-soaked and mangled. Within the walls the temple had been ravaged. Smoke drifted skyward out of the broken upper windows, and a sizable portion of the central domed roof had collapsed. The outbuildings, priests' quarters and acolytes' barracks had all been burned. The signs of battle and destruction were everywhere, but no signs of motion.

Lirah's heart squeezed and she hurried down the path with Ralenn now in the rear, hard-pressed to keep up with her as she ran. Lirah stopped between the granite statues bearing the visage of Anthos, they had been smeared with blood and marred by a blade. Bruist lay sprawled across the shattered beams of the gate. He had lost an arm and was nearly cleaved in half along his torso. Fodir was similarly mutilated. Gasping for breath between pounding heartbeats she scanned the inner courtyard. It looked like the acolytes had put up a bitter fight. The smell of blood was so thick she gagged. The bodies of people Lirah had known all her life laid dead across the yard along with many slaughtered livestock.

Lirah felt the warmth of the sun on her shoulders and turned to face the light, gasping for air. She looked up into the stone face of Anthos' statue next to her. The smooth white stone had been viciously hacked by some weapon. A savage hand had smeared blood in strange symbols on the statue's robes. Lirah focused on the face— hard lines and large eyes she was familiar with, neither happy nor sad. A perfect visage of eternal patience and calm. The sunlight shifted and dazzled in her tear-filled eyes. She blinked hard and for a moment in the shimmering light, Anthos smiled. Warmth and a sense of peace sank into her, and despite everything, she felt that somehow things would turn out right. She blinked again and saw nothing but the cold stone of the statue. Lirah realized that Ralenn had placed a reassuring hand on her shoulder, and he now stood just behind her. His warm strong hand helped to calm her further and Lirah managed to catch her breath and slow her tears. Lirah wiped her face with the edge of her sleeve and slowly turned back to face the carnage. She looked further down the path to the temple and saw something that made her cry out and run toward it.

"Lirah wait!" Ralenn called, running after her.

She ran through the burned and trampled garden to the shattered doors between the marble spires of the temple. She stopped over a partially burned corpse that lay in the doorway. His white and green robes were burned and stained with blood and ash. Another priest lay near him, also killed by the fire that had ravaged the temple. Lirah knelt over his body, the horror and pain threatening to crush her again. Not Gaileng!

*No, no, no. This cannot be...he was favored of Anthos...*Her thoughts raced and she tried not to see his face on the burned corpse, but no matter how she begged Anthos and all the Aashahl for this not to be Gaileng, she knew it was.

*Merciful Shepard, Paldrii, see his soul safely on high. Usher him to the halls of our Patient Father...*she prayed, hoping the Aashahl were listening. She felt like the world was spinning and she might just be flung off into a void of despair, alone with her sorrow. Lirah had never felt so lost. She was drowning, she couldn't breathe. Then Ralenn was by her side. Lirah felt his hand take hers and he gently pulled her up to stand near him. He pulled her close into a comforting embrace. She clung to him, he felt solid and safe. He felt like the only thing that could help her in this moment. Her first two sobs ripped out, sharp and savage. She let her face drop onto his chest and let all the pain flow out of her in hot tears and hiccupping sobs.

She couldn't say how long they just stood there. Lirah clung to Ralenn and wept until she could cry no more. She felt empty, but better somehow. She let her arms relax and took a step back away from the temple doors to sit on a stone bench. She let out a long deep breath. Ralenn sat down next to her.

"I'm so sorry Lirah...so sorry." His voice was soft and sincere. She wiped her face cleaner on her skirt hem.

"Sorry for crying all over you," she said with a shaky voice, realizing she had left a large wet patch of tears and snot on Ralenn's chest.

"It's fine, are you alright?" he asked. He immediately regretted the question. Of course, she wasn't alright. Lirah could hear the hesitation in his voice. "What can I do to help Lirah?"

Force Oliar to turn back time...stop the attack...save Gaileng, she thought. But instead, she said, "We need to take care of the dead. I'll need help."

Ralenn stood and held out his hand. "Show me what to do."

It took the better part of an hour to gather all the dead to where the pyre alter sat on the highest edge of the dell behind the main temple. Their progress was slow and interrupted by frequent tears as Lirah helped carry the dead who had been closest to her in life. Kuill, Detan, Itheil, Fodir, Bruist, Cailli, and Gaileng—so many dead. So many she had learned from and grown up with, dead.

Ralenn stood next to the pyre with an oil lamp in hand. The pyre alter was a wide, curved stone slab set upon rows of carved figures depicting many of the Aashahl, and it now held a host of bodies— old and young, male and female, the dead priests, acolytes, and disciples of the Anthosn temple. There were still many missing, but they had found no sign of the survivors.

Ralenn had only seen the pyre altar used once. It was a thing of magic that he didn't understand. Kail said they were a primal summoning gate for elemental powers, but Ralenn wasn't sure what that meant. On the other side of the altar was Lirah, she'd been sitting there for a while now. She had been noticeably quiet the entire time they had been tending to the dead priests and acolytes. Only speaking to say the prayers and the appropriate rites for the faith of the murdered Anthosn.

Ralenn found his stomach could not unknot itself. He felt sick and horrible, it was all so wrong and terrible. Lirah might never be the same. How could she? A guilty part of Ralenn was relieved that the smoke they saw was just from the temple, and he had convinced himself that Mirris' delay was due to her being with Kaileth. While they had worked, he tried to find signs of the attackers of the temple.

The buildings had clearly been looted to some degree, but not completely. A few broken weapons and a shattered shield were near the gate, and there were tracks. Large, heavy animal-like tracks that Ralenn could not place. It worried him, but he knew that Lirah would not leave until the dead were laid to rest. There was a chance that the attackers were still close, and there was also a chance that they were on their way down the mountain toward Allinth.

He examined the lamp in his hand again. It was made of brass and covered with ancient tok runes. Three wicks burned with a yellow-green flame. He held it at arm's length and slowly walked toward the altar just as Lirah had instructed him to do. A vapory haze hung in the air around the bodies, which seemed to be drifting up from the altar. Ralenn gently dipped the lamp's flame into the vapor then quickly stepped back as the vapor surged into a column of bright green flames. The heat was intense, but it produced no smoke or scent of fire. Ralenn placed the lamp back in its place within an alcove inside a large stone pillar at the edge of the altar.

Lirah sat on the far side of the dell, the pyre alter to her back. She couldn't cry anymore, she felt hollow and wrung out. The heat from the pyre sent tingles up her back as she looked out across the mountains.

Lirah had been raised in the Anthosn temple, but she would not have called herself an Anthosn. She had learned of many of the Aashahl here, though. Dannitar mother of the seasons, Paldrii mistress of the lost and guardian of the worthy dead, Jillii Everhope, Leshay'ar mistress of strife, Fiivan Son of the fast waters and mighty Frothvar Father of the high forests. Many took a highly active role in the lives of their followers, but not Anthos, not the Patient Father. Why? Why hadn't he intervened in this instance? Gaileng had to have been among the most favored of Anthos, he had to be! Gaileng was the high priest. He had all the blessings and marks of a favored of Anthos.

*Patient Father, give me the patience to bear this strife. Leshay'ar, grant me the wisdom to grow from this trial...*Her prayer faltered as Ralenn sat down next to her.

"Is there anything else we need to do, any prayers and such?"

There wasn't. Lirah had seen to the supplications to the appropriate Aashahl to see to the afterlife for the dead, but it seemed empty. She wasn't sure if that was because she never had fully believed in Anthos, or if it was just too much heartbreak to take in at once. She had physically seen manifestations of several of the lesser Aashahl, but never anything from Anthos. Gaileng had always told her that one could connect with Anthos if one could still their inner self. Lirah was not sure what he meant by 'still one's inner self.' It was hard for her growing up, and she had always felt like a bit of a disappointment to Gaileng and the other priests, though they would have never said such a thing. It was clear to Lirah, however, that there was a wildness to her that would never quite fit in with the Anthosn way of life.

Despite this, the temple was her only true home, not Allinth. And it was gone now. She could feel Ralenn next to her struggling to find something to say. There was nothing to say, not really. Just having him next to her was exactly what she needed right now, though she was not entirely sure why.

He was close to her on the little bench, thigh to thigh and without fully thinking about it Ralenn placed an arm around the curves of her shoulders and simply held her. The thick braid of her hair smelled of lilac and lavender despite all that had happened. The pleasant scent reminded him of all the time they had spent as children playing out fablettes among the lilacs of the temple grounds. He felt the gentle lines of her body press into him as she leaned into the embrace. Lirah took several deep shuddering breaths; her eyes locked on the expanse of the mountain before her. Ralenn studied her face, marking each feature, the flushed apricots of her cheeks, her full lips set firm in determination not to cry, her soft eyes, so full of sorrow his heart could have screamed at such an alien emotion in his dearest friend. He searched for the right words to express how sorry he was. How could he tell her how much he wanted to comfort her, how much he cared for her? Everything that came to mind seemed too small for this size of sorrow.

Lirah let herself be fully supported by Ralenn. Finding the moment to be exactly what she needed amid all the horror and loss. She smiled a little and again wiped her nose on the hem of her skirts.

Life is such a terrible bittersweet thing.

Again she looked out over the mountains, this time looking more to the northeast of the valley where Allinth lay.

"Lirah, I..." Ralenn started to say.

More smoke!

"Look!" Lirah interrupted him, pointing to fading gray columns of smoke. The thought had not occurred to either of them that the smoke they had seen from the glade near the sphinx cave had been from both Allinth *and* the temple.

"Allinth! Lirah, whoever did this must have gone to the village."

"What should we do?" She stood, the lean muscles in her jaw, neck and arms setting hard with resolve. Someone who did not know her would have thought she sounded like her usual, determined self. Ralenn, however, could hear the tears in her voice.

"We have to help. There will be wounded, I am sure," he said.

"I could gather all the healing supplies that I can. There has to be some left."

"Just so. If I leave Riidak with you, do you think you will be alright? I can run ahead and see what we are dealing with."

"Yes, I'll be fine." She straightened her skirts and frock and held out her hand to him. "Come on, we have more running around to do." She gave him a little smile. It was still sad, but resolute. He took her hand, and she pulled him to his feet, then they hurried off the pyre hill to the temple grounds.

"If anyone comes, run into the forest and head to the Falls of He'Aril. If anything happens and we don't find each other I will meet you there."

"Ralenn, I'll be right behind you, now go."

He nodded, gave Riidak a command to stay, and took off.

Ralenn's lungs burned, his legs ached, and his feet felt raw. The potion from the morning had begun to wear of and he could feel a deep weariness he had never known before. It was nearly six skains to Allinth from the temple, and he knew that on a good day it would take a full halfsun or more. Ralenn hoped that between running the whole way and the mostly downhill trail he could make it in half that time.

He forced himself to think of something besides running, and without meaning to he thought of Lirah. As he left Ralenn had smiled at her, and Lirah had given another small smile in return. He loved her smile, the heart shape of her lips pulling wide into a bow. He took courage from it. Ralenn had walked out of the remains of the temple and over to Riidak. He hated to leave but did not know what else to do.

"My friend you must guard Lirah. Let no harm come to her," he had said.

Riidak gave him a friendly nuzzle and trotted over to where Lirah was searching a storage shed near the temple. Then he had turned and started to run.

That had been hours ago, and Ralenn felt urgently that he had to get to Kaileth. He was retracing the path he took yesterday, but all looked different to him now. He soon came to the village greenhouses.

Almost there...just have to keep running a bit longer.

As he passed by, a shadow moved within a round window in one of the long, low, stone buildings. Ralenn slowed to investigate. He didn't want to leave a threat between him and Lirah. The form within the greenhouse was too big to be a man, and it had a long snout.

Ralenn moved closer to try to identify the creature. He left the path and made his way over to the trail that led to the door of the house. Ralenn moved within twenty paces or so of the door and looked down.

Those are the same tracks...

Large, animal-like tracks ran down the trail toward the greenhouse door. He thought he could hear something breathing, almost growling within when the door suddenly burst violently open.

5

A Life in the Balance

P ray not for prowess in all things. Pray instead to be used up like unto dry kindling in the birth of a conflagration that will outlast any single work of mortal hands.
Essays of the Divine

The door flew open and hit the wall so hard that the top hinge gave way. Stooping to avoid hitting its head, a Grishkah stepped out of the doorway, bloody sword in hand. Grishkii were semi-intelligent beasts that looked like a jackal or hyena with a fur-covered, humanoid body and elongated back legs. Their front legs ended in hand-like paws with short, hooked claws. They were large. Larger and stronger than most men. Kaileth had shown them and many other creatures to Ralenn in a book he kept at home.

The savage looking creature snarled and scanned around the area, sniffing the air. The Grishkah that now stood before Ralenn had short tan fur and a tattered hauberk of rusting maille strapped over its burly body. Out of instinct, Ralenn dashed into the shadows of several large currant bushes, hoping the jackal-headed beast hadn't seen him. The Grishkah was slow enough that by the time he spotted Ralenn a black-shafted arrow found its mark in his mailled chest. The Grishkah fell onto the path, howling and cursing in its savage native tongue.

A second, red-furred Grishkah came running through the doorway. With no time to fire his bow again, Ralenn drew his sword. The growling beast swung at Ralenn's head with a jagged sword, missing by only a few inches. As he ducked the blow, Ralenn slashed the leg of the Grishkah, sending him crumpling down onto the path in front of the doorway. Ralenn struggled to keep his breathing under control. After everything he had been through his body was threatening total exhaustion.

Looking around, Ralenn was shocked to see the tan Grishkah get back to his feet, thick blood spilling from his wound. He now came at Ralenn, who parried the first and second strikes at his body, then made a strong cut to the Grishkah's shoulder, just as he had so many times before sparring with Kail. The avertyyn blade rent the maille rings and flesh alike, and the Grishkah howled in pain but did not stop his assault. Ralenn cursed and hesitated only for a moment, shocked by the resilience of his foe. A strike from behind sent Ralenn stumbling into the mud off the side of the trail.

Idiot! Mind your surroundings. Again, he cursed his novice error and wished hard for one of the shields from the cache at home. He had mistakenly counted the red-furred Grishkah out of the fight.

Before Ralenn could get up, the tan beast was again upon him, but as the Grishkah raised his weapon to finish the conflict, Ralenn swung his sword as fast and hard as he could, cleaving both legs off above the knees. Aghast at the ease that the blade struck off the limbs, Ralenn scrambled back away from the sudden spill of gore. The crippled Grishkah dropped his sword as he fell to the ground, howling and thrashing wildly.

The red one was up again—he picked up the sword of his fallen comrade and attacked. Heart racing, Ralenn was back on his feet in time to instinctively block a slash to his shoulder and returned a thrust to the beast's heart, a move he had practiced a thousand times with Kaileth. The red-furred Grishkah only had a leather vest on, and so the blade of Ralenn's sword ended the creature's life with ease, gasping once before limply sliding to the ground. Ralenn forced his breaths to slow as he now turned to the tan Grishkah, who was writhing on the muddy ground. A stroke to the neck ended its suffering. Ralenn wiped his blade clean with the fur of his slain foe and sheathed his sword. He stood for a few moments. Watching for more foes but mostly working to catch his breath. He revisited the fight in his mind and was embarrassed at how sloppy it had been. Nothing like the perfect lethal motions of Kaileth in the sphinx vision.

Lucky once more, he thought to himself. *Brek loves a lucky fool, I guess.*

Reaching around to his back he pulled the Grishkah sword from the wooden base of his quiver where it had stuck when the beast had hit him. He looked at the sword and laughed a little. Kaileth would have had more than a few things to say about such a mistake.

"That was close," he muttered to himself. "I wonder if every battle is like this, just one slip away from Paldrii's grasp,"

Running into Grishkii this high on the mountain troubled him. He knew Kaileth had always thought the wolf creatures that had attacked when Epri was lost had been Grishkii. The people in the village didn't agree, but Kaileth was sure. If these monsters were now returned in numbers large enough to both sack the temple and take captives, then Allinth likely had suffered the same. With an increasing sense of dread Ralenn took up his bow, recovered his arrow, and ran down the road to his home of Allinth.

Ralenn's determined pace soon saw him the last skain from the greenhouses to the final slope down into the village. The scent of smoke was thick in the air. He stopped as the village came into view and dropped to the ground, seeking the cover of a shady aspen grove.

Frothvar's breath, it's too late. His pace faltered, and he felt his heart jump into his throat. There before him was the village he knew as his home, where the people he knew and loved dwelled. The once thriving community was now a scene of death and sorrow just as the temple above. Shops and homes were now hollowed by fire, burned and gashed bodies littered the streets. Ralenn could all but see the hand of death that had just crushed the life out of Allinth hanging in the smoky air above the village.

He carefully watched the village and mountainside for some time, looking for life, movement, or any sign that more Grishkii were still there, nothing. At last, Ralenn got up and ran down the hill and into the street. At every turn, signs of slaughter and death met his eyes. Most of the houses and shops were looted and burned. Everyone he saw was mangled and clearly dead. It was just as the sphinx had shown him. But Kaileth, where was he?

Ralenn felt numb now as he hurried down the street toward his home. His running feet on the muddy street was the only sound to be heard, that and the pounding of his own heart. Finally, he stumbled upon the sight the ice sphinx had shown him, and it felt as though his heart would burst in panic. There, upon the wet earth of the street, lay the motionless body of Kaileth. His form was surrounded by his slain foe with his back toward Ralenn, and atop his arrow-pierced figure stood Mirris, a crossbow quarrel lodged in her shoulder, guarding her fallen master.

"Kaileth!" Ralenn cried as he dashed to him. He choked back his fear and knelt to look at the two cruel arrow shafts sticking out of Kaileth's back.

"I am too late," Ralenn whispered as he placed his hand on Kaileth's shoulder. He had been too slow. How many hours were spent at the temple? Ralenn bowed his head, feeling hopelessly defeated. At the edges of his mind a crippling anguish threatened to swallow him whole. He tried to push it back.

Can't panic. Have to come up with a plan. What to do? What would Kail do? Aashahl above and below! Why is this happening?

Suddenly, and to Ralenn's great astonishment, he felt Kaileth's shoulder rise and fall with a long, shallow breath.

"He's alive!" Ralenn nearly sobbed in relief. Mirris was still looking at Kaileth, worry etched into her eyes. The bird's expression looked so human sometimes, and at this moment Ralenn was certain she felt the same.

"Mirris, can you fly?" Ralenn asked. He didn't bother trying to put the words into her ancient tongue, there wasn't time. Mirris said nothing, nor did she look away from Kaileth.

"Mirris, please, if you can fly, you must find Lirah and speed her here. She might be able to help Kaileth." Mirris' head darted toward Ralenn, and she fixed him with her eyes. Ralenn could see the emotion in them—fear, raging sorrow, even a little anger, he thought. He had never seen so much expression from her, and it startled him.

"Mirris," His voice cracked a little and he cleared his throat. "Mirris, he is not dead, Lirah can save him. She has healing supplies." Mirris looked back at Kaileth, then again at Ralenn, her eyes softer now. She stretched the damaged wing. The quarrel looked to be lodged deep, but not fatally so. She nodded to him once and took off flying toward the temple.

Ralenn watched her go, then, taking Kaileth under his arms, he picked him up and started to carry him toward their home.

***

Lirah was sitting on the black rock that Ralenn had sat upon the day before when life was so happy and simple. She had gathered a large pack of healing supplies, along with some of her personal items from her room—what was left of her room, that was. The fire had caused much of the temple to collapse as the wooden timbers that supported some of the stonework burned away.

"Just a day ago, only one day," she said again to herself, remembering the last time she had spoken to Gaileng. There was so much she would have said, so much she would have done had she known that was the last time she would see him alive.

But he is gone, and this is real, and there is nothing I can do to change any of that.

Without meaning to Lirah's thoughts drifted back to the past. Her life had been a carefree one. The priests were truly kind to her, and she enjoyed learning from them, even if she didn't take well to their more reverent practices. The others too, the acolytes, the disciples, everyone truly treated her well.

"And put up with my antics," she said aloud.

She could not remember her real parents, but Gaileng had loved her as much as any father would have, she was sure. This thought almost brought a fresh wave of tears from her. She steadied herself, placing a hand on Riidak's shoulder.

"Crying won't change anything, will it, Riidak?" She looked into the great hound's deep brown eyes and thought they looked as sad as she felt. She sat up. "Come here, Riidak, I need some comforting and it looks like you could use some too."

The four-legged guardian trotted over closer and sat in front of the black rock. Lirah leaned over and wrapped her arms around Riidak's thick warm neck.

"I'm glad Ralenn left you here. But I think our rest is over, we better catch up to him and see what happened in Allinth." She released the dog from her embrace and breathed deeply. Lirah hesitated to leave, though she was not sure why. A sinking feeling overcame her, and she knew that whatever her life had been before it would never be that simple and safe again. She was afraid of what was to come in the life ahead of her.

Ralenn needs you. The thought did not seem entirely her own, but she pondered it.

"Ralenn. There is no one else I'd rather face such uncertainty with than him..." She looked down and considered the hound's expression.

"Can I tell you a secret, Riidak?" A hint of her usual cheer started to creep back into her voice.

"I really care for Ralenn, more than he knows, I think." He had been her best friend ever since she could remember. But for a while now she would often catch herself wishing it was more than just a friendship.

"The problem is, I don't know if he feels the same. He can be so strange sometimes." Riidak only stared back at her with now smiling eyes. "Fine, be that way, but I know you care about him too, you silly dog."

Riidak's head turned suddenly, startling Lirah.

"What is it?"

The dog walked into the road and looked up, so Lirah also gazed skyward. The afternoon sky was a sea of perfect blue. Lirah searched the sky until she thought she could see a speck slowly circling. Moment by moment, it came closer to the ground until Lirah realized it was a bird. Mirris! The falcon slowly glided down onto the road and gently landed close to the path to the temple.

Lirah rushed to meet Mirris but came to a sudden stop when she saw the shaft of a crossbow quarrel running through the beautiful falcon's shoulder.

"Oh, Mirris, what happened? Where is Kaileth, and Ralenn?"

"Ralenn és amb Kaileth. Kaileth necechita la tevah ajuda."

Lirah's jaw dropped; she never actually expected the bird to answer her question!

"You can talk! But I...I'm sorry, I don't understand, Mirris." Lirah felt a little silly being less able to communicate than a falcon. How had she never known Mirris could speak? She knew Kaileth and Ralenn could give her detailed commands, but being able to answer in turn? She hadn't expected that at all. A part of Lirah acknowledged that for some time to come she should expect to face many things she had never supposed possible before.

"Well, I may not be bright enough to speak with you, but if you will come here, I can mend your wing."

Mirris' eyes flashed at Lirah, and she bobbed over to her. Lirah pulled the quarrel from Mirris' shoulder and, taking an herbal salve and some sulf-char from her pack, she applied it to the wound. The large falcon made no sound, but only watched Lirah work. A verbal incantation finished Lirah's healing efforts.

"There, Mirris. By tomorrow that should be mended up quite nicely." Mirris looked pleased by Lirah's work and spoke something to Riidak, who had come over to observe the repairs to his companion.

All Lirah could think about now was Ralenn. What would he find in the village? Riidak barked and the sound shook Lirah from her thoughts. He was on the road running, and he looked back as if he wanted Lirah to follow. She put on her cloak, gathered up her equipment, and ran after him. Mirris flew up and lit on his shoulders as the three of them started down the forest-lined trail toward Allinth.

* * *

Not all the buildings in Allinth had burned, and by the grace of the Aashahl, Kaileth's shop and their home were among those spared. Ralenn found Kaileth to be a heavy load, much heavier than he should have been, and his going was slow. He was unsure if it was his exhaustion or if Allitorii were heavier than humans of an equivalent size.

He passed through the smashed-in door to the shop, finding it in disarray. Signs of close and vicious fighting had been cut and hacked into the interior of the smithy. Ralenn made his way through the debris strung about the floor to the kitchen door and their home beyond. Ax marks on the door to the rest of the house confirmed Ralenn's suspicions. Kaileth must have locked up the house and rushed to fight in the street. The strong steel and wood door was covered with deep blade marks, but the door had held.

"Great," Ralenn said, as he looked at the locked door. "Now I will have to find the key." Ralenn put Kaileth down near the wall and started his search. The floor of the shop was a mess. Tools, charcoal, broken benches, and splinters of wood were everywhere.

Alpa, guide me, he prayed as he kept searching, then he had a thought.

Kaileth probably put it back into his pocket! Kaileth's pocket was soaked with blood, and Ralenn could not help but wince as he slid his hand inside. He felt the key and pulled it out quickly. Ralenn unlocked the door and pulled to open it, but it did not move. He examined the door closer. The hinges had been mangled by a weapon. Breathing deeply to stamp down his frustration and fear, he quickly found an unfinished plate-spring for a wagon and pried the door open.

Ralenn again picked Kaileth up and carried him up the steps and into the kitchen. The room looked much as it had the day before. It was strange to think how much the world around it had changed. Ralenn took Kaileth to his room and laid him in the bed on his side. This room was oddly in slight disarray— cloak stand overturned, the bed was not made, and some of Epri's things were on the floor.

That's strange; he always makes his bed...

Ralenn put Epri's mirror back on the shelves and took a closer look at Kaileth's wounds. He didn't dare pull the arrows out for fear of doing more damage with his inexperienced hands. Blood was still oozing out slowly from around the arrow shafts and running down Kaileth's back onto the linen of the bed. The bleeding was slow, but Ralenn knew it had to be stopped. He took his knife and cut some cloth from the curtains, then wrapped the strips of cloth around the arrow shafts and pressed it into the wounds, which seemed to stop most of the bleeding. Kaileth was still breathing in long slow breaths, with terrifyingly long pauses between. Each breath might be his last, Ralenn knew. But he was not sure what else to do, and he sat down tensely in a chair near the bed.

Suddenly overwhelmed with fatigue and exhaustion, a haze of weariness fell upon him, and he spoke softly to himself. "I hope Lirah hurries."

Weariness and emotion began to blur his senses. Ralenn still felt slightly numb, but at the same time he felt anger, fear, and anguish. How was he supposed to make sense of all this death? How did anyone make sense of such tragedy? Ralenn thought about when Epri was lost, and her father killed. It was a little less than four years, but her loss had profoundly changed him from boy to man. He had never been the same. He knew Kaileth still grieved for her. Ralenn did too, though his was the pain of losing the closest thing to a mother he had ever known.

Ralenn believed she would be found for the first year. He looked for her face in every shadow and thicket when he and Lirah would explore the forests. His dreams were haunted by her, calling to him. She seemed so real in them. How could she be dead? Yet she was—and with the passing years, he had learned to live with the awful truth of life without Epri. It was easier to lose himself in the forge and the drills, to bury his mind in work and repetition. Easier still to wander the forests than to face the grief that waited, patient and unyielding, at the edges of his thoughts.

Trying to push aside the memories of losing Epri, Ralenn wearily looked through a small round window. The light from the setting sun had begun to flow into the room. The blaze of orange turned the skiffs of cloud into golden ribbons woven across the sky, drifting to rest on the great stone walls of the mountainside. It looked so calm, so peaceful, as if there was nothing wrong in the world. He wondered how many unnamed and unknown villages had been burned and lost all while the larger world carried on as though nothing was amiss. Even great cities like Ell'Anoth, ravaged with only the orphans and broken-hearted left to remember before. Maybe the Aashahl only cared for the suffering and death of the innocent? The world surely could be rife with it.

Many care and watch over the worthy. Aashahl ever surround.

This thought, an answer Epri had given him on many occasions as a questioning boy, broke into the spiral of his dark thoughts and he found himself drifting into a soft veil of exhaustion.

Ralenn's gaze stayed fixed upon the sky, and he watched the first evening stars appear. His thoughts grew as distant as the stars that he looked upon. His mind was a ship tossed with the waves of a tempest, battered and driven by the winds of all that had happened. Without meaning to, his eyes started to close, and he drifted into a deep sleep.

The opening door swung into a low table and the noise of it stirred Ralenn from his sleep. His eyes shot open, and he grabbed for his sword.

"Ralenn, wait, it's me," Lirah reassured him, seeing his move to arms.

Ralenn took a deep breath and released his sword. "I'm so glad Mirris found you," he said tiredly. He still felt so totally depleted that his eyes struggled to stay open and focus on Lirah. On top of this his leg had started to throb where the sphinx had wounded him.

Lirah folded her arms and furrowed her brow. "Why didn't you answer me, Ralenn?" she asked with concern. "I thought you might have gone off and got mauled by a thryn'eke or something. I've been searching and calling you for ages!"

"I'm sorry, I guess I dozed off. I was worried that Mirris didn't make it with that quarrel in her wing." Lirah had now moved into the center of the room, between the bed and Ralenn's chair.

"She did, and now I'm here, but you need help. Paldrii's shadow! You've lost so much blood—again!"

Ralenn shook his head and looked over to the bed. Lirah followed his gaze to the form of a wounded man, laying still in the dim light. Ralenn motioned faintly toward him.

"I don't think he will live much longer, Lirah." His voice wavered, and she swiftly moved to Kaileth's side.

"Then I'll do my best to prove you wrong," she said, putting on her best brave face and squaring her shoulders. "Go and get clean water, fresh bandages, and some light."

"Right, will a candle work?" he asked.

"If it's bright, but a lantern would be better. Now hurry," she replied.

Ralenn jumped to his feet and headed out of the room. Limping more than a little.

"Hurry!" Lirah called after him. She then turned her full attention to Kaileth. She surveyed his wounds and knew that Ralenn's worry was not misplaced. It would take all her skill and a good share of luck to save him.

"Dannitar, give me the strength, Patient Father, help me to use it." She paused and squeezed the edge of Kaileth's blood-soaked clothes into a small bronze chalice she produced from her healer's bag. Filling it with Kaileth's blood she furrowed her brow and continued her supplications.

"*Felairtarh, Mistress of Slaughter and Death. You have drunk deeply this day. Your ewers are filled with the blood of the slain. Take this last cup and pass this one by.*" She clenched her eyes tightly shut and focused her thoughts on these last words, certain that of all the aashahl she needed to placate at that moment Felairtarh was the first. The cup in her hands grew warm, then hot and she struggled to not drop it. A long moment passed, and she couldn't keep from letting a whimper of pain slip her tightly pressed lips. Then it was done, the chalice cold and inert in her hands, and to her welcome surprise, empty of Kaileth's blood. Lirah had tried this supplication with animals before, carefully supervised by the priests at the temple, but never on a person nor in such a dire need.

Wish I had the chalice with me after Ralenn let the sphinx maul him; would have made that easier.

The greater powers now seemingly on her side, it was up to her to put everything else she had been taught into practice once again. Lirah let out an anxious breath and set to work, first carefully snapping off the shafts of the arrows a few inches from where they entered Kaileth's back and shoulder.

When Gaileng first brought Lirah to the temple, he found she had a natural ability of empathy, the most important trait for healers of Anthos, or any of the Aashahl. Because of this, Gaileng and the other priests had spent much of their time instructing Lirah in the arcane art of empathic healing, which would draw on the aid of arcane magics and the blessings of the Aashahl. It was to this discipline that she now turned to in order to save Kaileth.

Before finding Ralenn on the mountain, she had not had much occasion to put her knowledge to practical use in dire situations. But after a long day of feeling helpless with no way to undo the damage, she now felt empowered.

Here is something I can do! I can save Kaileth. No one else dies today!

She removed the blood-soaked bandages from his strong and surprisingly young-looking back. Kaileth's age was indeed a mystery. He was at least twice as old as Lirah, but he did not appear that much older than Ralenn, maybe two or three years at most. He did *seem* older though. Kaileth had an air about him of one with great wisdom and experience in life.

Lirah closed her eyes and held her hand over the arrow in Kaileth's shoulder. With eyes closed she could focus on her inner awareness until she noticed a tingling sensation coming from inside her. She focused on this as she had been taught and started to feel the sensation grow in her mind. She focused harder and started to recite the words of a prayer of power in her mind.

Anthos ja aashahl annah mulle tugevust tagasi nõuda selles elus.

The prayer was meant to focus the mind and secure the blessings of the Aashahl in the healing efforts. Lirah knew that there were healers who did not recite, but they were only the most powerful. This was only the third time Lirah had even tried to sense another's wounds.

Without hesitating, there was no time to second-guess herself, Lirah pushed her perception and feeling out of the bounds of her physical form and into Kaileth. A pulsing sapphire-colored tongue of flame formed in the palm of her hand and entered the wound in Kaileth's shoulder. He twitched as the energy penetrated his wound, and muttered something out of his fevered daze.

Lirah's face twisted in pain. She could feel the damage from the arrow as if it were her own, plus the increased acuity of a trained empathic mind made it all the sharper. Her breathing grew fast and labored. She moved her hand to the second wound and began chanting out loud, trying to keep her mind focused and attuned to Kaileth. She vaguely registered Ralenn reentering the room with the supplies he was told to find, but she ignored him. The shock of Kaileth's pain threatened to throw her out of the thaumaturgy, and it took all her mental strength to continue.

Lirah finished the incantation and turned to Ralenn as he stepped the rest of the way into the room. She felt shaky but could not help but feel thrilled by her success as well.

"This was the best that I could find, will it work?" Ralenn held out the curtains from his room, a large flask of spring water, and a crystal lantern.

She smiled wearily at him. "Yes, these will do fine." Lirah took the flask and lantern and set them down next to the bed. "Ralenn, cut that cloth up into strips as thick as your hand and thrice as wide as your chest. Try to keep them from getting frayed at the edges if you can."

"Alright." Ralenn drew his dagger and started about his assigned task, while Lirah considered her next option. She would have to heal the wounds from the inside out, and there was only one way to do that. First the arrows had to come out.

I sure hope this works the way the books claim. Lirah couldn't tell if it was a prayer or just doubt-ridden thoughts clouding her mind.

The sun was fully down for the night, and the shadows grew long inside the makeshift infirmary, cast wide by the light of the lantern. Ralenn lit some candles, and Lirah took the lantern and hung it on a hook in the wall over the bed. She then knelt by the bed and took hold of an arrow. She pulled gently at first, slowly increasing her effort. The arrow held firm. She then paced the room a few times and took a deep breath.

"Brek's piss." It was anger, not defeat, in Lirah's voice. "The arrows are stuck in the bone, and I can't pull them out."

"What are we going to do, then?" Ralenn had stopped his drape shredding.

"I can't get them out, but I'm hoping you can." Lirah gestured for Ralenn to approach.

"I don't know, Lirah, I'm no healer."

She could hear the apprehension in his voice, but there wasn't time to be sympathetic to his worries. "Well, I'm not strong enough to get them out cleanly, so you will have to do it. It's not complicated, just pull them straight out in one clean motion." She pushed Ralenn in front of her and toward Kaileth.

"I'll do my best. Is there any trick to it, or words I should say?" he asked timidly.

Lirah gave a little giggle, relaxing her shoulders a bit.

"No, but praying won't hurt. Just quickly jerk them straight out, alright?"

"Alright." Ralenn knelt by the bed and took hold of the end of the arrow in Kaileth's back. "Dannitar, guide my hand," he whispered. Then with a short powerful pull, he jerked the bloody barb from the wound.

Fresh blood ran from the gaping hole in Kaileth's back as Ralenn set the arrow shaft down and grabbed the next arrow in Kaileth's left shoulder. The light from the candles and lantern danced upon the blood-drenched skin, and Lirah noticed several scars on Kaileth's back and shoulder. Another quick yank saw the second dart free. Ralenn sat wide-eyed, looking at the wounds for a moment till Lirah placed her hand upon his shoulder. She could see him pale slightly.

"Wow, Ralenn, you have some skill. Have you considered working as a tooth leech?"

"What? No, not really."

Through a muffled chuckle Lirah went on, "With a pull like that you could pop any tooth out." Her smile grew larger. If she could keep smiling, she could get through this. She hoped her uncertainty and nervousness was not as easy to see as she felt it was.

I can do this...I can...I must, she thought, trying to keep calm and confident. When she had healed Ralenn's wounds she had connected to something, something powerful. His wound healed much better than a potion and a little sulf-char should have done. There was magic in that healing, and Lirah hoped she could call on that power again for Kaileth.

"Oh, thanks, Lirah," he teased, smiling back at her. A little of the sparkle returning to his dark eyes.

"I thought that you'd appreciate that," Lirah said, stomach fluttering at his gaze. Looking away she took her bag from her shoulder and kneeled by Ralenn's side near the bed. Breathing slowly to steady herself, she reached into the bag and took out several vials of enchanted herbs, a yellow potion, and a pouch of sulf-char.

"Lirah, did you notice the scar on Kaileth's shoulder?" he asked.

"Yes, I sensed that it was from the first time he was struck by an arrow," she said, still going through the contents of her bag.

"The first time? That must have happened before I was born then, because I don't remember Kaileth ever getting shot."

"Neither do I." Lirah opened a triangular tin filled with a thick, bright red fluid, Paldrii's Veil, then poured a small drop into each wound. Upon contact with the flesh, it sent sparks into the air.

Ralenn stepped forward, apparently worried at the dark red smoke, followed by crimson darts of flame coming out of the deep wounds in Kaileth's back. She guessed that he was a bit taken aback. He had never asked much about her healing skills, and she had never really brought it up.

"It is supposed to do that," she reassured him as the flames grew. They became about a hand's length long, and a distinct and unusual smell began to fill the room. Kaileth groaned and Lirah closed her eyes as she began to speak the lyrical words of another spell, until her hands started to glow with a pale blue light. It was working, the magic was there.

This is going to work, just have to keep the connection.

She focused on the energy she felt flowing from herself and accumulating in her hands. Lirah took a deep breath, then smothered the red spouts of fire with her glowing hands. A plume of purple smoke surged out from around her hands, and she felt herself, her very core, connect with Kaileth's wounds. The pain was more than anything she had expected; her breath caught, and everything went black.

Ralenn darted to Lirah as she nearly collapsed, and held her shoulders steady. Her entire frame was quaking as though she were in terrible pain. Sweat was dripping from her face, her eyes clenched tightly shut, her mouth moved as if speaking but no sound could be heard. Ralenn didn't know what to do, but he dared not speak for fear of interrupting the enchantment. Lirah was breathing fast and sharply, still shaking terribly. He looked down upon her back and could see small spots of blood starting to seep through her clothing over her back and shoulder.

The next few moments seemed longer than a lifetime to Ralenn as he held her. Fear for her life began to build within him, and he was about to pull her from Kaileth when Lirah jerked both her hands from Kaileth's wounds. She was still breathing heavy, but Ralenn could feel her body relax.

"Lirah, are you hurt? There...there is blood on your back." He didn't try to hide his worry. For several more moments she did not respond. Then, blinking hard, she turned her head to him and placed her hand upon his. Ralenn felt his heart jump. She smiled gently but she looked exhausted, dazed even.

"I'm alright, don't worry. I'm fine, just very tired." She paused to catch her breath. "Well, more like very drained." Ralenn had never heard her voice sound like this. It was a slow soft wisp between staggering breaths.

"But you're bleeding, Lirah."

She squeezed his hand as he helped her to stand.

"Yes, there would have been some, but it has stopped now and there are no wounds." She turned to face him. "You can feel for yourself if you like." Lirah's normal tone seemed to be returning to her, however, a cloak of weariness still clung to her. Lirah took Ralenn's hand and put it to the back of her neck, pushing it down under the top of her frock. He moved his hand over to the top of her shoulder and could feel no wound, just warm smooth skin. He felt his face flush a little and hoped it was too dark for her to notice.

"See, not hurt at all." She pulled his hand back out and pointed to Kaileth, "And look at Kaileth's wounds." She sounded pleased.

They both turned and observed Kaileth. At first, he thought it a trick of the light in the room, for there were no longer any wounds to be seen, only new scars that looked much like the old one upon Kaileth's shoulder. He was healed, and Ralenn felt such a relief that he almost shouted out loud in excitement.

"Lirah, this is amazing." He stretched forth his hand and felt the scars where the arrow shafts had been only moments ago. They were hard, and still hot from the spell, but definitely new flesh, no wound at all remained.

"Now all we can do is wait and pray." Lirah was putting her healing aids back into her bag.

Ralenn sat down on the edge of the bed and put his hand on Kaileth's side. Kaileth's breathing was now deep and easy. *He is going to be alright, we all are,* he thought.

Ralenn sighed deeply. Kaileth always knew what to do, and now more than ever Ralenn craved his guidance. Kaileth was a father to him, but he had always been different than the other fathers in Allinth. Kaileth was kind, always swift to guide and instruct, and slow to anger. More than slow. Ralenn could not think of a single time when Kaileth had lost his temper, or even raised his voice outside of battle drills. He loved Ralenn, of this there was no doubt, yet most in town saw Kaileth as more of a mentoring instructor rather than a father much of the time, always placing Ralenn's training and guidance as his first priority. Regardless of what others thought, Ralenn knew that Kaileth would always be there for him, and that he would always know what to do in the face of adversity. Everything that had happened today had proved that Kaileth was wise to train Ralenn so diligently and for so long. Ralenn had survived because of Kaileth's endless patience, because of his limitless desire to see Ralenn improve and learn. Ralenn was alive because of the way Kaileth showed his love for him. The love of a father, a guardian, and a warrior. Ralenn knew that once Kaileth was well he would deal with this crisis with his usual calm manner, and that they all would be alright.

He stood and returned to his place in his chair, sighing again in relief to see Kaileth whole again.

"Wait," he said, as he looked at the pile of bandages he had made, that now sat on the arm of his chair. "If Kaileth is well now, then what were the bandages and water for?"

Lirah turned a smiling face to him and answered, "They were mostly to keep you busy. But who knows, we might need them later if you two keep getting cut up like this." Lirah finished putting her potions away and turned to fully face Ralenn.

"And the water?" he asked with a raised eyebrow.

"You aren't going to leave all that blood on Kaileth, are you?" she grinned as she spoke.

"No, I suppose not," Ralenn said.

Lirah now tried to stand, but her legs faltered and Ralenn jumped to his feet to catch her. He barely made it in time before she fell.

"Lirah, what's wrong, are you alright?" He could hear an almost childish tone of panic in his voice, and he quickly tried to hide it with a nervous cough.

Lirah's voice was calm and smooth as she answered, "I will be. I'm just tired now. You see, to give that much life back to someone, not all of it can be made by the arcane or from potions, some must be transferred from the healer. I will be fine. I just need to rest."

"Are you sure? You look pale." He still felt a little panicked as he held her. It was too much to think of nearly losing Kaileth and then Lirah too.

Lirah gently moved his arms away but held his hands in hers as she spoke.

"I will be just fine, Ralenn, trust me. I just need some rest, alright?"

"Alright, if you say so. You can sleep in my room tonight."

Smiling, Lirah took a feeble step and again stumbled. Catching her in both arms, Ralenn easily picked her up and took her to his room, setting her on the soft blankets of his own bed. Surprisingly, she didn't object, and he could feel her relax in his arms.

The stars danced in the sky as the moon threw its light upon the still valley floor. Outside, the minstrels of the night were playing loud and clear—the cricket, the owl, and many others filled the air with Nique'shay's comforting lullaby. Lirah leaned her head back onto the soft pillow and looked up into Ralenn's dark eyes.

"Will it be safe to stay here, Ralenn?" she asked softly.

Ralenn smiled and gently touched her shoulder as he spoke. "I will make sure of it. Get some rest, Lirah, and I will see you in the morning." Ralenn walked to the door of his room but stopped and looked back at her. "Thank you, Lirah. You saved him. You saved us both."

The starlight spilled into the room and danced in her large smiling eyes as she looked back at him. Ralenn again felt his face warm with a blush. Had he always felt like this when she looked at him? He was sure that it was new, and he wondered what had changed.

"You're welcome, Ralenn. I've always been driven to heal. It's a deep part of me, I guess." She grinned contentedly at him and then closed her eyes, taking a deep breath. Her eyes opened once more.

"Ralenn..." she whispered. She hesitated and Ralenn thought he saw a slight change in her content expression. "Will you leave the door open?"

"Sure, just call if you need me." He slowly started out of the room and Lirah closed her eyes again and relaxed into the soft bed.

"I will, I always will," she said even softer.

Ralenn returned to Kaileth's room and cleaned the last of the blood and dirt from him before placing a wool blanket on him. He was breathing easy now, and it looked as though he were simply asleep.

Ralenn suddenly remembered Riidak and Mirris. He left the house and walked outside to where Riidak sat with his pack and armor still on. Mirris was on top of the sign that hung over the door, watching over the house of her master. Ralenn went over to Riidak and started to take off the pack.

"I'm sorry, my friend, I didn't realize you still had this load on you." He quickly removed the pack and armor and set it inside the shop.

"There, that's better, isn't it?" Riidak stood and wagged his short tail a little faster.

"Mirris, let me take your armor off." Ralenn looked to the falcon, but she shook her head and remained fixed in place, watching the surround. He knew better than to try to force anything on her. She was particular and only showed true affection with Kaileth.

Ralenn moved the pack deeper inside the shop, then went over and shut the door into the house where Kaileth and Lirah now slept. Walking back outside he looked up at the starry night sky. The terror of the day began to crash into him like waves, and his view of the heavens became blurred with a few tears.

"Why? What did Allinth do to offend you? What did I do?" Ralenn's questioning prayer, gently whispered, rose into the still of the night. He heard no answer.

At least Lirah and Kaileth were with him. He thought of how glad he was that Lirah was with him. He had so many happy memories of the two of them out in the woods upon imagined childhood adventures. These thoughts filled him with warmth, though there was nothing pleasant or heartwarming about this real adventure, nor the dark and uncertain future that morning would surely bring. Ralenn spoke to his feathered and furred companions, and, in their own tongue, asked them to stand watch, each in turn, and to wake him if anything moved. They understood, and Mirris, remaining on Kaileth's shop sign, started the watch. Ralenn again looked to the stars.

"Tomorrow will be better," he said. "Somehow, it will be better." With full confidence that Mirris and Riidak would keep them safe, Ralenn strode back into the scattered shop and made such a bed as he could in front of the door to the kitchen and slowly drifted into a deep sleep.

6

The Aya Dao'Tai

For thus is it written; they who seek the Tears for aught but the will of Anthos hasten thence to their own destruction. Many are they who take up the call of the Tears and lead away the covetous and the fool unto destruction in the realms of the ancient and bitterest of wars.
Essays of the Divine

The iron-clad door to the upper audience chamber slowly swung open, the great hinges groaning in complaint. Through the open stone doorway walked a proud-looking gray and black furred Grishkah. His especially fierce appearance and his gold and jade encrusted armor would have made him stand out in a pack of his fellows. He was now, however, alone.

The pads of his feet made little sound as they fell upon the floor, carrying him into the large rectangular room flanked with spectacular bookshelves. Two doors were set within these shelves, one in the middle of each wall, facing the other. A large stained-glass window, depicting a red-crested bird of prey rising out of the setting sun, was set in the wall farthest from where the Grishkah had entered the room. The Grishkah stopped and gave a low bow to a figure seated at the far end of a long black table lined by tall chairs.

The table was in the middle of the grand chamber and Rovik's broad figure was starkly silhouetted by brilliant colored light spilling through the window behind him. He sat in one of the large chairs with folded arms, carefully schooling his expression in a manner that he knew made him look wise and stern. He kept his appearance neat, his silver hair and thick mustache neatly trimmed. The features of his face were noble—square-cut jaw, broad chin, sharp well-proportioned nose, and a hard lined brow with just enough creases from time to speak of experience. Yet, not so many as to mistake him for an elder past his fighting days. Decades of campaigning had left his skin the color of tanned saddle leather and his hazel eyes a touch lighter than they were when first he took up the sword for his city. In his years as chancellor to the Aya Dao'Tai, he had found he could gain the trust of many thanks to his generally kind and understanding appearance.

"Hail Kiidarash, of the Fyskk, greatest of all the Grishkii" Rovik called out cordially, standing and taking a few steps over to where Kiidarash stood. The light revealed his garb to consist of lavishly embroidered olive-green robes, held at the waist by a wide leather belt from which an elegant sword hung.

"How did you fare in your task, Chieftain?" he asked as he walked over and sat on the corner of the table in a casual fashion, trying to put his guest at ease.

Kiidarash slowly answered in a low, snarling voice.

"Thhrra villrrhgge irss destrrohed, Shancellohrr Rrovich, anderr peeple writhh irrt."

Rovik smiled as he spoke again, "That is good, I hope you did not lose too many of your warriors."

"Thhosse whho feerll dirrd sso irrn glorriouss barhttle." Pride was evident in Kiidarash's voice as he spoke of his fallen comrades.

"What of the fugitive? The young man, was he killed or taken?" Rovik probed. This was the real reason he had hired these creatures, and he had to hide his impatience as Kiidarash took a moment to make his answer.

"Thhosse whho werrer not killrred arre being brrougght herrer. Ar-rgnd I harrve lefft warrriorrss ta ennssurrhe tat norr one esscaptt by hrriding."

Rovik smiled again in relief, came to his feet, and walked over to a door set in the center of the bookshelves to the left, motioning for Kiidarash to follow him. The Grishkah chieftain did so, and they both passed into the next room. Once both man and beast were in the room, Rovik pointed to several wooden chests and a long crate.

"I am glad that our collaboration has been so productive. I hope that this marks a future of increased cooperation between our two great peoples." He knew these Grishkii liked being referred to as a people rather than the usual derogatory terms most humans applied to their kind.

"As you can see," Rovik kicked the lid of a chest open to reveal its contents of gold and jewels, "the Aya Dao'Tai rewards her friends gen-erously."

Kiidarash gave a toothy smile and knelt next to the open chest, tak-ing a handful of gem-encrusted bracelets, greedily looking them over. "Yerrss, tiss I carrn see!"

Rovik took an elaborately decorated long sword from the crate and handed it to the chieftain. "She is particularly pleased by your devo-tion to her and your commanding leadership."

Kiidarash took the blade and held it aloft, letting the sunlight from the windows dance upon the steel. Rovik was sure it was the finest weapon his hands had ever held. Far better than the crude weapons the Grishkii fashioned themselves. At length, he again found his tongue and spoke.

"I shrrall not dissplesse herr, my lohrrd. We will grr corrntinue to serrve thhe Subjurrgett wirrth devorrhshnn."

"See that you do," said Rovik.

Kiidarash placed his arms across his chest, as was the tradition of his kind when making an oath. "Shancellohrr Rrovich. Mhy warrriorrss shrrall not rhrest till the Ayarr Dao'Tai'ss prrey irss ouhrrs orr errdead. Ssor swearrr I."

Rovik smiled and clapped his hands, and several men carrying litters entered the room through one of two curtained doors. "Return if the situation changes. These men will take your tribute to your caravan. I must attend to other matters now."

The men started to load the treasure onto their litters and leave the room. "Verry werrll Shancellohrr, I marrke my learrve terrn."

"Till next we meet, Chieftain, friend of the Aya Dao'Tai and ally to Subjugate."

Kiidarash bowed, then turned away from Rovik and left through the same door he used to enter the room, signaling for the treasure bearers to follow.

Rovik exhaled loudly in relief; he was glad that was over. Of the few good things he could say about the Grishkii, having a pleasing odor was not one of them. As the last load of gold left the room, a soft, elegant voice came from the curtain-covered doorway behind him.

"Paying tribute are we, Chancellor? I was under the impression we were hiring simple-minded creatures to do our necessary but messy tasks for us."

He heard the curtains part and turned to face the Aya Dao'Tai. She was a tall woman, taller than most men, dressed in a simple flowing white gown. Her skin was a very dark bronze, and a large ruby hung from a silver chain about her delicate lissome neck. Straight steely-black hair came to the tops of her shoulders, held in place with a simple circled of silver set with a rare sun fire opal.

Her face was all soft lines and delicate grace, yet her gaze devoured like a predator's, the contrast more striking for its undeniable allure.. The sclera of her wide, deep-set almond shaped eyes was a shade of red so dark only direct sunlight showed it not to be black, contrasting the luminous crimson of her over-large irises. She was beauty made dangerous, sensuality forged into power; the stillness about her seemed to thrum, as though even light and shadow awaited her command.

Rovik bowed lower than was comfortable, and the two of them returned to the larger room.

Rovik was the governor of the Anoth province, and he had served as the Aya Dao'Tai's chancellor ever since the capital of Ell'Anoth fell. He oversaw the mundane governance and logistics of much of the Dao'Tai Subjugate, while military matters and matters of security fell to the Dao'Tai generals. It was unusual for Rovik to deal in matters like this, but the Dao'Tai refused to directly deal with the Grishkii. Rovik knew he was kept out of much of the inner workings of the Subjugate, but his current position still made him an important pillar that legitimized the Aya Dao'Tai's reign to the people of Anoth. Besides, it wouldn't be long before that changed, he had long had his own plans in motion to secure a more influential position. A position that would gain him a more comprehensive view of the Subjugate's wider machinations.

He collected his thoughts as they walked, and once he stood near the end of the long table again, he spoke.

"Aya Dao'Tai Afyreen, they are indeed your servants. However, the Grishkii are an enormously proud race, and to make them seem like the controlling entity in our dealings will ensure their loyalty and continued assistance."

She did not acknowledge his logic as she gracefully strolled over to the large arched window, reached out a long-fingered hand, and pressed it to the cold glass.

"I never could bring myself to replace this window, there is something about it. It is simply too beautiful to destroy."

She quickly turned, causing an unusually large shadow to shift across the room. Rovik was used to seeing this and had trained himself to not react. He attributed it to her arcane powers, but he wasn't sure what caused it. She had always had an uneasy air about her, and her presence felt larger than it should have. He had tried to discreetly find out what magic could cause such a discomfiting phenomenon but never found any answers. She continued to speak, and he forced himself to listen.

"Don't you agree?"

"I do. It is exceptionally beautiful, and it serves you well," he said thoughtfully. She looked amused by this and nodded for Rovik to continue.

"Each time we cause your vassals to meet you here, they sit in this room, under that window, and are reminded of your power to both take and keep what you wish."

She smiled thoughtfully, her generous lips pulling wide as she returned to gazing out the colorful glass.

"What did the beast report?" Her voice grew deeper and commanding as she changed the subject back to the Grishkii's mission.

"The village where the fugitive lived is destroyed. All who were not killed in the attack are being brought here, and Kiidarash left warriors to make sure the boy is not hiding in the area."

"Very good, Rovik. It appears that thus far, our faith in the Grishkii is not misplaced. But I won't be satisfied till all the Anoth line is dead. Until we can ensure that line is broken, we cannot ensure safety from a rebellion. A leaderless people are easily cowed."

She seemed to fill the room with her too-large shadow, and anger was in her voice as she spoke.

"When our last assassins told us he had been found and they had slain him, they drowned the wrong boy. This time I want the task—"

Their conversation was interrupted by a page entering the room. He bowed very low and spoke. "Your Majesty, my lord, they assembled as you asked and await your pleasure."

Rovik shot a glance to the Aya Dao'Tai, who nodded. He then spoke, "Thank you, you may send them in."

Afyreen and Rovik took their seats: she at the head of the table where Rovik had been sitting when Kiidarash entered, and he to her right. A short time passed in silence. The first to enter the room was the Aya Dao'Tai's sorcerer Sethel, who sat to her left. Rovik knew that his increasing favor with Afyreen angered Sethel. The disconcerting man served as an advisor to the Aya Dao'Tai and managed certain spy networks. To secure a better position for himself in the Aya Dao'Tai's court, Rovik knew he would need to carefully edge Sethel out of the picture.

After Sethel, the rest of the nobility soon followed: High Dayrn Chalid, Threydn Drogemyna, Lady Re'alis, Ornurgr Nevicore, Dyne Biellah, and High Lord Rahdan Devick. They all stood next to their chairs, bowed or curtsied, then took their seats. This group of individuals represented the provincial governors under the rule of the Aya Dao'Tai. Before the Dao'Tai invasion, all of those provinces had at one time or another been sovereign states in their own right.

When the Aya Dao'Tai finally overthrew Anoth and her allies, she allowed the surviving realms to keep their forms of government in exchange for being subject to her laws and dominion. In return for giving powers of government to the Dao'Tai Subjugate, they were promised protection and a voice in the council. Any province, as the realms were now called, that disobeyed the will of the Aya Dao'Tai or did not pay tribute was quickly punished. This usually consisted of total invasion and occupation, followed by a complete extermination of the rulers. A new Subjugate governor would be set over the people, who would be made virtual slaves to the state. All property would be the Dao'Tai Subjugate's, and the people would be given back what their governor saw fit for them to live upon. This had been the fate of Dayrn Halor's land and people in the Freeholdn. So, to end the war and gain security, peace, and protection, the rulers and officials of the High Sun Realms surrendered their freedom and rights to the power of the Aya Dao'Tai. Before the fall of Anoth, there were over twelve independent realms from the Shellidack Mountains to the sea. There now were only six that still maintained their own rulers and a semblance of independence.

These last six rulers of the provinces now looked to the Aya Dao'Tai as she spoke.

"I pray you have found the past fourthmoon here in the city refreshing. I am pleased that you all were able to come; I appreciate the distance you must travel," she smiled.

Rovik knew well the several smiles that frequented the angles of her face. Most of the time a hard-cold edge stole away any pleasantness from the curve of her lips. Nearly as often, her smiles were laced with a savage lust for the suffering of others and a satisfaction in her role in this torment. A few rare times, however, he had caught her wearing a sincere expression. A small and reflective, even sad smile that hinted at distant bittersweet memories. This only added to his uncertainties about Afyreen's past. Regardless of the expression she wore, the members of her puppet council had always been sufficiently cowed by her.

"Now, let the ruling council of the Dao'Tai Subjugate come to order. We will first hear pressing matters, general comments, and issues. Tomorrow will be a full economic report, and the day next shall be reserved for specific provincial matters in order of precedence."

A page entered and passed each seated person at the table a lavishly scripted itinerary for the next four days, covering the three days of council and the final day of mandatory reverie. This last day was normally used to flaunt the power of the Dao'Tai before the remaining noble families of the realms. It was also one more day to catch the nobles in illicit plans or intrigue.

Once the page left the room the Aya Dao'Tai continued to speak.

"Very well, who has issue for this body first?" They all sat silent for a while, looking one to another, then one finally spoke.

"I do, Your Majesty." A short, thick man stood, clad in an ornate brigandine armor. His course ruddy hair and beard were streaked with plentiful gray, and the fair complexion of his wide, round-cheeked face was aged and discolored by the sun.

"Very well, speak, High Dayrn Chalid of Thenill and the Vagath'Oth."

"By your leave, my Aya Dao'Tai, I request the emergency support of Subjugate troops to assist my own in quelling a Grishkii threat to my lands and city. I would also ask that the lands bordering my own double their watch."

"*Your* lands and city?" She raised a hard disapproving eyebrow.

"What kind of threat are we speaking of, Chalid?" asked Rovik quickly.

"Forgive me, my Aya Dao'Tai, it is your province, of course." Chalid visibly paled under her glare, his voice growing thready as he continued.

"The threat is a substantial one, my lord. A garrison at a border outpost was destroyed, along with two half-troops of cavalry I sent to assist. And during my time here I received word that several mountain villages and farmsteads have been attacked as well." Chalid was clearly flustered as he sat back down. He hated formal affairs, and Rovik had found he was much more at ease and willing to talk after a few ales.

"With your leave, my Aya Dao'Tai," Rovik inclined his head respectfully. "I propose to send two tar'thyrts of heavy infantry supported by skirmishers to assist the Dayrn's forces and push the Grishkii out."

The Aya Dao'Tai gave a nod of approval to Rovik, so he continued, "And I would also like to send patrols into all neighboring lands to search for other Grishkii threats to the Dao'Tai Subjugate." He knew Afyreen would appreciate his efforts to expand her control, and he hoped such a move might gain him a few steps closer to their inner circle.

She smiled. "You have my leave to do so, Lord Rovik. Will this be enough, Dayrn?"

"Yes, my Aya Dao'Tai, I thank you," Chalid said. With that he leaned back in his chair, looking very much relieved. He was not a happy vassal of the Subjugate, but he would rather her men die than his own. The High Dayrn was known to keep the majority of his forces close to Thenill and his keep rather than sending them out on regular patrols. This left most of his vassals to fend for themselves against the dangers of the mountains.

"Are there any other matters?" Afyreen asked. "Nevicore, most worthy Ornurgr of your kin. I take it as a matter of course that you are able to offer the services of your cavalry to aid as Rovick has proposed?" Her voice thickened with false affection. A tactic Rovick knew she loved with the leader of their critical allies the Taivadeans. Nevicore was a thick-limbed, gruff-looking man of long sand-colored hair and a complexion carved by life facing the harsh sun and sea. He was as broad, but not as tall, as Lord Devick, and talked with a heavy lilting accent and a booming voice. As the Ornurgr of his people, he was the undisputed leader of the Taivadean Verr'Ords warlords and spoke with an aura of iron seemingly unaffected by the Aya Dao'Tai's manner.

"As you say, 'tis a matter of course, Your Majesty. My kin will serve, man and horse, shield and spear alike." He rose to speak, keeping his expression empty of emotion, giving a small bow as he finished.

"Ever to the point," Afyreen said turning her attention to the rest of those seated at the table.

"What next takes precedent this day?" she asked with a flourished gesture of her delicate hand, sunlight catching in the large ruby of her bracelet.

"I have cause to speak. I protest the incursion of Subjugate troops into my lands," said Lord Devick of Mantorah.

Rovik sighed inwardly, Devick always had been difficult to deal with. An idealist who continually skirted the edges of openly spurning the supremacy of the Subjugate. He was a large man, taller than most, with warm dusky skin and a muscular figure born of a warrior's up-bringing. He struck an imposing figure today clad in silvery maille with the dark blue and gold Mantorahn tabard pulled tight by his sword belt. He kept the black-brown balayage of his hair mid-length, just covering the tops of his ears down to the bottom of his strong neck. There was a handsome sturdiness to his face complemented by his thick, neatly cut goatee. Fire threatened from behind his black eyes as he spoke, the low, firm timber of his voice drawing all eyes to him.

"For eight months your soldiers have been occupying the city of Anuar, committing all manner of atrocities. Looting, murdering innocents, and even taking virtue from the women, and selling those whom they are done with to your slavers. The Camarilla Daradar of Mantorah has petitioned for relief multiple times to no avail. As the High Rahdan of my people I cannot let any more of your oppressive brutes into my lands! If there needs to be more patrols then my troops will see it done, but your soldiers are not welcome. They must leave Anuar and recompense is due their victims."

"Lord Devick, it is not your place to deny entry to them. You are subject to my rulings." The Aya Dao'Tai sounded calm, but Rovik saw her body go rigid with anger in her chair. He felt a chill down his spine as the anger in her voice grew. "That city was a haven for criminals and rebels; it was deemed a threat to the realms."

"If that had been the case then we would have taken care of the problem. But I think you simply needed more slaves for your farms and for your soldiers to prey upon."

Rovik was shocked; even Devick, difficult to cow as he was, knew it was not wise to speak to her like this. He hoped the Aya Dao'Tai would not do anything in front of the council.

"Lord Devick, please. Rumors are beneath us here. If you find my men so distasteful, then I will stay them from helping you. However, I will not be responsible for any mishaps that may befall you and your people due to your abrasiveness. We can discuss this matter at length later." The Aya Dao'Tai's voice was once again sweet, but there was a venom in her words that Rovik, and he was sure Devick, took note of.

"Thank you, Your Majesty," Devick said stiffly and sat back down. There was an uncomfortable pause, and the heat of the words exchanged still hung in the air.

Surprisingly, Lady Re'alis stood next. "The realm of Lea'Angleneth also denounces your claim to patrol our lands. Under the Treaty of Rule, Dao'Tai soldiers may only occupy the land of Anoth proper and any city, province, or realm under rebellion or breach of treaty. Lea'Angleneth is neither in rebellion nor breach of treaty."

Rovik froze. He might have expected a declaration from Lord Devick, but Re'alis? Lady Re'alis was an elegant woman of noble pedigree. Every aspect of her, from her long carefully kept light auburn hair, to her svelte limbs, keen figure, and refined speech and movements, was an example of grace and beauty. High sweeping cheek bones perfectly framed her deep-set dark hazel-green eyes. Her porcelain skin was currently a little flushed with emotion as she finished speaking. Rovik had never spoken to her much himself, but he knew her empathy for the common people, and their love of her, made the Aya Dao'Tai feel threatened at some level by the lady. He carefully looked to Afyreen, trying to gauge how terrible her reaction would be.

"Are there any others who decline my assistance?" The Aya Dao'Tai looked around at all those who sat at the table as if by her very glare she could turn them to ash. Her otherworldly eyes slowly moving from one person to the next. No one spoke.

"Very well, Lady Re'alis, Lord Devick, the security of your respective realms is yours to ensure." The lady bowed and took her seat, smoothing her dark red, almost black dress. Afyreen took a long, easy breath.

"I hope we hear that your realms have been well at our next council. Should aid ever be needed, you have but to ask for it." She smiled, but Rovik could see the malice in her eyes.

"Is there anything else?" Rovik asked. He wanted to get on to something less tense.

"Earre. I've a wee item, m'Aya Dao'Tai," said Drogemyna. He stood to speak and was only slightly taller than the high-backed council chairs. In contrast to Nevicore, Drogemyna was compact in frame. He wore a remarkably complex armored vest of metallic beads and bronze scales shaped to look like seashells. His garb was well suited for the warm air and salt spray of the sea, all light-colored linens and bronze fashioned in a manner to let you swim long enough to escape its weight in the water.

Drogemyna's arms were bare and darkened by a life on the decks of the mighty ships of Thalyphonie. Azure bands of geometric styled ocean waves were tattooed around the anchor-cable-like muscles of his upper arms. His lean sunbaked face cut a profile like the ram of a pentareme warship, angled, hard and marked by years of surf and savage shipborne warfare.

"Go on, Drogemyna, Threydn of Thalyphonie."

"By'in yer leave, threeyn murr of mi'merchant vessels be grrn'missing. I wuld yern perrmission ta send two diremes ina ta Subjugate serviss ta investigate thiss'n."

He struggled with the shared language of the continental realms, his Thalyphonic accent soaking through each word.

"Of course, you have it, and bring word of the result of the inquiry," she said, her tone relaxed, appearing the benevolent ruler once again.

"Aye, Yourrn Majest. Many thundering t'anks yours," Drogemyna inclined his head in deference as he finished and took his chair again.

"Now, does anyone else have a matter to bring forth?"

"I do, Your Majesty," Dyne Biellah spoke. She was a diminutive thing, standing only slightly higher than the tall-backed chair behind her. She was young, not much over twenty, sable-haired and doe-eyed. Her eyes seemed exceptionally large when compared to the slim features of her face. There was terror in those eyes now, and her smooth milky skin was even paler than normal.

"Please, speak," Afyreen said with a gracious smile. Rovik knew the Aya Dao'Tai was often amused by the timid airs of those who stood before her—though Biellah's unease was well justified. Once a lesser noble of her land, Biellah had been cast into sudden sovereignty when her great-uncle was executed for rebellion a few years past. The weight of the northern Freeholdn realms had fallen upon a maiden scarcely prepared for such a burden.

Biellah hesitated, swallowed hard, and managed to continue.

"Your Majesty, did my dispatch reach you?" Afyreen looked at Rovik, who shook his head.

"It would seem that we did not receive it." Biellah's pallor grew worse, and under her elegant dress she was shaking.

"The matter..." she stammered, "The problem is at the frontier..." she paused again and seemed wary to continue. All in the room hushed at the mention of the frontier.

For just a fraction of a moment Rovik thought he saw concern dart across Afyreen's face.

"I see, we will address that issue directly then." She gestured for Biellah to sit, then once again looked them all over.

"Is there any other matter the rest of you have for today?" No one spoke for quite some time. It was clear that fear, not respect, kept them all in such reverence.

Rovik stood. "If that is all, then this council is adjourned for now. Please see your schedules for your individual appointments. Refreshments are in the grand hall."

All the nobles stood, acknowledged the Aya Dao'Tai, and walked back out the door, except Biellah, whom Rovik motioned to stay by him. No one spoke until the door was shut, leaving the Aya Dao'Tai, Sethel, himself, and Biellah in the room.

Sethel spoke first in a seething voice, like the hiss of a snake. Snake, in fact, was a good word to describe the man. His thin, hard-looking lips barely parted when he spoke, making it seem like each word slipped out as smoke through a crack. He kept his head shaved smooth along with his gaunt face. It was hard to say, but he appeared just as thin and saccharine under his robes as his face betrayed. His beady wide-set eyes constantly flittered about, making it hard to speak with him undistractedly.

"What is the problem at the frontier, Biellah?"

She spoke with near panic in reply. "They breached it!" she squeaked. "The fight was desperate, but your army was just able to push them back. I don't know how long they will hold. They are attacking with renewed vigor, though I don't know why. I can send my little army, but against them I don't know what good it would do, not against the Akarii. If they escape the siege, what of my people? What will they do to us?"

"I see. Why did our army not send word?" Rovik asked.

"They fight even now, maybe their messenger is slowed. But I can't fathom why my messengers did not reach you." The dyne was now openly trembling. It was clear she thought she would be blamed, perhaps even executed like her uncle.

Afyreen rose and placed a comforting arm around Biellah and guided her over to the large window. The young lady shivered but did not resist. Her arm felt cold and hard as an icy steel band around Biellah's shoulders.

"Do not worry, Your Grace, you are not your predecessor, and I am sure you are not at fault here. We will send troops to secure the frontier today. Your people will be safe. Now go, rest from your journey, and enjoy the amenities of the city while you are here. We will seek news and counsel with you later if necessary. Be at peace, we will not abandon you."

Biellah smiled in relief, "Thank you, Your Majesty. You are so kind." With a graceful curtsy the dyne left the room. The Aya Dao'Tai, Rovik, and Sethel remained standing in the room.

"They are planning something, I feel it," Sethel seethed.

"Biellah and the Freeholdn Dynes?" asked Rovik.

"No, the bold lord and lady. Devick and Re'alis," Sethel snapped.

"What are they planning, do you think, Sethel?" Afyreen asked with an amused tone.

"They may be planning to break off from the Subjugate and open hostilities toward you."

"This would not surprise me, but how sure are you?" she pressed.

"Quite sure," answered Sethel with a sniff.

"Your Majesty, my information reports support his divinations," Rovik jumped in, glancing at Sethel.

"Both Devick and Re'alis have been building up and moving their armies. Whether or not they are planning something together is not clear, though."

Rovik hated trying to compete with the foul magics of Sethel's scrying for information. He didn't trust the means or methods.

The Aya Dao'Tai stood and walked back over to the window, blocking more of the light than her slender form should have. She laughed a little before saying, "Rovik, your information? Do I have an aspiring spymaster I was not aware of?" She laughed again, a hard musical sound, like bells falling down a spiral stair. It sent a chill through Rovik.

She continued, "It would be such a misfortune if something happened to the lord and lady on their way home, would it not?"

"It would indeed, Your Majesty," he answered gravely. Devick and Re'alis just didn't seem to understand that the more they resisted the Aya' Dao'Tai the more their people would suffer for it. Maybe it would be best for their realms if they no longer led them.

"With none of my peacekeepers in their lands, the Grishkii threat is a great one." She turned to Rovik with an expression of stone, but a smile in her flashing ruby-black eyes. She loved the intrigue of these types of plots. As much as she seemed to love anything in Rovik's estimations. Her eyes went cold as she addressed the sorcerer.

"Have the army put on heightened alert, but we will not move unless we need to. Sethel, I need to know exactly what they intend to do! They will be in the city for some time yet, do not waste the opportunity to learn something."

Sethel and Rovik both bowed and said, "Thy will be done, my Aya Dao'Tai." They then turned and left Afyreen to herself.

Truly it would be such a boon to have cause to pacify Mantorah and Lea'Angleneth, she mused with another small laugh. She instinctively sucked her teeth, her tongue lingering on their sharp white edges as might a predator considering prey. She let a smile widen and part her lips, thinking of the next phase in her given task.

"Soon all will finally be prepared."

7

Machinations

*P*uzzle not over long as to the goodness of one aashahl or the next. Know instead of their unknowableness and in this accept their will as it arrived on your path.
Essays of the Divine

Devick stood in the grand hall that was the center of the old royal compound in Ell'Anoth. The room was vast, hundreds of people could have easily fit inside with room enough to mingle and dance. Radiant white beams curved up from the tops of the high stone walls to form the cavernous, vaulted ceiling. Brilliant splashes of colored light fell in sheets from the stained-glass skylights near the peak of the ceiling, filling the long elliptical room with vibrant colors. A soft breeze flowed from a host of open doors on each side of the room, causing the drab banners of the Dao'Tai to flutter just enough to reveal the exquisite carvings on the walls of the hall. These ashy black banners had a large purple tear shape marked with a tok rune above a purple and a gold wave. They covered the walls, almost completely concealing the full nature of the original decoration underneath.

In the center of the hall long tables and chairs had been prepared along with a vast array of food and drink. Exotic items from the farthest corners of the High Sun Realms and beyond were prepared for the enjoyment of the Aya Dao'Tai's noble guests. Servants scurried to the tables, bringing their lords and ladies refreshment. Near the tables with the food and drink another six long tables were set parallel to each other. Each table was set and prepared with colors matching the realm and ruler who should sit there. A dark blue and sunset orange marked the table Devick sat at, slowly eating grapes one at a time as he considered those around him.

Had he been too brash with the Aya Dao'Tai? Was there any chance of gaining his people's full sovereignty back without war? Devick was sure he knew the answer to both. He looked up to his men sitting at the table with him. Their lives, just as so many more in Mantorah, depended on him and the choices he would make on their behalf. Devick that the Camarilla Daradar of Mantorah would only restrain their desire for complete independence for so long, with or without the approval of the ruling Rahdan.

Mantorah was ruled by its numerous Daradar, each with their own lands and vassals. The Daradar of Mantorah bent to the rule of the High Lord Rahdan, who may not own lands or vassals outside that which is granted by law. The Camarilla Daradar of Mantorah selected the family to provide the High Lord Rahdan but, should that family fail in their duties, the Camarilla selected a new ruler. Devick's family had held the ruling title of Rahdan for hundreds of years. The Camarilla of Mantorah had never found fault with their leadership, even during the crisis after the fall of Anoth. Thus, the prospect of being the Rahdan that let house Tolkol fail in its leadership duties was not acceptable.

Sheibrok, Just Hammer, guide me through this. How am I going to make this work? He hoped his uneasy thoughts were not visible on his face.

Devick was suddenly aware that he was being stared at. He looked at the man sitting to his immediate right, Captain Gairrle Dryton. As always, he was wearing his full harness of Mantorahn plate. The sharp angular cuirass and gorget with matching pauldrons and tassets made him look even more imposing than his natural size did already. Over his robust armor he wore the blue and orange tabard bearing the heraldry of his station and charge. The features of his face, hard angled, sturdy, and strong with broad cheeks, heavy brow and a bulwark of a chin seemed made with the same eye as his armor. Gairrle had an eyebrow raised in an interrogatory expression. Despite his brutish build, he was a soft-spoken man who had worked his way up through the ranks, and for the last eight years he had served as captain over the personal guard of Lord Rahdan. Devick had known him as a friend and confidant for all this time and more.

"Those are either the worst grapes you've ever eaten, my lord, or you are chewing on something much sourer."

Devick chuckled softly. "The grapes are actually very good; they might end up being the only thing about this season's council that does leave a good taste in my mouth."

"My lord, if I may, what troubles you so soon? I understood the preliminaries went well. Did the brief opening session with the Aya Dao'Tai go ill? Has there been any change in the other realms?"

Devick took a thoughtful moment to reply.

"There are a great many things that trouble me. The earlier exchange with the council is certainly among them, yet it is much of what was not said and what is kept from us that causes my greatest concern." Gairrle nodded in understanding and Devick continued.

"When I know where I stand and what I am up against I can win battles. Knowing my foe, where we will fight, their strengths, their weaknesses, who my allies are, and who they could be. Here, in this struggle, I have no such knowledge. Is Mantorah the only people who remember the way the realms were during the glory of Anoth, the way it all was before the invasion? Are we the only ones willing to pay the cost to return there? I just don't know, and every time I come here, I feel more uncertain in my estimation of the other realms and what the plans of the Aya Dao'Tai really are. I am certain, though, that she would not let Mantorah simply leave *her* Subjugate."

"Have you tried just asking the other rulers?" Gairrle suggested in his usual low, flat tone. "This would be the best place—no letters to be intercepted, no suspicious journey to another realm, just a few stolen moments..."

Devick had thought about this approach before but feared exposure or betrayal. Significant efforts were in place to ensure any mingling between the members of the council when in the capital were monitored by Subjugate agents. Being caught seeking such information here in the center of the Aya Dao'Tai's fist would be a death sentence on him and the men with him. Yet Gairrle was right, any other way could be even riskier. Devick took another grape from the platter and studied it.

"I think the time for subtlety and inaction have long passed, Captain."

"Indeed, they have my lord, truly they have."

The announcement of Dyne Biellah entering the hall halted their talk. The dyne still looked a little pale and upset as she and nearly two dozen of her soldiers and ladies-in-waiting entered the hall. He wondered if her large retinue helped make her feel more secure in her precarious position over the Freeholdn realms. Devick watched her as she took her seat at her table and nervously looked around the room. Her eyes met with Devick's, and he gave a gracious nod and friendly smile to her. She smiled back timidly and quickly turned her focus to the platter of fruits, cheese, and meats that one of her servants set before her.

"Another piece I might be missing could have to do with the frontier. The last time I heard it mentioned was the council before Biellah's great uncle was executed. And you should have seen the dyne's face when she spoke of it."

"Whatever it is, we need to know more, my lord," Gairrle said.

"Perhaps that is where the bulk of the Aya Dao'Tai's army is? If so, that would buy us time to prepare should war erupt." Devick barely whispered this as a servant came near to offer more drink.

While being served, he mused on the Aya Dao'Tai's army. The events after the destruction of Ell'Anoth puzzled Devick. After that battle, the might of Mantorah had been spent trying to hold the southern lines. Only a small defensive force stood between the Aya Dao'Tai's army and the lands of Mantorah, yet no attack occurred, and the bulk of the Dao'Tai army simply never came. Once the northern realms were all brought to heel a smaller force came to the Mantorahn Red Gates offering a conditional peace treaty. It was in reality a surrender, but Devick's father had little choice. With not enough army left to resist, and the razed kingdoms in the north as an example, capitulation seemed the only choice at the time.

Since then, Devick had become aware of many oddities in the Subjugate. Massive slave farms near Ell'Anoth constantly produced vast amounts of food—smithies were in continual production of armor and weapons, the entire Kray'Bahn plateau had been turned into a vast military logistics complex, large enough to support a gargantuan campaign. Yet, there was no word of open war, no massive battles. The supplies and goods were simply shipped away to the northeast.

This situation played to the advantage of Mantorah, as it left the Aya Dao'Tai without the power to occupy the realm since it was too far south and too large. To deal with a Mantorahn rebellion she would have to empty Anoth of its occupation force. Even though the surviving Anoth were all enslaved, leaving them with only their task masters and no army to keep uprisings down would be a huge risk to the Aya Dao'Tai. Devick hoped that if he could get another, maybe two other realms to declare their independence with his, the Aya Dao'Tai would have to accept it as she could not challenge such an alliance with her army busy in the north. Learning what this secret northern army was doing was critical, however. It had to be something that they could not simply leave and march south, otherwise a second slaughter like that suffered by Anoth would visit the southern realms.

There are always the Tears of the Aashahl, if we could find them again, somehow—it would make all the difference, thought Devick.

Devick understood little in exactness of the Tears of the Aashahl, save they were an arcane weapon that had been used to free the High Sun Realms of another invader hundreds of generations ago. Having such a weapon at Mantorah's command could change everything. After an hour or two the sun was nearly set, and most of the nobles had left with their guards and servants, leaving only Biellah, her personal guard, Devick, and Gairrle at the tables. Devick gave a nod and he and his captain rose and slowly walked across the echoing hall, entering a stone corridor that led from the grand hall to the portion of the royal complex where the guest quarters were. Rather than retiring for the evening as the others had, Devick remained in the corridor, with Gairrle not far from him. The spark-lighters had not made their rounds, and so the corridor was dark and shadowy as the first group of the dyne' attendants and guards made their way to their rooms. As they passed there was no sign they noticed Devick or Gairrle at all. Finally, the dyne and her personal guard passed by. Devick walked from his place of concealment and swiftly came up behind Biellah and her guard.

"Excuse me, Your Grace, but might I have a brief, private word before you retire?"

She stopped and her guards turned to face Devick, clearly surprised to see him. Biellah looked unsure. "I suppose so, my lord."

Devick gestured to a window casement nearby, but out of earshot from where they now stood. Biellah motioned for her guard to wait, and she and Devick withdrew to the casement. It was deep-set and wide enough to serve as a bench seat. Devick chose his next words carefully, not wanting to betray his true intentions.

"Your Grace, I could not help but notice how much concern you have over the matter at the northern frontier; is there any way my people might aid you? What is it that preys upon your fair mind?"

Biellah sat down on the casement as though she could stand no longer. Her hands fidgeted with the lace of her dress sleeves as she stared into her lap. Devick felt sorry for her. She was plunged into a world for which she truly had no preparation. She had been born and raised to produce an alliance of marriage within the Freeholdn, leaving her ill-suited for the dynamics of rule under the Aya Dao'Tai.

"My lord, I am not to speak of it. She forbids it." She let out a long low breath, "Yet I cannot keep it all in. I have no one in Kali'Kern whom I can trust, not really anyway. The other courtiers through the Freeholdn all seem to be just waiting for me to fail so they can take control. Others like Kali'Kar and Kali'Toreen want nothing to do with me at all. The army is loyal enough, but they hold little political power without the support of the other dayrns and dynes. The Freeholdn have no true united leader, we are without a Durnori and I...I have no one to turn to."

"I see." Devick nodded sympathetically though he was also surprised by her outpouring. "Then might I offer an understanding ear, Your Grace?"

Biellah looked up at Devick. It was clear she was agonizing over the choice. He truly felt for her. All his life he had been raised to rule and he found it a constant near-overwhelming burden. Yet here she was, thrust into a role and position far worse than Mantorah's with not half the preparations or resources that Devick took for granted. Devick placed a reassuring hand on her trembling shoulder. His touch was so much the opposite of the Aya. All warmth and comforting strength. Biellah's breath caught slightly at the gesture's sincerity.

"Your Grace, you will find no better friend and ally than the people of Mantorah. You can trust me, I assure you," he said, holding her gaze with his.

"I want to believe that, my lord, truly. Perhaps we can speak in a better setting, when we have more time?" she spoke, a little easier.

"At a place of your choosing and convenience, Your Grace, but soon, before too much transpires here."

"Yes, soon. I will call for you, my lord..." Her words trailed off as she stood. Devick stood also and bowed.

"A pleasant eve, Your Grace," he said softly as she passed by and returned to her guards.

She paused and turned. "And to you, my lord, a pleasant eve as well. And," she smiled warmly, "thank you, my lord."

Devick gave a second bow in answer and watched as she and her guards disappeared down the corridor. Gairrle now removed from his place of hiding and stood with his lord.

"What do you think, Gairrle?" he asked the captain.

"I would advise you, proceed carefully; she is young, and we do not truly know where her loyalties are. I will see that our usual aides bend their ears to learn all they can of her while she is here."

"And I will try to speak with the dayrn and lady when I can. The others I have little hope for. They are too entrenched in the Subjugate."

Gairrle nodded his head and the two walked silently as a sparklighter approached, setting ablaze the spark stone torches in the corridor. The torches' blue, semi-translucent crystal produced an odorless, smokeless flame that gave a bright blue glow to the hallway. Devick retired to his room for the night, hoping for a restful sleep before the busy morrow.

The next day was filled with accountings to the many bureaucratic arms of the Subjugate, reports, tax reconciliations, imports and exports, military strength quotas, and the general census. Nearly all these reports were altered in some way by the Camarilla of Mantorah. Some to hide the buildup of the army, others to conceal the numbers of military-aged men, the rest to conceal the southern trade. The Aya Dao'Tai tried to control every aspect of life in her Subjugate, but due to the size of Mantorah the execution of this was often left to Mantorah and a few inspectors.

Each of the nobles at the Subjugate Council made their reports at the same time to separate review boards. Any inconsistencies or shortfalls from the Subjugate's requirements resulted in harsher quotas and restrictions for the next season. Should a province continue to fall short of Subjugate requirements the ruler would be removed and replaced. Devick thought the reviewers brought extra scrutiny on the reports and counts of Mantorah this season, and by the time Devick was released by them, the sun was long set and all the other nobles had retired for the night.

Devick returned to his chambers, locked the door, and stood looking out over the city from his window. His chambers were large and connected to the quarters of his guard. Rich red tile and dark carved timbers covered the floor and ceiling, respectively. It was lavishly furnished, though if he looked closely, he could see a repaired weapon gash here and an arrow strike there on the dressers, wardrobe, and bed posts.

Devick thought he heard something, and he strained his ears to listen. The soft knock came again as a slip of paper shot underneath the door and into the room. Devick picked the paper up. In a simple script it read, 'Meet me upon the eastern bulwarks when Ailc rises.'

Ailc, the great eastern star. Must be Biellah. He chuckled, "How very mysterious of her." He sat down in a plush chair, trying to remember when that star would rise over the mountains this time of the year.

There was another knock at the door, but this time it was loud and confident. Devick opened the door and found an Anothn slave standing there in a footman's uniform. He had the markings of his caste upon his face, a curving arch from temple to temple across the forehead and two streaking blots running down over the cheeks from under each eye. This one was fortunate to have been tattooed and not branded, as some were. The Aya Dao'Tai imposed a caste system upon all in Anoth. Most castes only had to have a mark upon their body. The pleasure servants had marks on their shoulders, labor slaves upon their forearms with variations based upon the type of slave. The servitude class had their marks cut, tattooed, or branded upon their faces.

Most of the servitude slaves were the descendants of the army of Anoth. The ones who did not surrender until the end. Practically all the adults were killed when Anoth fell, but their families were taken for the servitude class, the lowest type of Anothn slave. Marked so they could not hide their station. Other slaves could potentially earn their freedom and so their marks were kept in locations that one day they might be able to conceal. This was not the case for servitude slaves. They were slaves for life. Should they try to escape or cause trouble, the tattoos would be branded over. Should their disobedience continue, they could be cut.

This footman was tall and thin, black-haired, and gray-eyed. His body spoke of hard work and harsh living, yet his face showed optimism and a small smile. He could not have been much older than fourteen, though. He smiled at Devick as he spoke slowly.

"Fresh linens for you, my lord? They come especially prepared."

"I have been expecting these, thank you." Devick took the bundle of cloth from the youth and took note of its great weight.

"Here you are, for your time and risk." Devick gave the footman a handful of gold verts, more money than a servitude caste could gather in years.

"Thank you, my lord." The footman bowed low and swiftly returned to the dark corridors he had come from.

Devick returned to his room and opened the bundle. Inside he found a leather satchel with the sun and sigil of Anoth upon it. Devick looked around the room.

Better make sure, he thought, looking over the room suspiciously.

He got up and made a search of the room for peepholes or false walls. After making certain no one was listening or watching, Devick returned to the satchel and opened it. Inside he found a set of maps, several letters, two journals, and a ring of large iron keys. A hastily scrawled note was attached to the keys. This was the seasonal package from the spy network known as the Sunshadow, predominantly made up of the remnants of the free army of Anoth. Now they worked with Devick, supplying information for a long-awaited liberation war. Devick helped fund and supply them in return for their aid in learning more about the Aya Dao'Tai and her people.

One of the journals was full of reports from all the general information that had been gathered. The second appeared to be a hasty copy of a Dao'Tai soldier's personal journal. The letters looked like intercepted courier posts. One had the mark of Kali'Kern. Devick opened it hurriedly. It was a letter from dyne Biellah to the Aya Dao'Tai. Skipping down past the lengthy and ingratiating introduction Devick read over the contents of the letter:

'...and thus, it is with the deepest regrets that I must inform Her Most Eminent Majesty, that the northern frontier was breached by Akarii forces at a great loss to your men. Your own soldiers are sending the detailed report, however, I also wished to make sure our Majesty was informed. The escaping forces destroyed a nearby encampment before heading northwest. I will do all I can to see that Kali'Kern and all the Freeholdn continue to support the efforts of your forces at the northern frontiers. Please rest assured that a complete investigation into the manner of the breach will be made, and that if any persons are found to have been at fault, they will be turned over to you regardless of their station...

The letter continued a bit more and then rambled off into placating statements about the merciful and powerful Aya Dao'Tai. The next letter that Devick opened and read was from a Dao'Tai Ty'kahl. It was in their own language; however, a small portion had been translated by the Sunshadow:

"...enemy assault was focused and sustained. Arcane weaponry was present en masse...No reason to suspect insurrectionist support...assault halted by Ikthii deployment...nearby village and supply camp supplied dzum...15,843 killed in battle, 346 missing in the blast, 4,964 wounded till death, 5,834 wounded.

233 vitae of defenses lost, 245 wagons and supplies captured, 43 chariots and crews destroyed. Total war force losses: 26,987.

Enemy losses estimated at 3,354 killed in battle, over 3,000 wounded. Approximately 800 escaped the siege frontier.

Forces sent to destroy escaping enemy element did not return. Presumed dead. Trackers have been dispatched.

New equipment and personnel request to follow:
Heavy infantry two demi-legions..."

The rest of the letter was a long and detailed list of needed supplies. It was certainly clear that whatever attacked the Dao'Tai army in the north did terrible damage and suffered only a fraction of the casualties the Dao'Tai did. This was certainly not the case when the Aya Dao'Tai's army marched on other realms. He next read a brief report of Sunshadow agents involved in other assignments, shadowing patrols, looking in to the attacks in the Vagath'Oth Mountains, etc. Devick continued to read over the items from the satchel for a long while until his own thought suddenly interrupted him.

Dyne Biellah!

He ran to the window only to realize it faced the wrong way to see the eastern sky. He packed the maps, letters, and other items back into the satchel, then donned his cloak. With the satchel hidden underneath, he left his room and entered the room where his men slept. Two men were awake and on guard. They gave a silent salute to their Lord as he entered. Devick returned their hail and swiftly came to where Gairrle was asleep on a low but comfortable-looking bed in the corner of the long bunk room.

"Gairrle..." Devick whispered. The captain did not move. "Captain Dryton," he said more sternly. At the sound of his last name Gairrle snapped awake, fully alert. He sat up and was surprised to find Devick kneeling by his bed.

"My lord, what is amiss?"

"I have a shimmer that I need to leave with you."

Devick passed Gairrle the satchel and he placed it under his blankets.

"I will keep it close. Did the agents find them before the attack?" Gairrle asked carefully.

"No, they arrived after, but they did indicate that there had been several survivors who went further into the mountains. It could be them. If anyone might have survived one of their line could."

Devick that finding a surviving heir to the throne of Anoth was personally important to him beyond the political implication, though Gairrle had never said why.

"Brek's piss, to be so close only to be disrupted again by her ilk. It is like they know what we are about before we do." Gairrle shook his head in frustration.

"It's that warlock-spawn at her side that does it, I am sure."
"Could be, but we will find them. The aashahl are with us in this, of that I am sure. And they are far more able than a peeping little sorcerer." Devick smiled in the dim light and Gairrle nodded in agreement.

"I am going to meet with Biellah. If I am not back in an hour or two seek me on the eastern walls, in the old bulwarks."

"My lord, should I not come with you? This could be a snare."

"No, I will be safe enough," he reassured his old friend.

Without giving Gairrle time to reply Devick stood and left the room for the corridor. He walked with haste but slowed when passing guards in an effort to remain inconspicuous. In just half a shade or so, he came to the dark eastern bulwark. These defenses sat high above the river. Their stone structure was one of the few that had not been repaired after the war. The cliff and river below made any practical assault upon the city from that direction impossible. The bulwark was sheltered from attack on all sides by smooth-cut stone forming a tunnel dotted with murder holes below and arrow slits in front. Here and there large sections of the bulwark had been blasted away by the Dao'Tai's attack long ago.

Standing in the bright starlight close to the middle of the structure was a small, cloaked figure. As Devick approached he could see the long curling locks of the dyne' lustrous black hair falling around her delicate neck and out of the hood of her cloak. She removed the hood, letting the starlight splash over her flawless alabaster skin and dark eyes, giving her an ethereal look.

"Your Grace, I am pleased you were able to meet me, though the time and place is rather clandestine."

"And so it must be, my lord, for talk such as this."

She was right, though Devick did detect a bit of a dramatic air in her voice.

Remember she is young and impressionable. Seems she wishes to live out a scene from a play; so be it then. He studied her face for a moment, waiting for her to speak again. She wet the smooth bends of her lips and gave him a vulnerable smile.

"You wanted to know how you could help my people and about the frontier?" Biellah seemed different here in the chilly night air. She sounded more confident now, as though the anonymity of night protected her. Or maybe it was the air of intimacy that she found empowering?

"I will tell you all that I can. I have to tell someone lest it burn me up from the inside. My great uncle and father both spoke highly of your people, and your father. So, I choose to trust Mantorah. I choose to trust *you*, my Lord Rahdan." She paused for emphasis as she watched him with a tentative glow growing in the starry pools of her eyes.

"I am honored, Your Grace. Please, continue."

"My lands and people are trapped. To the north there is the frontier, manned by the bulk of the Aya Dao'Tai's army. That is her great secret, my lord. That is why no one can travel to the Freeholdn past Frey'Kalimag. This army is holding back a more terrible foe than the Aya Dao'Tai herself, monsters that only live to prey upon the weak and innocent, the Akarii. So, I am left with little choice but to support the Aya Dao'Tai."

Devick suddenly realized why it was outlawed to speak of the fallen northern lands. Biellah was not old enough to remember Akaroche for herself. She only had what the Aya Dao'Tai allowed to be spoken to go by. The Subjugate had gone to great lengths to vilify the Akarii, and the dyne was not the only one who had believed. This was made all the easier by the reclusive nature of the Akarii before the war. Virtually no non-Akarii had ever been allowed within the hidden realm of Akaroche. So, with the might of the Subjugate bent on vilifying them it was no surprise most feared the arcane terrors of the north.

"Your Grace, did your father ever speak of the grand alliance?" asked Devick cautiously, not wanting to sound condescending.

"Well, yes. I remember a little. 'The Threefold Defense,' he called it."

"Yes, but did he ever tell you what it was?"

She took a moment to answer, apparently trying to remember the tales. "Yes, I am sure he did, but I do not remember what it was. Pray tell, my lord."

"The Threefold Defense referred to the three largest of the High Sun Realms; Anoth in the center, Mantorah in the south, and Akaroche in the north. Each of these realms, along with their smaller neighbors, formed an unbroken chain of alliance from Mantorah's southern frontier to the northernmost reach of the Akarii."

"How can that be? They are monsters to be sure. Creatures of unnatural might and power. Like the Xydarii" she said in disbelief. Her wide eyes searched his and he worked to maintain his calm expression.

"It is true. They are not exactly like us. Though they are nothing like the blood-lusting Xydarii. Much the opposite. I've seen the Akarii before the war as a small child. They are a beautiful people, not that different from us, though they do have a powerful connection to the arcane. Their army was smaller than Mantorah's, but second to none in the western realms in battle. Many of the towers, bridges, and aqueducts in your own realm were built by them long ago. It would seem that the Aya Dao'Tai has been doing everything she can to keep their survival a secret."

"So, she has worked to hide the nature and existence of an entire people? Why?"

"With Akaroche out of play there is no uniting power in the north to cause problems. Convincing the people that they are monsters keeps anyone from wanting to rush to their aid. Should a few other realms unite and break the siege of Akaroche, together they could liberate most of the north. That and the Tears together might force the Aya Dao'Tai to recognize their independence. Should that happen, the southern realms would be under less of a direct threat and could take similar actions. We all might rid ourselves of her completely, Aashahl willing."

Devick paused, realizing he had started to excitedly ramble on to himself. To let the weight of what he said soak in, he quieted and held his breath. If this were a trick, or if someone were listening in, it would mean death for them both. A long time passed, and Biellah watched the stars thoughtfully. Devick could not help but notice as her expression transformed into a blend of determination and squelched fears.

"I would love to be free again. Free from the Aya Dao'Tai, from the fear, the duty, from all of it." She paused, sounding weary.

Devick did not interrupt. He was again struck with how young she was to have so much weight on her shoulders, but he watched what seemed to be a visible change wash over her. She looked more determined and less fearful with each moment.

"I was born and raised for one reason, to please a dayrn and to strengthen my lands through marriage. I am no durnori, I am so dreadfully unprepared for these games where thousands of lives hang in the balance on the choices I must make." She turned her eyes back to him and Devick felt his chest warm. Whether she knew it or not, her expression was filled with a longing that was hard to miss. She wet her lips once more and continued to speak, slowly and more deliberately now, each word dripping from her full lips like dew from flower petals.

"I choose to believe you, my lord, about Akaroche. What you say makes sense, and the destruction that is blamed on them could easily be the pillage work of the Aya Dao'Tai's men."

She took a step closer to him now, carefully shifting her cloak to ensure her form was more illuminated by the starlight. She had worn a gown carefully cut to accentuate the most appealing aspects of her form. Under the bright light of the stars, it did just that, teasing at what remained concealed, begging to be fully removed. Devick started to take a step toward her but caught himself.

You might be young, but you know your craft well. Devick realized that she was trying to ensure his loyalty and commitment the only way she probably knew how. Devick swallowed hard and tried to ignore her mounting efforts of seduction. He had to admit that she was more prepared for maneuvering in the court then she would have led him to believe. It was a smart move, for she had no more reason to trust him then he did to trust her. Romantic entanglement was probably a small price to pay for support and security from her perspective.

"I know that what I imply seems impossible, but you can trust me, the Akarii are not monsters, and they will be our best ally in the fight," he said trying to keep his mind on the conversation rather than the closeness of her enticing form.

"I believe you, but what fight, my lord?" She seemed taken aback.

"Yes, a fight, a war, a struggle, whatever it must be. I do not think I can keep the Camarilla of Mantorah from seeking liberation, nor do I want to keep them. I simply want the effort to succeed. I wish to help those who might join with us. I want to help you. I want to help your people, and you, find freedom again, Your Grace."

Biellah drew closer to him. The moment seemed to lengthen as she placed her hands tenderly upon his chest. She took a deep longing breath and let it out softly as she looked up at Devick with her dark eyes. The long onyx tumbles of her hair perfectly framed her swan-like neck, drawing attention to the silver chain and single brilliant green stone that hung low between the curves of her shapely chest. Devick could see the hunger in her eyes and a part of him wished to just give in and kiss her. Such a kiss might ensure her loyalty. A little further than a kiss could grant more than simple loyalty. It could be the means to an alliance that he realized he wanted as badly as she might need it. He dismissed this thought, though he did not move away from her. *She has to trust me, but not for the wrong reasons.*

"My lord, I..." she trailed off as she glanced at his pleasantly smooth lips, her own trembling. He could see her chest rising and falling swiftly with her quick breath. Devick's mind swam in thought. If a kiss was the cost of this alliance, should he pay it? Even if it was a false kiss, born out of nothing but necessity and more than a little carnal temptation?

No. This must be done honorably or not at all. He took a small step back from her, gently taking her hands in his own as he lowered them, giving her a smile, hoping to look understanding. Again, the moment seemed to lengthen. The two standing still, searching the other's face, hands still clasped, not wanting to make a misstep.

She seemed to steady herself as she said, "My lord, I do wish my realm to be free. I simply do not know how to help you. There are ways that I could escape my situation personally, but I cannot see a path for my people." She lowered her head as she spoke, sounding a little defeated.

Devick knew that should Biellah marry another provincial ruler she would be free from her post, and someone else would be placed there. Suddenly he realized he was on more dangerous ground then he first supposed. He had no desire to mislead Biellah into a romantic attachment, especially since her marriage out of her station would place her province completely under the Aya Dao'Tai's power. This escape truly had to be the greatest of temptations for her. He let go of her hands and took her by the shoulders, drawing her gaze back to his.

"I know your situation is precarious, Your Grace, and I do not suggest you march in open war. What I ask is merely for similar support and information as you have trusted me with tonight. In return, I will do what is possible to help you and your people where you see the need most. I truly believe *we* can find a way."

Biellah turned and leaned out upon the cold stone of the bulwarks. The hard cool surface helping to calm the sudden sharp yearning for Devick's touch. A yearning for any sympathetic intimacy, she realized.

To just feel not so alone.

The light from the stars glinted off the river far below. Brightest of them all, Ailc shone high above the distant mountains. Devick noticed her breathing slow and she turned back to him. In the chill light of the stars, the curves and angles of her face looked like etched glass, sparkling with fragility. It was a stark contrast to the trembling youth that Devick had seen before the Aya Dao'Tai earlier that day. She looked more determined, as though she had found a new source of empowerment.

"My lord, let us see each other as allies in this cause, then. I will do what I can, and you shall do what you can. And together maybe we can help each other see a better dawn for both our realms." She pulled her hood back up and stepped back into the darkness of the bulwark.

"Well spoken, Your Grace, and so shall it be. I am truly grateful for your trust." He paused for a moment, "And for your friendship in this." Devick thought he saw her smile in the darkness.

"I am glad too, my lord. I am tired of feeling alone and having nothing to hope for," she said softly, almost to herself more than to him.

"I will be sending word once we are free of the city. For the rest of our stay, I think we should carry on as before," he said.

"You are right, no one must suspect that anything between us has changed. Good night, my lord, and...thank you." As she passed by him, she reached out and brushed the tips of his fingers with hers. The gentle sound of her footfalls on the stone drifted into the silent night, and Devick was not sure how long he stared into the stars after the sound of it had receded.

Do we have a hope? Is there a way that leads to something other than war and a final annihilation for our people?

He watched as the pale gold moon started to crest the distant mountains. The calm light spilled onto the landscape, bathing it in an echo of dawn. Devick's thoughts drifted to the first time he could remember watching the moonrise, his mother at his side. She had told him of the moon and its movements, of the reckoning of time and the shift in the seasons.

"Devick, do you know why we count the span of our days by the light of the night?" she had asked him.

"Is it because the moon is so large, Mother?" he had asked. Devick remembered her smile, the love that glowed in her eyes. He remembered her soft touch on his shoulder.

"In part, I think so. The moon reminds us there is a rhythm to both light and darkness. The moon teaches us to hope in the return of the light, it is a reminder in the darkness of the dawn to come."

Devick was not sure what she had been talking about so long ago, but he understood now, and he could not help but wonder if he would someday have the chance to explain the moon to children of his own. He stood, letting the chill of the night numb the ache that welled up in his heart. A cold tear fell from his face, striking the stone he leaned on. He reflexively wiped his eyes, not realizing he had been weeping. He forced his thoughts from the past and his desperate hopes for the future.

I must focus only on what I can do in the present.

Devick remembered what Gairrle had warned him about in the grand hall, and he worried that Biellah had read more into their exchange than she should have. Regardless, she seemed to understand and accept what Devick had told her, and she seemed to be ready to help. He turned from the night sky and slowly made his way back into the main part of the palace. Once back inside his room he lay on the soft bed, hoping for a few hours of peaceful sleep before the next day arrived.

"Lady Re'alis, I must speak with her next."

8

Lord and Lady

*U*nto the kindreds who strive valiantly in life, a place is prepared in the afterlife according to their deeds and desires. Brightness to brilliance and dark to darkness will be the measure of the eons next. For it is written death is aught but the portal of continuance.
Essays of the Divine

Devick awoke and sat up in his bed. It was the morning of his last day in Anoth. Soft burgundy light came spilling into the room, filtered by the curtain of the window. Rubbing the sleep from his eyes he swung his legs from under the blankets and walked over to the window of his room. He parted the curtains enough to see outside; the sun was just peeking over the walls of the palace grounds. This was his last chance to speak with Lady Re'alis. Despite his best efforts, no opportunity had presented itself during the rest of the council to speak with her or the dayrn. Frustratingly, time and time again over the last fourthmoon he had been unable to have any meaningful words with Re'alis. Having known her from their youth, he was surprised by this and wondered if she was deliberately avoiding him. Or perhaps, the Aya was working carefully to ensure no collaborations could occur between any of her so-called provincial rulers. From what he read in the

Sunshadow's espionage report on Dayrn Chalid, it was probably best that he had not approached him.

Inside the palace complex he and the other nobles were fairly free to move about as they wished though Devick knew they were watched closely. Movement within the city was different. In the city or on their way out of Subjugate-occupied territory a Dao'Tai escort monitored all activity. Approved conduct papers were needed for inter-district travel within Ell'Anoth. They were also not allowed to correspond or travel outside their provinces without permission from the Aya Dao'Tai and an escort, all of which would make it more difficult to speak with Re'alis before they parted ways.

Devick dressed, packed his belongings, and entered the adjoining room. He found Gairrle there along with a few of his men.

"Good morning, my lord. We have been told that we are to leave the complex at our leisure. It might interest you to know that the Lady Re'alis' men are preparing to leave. Our men are ready to depart at your command."

Devick smiled. There was a reason Gairrle held the high rank of captain without being from a noble house.

"Excellent. We will leave immediately." He handed Gairrle a letter, the only mark on it a simple half circle with two lines under it. "See that this reaches the right person."

Gairrle took the letter, "Right away, my lord. Serjent Rahim, ready the men and horses."

Gairrle and Rahim both gave a salute and left the room. Devick and the remaining guards made their way back through the long corridor to the courtyard of the royal complex.

The courtyard was large, several hundred paces wide, surrounded with high walls of stone in the very center of Ell'Anoth. The palace complex had been restored after the war and was used as a figurehead place of governance. The true capitol buildings of the Subjugate were in the Dao'Tai fortress of Taiw'Tai. On this bright morning, the courtyard was filled with horses, chariots, and wagons, all of which were preparing to leave the palace.

Devick made his way through the men hurrying about to saddle horses, fill wagons, and ready all things to depart. He came near to Lady Re'alis upon her Appaloosa mount. Subjugate minders walked the ramparts about and hosts of palace slaves and servants thronged near, any of which could be eager spies for their harsh Dao'Tai masters. It was not an ideal place to speak with her, but he was out of time.

"Lady Re'alis, I would be honored if your party would accompany mine for as long as our paths are merged," he said with all the polish he could muster.

Re'alis smiled with a warmth that mirrored the radiance of the sun in her long red hair. Her eyes shifted just for an instant to her captain of guards, who nodded, then made her answer.

"I would be glad to have you join with us, Lord Devick."

"You do me an honor; thank you, my lady." Devick strode over to his braydfar warhorse and, aware of the gaze of Lady Re'alis, nimbly swung into his saddle with one smooth motion and rallied his heavily armed escort about him.

The companies of Mantorah and Lea'Angleneth together made for a grand host both in numbers and colored pageantry. Bright banners displaying the heraldry of their realms danced in the morning air. Passing out the gates of the courtyard, Devick saw the dynes, Biellah and her small Freeholdn escort gathered. Their distinctive maille and placard armor harking back to happier times in the realms.

"Your Grace, Alpa go with you, may your journey home be swift and safe."

Biellah smiled affectionately and waved her hand in farewell.

"And may she place a safe road before you as well, my lord, till we next meet." Devick held much hope that his exchange with Biellah would result in a strong cooperation. He knew the Camarilla would be eager for a potential alliance with the Freeholdn. They might even seek to send agents and troops in secret to bolster any efforts to counter the Subjugate in the north.

Devick and Lady Re'alis' companies streamed out of the courtyard and into a broad street, then slowly made their way through the city. Devick hoped that by traveling with Re'alis he would have one last chance to speak in private with her. This moment would have to wait until they were free of Subjugate escort and observation, which would not occur until they were safely some distance from Ell'Anoth.

The streets of Ell'Anoth were already bustling with people. Great gold-colored stone buildings lined the broad cobblestone streets—high arching temples, great manors, and shops of all kinds. Throngs of people from all walks of life and from many lands filled the streets and walkways. They looked as prosperous and well-groomed as would be expected in such a large and well-built city. It would have been a cheery and welcoming sight were it not for the tokens of the Subjugate's iron grip.

Guards and inspectors were on almost every corner. Dark watch-towers dotted the cityscape, from which Dao'Tai minders would watch day and night every movement of the populace. The city had been walled within to form different districts, and one had to have papers signed by an inspector to move from one district to another. Thus, all the comings and goings of the people were monitored. Worse still was the condition of all the lowest castes and slaves. Before the Dao'Tai invasion there were no castes of people, but now all were set into a caste, and slaving was a thriving industry. Most were young, the remnants of the last free-born generations of the Anothn people. They trailed their owners with faces downcast, hauling their burdens in silent desperation. Slaves were needed to form the huge labor force that kept the Subjugate soldiers marching. This was the state of the whole realm. All aspects of Anoth were now marred by the oppression of the Aya Dao'Tai.

As Devick rode through the streets, his thoughts turned to his own lands and people. If the Aya Dao'Tai had her way, the fate of Anoth would be Mantorah's as well. They were stopped three times at checkpoints and had to present letters of travel from the Aya Dao'Tai in order to pass the inspectors before they were finally at the city's outer gates. The gates themselves were a wonder to behold. They were three men high, and wide enough for six horsemen to pass through with ease. Their size was not the sole source of their wonder, though, the material of which they were made was even more magnificent—black stone bound with avertyyn bands. The craftsmanship was so fine that almost no seam could be seen when shut and locked into place. The skill and lore that allowed man to work stone like this had long been lost in the abyss of time, the gates of Ell'Anoth being one of the last relics. The gates shone brilliantly in the sunlight as Devick drew nigh. Despite their enormity and mass, they were so perfectly hung on their hinges that a few stout men could move them into place without great exertion. The company soon rode through the great gates and out onto the road that led into the countryside. At the gates, a small group of Taivadean horsemen fell in behind Devick's men. Devick was glad to be out of the city but hoped that the gaze of the Aya's lackeys would not be so keen as to prevent his meeting with Re'alis. A short distance from the city gates the lady brought her horse alongside Devick's.

"When I was little, my father and I would travel to Ell'Anoth to watch the plays in the great gallery. You remember, we attended more than a few together. It was such a wonderful, beautiful place to visit then. I once looked forward to coming here with so much anticipation." She let out a long sigh, "But now I am so very glad to leave it far behind me. I always fear that I may never be let out once I enter."

"I too, remember the greatness of the realm. Anoth was ever the great protector and arbiter of peace, and Ell'Anoth its heart. A realm you could count on to come to your aid. Yet, in her hour of need almost all forsook her." Devick shook his head, remembering the events that colored his youth.

They both looked back at the Subjugate escort, then she turned to catch his gaze directly, a sharpness in her normally warm hazel eyes.

"I feel that the threats of the Aya will follow us this time, my lord. Beyond the normal escort."

"We will see you safe as far as our paths are one, my lady, I swear it."

"I am sure you will, Lord Rahdan. You are always so quick to heed the call of chivalry." She smiled congenially. "It does put my mind at ease to know we are under the guard of your sword." Devick wondered how much the last handful of years had changed the perfervid girl he remembered Re'alis as in their youth. Before the war, before the Subjugate, before all their lives were turned on end.

They rode in silence for a while. Their surroundings gently turned into a green rolling countryside with small mills and farms sprinkled about like the dew in a pleasant meadow. But the roving patrols of heavily armed Dao'Tai soldiers of the Subjugate were always about, going from village to village and making sure that the will of the Aya Dao'Tai was enforced. There was always a steady stream of 'lawbreakers' to fill the slavers' tents and to serve as targets for Subjugate arbalesters. They rode tensely past them, and midday was several hours past and the road had carried them beyond almost all signs of man.

Devick turned to speak softly to Re'alis, who was still riding at his side.

"My lady, I fear that our defiance before the Aya Dao'Tai will bring extra scrutiny upon us and our people." He worked to conceal the concern in his voice. It was not hard to guess at the Aya Dao'Tai's intentions toward them both.

"I was thinking over the same issue. I would speak to you more of this when we are further away from the heart of her lands, and her escort," she answered quietly, giving a meaningful glance behind her to the Taivadean soldiers following them.

"Yes, talk such as that can wait," Devick reluctantly agreed. She was right to be cautious, but there was much he wanted to discuss with her. Instead, he forced himself to change topics.

"I would much rather hear of your home and lands; how do they fare?" he asked sincerely. The summers spent there were truly high-lights of my growing years."

The two of them fell into speaking of more pleasant things. They talked of Re'alis' home in Lea'Angleneth, with its great colleges, high towers, and green alpine dells. The land of Lea'Angleneth was a small city-state amid the Vagath'Oth Mountains. Angleneth, the capital and the only city of any size, was on the isle of Angleneth, in the midst of Lake Akarr. Lea'Angleneth was a peaceful land that enjoyed a sub-stantial portion of its safety due to the limited mountain passes into the realm. Despite the small size, they were well-known throughout the realms for their scholars, engineers, advanced architecture, and mechanical marvels. Devick knew some about this, for many of the mechanical weapons of Mantorah were made by the artificers of An-gleneth.

They continued their light conversation as the road steadily ran on and the day dwindled to late evening. They followed the road as it made its way through the pleasant countryside. It was a quiet and peaceful journey, and they kept a good pace. The low setting sun cast a comfortable orange light upon the land and travelers as they slowed their pace to look for a place to lodge for the night.

A small grove and oak thicket lay a short distance from the road. It looked to be a suitable place to overnight. So, the troop chose to stop and make camp under the shelter of the shaded thicket. Large tents were brought from the wagons, and soon bright fires and good food warmed all within and without. The night passed in peace, ever under the watchful eyes of the Subjugate escort.

As the sun rose from his slumber, Devick was up early to find yeomen and squires of the company already busy breaking camp and preparing to continue their journey. Shortly after a simple breakfast they continued their travel. The road in this part of the land was wide and in good repair, allowing them to ride four horses abreast with the wagons in the rear, riders on either side of them. Re'alis and Devick rode toward the front of the column, side by side as they did the day before.

It was a pleasant day. The air was warm, full of birdsong and the sweet fragrance of earth and greenery. Pleasant conversation of many things between Devick and Re'alis passed the time well, and Devick found he greatly enjoyed her company. Several days more passed, with both the good road and weather holding. On the fifth day from the gates of Ell'Anoth the land was slowly changing, becoming steeper and hilly as they drew closer to the mountains. A few hours before high sun, as the lady was relating some tale of an exploit of her youth, Devick became very silent and still.

"My lord, did I say something amiss?" she asked, noticing his silence.

"The birds, they are no longer singing," he replied slowly. As Devick said this the riders of the vanguard came up the road toward them, calling out as they drew near.

"My lord! There is smoke and the sounds of battle from the village down the road!"

Devick's face took on a fierce, grim look, swiftly taking a mental inventory of his company's capacity for battle. The total number of armored men, their present armor and weaponry, the best place of defense, and the avenues for attack.

"My lady, would you please draw back to your wagons and men?" he asked sternly.

She glanced down the road, and for a moment Devick was afraid she would demand to stay, but then she sighed. "Yes, of course, Devick, but what are you going to do?" she asked.

"I am going to make sure there is no threat to you or our company," he replied grimly. Devick and his men were already dressed in habergeons and angular plate cuisses, as it was the Mantorahn custom to always be ready for battle.

Re'alis pulled rein and rode her horse back to where her men were. Devick and two and a half score of his warriors, spurred their warhorses and galloped up the road ahead of the rest of the company, half the Subjugate escort following.

They rode over a low ridge, and smoke could be seen coming from the houses in the distance, though the village was still more than a few skain off. Halfway between them and the village Devick could make out the forms of chariots and men coming toward them at a slow, steady pace. He recognized the banners of the approaching men. Devick halted the advance of his company and moved to give the road to the on-comers. As they drew closer, it was plain for all to see they were soldiers of the Aya Dao'Tai, the dark purple and black banners with their gold sigil were unmistakable. It was a considerable number: six war chariots, a wagon, over three hundred armored men, and a few others on horseback.

All the Dao'Tai soldiers wore a complex and well-made suit of armor. The plates were steely blue in color, etched around the edges and fitted with flute work up the back and chest, rendering them all but invulnerable. They wore steel barbutes and thick leathers under the steel armor. The color of the helm was the same as their armor, save a low ridge that ran along the top of the helm, starting at the nose and continuing over the top. This was colored to indicate the rank of the one who wore it. The faces of the helmets were embossed to resemble that of a roaring lion. Altogether, these warriors were quite imposing, to say the least. When they were within a spear cast from Devick they stopped.

Two of the mounted men came up to where Devick had stopped his men. These men were not Dao'Tai, but rather Taivadean, long-limbed and blue-eyed. Bright blonde hair spilled out from under their tall helms. The Dao'Tai were not a people who normally rode horses, and so most of the cavalry used by the Subjugate was Taivadean. The larger of the two soldiers, and the one who looked to be their captain, addressed Devick.

"Sir, whho arre yoo and whhat is yoorr purpose on tha rrud?" The man spoke with a thick accent and a condescending tone. Devick responded calmly.

"I am High Lord Rahdan of Mantorah. We are returning home after concluding business with Her Majesty the Aya Dao'Tai. This is her seal upon the safe conduct pass." Devick held the paper for him to see. The tall, well-armed soldier peered through the ocular of his helm at the seal.

Devick continued, "We saw the smoke and came to see if we could lend aid to someone in need. The rest of our company is still coming up the road with our wagons." The Dao'Tai captain signaled his troops to continue as the Taivadean spoke.

"Varry whell, all seems ta be in orrdur. As yoo can see, yoor aid is nut needed nowh." The men-at-arms and chariots started passing by Devick and his warriors. They all marched and rode in good order. Devick looked again to the smoking buildings and spoke, careful to use the Taivadean word for captain.

"If I may, Ordvyr, what was the trouble in the village? Should we be on our guard?"

The ordvyr chuckled, "Nah, tha woold-be rrebuls ave bun stomped back inna ta dust they arre." The last of the chariots went by and he bid his farewell, "Gud day m'Lord Rahdan, and peace ta yoor rrealm!"

With that the two horsemen rode away giving a salute to the Taivadean escort of Devick's company as they passed toward the front of the soldiers marching down the road. Devick and his men held their place at the roadside and waited for the wagon that brought up the rear of the war band to pass by.

The large wagon slowly rolled closer, and all could hear the distinct sound of clattering chains over the noise of the wagon's iron-bound wheels. Devick watched closely as the back of the wagon drew near. As it passed by it left a trail of dust, and within the cloud Devick could see the forms of people—men, women, and children of varied ages chained to the back of the wagon. All had the battered, forlorn looked of war-taken prisoners, and many were blood-covered and wounded. Some looked up at him with pleading in their eyes and tears upon their faces, but none of the prisoners spoke.

Patient Father, grant me strength. Devick ground his teeth together. *Put my feet to the path of justice for these people.* He continued to pray, and it took the majority of Devick's self-control to stay his hand from falling on these people's captors. However, he knew that now was not the time to avenge all the wrongs of the Subjugate. So, he and his men watched the sorrowful parade in silence.

Devick could not help but take particular notice of the last prisoner. She wore a tattered blue dress and was built as one who had worked and fought all her life. It was not her outward appearance that caught Devick's attention as much as it was the fierce and defiant look she had upon her face. She was not like the others, wholly downcast and defeated, but rather much the opposite. Defiance and an unconquerable heart showed through her bright eyes; she was an unbroken spirit.

She looked at him long, and Devick dared not break her fierce gaze. At last, the chains at her neck and wrists forced her to look away. The dust hung thick in the still air as the woeful troop of prisoners faded into the horizon. It was not the first time such a scene had passed before Devick's eyes. It was standard procedure for the Dao'Tai's soldiers to react in this way to any threat, be it real or contrived. They would burn and slaughter most of the village, then the young and strong would be taken as prisoners, while being called enemies to the Dao'Tai Subjugate. The sick and old would be left to bury the dead and tell the tale.

The sound of more wagons and horses from behind Devick announced the approach of the remainder of his and Lady Re'alis' company. He broke the silence and spoke to some of his men.

"Serjent, take twelve men and see if we can lend aid to the survivors in the town. We will await the rest of our company here. If we can lend no aid, come to us speedily, I would not have the lady exposed to such a scene of death and sorrow if we can do nothing to amend it."

"It shall be done, my lord," answered Serjent Rahim. He then gathered his men, and they sped toward the town, leaving the rest in a tense silence. Even men familiar with the sights of war such as these could not help but be upset, for they all knew too well the end that awaited those taken by the Subjugate—the arbalesters' posts, or the slavers' guild. With this dark thought in mind, they sat in their saddles, awaiting the rest of the company.

A few moments later the company reached them, and the entire troop continued along the road to the town. The choking smell of burned flesh and thatch raced to meet them once they were a bow's shot from the gate and the low wall that ran about the perimeter of the town. Pillars of smoke were again pouring into the sky, as ink cast into pools of blue water. A breeze had picked up, turning embers into flames once again. Beams of sunlight fell like streams of golden tears through the smoky haze, illuminating a half-burned temple of Alpa within the village. It was as if the aashahl herself were weeping over the slaughter. The town, all afire, could have been a sad tapestry hanging in some cold, lonely hall, remembering a past woe—but this was all too real. This was the hallmark of the Aya Dao'Tai's rule—death, slaughter, and the abuse of the helpless. Devick could feel his face flush as anger, sorrow, and frustration stuck in his throat, threatening to escape in a sob, a scream, or maybe both.

"Sir, shall we draw also?" the serjent nearest him asked hesitantly.

Devick released the crushing grip from his sword hilt. A grip he had not realized he had placed there.

"No, force of habit on my part."

Re'alis was again at Devick's side, and she spoke in a hushed voice, as if trying to not disturb the fragile calm that was in the air. "More victims of Subjugate justice?"

Devick nodded in response. "We best not linger, milady."

They rode on, Devick reverently considering the loss of life that must have occurred within the village walls. Soon, the clamor of horses' hooves at the gates of the village drew their eyes to the coming of the Mantorahn scouting party. They rode up to Devick to make their report.

"My lord, we have searched the town throughout and can find no one living. It appears that all were either killed in the fight for the town or were taken by the Dao'Tai." This news surprised Devick. The Dao'Tai always left a few to warn others against disobedience to the Subjugate.

This is not a good development. Devick was unsure what this new turn in the Subjugate tactics meant, but he was sure that this was not the last time he would be witness to such events. He took a few moments to make his reply.

"Very well, serjent Rahim, then there is nothing to be done save bury the dead."

"Nay, my lord, there are none to bury. It seems that the dead and living were burned with the buildings," said the soldier.

"I see. Return to your position in the column."

"Very good, sir," Rahim replied, and he and his twelve moved back into the lines of cavalry.

Devick had no desire to linger, so with the company all together once again they set out on their way. The lighthearted chatter of the day prior was not present now. All rode soberly with few words exchanged. Devick pondered the sights of the day, and the possible reasons for the destruction at the village they had passed. Re'alis remained silent. He could feel her eyes on him for long moments of time, but he was too consumed in thought to return her gaze.

The Dao'Tai were like no other people in the High Sun realms. The vast Subjugate army was made up of these large, dark-skinned foreigners, standing a head above the tallest of the men of Mantorah, thick-limbed and extraordinarily strong. All their natural characteristics made them elite soldiers. No one really knew where the Aya Dao'Tai and her unstoppable army even came from. Their entire people had swept through the land from the east side of the Vagath'Oth, but their homeland was much further away, past the Shellidack Mountains and the gates of the east. They had their own language like the people of the Thalyphonie Islands and did not mingle or deal with others unless they had great need. Stranger still was the fact that the Aya Dao'Tai was nothing like the Dao'Tai themselves. She seemed to be something else entirely. Physically she was vastly different from the Dao'Tai females, but she also had an unnatural air of power, she seemed to exude it like a tangible substance. Her Junoesque build, unsettling eyes and the way light seemed to falter around her were singular and unnerving.

And there is her shadow—nothing normal about that. Devick's thoughts were swarming, like a hive of bees.

When Devick first met the Aya Dao'Tai he was much younger. At first, he credited the darkness that seemed to surround her as a youthful reaction to the fear she instilled in him then. Now, however, Devick had outgrown his fear, yet the shadow about her remained, larger than it should have been and nowhere near to her actual physical shape. No, there was something more to her than one could gauge with the eye, he was sure. Devick only could hope that this unknown factor would not cause the doom of his people and plans.

Miljah was full of beings who possessed powers that mortal kindreds could only dream of. He could think of a handful, mostly legends really, yet others were all too real. The Drakes in the south, the Akarii, Shedim, Atha'Tarrii, Pali'andeo, Allitorii, the Aashahl; even the royal line of Anoth possessed traits that could only be attributed to an arcane connection.

Dark tears take me, she could be anything really! And I don't know enough to tell what kind of threat she might be.

Devick suddenly realized that he had spent all these years making strategies to defeat the Dao'Tai army, but not nearly enough time puzzling out the Aya Dao'Tai and her true nature. He had directed the

Sunshadow to gather every scrap of information on the army they could find; troop numbers, fortress locations—everything. They had not had the same success gathering information on the Aya Dao'Tai.

Devick knew that the Sunshadow only aided him because they needed the supplies and aid that Mantorah could provide. The leaders of what was left of the Anoth army had their own goals and plans in place, and they had been careful to keep those a secret, even from him. He was sure that a larger part of the army than anyone might guess survived and were operating in the shadows of the Subjugate. Devick was lucky indeed that they would risk exposure to get him information at all. His thoughts trailed off as again he could feel Re'alis' eyes upon him.

This time he returned her glance and tried to smile, though his mood was still dark. He realized that they had traveled some distance now, two or more skain. The rhythm of his horse and the depth of his thoughts had put any sense of time and distance far from his focus. Re'alis returned his smile and wet her lips, as though to speak, but she said nothing. Devick wondered how long she had been waiting for him to look up at her; a shade, maybe more? He could not be sure.

"Milady, I apologize for my solemn mood. I find myself consumed with..." He shot a quick glance over his shoulders where the Subjugate escorts rode, ever watchful. "I find myself consumed with introspection," he finished in a quieter tone.

"I understand. I think we both will be in better spirits with another score skain behind us," she said.

"Indeed, much better I should think," he replied. Devick shifted his weight in his saddle and looked again to the Taivadean escorts. The plates on their armor were a soft brown color as was their maille, both covered with a beeswax lacquer as a moisture protection. Their stormy blue eyes never moved from Devick and Re'alis, and they made no attempts to conceal their observation.

Patient Father, help me. No sense in trying to discuss anything important till we are far clear from them. Devick let out a long sigh and Re'alis gave him a look that made him wonder if she was reading his thoughts. They continued to ride quietly, allowing the countryside to pass by to the cadence and clamor of the horses and wagons.

9

Treason

Of the Aashahl there are many who seek aught save the bliss of the natural spheres of dominion. Should they lend mortal kindreds their aid, the wise take heed and listen. Giving thanks in due portion to their benefactors.
Essays of the Divine.

Devick had been silent for more than a halfsun now and Re'alis struggled to clear her mind of the awful sights and smells of the razed village. For a while she had put her mind to thoughts of their surroundings, hoping their beauty would displace the sadness she felt for the people they had seen that day. Dannitar had been generous this season and the landscape was verdant. The road had narrowed much and presently wandered its way through short scraggy trees, velvet grasses, and vibrant stands of tall-stemmed flowers. Some she knew; the hot crimson lythsyn, the dark red-violet blood-lilies, and the purple-black night snaps. Other deep blue and bright yellow flowers she did not recognize with their azure starbursts and sun-bright twisting petals, respectively. The air was pleasantly fragrant and filled with the industrious buzz of legions of bees about their work amongst the marvelous wildflowers.

Despite her best efforts her mind kept coming back to the village. She was not accustomed to seeing such things as burned towns and chained prisoners. She was no fool and understood that such things were common enough in the Dao'Tai occupied realms, but she had not been fully prepared to see it all firsthand. The idea of such events occurring in her own home was a growing concern. How long could she hope to keep the Aya Dao'Tai placated and out of Lea'Angleneth?

How long before they march on the High Lakes? How much longer can we hope to be ignored and left in peace?

She knew, all too well, that should war come to her realm on the Subjugate's terms her people had little chance of survival. Lea'Angleneth's walls of mountains would not stop the Dao'Tai armies for long. They needed to be resisted, defeated even, for any real lasting peace and safety. It had to start somewhere; someone had to stand up to the Subjugate's tyranny. Yet, she wondered if Lea'Angleneth could withstand the repercussions of such an act. She wondered if they would stand alone.

The people of Lea'Angleneth were under the same restrictions on travel outside their lands as every other realm, and under a heavy tax. Three-fifths of all her people produced was claimed by the Aya Dao'Tai. Under this burden the people of Lea'Angleneth turned their mechanical ingenuity toward efficiency and production increase. Clockwork marvels now harvested grain, tilled the earth, and powered the industry of the High Lakes Realm. In many ways, Lea'Angleneth was even more a wonder to behold than it had been under her father, though no other realms could benefit from their prosperity and innovations. The Aya Dao'Tai had banned weapons production, and their inspectors were keen to make sure there was no violation of this order. They were too late, however, to round up the clever minds behind Lea'Angleneth's singular war engines. Re'alis didn't know for sure, but she had reasons to believe they had all fled to Mantorah where they, and their work, could be more easily hidden. At least that was what she hoped had happened to them. They would need every advantage in the war she was growing certain would come, and there were few advantages as keen as Lea'Angleneth's war engines.

Re'alis closed her eyes and focused on the motion of the horse under her, the smell of the cool air, and the sound of the countryside they rode through. The air was cool, but not uncomfortably so. It would be colder at home still. The Anoth plains always saw the first thaw in Arah-Donar, the very start of the springtime.

It will still feel like Arah-Far at home, cool and barely a flower bud open yet. Her anticipation of being home grew a little brighter with that thought. She opened her eyes and cleared her mind of everything, save the beauty of the renewed greenery around her. With the snows long melted here and the warming showers, everything was bursting with life. Trees, tall grass, wildflowers and more all flourished around them as they rode deeper into the untamed marches of the land.

It does not matter how bad it gets, the Dao'Tai cannot destroy everything good and beautiful, Dannitar has seen to that. With that thought she smiled to herself and shifted her weight in the saddle, careful to keep her riding dress from snagging on any tack. She had plenty of time to think things through on the way home. Time to mark the best path forward for her people.

They made good time that day and set camp much as they did the night before. The Subjugate escorts kept a careful watch on both her and Lord Devick all the night. They continued to travel and camp as they may for several more days. Most of the time Re'alis rode near Devick. They talked a little, but the weather had soured, and a light rain made the days feel longer and dampened conversation. On the ninth day from Ell'Anoth the weather cleared again. Without a word the Subjugate escorts departed, returning to Ell'Anoth, much to Re'alis' relief. There were things she needed to discuss with Lord Devick away from their prying eyes.

The next day saw them turn their course to follow the steppes of the Vagath'Oth mountain range, almost due south. The tokens of spring were evident in the sweet air as the group passed along the western slopes of the tree-covered walls of stone. This part of the Va-gath'Oth was very steep and heavily wooded. Several great spurs of the mountains cut out into the steps marked by streamlets and fast run-ning waters. On the way to Ell'Anoth, this part of their journey had been frequented by many harts, birds, and even a boar that fell to their supper fires. However, on this passing Devick thought the land was unusually still and free of wild game.

Despite this, the mood of the party was much improved, and pleas-ant conversation passed the hours of day. The land was quite different now. The green hills and groves of trees had changed to sharp thickly wooded rocky ridges with streamlets cheerfully winding their way to-ward the Aril River. They traveled all that day, making a steady course for the crossing of the Aril River at Far'thonnin's Ford.

That night they made camp near the base of the mountain where the narrow gorge they had entered that morning widened into a pleas-ant green glade speckled with more of the wildflowers. Devick deemed they were far enough from the Aya Dao'Tai and her spies to discuss the matters that had been in the back of his mind for the last few days. The Taivadeans' departure was unexpected, but he was not about to waste such a chance to counsel with Re'alis. Typically, the escort would have followed them all the way to their respective realms. De-vick wondered if the Taivadeans were about their own agenda. Ac-cording to the reports from the Sunshadow, the Taivadeans were not as enthralled to the Subjugate as it might seem. Could this chance to meet with Re'alis at their departure be a deliberate move on their part to help? There was no way to know.

The tents were pitched in good order within a circling grove of trees not far from the road. Both horse and man took rest and food in the cool shade of the towering trees. After supper and the setting of the guard, Devick crossed the camp to Re'alis' tent. Nearly all their party had retired for the night, save the watch and a few lingering souls near the cooking fire awaiting a mulled drink.

Passing the Alabaster Guard with an exchanged salute, he paused recognizing a member of Angleneth's royal guard.

"Gallant Aireathyn, I wish to pass a word to your mistress this eve."

"As you wish, I believe my lady expects you, Lord Mantorah." Aireathyn bowed, his perfect white armor reflecting the firelight of the camp as he moved for Devick to pass.

Devick strode the last distance to Re'alis' tent and stood near her door for a moment. Devick knew that he would need to be clear with Re'alis. He would have to make sure she understood how much danger his plans would bring upon any who assisted, or even knew about them. His thoughts scattered, Devick suddenly realized he could see the vague outline of Re'alis as she moved within her tent. He could not help but admire her form for an instant before realizing that she could not have been wearing much more than a chemise. He quickly turned his head and waited a bit longer. Several minutes passed in silence. Devick peeked back and could no longer see her moving within the tent. He put his hand to the pole that made up the doorway and knocked upon it.

"My lady, I would speak with you if you are not too weary from the day."

"Enter, Devick, and speak," she said, sounding eager.

He walked in and found Re'alis now in a warm-looking fur robe, relaxed in a carved pack chair. Devick walked over to a simple stool, and she motioned for him to take the seat next her.

"My lady," he started, but he was quickly interrupted.

"Please, let us talk like friends and not acquaintances, we have known each other from childhood."

Devick smiled at her and started over, "Lady Re'alis." She let out a soft trickle of laughter at his relentless formality, but Devick continued.

"What I wish to discuss would be considered treason, so if you want no part of it, please say so." Devick hoped his voice reflected the seriousness of the matter.

Her face lost its mirth as she spoke seriously, "What does this issue deal with, Devick?"

*This is it then...where to start...*He thought in silence for a few moments, not looking away from Re'alis as he searched for the right starting point, the right words.

"War, milady, complete rebellion, and the hope for the destruction of the Subjugate. Among other things."

Re'alis sat motionless and quiet for what seemed ages to Devick as he tried to wait patiently for her answer. It was excruciating. Her face was a mask, a carefully practiced expression that revealed nothing. No shock, no panic, nothing about her face betrayed what she was thinking. Devick was starting to worry that he had been too bold, too open with her. Maybe he had guessed at her mind all wrong and maybe she was not the enemy of the Aya Dao'Tai that she had seemed to be.

"Treason indeed," she finally said slowly, as though she were feeling the words for their fit, like a new dress.

Devick said nothing as he watched her face for some hint as to her thoughts—the arch of the eyebrows, the line of the jaw—nothing. He began trying to think of a way to backtrack when suddenly there it was, a hint at the corner of her lips, the curling start of a smile threatened to break through her mask.

"Well," the mask fell into a generous smile, "if it is to be treason then let us both be involved."

Devick let out a sigh of tension that he felt relax his whole body. She was with him. He felt a wave of relief wash over him, just for an instant, before the gravity of it all came crashing back.

"Please tell me all that you will, Devick," she said.

Devick did not miss the excitement on her face, nor the anxiety in her voice.

"Thanks to the Sunshadow, I have learned that the Grishkii attacks throughout the Vagath'Oth are the doing of the Aya Dao'Tai."

She looked confused for a moment.

No sense in holding back anything now, he thought.

"The Sunshadow are what is left of the army of Anoth. They help me gain information from throughout the High Sun Realms and even further away on occasion. They are a useful ally. We can trust them."

"I see. Well, then what was the purpose of the attacks?" she asked.

"They were sent to find and kill one of the heirs of Anoth."

She raised an eyebrow. "The whole family was dead, I thought, killed in the sacking of Ell'Anoth?"

"Or so we have always thought, but what if someone lived? The Aya certainly seems to think it was possible." He could not keep the excitement out of his voice.

"The bodies of Anica and Kyrale were displayed in public after the Aya Dao'Tai took the city. They claimed the children burned alive in the destruction of the palace. But what if one of them survived?" He wet his lips and continued, "The Grishkii attack was centered on a village called Allinth; this was the attack Dayrn Chalid spoke of the first day of the council."

"Devick, this is very intriguing, and I truly hope they survived, but even if an heir to the throne of Anoth does live, how does this help us? One person does not upset an empire." Her voice had only the slightest hint of skepticism. Devick could not blame her, he knew how desperate it sounded; he could only hope to convey his many months of searching, hoping, and planning into something that made sense to her.

"We need a weapon and a rallying point, an advantage in the war that is sure to come. Having an heir to Anoth would bring many to our cause as the legitimate inheritor of the old alliances. More than this, though. After seeking as much of the old lore as I could, I have learned that the royal bloodline of Anoth can both unite the Tears of the Aashahl and counter the evil powers of the carrion reapers. I confess I do not know how, but it is well documented that they have an otherly power in this regard. Without such an advantage I fear that our cause is doomed from its onset." He paused, giving his words time to form again. She watched him with unwavering attention. Her warm hazel eyes fixed and heeding.

"I intend to find the heir, Patient Father willing, and together fight for the freedom of Anoth and all the High Sun Realms. I have a plan; it is a bold venture, yet I feel the wind of fate at my back and I must head it." He leaned back, hoping that some of that made sense. Hoping that it was not as impossible as it sounded when spoken out loud.

Re'alis finally looked away from him for a moment to the spark stone lamps that filled her tent with a warm light. She smiled to herself, and Devick could not help but look upon the graceful lines in her face with wonder. In the years since they were children she had grown into an elegance and beauty that were all her own. Her movements and the way she held herself demanded respect as a noble lady, but in her face, he could see the spirit and fire that had ruled her childhood. She finally turned her attention back to him, her face more than a little stern.

"Ah, is that all you wish to do?" she said cynically. "I thought you wanted to do something sensible, like unite the remaining realms to fight the Subjugate. Not an impossible quest to find a lost heir and a hope of some magical aid. Don't you think that if the royal line of Anoth actually had such power that they would have used it when the Dao'Tai first attacked? There is no way you could defeat her armies, Devick. Let alone restore the Anothn throne."

Devick felt a spark of defiance and he leaned forward to speak.

"The heir is not my only aim but a part of a greater plan. Yet even so, all my life I have longed for an honorable, noble cause to pledge myself to. A true struggle against a true evil. Aiding the Sunshadow isn't enough. After almost twenty years of watching a foreign tyrant rule over a people she treats like animals and doing nothing, I can stand by no longer. The last king of Anoth set out to find the Tears but he failed, and I do not think his children were old enough to use their ability to stop the carrion reapers when the kingdom fell. We must find the heir, and we must help find the Tears. That is what our hope can be placed upon. That and our own people's strength. We have allies in the north waiting for us to move. I have started the necessary preparations for total war and the Camarilla is with me. The Dao'Tai army *is* beatable. We *can* break them, with or without an Anoth heir or the Tears. With these, however, we spare our lands much loss and ensure a complete victory."

"Devick, you realize that going to war with the Subjugate will almost surely lead to the fall of your realm, don't you? Not to mention the potential retaliation from the Aya Dao'Tai on the rest of the kingdoms?"

Devick looked down for a moment, and then looked deep into Re'alis' captivating eyes. "I do. But it won't, trust me. The Aashahl are with us in this. Anthos and Sheibrok are with us, Alpa for another, after what they did in that village we saw, and perhaps many more. You have to trust that we can make this work. We can defeat the Subjugate. The land and all the kindreds, mortal and otherly, chafe and suffer and will fight back if only shown they are not alone."

Devick paused again to let the rising emotions drain from his voice.

"Even if I am wrong and my land falls, better we fall fighting as a free people, not as chattels to be oppressed in the name of a so-called peace. The Camarilla is set for war. Mantorah is set for war and the temples of our land send up an endless stream of prayers to the aashahl for victory. I am told all the portents are with us. I feel it in my heart that now is the time." He paused, but Re'alis seemed to want him to continue, so he did.

"We can do this impossible thing. I genuinely believe we can. I am not desperate, I am determined. I am not foolish, I have cause for faith, and for hope."

"What surety do you have that there is a living heir of Anoth, Devick?" she asked gently.

"The Aya believes an heir lives. She has sent assassins once to kill them, and again with the attack on Allinth. If she would risk causing an incident in her careful court then she must believe an heir lives, and that this presents a threat to her. She knows a living heir is a chance to unite all who would fight the Subjugate. With war we might buy time to find the heir and with them the power of the Tears, the power to defeat the Subjugate once and for all. The time is now, before any other realms are totally cowed and subjected, before one more innocent village burns. The time is now, my lady, and if not us then who?" He finished and wiped the perspiration from his brow. Re'alis again sat in somber silence, and he could practically see all the potential scenarios and responses flying through her mind.

Better not to interrupt; you made your case well enough, let her sort it out. Give her time to process it all. Anxious thoughts did not spur either of them to speak, so for some time silence filled the intimate space of the tent.

At last, she cleared her throat and spoke. "My dear Devick, so clearly I remember the young man at his father's side, his eagerness to impress and live up to his lineage. The times we spent together, talking and dreaming of how our two realms might be, under our turn as their leaders. Truly in these times I cherish the long walks we shared on the shores of Lake Akar." She again let a small musical laugh brighten her face.

"The ever-watchful eye of our chaperons keeping us in line." She paused, clearly remembering happier days. Our two lands have been allies in peace and war for more than eight hundred turns of the seasons, and if it is in one last struggle for freedom that we are destroyed, then let it be so. May Anthos and all the Aashahl welcome us to paradise for it." Her words were distinct and deliberate, with the full weight of her realm's fate behind them.

Devick held his head in his hands and let out a long sigh, then looked back to Re'alis.

"A part of me had hoped that you would abandon me in this so that you would be spared, but I am overjoyed that we are to strive together, my lady."

She smiled warmly, nothing held back, revealing the small dimples of her cheeks.

"I would have it no other way."

He returned her smile, and they shared more than a moment, just looking into each other's eyes. For the first time since the Subjugate had invaded, he looked upon her allowing himself to see her as the beautiful woman she was, rather than the regal leader of her realm. Her face flushed and Devick quickly found something else to look at for a moment. Not wishing to embarrass her. Memories of their shared past, how he had felt for her then, what he had once hoped might occur between them darted through his mind and he did not want any distracting thoughts, not now. She let a sharp breath slip between her lips as she ran her hands through her long loose hair, moving it to fall in a single coppery cascade over one shoulder.

"How should we proceed then?" she asked.

It took Devick a moment to realize she meant about the Aya Dao'Tai. He quickly gathered his thoughts and worked to speak with his normal calm tone.

"Well, the point of finding an heir to the Anoth line is to find and unite the Tears and give our armies a protection from the reapers. With them and the Tears, I am sure that other realms will join with us. We will also strip the Subjugate's army of its primary advantage, the dzum. Once we start the war in the south, we are set to send aid to break the siege on Akaroche."

Re'alis looked intrigued, and Devick was sure all this talk of ancient lands and powerful magics sparked her interest. He recalled that she was an avid reader of mythical treatise and ancient lore. The Tears were something of a very distant legend, like the origin of the Aashahl and the Atha'Tarrii.

"Are you sure that the Tears of the Aashahl are even real?" she asked.

"Yes, my lady, I am." He smiled, thinking Re'alis almost had a child-like look about her now, like she was waiting for a bard to tell the great tales of old.

"When the people of Anoth first came to this land from over the sea, the people here were divided and under the rule of a great and ancient evil, Ach'Juln. The king of Anoth, Tyralenn, as he was called then, gathered and united the Tears, and with their power was able to free the land and its people. It was a long and bloody war; however, they triumphed, and the forces of Ach'Juln were driven far into the east. The realms he freed became what we call the High Sun Realms. Anoth led them to freedom and enlightened them, bringing many out of the dark worship of Ach'Juln and the ignorance that his oppression had sown."

"Or so Anothn bards would say. Do the scholars of Mantorah see their past in a similar light? Could it not all just be an ancient story to justify Anoth's role in the High Sun Realms?"

Devick smiled, knowing she had read most if not all the histories that he had on the topic.

"Mantorah would not live under such a falsehood. Our scholars see these events as fact, my lady, as you well know, I am sure. Anoth helped heal our lands too, mediating an end to our archaic practices of castes and slavery."

"A fair enough answer. So, then Ell'Anoth was built, yes?" Re'alis asked.

"Yes, and so it was until the Dao'Tai came. Everything I have found is clear—only one of their royal bloodlines can find and unite the Tears."

"But the Tears, what are they, and where are they? How can we find them? I have only heard of the term Tears of the Aashahl, never anything useful about them. Though there is an incredibly old text out of the Tir'Luthryel that my father had. It had a lot of information in it, and I am sure my father said it spoke of the Tears. But he never let me read it, and I haven't had the time since to worry about leisurely history readings. Perhaps it could shed some light?"

"Surely it would. Everything I have is a translation of a copy of a memory it would seem. But a direct text from the Dark Realms...that would give us a better understanding of what we are looking for. Surely more knowledge is with the monastic orders at Kali'Anglen." This was exactly what Devick was hoping for, a partner in his efforts to find the Tears and defeat the Subjugate.

"I am sure they do if they will part with it. Even so, do you now know how to stop the reapers?" Re'alis asked, letting out a soft sigh as she leaned back in her chair. Devick rubbed his eyes and realized it must be getting late.

"It is said that the royal line of Anoth held a power within themselves to combat the ilk of the reapers. Something in their blood that does not fully manifest until adulthood. They are supposed to be able to stop the reapers from taking the dead and the living and turning them into dzum.

"As for the Tears, it is my hope that the heir will know their use. It was their forebears who last used them. All I know is that there are fourteen, and when united they are a powerful force for the one who wields them. Powerful enough to defeat Ach'Juln. Somehow, they were scattered again after the war with Ach'Juln, and there was not much recorded from that time," he said regretfully.

"So first we seek the heir and ready our lands for a long bitter war," she said with the heavy weight of determination and the hope of confidence. Devick looked up at her, and in that instant the relief he felt at having her as an ally was overwhelming.

"As for our other allies, and hopeful allies, I have already started to rally the other realms to us. The Sunshadow is still at our disposal, as is the Dyne Biellah and Kali'Kern. Through the Sunshadow we can continue to court the other realms that we dare to. But, as you say, we must first find the heir. Then I think we—"

A cry and the sound of arms clashing cut him off. The distinct sound of fighting came from the side of the camp nearest to the mountains and quickly drew close to the tent. Devick drew his sword and rose to his feet.

"Stay here, my lady!" he warned and rushed out of the tent.

"Devick!" she called after him as she too jumped to her feet.

As soon as he parted the door of the tent and stepped out into the night, he was met by a large black Grishkah swinging a crude mace. Devick managed to duck the first swing and blocked the second with his sword. In a quick glance he saw that most of his men were embattled. The Grishkah swung again but missed badly, and Devick rushed forward, pushing his blade through the maille and flesh alike. In quick succession, five more of the beasts rushed Devick and found their deaths at his hand.

Sheibrok, speed my blade, quicken my mind, he prayed.

The carnage of close-quarters combat was all around Devick as he slew three more Grishkii with relative ease. After years of soldiering, he had fought many kindreds and beasts. The Grishkii, despite their great strength, were not among the most skilled swordsman he had faced. A Grishkah swung a large halberd at Devick's neck, who quickly ducked and rolled past his attacker's legs, striking them with his sword as he passed. The Grishkah fell to the ground in a pool of his own blood. Devick came out of the tumble and looked about the melee. The Grishkii had taken heavy casualties and were falling back toward the mountains. Just outside the camp Devick saw a mounted horseman shouting commands in the Grishkii's tongue to the routed Grishkii warriors. He was clearly a man, but the poor light made any further detail impossible to see.

"Take him alive!" cried Devick, pointing his sword at the human rider.

A growl from behind took his attention from the cloaked rider. A Grishkah warrior attacked, but Devick parried the thrust with ease, striking off the head of the charging beast. But to his horror he saw five more of the monstrous creatures dragging Re'alis from her tent to meet another two dozen or so near the trees. Devick ran to her aid, charging the mass of Grishkah. He heard the snap of several slings from behind him as he ran, and he pushed hard, hoping his speed would make him a hard mark to hit as his mind focused solely on reaching Re'alis.

A slung stone struck the back of his head, sending a shock of dizzying pain through him. His vision blurred, almost fading out altogether. Stumbling forward, he met the lady's kidnappers, desperately trying to fight his way through them only to find his motions slowed from his injury. Trying to fight off the blackness that threatened to steal away his sight, he swung hard at the nearest Grishkah, cutting through the haft of his spear and deep into his neck and shoulder.

The Grishkah dropped dead at his feet as his nearest comrade struck Devick with an iron mace in the side. The blow set him off balance, but as he threatened to topple to the ground, he let the momentum turn into a thrust landing with lethal force in another Grishkah. Devick soon found himself nearly surrounded by them, and he struck out a few times a little wildly, trying to keep them at a distance. By now Re'alis was disappearing into the forest. He was out of time.

Devick charged forward trying to place his blows where they would do the most damage. Through the thick blood that was now hampering his sight he made out the shape of Re'alis running back toward the camp, pursued by more Grishkii. Devick managed to kill two more of the assailants with heavy, well-aimed strokes of his broad-bladed sword, only to be struck in the chest with a club. His legs were faltering, and he was having a tough time seeing through the blood that was running into his eyes. Another Grishkah slashed him across the shoulder, and then pommeled him in his back, sending Devick nearly witless to the ground. Re'alis' scream of desperation supplanted the sounds of battle for a terrifying instant, and the sound of it drew the attention of some of Devick's men.

Satisfied that he was dead, and with Re'alis once again in hand, the Grishkii fled the rallying Mantorahns. Devick tried to stagger to his feet but only made it to one knee. About him, his men fought bitterly against the band of Grishkii. Their fur-covered bodies lay strewn about the camp, along with several of the soldiers from Lea'Angleneth. Devick's men had formed up now and began to march in close order across the camp, killing all the Grishkii in their path. As they reached Devick he again strove to rise, but the unstaunched stream of blood from his wounds sent him falling to the grassy turf and into unconsciousness.

10

Stories from The Past

S hould one set to the deeps, first entreat Bok and Fiivan. Should one set forth into the sylvan, pray a boon of Frothvar and Dannitar. Seek ye the favor of each aashahl according to thy works and their sphere of domin-ion.
Essays of the Divine

Over a fourthmoon had passed since Ralenn bid farewell to Allinth and what was left of his home. It had been several days before Lirah felt safe to move Kaileth. During that time, they gathered the slain of the village, loaded them in a wagon and took them to the pyre altar at the temple. Ralenn had noticed other wagon tracks going from the town down the mountain, wide and deep. There were not enough bodies for all the people of Allinth to have been killed, so he surmised that they had been taken by the Grishkii. Ralenn knew that the slave market was so robust amongst the Dao'Tai that it was common for most raiders and hired swords to capture as many victims as possible to turn a profit.

Wary of returning raiders, Lirah and Ralenn had gathered what provisions they could and planned to leave the village. They managed to find several horses and one wool-ox that were left in the livery sta-ble. The wool-ox was not full grown, but still stood nearly as tall as

Lirah at the shoulder. Its curling horns swept around in a wide half circle. The golden-brown mane and woolly fur had just been sheared, making the fitting of the pack saddle much easier. A fully grown wool-ox could easily carry fifteen bushels or more of grain and pull thrice that in a wagon. They were common in the high valleys near Allinth.

After taking the remainder of the weapons from the secret cache in Kaileth's shop, they saddled the horses and loaded the wool-ox with their equipment and supplies, enough to travel the long slow path over the southern passes toward the Aril River and the He'Aril Falls. The wool-ox's large pack saddle easily held all their equipment with some room to spare.

Kaileth was still in a fever-induced state of unconsciousness when they had left the village. Ralenn found a small cart, and with a little ingenuity, he and Lirah fitted the cart to the harness of the wool-ox, which Lirah had named Doffle. The cart made a perfect mobile bed for Kaileth and helped speed their journey. He was now breathing easier, and his pallid skin was regaining some of its color. Lirah worried that the arrows might have had some poison on them, but she thought he would be back to normal within a few days or so if they worked to help him drink enough. She had been able to get him to swallow some water and a healing mixture of herbs the morning they left, and even more water in the last few days.

With Kaileth in Doffle's cart, Lirah, and Ralenn on horseback, and two more horses to spare, they left Allinth looking much like a small vagabond troop. Mirris found Doffle to be an excellent perch, with Riidak leading ahead as if he knew where they were going. For days they wound slowly up a narrow, hardly visible path, in a southerly direction. Ralenn had been most of the way to the falls last Rah'Thar and recognized the path; it was marked with cairns the entire way to the pass at Ect'ar. The steep rough path made for terribly slow going, and two rather violent storms had not helped either.

They spent the first night huddled together around Kaileth and Riidak in a snowy evergreen thicket. A fire that high on the mountain could easily be seen from the valleys below, and they both knew that no fire would make their chances of escaping other raiders much better, even if it meant spending a frigid night. So, Lirah curled up next to Doffle and Riidak. Doffle's wool was soft and warm and she managed to get some sleep. Ralenn slept little that night, in part due to the cold, but also out of fear they were being followed. He worried that burning the dead would betray their escape, but he could not leave so many he knew as friends in the streets to rot. As the cold, silent hours of the night passed by, he could see lights from time to time in the valleys below and felt this confirmed his suspicions. They wandered about the edges of Allinth and the lower valleys but never drew much closer. The lights disappeared a few hours before sunrise, and Ralenn hoped they had given up the search for more survivors from the village. It was a restless night, but he didn't tell Lirah what he had seen—one of them should get some sleep.

Their travel was further slowed by Kaileth's condition and the amount of snow on the ground. They had to strap Kaileth down to the cart to keep him from sliding out the back. Lirah had suggested that if they lost some of the equipment they might move faster, but Ralenn did not dare leave anything. There was no way to know how long they were going to be wandering the wilds—they might need every bit of the stores to survive.

Each snow-covered skain passed in stillness—the mountains were motionless, with an unnatural calm. The mountainside was so still that Mirris and Riidak had a hard time finding game to eat. Near the Ect'ar pass, Ralenn noticed a set of old tracks in the frozen crust. A frost lion. He chuckled to himself at the irony and hoped they didn't run into it. They kept a steady pace each day, stopping only to check on Kaileth and rest the animals.

Doffle seemed to enjoy the altitude and chill, he had no trouble hauling his load despite the depth of the snow and incline. Most of the way he dragged the cart more like a sled as the snow was so deep the wheels did not reach the ground. By the end of the fourth day, spent above the tree line, they had reached the pass and started down the mostly snow-free southern side of the sloping mountain. As they descended, a dense forest quickly rose to meet them. Amongst the familiar pines, hemlock, and fir trees Ralenn noticed short evergreens bearing broad-petaled translucent white flowers. Lirah identified these as Jillii's stars, stating they had some medicinal properties besides being good for tea. They gathered some of these flowers as they slowly progressed. For several more days the trail to the falls had been winding its way through the verdant forest toward the final passes to the southern slopes of the mountains. This descent made their way much easier and warmer. By the tenth nightfall after leaving the village, they made their camp by one of the many springs that fed into the Aril River above the He'Aril Falls. Soft tall grasses carpeted the ground in a wide-fanning delta around the rocky pool of the spring. The air was cool and gently scented by the dark wet earth near the banks of the stream as it rushed from its issuance to join the great river below. The distant thunder of the falls could be heard if one held one's breath and stood motionless.

Ralenn and Lirah hobbled Doffle and the horses to graze upon the greenery, loosed their saddles and loads, and set Kaileth under the shelter of a tree. Soon Ralenn had a small pit fire going. He sat next to Kaileth and the fire, chewing a dried apricot. He couldn't help but smile at the warm little fire as Riidak trotted up close and sat. Ralenn had been worried about the hound's feet in the skain after skain of snow, but no sign of ill effect could be found upon his massive paws. Ralenn's feet on the other hand had been totally numb for the last two days.

If I ever must trek through snow again it will be too soon! Riidak's eyes seemed to say the same thing. Ralenn's spirits rose some as he patted Riidak's strong shoulder and let the fire warm them both. The respite was short-lived, and his good humor faded the more he thought about their circumstances. He had no clear idea of what to do, where to go, or how to keep Lirah and Kaileth safe. He knew it had been right to leave the village; it was obvious they couldn't stay and wait for more marauders to find them. Lirah and Ralenn had done all they could think of, taken all they could find from Allinth and Ralenn's home; anything and everything that might aid them. Yet, even after all their efforts, Kaileth could still die—the thought made his chest squeeze tight.

Ralenn suddenly realized Lirah had been speaking softly for some time, and he wondered if she had been talking to him. He turned his attention to where she was lying on her back, just within the light of the fire, gazing up into the clear night sky. She had been somber during the trip over the pass, but now she was picking out constellations and calling their names when she did.

"Look, Ralenn—there's Alpa's Crown, and over there, see the Grand Drake? And just above it, the Twin Sisters. They're a matched constellation—one of red stars, the other of gold. Those faint crimson ones are the Red Sister, and those bright ones beside her are the Gold. Up here, you can see the red stars better than down in the valley. They're said to follow each other forever across the sky—reaching for the other, yet never able to embrace."

Lirah sighed wistfully, then pointed upward.

"That one there is Ean'Oich... and that one's Ailc... and that one is—"

"Lirah, what are we going to do now?" Ralenn asked abruptly.

"What do you mean?" Lirah was clearly shaken by the question.

"I mean what are we going to do, where are we going to go?" He turned to fully face her, searching her eyes. The worry there was plain—her brows drawn tight, the corners of her mouth trembling before pressing into a firm line..

"Well... we are going the only direction we can, I suppose." Her voice quavered—soft, unsteady—as she struggled to suppress the turmoil beneath.

Ralenn knew she had taken comfort from his clear decisiveness to leave the village; she assumed he had a plan as they had gathered their gear and left for the mountains. But now he was voicing all the fears and questions that she had probably been trying to drown in the depths of the night sky.

"I suppose you are right. I wouldn't go to Dayrn Chalid, and the Freeholdn is too far." He let out a long sigh. "The northern realms are full of Dao'Tai, and we will never get Kaileth over the Vagath'Oth to Lea'Angleneth."

"From what I heard, the acolytes say the Dayrn and Aya Dao'Tai are happy allies and the Aya Dao'Tai is especially nasty, vile, evil even. South seems best, I think." Lirah propped herself up on one arm and looked across the fire at him.

"The acolytes called her evil?" he asked with a smile in his voice.

"Well, more or less. Acolytes aren't priests, you know, they are—they *were* more martial and less reverent than the priests. Many venerated Arontarh or Sheibrok as much as Anthos."

Lirah's smile wavered. "I can't believe they are all really dead, all of them."

Before Ralenn could respond Kaileth gasped sharply and opened his eyes, sitting straight up against the tree he was next to.

Lirah jumped with surprise. "Kaileth, you're awake!" she squeaked in shock.

"Shayar's mercy," Kaileth coughed, clearing his throat, "I am." Kaileth looked down at himself and smiled.

"We feared you might never wake, Kail." Ralenn didn't care that his voice was thick and shaky. Kaileth was awake and seemed to be alright.

He hurried to him and offered him a flask of water. Kaileth took it, and after a few long drinks he started looking around at where they were.

"That same thought had crossed my mind as well." Again, he smiled, as if he was just pleased to be there, wherever he was.

He turned his gaze to Lirah.

"It would be my guess that I owe my life to you, Miss Lirah."

She scooted closer to the fire as she answered. "Well, I ate most of that brittle cake you had stashed in the kitchen before we left, so I think we are even." She smiled teasingly and continued, "At least now I know where Ralenn gets his inclination for injuries."

She then pointed an accusatory finger at each in turn, "You two have to be more careful. I won't always be there to piece you back together."

"I'm glad you found the cake; it would have been a shame to waste it. We are blessed to have you with us. But where are we?" His voice still sounded a little rough, and he took another sip of the water.

"A day or so beyond Ect'ar Pass, just north of the falls, I think," Ralenn said.

He felt so relieved now that they had Kaileth back. He would know what to do, where to go, Ralenn was sure of it. Regardless of how wrong everything was, Kail would make it as right as it could be and carry on. Just like he had done after Epri was killed. Ralenn suddenly realized how much he relied on Kaileth's calm, unshakeable resolve to strengthen his own and help him press on. How many times had he asked himself what would Kail do now? Where would Kail go? Ralenn realized he had made every choice since they saw the smoke because it was what he thought Kail would have done.

I came so close to losing you in the village, he thought.

"Kaileth, what happened at the village?"

Kaileth's face grew stern, and he spoke slowly, like the memory caused him pain to put to words.

"It was not pleasant." He paused for several moments, then took a deep breath.

"A bit after sunup on the day after I left you at the trailhead, I heard a cry and the sound of battle from the watchtower's direction. I took a weapon, locked the house, and left the shop. I soon discovered the town was under attack, and the gates were already breached. Many of the town watch were already slain, and a surging horde of Grishkii had poured through the broken gates. Archers from the watchtower felled some of the creatures as they ran in, but they soon set fire to the towers and many other buildings.

"I found a few of the town guards trying to get people into the broch at the village square. I fell in with them, and we strove to save those we could. But there was a great number of foes." Kaileth looked down at his feet for a moment, took another deep breath, and continued.

"It didn't matter how many we killed—there were more. Soon all the guards about me were dead, or close to it. I was left alone before the doors of the broch, so I shut them and held my ground on the stairs before the doors. I could hear the sounds of killing all over the town. The screams of a woman from nearby caught my ear and I ran to help. I thought the doors would hold out long enough to aid her.

"Two men were upon her; these were the first men I had seen among our attackers. The men saw me coming and prepared to meet me. They looked Adohr, but their equipment was plainly the Dao'Tai in make. They did not last long and soon I helped the young lady to her feet. It was Emis. I told her to stay close to me, and we started to sneak back to the broch, but more cries from the storehouse next to our home caught my attention.

"As we grew close, I heard the barking and yelping of the Grishkii, as well as the cries of women and children. I peered around the corner of the shop to see a pack of Grishkii loading people onto a wagon. They had breached the doors of the storehouse and grabbed everyone who had been sheltering there. I told Emis to stay put and ran to free the people from the wagon. I don't know how many Grishkii there were, but I was able to free the prisoners. No sooner had I finished off the last of those by the wagon, when another two score came running up the street. I was the only armed man between the Grishkii and the women and children behind me, so I rushed the mongrels, hoping to buy time for our neighbors to flee. Looking back now, it was probably not the best idea." He chuckled darkly and shook his head.

"I fought them for what seemed an eternity—there were many, a full war band at least. After some time, I found I had fought my way back to the shop. Emis was screaming a warning at me, but I didn't understand until it was too late. An arrow struck my back. I turned to face my attacker, but a second arrow hit my shoulder, and I fell to my knees. It was like a dream, everything slowed down. The screams of Emis sounded so distant. I tried to stand but couldn't. The wounds burned and the sensation spread along with a deadening of my senses.

Several Grishkii were trying to break the shop door open; one came near me to strike my head off, but as he raised his blade Mirris swept in and drove her talons into the Grishkah's neck. She was pulling with all her might, but a bolt came from behind her and sunk into her body. She fell to the ground, and the Grishkah again prepared to end my life, but then Emis ran into the creature with all her strength, knocking him to the ground. Just then the door to the shop gave way. Two more Grishkii came and dragged Emis away, and the promise of loot from the shop distracted my executioner as he ran to claim his share.

I faded into unconsciousness, too fast for loss of blood, maybe a poison, I'm not sure. Just before I slipped away, I think I saw a man walking toward me with a strange crest on his placard. It was not one that I recognized. And that is the last thing I remember." Kaileth let out a long sigh and let his head fall back to rest on the tree.

"Well, it sounds as if you have had just as pleasant a time the past few days as Ralenn did. Only you had lots of dog creatures, and he had one big cat," Lirah said as she poked the fire a little.

Kaileth sat up straight again and considered her. "So, you did follow Ralenn up the mountain."

She tried to hide the guilty look on her face. "Yes, I did, and it was a good thing, too! I was able to help Ralenn and—"

Kaileth laughed a little and interrupted her, "Miss Lirah, I thought you would follow him, as did Gaileng. We both knew better than to try to stop you."

"Well, apparently I was the only one who was not sure I should go," she said with a small huff. She sounded a little disappointed that she was so predictable, but they all knew she rarely did exactly what she was told to. More often than not she would reach the end state Gaileng wished for her, she just did it in her own way.

Kaileth adjusted the cloak that he was wrapped in and slowly looked Ralenn and Lirah over before speaking further.

"So now I would like to know what the two of you have been up to, besides sneaking away after friends on secret errands."

Ralenn and Lirah went back and forth telling portions of the events to Kaileth, who took great interest in all of it, asking questions from time to time. Ralenn noticed a look of comprehension dawn on Kaileth, but he did not interrupt, listening carefully to how the confrontation between the sphinx and Ralenn had transpired and Lirah's rescue. He looked relieved to hear that they had taken many supplies, dear personal items from the house and all the contents of the weapons cache in the shop.

"...so, after we loaded up, we followed the trail, and now we are here talking to you," Lirah concluded. Looking happy, yet exhausted to have finished the tale, she lay back down and looked to the stars once more. Mirris appeared at the edge of the firelight and slowly moved to stand near Kaileth, her great shining eyes fixed upon him. Kaileth clearly took comfort seeing her healed so well.

Ralenn and Kaileth continued to talk about where they might go and made plans for their next move. Lirah pulled a cloak over her and was soon asleep fast. Ralenn placed a blanket over her as well, then sat next to Kaileth.

"So that explains why that lion just walked away from being impaled by my spear. It did seem rather large," Kaileth said. He sounded more than a little amused.

"It did mention your attack, but I have so many other questions. It showed me things up there, and I think I might have died—or something close to it. Lirah brought me back somehow—it was like waking from a place that wasn't meant for me. Oh, Kail... I don't know what truly happened, or how to feel about what I saw. Everything I experienced while fighting the sphinx—none of it makes sense."

"I would have never sent you to face such a beast, Ralenn, not without more preparation. We are so fortunate that the split of the coin fell to us, and Lirah followed you. You did defeat it, Ralenn, you triumphed." Kaileth looked at Ralenn with unmistakable pride. "The Fates were in this."

"Maybe so, yet I would not call it a triumph, though I did kill it." Ralenn still felt a spike of fear when he thought about the fight.

"Things like this happen for a reason, Ralenn—you finding a sphinx instead of a frost lion, Lirah following you and saving you—it is no lucky accident, no, not in the slightest. Brek doesn't meddle with such important things, not really. Our great challenge is to seek the 'why,' so we might thrive from our tragedies. These events have the mark of the higher Aashahl's will. Even what happened to Allinth—I must believe there is a reason the Aashahl let such things happen. Some good *must* come from it."

"I want to believe that, Kail, but it is all too horrible! How could anything good come from such an awful thing?"

"We must seek out the wisdom, and it will take time, it almost always does. That is why Anthos, the wisest of the Aashahl, is also called the Patient Father. Patience and wisdom are connected. We would have had much to discuss if your rite had been the only event the last few days, but now—now, there is no real reason to hold anything back." Kaileth seemed to be speaking to himself. Ralenn waited for him to continue. He knew when Kaileth mused like this it was important to listen.

"I had a growing fear that the Aya Dao'Tai might have figured out who you were. I suppose that could have been the cause for the raid. I thought it might have been a random attack until I saw the two men..." Kaileth paused, clearly considering his next words. "Setting the attack aside for later, let's talk of the sphinx.

"What I told you of the rite was all true, it is the rite of passage from man to warrior, but there is another rite. A rite only a very few attempt; only the ruling house of Alliix, and of Anoth."

"What do you mean, Kail?" Ralenn asked.

"It is a long story to tell, but as we have nowhere to go for now at least, I will explain the more relevant portions. It all started with the founding of Anoth and the great migration of your ancestors. You recall that, I am sure."

Ralenn could remember the history lessons of his youth. To the best of his abilities, Kaileth had seen to it that Ralenn was schooled in all the subjects that anyone of a noble station would have expected their child to receive. Ralenn had never seen the sense in such an education for a blacksmith's apprentice, but he had paid attention. Old Anoth was once a great realm far across the seas. Their descendants came to the High Sun Realms and founded a new realm they also called Anoth. Kaileth had told him that he was from this Anoth, but not much more.

"Yes, I remember," he responded.

"Good, and you remember the tales of Ryvadale?" Kaileth asked.

"Yes. He was the one who led the people north to escape the overspilling of the seas and the arcane beasts from the south, right?"

Kaileth smiled. "Yes, that is him. He was warned in a vision that the wave was coming and was able to lead his people to safety. This vision came through the grace of the Aashahl, and the powers of the sphinxes. The sphinxes of that day were not as the one you fought, they were not tainted with evil then. The sphinxes were the first beasts to come north as they sensed the oncoming destruction of the sea wave. They foresaw the wave's coming years before its actual arrival, and so started heading north. Your ancestors learned to avoid the creatures, as their powers could be dangerous to the weak-minded, but the rulers of Anoth learned to harness the sphinxes' powers. For several generations, the rulers of Anoth worked with sphinxes as the oracles of the realm. The sphinx benefited from the comfortable place of honor in

Old Anoth, and the realm profited from the foresight of the sphinx. In those days, the creatures were generally peaceful toward man, often sharing their wisdom freely, or at the cost of an answered riddle or game of wits. There were wicked ones to be sure, however most were not.

The rite of rule was created to make sure the king of Anoth was safe from all arcane manipulation, and safe from the sphinx's total control should the creature prove treacherous. This rite required a ruler to face a sphinx in a challenge of mental strength. Defeating the sphinx resulted in the power to master the will of the sphinx and enter the creature's thoughts. Succeeding in the rite left the ruler able to protect their own will from manipulation and able to know the truth of others' wills. This talent was developed to the point where all the later kings worked with the creatures as an oracle. That changed after the wave and the destruction of Anoth, though. The Ikthii captured many sphinxes and bent them to their wills, forcing them to fight to dominate the land. Your people helped to defeat the Ikthii and their allies, but because all sphinxes are connected in mind, they all shared in the taint from the Ikthii's awareness, turning them into true monsters. So, the rite was changed from a mental contest only to combat to the death.

"During the war it was discovered that when one kills an ice sphinx, one gains a portion of its power to see the past, present, and future, and to feel the mind and will of others at times.

"All heirs to the throne of Anoth had to slay a sphinx in order to be qualified to lead the people. This became the great rite of passage. The kings had to be able to shield their minds from the powers of arcane creatures. The rite of the sphinx is the first step on the path to the crown of Anoth."

Ralenn's mind was spinning with the implications of what Kail was saying—killing a mythical creature, gaining the powers of the old kings—who was Ralenn to have a part in this?

"As you know, after Old Anoth was destroyed by the wave and the war with the Ikthii, your people fled by sea and came to the shores of this land. Here they found the realms engulfed in war and thralldom to a great evil, Ach'Juln, a fallen Aashahl, or so it is said. The king of Anoth once again needed to use the power given to him by the sphinx to find the Tears of Aashahl and unite them. After years of war and struggle, King Tyralenn united the final lost Tears and was able to lead both his people and their new allies to victory against the Ach'Juln, and freedom for all." Kaileth paused for a sip of water then continued.

"To thank Tyralenn they made him high king and arbiter over the realms. The powerful realm of Akaroche gave him and his people the lands that the city of Ell'Anoth is built upon, what we now call Anoth. The new Kingdom of Anoth held peace over the High Sun Realms and continued the tradition of the sphinx. This gave the kings powers of the sphinx to ensure the land was held free from Ikthii infiltration."

"But Anoth was overthrown. The royal family was slain, and her people enslaved by the Aya Dao'Tai," Ralenn interrupted. "What good were their powers if the royal line failed?

"They *were* all killed, weren't they?" he asked, eyeing Kaileth as he sat silently.

Kaileth smiled gently. "I had hoped everyone would think that they all were slain. But apparently the Aya Dao'Tai knows some degree of the truth."

Ralenn had long had his suspicions about his parents and the circumstances surrounding Kaileth taking him to Allinth. They had only grown greater the morning Kaileth gave him the new weapons and armor. Then the visions from the sphinx happened, which seemed undeniable, yet he still willed himself to not believe it. He couldn't *really* be from a royal house, let alone the line of Anoth! But the things Kaileth was saying...Ralenn was frightened of what the full truth would mean, but he couldn't stop himself from wanting to know more.

"You were there, weren't you? You were in Ell'Anoth when the city fell. You know."

Kaileth spoke with melancholy, "Yes, I was there." He paused for a moment and then looked to Ralenn, "And so were you."

"Kail what happened?" Ralenn asked, not sure he wanted to hear it, but at the same time knowing he had to. He took in a slow breath, hoping it would ground his whirling mind.

"Please, Kail, I need to know."

"You are right, it is time. Know, first, that I held nothing back to hurt you. I hoped that I could keep you safe."

All the unexpected events of the last few days flashed through Ralenn's mind. "I think I understand what you mean, but please tell me now. Everything. No more waiting till I am ready or older. No more not knowing who I really am. Who I'm supposed to be?"

Kaileth took in Ralenn's serious expression and began.

"I was once a part of the Allitorii Guard. My people were charged with the protection of the citadel and the heirs of Anoth, the nobility of Ell'Anoth, including your parents."

"My parents *were* nobles then?" Ralenn felt a thrill course through him at the confirmation of his long-unspoken suspicions. Nobles, nobles of Anoth, even! Why else would Kail have tried to hide with a baby in the mountains?

"Yes, but they were not just nobles, Ralenn," Kaileth took a breath and looked him in the eyes. "Your father was King Garadale, and your mother Queen Anica, and you, your brother, and your sisters were heirs to the throne. I was specifically charged by the king with the protection of your mother—"

"Wait," Ralenn interrupted. He felt almost dizzy at what Kaileth had just said. It couldn't be true, but Kaileth would never lie. He didn't know where to begin with his questions, there were too many! A son of the king, with an entire family. It was all hard to believe, it could hardly be more distant from the realities of how he had grown up and what he faced now.

"I will tell you what I remember, but please let me tell this in my way...I do not enjoy visiting these memories."

Ralenn nodded and sat still. Mirris seemed to sense Kaileth's distress as she shuffled closer, bowing her head somberly.

"Your parents were the rulers of Anoth, the Ale and Alev. I decided to not tell you of your past for two reasons: First, you not knowing meant that should the Aya Dao'Tai's sorcerers ever come they could not read your thoughts and discover who you were. Second, if you ever attempted the rite of rule and were not able to find and defeat a sphinx, then we could just go on living a quiet, normal life."

Kaileth breathed deeply. "But you did pass the rite of rule, and so it is up to you whether you want to avenge your parents' death, unite the Tears, reclaim your throne, and free your people, or not. If you don't, we find a new home, in the southeast maybe. Somewhere in southern Andohra, or Mantorah even."

Ralenn could not help but notice that there was a slight change in the way Kaileth spoke to him now, but it was hard to define.

"As for the past, after the city fell and your mother, sisters, and brother were slain, I found you and we fled the city. The old alliances crumbled once Anoth fell, and the Dao'Tai armies swept in like a dark storm. The Aya Dao'Tai knew that if any of the Anoth royal line survived, her rule would be threatened. So, I tried to hide you. I would have gone further to the east, but..." Kaileth paused, he seemed pained, and Ralenn knew why. Epri.

"That was when I met Epri, and she and her father took us to live with them. She would not have wanted to leave Allinth, and I was unfit for travel for some time. Thankfully, Allinth was well out of the way; it proved safe enough. However, judging from the attack on the village, it would seem someone else finally knows who you really are."

Ralenn looked up into the deep night sky, sorting out what he was being told. The stars looked very distant and calm, so peaceful set in their place in the blackness above—it was the exact opposite of how he felt inside. Emotions surged and spun like a whirlwind, each new gust threatening to undo him. Finally, as his eyes traced one of the constellations Lirah had pointed out, the twins he recalled, his mind found the eye of the storm inside and a question formed there.

"Kaileth, I must ask this question again, and this time I will have an answer. It is not fully your secret to keep anymore, I think."

"Ask." Kaileth set his face firm.

"What happened to my parents, my family? I know they are dead, but how? I *need* to know." Ralenn's voice grew sticky with emotion, and he cursed the tears that started to build in his eyes. His gaze locked on Kaileth's face and Ralenn knew that at last he would learn what had happened to his family.

"Very well. I always planned to tell you—the time just never felt right." Kaileth sighed and closed his eyes. Mirris withdrew into the darkness, leaving the two alone in the moment.

"As the Aya Dao'Tai marched toward your father's realm, he knew that he would have to rally all the free kingdoms together and possibly find the Tears again to stop this foreign invasion. After a few months of fighting, the eastern battle line had stabilized with the armies of Anoth, Andohra, Dashra, the northern Freeholdn realms, and Akaroche holding firm. This was less than a year before you were born, and nearly two years before the sack of Ell'Anoth.

Mantorah was beset by Adohr and Drakes on their southern border, but they sent a host to aid us, as did Taivadees. The alliance and Threefold Defense were working. We had stopped them, but we could not push them back. Lea'Angleneth warned us that the Dao'Tai were probing the mountain passes, and that should they assault in large enough numbers they could flank our battle lines.

Your father had become convinced that the key to finding the Tears of the Aashahl was in the west. After several visions, he felt that without them we could not defeat the Dao'Tai. Against your mother's wishes, he set out on a voyage to the Thalyphonie Islands, and from there to the home of my people, the Isles of Alliix. I think if he had known the queen was with child he would have stayed, but with the eastern line holding he took the risk and set out to unite the Tears. He left Queen Anica under my guard and left the people in the charge of Prince Kyrale and High Chancellor Rovik."

Kaileth let out a long deliberate sigh.

"No one ever heard from King Garadale's expedition after they left the port city Ji'Tahdiak in Taivadees. Six months after he disappeared, the Subjugate armies put their plans into action. We had thought we had stopped their advance in the east, when in reality they were just waiting. Waiting for more of their forces to arrive and march far to the south to cut off Mantorah. They overwhelmed our eastern defenses, and Akaroche was never heard from again. The Freeholdn army was slaughtered. A few months before your birth the Dao'Tai armies had crossed the Vagath'Oth Mountains—the dayrns either surrendered to the enemy or were annihilated.

"We had sent out the desperate call for our last allies to come to our aid, but most had been purchased by the Aya Dao'Tai with gold and promises of power and land. Those who were yet our friends, Mantorah, Dashra, Andohra, and a few others, still fought against them in their own realms. Dashra and Andohra were crushed and scattered. Kali'Kern and Lea'Angleneth were completely overwhelmed and their armies scattered. Mantorah faced an enemy force so vast that they had battle on every side of their realm. So, we met the forces of the Subjugate in battle near the west way with the few soldiers that were left from Andohra. We fought harder than any had before, and the first few battles ended in our favor. Soon the remnant of Dashra joined us, and we held them for months at the Vagath'Oth with the help of the Tyraneth warriors.

"It was to no lasting avail though. Not only did the Aya Dao'Tai have a much larger army, but they were also highly trained, well-armed, and of a kindred of men naturally bigger and stronger than any I have ever seen. The tide of battle turned against us, and we started to get pounded back toward the capital of Ell'Anoth. We did not make their advance easy.

"It took them another ten months of fighting to finally push our army back to the heart of our lands. We gathered all our remaining forces in the Dyvost Canyon, south of the capital in hope that the terrain would help us hold them there. The slaughter there was like none I have ever seen. Many thousands fell, and we thought at first, we could break the Subjugate army. We turned the Adohr on the Subjugate army's flank and broke the Dao'Tai in the center. Our armies fought with honor and pressed the attack, but strength of arms was not the Subjugate's only weapon that day.

"That was the first battle that I saw the desecrators, the Ikthii at work. With them on the field we stood no chance. Each fallen warrior from either side would soon rise again to fight for the Aya Dao'Tai. It was unwinnable. When our lines finally broke, the Tyraneth and the Allitorii fought a rearguard and saved us from a complete slaughter. I returned to the city with your brother, the royal high guard, and with what was left of the main Anoth army. The Tyraneth and the Allitorii who had covered our retreat did not return to the city. I still don't really know what happened to them—I lost many dear friends. Most of my kin were among them, my brothers, father and all my sisters."

Kaileth paused, and for the first time Ralenn realized that some, if not the greater part, of his reluctance to share the events of the past was due to how personally painful it was. Kaileth had lost everything too, hadn't he? His family, his home, everything he had once loved was gone. Then there was Epri and his new life, but Kaileth had lost her too. Ralenn found himself marveling at Kaileth, at the strength it must have taken, that it *still* was taking, to press on in good spirits even through all that had happened. Kaileth took a few more drinks from the flask of water. He set down the flask and wiped his mouth on his sleeve.

"During the siege of the city was when I first saw you. I had been on the battlefront when you were born. You were about four months old. Your mother loved you more than life itself and she had me swear to save you no matter what happened to her or the city. Despite the might and weaponry of the Dao'Tai, they could not breach the city walls. We all held out hope that your father would return with aid, or that Paladin Valskar of Syrah or Jovis of Lea'Angleneth would come, but no one ever did. They had their own battles to fight.

"After five months of siege the defenses were finally penetrated. No one really knows how the Subjugate troops got in. The walls never fell, nor did the gate give way to ram or engine, but I think the chancellor had something to do with it. He pressed hard for surrender and political appeasement, then disappeared as soon as the enemy was within the city. After a week of fighting in the city they had taken thousands captive. Pockets of the army fought on, throughout the city, in any stronghold they could find. Some escaped on the river and others fled into the countryside. What was left of the Allitorii was pushed back into the palace and trapped. We fought as hard as we could, but we could not hold them back. In the end, I failed in my charge from the king.

"I and several others fought to protect the entrance to the room in which your mother was barricaded. We slew our attackers till they were piled three and four high all around, but by midday there were only three of us still standing; the best of the Allitorii had been spent. We tried to defend our queen, and we held them—till they brought up archers. We were all hit by their first volley. My brothers were slain, and I wounded. Before I could get to my feet again, the horde surged forward, trampling us all as though we were dead. They forced the door and rushed toward your family. Your brother fought well but was no match for their numbers. The queen...she gave her life to protect you, shielding you with her body."

A glimmer of tears pooled at the corners of Kaileth's bright emerald eyes, and his voice began to quake.

"I managed to get up, and I slew or drove off all her attackers long enough for her to charge me to get you and your sisters out of the city, and to watch over you in her stead. She died in my arms, pressing you to my chest.

"With no time, I took what tokens I could of your heritage. I ran from that place to where your sisters should have been in the next room. The guards there had already been slain, and fire surged through their room. I could hear more Dao'Tai soldiers approaching from the hallway. Trapped between the flames and the Dao'Tai I was forced to flee. I could find no sign of your sisters, but there is no way they could have survived that fire, and there has been no word of them since. I spent much time when you were small seeking information about them, and it would seem that they perished in the fire.

"After I got out of that wing of the palace, I fought my way toward a sally tunnel in the western guard house. Once clear from the keep and palace my way was mostly clear of enemies, thanks to several Mantorahn regiments that fought to cover those fleeing from the city. I don't know how the Mantorahn soldiers got through the siege of their own lands, but because they did, I managed to get you out. I was nearly killed in the fight, and if Epri and her father had not found us soon after, we both would have died. She saved me—she saved us both. They took us to Allinth, and that is how we came to our life there."

Ralenn felt overwhelmed at all he had heard, but his mind was less turbulent. It felt like his mind was a pool of water that had just had a bucket of earth and stone dumped in. It was cloudy, but he could feel things settling in on the bottom. Filling in holes and fissures in his mind that he never realized had been there. He knew it would take time to make real sense of any of it, but at least now he knew. He had had a family, and they had loved him.

"Kaileth, has there ever been any word of my father?" Ralenn asked after it was clear Kaileth had nothing more to say.

"No. I am afraid that he was never heard from again."

Ralenn thought this over for a moment. "Then I am the cause of the attack on the village, aren't I?"

Kaileth answered calmly and with surety in his voice. "No. The Aya Dao'Tai is the cause. Her evil is the cause. I believe that the Grishkii were working for her. You must not blame yourself for the evil others send after you. We will have to keep moving for a time to avoid further attacks, I fear."

*It is my fault...In a way it is...*Ralenn thought of all the people he knew and cared about who were now gone or taken by the Aya Dao'Tai. He hung his head with grief.

"Ralenn, you cannot blame yourself. The Aya Dao'Tai would have come to scorch our home in one way or another, with time."

"But what are we to do now, where should we go from here, Kaileth?" Ralenn asked bleakly.

"Well, my prince, we make sure that those we have lost are remembered. We live that much brighter for each person we have lost. We love that much stronger, reach that much further. We live fiercer, and we fight harder every day to make sure their loss and their sacrifice is not wasted. As for a cardinal path, my prince, I think we should continue toward the falls. From there we can set out for Syrah, or Mantorah itself." Kaileth's usual steady tone had returned.

"Kaileth, please don't call me that."

"Call you what?" Kaileth asked.

"Prince. You called me prince."

Kaileth looked a bit perplexed. "But that is what you really are, Ralenn. The last prince of Anoth."

"I know that now, but I don't think I have earned that title yet. It sounds odd. I'm not ready for, or worthy of, such a title," he said. He immediately wondered what it might take to feel ready for that word, and if he even wanted such a thing.

Kaileth nodded his head. "As you wish. I will refrain from it, for now."

"Thank you. Kail."

"You are welcome. my—"

Ralenn glared at him.

"It was a jest." Kaileth smiled in a cheerful way, a smile Ralenn had not seen for such a long time. They both sat quietly, allowing the ripples of thought to settle in their minds.

Ralenn at last spoke, "Do you think it will be safe here tonight?"

"I have been asleep for…I don't know how long, so I think I will stand watch tonight, and I can promise it will be safe," Kaileth replied.

"I am very glad to have you back, Kail, so glad."

"And I am glad to be here. Get some sleep, we have a long road ahead tomorrow."

Ralenn curled up in his cloak next to Riidak and the fire and slowly let himself drift into sleep. His mind invented visions of his parents, his family, and all that Kaileth told him, until sleep finally took him.

Ralenn woke before the sun the next morning. The predawn chill still clung to the air, and small glittering stars were the only light to see by. The fire had gone out long ago, from the looks of the ashes, yet there was heat in them still. Kaileth stood gazing downhill toward the falls with Riidak at his side. Lirah was also awake, wrapped up in her cloak and a blanket, sitting on the ground next to the ghost of the fire.

"What is he looking at?" Lirah's voice was as soft as the cool morning breeze that gently bent the branches of the trees surrounding them.

"I am not sure, but it is too quiet," Ralenn said, noting the lack of birdsong that should have greeted the sunrise. Only the distant thunder of the falls could be heard.

Without turning around, Kaileth spoke. "You are right. There is something down there that nature does not approve of."

"More Grishkii?" Lirah asked.

"Could be, but that is not all, Miss Lirah," Kaileth said, still looking intently into the forest below.

Ralenn wondered what it could be when suddenly a sense of dread and foggy darkness filled his mind. It was a presence; not a sphinx, he could tell, but something that felt similar. Ralenn's breath stuck in his throat for a moment, and he had to focus hard to push the darkness out of his thoughts.

"It's not Grishkii, it is something more evil and foul," Ralenn said grimly.

"Those dog-faced beasts seemed evil and foul enough to me," Lirah said with a shiver.

Kaileth turned to face Lirah.

"That they are, but they are a natural evil. Ralenn is right, this is different; I have felt it before. Mirris should be back soon, and then we will know more."

"Kaileth, is that a light down there?" Ralenn was now standing next to Kaileth, and Lirah also started to stand up.

"Yes, I think it is. But that is not the light of the falls—that is a fire."

As Kaileth said this, Mirris came darting in from the lightening sky and lit upon the ground in front of Kaileth. She came close to him, and Kaileth knelt to hear what she had to report. The bird softly spoke into Kaileth's ear.

"There is a woman down there, the Grishkii have her, looks like they are going to interrogate her."

"A woman, out here?" Ralenn was surprised.

Lirah was at Ralenn's side now and she grabbed his arm with a surprisingly strong grip. "Well, what are we waiting for? Let's go get her out of there!" she demanded enthusiastically.

Ralenn was startled by her intense response, and that she had come up so close without him knowing it.

"I agree, but we can't just rush in. Kail, what do we do?"

"We cannot leave her to those beasts. We will leave the pack animals here and prepare for a rescue," Kaileth said firmly.

"Lirah, you are pinching my arm off," Ralenn teased. Though the action had startled him, he liked the comforting feeling that washed over him as she held his arm.

"Oops, sorry." She let go and gave his arm a solid punch that set him off balance. "Is that better?" she asked playfully.

"Yes, much. Lucky for you my maille was off," he grumbled, rubbing the smarting limb. Lirah gave him a mischievous smirk and wrapped herself up in her cloak.

Kaileth had walked over to Doffle's pack saddle and started to pull out his armor. It was similar to Ralenn's, but with more steel plates over the shoulders, chest, and spine.

"I see you made a good search of the shop, and my room," Kaileth said appraisingly.

"Didn't want to leave anything important," Ralenn said as Kaileth jostled his way into his aketon.

Ralenn and Lirah busied themselves with gathering their equipment as well. She picked up her bow and looked at it for a moment.

"Just so you both know, I am not sure I could shoot a man—dog monster, yes—man, I don't know." Lirah sounded suddenly nervous. Ralenn gave her a soft punch to her shoulder.

"Don't worry, Lirah, we'll be alright. You just stay safe so you can piece us together when we are done down there."

Lirah smiled back at Ralenn warmly, the smile touching each feature of her delightful face.

"Miss Lirah," Kaileth started as he adjusted his armor. "I fear that before our travels are done you might be faced with such a task. But for now, leave the men to us if it helps. I am formulating a plan of attack that should put you to a use you are comfortable with."

"Thanks, Kaileth. I'll be fine, it's just, the priests sort of skipped how to ambush monsters in my classes," she sounded more upbeat now and less anxious.

As the sun started to creep up, the three of them stood on the brink between night and day, staring down into the unknown of the dark forest below. Lirah and Kaileth started down the slope toward the falls.

Ralenn hesitated. He had a growing sense of foreboding coiling up like a knot in his stomach. He thought that after the sphinx he would never feel such fear again, but apparently, he had been wrong. He was not sure why he was nervous; he had fought Grishkii before. But this was something else. He could feel *something* down there. Ralenn shoved his foreboding aside and stepped into the fleeting shadows of night that still hung in the valley below.

11

An Agent of Sorrows

Miljah is in her sphere as are the greatest of the aashahl and their do-minions. Venerate her and treasure her gifts that they may lessen the hardships of mortality and impart unto thee the bounty found within her aura.

Essays of the Divine

Re'alis slowly forced her eyes open, only to find more darkness. Her head was throbbing in pain. All was hazy, her thoughts scattered and indistinct like reflections in a muddy pool. She could make out the shadowy silhouettes of trees as they passed by her, like dark columns of a great hall. Something warm was running down her neck. Blood. The slow steady stream gave her something to focus on. She tried to move a hand to the injury but found it was bound fast to the other behind her back. Re'alis realized she was moving, up and down, sharply bouncing on something hard. Each movement caused pain to surge from a dozen different points on her body.

The staccato rhythm of the pain began to clear her head. Under-standing grew. She was on the shoulders of a Grishkah. Her vision still murky, Re'alis could hardly make out the forms of her other captors in the dark shadows of the trees. A narrow path wound its way up the mountain, and the Grishkii ran with all their speed along it. The trees were so close that it was hard to discern where one ended and the next began as they flashed by. The occasional flicker of moonlight illuminated the path and the pack of Grishkii that ran upon it. They covered the trail in both directions, as far as the poor light would allow her to see.

The Grishkah that was packing her started to bark and whimper to the others, who slowed down for him. Presently her ears started to thrum to a new, building rhythm of thunderous pressure and sound. The Grishkah pressed on as the air grew cool and humid. The harsh impacts of the running Grishkah under her, and the cool wet air, aided in bringing her back to full consciousness. Fully alert, Re'alis recognized a powerful sound that she both heard and felt over the jostling of the running Grishkah. It was the crashing force from a great fall of water. There was only one fall that she knew of anywhere in the region that might make such a clamor as that she now felt. The He'Aril Falls. She was awestruck at the speed of the creatures; they had covered an extraordinary amount of ground in only one night to be close enough to hear the mighty falls. She was certain she had only been unawares for some hours, not an entire day or two. Whatever else she thought about the Grishkii, they were efficiently quick when they had to be. This would make it all the harder for her guard or Lord Devick to pursue her captors.

She gave the strength of her bonds a test, twisting her hands and ankles with all her strength. The leather bindings creaked and bit into her flesh, but they held fast. The Grishkii pack slowed their pace and made a hard turn down the path they followed. The ground cleared before them into a wider trail.

The sound of the falls seemed to drive life back into her aching body with each breath she took. The air had grown even cooler and the dampness was tangible. The scent of moss and moist earth drowned out the smell of the sweating Grishkah that carried her. The vegetation changed from the close trees of the deep forest to ferns, reeds, and other wetland growth. The path was all but totally overgrown with plant life, but as the vegetation grew thickest, they suddenly passed through and into a large dell.

Massive trees stood like stationed sentinels in the wall of thick reeds and ferns surrounding the broad glade of lush grass that they entered. At the opposite side of the glade was a great semicircle of black stone, as high as a good watchtower, gently curving out over the glade. Over the curved lip of stone, a cascading ribbon of water plunged into the deep pool that filled the stone basin at the cliff's base before continuing to run down the mountainside in a rushing torrent. The large drooping branches of the trees at the clearing's edge were brightened by a soft green light that radiated from the pool and cliff face. A unique algae gave the waters a sparkling green glow, and the entire place seemed to be such that one might find any number of the Aashahl taking rest there.

The marching beasts crossed the glade and came to a stop on the north side of the pool, near a great tree that stood apart from the rest. The Grishkah that carried Re'alis took her from his shoulders and tossed her in the grass at the foot of the tree. Re'alis hit the ground hard, though the soft grass helped to cushion the blow some. It was clear from his whimpering that he was glad to be rid of her load on his back. Soon all the Grishkii were scattered about the glade; some cooled their weary feet in the water, others set a watch and started to take off their heavier pieces of armor. From a leather pack that one of the larger ones carried, a dark-furred Grishkah took flint and steel and soon had a fire going.

Re'alis managed to sit up, just as several of her captors took her and began to tie her to the tree. The ropes bit into her soft skin as the Grishkii pulled the cords tight about her and the tree. She could not help but cry out in pain, and this seemed to please her tormentors—they pulled the cords a bit tighter. Re'alis clamped her mouth shut after her first cry and was prepared for this second bout. She held her body tight and tried to hold as much air in her lungs as she could, fearing they would tie the ropes too tight for her to breathe. They finished their work, binding her fast.

She relaxed her tense body and found the ropes still so tight that it took concentration for her to keep the panic at bay. She shut her eyes and prayed.

Patient Father, calm my fears. Leshay'ar, give me strength to face this strife. Mistress Everhope, Lady Jillii send aid swiftly to me...

Again and again Re'alis prayed for the aid of the Aashahl, the rhythm of her words helping to keep the cadence of her labored breathing calm and her mind clear. She had been raised to venerate all the Aashahl in their given spheres of influence and power. Now more than ever she hoped they were listening, and that she had not given them some offense or cause to now withhold aid. She continued to pray until the sound of a large horse approached.

As the rider came trotting into the glade atop a dark horse, an unnatural wave of terror and despair overtook Re'alis. It was more terrible than anything she had ever felt. Images of the attack on the camp, of Devick getting cut down, future tortures that awaited her, and so many more horrific scenarios filled her mind with a crushing sense of dread. She struggled to cry out, but no sound came. She fought to move, to form a thought free of terror. Gasping in an agony that was both physical and emotional, Re'alis felt herself falling into a nightmarish daze.

"I have that effect on so many," the rider said in a soft, genderless voice, dismounting.

To her great relief, Re'alis' terror seemed to lessen just as suddenly as it had been forced upon her. She took in a staggering breath, studying the approaching figure. In the growing light Re'alis realized what the rider was, and her breathing hitched again—a *desecrator!* Her father had told her fearful stories about the desecrators, carrion reapers some called them; they were foul necromancers. They acted as tools of the Aya Dao'Tai and were a terrible offense to nature and to the Aashahl. It is said they had traded their souls, spent their very essence away in order to gain power over death and the dead. Their kind had not been seen since the fall of Anoth, and Re'alis could only imagine what horrible plans this creature had for her.

This desecrator was more male in appearance than female, but there was a plainness, a neutrality to its long pale face that made gender an uncertainty for it. It was tall, more than the tallest man she had seen when it stood fully upright, by at least two heads. Its skin was a pale bloodless ashen color. The firelight reflected from the skin of the desecrator as if it was formed of fine porcelain rather than living flesh. Many small spiderweb-like cracks formed and unformed at the corners of the creature's mouth and eyes. As it spoke, these cracks would open and seal again with little spurts of black smoke and red flame. Any motion appeared to crack the surface of the carrion reaper's body for just an instant, releasing the foul miasma before healing shut. Re'alis tried to keep her fear from showing as she set her jaw and pursed her lips.

"My master will be so very pleased that I have found you, especially since Afyreen didn't think we could take you alive," the creature chuckled to itself, causing new longer fissures to form on its face.

"Ah, a slip of the tongue, I used a name...No matter, I am sure you will keep it to yourself." The creature chuckled again.

Re'alis could feel her face flush as her temper surged, pushing back the underlying fear that the desecrator had left in her mind. She swallowed harder than she meant to and coughed a little to clear her dry throat. Re'alis glowered at the still chuckling desecrator, her temper burning hot inside her pounding chest.

You are the daughter of kings, the defender of Lea'Angleneth. Act like it.

"How dare you attack my camp and take me captive! I am Re'alis Ta'Angleneth, rightful queen of Lea'Angleneth, and the ruling governor of the same. Appointed by the Aya Dao'Tai herself!" She took in a sharp deep breath, cursing at how much her voice was shaking.

"I have guaranteed protection from her and her vassals. Whoever sent you has made a—" She was interrupted.

"My lady, please, deception does not suit you. We both know that you are no great friend and supporter of the Aya Dao'Tai. Nor would she be pleased by your proclaimed title. In fact, you and the late Lord Devick were plotting against her this very night, were you not?"

"My business is my own," Re'alis snapped back. "And I will not discuss it with you!"

The desecrator came up close to her now, close enough that Re'alis was able to catch the sulfuric scent of the creature's unholy aura.

"My lady," he admonished softly, "is that the proper tone to address your host with?"

What could have been a smile crossed the thin lips of the creature, forming a split nearly from where each ear should have been. Acrid smoke surged from the split, burning her eyes and sending Re'alis into a violent coughing fit. The smoke cleared and the smile left its face leaving the lower half smooth and essentially featureless. Re'alis found this blankness somehow more disturbing than its insidious smile.

It took hold of her wrist with a cold hand. Unnaturally long fingers wrapped around her wrist and started to squeeze. A sharp, icy pain shot through her body. Re'alis struggled to catch her breath—the pain seemed to stab at every part of her person, and she let out a slight cry, which seemed to almost soothe the desecrator. It tilted its head back and closed its eyes, basking in her suffering. It sounded like it was starting to purr, like some perverse felid. The pain grew so intense that she was sure it would drive her wits from her, pushing her into complete madness. She screamed. The sound cut out of her involuntarily, raw, and jagged, leaving her throat stinging and tears in her eyes. Then the desecrator released her from its grasp and took a step back. She slumped into her bindings, letting them hold her up as she panted frantically for air.

"My dear lady, now you have tasted both options to a degree. You may either converse with me politely and tell me what I desire to know, or you may remain defiant and receive more of the...shall we say *experience* that I just released you from. The choice is yours. However, time is short so please decide with haste."

Re'alis gave the thing no answer. She couldn't have even if she wanted to, her body was still shaking with aftershocks of agony. Cold drops of sweat fell from her hair as she hung her head, trying to regain control of herself. A thought suddenly struck her like a lighthouse un-looked for—she would not survive this. There was no way this creature would let her live. It would kill her and probably use its abominable powers to pull her mind apart first.

Aashahl surround, please give me courage...Dannitar shield me in thy mercy!

"Now then, the main query that I would have an answer for is this: What is your and Devick's plan regarding the Tears of the Aashahl?" It paused, and Re'alis could feel it focus on her, the tangible dread seeping through her steely exterior. It took so much of her will just to meet the creature's gaze that no answer came to her.

*It is just the monster's power, just an illusion you can ignore. See through it...Show no fear and feel no fear...*She repeated the thoughts to herself determinedly.

"No reply? Let's see...Tell me then, more specifically, how many Tears do you already have? How many of the other little lords and ladies are conspiring with you?" Its voice showed no emotions as it spoke.

Again, Re'alis said nothing and concentrated on keeping her wits and her breathing calm. Her body still ached from the brief touch of the desecrator's hand. She knew she did not have the physical strength to endure a more grievous onslaught. The desecrator seemed to con-sider her for a long moment. Re'alis could feel its aura pull back, as though it was regrouping, reconsidering her. It ran two of its long spindly fingers over its jawline in a contemplative motion. Its face held so still that all the fissures and cracks sealed shut, erasing any signs of its mouth once more. She found herself again praying fer-vently for courage and deliverance from this abomination—though a small part of her, the part that felt the slowly growing panic at the edge of her mind, doubted any such deliverance was in the split of the coin for her.

A slow creeping smirk cut its way across half of the desecrator's face, sending a curling puff of black smoke rolling into the air. Re'alis watched as the other side of its face cracked open to match, and again a hideously wide smile gaped at her as it spoke.

"You *are* hoping to seek out the Tears? Truly. A desperate hope, to be sure, my lady. Desperate indeed. But rest assured they are real, and they are out there. But they are also dangerous. You don't have them yet, this I can see. Are you sure you wish to find them?"

She could hear the truth of its smile in its voice, and her temper grew too hot to hold in.

"I would seek the heart of the Dark Realms, Tir'Luthryel, if I thought it meant you and your mistress' destruction!" She cursed again at the frantic emotion in her voice.

Control. You are the lady of Lea'Angleneth, she thought, mastering her fury and fear.

"I was under the protection of Lord Devick of Mantorah at our camp. He and my guard will swiftly be here. They will be the death of you!" Cold hard-edged fury filled her voice. She would control her fear, she had to. Even if it took her rage unchecked to do so. The memory of what happened the first time this creature pushed into her mind was all too fresh. Re'alis would do all in her power to keep that level of terror and panicked dread from taking over again.

The carrion reaper looked pleased by her response, and it spoke with a slight titter.

"Perhaps they will. Yet, my lady, that is a distant and far-off hope. Truly you must know that I will have all the time I need with you before any help arrives. Cling to your fragile hopes if it helps. But know that your only salvation lies in swiftly telling me what I want to know."

Re'alis once again gave no reply, returning to her inner mantras of prayer and supplications. Streams of sunlight peeked through the towering trees. A gleaming solar band flooded over her in a wash of the new day's heat. This singular sunbeam found its way through the surrounding forest to fall upon her with its comforting radiance. Re'alis' battered and sweat-chilled shivering body calmed. She closed her eyes and focused on the sensation, the motion of her loose hair in the gentle breeze, the thunder of the falls. Dannitar at least had not abandoned her, and the peace of the merciful sister warmed Re'alis from within. She smiled to herself and prayed.

Mistress of Seasons, Lady Evernew, hear my thanks for your succor. May your realms ever increase Dannitar, Merciful Sister...

When Re'alis reopened her eyes, the desecrator looked somehow diminished before her. It had taken a few steps back to get clear of the sunbeam. Its aura of dread was less tangible. Its expression was hard to read through the spurts of crimson sparking flame and puffs of inky smoke, but it looked both surprised and annoyed at her.

"I will not aid you," she said. The calm in her voice was surprising even to herself. Green splashes of color danced over her beleaguered elegant form as the leaves of the trees flittered exultantly upon the crisp breeze of the new morning. The desecrator scowled, sensing its power had somehow been checked.

"Very well, *my lady*," it spat back at her, clearly annoyed. "I will have my answers one way or the other. Unfortunately, you will not survive *the other* for long. Yet I promise despite your rudeness; I will try to keep you alive. Most of my cohort would simply enter your mind and tear the knowledge from you, but I wager you are too strong-willed for that to yield much. At least not without breaking your body first. I find that physical pain incentives are much more pleasurable for me. I find it...recreational, one might say." It again gave a sadistic smile as it continued to speak. "There is a delicate balance between too much and too little pain to elicit the desired condition in someone. I suppose that you will deal with much before you shatter. Either way, I will have the information I need." The desecrator turned and spoke to the apparent leader of the Grishkii, then addressed Re'alis.

"Please excuse me for a few moments."

Slowly it raised its long arm and held its hand vertically in front of Re'alis' face. A sudden and terrible rush of nightmarish images crashed into her mind, and her body fell limp in the cords as she was sent into unconsciousness.

12

Mantorahn Steel and Alabaster Plate

T he force we name as fate is an entity unto itself. It moves upon both mortal kindreds and beings of power. The Aashahl are not immune to Fate's current, though they might keenly see the ebb and flow. They who embrace the course fated to them will surge past impossibilities should their courage hold. They who seek to hide from their Fate will surely suffer a daily death of heart.
Essays of the Divine

"Re'alis!" Devick's cry rang through the disarray of the camp.

His eyes searched his surroundings wildly for a moment. When his head finally cleared, he realized he was in a tent, and he immediately tried to get up from the bed he found himself in. A terrible pain shot through his side, bringing him right back down again, panting to catch his breath. The events of the night attack came trickling back into his mind. He let his head fall back onto the pillows of the bed. He groaned in pain as his head touched the soft pillow. It felt more like a horse kicking him in the head than a comfortable cushion. He moved his hand to the site of the pain and could feel a large gash on the back of his skull. His fingers moved along the careful set of stitches that now held the wound closed.

"Great. Just what I need, one more blow to the skull."

A yeoman entered his tent, his face forlorn, his brigandine and placard covered with blood and grime.

"My lord, you're finally awake! We feared you would pass in the first hours of your wounding," said the man anxiously.

Devick blinked hard, trying to clear his blurry vision. It was Yeoman Fythal speaking to him. Devick was pleased the young man had made it through the fight. He had known Fythal for some time now. He started his service to Mantorah as a servant to the master of Devick's baggage train. Fythal was keen to learn everything he could, and before too long Devick brought him into his personal company as a yeoman. Fythal was fair-haired and dark-eyed, with a golden-brown skin typical for most who hailed from the lands about Ha'Rooh in southern Mantorah.

"Where is Lady Re'alis? Where is Gairrle?" asked Devick.

"The lady is taken," he answered solemnly. "And Captain Gairrle is searching for the trail, my lord. But you must lay still, you need—"

Devick cut him off, "Get the apothatrist or chyrurgeon. We must set out after the lady."

"My lord, the apothatrist is slain along with five others, including the chyrurgeon. I have both their craft bags, though. I did my best to close your head wound..." Yeoman Fythal tried to explain the situation quickly before Devick attempted to get up again. Devick let out a deep sigh that again made his pain worsen.

"Then bring them, Fythal, and have the horses readied. Those who cannot ride will wait here."

"Very well, my lord. Will Sir Jayle or Captain Gairrle lead the rescue party?" asked Fythal, worry for his lord clear on the young man's face.

"You should know better. I will lead it! Bring my armor," Devick ordered.

"But, my lord..."

Devick raised his hand and silenced the young man. "My armor, Fythal, and the craft bags please."

"Very well, my lord."

He hurried out of the tent and soon returned with Devick's squire, Harrc. At his command, the two men started to change the dressing on Devick's wounds as best they could. It was clear to Devick that his initial care was frantic and hurried. Large swaths of blood-soaked tent fabric and pieces of a cloak bound his injuries. Captain Gairrle entered the tent during this process.

"Sire, you should not be moving around." His deep voice filled the tent as he spoke.

"I appreciate your concern, Gairrle, but I will be fine. Just tie these ribs up tight, strap my armor on, and I will be ready enough. Where is the captain of Lady Re'alis' guard?" Devick asked sternly.

"He and what is left of the Alabaster Guard have already gone after her."

Devick winced as Fythal and Harrc pulled the bandages tight.

"Oop, that feels tight enough."

Fythal secured the bandages with a good knot. "That should hold those ribs in their place, my lord." He looked the bandages over.

"Excellent, thank you." Devick ran his fingers over the stitches on his head.

" You might make a decent chyrurgeon. Now, Gairrle, you said her guard followed after her. Do we know where they were headed?" Devick did not want to waste a moment.

"Yes, my lord, the entirety of her Alabaster Guard. It seems they are headed toward He'Aril Falls," Gairrle responded dutifully.

"Very well then; we will follow after them."

Harrc was now fitting Devick's armor to him—hauberk, cuirass, and helm. He hoped he looked a more battle ready than he felt. The chest plate was a more decorated version than the mass-produced standard that armored the war hosts of Mantorah. A double-thick placard covered the upper chest in a slow sweeping delta joining a triple set of strong vertical flutes then ran from the waist to meet the reinforcement. A few broad faulds ended in large fluted tassets to cover the gaps from waist to thigh. Known as Rahmith plate, it was light, swift to build, and durable in battle. The design was born from the Subjugate war and had remained in production ever since. Devick's reinforcement placard was edged in brass and etched with a scene of the two peoples of Mantorah uniting in triumph. A common motif in his realm. The same style of decoration was upon his tall gorget, visored helm, and the rest of the harness. Maille fine as fish scales reached past his knees, partially covering the greaves underneath. The plates of his armor bracing his wounds relieved some of the pain, though it was still difficult to breathe deeply.

Once fully armored, Devick and Gairrle walked outside to their war horses and the waiting men. As Devick paused next to his destrier Mina, to let his eyes adjust to the bright morn. He rested a gauntleted hand against her neck, leaning on her for a moment's strength before speaking. Broad-shouldered and deep of chest, Mina was of the Breydfar breed— Mantorahn stock prized for their endurance and unshakable temperament in battle. The slightly smaller stallions of the line were often used to draw war wagons and chariots, while the mares like Mina stood out from among the noble breed serving as both palfrey and destrier when needed — so great was their endurance. Her coat was a storm-gray dappled with silvery splashes, like sunlight washing through passing storm clouds. Her mane and tail were pale as ash, catching glints of deeper golden hues when she moved. Scars traced her implacable flanks like old runes marking past battles survived. Though she, like all her kin, had been bred for the hardships of war, yet grace lingered in her every stride.

"Gairrle, what of the horseman that was marshaling the Grishkii?"

"He escaped, my lord, but I did gain a good look at him. For what it was worth. I couldn't say what marks or heraldry he bore. None that I knew, or were discernible in the poor light."

"Very well, it would seem our luck is foul. Let us hope that the lady's luck holds long enough for us to come to her aid."

Three score of warriors and horses, a full company of Mantorahn cavalry, stood in a half circle without the tent, all armed in like fashion as Devick and Gairrle, their tabards pulled tight by their sword belts. Without the semicircle of soldiers there were still men moving busily about, tending to the wounded, and preparing the camp to move on.

Devick and Gairrle walked to the center of their men and stood. The expressions upon the warriors' faces at seeing their leader alive seemed to range from relief to joy. The armor appeared to be doing its job, as his men believed him healed from his wounds of the night. In truth, Devick was not finding it easy to breathe, let alone stand, but his men were waiting for a command from their recovered lord. Devick took a deep, painful breath, and addressed his men.

"My brothers of the spear and shield, a simple choice is laid before us. Do we seek our home and the safety of Mantorah to tend our wounded and mourn our dead? Or shall we set out and answer the call of chivalry; the call of honor to avenge our slain and aid an ally?" Devick was doing his best to sound confident and inspiring between his sharp painful gasps for air.

"Our losses were grave, and there is no terrible dishonor in taking the more prudent course of action. To give chase to such a large force, small as we are, is a true fool's errand. As for myself, I choose to play the fool's part. I choose to follow our attacker! That they may know the bite of our steel. I choose to give chase and come to the aid of our ally, the Lady Re'alis. Let us loose the wrath of Mantorah on our foes!"

Devick gestured to Fythal, who handed him the reins to his horse as his men cheered their lord's words. Carefully, Devick took to the saddle, making sure that his agony-twisted face was not in view of his men. Gairrle mounted also. Noting the earnest faces of the infantry who had been riding in the wagons as they watched Devick rally the cavalry, he spoke to them.

"Brothers, speed is the watchword of this venture. To you it is left to see our wounded and innocents safely to Syrah. There is no dishonor, see our company safely to Syrah with haste and wait for us there."

The Mantorahn infantry nearby lifted their lances in salute to Devick and his knights. Among the mounted chevaliers, a few exchanged brief, silent glances—each bearing the same hardened resolve—before joining the salute, raising their lances high to honor their lord and those who would remain behind..

"Valor!" they cried as one, with the men-at-arms returning the gesture and cry.

"Lord Rahdan, we are with you no matter the cause," Jayle De'Vinor, a knight commander and senior veteran in the company spoke. His face was hard, almost polished-looking, like smooth stone. His sharp blue eyes shone bright as bare steel under the noon sun.

"And I with you, Uran De'Vinor!" Devick smiled at the old soldier, covering a wince as he spoke. Jayle bowed his head in deference to his lord, the vigor of the moment building into a tangible electric force.

"That our might shall render justice..." Gairrle started in a booming voice over the clamor of the excited horses and men.

"And mercy temper our wrath." Devick finished the line from the oaths of the Bronze Lance, the founding oaths of Mantorah unification. Though Gairrle was no highborn, sired to a noble house, he was one of the most gallant men Devick knew; the equal of Jayle or any other scion of the old houses. He felt truly blessed to have so many good man at his call. From lowborn page to lordly knight, each man was a fragment of Mantorah's soul—courage made flesh, devotion bound in steel. Devick steeled himself against the pain and raised his lance high into the sky.

"Valor and death!" Devick's voice sounded stout and strong. The soldiers of Mantorah took heart and met their lord's call, raising their lances with their beloved lord and made their reply.

"Courage and blood!"

"Fythal, find the serjent valorous and send him to me. Then see that our camp is cleared and make with all haste to Syrah," Devick said.

Fythal nodded and ran into the camp swiftly, making his way to where the serjent was directing the efforts to break camp. This was the first time Devick had traveled with this serjent valorous, though he knew that the man had only just advanced to the position. Within the armies of Mantorahn a serjent valorous was one of the highest ranks a common soldier could achieve, normally leading a escadron of sixty-four men. Though in rare circumstances they had been charged with leading much larger units of soldiers. Only consistent acts of the highest battle prowess and chivalrous leadership could earn the rank and title. Devick recalled the soldier's name as he approached.

"Serjent Valorous Vertk, you are in charge of the company in my absence. Take them to Syrah and wait for us there. We go to lend aid to our allies," Devick commanded. Vertk nodded and rendered a salute as he raised the visor of his sallet.

"Understood, sire. May Aseairpeth speed your hunt." His voice was rough and gravelly from shouting orders the night prior, and Devick was sure the man had not slept at all for some time now. He was also sure that no matter what Aashahl Vertk chose to venerate, he would execute his charge well. Devick returned the salute.

"May Sheibrok, the relentless defender, protect us all. We will meet you soon in Syrah." Devick dropped the salute, as did Vertk as he turned and started to direct his men.

Fythal still stood nearby, and Devick could read the young man's expression as easily as an open book under midday sun. He wanted to ride with the chevaliers. Harrc rode near to him, and Devick noted the flash of envy that shifted over Fythal's expression as the yeoman took his place near his lord. Devick gave a nod to Fythal, his face set firm in a fatherly aspect. Fythal's day would come sure enough. Everyone would have the chance to test their mettle before peace was known again in all the High Sun Realms. That much Devick was sure of.

Devick and Gairrle spurred their horses and led the way out of the camp. The rest of the cavalry turned and formed into two columns, one behind Jayle and the other following Devick and Gairrle. They all took off at a gallop toward the He'Aril Falls. Mantorah heavy cavalry, no matter the number, made for an impressive sight. Both horse and rider were armed and armored with the best their land could produce. The long lance, bright maille, azure caparisons, and gleaming plate made them all a shimmering spectacle of lethal force. Devick felt emboldened with his cavalry behind him.

However, despite the gentle gait of his horse, every time the hooves of Devick's horse fell, the pain in his side pulsed anew. The aching gash to his head and bruises all over his body caused some of his distress. Yet he knew that there was something else wrong with him. He had been wounded more than a few times upon the fields of battle and knew well the smart of broken bone and rent flesh. This pain was different. He was certain his ribs were cracked, but there was something else wrong on the inside. A deep, burning ache that made each breath an agonizing eternity. This mattered to him little though and if anything, only added to the urgency he felt to find Re'alis.

Turning out of the camp, they rode hard for a short distance through a clearing. Gairrle took lead following the tracks he had scouted out earlier. The troop came upon the trail left by the kidnappers and the Alabaster Guard. The trail was narrow but easy to follow, and there was no attempt to hide it. It left the open grassy clearing, plunging into the deeper forest of the mountainside. Not long after they had come upon the trail, the worsening terrain made them slow their pace. Devick would have welcomed this relief from his suffering, if it did not also mean that they would be slower in coming to Re'alis' aid. After many hours of steady progress, they were deep within the dimly lit forest. Now scarcely two riders wide, the trail was winding a course much closer to the Aril River. Thick moist air turned to clinging ribbons of fog amongst the greenery on either side of the path. All the host knew that, at their current speed, an ambush set by their foe would be a disaster. Devick counted on the Alabaster Guard having gone before them to mitigate such a risk. They had been moving as fast as the path would allow, and their mounts were showing slight signs of weariness under their full harness.

Gairrle came close to Devick and spoke quietly to him. "My lord, the animals will not be much good in a fight without a rest soon."

Devick nodded. Gairrle was right, they needed to stop for at least a little while.

"Very well. We will rest at the next clearing we come upon at the riverside," said Devick regretfully.

Gairrle bowed his head in affirmation and signaled the men to continue. It was not long before they came upon a place fitting for the men and horses to drink from the riverside and rest for a while.

"This will do," said Devick. "Captain, see to the array of the men."

"Yes, my lord," Gairrle nodded and went about his work. A short time passed before Jayle and the second half of the chevaliers arrived. The men and horses all entered the pleasant clearing of green grass with easy access to the river. The chevaliers got off their horses and led them to water and to crop the lush greenery. A serjent and a few others were standing watch rotating to the river side as others finished refreshing. Devick did not turn away the steadying arm of Harrc as he slipped from his mount and limped over to a tree alongside the river. He placed his back against the tree and slowly slid down till he was sitting near the water's edge.

"Harrc, see to my horse as well. I need to be still for a moment," he said.

"Yes, sire, is there anything else you need?" Harrc asked, a frown in his voice. Devick knew what he was really asking. Should you really be riding this hard, sire? Can you keep up this pace, sire? Will this not kill you, sire? The unvoiced questions passed between the squire and lord so plainly that Devick felt compelled to answer.

"Harrc, I am just weary from blood loss. I am well enough, and I know my limits. That is why you are tending my horse while I sit here."

He spoke slowly, trying hard to only sound tired, screening the pain from his words. Harrc's face flushed a little at his thoughts being so easily guessed and smiled.

"Very good, sire, I will tend to our horses."

He turned and led the horses further down the stream. The pain in Devick's side was getting worse, and he was having a demanding time catching his breath.

Do I know my limits? Or am I just determined to die in a fight rather than on the road to Syrah. Sheibrok, give me strength...We have to find Re'alis...

He tried to distract himself from the agony by staring into the water. The sound of the water was soothing, and he peered deeper into the clear flow. The sun played upon the smooth surface of the river and glinted off something under the water's edge. The sparkle caught his eye, mirrored silvery in the stream. Devick moved closer to see if he could tell what it was. He could see a long keen edge and dark handle—it was a sword.

Devick leaned close to the water's surface, reached in, and took the blade from the cool river. He groaned from the painful movement and rolled to his back, lying there for a moment to catch his breath. He held the sword up so he could see it more clearly. Water dripped from the cold blade and hilt of the sword; the drops felt refreshing as they fell upon his face. The steel held the sigils of the Alabaster Guard and a delicate script upon the blade.

Aireathyn, Gallant Serjent of Lea'Angleneth is my Champion. May my edge ever be keen in the service of justice and mercy alike.

Startled by this, he turned his head back to the water and searched more carefully. A little further from where he found the sword, he could see something else on the rocky river bottom. White and burnished bronze glimmered under the cold swift waters.

"Gairrle, come here, quick!" Devick struggled to his feet.

The captain and two others came running to their lord's side.

"What is it, my lord?"

Pointing with the sword taken from the river, Devick spoke, "I took this from the river, and there is something else beneath its waters."

Captain Gairrle directed his men to wade into the clear stream and pull it out. The two men did so. Whatever it was, it was heavy, and the men had to strain against the water's current as they drew it closer to the riverbank. With the assistance of a few more Mantorahn knights, they heaved what was now clearly the armored body of a soldier onto the riverbank. It was plainly one of Re'alis' Alabaster Guard. Yet this wasn't the owner of the sword, Aireathyn. Devick's men were taken aback when they saw how this man met his end. There was but one wound, but it was a terrible one. In the center of the dead guard's chest was a hole large enough for a fist to enter. It was burned clean through him, armor, and flesh alike.

"No blade could cleave a man like that." Gairrle said, his voice low and uncertain. Devick crouched beside the slain soldier, eyes narrowing at the blackened edge of the wound as he continued

"Whatever killed him carried corruption in its edge. This wasn't the work of mortal steel."

He rose stiffly, pain flaring like a blade beneath his skin with every effort to stand. Inwardly, he leafed through the memory of old tomes and half-forgotten lessons, searching for what could strike down a man so skilled, so armored. Every answer he found reeked of ill omen. "We should get moving Sire." Gairrle said quietly, unease tightening his voice.

"Agreed. We should not leave this man in this state, though."

"We will see to his burial," Jayle said solemnly, and a few other men commenced with the digging of a shallow grave.

The rest of the company went about to prepare the horses to continue up the mountain. All the while Devick's mind was turning over what could have done that to a man. It could not have been any weapon of steel. The remarkable white armor of the Alabaster Guard would turn any blade. He wondered what sort of being could cause so grievous a wound with the powers of the arcane. He deemed that only the ancient powers could have killed him in such a fashion. Something otherly. Something not of any mortal kindred. Captain Gairrle and the men had soon finished heaping stones from the river high over the grave of the guard of Angleneth. He came to where Devick was leaning on his horse and helped his lord into the saddle.

"Lord Devick, what could have done that to the man?" Gairrle asked carefully, keeping his voice low.

Devick paused for a moment and considered his answer. "I think that you and I both have an idea what killed him. And if we are right, then we know who sent it."

"Yes, my lord. But why would the Aya Dao'Tai—" a shout from Jayle near the edge of the clearing cut the captain off.

"To arms; someone approaches!"

"Sir, it looks to be the lady's guard approaches!" another chevalier cried nearer to the path down which the newcomers were walking. Jayle squinted, scrutinizing the interlopers. Devick and Gairrle turned their view to the direction of the call. There they saw a group of men afoot coming down the trail that led toward the falls. Soon all could clearly see the distinctive armor and colors upon the approaching men's tabards; they were of Lea'Angleneth. It was the Alabaster Guard. For a moment Devick felt a wave of relief at seeing them. Surely this meant good news. Yet, there was something amiss. Jayle leaped into his saddle, clearly thinking something similar. He and those with him started riding from the far side of the clearing.

As the Alabaster Guard came closer to the clearing, Devick could see blood splatters upon their garb. Terrible holes in their pearlescent plates of armor. He made to point it out to his captain, but despite being a man of no few winters, Gairrle's eyes were still sharp and clear. Gairrle looked the oncoming men over closely as well, and they both noticed the faces at the same time. Their eyes were wholly black, filled with the abyss of death.

"Look to their eyes!" Gairrle cried. "They are dead, they are dead!" Gairrle's deep voice boomed, filling the clearing.

"To arms! Get to your mounts now!" shouted Devick as he gathered his reins and moved his horse forward toward the approaching lifeless men. Men taken by a carrion reaper. Jayle and those with him started to thunder across the clearing building into a charge.

The remainder of the Mantorahn cavalry were mounted and had just formed up as the guards of Angleneth entered the clearing by the river. Devick took his shield from its place on his saddle, but the pain of his wounds would not allow him to carry it very high. The lord of Mantorah held his lance aloft and called to his men, an eye on Jayle so as to time their start to merge with his band.

"Couched lances! At my start!" ordered Devick.

"But, my Rahdan, they are our allies," stated a chevalier close to Devick's side. The apprehension in the soldier's voice was easy to hear.

Devick turned to him and spoke flatly: "They are taken by a carrion reaper. Now is not the time to explain. They are not men, not allies. Trust me."

With a cry, lord Devick lowered his keen-edged lance and spurred forward, leading the thundering charge into what had once been men. His troops followed, merging into Jayle's charge as they crossed the clearing as one. Lance and spear tore through surcoat and maille — yet where the blows met the pearlescent white plates of the Alabaster Guard's harness, they glanced and skittered away harmlessly casting fitful showers of sparks into the air.

Even defiled by the curse that had bound them to false life, the royal armor of Lea'Angleneth was a marvel to behold: alabaster steel worked to a luminescent opaline sheen, chased with gilt and deep blue filigree bearing the sigil of Re'alis' noble lineage. Despite the pall of corruption, the radiant armor gleamed like bone in moonlight still.

Devick and his men drew rein and wheeled about as one to launch another sweeping attack. Many of the cursed Alabaster Guard had been slain, yet more than a dozen still stood, shambling in a ragged line before them.

"Second death take you all!" Jayle bellowed as his charger lunged forward into a rearing dash at the foe.

"Valor!" cried Devick's chevaliers as they launched after Jayle in the second charge. For his part, the wounded lord gritted his teeth against the pain and pressed Mina forward. The great mare obeyed without hesitation, her storm-dark coat flashing silver in the light. Together they drove through the cursed Alabaster Guard, Devick ensuring his blows missed their marvelous armor. Devick and his company came to a second halt near to where the first charge had started; horses and men drew heavy breath. A haze of churned earth and grass pollen floated in the air about them all. Someone sneezed hard, breaking the eerie silence that had formed like hoar frost over the moment. Their foes had been slain, it seemed, many pierced with more than one lance. The Mantorahn warriors and their lord looked sadly at the fallen men of Angleneth. Sorrow for lost allies soon turned to horror, however, at the sight of several of them getting back up. Despite their missing limbs and the spears lodged in their bodies, the walking corpses turned and ran with startling speed at Devick and his men.

Devick struggled to catch his breath. But before any could detect the hesitation of command, Captain Gairrle drew his sword and called to the men. "Draw steel, form up!" Jayle echoed this to his half of the host. With swords and war hammers in hand, they charged the living dead, again. This time, one of Devick's men was swept from his mount when one of the enemies leaped over the horse's head and tackled the lancer with full force, sending them both to the ground and knocking the lancer's helmet off. Devick was shocked to see Fythal scrambling to his feet. The yeoman must have followed with a slain lancer's mount and harness from the battle at the camp.

Fythal quickly took up his war hammer from where the force of his fall had flung it and engaged the guard who had knocked him down. He swiftly dealt two blows to the guard's head and neck that would have slain any foe. Yet the cursed guard stood his ground and returned the attack. Fythal caught the blow on the langet of his war hammer, but the unnatural strength of the possessed Alabaster Guard cut through both langets and the hammer's haft, striking him in the shoulder and driving him to his knees. The guard raised his sword to deal a death blow to the yeoman just as a third charge swept the field.

Devick saw Fythal's peril and changed his course to come to his aid. Devick's powerful warhorse swiftly carried him to the fallen yeoman. With an excruciating lean in the saddle Devick swung his sword with exactness, his blade taking the head clean off the guard. The strike was just in time to stay the killing of Fythal. As the last cursed guard fell to move no more, the Mantorahn cavalry gathered close to their lord.

Fythal got back to his feet. The wound to his shoulder was a severe one, but his well-fashioned armor had saved him from death. He looked at Harrc, tall in his saddle, his lance resting easy on his shoulder. It seemed to take Harrc a few moments to recognize Fythal in the armor he wore.

"Fythal? Not bad for your first tilt, not at all. You felled at least two." Harrc sounded genuinely impressed.

"Fythal, can you yet ride?" Devick asked with concern between staccato breaths. He was proud of the courage of his yeoman, but this was not a place for the untrained.

"I can, my lord, and I beg your mercy for wearing the garb of a lancer, but I could not stand by with the wagons again." He hung his head, knowing that his punishment could be severe.

"To wear a lancer's raiment unearned is a grievous offense, Yeoman." Gairrle's voice was gruff as he spoke. "Yet I, for one, think your actions earned at least one day in it."

"As think I," added Jayle.

"As think we all, Fythal. Now we will see to your wounds, and send you back to the camp to guard the company."

"Yes, my lord, and thank you for my life," Fythal said, his eyes grateful.

"See that they indeed make all haste to Syrah. And Anthos speed your journey," Devick said. He smiled and waved Fythal off to be tended to by another chevalier. Before long, the wounded yeoman mounted his horse and spurred hard toward the camp.

"See you in Syrah!" Harrc called after him as he rode into the thick trees.

"We must hurry...to Lady Re'alis. If she...has been taken...by a desecrator, then we don't have much time." Devick's words were slow and jerky as he tried to catch his breath.

"We will find her," Gairrle said confidently. Devick's eyes spoke thanks to his friend.

"Uran Jayle, lead us on," Devick called between his heaving.

"By your will, my lord!" Jayle led his half of the chevaliers onward out of the clearing and toward the falls, Devick and the rest following. The slope of the path grew steeper and the trees closer together. Devick was starting to feel panic creeping into the corners of his mind. It would take some hours more to reach the falls, hours Re'alis probably did not have.

"Relentless defender, guard her."

13

Smoke and Flames

*M*any *are they that decry the spheres of Xydrii, Felairtahr, and Arontahr; being of great passions, primal and warlike in nature. Yet no evil here dwells nor jubilation in wickedness. Look unto Drashtaa for such petty sins and shun all who venerate such.*
Essays of the Divine

The bright sunlight surged into Re'alis' blinking eyes as she forced them to open. For an instant there was just the pure searing light. Then the pain returned. Pulsing tides of agony emanating from her arms and legs. Muddled and confused, she searched for the cause of her suffering. She had been tied with her arms and legs stretched apart between two trees that stood at the edge of the glade by the falls. Her memory came crashing back, and her head throbbed terribly as she looked about to see where her kidnappers were.

It must have been late afternoon now, and the bright sun shone low through the treetops. Her eyes fell upon a stone just to her left. On its smooth black surface lay an assortment of what must be instruments of torture. The fire that the Grishkah had started earlier was now a bed of hot coals, in the midst of which were several glowing-hot branding irons. Re'alis could feel her heart start to race as she realized that these were meant to be used on her.

The Grishkii were huddled up in packs here and there, chattering to themselves and giving her the occasional glance. However, the carrion reaper was nowhere to be seen. She looked about the falls and the wide green dell but could not see it anywhere.

She was about to breathe a sigh of relief when wet gurgling sounds caught her ear from behind. She twisted her neck around but could not quite see what was happening. She could make out the shape of what had to be the desecrator. He was doing something to a form lashed to a tree. Re'alis couldn't see what was tied to the tree, it was on the side opposite her. The sunlight reflecting from a white helm at the tree's base drew her gaze, and she recognized the helm of Leovello, captain of her Alabaster Guard. A man whom she had known her whole life, he having served her father before her. Her guard had come after her, only to fall victim to her captors. The thought of him being tortured and slain at the hand of such a creature infuriated her, and she cried aloud—half sobbing, half screaming with rage.

"Stop it! He knows nothing you want. Stop it!"

The desecrator leaned from around the tree and looked up from his task, smiling widely at her. "I know that *now*, my lady, but one must avoid jumping to premature conclusions." His words only made her fury burn hotter, but there was little she could do save buy time for help to arrive. Surely Devick and his soldiers would not be far behind her Angleneth Guard? He had promised his sword in her protection, after all. Her mind clung to this thought.

"Devick and his forces will follow after me, and when they arrive, they will destroy you." Re'alis pulled against her bonds as she spoke.

"My lady, I doubt he will find you, mostly due to the fact that he is slain. As for your guards, they are also slain; I personally have seen to that. So, unless you suddenly have changed your mind and are willing to truthfully converse with me, we have little else to say to each other. I will use you for my amusement and be done with this affair."

Re'alis gave it no reply. She had seen Devick fall, but dead? He could have survived—he had to have survived. Even if he was slain, surely his soldiers would see his word upheld and those under his guard protected? Or had they all been killed and driven off? She was not sure. The battle at the camp was so chaotic. She had retrieved her own weapons in the tent and managed to kill several Grishkii before they cut through the tent and overwhelmed her in numbers. She had fought hard to escape, and nearly succeeded, until a blow to the head blackened it all. It had been hard to tell who had the upper hand when she was taken.

The desecrator left Leovello's ruined form on the tree and confronted Re'alis as he spoke, his aura of dread setting around her once more

"Listen, my sweet, you do not have to share your captain's fate. You still have the choice to freely give me what I need to know." It politely wiped a spatter of blood from its face as it talked to her.

"There is nothing you can offer that will gain my help. You will have to kill me. I will not aid you, nor am I a puppet to dance at your whim as you are for your mistress." This seemed to irritate the carrion reaper, to Re'alis' great satisfaction. It caught her by the throat, and the same icy pain from before again shocked her body.

"I still could simply enter your mind and crush it, rip what I need to know from your fragile intellect!" It let her go and took a step back, breathing heavily, jets of black smoke spurting from the large cracks that had formed around his eyes as he glowered at her.

"Then do so!" Re'alis snapped back, her face flushing hot. "Or lack you the power of the greater of your kin? A small expendable thing sent on a fool's errand!"

Somehow it looked abashed by her accusation. Re'alis realized she had struck a sore spot, but she was not sure yet how to exploit it to her advantage, though she had a mind to try. If no help was coming perhaps angering the monster enough that it swiftly killed her was the best she could hope for? This dark course of thought cooled her temper.

"Do what you will. I will not yield any answers to a soulless mongrel!" She glared as imperiously as she could, lashed to a tree. It stood staring at her with narrowed eyes for some long time in silence, slowly regaining some of its haughty calm before speaking. Re'alis gave thanks for each moment she stole back; moments Devick might be drawing nearer to her.

"Oh, come now, name-calling again, are we? That is not very befitting of someone of your pedigree and class. Now before we start exploring your relationship with suffering, I will ask you one more time—what were you and the Mantorahn planning, in detail, and who else is plotting with you?"

Re'alis held her head high and said, "I will tell you nothing. I am a free-born woman of noble birth, and I do not answer to a slave of the Aya Dao'Tai." She blessed the Aashahl for keeping her voice steady and calm. She watched its face for a response, and thought she found one in the subtle changes in the cracks and fissures around its eyes. They were finer, like infinite branching lines of a plant's roots spidering away from the black orbs. Almost like it was trying to hold back an explosion.

"And what would you know of slavery, my sweet? What would you know of true liberation?" it hissed.

"I know more than you might think. And of this I would gladly tell you all," she said, hoping to drag this exchange out as long as she could. Maybe Devick would come in time?

"I know what it looks like to be enslaved, to have power over pain, the suffering of others as the only things left to you. Tell me, how long has it been since you were given leave to act as you wished? Kill as you wanted to for reasons of your own?" She hoped she was guessing in the right direction.

Its face smoothed over in contemplation; all the marks of a mouth sealing shut again. Re'alis mustered all her nerve to not wither under its unblinking eyes as it seemed to peer right through her. At last its mouth split reappeared, glowing cinders and shadowy smoke as it spoke.

"I understand the gambit that you play. No matter, though, none come to aid you. So tell me, then. Why should you care over my plight, my sweet? Would you offer a better bargain? Would you be any better of a mistress than her? I think not. Power comes at a price, my lady—this you know, as do I. You might command armies, live in your lofty towers, dine on the best fruits of your lands, but you are no freer to do as you will than I am in my role. Your service and love for your people are ever the same as any thrall's iron chains or the strongest cage of the guild. You, my sweet, are a slave to your compassion, and that is why my master will destroy you all. That is why I choose to serve her—she is power, she is eternal, and she will reward her servants well!

"You have no concept of what you oppose, do you?" It sounded amused. "You have no idea what powers and spheres she is allied with, what forces she can command, and what forces she answers to—do you, my sweet? Do you?" Its voice was becoming more animated; it spoke louder and faster. Slits and cracks raced across its face. Its expressions ranged from elation, to terror, to limitless anger. It paused, and Re'alis knew she must answer.

"And what if I do know her true nature and I simply do not care? What is a little power to a host of spears? What good are allies if they abandon you in the heat of the fight? She did not have the strength to lay waste to us all in her prime, and she does not have it now. Mantorah and their allies are stronger now than ever, and we will throw off her yoke. Why are you and your kin frightened to do the same?" she spat, tilting her chin up defiantly.

"We are...we are not frightened, we are wise, we know. Why would we forsake the cherished of our maker? Why would we threaten to sour the very source of our creation? No, my sweet, you are mistaken, so very much so. We are serving, yes, obeying, but we are not slaves—not thralls bending ourselves to a lesser being. We are serving our better, and we will be blessed for it. A place at the right hand of the master of the New and Final Order is prepared for those of our number. Can you say the same for those you serve? Will they see that you thrive and survive every age and any threat? I think not. Your petty vassals will leave you to die. They would kill you themselves if they thought it would give them a better split of the coin! I see now that my patron has nothing to fear from you, my lady. You are an idealistic fool, passionate and driven, but so ignorant to the powers set against you. I do not need to know what you and the Mantorahn were planning, I do not need to know what you hope to achieve. You have no Tears. You have no hope. You are no threat. Yet you must die as my master commands, this is still clear."

The desecrator walked to the stone and took a long, hooked knife from the assortment of instruments that lay there.

"If I must die, then for the sake of obedience surely you could tell me of my folly? Of the true nature of your master? I would know my error for what it is. I would know the power of your master." She tried to sound both commanding and resigned to her fate at the same time.

It considered her again for what felt like an eternity, face expressionless. She could feel its aura touching her mind, peering into her. She filled her thoughts with her genuine desire to know of its true master. She realized that, should she survive this, the information gleaned at this moment could be of use. So, she shaped her thoughts, camouflaging her desire for life and escape with the yearning to know of this greater power that the reaper spoke of as its master and liege. It stood there long enough for the sun to spread further into the trees. Her arms and legs were numb now, and the dull ache seemed to be seeping now into her very core. Finally, it spoke.

"Very well, I will show you what it is to know my master." Without another word its long arm shot out, driving the knife it held into her chest with a thick wet crack. Before she could scream an icy cold stole away her breath. Images began to flash before her eyes—places, faces, impossible creatures. Her mind burned with the vicious influx of impossible scope. Then everything went black.

***

Lirah could still hear the strange soft voice speaking. It had an uncanny quality that defied explanation. Earlier she had heard a woman shouting, not in pain but in anger. From her position Lirah could now see a very tall figure in dark robes standing near a woman tied between two trees. There were also about a dozen Grishkii in view. She looked over to where Ralenn and Kaileth were. About a bow shot further along the perimeter of the glade, they were both still slowly crawling toward the edge of the thick vegetation. It had not been extremely hard to sneak up on the falls. The reeds, grass, and shrubs made a virtually impenetrable wall. It had been slow going, however, as they tried to make no sound. Thankfully, the pounding thunder of the falls obscured the few missteps that were made.

Lirah's hands were shaking as she took an arrow and fit it to the string. Ralenn had given her his bow and a few of his arrows. He said to only use his arrows in an emergency. Lirah looked again to Kaileth and Ralenn. Kaileth gave her a nod, and he and Ralenn took up crouching positions near the edge of the glade. Lirah pulled the arrow back and could hardly believe how light the draw of this bow felt. She would not have thought it more than a practice bow if Ralenn had not briefly explained its nature. Lirah took a deep breath and carefully aimed at the tall cloaked figure. She felt an aura of fear and dread emanating from it. As the tall figure turned toward the bound woman, Lirah could see some kind of knife in its hand. They were talking to each other, but Lirah couldn't hear what they were saying now. She felt hesitation to fire at the tall figure build like a swelling knot in her throat. She looked back and the knife was no longer in the figure's hand.

I can do this. We have to save her.

She let out her breath and released the arrow.

The arrow tore through the still air and struck the tall figure in the throat. A sharp sound like cracking stone rang out and the tall figure coughed out black smoke and ash, but it did not fall. Lirah saw darts of angry flames flicker around the arrow shaft. In less than an instant the arrow burned in half and the fletched end tumbled to the ground, still smoldering on the now burned-off end. The wound sealed in a spout of embers and murky smoke, and Lirah realized what this figure must be. Gaileng had told her of the awful Ikthii, the desecrators that had turned the tide in the war. It raised its hand toward her, the source of the arrow.

Lirah saw something glitter on the wrist of the cloaked figure. Her instincts screamed for her to jump, and she did just in time. A stream of crimson and inky smoke shot out from the desecrator's raised hand and smashed into the sloping hillside of vegetation where Lirah had just been. Ralenn and Kaileth were both already darting into the glade when the light from the thing's attack caught their eye. They had all initially planned on the men driving off the Grishkii while Lirah was to take down the cloaked figure and cut the woman free. This changed things, she was certain.

"It's a desecrator! We need to take it first!" Kaileth shouted as he turned to charge the now grinning creature.

A cloud of sooty smoke burst from its body and started to swirl in a black obscuring wall. The Grishkii were rushing toward them, and Kaileth and Ralenn dashed into the smoke—the Grishkii did not follow.

Lirah watched them both disappear into the smoke and for a few moments she did not know what to do. The Grishkii were just standing around the swirling fumes waiting. They did not seem to know she was there. She looked over to where the red dart of smoking flame had hit the hillside. Everything it had touched was now smoldering ash. The earth where it struck looked like dark green glass. Suddenly someone yelled inside the smoke. A burst of red light illuminated the figures inside as a form was sent flying out of the smoke and into a tree. Kaileth slumped motionless at the base of the tree, the chest of his maille shirt smoking.

The smoke was thick and caustic. Ralenn felt a tangible resistance against his movement, like trying to run in chest-deep water. There was also a force pressing on his mind. It felt dark and hateful, full of terror and depression. It also felt familiar. Something his mind had brushed against in the chasm of the sphinx's thoughts.

The inky torrent burned his eyes and stung his face. Ralenn was not sure if he could fight at all in such a blinding stream of cinders and ash. A sudden shift in the currents of smoke darted past his side. He turned to face it, slow to strike out for fear of hitting Kaileth. Again, a current, as though something or someone rushed quickly by him. Again, he turned, only to see the spinning smoke. A few more times the current shifted, and each time the apprehension and anxiety built within him. His ears hummed with the rush of the maelstrom he stood in, and his emotions seemed to be spinning just as much. A tidal pendulum of what felt like his own nerves, mixed with something else. It was hard for him to sort out and he struggled trying to catch his breath and calm his tumultuous mind.

Calm—seek the calm. Aashahl surround—help me.

He shut his stinging eyes for a moment seeking to slow his thoughts. Ralenn forced his mind back to the countless lessons at Kaileth's side. Lessons in self-mastery and discipline. Suddenly he realized that his thoughts were calm, but there was something else, something not his own.

Ralenn gasped as he felt Kaileth fly past him, struck by some kind of hot flaming blast. In desperation, he swung his blade into the sulfuric smoke. He thought he heard something laughing, but the sound came from all around him. He swung his sword a few more times at what he felt might be the source of the laughter. The blade found nothing to bite into, cutting an effortless path through the sooty murk. Resetting his thoughts, he again focused on the other feelings in his mind, the presence he felt. He took a few steps toward it and it felt stronger.

He tried harder to focus, to isolate this outside influence in his thoughts, and his mind started to give it a shape. Ralenn took a few more steps toward the presence in his mind and it felt as though he was stepping out of the blinding smoke. Soon he did not notice it at all, nor the ground under his very feet; he was enveloped in the presence as his physical body had been by the smoke. He tried harder to bring the force of his mind into focus and a form started to appear in the blackness.

A terrible smiling face suddenly loomed in front of Ralenn, scarlet sparks and flames spouting from the racking edges of its mouth. He swung his sword and opened his eyes only to realize the creature was more than twice his sword's reach in front of him. Before Ralenn could sort through the confusion within his mind the creature held a hand toward him. A bolt of red liquid fire smashed into his chest, and he felt his body rushing through the air.

Searing heat licked up to his face, Lirah's scream echoed in his ears, and the smell of burned hair and burning cloth filled his nostrils as he crashed into a large patch of reeds and a squat tree. Ralenn gasped for air. The thick vegetation had tempered his fall, but the impact was still brutal. His back burst with pain, as did his head. Ralenn looked down to his chest, expecting to see a hole straight through his body. Instead, he saw a smoldering hole burned through the leather jerkin he had put on to help silence his maille. To his surprise, the maille was untouched. Steam rose from between the links of dark metal, the sudden heat causing moisture trapped in the singed aketon to be released.

Ralenn took stock of his surroundings and saw that Kaileth was back on his feet now and fighting desperately to hold back over a dozen Grishkii. Lirah was running back up the hillside, firing arrows down at a group of Grishkii that were giving her chase. Ralenn struggled back to his feet as she felled her last pursuer. She looked at him with an expression of wonder and relief, then gestured frantically to Kaileth.

Ralenn took a deep breath and ran toward him and was just missed by another bolt of cindery flame as it shot out of the still undulating cloud of smoke. He slashed and hacked his way through the pack of Grishkii to find Kaileth in the center. There were far more of them than they had first thought. Mirris had only seen a dozen or so; more must have arrived after hearing the battle. The carrion reaper had been a complete and horrible surprise.

"I think we miscounted, Kail," he spoke as he blocked a halberd and killed its wielder.

"That desecrator..." Kaileth grunted as he kicked a dead Grishkah off the end of his sword. "We have to kill it, and fast, or our foe will be legion!"

"Kail, I can see it in the smoke..." Ralenn trailed off as he had a thought. "I'll take care of it," he said quickly. Ralenn could hardly believe what he was saying, but something made him feel like he knew how to counter the thing, and there was no time to argue.

With smoke still drifting from his burned clothing, Kaileth looked Ralenn in the eyes for an intense moment. Ralenn felt a rush of feelings from Kaileth, much more than he would have guessed could come from his stoic expression.

"Go, do it," Kaileth said grimly.

A woman's yelling cut through the sounds of battle.

"Look out!" the voice shouted from somewhere beyond the smoke.

The voice was followed by another stream of red flame that rushed toward the two men. It burned through the Grishkii in its path as it streaked toward Kaileth. He dropped to the earth just in time to avoid getting hit in the head. He tumbled like an acrobat across the ground, regaining his feet and simultaneously delivering debilitating cuts to the legs of several Grishkii in a sweeping stroke.

"Go, destroy it!" Kaileth called out once more. He sounded more desperate this time, though his expression had not changed.

Suddenly Riidak was there, carving his own path through the Grishkii, followed by Mirris who ripped with keen talons at their necks.

Ralenn charged through the gap they made back toward the desecrator's black cloud.

Inside the smoke Ralenn shut his eyes and focused his mind, this time intently searching for the desecrator. He could feel its presence shifting around him, slithering away from his sight, until—there it was! A shimmering image in the blackness. He forced his will outside himself like a swiftly cast spear, pinning the desecrator in his mind's eye. Shock, terror, surprise then a sense of keen recognition echoed into Ralenn's thoughts from the carrion reaper's inner mind. It again tried to debilitate Ralenn with its aura of terror. Ralenn batted this effort aside as he gained confidence in his strength of will. It seemed to Ralenn that he could both see the physical world around him along with a second strange ethereal reflection of the real world, colored with emotion and thought. In this second realm the desecrator looked frail and sickly, hollow and without force or might. Ralenn felt a surge of power from within himself, his eyes narrowing in contempt of this pathetic monster.

He could feel the anger and rage of the creature as it again raised a hand toward him. He was expecting it this time, however, and he dashed forward with a cry that sent a wave of ethereal force before him, driving the smoke away in a bow wave. In an instant Ralenn's sword was striking down on the reaper's arm with all his strength. His sword rang as it cleaved the arm of the desecrator off just above the elbow. All the spinning smoke instantly stopped and fell to the ground in a rolling plume of sooty ash. The desecrator shrieked in terror and surprise.

Ralenn looked at his smoking blade, then to the reaper who had fallen to a knee nearby. Ralenn raised his sword for another strike, letting his grip on the ethereal sight slip for a moment. The desecrator's head jerked toward him, sensing the lapse as it quickly raised his remaining hand toward him. An overwhelming blackness surged into Ralenn's mind like a tidal wave of filthy effluence. He stumbled and fell to the earth, struggling to fight off the assault. It was like the attack of the sphinx, but remarkably stronger. The vision flared, exploding into violence and wicked sharpness — the final attack of a cornered animal.

Ralenn heard a sharp crack through the blackness, then another, and the darkness in his mind was sucked away in a rush of clarity. He was able to force his eyes open in time to see the reaper struggling to stand as a third black avertyyn arrow smashed into the face of the creature. Each arrow sent out large cracks across its face that leaked smoke and fitful red flame. The awful creature looked at him with a broken face, its expression twisted by the damage from the arrow.

"It'sss yoou." The desecrator's ruined mouth hardly formed the words. It made to speak further but Ralenn intervened. He swung his sword and severed the reaper's head from its too long neck. A fountain of sooty smoke and blood-red ashes spewed from the wound and the head fell next to the crumpled body. The skull cracked and shattered, spilling black ash on the green grass. Ralenn had little time to savor this victory as more Grishkii came charging at him from the far side of the glade, the absence of the smoke storm revealing him to them.

Re'alis opened her eyes to find a scene of chaos and death around her. There were dead Grishkii upon the green grass; black soot and ribbons of black smoke seeming to come from a crumpled heap in front of her; two men, a war hound, and a battle falcon frantically fighting the hordes of her captors. She was not sure she had fully awoken from the dark dreams and blurry visions that had driven her senses away.

The dagger! Suddenly the memory of the sharp pain as the carrion reaper plunged its knife into her came back, and she looked down to her chest. There was no wound. She looked all around her and could see no evidence of the knife or the wound. Had it all been a dream too?

A gentle hand took hold of Re'alis' shoulder, cutting through her confusion. A soft female voice spoke into her ear from behind.

"I'm going to cut you down, hold still."

Re'alis turned her head to see a young lady, dressed mostly in simple white and gray, leaning up against one of the trees that Re'alis was tied to. The young woman drew a dagger and started to sever the cords that were galling at Re'alis' wrists and ankles.

Yet as the blade bit into the first cord, a Grishkah rushed from the center of the melee swinging a jagged sword. The young woman darted out of the weapon's path and slashed at her attacker's arm as it passed. The blow found its mark, but her blade turned when it struck bone and she lost her grip as the Grishkah's ruined arm lost its sword. The girl quickly snatched the dagger back up, but not before the Grishkah grabbed her, pulling her away from a helpless Re'alis.

Lirah spun and twisted, slashing at the Grishkah's shoulder and neck. Panic and fear surged within her, speeding her attacks. The creature howled in pain as the dagger bit into it again and again. She crawled out from under it only to feel its large, clawed hand seize her thigh and jerk her back. She shot the dagger out for another attack but this time the Grishkah caught her by the wrist. She took hold of the dagger with both hands now and tried to free her wrist. Her arms shook, and the Grishkah slowly forced her hands, still holding the dagger, toward her own chest. The Grishkah wrapped its clawed hand around both of Lirah's in an inhumanly strong grip. Fortunately for Lirah, his other arm hung uselessly at his side from her earlier attack, otherwise there would be no struggle at all. Even with just one arm the Grishkah was overwhelmingly strong. She gritted her teeth, her breath coming in puffing spurts of extreme effort. She arched her back, driving her shoulder blades into the earth, pushing with all her might. The Grishkah's wide fanged mouth pulled into an ugly smile above her, knowing she had not the strength to escape. Lirah's arms were slowly forced closer and closer to her chest. Consuming panic and the slow descent of the blade nearly drove all her senses from her. She struggled frantically. Trying to resist the creature's strength. But it was no use, and her trembling arms gradually dropped to her own breast.

Dannitar, help me!

Her breathing reached a frantic pace as the dagger closed the final distance. Her eyes grew wide with terror, unable to look away, fixed on the reflective surface of the dagger's uncaring edge. Lirah screamed as the Grishkah pushed her dagger into her chest. The pain was more than anything she could have imagined, her scream a brutal expletive of fear and anguish. The creature snarled with delight as warm blood rushed from the wound, the blade cutting its way toward her lung. She could feel the steel grind its way past her ribs, and she shut her eyes, unable to catch her breath; hot tears streamed from the sides of her face. She tried to push harder. To stop the dagger from getting any deeper. Lirah could hear Re'alis screaming for help, then her cries suddenly stopped. An overwhelming impulse to force the blade out took hold in her mind.

A profound, instinctive, and new source of determination flooded into her. Lirah tried harder to push the blade out and she felt a sudden flow of new strength rise to meet her need. Feeling as though she had a second wind, Lirah again pushed with all her might trying to force the dagger out of her body. She burned with the effort. Sweat mingled with her tears and blood. Suddenly Lirah realized it was not the effort of her muscles that caused the burning feeling. More than a little confused, Lirah could feel warmth and heat pouring from her wounds. In shock Lirah opened her eyes; this was not the heat from the running blood, but the heat of flames.

Something within her had been awoken by her desperation. She had unintentionally started to heal herself as fast as the dagger was cutting. The Grishkah pushed harder and Lirah pushed back with both her shaking arms, and then added a healing surge of new flesh and bone. A frantic mix of ecstasy, pain, and determination flowed through Lirah as she felt her entire body turn hot. Sparks and cerulean spurts of flames shot out of the wound in her trembling chest from around the edges of the dagger. She screamed in agony as she and her attacker reached a stalemate. She could not fully push the Grishkah off of her, and it could not push the dagger any further into her. It pushed with all its strength, but she was re-healing the wound as fast as it could be cut. The result was a continual sensation of the dagger ripping into her chest. She struggled to keep up the shield of healing energy, but she could feel herself waning. She didn't even understand how any of this was possible. Exhaustion rapidly flooded her mind and she waivered.

If I give out that dagger will kill me...

A rib cracked and the blade sank in through her lung and threatened to pass out the back of her shoulder. She coughed, frothy blood running from her cooling pale lips. Time seemed to stop, and then, so did her breathing. Only the pain kept her aware and focused. She could feel the dagger's edge cutting her flesh and bone, then the flesh forming anew, pushing the blade back only for it to cut through the new tissues again and again. Lirah felt detached now, adrift in a flowing current of warmth. She searched herself for more power, another reserve to pull from—and there it was! Subtle at first, then, as she reached out toward it, she realized that it was vast, like a dark sea under a starless night. She pulled on this source of life, just a little, just enough. Lirah was not sure what it was, but as soon as she connected fully to it, she could feel a scorching rush of strength flow into her and her underlying panic melted away.

Re'alis' eyes grew wider in horror. Blood pooled and flowed around the young woman in an unfathomable amount, yet she struggled on, tears flowing from her tightly shut eyes. Re'alis noticed that the grass seemed to be growing, and several flowers sprung up in the growing patch of blood-soaked earth. A macabre garden of blood-spattered newly grown wildflowers and ferns cropped up in mere seconds. What she was watching was beyond belief, and several moments passed before she was able to call out for aid again, astonishment staying her tongue.

"Help! Help her!" Re'alis screamed to the men battling the Grishkii. Her cry was smothered by the sound of battle, and she watched in agony as the Grishkah continued to drive the dagger into the young woman.

"Please help!" she yelled with all her might, voice growing haggard, but this time, they heard.

Ralenn and Kaileth fought their way to Lirah. In a panic-fueled stroke Ralenn cut the Grishkah practically in half, sending its body flying aside in a wash of viscera, the avertyyn blade finding nothing to slow its biting path. Lirah relaxed, dagger still in her chest, as the pressure from the Grishkah stopped. Ralenn watched with hesitation as the dagger slowly pushed its way back out of the wound in a fountain of azure flame. The dagger popped free, and nothing but smooth skin was visible in the blood-soaked hole cut into her clothing.

Lirah was finally able to take a deep breath again, and she opened her eyes to see Ralenn's panic-stricken face looking down at her.

"Lirah, are you..." he trailed off, his voice shaking.

She took stock of herself. She could feel the force she had drawn on recede, and a sudden weariness set in. Her clothing and the earth beneath her were soaked in her blood. A bright orange and pink lily happily bobbed just above her face in bizarre juxtaposition to the gore. Lirah felt detached, cold, and dizzy. Yet she lived. She smiled softly, moving her hand to lazily touch the flower.

"I am. I. I am alright, Ralenn. Help me up."

He took her hand and pulled her from the bloody earth. Her once mostly white clothing was a dark red, blood still dripping from her. It was a disturbing sight, to say nothing of the smell of so much gore.

"Ralenn!" Kaileth called in a commanding tone.

They both looked up and saw yet more Grishkii charging at them. Lirah stumbled forward. She picked up the dagger that had almost killed her and quickly cut the woman free. Re'alis collapsed, her legs numb and feeble after hours bound. Lirah knelt near her, still trying to muster her own strength.

"Are you alright, can you walk?" Lirah asked softly, barely able to speak. She was exhausted!

"Yes, but your wound?" The woman spoke in a worried tone. Lirah smiled and parted her clothing where the dagger had been. There was no mark at all.

"It's healed. Can you shoot a bow?" she asked.

With no time for debating wounds, the woman nodded, and Lirah led her away from the battle to where she had placed her bow and Ralenn's, along with their arrows. Lirah was glad for Ralenn's bow, as she was not sure that she could have drawn a normal one in her present state. They both took a bow and started to fire into the Grishkii that swarmed Kaileth and Ralenn.

Mirris screamed as she smashed, talons first, into another Grishkah, crushing its skull as she drove it to the ground. Riidak looked more like a bear than a hound as he fought, biting at throats and smashing Grishkah weapons aside with his large, armored paws. Ralenn and Kaileth moved in a lethal harmony, a lifetime practicing together on display. In a dance of steel, they fought, felling Grishkii with nearly every stroke. The creature's crude armor could not withstand their avertyyn blades.

Ralenn was gasping for breath as sweat poured from his brow. He did not think he could fight much longer, not like this. He looked to Kaileth. He didn't seem tired at all. His face was set with a dark, determined expression as he fought. Despite their furious fighting the Grishkii still came, barking and howling with excitement. Deadly arrows flew from the bows of Lirah and the woman she had freed as Ralenn, Mirris, Kaileth, and Riidak were slowly forced back toward them. Soon they were in a semicircle, their backs to a tight stand of huge trees. There was nothing to do but fight and hope that the Grishkii would fall back at the sight of so many of their dead.

Ralenn looked back to Lirah, who had retreated with Re'alis behind them, and his expression begged her to run. She shook her head and pulled an avertyyn arrow from her quiver. It seemed to Ralenn that the thunder of the falls suddenly got louder. He looked around the battleground and realized the sound was not the falls but the thunder of horses.

"Devick..." Ralenn heard the woman gasp.

Lord Devick and the chevaliers of Mantorah burst through the thick vegetation, filing out into the glade to form a battle line in a fluid stream of armor, horse, and grim warriors. Two amongst the host wore brilliant white and bronze-trimmed armor. His armor distinct, the leader of the Mantorahns gave a cry, and lances lowered in a charge. They crashed into the back ranks of the Grishkii with an unstoppable force, trampling as many under hoof as they cut down with their blades. Jayle led a dular of cavalry to the right side, and Gairrle led another dular left. Devick took the center with the remainder of his men and two Alabaster Guard survivors they had encountered further up the trail to the falls.

Lances, spent swords, and hammers were put into use by Jayle and Gairrle's men, keeping any Grishkii from escaping. Devick gasped in pain with every stroke of his sword, but he had to keep going. In a few moments of furious fighting, Devick had reached the besieged party at the center of the Grishkii pack. A warrior by his look near Re'alis gave Devick a salutary flourish of his black-bladed sword and spoke.

"Shayar bless your arrival."

Devick considered this man and his companions for an instant. He knew their weapons and armor and wondered at their implications. Yet now was not the time for introductions. It was clear they were fighting to protect Re'alis and that was enough, for now. Aireathyn and Ercoln dashed to Re'alis, their long silvery halberds ready to defend their lady and redeem the honor of the Alabaster Guard. Devick looked to Re'alis, and she was clearly filled with joy at the sight of her men returned to her. Yet he noticed her torn and bloody gown and grimaced. With her guard at her side, Devick turned back to the fight at hand.

More Grishkii entered the glade. Without the advantage of lances and surprise Devick knew it to be folly to fight Grishkii on horse in a melee. The monsters' size and strength meant that they easily gave battle to a rider, with the rider at the disadvantage in both speed and agility. At his command, Devick's forces dismounted and formed a shield wall around Re'alis and the others. Their mounts were taken to the rear in pairs by the lighter armored lancers. Devick gave Jayle and Gairrle each a knowing look in turn and they took command of the shield wall, each man moving to the center mark of the two halves of the battle line. Devick took his place to command the center of the formation of Mantorahn soldiers and waited for the next charge of Grishkii. Somehow, they were still terribly outnumbered. There must have been two hundred fresh Grishkii in the glade now.

The Grishkii formed ragged lines and charged. They smashed into the shields and spears of Devick's men, but the men held. Shouts and the clamor of battle rent the air. On every side the Grishkii attacked and the men of Mantorah held. Devick knew his men would hold as long as their strength did, but their hurried flight had left them precious little of that, and the size and strength of the Grishkii made up in part for their lack of skill. Shields started to crack, men cried out, and the heavy blades of the Grishkii crashed into their armor. The line did not falter, but it did grow smaller as the wounded were pulled back to the center.

A shrill sound suddenly cut through the chaos of the battle and Grishkii began to fall in large numbers, long arrows, almost spears, jutting from their bodies. The Grishkii turned to face the new foe in confusion, with many more fleeing in terror only to die pierced by javelin and arrow shaft. Devick caught sight of several flashes of colorful armor and tall warriors darting in amongst the now panicked Grishkii. He ordered his men to press the attack, and the two warriors who had been with Re'alis advanced with them. Aireathyn and Ercoln stayed with her, wearily watching for any threat directed at their charge. By her command they entered the fray in a lethal blur of avenging blows from their weapons. They slew with a fluid grace that spoke of the refinement of their armor and weaponry. A deadly testament to the elegance of the realm the served.

Devick could now clearly see a large number of the outlandishly armored warriors rushing from the vegetation. Soon, the Grishkii were the ones that were surrounded. With the aid of the new group of warriors it did not take long to slay the remaining foe. Two of the exotically dressed warriors ran from where they had just killed several large Grishkii to where the strange form of smoke and ash lay. The first warrior lunged at the pile with his spear, yet as the blade struck, it turned, as though the odd heap was made of iron shards. The second warrior approached. The warrior uttered something under his breath and with a powerful thrust pinned the form to the earth with his spear. He then called back to the others of his company in what Devick thought a beautiful, but alien language. Then he violently crushed what looked to be part of a head with the heel of his boot. An ear-splitting screech and wisps of smoke rose from the form as it crumbled further, now only a hollowed white shell, covered with black tattered cloth, filled with yellowed bones and gray ash.

14

New Sight and New Friends

*J*illii is to the sorrowful an everspring of kindnesses. Look for her hand in the smallest measures of mercy in this world. Know she is mindful to ease the mortal sojourn, seeking the smaller acts beneath her mother's cares.
Essays of the Divine*

For a time, all stood in silence as the smoke slowly drifted skyward. With the more obvious foe dispatched, would combat resume between the three disparate parties, or were they in fact unlooked-for allies in this wilderness? Devick's mind tried to process the situation, but his wounds had taxed him to the limit. He felt his mind wander; his limbs felt cold and sluggish. The only thing he could fix upon was her, Re'alis. He saw her leaning on a spear and breathing heavily. Brek had been with them, Aseairpeth had sped them on. They had made it, but she was not unscathed. He examined her face with concern and worry. Her clothing was ripped and tattered, her body was shaking, and blood oozed from wounds at her ankles and wrists. Compelled, Devick moved to her as swiftly as he could. Gairrle called after his lord, but Devick didn't seem to hear. Aireathyn and Ercoln both bowed to Devick as he approached, knowing they owed the lord of Mantorah for their lives and for returning them to their place of duty at Re'alis' side.

"Lady Re'alis, are you alright? I feared the worst."

The smile she gave in reply illuminated her face, and she embraced Devick, who was surprised by the sudden show of emotion, and somewhat pained as she wrapped her arms tightly around his wounded side.

"It told me you were dead; I am so glad that was a lie. I knew it was a lie, I felt it so, I prayed for it to be so. Oh, Devick, you came for me." Emotions threatened to spill out around her words. Devick returned the embrace, carefully clearing some of Re'alis' tousled hair so he could look more fully into her face. The moment slowed and for an instant he forgot the pain of his body as she looked up into his dark eyes, the delicate features of her face filling with warmth, desire even. Noise and clamor grew from all who were now in the glade. The gravity of the situation returned with force. She released him from her arms and quickly regained her composure.

"I am fine now, thanks to you and our new friends. But you, you fell at the camp! Even I feared..." she trailed off, turning him this way and that with gentle motion, looking him over for obvious wounds. Devick tried to smile, but his injuries were starting to gain the better of him.

"I was struck, but I am well enough now. The better even, since you are safe with us again."

Captain Gairrle walked up and spoke in a hushed tone.

"We are relieved to find you safe, my lady, nevertheless we should address our present situation, sire."

Jayle and the other Mantorahn cavalry were back in ranks eyeing the strangers with caution.

"You are..." Devick's breath caught painfully for a moment, "right. We need to find out who our new friends are, and what they are doing here."

"Lord, we will not leave her side," Aireathyn said reassuringly.

Re'alis nodded, and Devick followed her gaze as she turned toward her other rescuers. At the edge of the glade, where the grass met the wide pool beneath the falls, stood the two men and the young woman who had fought so fiercely to defend her..

Theirs should be an interesting story, Devick thought, raising an eyebrow to Re'alis.

Lirah sat on one of the many large black stones that surrounded the water. The soft glow from the falls gently illuminated the area she sat in, the shadow from the towering cliff of the falls placing the entire area in the shade. She was resting and trying to make sense of what had just happened to her when Ralenn came and sat next to her. He placed a reassuring arm around her, trying to avoid the soggier parts of her clothing.

"I don't know how you did that with the dagger, but I sure am glad that you did it." His voice was still shaking with trepidation.

Lirah tried to give him a smile, but even her face felt too exhausted to do that much. She leaned into his embrace and took a slow deep breath, feeling the comfort of his steady heartbeat.

"Ralenn, I suddenly feel like I don't really know what I am...does that make sense?"

Ralenn didn't answer, so she continued to speak softly.

"It frights me, yet excites me at the same time. There was so much death, and blood...I don't know if I will like who I will become to face all this." Lirah struggled to put words to everything that she was thinking. Her mind was full of confusing thoughts. And what did Ralenn think? He was just sitting there, quietly holding her.

He must think all this is making me go crazy. He might not be wrong...

"I should be dead, Ralenn, that Grishkah killed me. I even stopped breathing."

"But you didn't die, you survived." Ralenn's voice was calm.

"But how? People don't survive things like that! Not normal people, there was too much blood. There still is too much blood, I stink with it." Lirah could feel tears washing little streams through the blood and dirt on her face. She watched as the little clear drops fell alongside a few drops of blood into the surface of the pool.

I must look like a monster...

"I feel like a stranger to myself," she admitted quietly. "Losing our home was terrible enough; am I to lose who I am as well?"

Ralenn's gentle touch interrupted her thoughts, distracting her as his hand softly turned her chin and face up to look at him. A warm smile was in his eyes as he spoke.

"I know you, Lirah, you are kind and selfless, and fiery and sometimes reckless in all the best ways. Nothing that happened today changed that. We both have faced some impossible things since we left home. Since we lost home. We both have found new strengths to get through these awful trials. That doesn't change who we are, only what we are able to do. We need to trust fate will shape us for our purpose. We can trust each other. We just need to stick together. We will get through this, Lirah, I promise."

"I hope so, Ralenn. It feels like we will when you're near. That much I am certain of." Her reply surprised Ralenn. He was not sure what he expected her to say but it had not been that. She brushed back some of her matted hair and she finally let herself smile. Cool moist air whirled around them from the churning water of the falls. Her hand found his, holding it fast as she blinked away newly formed tears. Lirah let out a long slow tremulous breath. It felt as though she had been holding it since the fight ended. A part of her still awaiting the lethal finality of that dagger within her breast. Ralenn could sense the intensity of what Lirah was experiencing next to him. Sorrow, fear, desperation, and something brighter. Hope. He held her hand with tender strength.

The cool air felt good on Lirah's face. She puffed up her checks, pushing out another, deeper deliberate breath, and with it she expelled the greater portion of her darker thoughts. Her aching body relaxed a little more. She let her mind go, not thinking about anything, save the sound of the falls' rushing water and Ralenn's strong hand in hers. The force of the waterfall was tangible here. The air vibrated with it. She let its energy and rhythm fill her mind with its cleansing cadence. Then, suddenly, there it was; without trying, she was again aware of the latent force she had drawn upon earlier to save herself. She could feel it all around her. In the air, the trees, especially in the water. It felt like a warm golden light, though she could not truly see it. She wanted to ignore it at first, to run from it; but how could she run from her own mind and feelings? Instead, she focused on it, as before, though it was easier now without the panic from the attack and the pain of the dagger.

She slowly became more aware of the earth and stone under her, then the water and mist from the falls. The water almost seemed to glow in her mind, bright and flowing. She pulled her awareness closer to the life force. It felt like she was brushing cobwebs off her mind's eye now, to see the world around her in a completely new way. She could see, or feel, the outline of Ralenn's form, his beating heart, and the life force within him. He felt bright, but not as bright as Kaileth, who was coming near. Then she felt a brightness that far outshone both Ralenn and Kaileth. It flew into her awareness and came to a stop on the rocks near her. She opened her eyes with a start to see Mirris eyeing her inquisitively on a large black rock, backlit by the glowing falls. The large bird raised a feathery eyebrow, and Lirah could swear that she could feel the bird thinking about her. She felt warmth when she focused on Mirris, like a smile. She closed her eyes again and reached out in her mind toward the falcon. Again, a powerful surge of brilliance pulsed from where Mirris stood. It felt like the sun on a scorching summer day.

How could she have so much...life?

Lirah tried to gently push into the dazzling energy with her mind, unsure what it would do to her or Mirris. She searched for Mirris from within the light, and as she did, she sensed the energy from Mirris change, becoming more focused on *her*. Lirah was suddenly aware that she could feel emotions that were not her own. Each new pulse of energy from Mirris washed over her, feeling like...

Love?

Lirah jumped a little as Kaileth's deep voice sounded next to her, dropping Ralenn's hand as she opened her eyes.

"Miss Lirah, how are you feeling?" His voice sounded concerned, yet there was also a hint of curiosity. Ralenn and Lirah both turned around to face Kaileth and Riidak.

"I am not sure, to be honest," she answered a bit breathlessly, still bewildered by what she had just experienced. "I *feel* well enough, but...I just don't know what to think about it all."

"Battle of any sort is unsettling, as is coming so close to death," Kaileth said soberly.

Lirah nodded, but that was only half her worry. Kaileth stood considering her and Ralenn for a time, and she avoided his gaze, not wanting to discuss this matter as she didn't understand it yet.

"It is in these extreme moments of crisis that we are often forced to face what and who we really are. Take heart, Miss Lirah, your actions make Gaileng proud in the halls of the Patient Father. I am certain that it was not just chance that saw you safe from Allinth with us. This trial is your fated path. And we are alive thanks to it."

"I feel like I was meant to be here too," she said, surprising herself by the conviction in her voice. "But that doesn't make all this any easier to face." Tears once more filled her eyes. Lirah shook her head, frustrated at how distressed she truly was. She dared not wipe them away for fear of only smearing the bloody mess that was the rest of her across her face. As if he knew her thoughts, Ralenn offered her a square of blue linen for her tears.

Kaileth continued in a reassuring tone. "Such knowledge rarely does. However, you can have faith in yourself and in the fact that you are meant to be here facing these trials and growing from them. You are much stronger than you know, Miss Lirah, don't be frightened by that. Trust the goodness of your revealed nature. Gaileng always did."

Lirah nodded but said nothing. To speak was to risk letting the overwhelming sob that had built in her throat escape. By all the Aashahl she hoped Gaileng was proud of her. It hurt so much to think about him being gone. She had never heard Kaileth speak in this manner. He had always been kind but mostly reserved. She looked at Ralenn and suddenly realized she had covered him with blood. It was smeared in a macabre outline showing clearly where her arms had been wrapped around him. He smiled and held up his hand, which was also covered in her blood.

"Oh, Ralenn, I'm sorry! I forgot about the blood!" she exclaimed, coming closer to examine the damage to Ralenn's clothing.

He just laughed a little and pulled on a burned and tattered piece of his raiment.

"You can do little harm at this point. That fire blast sealed my outfit's fate," he said. And he was right. His jerkin had a large hole straight through it and was torn and cut in several more places. Well beyond any means of repair. There was a commotion from the other side of the pool that drew their attention. The few of the band of outlandish warriors were gesticulating and speaking passionately in their native language. They were an impressive sight, each so colorfully unique in hair and eye color, their armor, and weapons strange and ancient-looking, all bronzes and earthy shades of dark greens and leathery browns. It struck Ralenn that they also were all of a roughly uniform height, being slightly taller than himself and Kaileth it seemed, at this distance at least.

"They are Tundraihn," Kaileth said, answering both Lirah and Ralenn's unspoken question. "They come from the far southeast. They are not human kindred. Nor mortal kindred, for that matter, and can be dangerous. The others are from Mantorah, and the lady from Lea'Angleneth, I believe..." His words trailed off for a few moments.

Ralenn and Lirah looked at each other as Kaileth's expression grew contemplative.

"No, there is no doubt that we were all meant to come here. The Aashahl are at work in these events. We stand in the palm of fate's hand. Shayar guide us all that we can each rise to play our parts. Please stay here while I speak with the Mantorahns." With that Kaileth gave Ralenn's shoulder a squeeze and walked toward the group of soldiers.

Devick watched as one of the strangers approached. To his shock he saw the man was clearly one of the Allitorii. The Allitorii warrior bowed to the lord and his companions as he spoke.

"Mier fes Dular Du'Bre, Lords of Mantorah, I am Kaileth Hirradahn Jul'Epri, of Allinth. We saw the fire from the ridge, and upon discovering your situation, my lady, we came to lend aid."

Devick was impressed by this Kaileth's confidence and dignity, and he managed to smile as he spoke.

"It seems that we owe you a great debt, though I am surprised to hear that you are of Allinth. We have heard that the village and lands about have been lost to raiding Grishkii. It is good to see that some survived." Devick took a step to the side to introduce those with him.

"You apparently already know who I am, Master Harridan. Allow me to introduce my companions. This is Lady Re'alis of Lea'Angleneth and her guardian of the Alabaster Orders, Gallant Serjent Aireathyn and Gallant Ercoln, Uran Jayle De'Vinor, and Captain Gairrle of Mantorah."

Kaileth again gave a bow. "The eyes of Shayar brighten at our meeting. An honor to meet you all." He gestured to where his companions still sat. "I am accompanied by my apprentice Ralenn, and a priestess of the Anthosn Order, Miss Lirah. Please excuse them for the present, as this was their first such ordeal, and they need a moment of pause."

"Completely understandable," Jayle said, taking note of the large amount of blood on the young woman.

"Is the priestess going to be alright, Master Hirradahn?" Re'alis spoke with concern. "She was...that is, her wounds...How is she yet alive?"

"My lady, she is a healer of no small skill, though she might not admit that herself. I assure you her body is well healed from the fight. It is her essence of will that will need some time to recover, I believe."

"And what of you and your apprentice?" Gairrle spoke now, and mistrust was evident upon his face. "How does one from an isolated mountain village gain arms and armor as you now bear?"

It was a question Devick was also keen to know the answer to. Though he did not feel as much distrust for the man as Gairrle apparently did, not after seeing how he fought for Lady Re'alis.

"Noble captain, I assure you that my claim to this attire is honorable and earned; suffice to say it is from my prior profession."

"I see. And the others with you?" Gairrle gestured toward the strangely dressed warriors on the other side of the glade.

"They are not with us, but seem to be another band that fate brought here in the nick of time."

"They are Tundraihn, are they not?" Devick asked, though he was not sure why. Kaileth looked younger than he and could not possibly have had a chance to interact with the Tundraihn under the Subjugate's rule. And yet, he commanded a respect due to a seasoned lord. His eyes spoke of long years and vast knowledge.

"Yes, they are of the Tundraihn, my lord. It is a war band, not the more common hunters. For them to come this far north into the mortal realms is unheard of, sire."

"I have heard unsettling things about them and their forest lands." Jayle eyed them warily.

"I don't think they mean us any harm, my lords," Kaileth reassured. "I would guess their hatred of man is overemphasized in our lore."

"They helped us in the fighting and have had plenty of time to either leave or attack." Re'alis said.

"Very true, my lady. Master Hirradahn, would you accompany us to greet them?" Devick held out a hand to Kaileth, who took it in a firm grasp.

"I will, my lord."

"Excellent. Jayle, come with us; Gairrle, if you would, see that our company is prepared to remove our wounded and return to the road to Syrah." Gairrle nodded and Devick left with Jayle and their new acquaintance, Kaileth, to speak with the Tundraihn.

Re'alis eyed Devick as he walked away. "Gairrle, you have to tell me the truth," she said as they began walking to the group of Mantorahn cavalry.

"Of course, my lady, but of what?"

"Lord Devick, his wounds. How bad are they? I saw him fall at the camp, and I can see his pain now. What injury is he hiding?"

Gairrle swallowed hard and looked away, but she gave him her best flat stare, the one that demanded answers, and he relented. "My lady, his wounds are grave. We tried to stop him from coming, but he would not stay. He could not be kept from coming after you. With our apothatrist and chyrurgeon dead in the battle, there was little we could do for him."

"I see." Re'alis thought for a moment as she watched Devick approach the Tundraihn. She could see him favoring his side, and she now noticed his coloring was wrong.

"Well then, Captain, it would seem that your lord is in need of a healer."

With that Re'alis took the tabard that Gairrle had taken out of a saddlebag and put it over her stained and torn chemise, then with her two guards trailing after her, she marched toward the young man and woman on the rocks near the pool. They did not notice her approach.

"Excuse me, Priestess Lirah," Re'alis said. The two companions spun to face Re'alis as she spoke. Both clearly taken aback by the lady's intensity and her two white-armored guardians, one at each shoulder.

"I fear that I again need your aid." Re'alis spoke softly, but urgently.

"I am always eager to help how I can. What do you need?" Lirah said.

Re'alis sighed inwardly in relief.

"It is the Lord Devick. In the battle during which I was captured, he was wounded badly and has yet to be tended to. Our healers are dead, and I fear that he will perish as well without aid. He is ever so dear to me. Master Hirradahn says you are a great healer. Is there a way you could help him?"

Lirah seemed to hesitate.

"She is a gifted healer, my lady," the young man said. She believed Kaileth had called him Ralenn. "But she needs some rest herself before—"

"No, I will be alright," Lirah interrupted him. Re'alis noted the squeeze she gave his hand as she stood up.

"How bad is he hurt, my lady?"

Re'alis gestured to where Devick was clearly having to lean upon his spear to stay upon his feet. Even in the fitful light of the glade it was plain to see he was not well.

"Lirah, he looks pretty bad off, are you sure you have it in you to help him so soon after you revived yourself?" Ralenn asked. Re'alis thought it was kind of him to care for her, but she had no time for hesitation. She was relieved to hear the young woman's answer.

"Yes, I am sure. I can help him, Ralenn. I will be fine. I must at least try." She gave him a look and Re'alis bit back a smile at the poor boy's expense.

"Oh, thank you, Priestess, thank you. Stay here, I will go get him." With that Re'alis rushed over to where Devick had just started talking to the Tundraihn.

"Ralenn, go with her and see what Kaileth is saying. I don't—" Lirah didn't finish.

"What is it, Lirah? Are you sure you will be able to safely heal him?" Ralenn didn't want to undermine her confidence with his own uncertainty, but he had to be sure.

"I can. I just know it. I can do it. I think that maybe this type of...this type of healing was what I was made for. Maybe it's why I was saved from Anoth and why I was raised by Gaileng and why I followed you up the mountain. I can do this. But I will have to focus. I am tired and frightened and so, so scared of tomorrow. But this I can do. It will be easier at least, for this time I think if all I have to think about is the task at hand. Does any of that make sense, Ralenn, or am I talking in a circle?" Her eyes searched his, and Ralenn could feel her earnest need to heal this lord of Mantorah. It was fierce, burning like a star with in her. His newfound second sight could not help but see it like a brilliant jewel hung around her svelte neck. He would be a distraction. He understood.

"I will just be over there should you need me, Lirah. Dannitar fill you with her grace." Lirah smiled tenderly at him and Ralenn hurried after Re'alis.

"Excuse my interruption, my lords and sirs, but Lord Rahdan Devick has wounds that must be tended to or the Camarilla of Mantorah will be seeking a new High Lord Rahdan." Without further explanation, Re'alis took Devick by the arm and firmly led him away. He let out a gasp in pain but did not object. Ralenn stayed by Kaileth's side as the lady marched Lord Devick off to Lirah. He had a feeling the two women were going to get along very well.

"Rahdan Devick does have a serious wound," Aireathyn stated, having stayed as well.

"When he and your company found us it was clear even then he was wounded, and that was many hours and skain ago."

Kaileth nodded. "Then it is well that Miss Lirah will be helping him. He is in good hands under her ministrations. Please, continue," he said to the Tundraihn that had seen speaking before the interruption. The Tundraihn took little heed of this intermission and continued with a smooth, powerful voice.

"I am Orodan, leader of Eolai'Mahtair Telistia's Farseeker war band. As I told your lord, I am looking for a band of Grishkii and Srellites, some eight score strong, heading toward the Taiw'Tai Fortress with Tundraihn captives taken in a raid. We would be grateful for any aid you could lend."

Orodan was taller than Ralenn by half a head, with long, silvery hair. His angular, dark bronzed face looked as young as Ralenn's, though sterner and wiser. Orodan's eyes were the most fascinating part about his appearance; they were a luminescent gold, with such large irises that they left no white showing—like those of a bird. His lean, muscled figure was dressed in what looked to be a shirt of dark green and black scales, almost like leaves, which came to a point just below his knees. He was also armed impressively, holding a long bronze-bladed spear in his hand, and a great quiver of javelins, or perhaps extremely long arrows, hung from his back. A wide blade was strapped to his elaborately woven belt and near it was a long bronze rod with an odd socket on one end.

Ralenn knew the Tundraihn to be a wild people, wary of any who were not of their kind. They supposedly lived far to the southeast in the great forests where they could avoid the other kindreds of the land. Kaileth had told him the Tundraihn lived five times as long as any human, and possessed other arcane blessings, though Ralenn had always thought some of that to be mere rumors. Some said they could see in the darkest of night and run forever; others claimed they were more animal than man, savage and dangerous; yet others still claimed that they were immortal and could speak with the trees, rivers, and rocks of their lands. Regardless, Ralenn was sure now as he looked over the band of Tundraihn warriors that they were indeed creatures of magic that possessed traits no human did. They had an aura that was produced by more than just their strange and vibrant armor and clothing.

A long moment of silence passed, Orodan slowly looked over Ralenn and those near him. His gaze was deliberate and thoughtful, and Ralenn sensed a power in his eyes. They felt warm, wise from ages of life, and yet there was an intense passion behind them, a wildness. He shook his head slightly, not wishing his second sight to manifest here. Ralenn prayed he would have time to process his suddenly revealed abilities and to talk to Kaileth about them before they become a problem. If Kaileth had not shared so much with him the night before on the ridge top Ralenn would have been as troubled as Lirah was with her surprising powers.

Jayle finally spoke: "We will assist you as best we can."

"Information, that is what I need. Thanks to the Dactyls' unexpected hospitality, we have traveled *through* the mountains in the hopes of cutting off our enemy's retreat. This, however, also caused us to lose their trail. Have you come across any signs or word of a force such as I have described passing through your realms? We had hoped that the force here was our quarry, yet this was not the case. This band was Grishkii only, and there were no signs of the ikthii with the foe we seek."

Jayle paused for a moment before answering . Among Lord Devick's retinue, he was likely one of the few who had encountered a Dactyl and lived to remember it. They were perilous to all surface dwelling kindreds. Tales abounded of unfortunates whose memories were stripped away, or who returned from the southern Vagath'Oth mountains aged by years, with no recollection of what had befallen them.

"No, No band of Srellite and Grishkii has been noted in our realm."

"Nor ours, Master Tundraihn. Though we are many halfmoons removed from fresh news in Lea'Angleneth," offered Aireathyn.

"What road were they taking?" asked Kaileth.

"They were last seen heading north along the Aril River, through the Rividall Plains," said Orodan, who turned his gaze to Kaileth and Ralenn.

"Have either of you crossed paths with these creatures?"

Kaileth answered, "We have not, Master Orodan. We are refugees from Allinth and came upon this place only by chance. Our village was destroyed by Grishkii, but there were no Srellites with them, and they did not come from the river."

"I see," Orodan said with a sigh. "It seems the country is rife with their ilk, save those we seek."

Ralenn thought he could sense despair growing in Orodan, and for an instant, images flashed into his mind: an immense forest, fighting in the trees, and a beautiful woman. Ralenn shook his head again and tried to clear his mind. Ralenn knew somehow that the vision was of the raid Orodan spoke of. It seemed the gifts of his bloodline would not be fully denied. But before he could understand what he had seen in Orodan, a deep voice brought Ralenn fully back to the conversation.

"They would have to get past Syrah," Jayle pointed out. "I do not think a band the size you are seeking could get past our patrols unnoticed."

"You are most likely right," Kaileth acknowledged. "A large number of hostiles could not get through the Mantorahn frontier very easily without being spotted or engaged."

"If that is the case, then may I inquire as to the hospitality of Syrah? That is, would they be willing to lend us aid in our search?" asked Orodan.

Jayle answered without hesitation, but there was a hint of surprise in his voice.

"Syrah's gates are open to all who are friends of Mantorah, but I have not the authority to give you more men. I am sure that Lord Devick would be glad to assist you once we reach Syrah. The paladin would also be pleased to lend you aid, I am sure."

Ralenn was shocked that a Tundraihn would so readily ask for help from humans. Even Kaileth looked a little surprised. The Tundraihn were known for not being very social, and they rarely left their homelands. If they did, they usually treated those who were not of their kind with contempt. It was said they saw humans as short-sighted, greed-driven destroyers. It was also out of the ordinary for them to be so forthcoming concerning their errand. As their conversation continued, Ralenn noted one of them leaving their party to approach Lirah. He kept a wary eye on him as best he could while still lending an ear to their plans.

Lirah looked up as one of the Tundraihn walked over to where she and Lady Re'alis were tending to Lord Devick's wounds. She could not help but stare for a moment. She had never seen anything like him. Nothing about the Tundraihn seemed ordinary. He wore a large dark green cloak and a soft brown tunic. He was not as tall as some of the other warriors, though still taller than a good longbow. His hair was dark, yet in the sunlight she saw it gleamed a deep maroon, falling just over his broad shoulders and framing a narrow, thoughtful face. He wore little armor and carried no sword, but there was something commanding in his bearing. Instead, a large beaded pack hung across his back, and in his right hand he held a short spear. Lirah wondered at his place among the band. Ercoln watched him warily as he spoke.

"I am Tyllidus. I may be able to help you save his life." His words were slow and calculated as he spoke. Lirah had never thought she would see a Tundraihn, and she was a little stunned that one was now in front of her, offering help. She stared in wonder into his eyes. They had the same look as a bird of prey. Lirah looked deeper, and it seemed that there was something familiar there...She suddenly realized that he was smiling at her and she dropped her gaze.

"I would welcome any aid, my lord," she said timidly.

Tyllidus knelt next to her and Lady Re'alis, who subtly motioned for Ercoln to relax.

"I am Tyllidus, no lord, only Tyllidus. Now what is the damage?"

Lirah blushed a little as she replied, "I was about to find out."

She held out her hand, showing him the soft sapphire flame radiating from it. She gently lowered it to Lord Devick's bruised and discolored side. As it entered his body, Lord Devick took a sudden, abrupt breath, and then his eyes rolled back into his head.

"Miss Lirah, is that supposed to happen?" Re'alis' voice quivered as she held Devick's limp hand.

"Oh, yes, my lady," Lirah said between labored breaths. "I am trying to...feel the injury. I have to take on a part of it so I can know what needs to heal."

Tyllidus was pulling out a variety of oddly shaped bottles and herbs wrapped in an assortment of iridescently colored leaves. Lirah started to breathe erratically, and her eyes snapped shut. She quickly pulled her hand away.

"What is it?" Lady Re'alis asked.

"How grave?" Tyllidus asked.

Lirah let out a slow breath, trying not to sound panicked.

"I do not know how he was able to walk at all, let alone ride and fight. He has broken ribs, yes, but one of his organs is...burst. He is bleeding...on the inside. He is bleeding a lot." Lirah was working to slow down her breathing as she noticed Lady Re'alis' was speeding up.

"Is there nothing you can do?" Tears were slowly welling up and rolling down the lady's cheeks, running into the cuts and scratches left by her captors. Re'alis felt spent. She had no more strength left for new tragedy this day.

"I will do my best, my lady, but I can only take so much from him." Lirah was not sure if she could pull enough from her new, strange, deepened power to replace all the lost blood and heal the wound. She was sure it was possible after her experience, but she was not sure she could tap into the life force of Miljah again. It was that same well of power she had drawn upon when the Grishkii's dagger pierced her—she was certain of it. Gaileng had taught her such things. What she was not certain of was whether she could summon that depth again, or survive it if she did. Tyllidus held out his hand to Lirah and, in a calm tone, said, "I believe that we may be able to save him if we combine our efforts."

Lirah's confusion must have been obvious. Tyllidus continued.

"It is clear that you are an arcane healer of some skill, yet you have not worked with another healer?"

Lirah recalled her training with Gaileng at the temple. He had taught her how to use a portion of her power, but he had taught her from books and tomes, older than any other the temple held. Books only. She had been the only one who could use the arcane to heal. Gaileng told her that her mother was a healer too, but aside from this apparent hereditary connection Lirah had never been sure where her abilities came from, let alone how to combine with another healer like herself.

"I was the only empath at my temple, I have never even met another." This last bit she said more to herself than to Tyllidus. Lirah was not sure what to think. She hardly understood what she did when she healed. Aside from the recent healings of Ralenn and Kaileth, she had never attempted to heal any truly critical injuries. She had practiced on simple broken bones, shallow cuts, and mild illnesses, but the rest of her skill was a largely untested theory from her studies. Lirah suddenly found herself wishing that she had taken those studies more seriously. Tyllidus placed a reassuring hand on her shoulder. It was warm, inhumanly warm, yet not uncomfortable. He smiled as he spoke.

"It is simple enough; just as you seek the wound in the fallen, we first seek each other. We seek for the power within each other, the essence of us. Focus on it, on its rhythms, try to match it with our own, then, when our rhythms are synced, we can reach out together as one and address the wounds."

"I...I am not sure." She looked away. What if she did it wrong? She might worsen Devick's injury. But what really made her nervous was the thought of baring her inner self to such a complete stranger. He took both her trembling hands in his and warmth surged up her arms. She turned and found him smiling at her, his expression confident and firm.

"We can do this, believe in yourself."

"Please, Miss Lirah," Re'alis begged quietly. "You have to try."

Lirah nodded and closed her eyes. With hands still clasped she reached her senses out to Tyllidus. For a moment there was nothing, then she could feel surges of warm energy. With her eyes closed it was like she could see them, bright waves of colorful light emanating from Tyllidus. The pulses came in a harmonic pattern, and as she focused, she found herself matching it, then she added her own pulses to the pattern. Soon an undulating symphony of light and energy flowed through Lirah and Tyllidus. It was as if she joined with him in some way, as though she touched the essence of his being. She felt power rush through her until she could no longer distinguish his pulses from hers.

"Now." The voice was Tyllidus' and yet hers also. It sounded in her mind only, but she knew what it meant. She moved her focus from the pulses into Devick. Pain burst into her body, and she flared her pulses hard. Yet underneath the life force of Tyllidus and her own, Lirah felt herself drawn to the deeper, slower rhythms of Miljah that eclipsed all else in depth and magnitude.

Ralenn was looking around while Kaileth, Orodan, and Gairrle were talking about possible routes to take to Syrah. He had never seen so many noble-looking warriors in his life. He turned his gaze to the group of Tundraihn and noticed that quite a few of them were females. They looked just as battle ready as any of their male comrades, and in some respects even more fierce. A flickering light drew his attention back toward Lirah. Ralenn shielded his eyes with his hand and could see Lirah in the midst of the intensifying light. She had her hands clasped with one of the Tundraihn, the one that had walked over there earlier. They held their hands over Devick's body, and soon some type of a crystalline haze formed around them, emanating from their hands. The light's rays soon had the attention of everyone in the clearing.

The light's intensity quickly became greater than the sun overhead, and the onlookers were obliged to shield their eyes. Ralenn and Kaileth slowly started to walk closer to Lirah, and they were followed by Orodan and Gairrle. The light formed into an oscillating orb, and Lady Re'alis and Ercoln stumbled back out of its reach. The orb seemed to solidify for an instant, then, with a crack like thunder, the sphere burst into a thousand glittering shards of energy that crashed upon the black stone of the falls and green grass of the glade before fading away. It was dark now, or at least the sunlight seemed dark when compared to that shattered globe of light. Lirah and the

Tundraihn could again be seen next to Lord Devick. They both appeared to be out of breath, but Lirah was smiling. She stood up shaking, but she appeared to be unhurt. Ralenn dashed to her and broke the silence that had fallen upon all in the dell.

"Lirah, what was that, are you alright?"

She giggled tiredly as she answered him. "I am not sure. I think it was me, but...Tyllidus?" she turned toward the Tundraihn questioningly.

"All of the energy was you, Miss Lirah. I would not have guessed you possessed such power."

Lirah gave a broad smile. "Neither did I."

"I believe that all I did was help you channel it correctly," Tyllidus said, smiling back at her.

It was clear to Ralenn that this Tyllidus was intrigued by Lirah. He stood regarding Lirah with an expression that was hard to read in his unusual eyes. Yet Ralenn was sure he could guess his mind, his burgeoning otherly senses brushing the Tundraihn's surface thoughts. Curiosity, awe, and desire. Ralenn thought he felt a hunger burning in this Tundraihn. It was unsettling, and Ralenn tried to dismiss it as simple jealousy. However, he had a suspicion that he was actually feeling these emotions coming from Tyllidus. Since the fight with the sphinx this sudden connection with others' motivations and thoughts was happening more often. The struggle with the desecrator had been the storm that burst the dam, apparently unlocking the gifts of the sphinx Kaileth had alluded to.

"Well whatever it was, did it work?" asked Ralenn. He was worried a bit for the lord, but he mostly wanted the roving eyes of Tyllidus to shift from Lirah.

"Uh, yes; from what I can sense, he is fine now. In fact, a little better than normal." Tyllidus started to put away his equipment.

"When will he wake?" Lady Re'alis asked, having returned to Devick's side as soon as the light was gone.

"Well, if he acts like everyone else I have healed, it will be a day or two," Lirah said.

"I concur, Miss Lirah," Tyllidus was again looking at her, but with a more guarded expression. Re'alis knelt at Devick's side and took his hand for a moment. Ralenn wondered how close the lord and lady were; she seemed very concerned for his safety. Re'alis gently released his hand and turned a smiling face to Lirah and Tyllidus.

"Thank you, thank you both," she said emphatically, face slightly flushed.

Lirah gave a small curtsy. "I am happy I could help, my lady."

Jayle spoke next, looking a bit bewildered. "If Lord Devick is going to be recovering for the next few days, I propose that Captain Gairrle should take charge of the men. As the lord's chosen captain it is right."

"With your leave, my lady?" Gairrle added.

"Yes, of course," Re'alis agreed.

Gairrle turned to Orodan and Kaileth. "We are going to make with all speed to Syrah. You are welcome to accompany us," he offered formally.

"If in Syrah we may have word of our prey, then that is the path we will follow." Orodan nodded, turned on his heel, and strode over to his men.

"What about you, Master Hirradahn?" asked Jayle.

"We were planning on heading there ourselves," said Kaileth.

Gairrle smiled as he spoke. "Good, there is safety in numbers."

Orodan quickly returned, "I suggest we leave with the sun on the morrow. My band needs rest before the final run." Orodan did look weary, and Ralenn wondered how far they had pursued their enemy.

"A rest will be good for all," replied Gairrle. With that he and Orodan left Jayle, Kaileth, and Ralenn alone.

"It seems that you are no stranger to a fight," Jayle stated flatly. His hard eyes spoke of questions for Kaileth. Ralenn tensed, unsure of the man's implication.

"That is a fair statement," replied Kaileth, bowing his head respect-fully.

"It will be good to have you with us, Master Allitorii."

Ralenn looked to Kaileth in alarm, but Kaileth gave an almost im-perceptible shake of the head. As Jayle walked away, Ralenn wondered if they had already revealed themselves too much to these strangers. They had been allies when confronted by the Grishkii, but now would that remain the case? Should all the truth be found out, what would that mean for an heir of Anoth, his lone Allitorii protector and a miraculously powerful healer?

15

The Falls

The Otheäil, Shedim, and those sired by the Aashahl are to be considered of the same order as their divine parentage. To know the fullness of their mind is not for mortal kindreds. Seek ye instead a harmony and liberation from the doomed taboos in their otherness. Know they have the extra care of their makers close at hand.
Essays of the Divine

Several loud splashes suddenly awoke Ralenn. After it was decided that they stay put to rest through the night he had removed his armor and found a secluded spot near the falls, away from the glade and the others. He thought the splash might have just been in his dream when another splash sounded, and he sat up to see what was going on. A dark tan streak of a body shot past him from the top of the falls and plunged into the deep shimmering pool. The female Tundraihn were diving off the falls and into the water. Several of them were swimming around and calling up to their companions who had not jumped in yet. Ralenn blushed and turned away as he realized they were not wearing any clothing.

"I wondered how long you were going to gawk at them." This statement was accompanied by a firmly placed kick between his shoulders. Ralenn tumbled to his side and saw Lirah looking down at him. She was frowning a little, but Ralenn knew it to be her jest frown. She sat down next to him.

"I was not gawking; I turned as soon as I noticed."

"Sure, you did. But I did not come over here to harass you, I came over here to run you off."

"Run me off?" Ralenn said, confused.

"Yes, unlike the perfect-bodied warrior creatures of mystery that you were staring at, I am a pale-skinned boring woman, and I do not wish a male audience as I bathe. This is the easiest place to enter the pool. So shoo, please." Ralenn did not argue, though he did shoot her a playful smile as he rose to leave.

"Enjoy your bath, my boring lady."

Lirah stuck her tongue out at Ralenn but lost her scowl in a smile as he left. She slowly started to remove her blood-caked clothing once she was sure she was alone. As she started to remove her last boot, she realized she was being watched. Four female Tundraihn faces sat bobbing up and down as the warriors treaded water and watched Lirah. They looked like mystical ilysh in the pool. All too ready to lure away the unsuspecting to a watery doom. Their long vibrant hair shone in the last of the day's sunlight, revealing brilliant reds, dark blues, metallic golds, and blacks. Their faces were varying shades of deep bronze and their large eyes watched Lirah with a fierce intensity. Lirah froze, not sure what to think. Finally, one blue-haired and green-eyed female swam to the rocky pool's edge and rested her strong arms on the cold stone.

"Sister, why do you travel with and play thus with the akah?" Her voice was soft, and she spoke with a slow deliberate pace, the words were alien upon her tongue.

"The akah?" Lirah questioned.

"Yes, the male, the akah who you dismissed."

"You mean Ralenn; that is his name."

"Yes...Ralenn," the Tundraihn spoke his name dismissively.

"It is clear that you want him, sister, why not simply take him for your own? We would help you should you wish it."

Lirah blinked several times rapidly, in surprise before having to squash a giggle from escaping as she pictured this band of exotic naked women helping her to *subdue* Ralenn for her benefit. Was it truly so obvious that she cared for Ralenn? Was it so easy to see that she did want him? Though perhaps not in the way she suspected the Tundraihn was referring to.

"Where I am from, we do not take people as you say. There is more to it. There is supposed to be love...selfless love that's shared..." Lirah trailed off, not sure how or even if she wanted to explain further. "It is just not our way," she finally said, looking back to the Tundraihn.

"So it would seem. In sooth, your power would do better mated to another, one of our fellow kindreds and cousins."

The Tundraihn paused in consideration for a time and Lirah was unsure what to say or do next. The females seemed wilder, feral, and less human-like than the male Tundraihn. Their features a little sharper, their expressions fiercer, bright eyes that promised a perilous intensity in whatever actions they might take.

"Ealë is what I am called, sister."

"Lirah, I am called Lirah," she replied.

Ealë smiled and offered a hand. "Lirah, come. We will help you clean the death from your body."

Lirah hesitated for a moment, wondering if it was safe, yet despite their differences she found herself sensing kinship with them. They felt familiar somehow, and before she knew what she was doing, Lirah took Ealë's hand and entered the pool. Ealë and the others smiled and started to swim toward the falls. The cool water felt soothing on Lirah's tired feet and achy body. She closed her eyes and took a few deep calming breaths before swimming deeper into the pool.

Lirah followed Ealë and the others, as they swam around and behind the curtain of falling water, to the rocks at the base of the cliff. There Lirah saw over a dozen more female Tundraihn sitting on the stones and at the pool's edge. They were washing and tending to each other's long hair. Each of them had long flowing hair that must have been tightly braided upon their arrival to the battle, as Lirah had not noticed it until now. Each of them that Lirah looked upon had the most striking colors of hair and eyes—iridescent reds and blues, deep and brilliant greens, vivid whites, and golds. They reminded her of flowers. Many of them also had pale silvery tattoos in elaborate curved patterns on their dark skin.

Ealë came to a stop near a shallow part of the pool and gestured for Lirah to join her. Lirah pulled herself mostly out of the water and turned to face Ealë and the others. They were all busy with a variety of ornate combs and brushes. Others were washing in the spray of the falls. Ealë handed Lirah a small glass vial.

"Here, sister, this will take the smell and stain of death from you; go." She gestured toward a stream of falling water.

"Use but a few drops and clean."

Lirah took the vial and thanked Ealë, then she carefully made her way over the wet stones to where a separate stream of water fell from the larger falls above. She now stood well behind the main fall of water; the cool mist filled the air in great billowing clouds. The high arching stone ceiling was glowing even in daylight with soft emerald light. The mist was so thick that Lirah could only just make out the shapes of the others in the glade outside. Lirah held out her hand to the translucent ribbon of falling water before her. She slowly let her fingers enter the water, splitting the ribbon into smaller rushing streams. To her pleasant surprise the water was warm. Not overly so, but just warm enough to be pleasant.

Lirah smiled and slid her arm, then shoulders into the water, letting it flow down and around her body. She could feel the water running over her, rushing down her back, over her chest, wrapping around her legs. She was aware of the energy in the water; she could feel it with more than just her skin. The life blood of Miljah. The water felt rejuvenating, and she could feel a healing strength flowing through her just as the water flowed over her. Lirah reached out with her newfound will just slightly and was able to fully sense the life force that was in the water. Lirah wondered if the water felt warm to her because she was connected to the vitality in it, absorbing the strength as one would soak in warmth from the sun. Maybe it was only warm to her? She opened her eyes and held out her arm, watching the water flow down her shoulder and run in a dozen little streams down her muscles and curves to fall onto the stones at her feet.

How have I not felt this before?

Lirah thought back to all the times she could remember healing and using her gifts. She had always just focused on pulling strength from herself. She had never before tried to pull on the world around her. Yet, as she thought back, she realized that she *had* been aware of it, at least a little. When she had healed Ralenn on the mountain, she *knew* she hadn't done that all on her own. There had been something helping her, some kind of energy that she had thought of as a blessing of Dannitar at the time. Her mind reflected back on moments when she realized she had touched the power and energy that she was now fully aware of it as it flowed around and through her.

As the strength of the water continued to revitalize her body and mind Lirah ran her fingers through her long hair, working out the tangles and clumps of blood. She felt alive in a way that was like nothing she had ever experienced before. No longer frightened by her new awareness, Lirah let her worries, fears, and hesitations wash away—like a dreamer awaking from a lifetime of slumber, Lirah suddenly was filled with a connection to all the life and elements around her. Lirah let herself drift, enveloped in her unfettered expansion of *life.*

This is exultant!

After some time, she pulled back and soon only felt the warmth of the water again. She examined the vial she still held and found it contained a light green liquid. She opened the cork stopper and let a few drops fall into her hand. Immediately a pleasant floral scent rushed up from the open vial and her hand. She realized that it was the same smell that surrounded her in the mists. Lirah started to clean the rest of the matted blood from her hair and body, the sweet-smelling soap and fast-falling water washing the last visible traces of the day away. She breathed out in release and let her mind wander again as the falling water massaged her shoulders and back. She had been very sore and tired from the strains of the last few days. Her blistered feet and wind-chapped lips, bruises and cuts had all been present when she entered the water, yet now, all were gone—healed. Lirah continued to wash and enjoy the water for a time. Eventually her mind returned to the Tundraihn and Ealë's comments.

She called me sister, but not just sisters as women, as kin.

Lirah pondered this as she watched the Tundraihn washing and grooming nearby.

I wonder...

Lirah closed her eyes and reached out, seeking the life that flowed within the others. She could not see their forms so much as feel them—brilliant auras that shimmered like halos of living light. The Tundraihn women radiated warmth and color, their energies twining and pulsing in quiet harmony. Lirah turned her awareness inward, tracing her own life's current, then Ealë's, and then another's nearby. Their essences were akin, familiar—like notes from the same chord. She sensed that they, too, felt her presence, though not as sharply as she felt theirs. To them, her touch must have been like ripples spreading across still water, softly brushing against the edges of their light. The thought unsettled her, and as her unease returned, the connection faded like mist from the surface of a pond. Ealë was now coming near. "You called to me, sister, are you finished bathing?" Ealë's voice was smooth and pleasant as she spoke. Lirah nodded in affirmation, heat touching her cheeks as she realized her probing had not gone unnoticed.

"Come then, sister, let us tend to you, as is our way."

Lirah was not sure what that meant, nor if she was totally comfortable with the prospect of a shared bathing activity. However, she still felt the connection to Ealë and the others that was hard to deny. So she swam back to the main part of the cavern. Ealë helped her from the water then gestured for Lirah to sit and Ealë and several others began to braid her hair and sing softly. Their native tongue was well-suited for song, as it seemed to flow from word to word, forming an uninterrupted stream of melody. Ealë and the other Tundraihn nearby joined their voices in harmony, filling the misty air with their melodic song. Lirah was soon able to hear the pattern in it, and thought it sounded like a spiritual mantra or ballad. Ealë and a few others would sing a section of song, then the rest of the Tundraihn would repeat it and then also sing a few lines that only they sung. Then Ealë and the first to sing would sing anew, and the others repeat again, verse after verse. Lirah closed her eyes and listened contentedly as Ealë and her sisters' deft fingers worked Lirah's hair into countless intricate braids.

Time sped away. Without noticing when she started, Lirah was now singing with the Tundraihn. As she had slowly relaxed, she again connected to Ealë and now was not only singing, but also she understood the song. It was a story, or a history rather. A history of their people. Their wars, their struggles, and their dealings with the Aashahl. Suddenly Lirah realized that the singing had stopped and Ealë was looking at her intently.

"Who are you in sooth?" Ealë's voice was still soft and pleasant, but her face was hard and questioning.

"I am Lirah, nothing more, Ealë." Lirah was not sure what she meant.

Ealë continued to look intently at her. Searching Lirah's eyes with her own. "And why take this guise? Be you here as a test for your daughters?"

"Daughters? What do you mean?"

"You are an acolyte of Syrnii are you not? One of her scions? Sent here to observe and test us as we venture so far from home?" Ealë said.

Lirah recognized the name Syrnii, to a degree. Gaileng had taught her about all the greater Aashahl, but they had not spent much time on Syrnii, Mistress of the Forests. Lirah had no idea what Ealë thought her connection was to Syrnii, though, and as she searched for a reply Ealë spoke first.

"We felt your power, your touch on our minds, and your supremacy over death. We see how Miljah heals you and is pulled into you. Now I think I see why you are with the akah. Do not pale, otheäil, we will not reveal you." As she spoke Ealë took Lirah by the hand and kissed it, she then turned it over and closed it around an object.

"A shield for your sojourn on Miljah. Talla thulle otheäil tä Syrnii güi dä julti. We are ever your servants should need arise, otheäil tä Syrnii." Ealë stood and bowed slightly before slipping back into the water and swimming toward the far side of the pool, where most of the Tundraihn were gathered. Lirah sat still, trying to make sense of what Ealë had said.

Talla thulle otheäil tä Syrnii güi dä julti...What does that even mean, and what is an otheäil?

Lirah opened her hand and looked at what Ealë had given her. It was a pair of ear cuffs. Elegant silver wire set with glittering gems that formed a gentle curve to follow the outer edge of the ear. In the middle of each cuff was set a larger stone. One cuff held a blue stone and the other a green one. They were fashioned so that once on the ear the large stone would sit in the widest part of the ear, suspended by the silver setting. They were delicate and beautiful.

Lirah turned them over in her hand a few times, wondering at their intricate design. She now noticed that they were strung on a simple silver chain, so for now she clasped the chain around her neck and stood up.

She was alone now, the Tundraihn were on the far side of the pool getting dressed back into their armor. Lirah guessed by the light in the glade that it was now late in the evening. She carefully made her way around the black stones back to the grass at the water's edge where

Ralenn had been sleeping earlier. There she found her clothing. It was still covered in blood and grime.

"I did not spend hours getting pampered to put those back on."

Looking at the bloody clothing Lirah remembered she had left the soap Ealë gave her on the stones, and she hurried to get it. Soon, with the soap in hand, Lirah was busily washing her clothes, working hard to get them clean. Thankfully, the soap worked wonders on the blood-stains and the white and gray of her clothes was soon mostly visible again, ending up a light burgundy color. Lirah thought the new color was nice if you could ignore the disturbing source of the dye. All of her clothing still being very wet, Lirah looked for something to cover herself with. Ralenn had left his pack when she had run him off. She opened it and helped herself to a long tunic. It was far too large and hung past her knees.

Just right, and it even smells like him. She grinned, feeling so much re-vived that she could have danced.

By now campfires were set and both the Tundraihn and soldiers of Mantorah were preparing their meals. Lirah could see Ralenn and Kaileth along with several others near one of the fires. Lirah wrung out her clothes as best as she could. She searched for a small fire to dry her clothes by. She soon saw Re'alis and a few Mantorahns near a fire that was apart from the others, and she quietly approached. She hesitated outside the edge of the lady's fire, unsure if she should intrude. Re'alis waved her to approach, though, so Lirah gave a bow as she spoke.

"My lady, would it be much trouble if I were to dry my things by your fire? I am not fit to be seen, I fear." Lirah raised both arms high-lighting her revealing attire.

"By all means yes, please join me." Re'alis smiled kindly. "Captain Gairrle, Aireathyn and Ercoln, if you could offer us both a measure of privacy. Lirah had not noticed her guard watching nearby. They bowed and withdrew further, Gairrle going to see to the posting of sentinels. Re'alis was not much better dressed than Lirah, still wear-ing only a tabard over her torn chemise. Near the fire Lord Devick lay unconscious on a bier. Lirah started to array her clothes on a fallen tree near the fire to dry. Re'alis sat on the end of the tree watching Devick slowly breathe. Lirah spoke as she finished her work and sat down near the fire.

"Don't worry, he will mend, my lady, you will see. He just needs sleep now." She hoped her words gave the lady some comfort. She seemed distressed by his stillness.

"I believe you, yet I cannot help but worry over him. I have known him long and count him as a close friend." Re'alis did not look away from Devick as she continued. "I will be forever in your debt, Priestess, for saving him."

"My lady, please, you can call me Lirah, just Lirah."

Re'alis smiled warmly. "Lirah, then, thank you."

"You are very welcome, milady, but there is no need to thank me. I only did what had to be done."

"Perhaps so. Truly you are a more capable healer than any I have ever seen. Later, I would love to learn of your knowledge and abilities. But for now, I feel spent and weary. Too spent to even care to wash." Re'alis laughed sadly at herself. Lirah didn't know what to say and so they sat still for a time watching the fire till Re'alis again spoke.

"The Tundraihn, did they do that to your hair?"

"They did, milady; they also gave some of their soap to me." Lirah held out the vial of soap.

"That explains the extraordinarily pleasant fragrance about you."

"I am so sorry, I should have offered it sooner. You are welcome to use it, milady. There is plenty to spare, as only a few drops are needed."

"No apologies, this has been a flustering day. Perhaps I am not too spent after all to wash a little before the sunset." Re'alis sounded more cheerful as she said this, and Lirah happily handed her the vial.

"If you go over there where the grass meets the edge of the pool and the black stones, you can walk behind the falls and have some privacy."

"Thank you, Lirah." Re'alis arose but hesitated as she looked upon Lord Devick.

"I will watch over him, milady, don't worry."

"Thank you." She then started toward the falls but again paused and turned back to Lirah.

"Re'alis, for you, I am simply Re'alis."

Lirah nodded and smiled brightly as Re'alis continued to the falls.

Sunlight filtered through the tall trees at the western edge of the glade. Lirah sighed deeply and leaned back against the tree. The cool blades of grass gently caressed her bare legs as she stretched out a little and let the last of the day's light warm her. The last halfmoon had been such a whirl of terror and relief all at once. She was not even sure who, or what, she was anymore. Neither was she certain of what tomorrow would bring. Yet somehow, she was at peace. She looked about the glade, not knowing what she was looking for until she found him—Ralenn. He was sitting near Kaileth. Somehow, he seemed to feel her eyes on him, and he turned and looked at her. He smiled as their eyes met. Lirah smiled back and blushed a little as she pulled the collar of his tunic to better cover her bare chest.

Tomorrow will turn out alright, I think.

16

Justice of the Realm

*M*any are they that espouse striving for the singular patronage of an Aashahl. Seek the wisest counsel in this, for singular veneration does not necessitate one shun another.
Essays of the Divine

The short-curved limbs of the steel crossbows groaned as the thick dark fingers of the Dao'Tai arbalesters drew strings into notches and placed bolts ready to fire. Jahllia watched. A normal man would have needed a mechanical advantage to set those bows, but not the Dao'Tai. They raised their weapons and took aim at the line she stood in—a line of shaking figures silhouetted against the setting sun.

The rays of amber light seeped over the stone walls of the court-yard, revealing her fear-stricken comrades. Their garb was simple; they had all belonged to the same small village. Jahllia tried to be an example for them, standing tall in her favorite blue dress, now stained by the blood and dirt from the road. She would not quake with fear before these murderers. The Dao'Tai had arrayed her and her comrades in a row, each chained to large poles set into the ground. The poles were marred by countless holes and spatters of dry blood, the tokens of other evenings such as this. The heavily armored soldiers held their aim and waited for the command to fire. Jahllia knew it was quite common for executions to be carried out at the imperial fortress of Taiw'Tai. Generally, with a large audience. According to the law of the Subjugate, traitors to the realm were to be shot by a company of new arbalesters and left to slowly die in the night. The Aya Dao'Tai thought this a fitting punishment for traitors. The novice executioners generally did not kill with one bolt; most who were hit suffered greatly before they finally bled to death. It was not common, however, for the Aya Dao'Tai herself to be in attendance, as well as Chancellor Rovik.

Jahllia had spent most of her life dodging just such a death, all while doing everything she could to resist the Dao'Tai as a cell leader with the Howe Keepers; an Anothn resistance movement. It wasn't always like this. Her earliest memories were happy ones. Her family had owned a farm near the Anothn border with Andohra. The deep forests of the mountains pushed down into the rolling countryside and made for a childhood filled with exploring shaded paths or running in sunbathed fields. When the Dao'Tai started their purge of Andohra, Jahllia's family was out of the way of the actual fighting. She knew there was war. Her parents talked about it nearly every day. The debate to flee south or stay put and pray for a swift end to the fighting was a daily occurrence.

Her family decided to stay for the rest of the season at least. When the first group of Andohrase refugees crossed their fields, her parents could not turn them away. The days passed and more Andohrase came trekking out of the mountains. Their numbers grew into the hundreds. Their eyes held a distant ache that Jahllia was now all too familiar with. Faced with the plight of the refugees, Jahllia's family turned from farming to helping the Andohrase south. Her father's host of large wagons made trip after trip from their farm to the Mantorahn frontier near Syrah.

This continued for some time before the Dao'Tai discovered the secluded farm and descended upon it in force. Jahllia's father, her two elder brothers, and most of the farmhands were slain in the raid.

Only Jahllia and her mother—newly with child—escaped the slaughter. They fled through the fields and did not stop running until the horizon gave way to unknown forests.

Days passed before a temple of Alpa took them in. Seasons followed, and within those quiet walls her mother bore a son, whom she named Jayin. For a time, they knew a fragile peace while the Dao'Tai consolidated their rule. Winters and summers passed in measured rhythm, and Jahllia began to believe they had at last found safety.

But the illusion did not endure. One night, without warning, the Dao'Tai found cause to sack the temple. Jahllia's mother was killed in the assault, buying time for Jahllia and Jayin to flee once more. That night ended her childhood; she left it behind with her mother's body, and from that moment on, her life became a struggle simply to endure.

They made their way to Ell'Anoth and began their new lives as street urchins —always a breath from death, whether by hunger or the blade of a Dao'Tai soldier. In time, Jahllia and her brother fell in with a band of rebels, each driven by their own deep wounds and need for vengeance against the Dao'Tai. For Jahllia, that purpose hardened her; it honed the grief that had once hollowed her into something sharp and certain. For the first time since war had shattered her family, she felt she belonged. She had a cause, a family of sorts, and a reason to live—to repay every drop of blood spilled by the Dao'Tai tenfold. That same fire had carried her here, to the death she had always known would one day find her.

The captain of the execution detail, a non-Dao'Tai collaborator, looked a bit nervous to have the Aya Dao'Tai herself overseeing this execution. He swallowed hard and cleared his throat as he took a parchment from the case that hung from his side. The air was so still that the sound of the paper unrolling echoed within the walls. The captain held the large sheet at arm's length before him and began to read from it a list of charges.

"Before you die, the law of this land requires that your charges are read to you. According to the established protocols for interprovincial travel of the lower class, you are all hereby charged with traveling from the Heod province to the border province of Gie'Kia without the due papers and endorsements. The persons: Begga, Vestad, Vestod, and the woman in the blue dress, are also charged with possession of illegal arms; namely, two dozen spears, one dozen long swords, three short swords, two long bows, and eight unregistered daggers. The woman in the blue dress is additionally charged with having no identification papers and withholding her name from officers of the Subjugate. All other persons taken are charged with resisting arrest, aiding, and associating with weapon smugglers, cooperating in treasonous activities, and plotting against the Aya Dao'Tai herself. This is your last chance to admit your crimes and die free of guilt in the eyes of the Aya Dao'Tai that she may make your path to the afterlife swift."

Most in the line of condemned were either weeping or said nothing in reply. They all knew well that nothing they could have said would save them from their fate. The captain of the arbalesters was still waiting for a response when Jahllia turned to look at him directly. Her simple blue dress was tattered and muddy around the hem. Her short sunset-blonde hair was matted in places with the blood of her comrades who hadn't survived the arrest. She was only a bit taller than her brother Jayin, the boy she stood next to. Her hard life had left her thin and strong. She tensed as she stared down the men who would be her killers. She did not cower. Instead, she put on her most defiant face.

"How then do you plead?" the captain asked.

She glanced at the captain, then turned her gaze to the balcony of the tower opposite where she stood. There, high above the courtyard, the Aya Dao'Tai and her chancellor stood watching. The Aya Dao'Tai did not appear to be paying any attention, musing over the view of the fort afforded her by the perch. Chancellor Rovik was watching, however, and Jahllia gave him the full intensity of her gaze.

She finally answered, shouting, the words hot with anger.

"We do not recognize your bloody rule! But since we're going ta die—yah, we were try'n to fight against you-n-yours. I was seeking ta end your rule! I was seeking ta end you!"

A few of the arbalester's arms began to shift under the weight of their heavy crossbows. Some of the other prisoners nodded in agreement with Jahllia, taking courage from her words. The captain hastily shoved the paper back into its pouch and pulled a short, iron-headed club from his belt.

"How dare you cast your vile eyes upon the Aya Dao'Tai! How dare you speak of her demise!" he barked, raising his weapon.

Despite the chains that leashed her to a pole, Jahllia stepped up to face him, only to meet the club crashing into her. She let out a cry as the iron club struck her in the head and drove her to the ground, manacles biting into her wrists. The captain raised his weapon to strike again but was halted.

"Hold, Captain!" the chancellor shouted.

The captain turned to the balcony and looked at the Aya Dao'Tai, who was now paying close attention. There was a chuckle in her voice as she spoke.

"Yes, Captain, hold. Let her speak, I am...intrigued. Yes, let her continue."

"Your will be done." The captain signaled for the arbalesters to lower their crossbows, and a few of them let out a sigh of relief as they slowly lowered their weighty weapons. Aya Dao'Tai Afyreen leaned onto the stone bastion that surrounded the balcony and casually rested her head in her hands.

"Tell me, what is your name, *woman in the blue dress?*"

A torrent of dark-red blood rushed from the gash in Jahllia's forehead. She cleared the blood from her eyes and rose to one knee to make answer to the woman she hated.

"Hah! And why would I give it ta my murderer? Why should you 'ave the pleasure of knowing any of the names of your victims? You're not worthy of our names!"

The crack of the iron club smashing into the small of her back echoed off the wall of the courtyard and made the boy next to her wince. Jahllia was again face down in the earth, coughing and struggling to regain her breath, but she looked up and spat into the ground in front of her. The Aya Dao'Tai raised her hand to stay the captain and she spoke.

"I like to know my enemies, and you seem to harbor a great hatred for me, so I will have your name!" She was now standing fully upright, gripping the stone tightly, with both hands partially cloaked in her shadow. The impatience was growing in her voice, which made Jahllia smile.

Jayin stooped and spoke softly as she struggled to get to her feet.

"Jahllia, please, just tell her your name."

Jahllia swore under her breath at herself for getting Jayin mixed up in all this. She was ready to die, but he was too young. She strained to rise to her knees and again wiped the blood from her eyes and face.

"I won't amuse you anymore; Paldrii's piss upon you and all your lot," she said, her voice growing soft. Tears cut clear paths through the blood as both ran down her face. She turned from the balcony to face her death, wiping the blood away from her thin lips.

"Very well, Jahllia. I have what I wanted—Captain, proceed."

The captain returned to the line of arbalesters and ordered them to the ready.

The captain drew his falchion, raised it above his head, and then swung it down to his side. The scream of the bolts through the air shook the evening as they sped from the string and found their marks.

The sun was nearly set now, leaving the courtyard in shadow. The fallen forms of Jahllia and her companions were the only things remaining in the courtyard, still chained to their posts. It was normal procedure for the guards to leave the bodies so any that were wounded would expire in the night. It also gave a chance for carrion birds to desecrate the corpses or chyrurgeons to carry off subjects for study. Not long after the soldiers had left, the stars came out to paint upon the night's smooth, dark canvas. The earth felt cold under Jahllia's body, save for the warm pools of blood. She could feel the life leaving her as she lay on her back peering into the heavens.

I've killed us all, Jayin...I am so sorry.

Silent tears filled her eyes. The plan had been too ambitions. Too many had become involved, and this was the cost. A bolt shaft was lodged in the left side of her chest, and another had passed clear through her waist. It was difficult to breathe. Jahllia knew from tending others' wounds that she would be dead swiftly. She looked up into the night sky. The stars were always so beautiful, and they seemed even more so to her now.

At least I can see where my soul will be soon, she thought. *Lord and Lady of Night, see us all home...merciful shepherd guide us to paradise...she* prayed, surprising herself as she did so. The Aashahl had shown her no love in life; why would they now in death? Yet, she could not help it, at least for her brother's sake if nothing else.

Nique'Shay, Dar'Nique'Tar, see us safe to Paldrii's keeping, guide our souls with your dance and song to the fold of the merciful shepherd. Patient Father, forgive our wrongs. Leshay'ar, bolster those we leave behind...she prayed, trying to remember the order of ascension, the correct names, and phrases to aid in her brother's flight into the heavens. She prayed on. The dark twins of the night had been the only aashahl who had ever seemed to take an interest in aiding her in life.

Her sight was growing blurry, but she could see the clouds of a storm starting to roll in and blot out the stars. Slowly, with effort, she turned her head to where Jayin was lying next to her. Her eyes found the shafts of death jutting out of his small body. He had reached out toward her as he fell, and she now managed to touch him. Her fingers were trembling as they slowly took hold of his hand. It was cold, deathly cold. She closed her eyes. She knew what dead hands felt like, she had felt them on too many friends and family. The sorrow hurt too much to cry, though she desperately wanted to.

"Lord of Dance and Lady of Song, see that he finds it safe ta Paldrii's fold. Guide 'im through your dancing lights, through your darkest nights...see him safe ta the merciful shepherd...safe in Paldrii's keeping..." she muttered under her breath. "And if you don't then may the Patient Father damn yah all with us that you've forsaken here!" Her voice failed her, and she was forced to continue her praying and cursing to the Aashahl in thought only. If only she had taken greater care, or left Jayin at the camp this time. None of that mattered now. Her family would finally be together in death as it could not be in life.

She grew colder and could not tell how much time had passed. She looked again to her dead brother, only a boy.

I'll be with yah soon, she thought, drifting into the black sky.

* * *

The gate squeaked as Tellig pushed it open, and Esea cursed him quietly. They moved together as shadowy figures from body to body across the courtyard, checking each fallen prisoner for signs of life. Tellig found the woman in the blue dress, and whispered to Esea.

"This is the one, this is her, I-I-I just know it." Esea moved up alongside him, cloaked in the darkness.

"Yes, Tellig. Yes, that appears to be her."

"He... he will be pleased with us, won't he? Won't he?" Tellig's voice rose as his excitement grew. The master would reward them.

"Hush, you fool! If the guards catch us it will be us in front of the poles."

"Sorry, sorry. I-I am just...L-look, Esea! She is still alive."

The murmurs of the approaching storm could be heard now, thundering across the sky, so they began to move more quickly. Esea took a large sheet of thick, stiff cloth from his shoulders and handed an end to Tellig.

"Come, help me get her on this."

The two stretched the cloth and laid it upon the ground next to the woman. Esea held his hands over the material and muttered a short incantation. The cloth trembled and then became stiff as a slab of stone.

They then quickly removed the manacles using a small key Esea produced from a pocket.

"Grab her legs, Tellig, and be careful."

"I w-will be."

The two gently slid her onto the sheet. She seemed to smile as her eyes fluttered open and closed again. Tellig shuddered. The two men took hold of the ends of the cloth litter and started for the gate.

"Esea, I-I-I don't think that she's breathing," Tellig said quietly, alarmed now. They might have gained a reward for retrieving her, but they would certainly be beaten if she died.

Esea looked over his shoulder. "You're right, we must hurry then."

They rushed out of the courtyard and turned down an alleyway where a cart and horse were waiting. The two hid the woman's body in the cart and then headed out of the main fort. They made their way swiftly, cutting down alleys and side streets to avoid patrolling guards. Thanks to several endorsed let-pass papers they were through the checkpoints of the fortress and outside the main wall when the storm began in earnest. The rain was falling fast and thick as the cart hurried through the maze of tents and wooden buildings, then came to a halt next to a large stone guard tower that overlooked the river. Esea and Tellig jumped from the seat, took the woman's lifeless form from the cart, and dashed through the rain. They came to the entryway of the tower and knocked on the door. It swung open in an instant and they were met by a tall woman holding a lantern in her hand.

"You are late," she said tersely. Esea started to speak but was cut off by the woman.

"Get her inside, now! She does not have time for your excuses and the chyrurgeon charges by time."

The two wet men nodded, then entered the tower quickly. The woman peered into the night for a moment, then silently shut the door behind her.

17

Councils and Regrets

Beware indulgence in self-pity. For there are those among the powers of Miljah who would have you dwell there always so as to share in your exquisite suffering. Instead, sorrow when in its season but ever seek out the spring.
Essays of the Divine

It felt like Rovik had been running down this dark corridor forever. The door out could not be much further ahead. Sweat ran down his forehead, stinging his eyes. His hands felt shaky and feeble on the handle of his sword.

"Have to keep running...I have to get away..." His words sounded weak and thin.

"Where is that cursed door?"

The crashing sound of armored feet echoed off the dark stone walls behind him. They were getting closer. Flashes of lightning blasted through the high windows before him. Tokens of the approaching storm. The air was thick with moisture and latent energy. He had to hurry, he knew it, but his body ached for him to stop, to rest and simply let oblivion come for him. The crashing footsteps drew closer. He ran. With all the speed he could muster he ran on past column after column, window after tall narrow window, but the door never came.

"Must be only a bit further..." he panted, begging his legs to keep up the pace.

There at last, revealed by another flash of lightning, was the door. He sheathed his sword and grasped the handle in building desperation and pulled. As the door started to open, he risked a glance behind him. Inky smoke, black armor, and bright glowing eyes filled the corridor in a rolling tide of imminent death. He cursed and hurried to force the heavy door open. The ancient hinges popped as Rovik strained and jerked the door fully open. Then pain—a sudden sick, aching pain shot into his stomach and radiated throughout his exhausted body. Instinctively his hands darted to the dagger's hilt that now sat buried in his gut up to the quillons. The slender hand that placed it there now gently lay upon his pounding chest. Her eyes were so blue, like burning stars, bright and beautiful, cold, and dangerous. Her face was calm. It held no visible malice. Without a word she pushed and Rovik felt compelled to step back into the corridor. He tried to speak, to ask why, to ask anything, but the pain robbed him of the breath and words. He could smell the hot steel and burning sulfur behind him, and in that moment, he was sure there was no escape.

The first avertyyn claw burst through Rovik's shoulder from behind, picking him up off the ground before throwing him into the wall. He hit his back hard and suddenly all the pain was gone. He felt nothing. The girl in the doorway never broke eye contact with him and he wondered that she did not flee the terror that now filled the corridor around him. Rovik could hear his bone breaking, his flesh tearing as his attackers descended upon him; yet she never looked away. Her dress drew his attention as it came spilling out of the doorway into the corridor. It was made of the deepest blue, trimmed with the colors of a setting sun. The girl with the blue eyes took hold of the door's latch and pulled, sending the layers of her elegant dress spinning to reveal the white, silver and gold colors underneath.

"It is not too late; each choice is a new start."

The door slammed shut and Rovik wondered at her words as another claw tore into his broken body. He was not sure when it left. A few minutes, an hour perhaps. He still could not feel anything but the warmth of his own blood running under and around his face on the cold stone floor. His eyes vacantly scanned the dark sky beyond the window near the closed door. Lightning rolled through the black clouds, and with each flash the image of the girl with the blue eyes cut into his mind.

"Choose!"

Rovik sat up gasping for air as though he had been holding his breath for some time.

"A dream...only a dream..." he said aloud, and hearing his words grounded his spinning mind. Yet the word still echoed in his thoughts, "*Choose.*"

Choose what? he thought. What was there to choose? More lightning lit up his actual window, and again the face and eyes of the girl danced through his mind.

"She has the same eyes...It is the same one, the same girl..." he whispered.

The feeling he had when he looked into her eyes was strange and terrible. It was as if she knew. As if she knew all that he had done. He turned and sat on the edge of his bed staring across his dimly lit room.

It was the only course of action I could take, he thought for the thousandth time. *Had I not done it many more would have died in the battle. It was the only choice...*

This was not the first time such a dream had troubled him. Normally the door was simply locked; it had never opened in previous iterations of the nightmare. It had certainly never had the girl with the blue eyes in it waiting to stab him, then comfort him. Had she been comforting? Rovik tried to hold on to the dream. Her words, her dazzling dress, the dagger; he had felt comforted by her somehow. She had been his doom in the end, but also his release. Did the dream mean something? Was it a message, a sign from an Aashahl? Or just his own guilt and troubled mind bubbling up to haunt him again? He couldn't guess. Rovik ran his hands through his hair and shut his eyes as tight as he could.

"This is better...It is. Things would have been worse..."

He let his gaze travel across the large, richly furnished chamber. Once, it had belonged to the royal family of Ell'Anoth; now it was his, a reward for loyal service to the Aya Dao'Tai. Yet a part of him could never shake the sense of being watched, as though the room itself remembered its true masters and knew he did not belong. He stood and walked to a large basin set in an ornately carved wooden stand. From a pitcher on the stand he poured water into the basin and proceeded to wash the night from his eyes. He would need to be clear-minded this day. The Aya Dao'Tai had called for a special council with her Dao'Tai generals. It was odd for Rovik to be summoned, as usually they normally did not include him in military gatherings. Rovik knew he was only one of the many cogs in the Subjugate machine, and he wondered at her larger game.

Rovik had been overseeing the ordinary operations and business transactions in the province that once had been the Kingdom of Anoth. As the chancellor of that fallen realm he gave a sense of legitimacy to the rule of the Subjugate. Of late he had been tasked with additional duties, such as dealing with the Grishkii. Many of these new duties were passed off as unrelated, but he felt there was a connection between them all. He had been trying to put the pieces together himself, to little avail. She was clearly still obsessed with the idea that there was a surviving heir to the Anoth throne, and she was set on killing them. Events like the destruction of Allinth proved that.

Yet there were other things, secretive caravans from the east, the massive army she kept in the north besieging Akaroche, and the constant spy activity in the far south. The caravans caused some problems, as Rovik had to see that no one stopped them and that no one saw them, outside of the guard. They only came on the moonless nights, and he had no idea what or who was in them. Similar caravans of wagons also streamed into the fortress by night from the docks. He did not know what their cargo was or where it came from. It was unloaded from large and unusual-looking ships. Rovik had never seen their equal for design and workmanship. This had only been occurring for the last six months or so. He knew better than to ask, but all he had been able to gather was that they were from far western isles.

He continued to ponder these events as he got dressed. It was maddening. There had been many other unusual and secret things going on. Raiding parties had been sent into the south and east. Rovik knew of them from the supply requests he handled. What they were after he did not know, again. In all these cases, Rovik only negotiated the logistics and compensation for the jobs. Sethel was the one who oversaw the execution of these different operations, and Sethel only reported to the Aya Dao'Tai herself.

Once fully dressed and ready for the day, Rovik left his room and walked down the corridors of the keep that had once been the palace of the king of Anoth. It was now mostly used as an administrations building. The Aya Dao'Tai did not live in the old palace. Her palace was built by her soldiers across the river within the walls of the Taiw'Tai fortress.

"Good mornin,' milord." The maidservant's greeting startled him.

"Hmm, what? Oh, yes, good morning, Milda."

She smiled and curtsied. "Beg pardon, milord, I didn't mean to startle you. Do you care for anything for breakfast?"

"Yes, but I have to be to a meeting here shortly, so be quick about it. Have the stableman ready my horse," he said distractedly.

"Yes, milord, right away," she said, dutifully bustling out to run her errands.

Rovik made his way to a small dining room in a tower that overlooked the river and city below. This was one of his favorite places to be in the morning. He took a seat at a small table and looked out the window onto the scenery below him. The keep of Ell'Anoth was perched atop the sheer cliffs that made the western bank of the river.

Upon the eastern side lay part of the city of Ell'Anoth, and a short distance beyond her walls the fortress of Taiw'Tai was built. The sun fell upon the land in golden columns through the scattering clouds.

Rovik found his thoughts turning to the city of the past, before the coming of the Dao'Tai, but he was saved from reliving sorrowful memories when several servants entered the room bearing platters of cold ham, fruit, bread, and a flagon of new wine. All these were quickly set before him, and the servants left without saying a word. He ate hastily in silence, a lone man solemnly gazing out over the city. About the time he finished eating Milda entered the room and gave a small curtsy.

"Milord, your horse is ready."

"Thank you, Milda, that will be all." He stood up and started to leave.

"Was the food adequate, milord?" Milda's voice gave away how eager she was to please.

"Yes, it was fine, thank you." He smiled a little and walked past her out the door. It took several minutes to pass through all the halls of the palace and finally make it to the stables. The stables were exceptionally large. They were once home to several troops of Anothn cavalry as well as the horsemen of the Allitorii. They were now almost empty and in need of repair. The Dao'Tai soldiers used horses very little, usually only for their chariots. They kept their animals within their own fort, so the only horses in these stables were Rovik's and those of a few servants who worked for him. Walking past one empty stall after another, he finally came to his horse.

He found Takah saddled and ready to ride, but out of habit he checked the tack just to make sure all was in order. He smiled and patted the large animal fondly. Takah had been a gift from— He cut off this line of thought.

No, she is gone now. Can't think of it.

Takah was getting old, but not so old as to no longer bear his master about the city.

He climbed up into the saddle and slowly rode out of the stables into the yard without. The sweet scent of the air after the night's rain greeted him as Takah trotted along the cobblestones. His mount carried him out of the palace grounds and onto the streets of Ell'Anoth. The horse and rider both knew this trip well. The Aya Dao'Tai held all of her more secretive meetings within the walls of her own palace and fortress. Rovik let his mind wander as his horse led the way.

The streets were full of people going about from place to place carefully monitored by Subjugate agents. Though the city dealt richly in trade, the taxes upon the people were so high that they saw little profit. In fact, most were only able to meet the bare necessities of life. Rovik looked at these people as he passed and recalled how different the city was under the old king and queen. The streets seemed to be bright and cheerful then. The people were well-dressed and had happy countenances. One would not recognize the old and new Ell'Anoth for the same place were it not for a few landmark buildings. Rovik could not help but ask himself if these people really were better off this way. Was what he did the only option?

Rovik quickly squashed that thought. *Yes, it was the only way,* he thought firmly. *The only way to save the people and myself from death. I just wish she would have come with me...She didn't have to die.*

He could remember that day so clearly, the argument they had, her child crying. He had left with so much anger over her stubbornness. Her husband was dead, why could she not see that? Why would she not give up hope and do what was needed to ensure survival?

"Papers, Lord, I need to see your papers or a Subjugate signet ring." The gatekeeper looked up at him, waiting for a response. Without him realizing it, Rovik's horse had carried him right to the outer gate of the city. The gatekeeper spoke again, this time a bit louder, "Chancellor Rovik, may I see your papers or ring, please?"

"What? Oh yes, here it is." Rovik held out the hand that bore the ring of the Aya Dao'Tai's chancellor.

"Thank you, my lord." The guard nodded, and the gates were opened for Rovik.

He rode quickly now to make up for the slow pace with which he had made his way through the city. Once out of the gates he took a course that followed the outer wall of Ell'Anoth till it broke away to the northeast. He spurred his mount to a canter and soon came to the drawbridge that led into the eastern side of the river. The signs of the Subjugate occupation were even more blatant upon the eastern banks. A labyrinth of tents and shoddy wooden structures covered the ground. They housed everything from merchants and stores to slavers and mercenaries. The collection of sad buildings stretched from the river's edge to the stone walls of the fortress of Taiw'Tai. Rovik hated having to run through this gauntlet of humanity at its worst. He quickened his pace as he came under the shadow of a small tower and entered the widest of the streets that snaked their way through the den before him.

There were no cobblestones on this side of the river, and his horse's hooves sank into the rain-soaked road. At every turn he was met with merchants selling their goods, slavers auctioning their thralls, and all manner of loud and distasteful displays of greed and lust. The stone of the fortress's walls soon loomed ahead of him. Rovik slowed his horse and hailed the gatekeepers. After they looked to see who it was, they asked for his certification and his business. Rovik gave the appropriate answers, and the gates were quickly opened for him. The ponderous gates swung open before horse and rider, and soon he was within the walls of the fortress of Taiw'Tai.

The fortress was tremendous in size, almost as sprawling as the city of Ell'Anoth. Her walls were made of angular blocks of slick dark stone. The edges were so finely cut that they fit together with hardly a visible seam, and they did so with no mortar. The stone itself had been brought down river from the northern ranges of the Vagath'Oth. Overshadowing the walls were towers made from the same stone, and atop these an overhanging parapet afforded the defenders a direct view of the walls below. It had taken vast numbers of slaves to cre-ate this fortress over roughly a span of ten years. Nearly every man, woman, and child from the fallen kingdoms of Anoth, Dashra, and Andohra worked on it—a final monument to their defeat. What was left of these people were still serving as slaves for the Subjugate's use.

Rovik was now passing through the rows of immense barracks that housed the Subjugate soldiers. Despite having many soldiers abroad, nearly half of Afyreen's army was housed within Taiw'Tai. At the center of the barracks, stables, and the other buildings that filled the fortress walls were the citadel and the palace of the Aya Dao'Tai. The spires of the palace were so tall that they could be seen above the fortress from the west bank of the river. They looked like the spikes of a wicked crown atop the practical square lines of the fortress complex.

Rovik brought his horse to a halt within this structure's shadow. The palace consisted of a low wall surrounding a massive stone dome and five towers. Four of the towers were built facing the cardinal directions around the outside of the dome. The fifth tower was built into the center of the dome and rose from there high above the other four. Atop all five towers were strong bulwarks and curiously fashioned sculptures. As he waited underneath the imposing palace, a short and poorly dressed man came running up to Rovik from the gatehouse. He was a stable slave. He took the lead rope of Rovik's horse, and the lord got from his saddle. With no words exchanged, the small man led the horse away to a stable that stood on the east side of a long barrack. Rovik looked after him for a moment, then slowly walked toward the palace that was before him. The closer he got, the heavier his feet felt. The air itself seemed to hold still from the very dread of this place.

He came to the doors of the outer courtyard and knocked upon the painted wood. He stood for a moment before the doors swung open to let him in. Before him, under a lavishly carved portico, was a wide paved path that led through the lush and exotic gardens sheltered behind the wall. The gardens were incredibly beautiful, despite their location; fountains and exquisite statues of Sylphs, Shedim, and other beings of ancient magic punctuated the vegetation that hung from the walls and beams overhead. The air within the gardens was thick with the aroma of wildflowers and nectar. It was the finest garden he had ever seen. Rovik often wished that the residents of this cantonment were as beautiful and peaceful as this garden that lay in its center.

He crossed through the pleasant plants and flowers to a tall door set into the exterior of the copular-shaped palace. At either side of the door stood heavily armored guards. They gave nods to the lord as he approached and opened the doors for him. Rovik took a few steps into the vestibule and stopped to let his eyes adjust to the poor light that was filtering from narrow windows on either side of the door. Echoing footsteps could be heard from the columned corridors beyond the room Rovik now stood in. A richly dressed servant came walking toward him from the inner halls of the palace. She spoke to him in a low calming voice.

"Chancellor Rovik, the Aya Dao'Tai is awaiting you," she smiled, quickly turning to walk back down the passage she had just come from. Rovik quickened his pace to catch up to her. He had never seen this servant before, and she was clearly not Dao'Tai or Taivadean. It was unusual for Afyreen to keep a non-Dao'Tai servant inside the palace who was not marked as a slave.

"Have you been in the palace long?" Rovik asked.

"No, my lord, not long at all," she replied, clearly surprised by the question.

"Well, it is good to see a pleasant smiling face here." The woman again smiled at him and Rovik caught the slightest blush in her dark-freckled cheeks. Soon the two came into a large open hall; the ceiling arched high overhead. At the center of the expanse stood the base of the fifth tower that could be seen from outside, coming from the center of the domed roof of the palace. Surrounding this tower was a circular skylight. Everything about this room was on a grand scale—an entire mansion could have fit into this hall.

The light from above illuminated the dark red stone of the pillars and archways. All was slick and smooth as glass, save the sides of the tower's base. Around the bottom, a series of arches and doors stood, and above these were images of the Aya Dao'Tai carved into the stone. Each one portraying her with a different expression and garb but always surrounded by ebbing swirling smoke. Each seemed to depict her in roles that normally were reserved for the Aashahl; creating life, taking life, guiding the stars in their path, causing the seasons and harvest to come.

"I may go no further, my lord." The fair servant bowed to him and hurried down another corridor that opened into the great hall. He set out to cross the huge floor. The reliefs of the Aya Dao'Tai seemed to gaze out over the open space below, as if watching all who would approach. The tiles of the floor rang as Rovik's boots fell upon them, and the sound reverberated throughout the arched heights of the hall. He stopped in front of the largest of the doors at the tower's base and reached to open it. The latch, however, turned from the inside before his fingers could grasp it, and the door opened slowly. The light in the doorway was just enough to tell it was a woman, but not much else.

"I am not one who should be kept waiting, Rovik," Afyreen said. Her voice rang shrill in the still air of the room.

Rovik bowed low before her. "I apologize, Aya—"

"I also do not have time for excuses." She abruptly stopped him, but the anger in her voice had lessened. "Come with me quickly, the others await us."

She turned and headed into the tower, and Rovik hastened after her. She moved nimbly and swiftly down the hallway, and then up a spiraling stair. The light of lamps was all there was to see by, yet it was enough for Rovik to tell that she wore a thin, revealing gown. She often dressed scantily in her palace. It was common among her people, or so he had been told, though Rovik still found it was always a little unnerving. He thought maybe that was the point.

He quickly averted his eyes and continued up the stairs. They passed door after door, and still they climbed higher. Finally, as Rovik was starting to grow weary, she stopped before a door, opened it, and walked into the room with Rovik close behind her. The room they now stood in was large and well-lit by several windows set high in the walls. This was the private council chamber of the Aya Dao'Tai. Rovik had only been here on a few occasions. None of which were very pleasant ones. The walls were hung with plush burgundy fabric, and a great gilded chandelier was suspended from the ceiling over an elegant table in the center of the room.

Several people were already seated in a few of the chairs that sat around the table. Rovik knew some of them, but there were a few that he had never seen before. One of the strangers stood in a shadowy corner, aloof from the rest, who were talking to one another in hushed voices. They quickly noticed the approach of the Aya Dao'Tai, and all stood and made obeisance to her. She then walked to the head of the table and motioned for Rovik to be seated at her side. He did so, and the others again took their seats. All save the one that stood veiled in shadow, they remained where they were.

Rovik quickly took inventory of those he knew and those he did not. Sethel was there, as well as the three leaders of the Dao'Tai armies: Zeffyd, Hath'Kii, and Dak'Jec. Ornurgr Nevicore was there also, and then there were two others he did not know. The two strangers sitting at the table were very outlandish in dress and features. They were both dressed in finely woven robes and tunics, the cloth of which shimmered as it caught the sunlight from the windows. Their skin was a deep brown, and black freckles were sprinkled around the bridge of their noses and their cheeks. He assumed they had to be from some region of the eastern isles, but he was not sure. With those who wished to be now seated, Afyreen cleared her throat and began to speak.

"Now that we are all gathered here let us get directly to the matter at hand. The matter of war." Rovik started slightly in surprise at her words.

"It is time to consolidate our power. We now have the support we need from Drashtaa to do this."

Rovik was truly shocked, though he did his best to conceal it. He remembered the old tales of Drashtaa, a being said to have once been among the lesser Aashahl. Drashtaa had possessed all that any spirit could desire, save one thing: the love of a mortal chieftain's daughter. She loved another and despised Drashtaa for his vanity and pride.

Mad with envy, he slew her lover and took her by force. For this crime, Anthos cursed him, stripping away his form and his divine power. The legends say he endures still, feeding upon the greed and corruption in the hearts of men to sustain what remains of himself. In time, he became the monster of fables—the taker of the selfish, the prideful, and the damned.

But this was little more than a legend used to scare children. Or so Rovik had always believed. Afyreen continued.

"In addition, we again have the full aid of the lesser drakes, Adohr, and the Srellites. Chancellor Rovik, we will need the continued full cooperation of the Grishkii tribes as well." Rovik was still trying to process all she had so casually said and did not answer immediately.

"Rovik?" she prodded. He replayed what she had said to him quickly in his head and stumbled to make an answer.

"Yes, Your Majesty, they will be more than willing to aid us." Afyreen smiled and continued.

"Excellent. Now as to the Isles of Thalyphonie. Threydn Droge-myna believes his intentions for subtle resistance are unknown to me. He will realize his folly as your revolution sweeps him aside."

She addressed the two brightly dressed men who sat at the far end of the table. They made their reply with stammering words. It was clear that they were not yet fluent in the common tongue.

"Aya Dao'Tai...w-we ready to make battle...for you," one said, then quickly turned and looked to the other as if to see if they had spoken correctly.

"Wonderful, we will reward your service greatly and Thalyphonie will be yours ever after." She turned to one of the Dao'Tai.

"Ty'kahl Zeffyd," she said formally, using the title for lead generals of the Dao'Tai armies. "You are to coordinate with our allies and lay plans to achieve our goals. Here are the tasks first at hand. The realms of Lea'Angleneth and Mantorah have had too much autonomy for too long. They both have made it clear that they are in opposition to us and my rule. Re'alis is to be the first to fall. I want Lea'Angleneth crushed, totally and completely; her people slain to the last or enslaved; her cities and villages destroyed," she said with a harsh and vicious tone.

Ty'kahl Dak'Jec answered. "Great Aya, our forces will be ready to destroy Lea'Angleneth. If we may?" Afyreen nodded and the Ty'kahls stood and laid several maps upon the table before her and the others. Rovik thought it interesting that the Dao'Tai always referred to Afyreen as Great Aya.

The Ty'kahls were now explaining to Afyreen the best ways to assault Lea'Angleneth while keeping Mantorah from coming to their aid. Rovik said little and simply observed as the plans were made and came together. It would be a two-fronted assault. The main force would move along the West Way to Thenill. The city would be taken, and from there they were to sweep the Akarr Valley south to Lake Akarr. There it would besiege the Isle of Angleneth. A secondary force of Dao'Tai soldiers, supported by the Grishkii, would head south to Syrah to cut off the road north—thus, stopping Mantorah from sending aid.

A third host of Srellites and Grishkii were to join forces with the Dao'Tai that were already in the Vagath'Oth. They were the same Dao'Tai that Afyreen had sent to Chalid to help stop the Grishkii raids. This army was to march in secret to the southern pass by the

Aril River. There they were to stop any escaping refugees, and they were to see that Mantorah could not come to Lea'Angleneth's aid by that road. Thus, the entire realm of Angleneth would be surrounded and cut off from help. Afyreen smiled as she sat and listened to the well-made plans of her Ty'kahls.

Rovik was not used to feeling like this; his mind was a blur. The people of Thenill had done nothing to deserve such slaughter, neither had Lea'Angleneth really. Lady Re'alis might be defiant, and she should be removed from power, but the total slaughter of her people? That was not even legal by the despicable laws of the Subjugate. But what was he to do? If Afyreen was set to go to war, then there was nothing he could do. It was better to be on her side and behind her armies than in front of them. The council of war lasted for several hours as each at the table was given a specific task to complete. The men of Thalyphonie were given free charter to raid the Mantorahn coasts, with help from Ornurgr Nevicore and the Taivadean Navy. Rovik was to see that the Grishkii would cooperate with the plans and the navies were supplied with adequate slaves and equipment for sustaining battle. Their goal was to destroy the Mantorahn Navy and blockade the Mantorahn ports. During the entire meeting, the figure in the shadowed corner never moved, nor did they speak. Finally, as the sun was reaching its meridian, all the details had been worked out to include reinforcing the northern frontier, and the Aya Dao'Tai stood and addressed all who were present.

"There is one last matter, an heir of Anoth is rumored to have survived. Our spies are uncertain if these stories are just wishful thinking being spread by the hopeful or simple talk of the idle peasants. A real or false heir could cause us problems. Should any of us encounter anyone who could be or claims to be the heir they are to be captured, if possible, killed if that is the only option."

Nevicore and Rovik looked at each other, then to Afyreen with puzzled looks upon their faces.

"Surely, Your Majesty, he was slain with his family?" Skepticism was clear in Nevicore's voice.

"So we have always thought, but recent events have led me to think otherwise." Rovik knew she was certain that the child had survived, though they never had any real proof. With a dominating glance, Afyreen looked around at all who sat before her and spoke again.

"Now, unless there is anything we have overlooked, you are dismissed. All of us have much to be doing."

With no further words Nevicore, the Thalyphonieans, the Ty'kahls, and Rovik all stood and walked for the door. Rovik was last to leave and, turning his head to glance behind, he saw the stranger in the shadows take a step into the light. He could hardly trust what his eyes saw. For unless he was greatly mistaken...

Ikthii!

He had been assured by the Aya Dao'Tai that she was no longer in league with those abominations. The door shut behind him, but Rovik lingered with his back to it. He peered through the keyhole to confirm, and there was no mistake about it, the figure that stood in the shadows was a carrion reaper, one of the ikthii. When Rovik had first started to deal with Afyreen, she had vowed that she would no longer work with the creatures. This was clearly not the case. After the war they had devoured entire villages with no cause other than their lust for death. Rovik had worked hard to convince her to distance the Subjugate from the ikthii. He had counted this success as one of his biggest atoning achievements. Countless innocents surely had been spared by his efforts to keep the carrion reapers from actively working with the Subjugate. The sudden revelation that Afyreen had simply hidden her cooperation with them shocked Rovik to his core.

What else has she lied to me about? How much do I really know about her plans at all?

The others had disappeared down the stairs by now, so standing by the door alone Rovik pressed his ear to the timber and strained to listen to what was being said within. One voice was clearly Afyreen's, and the other was low and sounded male. This one was speaking now.

"Aya Afyreen, let us have the denizens of Thenill. If we take them, we can use them in the battle against the men of Lea'Angleneth. Thus, sparing your soldiers from suffering great loss from the mechanical weaponry of the Lake Isle dwellers." Rovik could hear the empress make her reply, but her words were soft and muffled by the wood of the door. A third voice now spoke, this one recognizable as Sethel.

"This may be true, my Aya Dao'Tai. The Freeholdn surely cannot muster a sufficient army to resist our march, but Chalid may object to our attack on Angleneth, thus completely removing him and his people could benefit us and avoid future problems."

The reaper spoke again: "And what of the Tears? Have the Xydar female or Jendayi given us anything as to their location?"

Sethel answered, "No, they have given us little more than screams, but we have one of the Tundraihn coming to us. She should have the knowledge the other two apparently lack. However, some good has come from taking the Xydar and Jendayi."

The Aya Dao'Tai made a quiet reply and Sethel continued.

"Yes. Thanks to the secrecy in which we took them captive, the Xydarii and Jendayi are now on the brink of war, each blaming the other for their lost royalty. This should keep the Xydarii trapped within the Dark Realms." Despite the thick timber of the door, Rovik clearly heard the cold laughter of Afyreen.

The reaper spoke again. "Aya, you are right to find joy in this; for we need only to keep our enemies complacent or fighting each other to ensure our victory." Rovik stepped back from the door. The sound of the reaper's voice was drawing closer. The eavesdropping chancellor started down the stairwell and ducked into the first doorway he came upon. With his back to the cold stone he held his breath and listened. If Afyreen knew he had been listening, she would deal sorely with him.

He soon heard the sounds of the door opening from the stairs above. Echoing fragments of conversation drifted down the stairwell, and Rovik could practically feel their eyes upon the dark doorway where he now took refuge. The conversation lulled for a moment, then the door was pulled shut again. Rovik breathed a sigh of relief, but suddenly the latch of the door next to him clicked, and someone stepped rather loudly through the doorway.

Out of fear of discovery, Rovik swiftly took them off guard and with one arm pinned them to the wall, covering their mouth with his other hand. Light from the now open door flooded into the doorway and stairs, revealing this person to be the pleasant maidservant that had shown him into the palace earlier. Their eyes met and she must've seen the desperation in his. Without speaking a word, they understood each other. As he slowly let her go and uncovered her mouth. The upper door was open again and Afyreen's voice called down.

"Sificah, is that you?"

The maidservant stepped past Rovik and answered her mistress. "Yes, Aya Dao'Tai. I was just on my way to—"

"Well, get back on your way, then," Afyreen snapped.

"Yes, Aya Dao'Tai." Sificah bowed to her, then walked back through the door, taking Rovik by the hand as she passed, leading him along after her. Once in the room beyond, she shut the door behind him and turned to face him. He was searching through the scattered thoughts within his head, trying to make some excuse to give her that would keep her from asking too many questions. Before he had any response formed, she spoke.

"Chancellor, you overheard something, didn't you? Something she didn't mean for you to hear."

Rovik chose his words slowly and with care. She clearly was smart, and he did not wish to insult or anger her. If he did that, she might report him to the Aya Dao'Tai.

"I am chancellor of Anoth. The Aya Dao'Tai holds no secrets from me. I simply did not wish to be seen taking my time down the stairs." This explanation did not sound as good aloud as it had in his mind.

For some reason, this servant made his usually quick mind and sharp tongue grow slow and dull.

"That is not what I saw in your face in the doorway. No matter what you say, I could see that you heard something terrible." Rovik tried to say something, but she cut him off.

"Milord, I am but a servant here, I don't stand in a place where I can make much of a difference. But you can. You need to choose, but please don't waste the risk I took to conceal you." She spoke with sadness in her voice, and before he could respond she left down the hallway, leaving Rovik alone. Rovik reopened the door to the stairs and peered into the darkness. Hearing and seeing nothing, he quietly made his way down the spiraling stairs and back out into the main hall of the palace. He picked up his pace and soon was through the gardens and out of the palace entirely. Once through the outer gates, Rovik could see the plans of the Aya Dao'Tai already being put into effect.

Companies of marching Dao'Tai soldiers were leaving the fortress through the main gate and heading out to staging areas that had been chosen by the Ty'kahl in the council. One thing was certain to Rovik; with the speed that Afyreen's plans were being put into effect, both Lea'Angleneth and Mantorah were going to be caught off guard. Thousands would die as hundreds of border villages burned. For Afyreen had made it clear that few were to be taken as prisoners.

There is nothing I can do! He shouted within himself, not daring a misstep here under the watch of so many eyes. Rovik took a few deep breaths as he stormed off toward the stables that held his horse. He had to get out of this fort, away from the reminders of war and the slaughter of innocents to come.

Afyreen was now alone in the council chambers. She leaned over the long table wrapped in her shadow, turning through the maps and lists of assets.

"Soon, we will have what we need," she whispered gently. "Very soon our separation will be at an end." A broad warm smile curved her broad lips as tears threatened to fall from the sable-red of her eyes.

The chamber door creaked opened and Sificah was marched in, followed by two guards; they stopped a few feet short of the long table in the room's center.

"Aya Dao'Tai, you asked to see me?" Sificah's voice was trembling.

Afyreen stood up and took a few steps over to the head of the long table, clearing the moisture from her eyes. She stood with the sunlight bursting through the windows, throwing her shadows wide over Sificah. She knew the effect would make her look wreathed in both darkness and flame. Sificah was now visibly quaking in the hands of the two guards. It was never a good thing for a servant to be asked for by name to come before the Aya Dao'Tai. Afyreen took a few more steps toward her fear-stricken servant and spoke.

"Sificah, you have not been with us long have you?"

"No, Your Majesty, not long."

Afyreen drew closer to Sificah, close enough for the scent of the servant to reach her. Slowly, she stretched forth her hand and gently caressed Sificah on her cheek. Terror at what may be in store for her filled Sificah's face at the touch, and Afyreen smiled inside. The girl's soft face felt fragile under her cold, hard hands, and Sificah shut her eyes tightly as if bracing herself for the assault she deemed imminent.

"You are pretty for a maidservant, age notwithstanding. I like to surround myself with beauty when I can. It is too bad you were not born to a higher station. You could have perhaps been an official mistress of, or even the lady to, some great lord." Afyreen's voice was soft, yet there was venom in the words. She withdrew her hand from Sificah's face and turned her back to her, still speaking.

"Who were you concealing within the doorway?"

To her credit, Sificah did sound innocent and calm. "I was hiding no one, Your Majesty. I was—"

Afyreen turned sharply and seized her by the throat. She was too angry to even feel satisfaction at Sificah's terror at her incredible speed and steel grip.

"Do not lie to me, slave! I know you were with someone, and they were spying on my dealings. Now you will tell me who it was, or you will suffer for your silence."

Sificah was gasping for air and desperately clutched at Afyreen's wrist.

"Please...I was hiding no one."

Afyreen raised her slightly up with her single arm and smiled as she looked into her servant's eyes. "Do you think you can lie to me? We sensed the presence of both of you. In fact, Sethel even suspects that you care for the one you are now sheltering with your lies. One of the stable hands perhaps?"

The terrified servant was now losing consciousness, but just before she did Afyreen released her grip, and Sificah fell in a heap on the cold stones of the floor.

"I asked you twice, and that is double the patience I have with most, so count yourself lucky. Guards, take her to Sethel and his...associates. See if he can pry anything from her. When they are finished send her along with the other two to the slavers' guild. See if they can find a use for her. And buy a replacement, a pretty one."

Sificah tried to speak, but she was only sputtering incoherent nonsense, and Afyreen sneered. The guards grabbed her by the arms and under her shoulders and dragged her out of the room, leaving Afyreen alone once again. She stood silent for a while, and then spoke to herself.

"It is a pity, really, she had such a pleasant smile."

Afyreen turned back to the maps and papers that were atop the table and focused on her plans for the near future.

18

Of Self, Rain, and Riding

There are quarters of this realm that draw the eye of the heavens. Seek ye therefore a life in a place of your own making and embrace the whims of those of the spheres above you with meekness.
Essays of the Divine

Ralenn had never been so damp and miserable in his entire life. It had been raining since they left the falls almost four days ago. At the insistence of the Tundraihn they had only stopped once to find shelter when the storm was at its worst. He could hardly believe the speed the Tundraihn warriors could travel at. They were all on foot, and yet they kept a pace that had the horses trotting. The truly impressive part was that it seemed they could have gone faster were it not for the weather, darkness, and Lord Devick's litter. Had they wished it, these tall warriors could have easily outrun the horses over distance. Even at their slowed pace the horses were straining to keep up. The Tundraihn would go far ahead and then they would be forced to wait for the slower horses and men to catch up. Ralenn was sure much more of this would either be the death of the horse or of himself. The horses of the Mantorahn soldiers seemed to be well enough. They were of a stature and strength unlike any Ralenn had ever seen. Kaileth had told him they were Breydfar horses; bred for battle and endurance beyond measure. This explained why Doffle and the horses from Allinth struggled to keep the pace.

The company had been winding their way down and out of the mountainside all day prior and into the first watches of the night. All throughout the rain-soaked night they had made their way through the thick forests that surrounded the last foothills of the mountains. They relied on the Tundraihn heavily that night as the poor light did not impair their ability to navigate in the darkness. The way had been steep and winding in the dark stormy night. Now their surroundings had changed to that of rolling hills and sloping ridges as they traveled through the skirts of the Vagath'Oth Mountains. The sun finally started its ascent, breaching the banks of the storm clouds with its glowing rays. Ralenn felt a surge of relief as the first orange beam cut through the breaking storm clouds.

Their path of travel followed the Aril River most of the hurried journey, and the sound of it roaring with rainwater had given them a mark to steer by in the starless, storm-thrashed nights. Ralenn looked around to see where Kaileth was and soon spotted him leading his horse next to Orodan. The two were speaking with each other in hushed tones, and both had serious expressions on their faces. Ralenn made a mental note to ask Kaileth about their conversation later. Ralenn stretched and leaned back in his saddle to soak up some of the warmth of sunlight falling upon him.

With the new light, Ralenn looked back to the horse that carried Lirah. He had made her take his cloak two nights ago when the storm was at its worst. She now appeared to be fairly dry in the early morning light. She caught him watching her and gave a warm smile. Ralenn wondered at her. The sunburn and wind chap were gone after that first night at the falls, and since then she did not seem to be as weary and sore as he. He was not sure if her new increase in powers had something to do with this apparent rejuvenation, or if she simply was bearing their hardships extraordinarily well. After she healed him at the sphinx cave, she had been weak and weary, yet now she had brought herself back from the brink of death and healed Lord Devick with no outward toll.

"You look frozen, Ralenn. Maybe you should have kept this enchanted cloak of yours." Lirah's cheerful voice was untouched by the chill of the night.

"I am not as cold as I may look," he said through chattering teeth.

She laughed, "Oh, I am sure! But are you as wet as you look?"

Ralenn couldn't help but laugh despite himself.

"Yes, I suppose I am as wet as I look. I may be even wetter than I look. That storm had more than its rightful share of rain."

"I know! And all these people are in such a hurry they couldn't even stop for a moment. It would probably have been better for Lord Devick if we stopped for a bit. I am surprised that he is still out. He was hurt very badly, but how do you sleep through days of rain and bouncing between those huge horses? He just needs more time, I think. At any rate, your cloak hasn't let a single drop of water through it. You still don't know where Kaileth got it, do you?" asked Lirah suddenly amidst her chatter. Ralenn had to catch up with her fast speech before comprehending the question she asked him.

"The cloak? I don't know, I had never seen it before he sent me up after the lion."

"Hmm, well I would guess it was made by something magical, like the Atha'Tarrii or something like that. Gaileng told me all about the Atha'Tarrii, and the Shedim, and all the..." Her words trailed off, and sorrow filled her face.

"I keep forgetting he's really gone," she said softly. "I think of how exciting it will be to go home, burst into his chambers to tell him of all that we have done, only to remember he is dead."

Ralenn strove for something to say to comfort her, but nothing came. Without really thinking about it he reached over to where she sat atop her horse and placed his hand gently on her shoulder.

"Gaileng will always be watching over you, Lirah."

She turned to Ralenn, placed her hand on top of his, and gave it a warm squeeze.

"I hope so. I just wish we could have saved him. It is strange, though, all that has happened over this halfmoon or so seems like a dream, like fog covering the mountain valleys. I keep waiting for the sun to come up and melt it away. I keep waiting to wake up from the dream. But I won't, it is all too real. I fear that this is only the start of it too. I don't see us settling down in a nice new little village any time soon." Her words felt heavy in the silence that followed them. Ralenn was not used to Lirah being so serious.

"You're right, I think. But I also think that we can make it through this together." Ralenn was surprised by his optimistic response. He was not feeling very hopeful at the moment. In fact, he was feeling more tired, spent, and gloomy than he ever had, but she didn't need to hear that. Lirah interrupted his introspection.

"That is why the Aashahl give us good friends to travel through life with, they help keep you going. Not to mention how often some of them need to be patched." She reached over and gave Ralenn a stout punch to his shoulder. The shock of it drove away the beginnings of his self-pitying and he forced a smile on his cold face.

"Alright! Yes, we are lucky to have you with us, Lirah! I, for one, would not be in such a good mood if those claws were still stuck in my leg," he grinned at her. "Or alive at all for that matter. Kaileth wouldn't be with us either, and Mantorah would be without their lord."

Ralenn looked at her with some of the awe he felt during the healing of Lord Devick. Ralenn was realizing there was a side, a power to Lirah that somehow, he had not noticed through all the years of knowing her. It was also apparent that the female Tundraihn considered her to be different. They had welcomed her in their midst at the falls and always gave her special salutations if they came near. In some ways, Ralenn felt that he was getting to see who Lirah really was for the first time now.

"How *did* you heal him, Lirah? I thought there were no longer any arcane empathic healers, but that is what you did, isn't it? You said you must use your own life force to heal. Don't all empathic healers heal that way? So, shouldn't wounds as bad as his have drained you till death? Unless you are an arcane empath, that is..."

Lirah seemed to ponder over his question as they rode along silently for some time. Her expression spoke of deep introspection. She started to speak but hesitated and swallowed hard before starting again.

"You are right, Ralenn, what I did for Devick and myself would kill an empathic healer, even one of the most powerful..."

"So how did you do it? Was it the presence of the Tundraihn?"

Lirah spoke slowly, as though she was having to search out each word one at a time.

"No...it was not that...Ralenn, I am not an empathic healer...It seems I am something else. An arcane empath maybe? I don't know. Something the Tundraihn call an 'otheäil tä Syrnii'..." She paused again and Ralenn waited silently.

"I believe it is a type of arcane healing power. Gaileng only spoke of such things a few times. Syrnii is one of the Aashahl, the Mistress of Forests some call her. The priests said she is the maker of the Tundraihn..." she trailed off again. They rode in silence for several minutes until Lirah excitedly spoke again.

"It was like nothing I have ever felt before, Ralenn. Yet it was familiar. I found another source of life to draw from. Another source of healing and strength. For an instant, I was aware of everything around me—you, Lord Devick, the Tundraihn, everyone. But not just people, I could feel the stone, the trees, and the water of the falls, too—everything. I could...*feel* all of it, like it was a part of me. It was as if Miljah's life force was one with mine. So, I used it, I think. At least that was what it felt like. I used life force from Miljah to heal him. Don't ask me how it worked, though."

Ralenn stared at her, stunned at her response. Ralenn knew some of the nature of the Aashahl and the spirits in the world, but this was the stuff of myth and legends. Yet legends come from somewhere, don't they?

"Don't look at me like that! I don't know how it happened; it just did!" Lirah said defensively. Quickly realizing he was still staring wide-eyed at her he flushed and schooled his expression.

"However you did it, we were blessed to have you there. Lord Devick would be dead by now if it hadn't happened," Ralenn reassured her. "And you would have died by the hand of that Grishkah."

She smiled, seeming mollified, and her voice now took up her familiar teasing tone.

"While we are on the subject of newly exposed skills, where did you learn to sword fight like that? You danced circles around those big Grishkii."

Ralenn chuckled as he spoke. "You already know that. Ever since I can remember Kaileth has taught me to defend myself. He would have me fight him all the time. You remember he always said we had no right to make swords if we could not use them."

Lirah looked at him as if to say something skeptical, but her expression quickly changed to a simple smile.

"Alright, if that is what you say, I believe you. But it looked a lot more like you were born to fight. It was more than what you could get from practice. Maybe it's in your blood and your father was a soldier or warlord or something...Maybe a sh'tar even?"

Ralenn was careful to keep a straight face. Had Lirah overheard what he and Kaileth had spoken of that night above the falls? He was not sure, but who else could he talk to? She was his best friend.

I should just tell her, she should know...

Lirah watched him with curiosity as he struggled inside. Ralenn looked around at the others near them. Several Mantorahn soldiers were a few dozen yards behind. Riidak trotted ahead. No one was within earshot.

"Lirah, I know who my parents were..." he paused. Lirah said nothing, only nodding for him to continue.

"My mother was—" It seemed hard to say out loud.

Why is this so hard? Just tell her your father was the king of Anoth, your mother the queen...

He took a long deep breath. He truly had not come to terms with who his parents were himself yet.

"You don't have to tell me, Ralenn, it's alright," Lirah said understandingly.

Ralenn looked at her, expecting to see hurt on her face, but her features were calm and friendly. She had shared her personal experience of healing, something so new and foreign to her that she didn't understand. That gave him courage to share his own troubles.

"No, I want you to know, but please keep it to yourself. I am not sure what to think of it all myself yet." He took one more breath before saying, "My mother was...Queen Anica, of Anoth. My father was King Garadale."

He couldn't believe he had just said those words. Finally speaking them to someone made the rest come out easier.

"My mother was killed when Ell'Anoth fell, my father was lost at sea. My siblings are dead, too, which makes me the cursed heir to the lost throne." Ralenn seemed to be more telling himself these facts rather than Lirah. He looked off to the horizon, expecting to hear some sort of exclamation from her, but she was silent. Unsure of what to say next, he went back to her original question.

"As for the swordplay, I was just trying to protect my friends. If it looked like I knew what I was doing, then it was just luck. Brek's mercy for sure..."

Ralenn met Lirah's gaze. She didn't look shocked, or even surprised, she looked a little sad.

"Ralenn, I am so sorry they are gone. I am sure they loved you dearly."

Without knowing it, Lirah had struck on what he had been feeling, but did not want to confront—sorrow.

They are all dead. I will never know them...My brother, sisters, father, and mother. I had a family, and they are all gone now...The Subjugate killed them. She killed them.

A part of Ralenn had always hoped to find out that some of his family had survived and had just been separated from him in the chaos after the sack of Ell'Anoth. A darker part of him had always whispered of their death. This part of him no longer sorrowed for their loss, but now shrieked for revenge. Ralenn pushed that thought from his mind, startled at how quickly his sadness had turned to anger, hatred even. Fury at the person who caused the murder of his family, the Aya Dao'Tai.

"Ralenn, are you going to be alright?" Lirah asked softly, her voice full of concern. He looked up to her, realizing his trembling hands had a white-knuckled grip on the reins. He let out a long deep breath and relaxed, clearing his mind.

"I will be," he said after a long pause. "I just need time to let it soak in. Everything since we left home has been just...just impossible. It's all too much."

"I think I understand, just please don't hurt by yourself, not when you don't need to. I am here for you, even if all I can do is listen." She smiled so genuinely at him that he felt her warmth as a near-tangible force and wondered if his second sight was at play.

"Thank you, Lirah, it means a lot to hear you say that. I just need time, I think."

She nodded. "I won't tell anyone, just don't bottle it up, alright?" She gave another disarming smile, the pleasant curves of her cheeks pulling wide and Ralenn could not help but smile back.

"Also, don't expect me to start calling you, 'Your Majesty.'" She gave him a wink and Ralenn leaned back further in the saddle, stretching his sore legs and grinning as the sun started to feel warm on his skin.

Their conversation was halted by a shout from Gairrle. Ralenn could see several Mantorahn soldiers come running up. They reported to Gairrle, who then walked over to Orodan and Kaileth and spoke to them. They all nodded in agreement. Orodan cried something in his native language, and soon all the Tundraihn took off with amazing speed in the direction the Mantorahn scouts had come from. On signal from Gairrle, the rest of the party, including Ralenn and Lirah, sat motionless for the better part of half an hour. Captain Gairrle was pacing back and forth next to Lady Re'alis and the litter that carried Lord Devick.

They were stopped in a wider spot in the labyrinth of tall, wide-bladed grass and thick scrub oaks that filled the space between two tall rocky ridges. Their path was not marked or manmade, but simply the course of least resistance in the direction they needed to go. All that night and that morning they kept close to the river where very thick trees and undergrowth grew. Here the trees of the forest were gone, and only a few scattered oaks and cottonwoods remained, dotted here and there amongst the tall brush that surrounded them. Mirris had been aloft ever since the storm had broken, ranging far ahead. While poor Riidak had to trudge along under his own power. As they waited in this reprieve from the forest, Ralenn tried to guess what might have been found by the scouts ahead while he helped Riidak to both food and water. Jayle and the scouts had been several hours at least in front of the main body of their company. As he was thinking it over Kaileth rode up next to where Ralenn and Lirah had dismounted and spoke softly to them. He had been talking with Lady Re'alis and her guards.

"There is evidence of a battle ahead."

"A battle between who?" Ralenn asked.

"It looks to be between the Grishkii and the Srellites. There are several wounded Srellites left, and the Tundraihn have been allowed a head start to see if it is the band they seek. We thought it best not to be seen by the Srellites together, or to slow the pace of the

Tundraihn. It is best if our enemies do not know we are working with the Tundraihn. Orodan has also entrusted us with the knowledge that their queen's daughter is among those taken."

"You mean their priestess?" Ralenn asked in surprise, remembering the beautiful woman he had seen in his mind back at the falls.

"Technically she would be the high priestess to Syrnii. They feared to tell us at first, but he felt we needed to know now. I think they may need more of our help than they wish to admit to. She must be more than just the heir to a throne," Kaileth said thoughtfully.

"Kaileth, why would Grishkii and Srellites, whatever they are, take the high priestess from the Tundraihn?" Lirah asked.

"At this point I would guess they were paid to kidnap her. It is not like them to take anyone alive, they are more prone to eat their prisoners."

"I don't even know what a Srellite is." Lirah looked perplexed as she spoke.

"Miss Lirah, a Srellite is not something you ever want to meet in person if you can help it, so I consider it a blessing you have not yet. However, you should know of our enemies. Srellites are from the deserts and wilds in the south. They are akin to drakes in a fashion, though much, much smaller and without any form of magics. They are like men in shape, but their skin is thick as saddle leather and about the same color as the stones of their desert home. Scaly would actually be a better description of their hides. Many of their traits are drake-like, especially their eyes. They are very strong and very cunning and eat a great deal of raw meat. Not the kind of creature you will ever want to meet alone."

"They don't sound pleasant," she said, shuddering. "Still I'm surprised my studies missed them."

"They are a relatively new threat in the northwest. Not much is really known about them, and there are certainly no books on them that I know of. I think it's safe to say we will see at least their corpses this day." Kaileth turned his head to the side just as Riidak alerted to something.

"Some of the Tundraihn return."

As Kaileth finished saying the words, two of the Tundraihn warriors entered sight and ran up to Gairrle and Lady Re'alis. The four shared quick words, and then the two tall warriors left the captain and lady, running back down the same path they had just come from. Ralenn continued to watch as Gairrle and Lady Re'alis consulted closely together for a moment longer. Ralenn had just finished applying a special salve to Riidak's tired paws when Gairrle raised an arm and signaled for all the company to head out down the gently sloping ground.

"Back in your saddles, then," Kaileth said, with just a hint of a smirk on his lips.

"I guess so, but I seriously doubt our horses can go on much longer like this," Ralenn said as he and Lirah both got back on their mounts.

"Not to mention that I am no dispatch rider myself, and may never walk normally again after," he grumbled. Lirah laughed, as did Kaileth, but he was serious. Ralenn hurt in places and ways that he never thought possible. Some of the damage had to be nearly permanent, he was sure.

"You could always run for a while." Lirah offered as she eased into her saddle, as though it was the most comfortable place she could be.

"I have to ask, how are you not hurting right now? You were no more used to riding than I when we left home," he pointed out. Lirah looked thoughtful for a few moments as they started to ride down the trail again.

"I don't really know," she finally said lightly. "I am sleepy, and more than a little hungry for something other than soggy bread and mushy fruit stuff, but other than that I feel rather good. I did sleep really well at the falls."

"Lirah, that was days and days ago. Since then, we have only rested once," he said, a little befuddled at her apparent ignorance to her own unnatural stamina.

"I know, I guess I really didn't think about it. I should be worn out, I suppose, but I'm not..." She looked surprised for an instant, then held her hand out as though she expected to see something in it. Her expression went flat, as if she was suddenly lost in deep thought.

"Lirah?" he said, a little worried at her blank expression. She didn't respond.

"Lirah, are you alright?" he asked again a little louder.

"Wha—oh, yes, I'm fine, sorry. It's just...it's just that I think I am still pulling strength in somehow, like it is my new normal?" she said, seeming to ask the question of her surroundings rather than Ralenn.

"Well, if you figure out how to share let me know," he said much more tersely than he intended. Kaileth carefully listened at a distance to the exchange as Mirris took a morsel from his grasp, her talons clutching the tall cantle of his saddle. They picked up speed and Riidak fell to the rear with Doffle and the pack horses.

The path narrowed and Ralenn let Lirah pass into single file without further talk. Ralenn felt more than a little ashamed at how bothered he was that he was so much weaker than Lirah. He had always aspired to be the equal of any warrior in body and mind, training for countless hours to build his stamina, strength, and agility. Now, on his first real try he was cold, wet, and worn out. He had to admit that he was more than a little jealous of how easily Lirah seemed to shrug it off, regardless of what innate abilities she used to do it.

You are being silly, he admonished himself, and he knew he was. He was lucky to have Lirah with him, and luckier still that she had the powers that she did or else they all would be in bad shape—he, Kaileth, and Lord Devick would all be dead.

The maze of grass and bushes slowed progress. The lead mounts and their riders were having to literally push their way through the walls of dense vegetation. While the Tundraihn seemed to slip through it with no evidence of their passing, the cavalry of Mantorah methodically broke trail. The hooves of their horses had been pounding the path for some while when a true trail, probably one used by herdsmen of the hills, appeared before them. The troop of men and horses rode out on it and finally were able to ride free and fast. Lirah quickened her horse, and Ralenn followed, hastening their steeds to come up alongside Gairrle and Lady Re'alis. Kaileth was again talking with Gairrle, and soon Lirah was speaking with Lady Re'alis. Ralenn's position put him in earshot of either conversation. However, Gairrle and Kaileth's topic seemed more relevant to what Ralenn was wanting to know, so he turned his full attention to them.

"Captain, are we to expect more trouble ahead?" Kaileth inquired.

"Nothing more than slain foes, and perhaps some information the Tundraihn needed."

"I see. So, the Tundraihn have finished with the survivors, then?"

Gairrle weighed his answer carefully, "Yes, they are...finished, as you put it. They wanted to question the Srellites but thought it unwise to reveal all of our company."

"Indeed, that seems wise. If what I have heard is true, then at times the Subjugate's sorcerers have the ability to see through the eyes of their servants."

"You speak the truth, Kaileth. However, such things are not common knowledge."

Wariness grew in Gairrle's voice as he continued to speak.

"Only one who has had much dealing with the Subjugate, or one who was in her service would know this power."

Kaileth smiled. "Captain, you are right to be suspicious of a total stranger. Especially one met under such curious circumstances. However, I assure you I gained my knowledge of the Aya's ways through many battles with her armies. I have fought her from the Gates of the East to the very palace of Ell'Anoth. I would deem that there are few who have fought her as hard as I and my long-dead comrades."

Ralenn could not keep a wide grin from his face at the look of submission that Gairrle wore.

"It was not my intent to impugn your honor, sir," he said humbly, inclining his head to Kaileth.

"You did no such thing. It is good to be wary at times such as this. I do, however, want you to be certain that you have no stronger ally than myself when it comes to opposing the Subjugate."

The three rode in silence for a time. Both the Captain and Kaileth looking contemplative.

"So, I take it you believe that this attack on us was the work of the Subjugate?" Gairrle asked.

Kaileth was quick to reply. "Was it ever in question? I cannot see how it could be anything else. There has never been trouble with the Grishkii in these lands. Not like this. Some stolen cattle, a raided farmstead perhaps. But villages destroyed, and an attack upon an armed camp? Fighting to the last to capture a single prisoner? Grishkii would never act so boldly were it not for an outside force working on them. The presence of the Ikthii proves the Subjugate is behind it of itself."

"I agree. Lady Re'alis told me a little of her interactions with it. There is no doubt of what that creature was. When you were speaking earlier to Lady Re'alis and myself of the attack on your home, you mentioned seeing a man with the Grishkii. Can you remember what he looked like?"

Kaileth thought back to the events in the village. "He was tall, but not built as the Dao'Tai. His tabard bore a curious heraldry. It looked like a tree cleft in twain. There was something over the split in the tree, but I cannot recall what it was."

Gairrle seemed to consider Kaileth's words carefully before answering slowly, "Could it have been a hooked dagger?"

"Yes, I do think it could have been. All I remember about it for sure was that it looked like the cause of the tree's sundering. I can't say that

I have seen it before. It wasn't Freeholdn or Taivadean—of that I am sure." Kaileth tried to recall more but failed.

"If that is the case, then not only were we attacked by Grishkii under the same command, but the Subjugate is without a doubt the instigator of these assaults. For what cause she attacked your village, I could not guess. However, it is no secret that she does not care for my lord, nor Lady Re'alis." Gairrle was worried. Unsettled by the almost death of his lord and the events of the last few weeks.

"I believe there is much moving that we are not aware of yet, and I fear that death and further enslavement will be the cost of our ignorance," Kaileth said, sensing the captain was debating sharing more.

"How right you are. The men bearing the sigil of the split tree—it has been reported to us that they are part of something called *the Sundering*. Trusted agents in several realms have seen them: observing, directing others, but never taking part themselves in the deeds they command."

"Another actor in play? Agents of the true foe perhaps? This is curious and disturbing news. The Aya Dao'Tai is far too cunning to make such an open attack on the rulers of other lands unless she is expecting support in the war she surely knows will ensue." As Kaileth finished speaking, Ralenn realized that all around them were silent, including Lirah and Lady Re'alis.

Re'alis leveled her gaze on Kaileth.

"It would seem there is more to you, blacksmith of Allinth, than I was first aware of. You speak as one who knows our foes from harsh experience. I also fear that the Aya has many things planned against us. However, her failure to take me and kill Lord Devick has disclosed at least a part of her plans. The desecrator was not guarded with what it shared with me. The questions it asked were illuminating to the scope of the game the Aya is playing. Hopefully, there will be enough time for us to rally against her plots and defend ourselves." Kaileth bowed his head in agreement to the lady's words.

"Don't forget the Tundraihn," interjected Lirah. "The Subjugate has been busy in their lands too, and making them her enemy can't bode well for her at all. Perhaps they can aid us as well?"

"Yes, Miss Lirah." Kaileth smiled at the exuberance in her voice as he spoke. "The Tundraihn are not ones to leave a debt unpaid. I am sure that if we can aid them in their rescue, they will aid us if they can. And I would like to learn more concerning what the Dao'Tai have been up to in the south from Orodan if the chance presents itself."

"As would we all, but I think he will be slow to sit and counsel with us while his people are in the hands of the Srellites and Grishkii," noted Gairrle. Everyone nodded in agreement and silence followed. Eventually Re'alis and Lirah again took up their previous line of conversation.

Lirah could not help but stare a little at Re'alis. She was the kind of person Lirah read about as a child—ladies living in beautiful palaces with knights and serfs at her every call. Even under their current destitute circumstance, Re'alis could never have been mistaken for anything but the highest-born lady. Her posture and bearing commanded respect and her every motion was pure refinement and elegance. To Lirah she was an embodiment of regal loveliness.

"It is good to see you fared the night's storm so well." Re'alis' voice was soft and kind as she spoke. "I must thank you again for lending me your soap at the falls. I didn't realize how filthy I had become. I also owe you much for your aid in that fight, and in saving Devick."

Lirah's face flushed slightly. "My lady, I am happy I was able to serve in some capacity."

"Lirah, you did far more than simply serve, you helped save me and Devick. You have earned my trust and friendship. You are a true friend of Lea'Angleneth. There is no need for you to speak as a servant. You are clearly a powerful disciple of the healing arts and must also be a favored of Dannitar."

"Oh, my lady, I don't—that is, I only tried to help as best I could; praise be to the aashahl that it worked out, but I don't feel very favored by anything after all the awfulness that has happened. Helping others has been the only thing that has made all the terribleness bearable."

Lirah felt a melancholy threaten to settle on her but Re'alis would have none of that, her kind voice luring Lirah back from her darker thoughts.

"My dearest Lirah, Is there any truer mark of discipleship to the divine than sacrifice in the service of others?"

Lirah smiled widely at the kind words of Re'alis, and the two continued in friendly conversation of Lea'Angleneth and Re'alis' home, Lirah's knowledge of the arcane, and many other things. They rode on for some hours and Lirah found Re'alis easy to talk to. She asked the best sort of questions and listened to every word of each answer. It was nice to have someone to share the happy memories of her old life with. Her time in the Anthosn temple under the tutelage of Gaileng and the others, summers in the high forest with Ralenn. Harvest festivals and the innocent beauty in the simple life in Allinth. Lirah was explaining one of these instances to Re'alis, who listened intently.

"...Gaileng told me so many times that if I spent half as much time practicing to be a proper lady as I did running around the forest that I..." Lirah trailed off as the images of Gaileng's dead body came flooding back to her mind. Re'alis smiled sadly; she knew of the recent destruction of Lirah's home.

"Lirah," she spoke with earnest empathy. "What was he like, your Gaileng?"

Lirah sat quietly in the saddle for a while. *What was he like?* She thought over her memories of growing up under his care. Unlike Ralenn, Lirah had never really had any hope of finding her real parents. Gaileng made it no secret that all her kin were slain in the sacking of Ell'Anoth. Gaileng, Bruist, Fodir, Theatta, the others, they all were her family. Now with them all gone a part of her had been lost. Gaileng especially. He had always been there, waiting for her to get back from the forests and mountains with new stories of her small adventures. He would listen to her tales of newfound meadows and the activities of deer and birds as though they were the most important things he would ever hear. He would spend hours helping her with her studies, never getting upset at her mistakes or lack of concentration. He was steady, dependable, he was...

"He was loving, my lady, selfless and caring. Reliable as the sunrise and just as warm." Re'alis listened as Lirah continued to quietly speak, slow hot tears pooling in her eyes.

"Gaileng was my refuge. He taught me that patience, love, and a kind heart were more powerful than anger and hardness ever could be." Lirah smiled through the tears, thinking of all the times he had talked with her about such things.

"He would often take me to a place where the Aril cut a slot right through a rock cliff face. The stone was so cold and hard there, black as avertyyn, but there were also a few trees and a nice thicket, covered with beautiful flowers. We would sit near the water and just listen sometimes, until I got antsy. Other times he would have me read or we would talk about things. The last time we went there I finally understood why he loved that place."

She paused and looked toward Re'alis. "It was a peaceful place where it was easy to listen to Miljah, a place to listen for the Patient Father, or any of the Aashahl, I suppose. But also, I think that place was like him. The soft running water, deep and steady, had slowly—patiently—cut through even the hardest black stone; and there in its path, the trees and flowers grew. I guess that was what he was like, he was the steady stream that made sure the flowers could grow..." Lirah trailed off again. She was not sure where she was going with all this, but it felt good to talk about him to Re'alis. It was right to remember the good, to remember the man he was.

"His steady kindness shows in you, Lirah. I think he would be proud of all you've done through all this trial."

I hope so, Lirah thought.

The tide of melancholy finally swept over Lirah as she let herself feel his loss and remember the loving years spent learning at his side. She wept silently, but not wholly in sorrow. A soft smile brightened her tear-stained face.

"He would want me to be happy," she said at length. "He is finally with Anthos, called home to paradise, I am sure. He would want me to be happy for him."

Lirah turned wet, smiling eyes to Re'alis. "I suppose, my lady, that death only really wins if we forget the joy of having known the lost."

Re'alis leaned in her saddle and put a reassuring hand on Lirah's shoulder.

"You are so very right, Lirah."

They both smiled now, and Lirah felt as though a great weight was taken from her heart. Lirah let her eyes and thoughts wander in the dazzling sky. Bright silvery clouds in billowing majesty parted into dozens of isles of white in the sea of blue. The storm was well spent above them and it looked to be the start of a new and pleasant day.

Before their conversation could pick back up again several Tundraihn warriors, including Ealë, stepped out from the thick brush that lined the path and started walking alongside the horses. Ealë looked up and smiled at Lirah but said nothing. They soon saw the rest of the Tundraihn warriors scattered about a clearing that looked to be the intersection of three ill-repaired roads. There on the ground and amongst the grass were many bodies, Grishkii as well as what she assumed to be the Srellites Kaileth described. All had been slain in very violent ways. Lirah looked down from her saddle at one of the Srellites. It was as Kaileth had described. Its large, lizard-like eyes stared up at her from its reptilian face. It was not a friendly-looking creature. The company slowly rode their horses through the mess into the center of the crossroads where Orodan and Jayle stood. Orodan looked up to Captain Gairrle as they all approached, and addressed them all.

"It is good you have arrived. We were considering heading out alone. We learned some from the wounded Srellites. Apparently, a dispute over what to do with the prisoners arose after their human overseers died during a wolf attack. The Srellites wanted to sell their prisoners to the In Kind Mercantile slavers, but the Grishkii remained set to turn them over to the Aya Dao'Tai. They fought, and the Srellites were the victors."

"If they won, why did they leave any surviving Grishkii?" asked Re'alis.

"The wounded we spoke with were not Grishkii, they were Srellites. They do not care for their wounded as we do and had left them to die. Fortunately for us, they had enough life left to give us some valuable information," Orodan said flatly.

"If the Srellites are taking your people to these slavers, then our chances of rescuing the Eolai'Mahtair are now greater than if they had taken her to the Dao'Tai fortress," Kaileth said.

"Not only that, but we do not think we are far behind them now, perhaps a day, no more than two. Our success would be greatly aided if one who was familiar with this land and these slavers could accompany us. We would be in their debt, and that is no small thing." Orodan stood hopefully, waiting for a reply. Captain Gairrle looked to Jayle, who stood next to Devick's litter trying to keep Doffle from licking the lord. Jayle pushed the animal back and spoke, handing the lead to Harrc.

"Captain, this company is yours to command," he said a bit sternly to Gairrle. The older warrior seemed worn thin by the last few days.

Gairrle nodded curtly and turned to Orodan.

"Master Orodan, I would send any aid at my disposal, but I unfortunately have none. I must see my lord safely to Syrah. I'm sorry. I can send a few of the men in my charge with you, but their knowledge of what lies before you is limited."

An uncomfortable silence followed the captain's words. Orodan's expression was hard to read. Lirah looked from face to face of all who were about them. Her eye settled on Kaileth, and she thought he looked deep in thought. Lirah looked to Ralenn and saw he was watching him as well. They both waited, and soon Kaileth broke the silence.

"I would be honored to assist you, Orodan, if it is acceptable to all." Orodan looked pleased at this, and he looked to the lady and captain for their response.

"You are free to go wherever you wish, though the safer road is to Syrah," said Re'alis with concern.

"If Kaileth is to go with you, then I would ask that I might go also," Jayle said. "More soldiers will be of little value. If anything, they would be a hindrance, seeing that the Subjugate wishes the death of Lord Devick. They would draw her eye to you quicker. Yet, Mantorah should see that this deed is done, and I have been there before." Gairrle nodded in agreement with the knight commander of house De'Vinor, as did Orodan.

"I would be happy to have you with us, sire. The road to Syrah is yet long and not without peril. The blades of all might be needed to keep the rest of your company safe, Captain Gairrle." Kaileth added.

"So be it," Re'alis said reluctantly. "We will continue to Syrah, then. Orodan, should we look for your coming after you have recovered your people?"

"You would be welcome in our lands, and it would ease all our minds to see you all safely returned," Gairrle suggested.

"When we are successful, we would welcome hospitality and a safe place to rest from our hastened journey. My lady, I apologize for not telling you the full nature of our errand into your land, and for any abruptness I may have treated you with. Rescuing the Eolai'Mahtair is my utmost priority. I assure you, when we return to our lands, favorable tales of your kindness and hospitality will find the ears of our people." Orodan gave a small smile as he spoke. It was the friendliest and most open gesture they had seen from him thus far. Aside from Tyllidus and Lirah's encounters with the females, Orodan was the only Tundraihn who had openly spoken to anyone outside their own numbers. It was easy to see the mistrust and watchfulness that most regarded their human companions with. Orodan had been polite, but reserved, usually speaking with a flat expression.

The Tundraihn now stood in a half circle behind their leader, their delving eyes searching the faces of Jayle, Kaileth, Ralenn, and Lirah. A few exchanged quick words in hushed tones. The way the light was falling upon their hard, angled features made them look more like bronze statues than living beings. Ealë quietly slipped up next to Lirah and spoke in a hushed whisper.

"It is the will of Syrnii that you go with us, sister. I am pleased also." She looked around to make sure no one heard and then moved back toward her kin. Lirah smiled and did wonder at the Aashahls' hands in all this. Was she fated to be on this path, or just a victim of a chaotic world? Lirah knew that it was hard to tell. Gaileng and the other at the Anthosn temple all believed that the Aashahl could take a highly active role in the lives of mortals. Some even took on the guise of mortals living among the realms without anyone knowing. They could choose champions, or curse enemies, or help their faithful. Lirah was not sure what she believed. The last few days seemed cursed, to be sure, but there were also signs of aid as well. Lirah could not dismiss the fact that her sudden surge in healing ability had come just when it was needed most.

"Kail, what about Doffle? He is too slow to go with us, but we can't just abandon him."

"Captain Gairrle, if you could take our pack animal and the goods we will not need with you, I would much appreciate it," Kaileth said.

"It will be done. They will await your return. And in the meantime, we will prepare Syrah for war. For if what we all think is happening is indeed afoot, then war will first come to her gates."

As they made preparations to split their party, Re'alis found a moment to speak to Lirah.

"Miss Lirah, before you go, what of Lord Devick?" Re'alis' face showed the concern she still felt for Devick's well-being.

"Don't worry, my lady, by the time you get to Syrah, Lord Devick should be awake and well," Lirah said confidently, hoping to set the lady's worries at ease.

"You would be welcome to accompany us Lirah. The Tundraihn already have a healer with them, and I would feel better knowing you are near should Devick need you." Re'alis' voice was sweet and sincere. The Tundraihn had already gathered themselves and quickly started down the road following the tracks of the Srellites. As Ealë passed she paused for a moment to place a hand on Lirah's shoulder, apparently not caring if Re'alis overheard.

"Come, sister, the Fates call."

Re'alis looked more than a little surprised by Ealë. Lirah considered her choice. Though she already knew what path she would take. She looked from Ralenn to Kaileth, Kaileth to Mirris perched upon Doffle's shoulders, Riidak excitedly prancing around the wool-ox's tail. Harrc still held Doffle's lead, and he smiled at Lirah as their eyes met. Ralenn followed behind Kaileth, slowly riding after the Tundraihn, but both looked back, awaiting Lirah's choice. She knew she would always follow Ralenn, and her heart thrummed at the realization.

Lirah turned her horse to the trail westward.

"My lady, Lord Devick will be fine, I promise you." She smiled gently at Re'alis. "But how can I let my friends go off into danger without me? Ralenn and Kaileth are all the family I have left. I just can't leave them, and they are quite accident-prone," Lirah said a little more loudly, shooting Ralenn an impish grin.

"Of course, Miss Lirah," Re'alis said, amused. "And I have no wish to separate you from those whom you love. I do wish you to know that you will always be welcome in Lea'Angleneth."

"Thank you, milady, truly." Lirah smiled and bowed to her.

"On condition that you call me Re'alis." Re'alis smiled also. "Be careful. Grace of the aashahl go before you all!"

Lirah smiled the brighter as she replied, "And before you also. I will be careful. After all, Lord Devick has yet to grant me a wish for saving him. Mantorahn lords can do that, right?" This made Re'alis laugh out loud, and she winked conspiratorially at Lirah, who then turned and rode to catch up to Ralenn, Kaileth, and the Tundraihn. After a short distance, she turned and called back to Harrc.

"You better take care of Doffle for me!" Harrc waved and chuckled to himself.

"You best take her seriously," said Re'alis sternly.

"Milady?" asked Harrc, a bit confused.

"My good man, that was clearly a threat!"

19

Rovik

When it shall be that another hast done aught to wrong you dismiss your bile swiftly. Puzzle out the meaning of the act and in equal measure take acts to protect from another offense. Yet show mercy to the offender lest wrath doom thee to become that which you despise. There are many dark and fallen ones who seek to prey upon the unforgiving and enraged.
Essays of the Divine

Rovik sat limply in the saddle of his horse as it slowly wandered down the wide cobbled street. Thoughts rushed through his mind, and he felt like he would unravel at any moment—the dream, the fresh talk of new wars. He felt sick, and his stomach threatened to empty itself.

Choose! Again, the word blasted through his thoughts, but not in his voice, not the girl with the blue eyes anymore, but Sificah's voice. Powerful and thundering in his thoughts.

Choose! This time it was louder, a blend of the blue-eyed girl and Sificah. He shut his eyes tightly, breathing in staggered, shallow gulps.

"It is not real. It was a dream. Just a dream. You *have* chosen, you chose to survive," he whispered, hoping hearing his thoughts aloud might make them feel more reasonable. They didn't. The turmoil within himself churned as all the ignored guilt of the last twenty years or more came rushing back into his mind in a tide of regret. Regret and shame.

'Open the spillway gate, I have made up my mind.' That was what you told him, you stupid fool, you chose true enough that day.

Again, he returned to the day Ell'Anoth fell. The day she was killed. The day he doomed the people to an enslavement he did not foresee.

The day I chose to betray them all, and for what? For this?

Rovik shook his head in a hopeless effort to cast off the crushing shame and despair that closed around him.

I did what I had to; what had to be done to save lives. It did save lives. To fight on would have meant death for us all, why couldn't she see that? We were defeated, besieged, trapped!

The sounds of the street grew louder as his horse continued slowly to carry him back to the palace. Rovik noticed nothing, lost totally in his own shattered cognizance for a time. This was not the first time such a frantic state of mind had threatened to drive him into self-loathing madness. The darkness of his own regret was always lingering in the back of his thoughts. Lingering in the same corners where he kept the memories of Anica.

A sudden bolt of clarity rushed through him.

"It is her. Both of them." First the girl with the blue eyes, and now Sificah had touched the parts of his mind where he worked to bury Anica's loss. Where he hid the love he had felt for her. The horse came to a sudden hard stop, snapping Rovik's head back and jarring him to an awareness of his surroundings. A robed figure stooped in front of him, desperately trying to pick up a large spilled basket of yurbs and shallots. The crowd that now flowed around the crouched figure and Rovik took no notice of them as they hurried to their homes. Simply reacting, Rovik got from his horse and knelt next to the person, who he could now see to be an elderly woman. In a few silent moments, her basket was again full. His hands swiftly recovering her fallen produce.

"Thank you, sire, that would have taken me some awful lot of time, and when you are my age you count every shade and jot."

Rovik only smiled and gave a courteous bow as he took back to his saddle. The old woman smiled and waved, the sinking sun catching the blue light in her eyes. Her brilliant blue eyes.

The same eyes!

Rovik turned sharply in the saddle, looking behind to where the old woman had been standing. She was nowhere to be seen. Rovik stopped his horse and searched the crowd. They passed by him in relative silence, faces downcast, most returning from a hard day's labor in service to the Subjugate. The woman was gone, lost in the crowd somewhere. Who was she? Without warning Rovik's mind flooded with moments of the past, clear as the day they were made, and he heard the conversations of that time some two decades past.

"Look to Thenill! Her walls still stand, her people free to live as they choose. Yet also consider Dashra, Anica. Their homes burned, their people and army slaughtered almost to the last. There is no victory over the Subjugate. If we just acknowledge their sovereignty over us, we can live on much as we do now. No more war. No more death for the people."

"No, Rovik. Anoth will not trade domination and foreign rule for so-called 'peace.' We are a free people, and we shall fight on to the last as such. Our allies will come, Rovik. We are not yet alone in the war. There is still hope. So long as Anoth stands others will rally to us. Should we kneel they too will bow to the Subjugate. Do you not see?!"

That was what she had said. Anica was so stubborn, so unyielding. And that had been what he had loved about her. Rovik replayed that moment again, and again. What could he have said differently to help her see? Surrender was not defeat—it was survival. Yet, he also knew that no amount of debate nor argument could have changed her mind. If he had only known how close the Mantorahns were, how much of Andohrah's army had survived. But how could he have known that? At the time, all seemed lost and defeat assured. About a month after Ell'Anoth was taken Rovik learned that a massive army had landed by ship from Mantorah and joined forces with large numbers of Andohrase and Taivadean soldiers. They had been a fourthmoon away from Anoth when the Dao'Tai took the city, and upon learning that the city had fallen they disbanded and returned to their homelands. The north had fallen with Anoth's demise.

Coward...

The word echoed in his thoughts almost continually. And in the fleeting moments of honest retrospection, he knew he was. He had been afraid, afraid of a siege, afraid of the Dao'Tai, of death, of the ikthii. Afraid that Anica would never accept her husband's death and choose to be with him. He was still afraid.

A fool's hope! A fool indeed.

Rovik chuckled darkly to himself, accepting that he was both a coward and a fool. No sense in denying it. But what now? Again, he was faced with the knowledge of impending doom for a faultless people. Nothing? After all, he could not stop the Subjugate's mighty army, nor change the mind of Afyreen. Even trying to question her actions could get him swiftly killed, or worse. He knew the ikthii took special pleasures from torture. But what if he was killed? What if he did die trying to do something good, something selfless? Would that tip Brek's coin in his favor? Would that shift Paldrii's rudder toward the heavens and Anthos' halls? Could he be both brave and a coward, both a fool and selfless?

Rovik had no answers for himself, but he did know that this time he could not simply sit by and let the Subjugate's plans roll forth unmarred. He had to act, to do something that would make Anica proud, something that would make himself proud. Something that would make him a little less of a coward. Rovik straightened in the saddle and took a firm grip on the reins of his horse. He would have a lot to do in a short time, and secrecy would be the key. He leaned forward in the stirrups and his horse sped off fast as he could through the throng that still moved in the streets of the city.

***

It was dark, well after midnight, and the cool air stank of human waste and rot. Rovik had taken the greatest of care as he left the palace, ensuring he was unseen and unfollowed. He still was not even sure what he was hoping to accomplish, but he had to find them—*The Sunshadow*. Rovik hoped he could find an agent of the secretive group. He knew from reports of their activities that they often took refuge with the servitude caste in the city. He hoped they might know how to get his knowledge of Afyreen's plans to the right people if he could find them in the scurry. The scurry, as it was now called, had once been a clean and bright quarter of Ell'Anoth. It was mostly populated by the families of the garrison and the tradesmen who outfitted the Anothn army for war. The homes were modest but well cared for, and the small gardens and shops were well kept and pleasant.

It was now the fundamental opposite—a place of disease, filth, and misery. The scurry was still the home of many of the once-defenders of Anoth and their families, now only recognized as the *scur*. The scur were the servitude caste and slaves of the Subjugate. To kill, rape, or mistreat a scur was not a crime in the city. You would have to pay for the scur, but you would not face Subjugate justice. If one wished to take a scur female or wanted a male for a living weapon target, one was free to do so, so long as the current owner was compensated. Those of the scur who had no private owner were the property of the Subjugate, and so the local Dao'Tai officers would have to be compensated for any permanent damage to a scur.

The scurry was ironically about the safest place for them in the city. Thanks to the terrible living conditions, most stayed away from the area. This gave the scur some respite from their oppressors. For the most part the Dao'Tai left the scurry alone on the order of Afyreen. Rovik knew that she recognized their need for their own space if she wished to stave off an organized revolt. The scurry was large, easily a fifth of the city, and it housed many thousands of the scur. Dozens of Dao'Tai watchtowers surrounded the area, and roving foot patrols wandered the streets and alleyways. These Dao'Tai, however, were under strict order not to mistreat the scur, and for the most part they obeyed.

Rovik was carefully peering around a building, trying to see where the guards in the closest watchtower were. Seeing that they were on the far side, he quickly made his way from shadow to shadow across the street and closer to his destination, a tavern located deep in the scurry. Rovik knew that the tavern keeper had been a Sha'Tar in the Anothn army, commanding over a hundred soldiers. If anyone might know how to get a message to the Sunshadow, KaTyle would know.

The tavern had once been barracks. It was a three-storied structure made of stone and large timbers. Part of the third floor had been burned in the sacking of Ell'Anoth, leaving the upper corner of the building crumbled. The scur had not been allowed to repair any damage from the war. The building's narrow windows were shuttered and dark as Rovik drew closer. He walked swiftly up a narrow alleyway to the small back door of the building. He had been here many times before in the past, visiting the barracks often as part of his duties before the fall of the city.

Taking a key from his pocket, he hoped the locks had not been changed. Rovik quickly searched the dark alley for signs of someone watching. He turned the key and the door opened. He was standing in a dark storage room. From the smell, it was serving as an ale cellar. Several huge casks sat in the corners of the room, with several smaller ones tapped and ready. Soft light filtered around a closed door on the far side of the room. Rovik approached carefully, knowing that KaTyle would likely kill him if this didn't go right. To his surprise he could hear hushed voices in the room beyond the closed door. Not knowing what else to do, Rovik cautiously knocked on the door. The speaking stopped and the air hung all too still for a few moments. Rovik knocked again, this time a little louder.

"I'm looking for Sha'Tar KaTyle, I—"

A thick arm shot around Rovik's throat as the door suddenly opened and he found himself dragged by the neck into the room beyond. He knew better than to struggle, but the sudden terror and panic was hard to deny. This was exactly what he was afraid of. They might just kill him out of caution without hearing him. They might also just kill him for who he was. Rough hands quickly searched and found his small dagger and leather pouch. These were removed before the arm was taken from his neck and Rovik fell coughing, sprawled on the well-worn stones of the tavern floor.

"You realize that it is death to speak the old names of the realm?" a voice asked from the corner of the dark room.

"In fact, we would do well to turn you in for speaking them, the reward is no small thing to ones as poor as we."

Rovik turned over and slowly stood up to face two large men. Both wore rough and simple tunics and chausses, and both had stout cudgels tucked in their leather belts. The raised shoulders and harsh expressions served to discourage any brash actions on Rovik's part. Dim light from a wood and skin lantern threw long shadows across what was clearly the main tavern hall. Long tables and benches sat in rows, and a high bar on one side of the wide, low-ceilinged room. The shadowy form of another large man leaned against the farthest corner of the room. Rovik could feel the hot glare of this man, and he again spoke.

"It is either great foolishness or great need that would bring you to my door in the middle of the night."

Rovik straightened his stance and cleared his still-aching throat.

"To be honest, it is both, along with a fair measure of desperation."

From the man's sudden change in posture Rovik had not been the only one surprised by his honesty. KaTyle left the shadows and took a seat at the end of the table nearest to Rovik. He motioned for the other two men to back off before gesturing for Rovik to join him. Rovik sat stiffly on the hard bench, trying to steady his shaking hands under the table.

"Why are you here, Rovik, and why should we not kill you and feed your body to the errvts?" KaTyle's voice was smooth and deathly calm.

Rovik hesitated to answer for a moment. Why shouldn't they kill him? By their estimation, and his own, that was what he deserved.

"I have knowledge, information that can make a difference for thousands of people," he said, careful to school the anxiety in his voice. He was only successful in doing so because of his years of practice in speaking with the Aya Dao'Tai.

KaTyle said nothing and gave a gesture for Rovik to continue.

"The information needs to get outside the city, to those who can use it, but I cannot get such a message to them myself, I am too closely watched. I need help. I need your help, or maybe the help of others that you might know."

KaTyle seemed to relax a bit and he let out a long sigh.

"Tell me everything, Rovik, every little detail, like your life depends on it. Because it absolutely does."

KaTyle's voice was cold and sharp as a sword blade, and Rovik knew without a doubt that he meant every word. So, he started with the details of the attack on Allinth, and explained every aspect of Afyreen's plans, the order of battle, the rumors from the Freeholdn, and what he suspected would happen in the south. It took some time to detail it all, but KaTyle's attention never wavered, nor did he interrupt. He listened as though each word was being chiseled into a stone slab within his mind. When Rovik finished explaining what had finally led him to seek out KaTyle, nearly three hours had passed. KaTyle sat, clearly pondering it all for some time. The room was dreadfully still. Rovik could all but see KaTyle weighing all that had been said against the litany of his past sins. Finally, KaTyle rubbed his eyes and looked up at him.

"Rovik, did you have the spillway gates opened?" A weariness permeated his voice as he asked the question. Rovik took a moment to measure his response, knowing that death might meet him no matter what he said.

I have chosen.

"Yes," Rovik said firmly, and for the first time without any excuse or justification. "I had the spillway opened."

KaTyle looked him hard in the eye and Rovik did not look away. He wanted—hoped—that somehow KaTyle would see the anguish this knowledge left within Rovik.

"Very well," KaTyle said flatly as he stood and walked to the bar. Rovik watched, still not daring to move as KaTyle poured himself a mug of ale and drank it in a few gulps. He wiped his mouth and short gray beard with his apron before rejoining Rovik at the table. By now the other two men were both sitting at the bar, still carefully watching Rovik's every move.

"I can get this information to the people you are seeking, but I want to know that you are committed to the right side this time, Rovik. I want to know you would die for your people this time."

"How? What can I do to prove this to you?" Rovik desperately wanted to prove it to himself as well.

KaTyle smiled and chuckled dryly to himself.

"You can get my sister out of the Subjugate's hands."

20

Mountains to Plains

S *trive with all your vigor to build a bulwark of wisdom within yourself that the falsities of the fool do not cause you to stumble onto mournful paths. The Fates hold no kindness for they who sin out of ignorance. Wield your agency with prudence and deliberateness.*
Essays of the Divine

Everything ached—legs, back, arms, shoulders, and a pounding head—everything begging for rest. The horse's labored breathing and staggering gait told of its fatigue as well.

I can't believe how far we've come, Ralenn thought as he adjusted his weight in the stirrups for the thousandth time. The leather groaned, as did he, stretching his sore legs and standing in the saddle. It still hurt, but at least it was in a different area. For countless hours, Ralenn had been going back and forth from standing, sitting, and leading his horse at a steady quick pace. Every option he had was painful, and his mind and body yearned for rest and sleep. There was yet no rest to be had, not till their goal was in sight.

He looked back to Lirah. She noticed his eye and smiled warmly, if not a little sleepily at him. She seemed to still be bearing their rushed journey with little physical toll. Kaileth and Riidak held their place toward the front of the party with the Tundraihn, with Mirris flying overhead. The road they traveled down made its winding course to the northwest, and by mid-morning the mountains were turning into purple silhouettes on the eastern horizon.

The troop of Tundraihn warriors moved at a steady jogging pace, causing Ralenn to regularly coax his mount up to a canter to catch up with them. He was not sure how long his horse could keep up, they had neither stopped nor slackened their pace. The Tundraihn did not seem to tire at all. In fact, Ralenn thought they were actually starting to speed up. He was not used to riding very much at all. In Allinth there was no need to ride. Only traders and messengers who left the mountain village rode very far. Ralenn slowed his pace and let his horse rest. Soon Lirah pulled up next to him.

"Lirah, are you doing alright?" he asked.

She looked up at him from the road. "Yes, I'm alright, but my legs are getting a bit worn out." She paused. "And my bottom is getting really sore," she whispered, not wanting everyone to overhear.

"Same here. I can't believe how long these people can move like this! Any man would have given out long ago." They both slowed their pace and quickly were left at a distance from the rest of the party.

"Strictly speaking they are not any man, they are not even humans..." she answered, but her words trailed off.

"Lirah, when we first saw them at the falls you called them Pali'andeo. What does that mean?" Ralenn asked. They had not really talked much since their conversation the day before. He hoped now that some conversation would also take their minds from their current discomfort.

"Oh, it was part of a legend I remember the priests telling me when I was little," Lirah said thoughtfully.

"What was the legend?" Ralenn's curiosity was piqued now.

"It is long, and I don't remember it all. It is one of the origin epics. They are a large set of stories and the oldest of legends compiled into a single chronological tome. Gaileng was very proud of his copy of it. As proud as he was of anything, that is. He said he had to travel to all the Anthosn temples in the realms to compile it. Even the one near the Dark Realms. But basically, it starts a very long time ago, when Anthos and the Aashahl made Miljah, the heavens, and all that was in them. There were lots of Aashahl then. They liked to walk Miljah and enjoy what they helped create. Over time other living things were made by Anthos, like men. Anyhow, a bunch of the Aashahl fell in love with some of the people that Anthos had made to live on Miljah"

"Wait, you mean something powerful and magical as an Aashahl fell in love with mortals? Is that possible?" Ralenn interrupted.

"I don't know Ralenn. Love does strange things to people, and apparently the Aashahl are also subject to its power. Anyway, it's just a legend, so who knows how much is true?

"Right, what happened next then?"

"So, these Aashahl wanted their mates and children to live with them forever as immortals in paradise."

"But that would never work, surely?" Ralenn again interrupted questioningly.

"I would tell you if you would let me," Lirah said with mock exasperation.

"Sorry," he said sheepishly.

"Good. So, like I said, these Aashahl wanted their mortal companions and children to live with them forever. They brought them to the heavens and tried to hide them from Anthos and the other Aashahl; others still hid them on Miljah, but they of course were found out. They were taken and a council was held to decide their fate for bringing mortal kindreds into heaven and mixing the blood of the Aashahl with the created. Many of the other Aashahl wanted them banished and their mates and children killed.

"Anthos, however, saw their hearts and had mercy on them. He gave them a choice: either be banished from the heavens forever to live a life with their mortal companions, or they would have to relinquish their ability to visit Miljah and the mortals would be sent back without them. Should they keep their divine powers they would never see or be with their mortal loves again. Should they choose exile they would also have to give up most, if not all of their powers, and possibly their immortality along with it."

"What did they do?" Ralenn asked. He could not help his curiosity; he felt like he had when Epri told him stories as a child.

"They chose to forsake heaven and their powers to stay with their beloved companions. So, they were exiled from heaven and given the name of Pali'andeo, I think it means fallen one, or fallen from heaven, or something. Anthos took most of their powers, yet some were retained. They were so intrinsically imbued with the arcane power that even Anthos could not fully strip them without also un-making them. Still, they were greatly diminished and forever exiled from their home with Anthos and their Aashahl siblings. As time went on the Pali'andeo experienced both the joy and bitterness of living in a mortal world. They had children, and the Pali'andeo became peoples after their own kind. They were supposedly a very exotic, powerful people, having inherited some of the diluted attributes of their Aashahl ancestors. Some became nations and founded realms, and others were wilder and populated the untamed corners of the world.

As more time passed and the Pali'andeo increased in numbers, a few of the Aashahl thought this punishment was not harsh enough, and it infuriated them. They sought to destroy the children of the Pali'andeo, and so they inspired hatred between their descendants. Wars erupted between the different Pali'andeo races. Fear of the power of the Pali'andeo caused the mortal kindreds to also start wars, and for a time fear and chaos covered the land. Some of the Pali'andeo races were almost exterminated. Others resolved their differences and ended the strife. The kindreds that were still led by the original Pali'andeo, and fallen Aashahl, eventually met in counsel, recognizing the hand of another Aashahl in the chaos and wars. They made a pact to stop the bloodshed and give the mortal kindreds a wide berth, so to speak. They also banded together against the kindreds of the Dark

Realms, besieging them for thousands of years." Lirah blew out a long whistling breath.

"There is a lot more, but anyhow supposedly most of the ancient, magical, and long-lived beings you've heard of are the Pali'andeo or their descendants, called the andeo. The Akarii, Ilysh, eastern giants, Shedim—all the creatures and people like that are supposedly andeo. Except the Atha'Tarrii and the spirits of Miljah and nature, they are different. Divas are something else too. It is sort of confusion and possibly mostly myth as well." She shrugged.

"That is what I remember from the tome. I only read over it a few times. It was very detailed, but all those things happened at the beginning of the world, so it is hard to say how accurate it is." She paused and took a drink of water from a nearly empty water skin.

"The Tundraihn are a lot like the descriptions of one of the races descended from the Pali'andeo, from the Aashahl Syrnii specifically. I just assumed they were a myth, but Gaileng had me learn a bit about them regardless. He said they were creatures who were tied to magic and the powers of the arcane in ways that humans could not be, and that I could learn much about the arcane from their stories and legends whether they were real or not." Lirah finished with her tale and looked up to find Ralenn staring at her.

"And you said that you didn't remember much!"

"Well, I don't! There was a lot more that Gaileng tried to teach me, but I didn't pay enough attention. It all seemed so ancient and...and too colossal and great for me," she said, looking down at her hands.

"Too great for *you*, Lirah? Do you remember the things you've done since we left home? You seem to have more power than the Tundraihn healer, and according to you he's some descendant of an Aashahl! So, I think you are colossal enough."

Lirah laughed pleasantly, "You're calling me colossal?"

"That didn't come out right." He felt his face flush.

"It's alright, I understand what you meant, Ralenn." They smiled at each other and laughed again. Soon Ralenn's horse started to breathe irregularly. He slowed further and gave the horse its head.

"I fear my horse is totally exhausted," he said worriedly. "Lame, even."

"I'll stay with you, then," Lirah said.

The two slowed their horses' paces to a near stop. Within a few minutes and after a few turns on their path, the band of warriors, along with Kaileth, were out of sight.

"Now what, Ralenn? What if they leave the trail?"

"Their tracks should be easy enough to follow," Ralenn said, trying to sound reassuring. But truthfully, he was concerned that their speed of travel would make the point irrelevant. They both dismounted and slowly led their horses for a while. Their fatigued mounts plodded along, following the trail as they walked in silence. Thankfully tracking the Tundraihn became unnecessary, for they soon caught up to them. They had stopped by the side of a slow-moving stream.

Jayle was checking the shoes on his horse, and Kaileth had dismounted and was kneeling by the streamside with Mirris close by. The Tundraihn were also quenching their thirst and cooling their feet. Riidak was in the shallows of the water and looked very pleased to be there. The sound of the cool water churning around smooth stone at the stream's edge sounded as welcoming as an old friend's laughter to them both. It was now getting close to the heat of the day, and they needed water and a break from the saddle. Soon they all were resting their feet and horses by the cool water. As Ralenn was lying in a soft patch of grass and ferns, a shadow fell over him, and Mirris swooped down and lit on the earth close by him. Lirah had both her feet in the stream as she leaned back and watched Mirris approach.

"Of all the times I wished I could fly, Mirris, this is one of the greatest." Lirah laughed a bit, rubbing her backside as the great bird quenched her thirst in the refreshing stream. Ralenn relaxed further on the soft grass and closed his eyes for a moment. He let his mind drift. Suddenly something slammed into his shoulder.

"Ralenn, wake up!" Lirah was giggling as she spoke. "We are getting ready to go."

"And why is that funny?" He stretched, realizing he had fallen asleep.

"It's funny because you were snoring."

Ralenn looked around at those near as he spoke. "I was?"

Jayle nodded. "Make of a good soldier, that. Sleep where and when you can, lad. A rest I am sure you earned, but come, we must be off."

Few words were spoken among the group as they had rested, and not even an hour was fully spent as they continued their march. The weariness had only just left Ralenn's body as he slid back into his saddle, and he dreaded the return to it. With Kaileth leading now their course took them in a more westerly direction for several hours, and by midafternoon the lay of the land had quite changed from the slopes and forests of the mountainous bluffs. All around them was now green headlands, spotted here and there with thickets of brush and a few squat trees. The trail of the Srellites was easy to follow in the tall grass by the waterside. They crossed a brook at a shallow ford and picked up the trail of their quarry on the other side, heading more northwesterly now. The trampled path in the grassy turf seemed to stretch on forever into the distance as the sun began to sink into the far western horizon.

The Tundraihn's pace had slowed now, whether due to weariness or for caution's sake, Ralenn was not sure. But they did not seem fatigued. Ralenn and Lirah both dismounted again and walked with their horses alongside Riidak and Mirris, who was now atop Riidak's shoulders. Kaileth was still with Orodan at the front. On and on the troop marched, their pace never slower than an uncomfortably swift walk. The land started to slope downhill eventually, and soon stars could be seen taking their place in the sky. Hours passed, and Ralenn and Lirah were once again in the saddle riding quietly side by side.

It had been a warm day, and the speed of their travel had made the heat seem worse. Now that the sun was in total retreat, a gentle breeze began to bend the grass and cool the weary travelers. Ralenn was spent. Each fall of the horse hoof was just enough of a shock to keep him from falling asleep where he sat. Sores had opened on his body from the saddle, and blisters covered his feet from the turns he took walking. His eyes burned and his body ached for sleep. They had not stopped for rest since the stream. His water skins were empty again. If Lirah was half as hungry, thirsty, and worn out as he was, then they would both need to take a long break soon.

He looked at Lirah; she seemed tired, but not dreadfully weary. She had seemed almost fully rested after the pause by the stream. Ralenn did not fully understand what an arcane healer was versus an empathic healer, but he was certain that Lirah had changed after the fight at the falls. Based upon their lifestyles back in Allinth, Ralenn should have been the hardier of the two, and not just because he was a male. He spent countless hours on his feet working at the forge, training with Kaileth or running after swift game in the mountains. Though Lirah did often join him, she had also spent many hours studying books in the temple. She was never slow nor easily tired when they went together to hunt and explore the mountains, but not like this.

"Ralenn," Lirah's voice was barely audible over the fall of horse hooves.

"We have traveled further today then I have ever traveled in my whole life. I never thought I would go so far from home." She sounded tired but cheerful.

"I am sure we have. We must be getting close to the great bend in the Vryl'Bahn River, the one by Ell'Anoth."

Ralenn could remember well the tattered map that Kaileth had kept in his room. Many times, as a child, he found himself staring at it, imagining all the great people that must be in the vast lands wrought with ink upon the map's surface. Ell'Anoth had often been the focus of his daydreams, the city looked so grand on the map. It seemed to make more sense now, all of his childhood daydreaming, and the strange lure that part of the map had. Ralenn was now closer to that city than he had ever thought he would be, and he found himself dreading it. Within that city were the echoes of a past that he was still coming to grips with.

"Ralenn, look!" Lirah whispered nervously.

Her voice recalled him from his thoughts. "What?"

"Look up there, there are lights!"

Ralenn peered into the night and saw a light on the horizon.

"It must be the camp." Ralenn realized he must have been lost in his memory for an awfully long time. Judging from the position of the moon, it was now some hours past midnight.

The grass was tall here, all the way past Riidak's back and clear up to the belly of Ralenn's horse. The presence of reeds and other wetland vegetation signaled that the river must be close.

"Lia'ti freath tä allitor adai ti dridres shea'jul, ti akah'dri."

Neither Ralenn nor Lirah had heard Ealë's approach, but she now stood close. Ealë smiled up at Lirah, then turned a flat expression to Ralenn before returning to the shadows of the tall grass.

"What did she say?" Ralenn questioned.

"Kaileth wants us to dismount, I think we need to be quick about it too."

Once off their mounts, the height of the grass and reeds effectively hid the lights of the camp from their view.

"Lirah, I didn't know you understood Tundraihn."

"What do you mean? I don't," Lirah whispered in reply.

"That warrior, she spoke to you in their language. I didn't understand a word of it."

"No, she...she was speaking in Tundraihn?" Lirah stammered a little as she spoke

"Yes, it sounded beautiful, but totally unintelligible." Ralenn watched Lirah's face carefully as he spoke.

"You understood her, didn't you?"

Lirah paused for a while as they walked together through the grass. "Yes, I did. I heard and understood her just as easily as I do you now."

"But how is that possible without having learned their language?" Ralenn was confused.

"I think I know how, but it is hard to explain." Lirah looked up into the starry sky. Ralenn could see tears threatening in her eyes and her breath was shallow and fast. She kept clenching and unclenching her fists. Ralenn worried he hit a nerve with something he said.

"At the falls, I felt a connection to Ealë, and the other Tundraihn. Like when I heal someone, but it was different. I was able to understand their songs, and I guess I still have enough of a connection to Ealë to understand her words..."

"You guess?" Ralenn questioned.

"That is all I can do, Ralenn. I don't understand what is happening to me at all. I am trying not to lose my grip and come apart over it." Her frustration was easy to hear.

"I'm sorry, Lirah, I just want to understand so I can help you. So I can be there for you. Remember, we can get through this together. I still think so, no matter what struggles we deal with inside or outside ourselves."

"I know, it just is too much too fast. Right now, I just want to get through this without losing my mind, then we can pause and search for the why and how. I just need you to not treat me like I'm different, or someone you don't know. Please, no matter what happens I need you to treat me just as Lirah, simple Lirah from Allinth. Can you do that?" Her voice was pleading and the threat of tears in her eyes grew.

"I can, Lirah, I promise." She smiled and took his hand tightly in hers.

"Thank you, that is all I need, I think." She gave his hand a squeeze and slowly let it slip from her grasp. They still followed the foot-carved path through the plain as it gradually sloped upward. It was soon apparent that they were headed up a steep rise in the earth, like the backside of an abrupt ridge. Ralenn put his head down and trudged up the hill till he almost bumped into several Tundraihn standing before him. He looked up and saw the whole company had stopped at the crest of the ridge that ran in a half circle, forming a border around the large, dish-shaped lowland below.

On the far western side of the lowland plain, atop low cliffs, shone the lights of a large city. In the plain before them, many fires and lights illuminated a labyrinth of tents, wooden structures, adobe, and stone buildings of all manner of shapes and architecture. The collection of buildings continued all the way to the banks of the river to the north and west. At the center of this hodgepodge of structures, an immense arena had been carved into the bank of the river where it bent from its southerly course and headed west toward the ocean. The bend in the Vryl'Bahn River formed the eastern and southern border of the city of Ell'Anoth and divided it from the Taiw'Tai Fortress to the east and the slavers camp to the southeast. Ralenn made his way to where Kaileth stood and whispered anxiously.

"Is that the...slavers' camp?"

"Yes. At least it started as a camp, but as you can see it is a city now. A horrid city, where men can indulge in the excess of all their lusts."

Ralenn was bewildered at the sprawl of buildings before him.

"I had no idea it would be so...large," he said slowly.

"Don't worry, we are not going to attack the entire camp. Stealth will be the better course here," he reassured. Lirah came up next to them.

"That place is massive, Kaileth, how are we going to find one person in there?"

Kaileth let a determined smile streak across his face.

"There is only one place they would take Tundraihn in there, we only have to devise how we will get in without commotion and then get out without being discovered." Orodan stood nearby listening as Kaileth continued.

"First we need to get in sight of the main gate and observe the entry and security measures. That will dictate how we get in. If memory serves, there is a place we might hide, yet also be able to see the gates."

Kaileth looked to Orodan who simply nodded in approval.

"Perhaps we should have brought more men from my company; should a fight break out we will be hard-pressed to escape." Jayle spoke with a hardness, and Ralenn had the distinct impression he'd seen too many battles go poorly.

"We will avoid such a fight at all costs. I think a way will be opened to us if we are not overly hasty and plan well our actions. Come, let us leave this high place and find the gates."

No one spoke further as the company slipped off the ridge, following Kaileth toward a large grove of trees. The grass on this side of the hill was even taller, and soon the stars were difficult to see overhead. Lirah stuck close behind Ralenn and Kaileth. She felt both excited and nervous as they drew closer to the lights of the camp. Her mind was trying to make sense of so many people in such a large place. Allinth had been the only village she had ever been to, and to see such a massive city truly astonished her. Her excitement was interrupted by a sudden horrible smell. Her stomach churned and she quickly pulled the front of her frock up and over her mouth and nose. The sweet fragrance of Ealë's soap came just in time to stave off a gagging retch. Several of the others were coughing and gagging on the smell around her. The Tundraihn quickly tied cloths over their faces in an effort to stifle the smell.

"Kaileth, what is that awful stench?" Lirah's muffled voice asked.

"That would be the cesspools from the city. All the filth, dead bodies, and the like from the slavers' camp is washed out into them. The stench won't be as strong inside, I think."

Apparently, people don't have a sense of smell here, thought Lirah. Soon they started into the grove of trees and the smell waned enough that Lirah took the cloth from her face. The trees were short but thick with strange stringy leaves, more like thick knotted hair that hung in sprawling clumps from the spindly mess of branches. However odd the vegetation was, it did serve to obscure all the lights from the slaver camp and the stars above, completely hiding the company from any unfriendly eyes. Lirah took a guarded deep breath and the last of the Tundraihn entered the trees.

"Rest quietly here," Kaileth whispered to Lirah and Ralenn. "Orodan, let us take a look further on near the gates." Orodan agreed and the two of them quietly disappeared into the thick vegetation. The trees had a salty smell about them that thankfully smothered some of the stench that drifted from the nearby slavers' camp. Ralenn plopped down on the spongy ground with an exhausted sigh. Jayle sat nearby.

"Best catch another nap while we can. This could be the only rest we have for a while again." The knight spoke with a hint of fatherly concern.

"I won't argue with that advice, sire. I won't be worth much in a fight, tired as I am now."

"Aye, that is the life of soldiering at times. March till you are ready to drop, stealing rest where you can. Though I must admit this run has me spent as I have not been for years." Without another word Jayle leaned back against a stumpy tree and closed his eyes. In seconds he started to snore slightly, and his breathing slowed. Ralenn closed his eyes as well.

Lirah watched as he relaxed and drifted off to sleep. She could feel his exhaustion if she focused on him. He was right, his body was spent and would not be much use in a fight. After making sure he was asleep she carefully drew near and took his hand. It was cold and clammy. Trying not to wake him Lirah opened her mind and found the latent power in the earth around her. It was not the same as the falls. It felt more distant, almost asleep. It took some effort and concentration to draw upon it. Yet after several moments of focusing she began to draw strength into herself. The rejuvenating flow pushed her fatigue aside and invigorated her mind. Now feeling more in tune with the land she began to push the restorative pulses into Ralenn.

Minutes passed and soon his hand felt warm in hers. She let go and opened her eyes. Ealë was standing over her, watching. Before Lirah could speak she left quickly, walking off and into the thick trees around them. Her expression was hard to read. Lirah let go of Ralenn's hand and performed the same restoration on Jayle before she found a place to sit down nearby. She leaned up against a soft grassy rise in the earth and tried to relax and rest. Tyllidus approached, but Lirah was not in the mood to talk to anyone. Though she felt perfectly fine physically she was tired emotionally and needed some time to herself. She quickly closed her eyes and feigned sleep.

The Tundraihn healer stood for a time and watched her. Lirah could feel his eyes on her and was tempted to reach out to him and connect with her newfound powers, yet she did not feel the same closeness that she had felt with Ealë and the other females at the falls. Before she realized it, he was gone. Lirah kept her eyes closed until sleep truly did find her.

21

Two Fools' Gambits'

*I*n time of harvest make your obeisance doubly so to Dannitar and they of her house that your works might be consecrated in her sight and for your sake.

Essays of the Divine

Kaileth peered through the thick vegetation trying to make out the shapes in the haze before him. He could hear the slow steady breathing of Orodan close by, though he could not see him through the grass and shrubs that they both were lying in. They had slowly crawled for a significant distance before the undergrowth beneath the squat trees thinned enough to make out the outline of the palisade and earthwork wall that surrounded the slavers' camp. Once they could see the walls they continued to crawl slowly and quietly until the gates were visible. A thick fog hung in the air, and from the smell Kaileth deemed that it was mostly smoke and fumes from the bathhouses inside the camp. Orange light spilled through small gaps in the palisade walls, throwing plumes of light fitfully about in the gloom. In this light he could see many guards. Kaileth knew from their rudimentary armor and weapons that they were soldiers of the In-Kind Mercantile. A powerful merchant guild organization that had shifted a large part of their trade to slavery under the Subjugate. Nearly a dozen of them were standing near the gates and in the low towers that flanked the gate.

"This place is larger than I had thought, and full of potential foes. I do not think a group such as ours will be allowed in, nor would it be wise to fight our way in," said Orodan in a hushed whisper.

"There could be another way," Kaileth proposed. "Perhaps the river; there is no wall there, and we could slip in unnoticed."

"Yes, but should a battle arise upon our discovery, it would put the ones we seek in great danger without a swift escape. We cannot take that risk," Orodan said.

Kaileth knew he was right and watched the gates, thinking in silence for a time. There was only one gate, and many soldiers within the place. Kaileth knew that though they might be able to sneak into the city via the river, they would not be able to get out that way without the possibility of a fight. Should a band of warriors such as Orodan's be discovered, the Subjugate army would be called before they would escape.

Presently, a small group of people and horses approached the gates. As they neared, Kaileth and Orodan heard raised voices, and soon a few guards from the gates left the palisade and approached the newcomers. After a few moments, the guards inspected the people whom Kaileth could now see were chained together. A swift inspection followed, then the troop of prisoners and their captors were allowed into the camp. Kaileth looked to Orodan, and his expression confirmed that he was having the same thoughts. They both carefully started the long slow crawl back to the others to finalize their plans.

Lirah awoke to Jayle's firm hand on her shoulder.

"Miss Lirah, Kaileth is back. There are plans to be made."

She sat up and rubbed the sleep from her eyes. Yawning, she looked up at the sky. Dim stars still glittered here and there, but the morning was not far off.

I must have been out for hours, she thought as she stretched her stiff limbs. Ralenn was already up and looked to be very much physically renewed due to her discreet ministrations. She smiled to herself as he waved for her to join him and the circle of others he stood near. Orodan, Kaileth, Jayle, and a few of the other Tundraihn now stood in a circle. They were all talking quietly. As Lirah approached, they stopped and regarded her for an uneasy moment. Kaileth finally spoke.

"Miss Lirah, we believe we have a plan to enter the camp without a fight or alarm."

"That's great, Kail! What are we going to do?"

Ralenn gave him a hard look and folded his arms. Lirah could not help but notice his sour expression. Her excitement was building, and quickly. This would be different than the panicked horror of the fight at the falls. She could feel it. This morning would entail stealth and deception. Her mind danced with anticipation at helping the people in the slaver camp, saving the Tundraihn priestess and other such deeds. Kaileth's voice drew her focus back.

"We have watched several groups enter the camp. At the gates, the guards inspect the captives being brought to the camp, and the bands we watched were then allowed to enter. They all had female prisoners or men of sound body. If we array some of our band in like manner, we should be able to enter the camp as well."

"So, all we need to do is make it look like we are slavers and we sneak into the city," she said, the anticipation building once more.

"Precisely, as the only non-Tundraihn males—myself, Jayle, and Ralenn—could pose as slavers. We would then take you and a few of the Tundraihn as slaves and enter the city. Too many Tundraihn would attract unwanted attention."

Lirah could tell Kaileth was searching her face for a reaction. As he continued, she tried to remain as stoic as she could.

"Once we are inside, we will stealthily discover the location of the Tundraihn captives and then carefully sneak out of the camp."

"I am still not sure we will be able to leave the way we came in. The guards are sure to question us leaving with more slaves than we entered with," Jayle said thoughtfully.

"True, and a fight near the gates would bring the nearby slaver garrison upon us," added Orodan.

"What about the river then? Could we escape that way?" asked Ralenn.

"We could. However, should we be discovered during the escape we would be lethally exposed in the water," Kaileth replied seriously.

"My people could cover the escape from the other side of the river. We could also have some of the scouts swim across and lie in wait to protect you as you made for the water," Orodan said.

"There is also a fishing village on the river near here. With care you could find and use several of the fishing boats. It would hasten our escape." Kaileth sounded confident. Everyone stood quietly for a moment, each pondering the planned infiltration and escape.

"I do not think we will devise a better plan," said Jayle at length. "Least, not in time for it to be of any good for the ones in that camp."

"Let us prepare swiftly while the sky is still dark," Kaileth added.

Orodan and the other Tundraihn agreed and they quickly set out to prepare. Kaileth, Lirah, and Ralenn stood together for a time.

"Lirah, are you sure you want to come with us?" Ralenn asked quietly. She immediately felt her ire rise at what his question implied.

"And why wouldn't I? I've come with you this far, haven't I?" Lirah shot him a fierce glare.

"I know, it is just that I am not sure—"

Lirah cut him off, trembling with a sudden hot anger.

"Not sure, what? Not sure I can handle myself in there? Not sure I can keep up with you?"

Kaileth watched with an amused expression as Lirah continued to berate Ralenn for a short time.

"Who has kept you alive? Kaileth too? You might be the one with the ancient armor and hero's sword, but I can hold my own, Ralenn." Kaileth interrupted before she could really get going, though.

"I would not underestimate her, Ralenn. Out of the three of us, Miss Lirah has needed the least tending to. I think she has proved to be the hardiest of us all. That wound from the falls would have killed either one of us. Yet, here Miss Lirah is. We will need her skills inside that place, I am sure of it. Who knows the state of the captives? Lirah could be the only way to get them on their feet."

"I just don't want you to feel like you have to go into that awful place just because we are. That's all. I know we would not even be here if it weren't for you, Lirah. And we have no right to place you in danger again and again."

Lirah stopped and glared for a moment longer. She had reacted sharply, she knew, but why had she? She searched her emotions, trying to put her finger one what really had set her off.

They can't leave me behind. They are all I have left. I have to keep them safe.

The realization that her fear of losing Kaileth or Ralenn was the true source of her anger calmed her some, though she still knew that Ralenn didn't fully understand how close to death he and Kaileth both had been. Nor did they really understand what changes Lirah had been facing in herself. Her connection to Miljah, others—whatever it was, was hard for her to comprehend, let alone explain to anyone.

How long will you see me as just a little girl, with scraped knees from playing in the woods? We have grown up, Ralenn. Lirah felt the flush drain from her cheeks. She relaxed her shoulders with a sigh.

"Ralenn, I will be fine. We are all going in together, and I am not helpless."

"I know, Lirah, it's just...I worry about keeping you safe after the fight back at the falls. You are alright, but you nearly died. You kind of did die, or at least got caught between life and death. It took an act that I would have thought only the Aashahl themselves could do to keep you alive. What if something like that happens again? Will you be able to un-die again?"

Lirah hesitated for a moment. Would she be able to do that again? She felt, just a little, for the connection to the life force around her. *There it is.*

"Yes, I think I can, Ralenn. But this isn't going to be an open fight. You don't have to protect me."

"Physical danger aside, Miss Lirah, there will be sights and things in that den that no young lady should have to witness, I am sure," Kaileth added.

"But it would be better if I came, wouldn't it? More convincing to the guards if I am one of the captives, wouldn't it, Kail?"

"Yes, and I am also certain that we will need your healing abilities when we find the Tundraihn priestess."

Just the thought of people needing her aid filled her with a consuming urge to help. Like it was a compulsion not wholly her own. It was strong enough that Lirah was frightened a little at the intensity. Yet, with this feeling came a surety that there were people in that camp that she could help. People only she could save.

"It's settled, then. I guess you will just have to accept that I refuse to be left behind." Lirah gave Ralenn a solid elbow in his ribs as she spoke.

"As often as you need a healer, I am surprised you would dare do anything without me on hand." She smirked and started toward her horse, feeling Ralenn's eyes on her.

"She will be safe, Ralenn, safe as any of us will be," Kaileth said reassuringly.

"That is what bothers me, Kail; none of us are safe. We are about to sneak into the heart of the slavers guild to rescue a Tundraihn priestess. We are only a few dozen skain from the Aya herself."

"We will get through this, Ralenn, we will stay together, and we will make it out of the camp." Kaileth sounded very sure, and Ralenn took some comfort from his confidence. "Go, get ready and make our mounts ready. I need to give Orodan directions to the village." Ralenn walked over to where Lirah seemed to be examining herself thoughtfully.

"Well, I guess I need to look like a slave girl, huh?" Lirah said as she looked on her attire.

She seemed less annoyed with him now, so he decided to press his luck.

"Are you completely sure you want to go through with this? What if something goes wrong and you get caught in there, or worse?" Ralenn tried to not let the worry through in his voice.

"Then it will be *your* turn to save *me*." She smiled and started to take off her cloak, belt, and frock.

"Do you want me to go while you get ready?" asked Ralenn, not wanting to make her uncomfortable.

"No, you are alright for now." Lirah was now trying to rip a hole in her skirt.

"I actually think I need your help," she said, holding out the hem of her skirt. "Here, can you make some tears in my blouse and skirt? Make it look like I tried to get away, but my clothing was caught or something."

Ralenn came closer, knelt at her feet, and took hold of the soft cloth of Lirah's skirt.

"How large of a rip do you think?"

"Pretty big. I need to look convincingly tattered."

Ralenn took hold of the cloth and ripped up toward her waist but stopped after only a few inches.

"Oh, come on, Ralenn, I know you are stronger than that." She placed her hand about halfway down her thigh. "Here, tear it up to here, alright?"

"Alright," he replied and ripped the cloth to where she had indicated, exposing her tight-fitting leggings. He blushed a little, but Lirah took no notice.

"Perfect! Tear a few more down at the bottom, and a few on my blouse, and I should look the part!" Lirah said. He took the skirt and ripped it in a few more places, then stood and tore a few smaller spots in her blouse as directed by Lirah. She looked down at their work and smiled.

"There, that looks good."

She now took her braided hair and let it down. It took some time to undo the delicate work of the Tundraihn's hands.

"I will have to ask Ealë to teach you how they braided my hair. I really like how they did it. Here, help me with these."

Lirah placed several of the intricate braids of her hair into Ralenn's hands and they both set to undoing them. Soon a cascade of copper-brown fell in waves as her hair flowed to her slender waist. Ralenn was struck by how pleasant her hair smelled, an exotic flowery scent, alluring but also curious somehow on Lirah. As she finished picking apart the last braid, he looked at her, realizing that she was different somehow. *They* were different. He couldn't say what, but something had started to change between them, maybe it had already changed, and he was catching up. He had always cared for her. They had been friends all their lives. This feeling was more. More intense, more specific than general friendship. She was still his best friend and at the same time he felt that she was more of a mystery than ever before. Lirah stooped and took some earth in her hands and smudged it on her face and arms. Finally, she took her hair with her hands and tossed it around a bit to give it a distressed look.

"That should do it," she remarked. She pulled a bit more hair in front of her face and peered through it, placing her hands out as if she was ready to be chained in a dungeon.

"Please, don't sell me, sir," she said with a half-smirk on her face.

"You look the part, but I don't think that smile will convince the guards. You are having too much fun with this," Ralenn admonished. But he couldn't help but smile back at her eagerness to assume her role in the plan and her relentless cheerfulness.

"Don't worry," she said. "I will seem upset when it's time. I am just excited; we are going to save a Tundraihn princess!"

"Priestess actually, who is in the middle of a slaver fortress filled with evil men."

"Alright, mister gloom, I will be careful when we go in there, alright?" She moved her hair from in front of her face and stood thinking for a moment. She looked over her finely made boots and leggings.

"I don't think my captors would let me keep such nice things," Lirah said as she began to unlace her tall leather boots. With the boots off, Lirah started to slip off her leggings, the dim light running up her shapely thighs and down the curved muscles of her calves. Ralenn blushed and turned away, leaning against a nearby tree. With all the tears in her skirts and blouse there was not much covering her legs and chest. She seemed oblivious to how much of her body was exposed.

"You clearly spent too much time with the Tundraihn at the falls." Ralenn said over his shoulder. Lirah giggled in response, throwing a boot at his back.

"So you were peeping at us then!" She laughed back at him.

Now turned, Ralenn could see Orodan, Tyllidus, and the Tundraihn second-in-command Kyleeal were having an intense discussion. Tyllidus seemed very upset, especially so, for what Ralenn had seen of their kind in the last few days. Tyllidus stormed off, leaving Orodan and Kyleeal shaking their heads. They spoke for a moment longer before Kyleeal started leading the Tundraihn host out of the glade.

"Best hurry, Lirah, I think the others are about ready to go."

"I'm done now!" Lirah called. "How do I look?"

Ralenn came from behind the tree and stopped to look at Lirah. The glittering light from the moon and stars sparkled upon her smooth skin as she stood barefoot, wearing only her short tattered skirt and her blouse that was now torn off a few inches above the top of her skirt. Ralenn could not help but stare. Her flowing hair fell about the enticing curves of her freckled shoulders and on down toward the tight form of her bare waist and legs. Her laughter caught him by surprise.

"Do I really look that bad?" she asked. "You're making an interesting face."

"Oh, no, I was just thinking..." Ralenn's words trailed off.

"Thinking what?"

Ralenn could feel his cheeks flush red and was grateful for the darkness.

"I was just thinking how pretty you look in the starlight," he blurted out.

Lirah laughed out loud. "That was not exactly what I was going for, but at least I should sell for a good price, right?"

"You would, but we aren't going to let them sell you. We just need to find the Tundraihn priestess."

"I know, Ralenn. I know you won't let anything happen to me." She placed her hand on his shoulder reassuringly.

"Are you two ready?" Kaileth asked, approaching them in the darkness.

Lirah and Ralenn turned about as he walked up to them, followed close behind by Orodan, Ealë, Jayle, and two other Tundraihn.

"Yes, we're ready," said Ralenn hurriedly as he took a step away from Lirah.

"Miss Lirah, you look the part very well," Kaileth said approvingly.

"Why, thank you," Lirah said cheerfully. "I just hope the guards will buy it." Kaileth gave her a nod of affirmation.

"I fully expect they will," reasoned Jayle. "This is a good plan, we'll push our way through any hick-ups, I am sure."

Orodan and his soldiers had also made themselves look like war-taken thralls, with their armor gone and clothing torn.

"It has been decided that myself, Ealë, Irem, and Shytov will assume the guise of thralls," Orodan stated. Ealë and Irem were barefoot, with all of their armor and most of their clothing gone, leaving only a small covering for the chest and waist. Ealë looked like someone had hit her a few times in the face, giving her a cut lip and eyebrow. Shytov and Orodan were just as battered and exposed, both wearing only a covering about their waist.

"Seeing as you are of the same race as the ones we seek, we should be taken to where the other Tundraihn are." Jayle said with a nod of approval.

"I believe that will be the case," Kaileth said. "Now we need to tie your war gear to Miss Lirah's horse, and then you five will need to be tied together."

As Kaileth spoke he handed Ralenn a coiled rope and gestured for him to begin to tie his comrades together. Ralenn bound Orodan first, then Shytov, Ealë, Irem, and Lirah last. By the time Ralenn finished, Kaileth had Lirah's horse prepared. Jayle was already mounted, and he took the lead rope that was tied to Orodan's neck. Kaileth and Ralenn also mounted their horses. Kaileth rode close to Jayle, with Ralenn in the rear behind Lirah. The rest of the Tundraihn had already left for the fishing village, so there were no farewells to make. Kaileth led the little troop from the grove of brush and trees. It did not take long to reach the road that led down to the gates of the camp.

Ralenn looked toward the star-speckled sky as his horse cleared the trees. It had to be very early morning, he thought, perhaps even only a couple hours from the sun. He yawned; he was growing sleepy, yet somehow his brief nap in the trees made him feel renewed. His sores and blisters were gone. He rubbed his eyes and looked down to Lirah, who was in front of his horse. She seemed to feel his eyes, and she turned to him and smiled. She looked weary as well, but there was something else in her expression. It was a look he had seen in her eyes before, though he was not yet sure what it was. A fierceness and determination maybe?

They made their way down the road for nearly half an hour, and soon the gates were before them. Kaileth brought the group to a stop several paces from the entrance to the camp and there waited for the guard to come forth. A commotion could be heard from the guard shack within the walls, and soon a half-dozen or so armed men came out to greet them. They formed a semicircle around Kaileth and Jayle, and the largest one in the center spoke in a rough voice.

"What business 'ave you with us?"

Kaileth responded calmly, "We have just arrived with our thralls for your markets."

The apparent leader of these guards made a throaty noise in reply, then moved to inspect the five bound figures.

"As you can see, four are Tundraihn warriors, good for the arenas. And the fourth, she is human and would be good for—"

The guard interrupted him. "Humph, I know what she is good for."

He started looking over the slaves-to-be. He tarried long, looking over, and even touching, Irem.

She gave a harsh glare and pulled away from his advances.

"Haven't seen too many of this kinds' woman-folk," he said, moving on to look over Ealë.

"They are more spirited than most," Jayle said.

"Looks like this one already gave you some bit of trouble," the slaver guard said, noting Ealë's damaged face as he started to handle her.

"See that you don't despoil our goods before we get our money out of them," Kaileth demanded.

"Of course, meant no harm," he muttered.

The guard let Ealë go as he started to approach Lirah, but Riidak leaped from the shadow of Ralenn's horse into the guard's path and growled. The man quickly stepped back from the war hound. Kaileth called the dog to his side, and Riidak slowly obeyed, still growling and eyeing the guard. Ralenn silently blessed the hound for protecting Lirah from the man's wandering hands.

"Best if you keep your hound on a short leash," said the guard, visibly shaken by the size and aggression of Riidak. "Most here won't think twice about answerin' his growl with a blade."

Kaileth chuckled a bit as he answered, "Yes, that they may, but it would be their folly. I will, however, keep him close. I do apologize if he startled you, but it is his job to see that my goods are not spoiled. I am sure you understand."

The guard nodded to Kaileth, then continued with his inspection of Lirah. He stepped close to her and moved the hair from her face with a short club. The guard stood looking at her for a moment, then took hold of a length of her hair and held it close to his face, smelling it. Ralenn felt anger rising in the pit of his stomach, watching her being scrutinized. He did his best to look nonchalant, though, his only outlet to grip the reins tighter.

"Humph, could be wrong, but I would place coin to say she is not human. She is more akin to these othern, tho' it's hard to see. You don't even know what you have caught! Take them in, and good fortunes at the market."

"Is there a particular booth we should see for selling thralls of such unusual kindreds?" Kaileth asked.

"That there is, lord," replied the guard. "The arena masters, they will pay the best for all four of them."

Kaileth bowed his head to the guard and started forward. "I thank you, sir," he said as he passed the guard captain.

"Humph, enjoy your stay, lord," said the guard. "Oh, and watch yern weapons. They are likely to come up missing, fine as they are and all."

Kaileth gave the guard a nod and coaxed his horse forward. He passed through the gates with Riidak at his side, followed by Jayle and the others. Ralenn could just hear Mirris as she flew back and forth over their heads. The gates closed behind them with a dead-sounding thud, shutting them within the mass of In-Kind Mercantile's hive of hedonism.

As they entered the city a tumult of sounds immediately greeted their ears, but Ralenn hardly noticed.

*What did he mean, not human? Lirah's as human as I am, surely...*Ralenn shook the guard's words from his head. He looked around as they passed from the gates into the dimly lit streets. The filth and mud-covered lane they traveled was a true reflection of the character of most that lived and did business here. Ralenn could not help but feel bad that Lirah and the others were now treading this muck barefoot.

Many shadows were cast from lanterns that hung on poorly made poles here and there along the sides of the muddy road. As Ralenn's eyes adjusted to this dim light he could see the make of the buildings they were passing. Most looked like huts made with great haste and little care for craftsmanship. These had clearly been occupied much longer than they were designed to be. In the midst of these bracken huts were buildings of sod and mud brick. Some of these even had two stories with round windows set high in the walls. From these windows, silhouetted figures watched the passing of Ralenn and Kaileth with their apparent slaves. There was clearly an ongoing effort to replace the ramshackle structures with proper timber and plaster, even stone buildings. Yet the predominance of these outer rings of habitation and trade were of the cruder make.

Sounds of debauchery and riotous living hung thickly all around the tents and buildings of the camp, There was a surprising number of people making their way in the muddy streets at this hour. In the poor light, it was hard to tell who anyone was, but from their armor and the equipment upon their animals of burden, many of the passersby were obviously slavers returning from the market and arena. Others looked like possible nobles or wealthy merchants from many different lands. There were also many Ralenn deemed were embarrassed to be there, for they tried to hide their faces and moved about as if they feared they were being followed.

With Kaileth in the lead, they slowly made their way further through the maze of streets and alleys, steadily getting closer to the arena at the camp's center. Larger stone and timber buildings became more common. Several wider streets appeared to be paved, even, leading toward the river and the actual Dao'Tai Fortress to the north. Ralenn looked at Lirah often to see if he could get a glance of her face and guess what she was thinking. He had been unsuccessful, though, for from the time they entered the camp Lirah had kept her head hung down as one overwhelmed with despair. She certainly looked like someone who was bound for the miserable life of a thrall.

After several minutes, their course took a sharp turn in front of a long wood building. As they drew closer, Ralenn thought he could guess what business was run there. A spacious porch, lit with red lamps, ran down the length of the building. Many women, scanty of dress, were loitering about, doing their best to look appealing to all who passed by. They waved and called after the group promising unforgettable indulgences under their skillful care. Kaileth and Jayle politely ignored their clamors. Ralenn was glad for the poor light as it hid his blushing cheeks. Never had he heard such things!

Soon after passing the large, porched building, Ralenn saw a series of larger buildings drawing near. He recognized these as the same buildings he had seen from the hillside above, the buildings surrounding the arena. The number of people in the street had lessened, only slavers and their thralls came to this area of the road. Kaileth brought their little troop to a stop in a shadow cast by a tall timbered house within bow's shot from the gates to the arena. He dismounted, and Ralenn did likewise. Kaileth motioned for no one to speak, and they stood in the darkness and watched the buildings ahead.

The arena was circled with gated barracks and holding cells. These were made of stone and large timbers. At the gates stood heavily armed guards holding the leashes of several muzzled hounds. Kaileth and Ralenn watched, as did Lirah and the others, as groups of slavers and their captives approached the guards. The groups of slavers were stopped, and the guards brought their hounds forward. Ralenn and the others watched closely as they sorted the captives into several groups and then led them into the barracks behind them. The slavers remained outside the gate, and in a short time a tall thin man emerged from the gates and gave the slavers a large roll of paper. With the papers in hand, the men left the guards at the gates and returned up the street. Two more groups of slavers and their captives were dealt with in like manner.

"What are we going to do, Kaileth? It does not look like they'll let us in there," whispered Ralenn. Kaileth stood silent for a moment, looking at the gates and guards, then replied.

"It will be up to those who can get inside to find the ones we're looking for. I feel the Fates with us in this." Kaileth sounded totally confident. Jayle frowned deeply, shaking his head at it all. Ralenn did not like the thought of Lirah getting sent into that place and opened his mouth to say so, but Kaileth stopped him with a raised eyebrow. Ralenn knew he was asking for better suggestions, and he had no alternative to propose, so he held his tongue.

"I can't see a better choice," Jayle commented. "Nor is it probable we can sneak in there."

"I agree; we cannot risk a fight within this place." Even dressed as a slave, Orodan's words sounded commanding as ever.

"We will find them, but I deem we will also need assistance to get out."

"Kaileth, could Mirris follow us from above, then let you know where they take us?" Lirah asked, looking at the bird that was now upon the ground near Riidak.

"That way we could figure out how we could get you, and maybe even get word from you about where you are going," Ralenn followed Lirah's train of thought.

Kaileth stroked Mirris' feathers as he replied. "Yes, she could do that. I feel it would also be wise to send her now to survey the compound for possible exits before you are stuck in there." All agreed, and after Mirris received instructions from Kaileth she flew into the dark sky. All eyes watched her disappear from sight and the group stood in silence, awaiting her return. After some time, Kaileth broke the silence.

"Once you are inside, we will need to wait for Kyleeal and the boats before we come get you. Otherwise, we will be caught on the banks of the river with nowhere to go."

"How do you intend to alert us that it is time?" asked Orodan. "With all the noise and commotion of this place, a signal will not be heard."

"Perhaps Mirris could be the one to alert you once you are inside," Kaileth proposed. "However, there will be a chance that she cannot reach you."

Ralenn spoke up. "If Riidak and I were to wait outside the barracks, Mirris could let us know that Kyleeal is here, and he could let loose with one of his howls. If we are close to where they take you, it will definitely be heard over whatever noise this place may make."

Mirris now swooped down from the black sky, startling them as she landed close to Kaileth. Kaileth knelt and began to speak with Mirris in her own tongue, and he seemed pleased by what she told him. He smiled as he spoke.

"There is a large doorway at the western side of this place, facing the river. She says there are only two men and one animal there, and the light is poor. The river is a short distance further to the west."

"Truly, we are fortunate to have your assistance, Kaileth. One who knows the ancient language of nature's creatures is a wise and prudent friend to have," said Orodan solemnly.

"Indeed, there are few even among our people who know the tongues of nature," agreed Shytov.

Kaileth smiled and bowed his head a little before continuing. "The aashahl guide those who serve their will, my friends. This is what we will do. Jayle, Ralenn, after they are taken inside, Mirris will go to you first and let you know where in the barracks they are being held. Then she will fly to me. I will go to the riverbank to clear it of foes. Once I see Kyleeal coming, I will send her back to you two. Listen for Riidak's howls, Orodan, they are quite unmistakable. When you hear them, make your escape, and Ralenn and Jayle, you help however you can from the outside. Then we all make for the west door and the river. We will have time, and from what Mirris saw we should be able to swiftly fight our way free." Everyone seemed to agree, and so Kaileth,

Jayle and Ralenn returned to their saddles. Lirah hung back to speak to Ralenn just as they started out into the light again.

"You had better be careful out here. I don't want to get stuck in there because you got hurt again and I was not there to heal you." Lirah smiled, trying to lighten the tension as she spoke.

"We will be. You just be careful inside there, it doesn't look like the best of places to stay."

"Just don't do anything stupid trying to get us out. I just...I couldn't stand for anything to happen to you—you are all I have left."

Ralenn wanted to say something reassuring to her but they were now too close to the gates.

"Oy there! Off yer horses and take hold of yer dog!" was the call as several guards came out from the iron gates. The foremost, dressed in a dark tunic and dirty red cloak, was speaking.

"Now, these five the ones yer sellin'?"

Kaileth had just taken hold of Riidak's armored collar as he replied. "Yes, good captain! These are the five to be sold, and they were not easy to take."

"I am sure they weren't, but our dogs be the judge of their worth. Line 'em up fer us, and we will see what they are and what we ought be givin' you fer 'em."

Jayle took the rope from the horn of his saddle and pulled Lirah, Ealë, Irem, Shytov, and Orodan forward into a line before the guards. Lirah looked up at the guards, and Ralenn could see tears streaming down her face. It took all the self-discipline Ralenn had to stay himself from rushing to comfort her. She truly looked the role of a slave bound for the markets. The In-Kind guards led their hounds one by one in front of Lirah and the others. The first hound, with its drooping cheeks and floppy ears, simply sniffed the air around the prospective slaves. Ralenn noticed that each one of these hounds had a symbol painted upon the leather armor on their backs. One by one, each of these dogs passed by doing nothing more than smelling the five bound captives.

"Well! It would seem you got yourself some prizes here," the guard with the red cloak said excitedly. "It's pretty clear what you have here, but we have to make sure you didn't change their appearance or scent with some sort of trickery."

"Please, take your time. I want to get my money's worth out of them," said Kaileth. Ralenn was impressed with how convincingly Kaileth played the part of a slaver.

One of the guards brought out a dog with a big green leaf painted on its armor. As this dog started down the line it paid no more attention to Lirah than any of the other dogs did. However, as it neared Ealë it started to bark and howl excitedly.

"Ah, it's what I thought, you have a few forest fey here," said the guard appreciatively. The dog moved from Ealë to Irem, then Shytov and Orodan, reacting the same to each.

"Four forest fey! Ha! You've had a long journey to bring these here, and from their looks they're from the forests of the south."

"Indeed, you could say we had a long journey," replied Jayle.

"I hope that our efforts in gaining these exotic creatures is reflecting in our payment." Kaileth added.

The guard chuckled, "I am sure you do."

Ralenn did not speak for fear of saying something wrong. So, he quietly held the rope that Lirah and the Tundraihn were tied to as the slaver-guard took a green stick of chalk from a pouch at his side and started to draw on the face and chest of Orodan and the other Tundraihn.

"I have seen more of these forest rats of late than I have in all my days past. Hells, I've seen more this day than me and me father's father have even seen long as we've been in this trade!"

He grinned to Kaileth and signaled for the next dog to come forth. It soon emerged from the barracks gate and once again the animal had no reaction to Lirah. The guard looked perplexed as he spoke.

"Hmm, it would seem that you have a most rare one here; I've a hunch as to what she is though."

Another hound was brought out, bearing half of a red broken heart on its armor. The poor animal looked half-starved to death as the guard from the arena barracks led this last hound up to Lirah. Barking and howling echoed over the din of the camp as the hound erupted with excitement. The guard pulled hard on the animal's leash, and Lirah reeled back from it as it lunged up at her.

"Ah ho! Sure as I be thinkin,' she's a heart-mender, she is!" The red-cloaked guard seemed particularly excited at this discovery.

"Hmm, from yer faces I deem you've never heard of the heart-mender as we in the trade call them," said the guard to Ralenn.

"No, I haven't. I have—" Ralenn caught himself before saying he's known Lirah since they were children. He censored himself as he continued to speak. "That is, I thought she was just a girl when we took her."

"Ha, girl, yes," laughed the guard. "That she is, and a pretty one, too. But she is a heart-mender sure as my cloak is red. I have seen one other in my life. I was of a mind to get rid of that dog, seeing as we never use it."

"Fortunate for us that you did not, then," Kaileth said.

"Yes, she will get ye a good price, that is fer sure. Now just give me a few moments to draw up yer voucher papers, and ye can get on your way to soon be the richer!" With that the red-cloaked guard nodded, turned, and hurried back into the barracks, leaving a few guards to watch the gate.

Orodan looked to Kaileth, then Ralenn and gave a slight nod, as if to say, *Here we go*. Within a few minutes the guard captain came running back, red cloak trailing behind him. In his hand he carried five small scrolls, each tied with a small strip of cloth. These he handed to Kaileth.

"There ye be! Take these to that big building ye passed on yer way here, the one with all the red lanterns about it, with the big portico running around the front of it. Ye can't miss it. Go in there and give those papers to the guard inside and he will see that ye get yer pay."

The guard smiled and took hold of the rope Ralenn was holding, who tried not to look reluctant as he let it go.

"Pleasure doing business with you," Kaileth smiled.

"Oh, likewise to ye!" With that the guard captain jerked on the rope, causing Orodan and all those tied to it to lurch forward and follow him as he entered the barracks.

Ralenn stood motionless and watched as Lirah entered the shadows inside the gatehouse. She stopped for a moment and looked back to Ralenn. Their eyes met and she gave him a small smile. Before he could return it, the rope around her neck drew tight and she was pulled along into the arena barracks. The iron-barred gates clanked shut behind her. Lirah and the rest of their comrades were now out of sight.

"Come, we need to be off." Kaileth was already back in his saddle looking down to where Ralenn was still standing.

"Back to that building, then," Jayle said, looking down the way they had come. Ralenn climbed onto his horse and the three men started back through the street, followed closely by Riidak. After they had some distance between them and the arena gates Kaileth spoke.

"Do not fear for them too greatly, Ralenn," he said gently. "The men of this place will not damage nor spoil thralls of such great quality. They will treat Lirah well enough."

"I hope so, Kaileth. I still wish we had a better way to do this."

Kaileth smiled comfortingly, "She will be well. In fact, she could be safer than we. Shayar is with us, I can feel it."

Their horses soon carried them back to the building the guard had spoken of. The crowd in the street had thinned down to only a few people, and the camp was somewhat quieter. Most of the women they had seen earlier upon the porch were gone also. Ralenn again yawned and rubbed his eyes as they dismounted in the street and started toward the building. He guessed the sun was not far off, but somehow, he was not as tired as he knew he should be. The red lamps around the porches cast their light in streams onto the street, giving everything a bloody appearance.

"If you would wait here with the horses, Jayle and I will go in and see what I can learn from the patrons here," Kaileth suggested. He handed Ralenn the reins to his horse and started up the stairs into the building. "Perhaps we can even turn in these vouchers!" Kaileth winked. Jayle chuckled a little at this.

"Yes, but we should probably give a share back to the ones we sold to get it." Ralenn grinned as he said this, as did Kaileth as he walked through the entrance.

Ralenn felt a little better now about leaving Lirah with the In-Kind soldiers. She could take care of herself, and she seemed to be a prize to them, so they wouldn't treat her poorly, he hoped. She was also with the Tundraihn. Ralenn recalled the times in the not-so-distant past when Lirah had come to his aid. She always seemed to show up right when he needed her most. He hoped that he could return the favor now.

The camp had grown even quieter as the dawn drew nearer. Ralenn leaned back onto the wood of the stairs and let his eyes wander into the depth of the stars above him. They all sat glinting in their places, calm and still, slowly fading away in the growing dawn. The calm of the sky was comforting. Though all things about him seemed out of control and amiss, as far as the heavens above were concerned, all was right and on course.

*Jillii, guard her...*he prayed quietly.

22

A Little Fight Left

Take up the shield of Alpa ere you leave hearth and kin behind. Take her care upon you as a cloak to shield you as you wander in untended lands. Be it unto the lesser as unto you in her sight and strive to speed others on their path with charity of heart.
Essays of the Divine

Pain shot through her head as she forced her eyes slowly open. The air was thick and hard to breathe. She coughed, trying to ease her breathing, but this only caused more pain. She blinked several times, but her vision was still blurred. Something was sticking her eyelids together, so she tried to brush it away. Jahllia attempted to move her hand, and a stabbing pain rushed through her side as she did so. Something was biting into her wrist, and she found it was bound with a cord to the bed that she now realized she was in.

Where am I? Oh, Paldrii take me, I hurt! she thought.

She held her face up as high as her throbbing head would allow and just managed to get her hand to meet it. She found her face was crusted with blood and dirt, which she brushed clumsily away from her eyes. She looked at her arm and saw a thick metal ring clamped around it. Letting her hand rest upon her neck she felt another thick steel ring. This triggered the memory of what must have been the past day or so to return to her mind. Jahllia let her arm return to the bed as she strove to re-catch the breath her movements had just taken from her. She was surprised to still be in so much pain; she thought death would have taken her long ago.

Slavers. I've been taken by slavers.

With her eyes a bit clearer now she surveyed the room she was in. The ceiling was low and dark, and the only light came from a lantern that hung on the wall outside of what Jahllia could now see were bars. She was in a prisoner's cell. The room was just big enough for the bed that she was lying upon and a small stool in the far corner that had a bunch of cloth on it. Her vision swam and she lowered her head again, taking several moments to catch her breath.

Jahllia's thoughts turned to those whom she guessed were now long dead. Begga, Vestad, and the others had been the only family she and Jayin had known since their parents died. The reality that her brother was now gone suddenly sunk in. Jahllia's heart flooded with waves of sharp raw sorrow and guilt at his loss. She had promised her mother she would keep him safe. She had promised, and she had failed. She turned her head away from the light and let the gulf of sadness and grief in her heart burst from her blue eyes in torrents of hot tears, washing some of the blood and dirt from her face. Her body and mind were so weakened from agony and heartache that soon Jahllia cried herself to sleep.

She awoke again sometime later with a strange calmness in her. Her mind was clear, save for the agony that she still felt. A life of hardness and loss taught her to focus on survival. She had survived her parents' murder, her home's ruin, the sack of the temple, numberless assaults, and struggles with Subjugate soldiers. Now with the last of her family gone she was more determined than ever to survive, even if only to defy the Aya Dao'Tai and her sentence of death. Escape and survival would be her act of rebellion now. Jahllia gathered her thoughts, centering her resolve.

I have to get out of here. She again looked around the room, but this time realized that it was not just cloth on the stool in the corner, it was her blue dress. Jahllia looked down at herself and found that, save for the bandages around her wounds, she was naked. The thought of her enemies seeing her naked and unaware made her face flush with anger. She had to get out, now!

With much pain, Jahllia sat up and put her back against the wall behind her. She was now closer to where her restraints connected to the foot of the bed. This gave her enough slack to get the leather bands to her mouth, where she started to chew. The leather was old and tasted horrid, but it started to give way to her teeth, and within a short time, she was free. However, when she tried to move, she found that the extent of her wounds was almost as good as chains at keeping her in the bed.

She struggled to her feet and took a few shaky steps toward the stool before she fell to her knees with a cry of pain. She remained on her hands and knees for a few moments, regaining her composure, then crawled the last few feet to where her dress was. Jahllia took it from the stool but did not find her short leggings or brogues. With her dress in hand, she leaned against the wall and put the bloody and tattered garment back on.

After another respite she crawled over to the bars of her room. Jahllia propped herself up in the corner opposite the stool and examined the door and bars of her room. The door and bars alike were made from wrought iron and set deep in the cold stone floor. The lock on the door was large, and Jahllia had no tools to pick it open. There was, however, almost enough room for her to squeeze between the bars, if they were just a few more inches apart.

She leaned her head back against the wall and stared at her bed, thinking of how she could get away. She still was not sure where she had been taken, or how long she had lain near death in this cage. Regardless, Jahllia was certain that it was not anywhere she wanted to be. As she stared at the leather straps hanging from her bed a thought came to her. She moved back to her bed and took the straps from the wooden frame. Jahllia then made her way to the stool and turned it over. She found several of the stool's legs to be loose and removed one of them. With stool leg and straps in hand, she returned to the corner of the room by the bars and again sat down.

Jahllia now took hold of her short blue dress and pulled it up toward her waist, exposing the white linen lining underneath. She found a hole and started to tear the lining out, about halfway up the length of the dress. Soon she had a large loop of cloth from her underskirt.

After a few more minutes of resting, Jahllia slid up till she was standing against the wall again. She took the leather straps and the piece of her petticoat and wrapped both together around the middle of two of the bars of her cell. She tied it off as best she could, then placed the stool leg in the center of the cloth and leather and began to twist it. Doing so caused a new deluge of pain from the wounds in her side and chest. Again, she twisted, but the pain was so great, and her strength so spent, the bars hardly moved. She gasped for air and used all her might to continue turning the stool leg without crying out. The cloth and leather slowly began to twist and pull the bars together. With each turn, the pain grew worse, and Jahllia found it getting harder to breathe.

"*Nique'shay, give me strength,*" she prayed in a gasping whisper, tears filling her eyes. The faintest chitter of soft laughter sounded from the shadows behind her. Jahllia turned her head quickly to look behind her. She saw nothing in the room. She turned back to the bars and twisted the makeshift windlass. The shadows around her grew deeper. The soft cheerful voice filled her ears. She clenched her eyes and hoped that whatever power was upon her now was there to aid her. She drove through the pain, and within a few minutes the bars had bowed the few inches she needed to pass through.

Seeing this, she collapsed onto the floor panting and shaking. She was alone. The room still and silent. Whatever had helped her was gone. *Thank you...*

She was surprised no one had come to check on her with all the noise she had been making, but she was not going to wait around to see where her captors were. Jahllia crawled back up to the bars and used them to get back to her feet. She started to step through, and, small though she was, she had just barely bent the bars enough to get through with a tight squeeze. Jahllia stuck her head out the bars to look down the length of the hall. She saw no one, so the rest of her followed, and with a little painful wiggling she was out of her caged room.

The sound of her bare feet softly echoed off the stone of the hall as she slowly slid along the wall, heading away from her room. There was no light in the direction she was going, and soon she was forced to feel her way down the dark hallway. Her eyes soon adjusted, and she could see wood doors here and there along the hall. At the far end, a light shone through a hole in the ceiling over a flight of stairs that led up into the light. *That has to be the way out,* Jahllia thought to herself, and she continued to slowly move toward the light, using the wall for support.

When the stairs were finally at her feet, she looked up into the light that flooded into the hall and saw it came from the open stairway above her. Jahllia crawled up a few steps and listened for anyone in the room above. She heard nothing, and so she continued up the stairs. As she neared the edge of the floor above, she stopped and peered up into the room. It was large and round, well-lit by many candles and large lamps.

The sudden sound of boots on wood had her frozen in the shadows of the stairway in fear. She held her breath as she heard a door open, and two Dao'Tai soldiers entered the room. She could see their shadows from where she hid as they dropped something on a table, then tromped up the stairs of the larger room, leaving her alone again. She let out a gasping breath of relief and slowly sat down on the stairs. She listened and looked out the high windows for a long time. It had to have been very late in the night, maybe early morning she guessed by the stars that were out. She continued to listen. There was no sign of anyone. After watching for several more moments Jahllia slowly crawled up into the room.

The wooden floor was rough and splintery, so as soon as she could, Jahllia made her way to the wall and used it to stand, rather than continue crawling. She could now see that there were several tables and chairs in the room. All seemed very still to Jahllia. Far too still. Though if it truly were as late in the night as she guessed the house was probably all asleep. There were only two doors in this large room besides the one leading down to her cell. The one farthest from where she stood was open, and through it she could see more stairs going up. A trail of mud led from the closed door to the table where the soldiers had left their load, then up these stairs, confirming the path they had taken.

That's the way out, then. Nique'Shay, cloak me.

She staggered toward the door, trying to keep her shaking legs under her. Upon reaching it, she again stopped and listened. Not a sound came from the room on the other side, so with great care Jahllia raised the latch and began to open the door. The room on the other side was dark and small. She took a few steps into it and saw it was an entryway and coatroom.

Cloaks hung on a row of hooks on the wall, and a rack next to a small door held several staffs and weapons. Deciding this must be the more likely way out than the continuing stairs in the other room, Jahllia hurried as fast as her wounds would allow to don a cloak and move to the door out of this place. The cloak felt soft and comforting over her cold, battered shoulders, as if it could shelter her from her foes. She started to open the door, but the weapons rack caught her eye, in particular a long knife, belt, and a small hand-crossbow. She eyed them for a moment, quickly strapped the belt around her small waist, and tucked the knife and bow into it, then hid them both under her cloak.

The latch felt cool in her hands as Jahllia slowly opened the door and looked outside. A rush of refreshing night air greeted her, and the sight of a large Dao'Tai soldier's back. He turned to face her and before he could utter a word her instincts overpowered her pain. The dagger was out and had already found its place in the side of the soldier's thick neck before she had taken another breath. Gurgling, the soldier tumbled backwards into the doorway, falling across Jahllia. She gasped for air as the bulk of the soldier both smashed her to the floor and caused shattering pain to surge from her wounds. Fighting back panic, she struggled to get out from under the dead body.

Now you've done it, you fool! Dark tears take me, he is so heavy!

Continuing to curse herself for getting into such a predicament she continued to fight to get out from under her victim's mass. His weight seemed impossible to move. Minutes passed and soon she could hear boots coming back down the stairs in the other room. Frantically she tried to get the dead soldier off her, but it was no use. He was far too heavy for her in her wounded state. As the sound from the other room drew near, she managed to pull the knife from the dead soldier's neck. She then did her best to hide herself under the soldier's cloak and her own as the door to the entry room opened.

Peering out from under the cloak she could just see the boots of another soldier as he entered the room and saw his fallen comrade. Fortunately, the poor light made it difficult to see, and so Jahllia was undiscovered. The soldier spoke in his native tongue and seemed to be jovial in his tone. He took a few steps closer to his fallen comrade and Jahllia could smell the wine on the soldier. The soldier again spoke and this time he kicked the dead soldier with his foot.

Seeing as there was no reply the soldier then knelt and rolled his dead comrade over, freeing Jahllia. He stooped, shocked for a moment, and that was all the time she needed. Again, her knife darted to find its mark. A well-practiced hand drove the steel edge through the eye of the second soldier and he too fell dead next to the first. Jahllia rose to her knees, taking a few deep breaths. She then crawled out the open door and down a few steps where she again rested for a time.

It won't take long for those two to be discovered.

She checked her surroundings but did not recognize where she was. A maze of buildings, streets and alleys lay before her. The sky was clear and dark, but there were not many stars set in their places. She peered into the darkness and found no one in sight, though in the distance sounds of people and movement could be heard. Leaning against the steps for a moment, Jahllia took a deep, aching breath, pulled the hood of her cloak over her matted flaxen-blonde hair, and stepped into the street.

Cold mud squished under her feet as she took each slow quivering step across the road. Raising her head, she saw a dark alley and hoped to find shelter there from those who might come after her. Once across the street, Jahllia caught the edge of a barrel at the entrance of the alley and leaned against it to catch her breath. She had only been resting for a few moments when three figures burst through the doorway Jahllia had just gone through. They stood in the light for a moment, then one of them spoke.

"Th-th-there she is. By-by the barrel, Esea."

"Yes, I see her too, Tellig. I can't believe she is sta—" The second man was cut off.

"Booth duv yoo shut up and leet's cahtch'er!" a third man snarled. He spoke with a thick accent that sounded rough and cruel, and somewhat familiar.

They all three started running after Jahllia, who did her best to flee down the narrow alley away from them. She was too wounded to run for long, and soon she staggered and fell into the mud. Before she could get back up, a crushing hand took hold of her shoulder from behind and flipped her small frame up into the air. She landed on her back with a thick slapping sound and a splash of filth and dirty water. The impact knocking the wind out of her.

She looked up and saw a large man standing over her. It was too dark to see his face, but from his voice Jahllia knew he meant her no good.

"Yoo wun't surrvive te leyson I'm about ta give yoo, yoo little wretch!"

Jahllia still had not regained her breath when he stooped and grabbed her under the arms and picked her clear off the ground. She made a feeble attempt to free herself from his clutches. However, his crippling grip was pressing into her wounds, and his fingers felt like nails being driven into her body. Her movements to escape enraged him even further.

"P-p-please, master, don't hurt her anymore," said one of the other two men who had come running up behind her captor.

"Oh nooh Tellig? Shey iss mine, an I will do ashh I will wit mah property!"

Hearing herself being referred to as property caused Jahllia's temper to flare. Pushing through the pain, she managed to kick the man in the stomach, though it was no harder than a child might have kicked.

"Ah, still 'ave sum fight in yoo, eh?" growled the large man. "Well, I cahn drive tat out duv yoo!" Then Jahllia's captor started to squeeze her wounded chest and side, causing her to scream out in pain. He then threw her into the side of a building, laughing darkly. Jahllia was almost knocked out by this, and she lay in a heap at the base of the building's wall. Hardly moving under the muddy mess of the cloak that obscured most her form.

"I mah not be ahble to breek yoor spirit, baht teer iss one thing I cahn tik from yoo tat yoo can't git back." His threat dripped with vicious intent as he started toward her again. One of his servants abruptly stepped in front of him.

"Master, please, she is wounded and will die if she doesn't get more care soon. The chyrurgeon will be back here this morning. Let's just get her back to the house. You can have more satisfaction if we get her into better health."

"Know yoor plass, slave!" raged the large man as his fist slammed into the servant's face, sending him to the ground. The large man laughed again as he came up to Jahllia and took her by the leg, pulling her away from the wall.

"He iss right, I hahd better git whaht I want froom yoo beforre yoo die. I've alreedy spent goood coyn keping yoo alive, tis time I git a returrn foor my—" The mechanical clank of a crossbow trigger cut his sentence off.

"Miljah...drink...your blood..." Jahllia's words were little more than a whisper as her attacker fell to the earth without making a sound.

The moon was slowly rising in the sky, and a beam of soft light fell into the alleyway, revealing a crossbow bolt in the face of the large Dao'Tai man at Jahllia's feet. She knew him for certain now; it was the sub-officer of the execution detail. The other two men rushed over to their fallen master; it was quickly evident that he was beyond any aid.

"N-n-now what do we do, Esea? She k-k-killed him!" The man named Tellig sounded panicked as he spoke.

"He was going to do the same and worse to her, Tellig," said the one called Esea. They both spoke as if she could not hear them at all.

"C-c-can we just go back t-t-to the house, Esea?" asked Tellig. He clearly did not want to be found with the dead body of their master.

"I'm not sure what we should do. We can't go back; they will think we killed him. No one will believe that a girl in such terrible shape killed the sub-captain, Tellig." Esea sounded calm as he spoke.

Tellig, however was sounding very scared. "Then what are we to d-do?"

Before Esea could answer, the sound of men and horses met their ears. They quickly turned around to see In-Kind guards at the entrance of the alley.

"You two, stay where you are!" shouted one of them. Several men on foot ran up to where Jahllia, Tellig, Esea, and the Dao'Tai sub-captain's body were.

"What is going on here? We had reports of screaming," asked the slaver serjent. Before Esea or Tellig could answer, one of the guards next to Jahllia spoke.

"Sergeant, we have a dead Dao'Tai, looks like a soldier."

The serjent barked a laugh. "Are there any other kind?"

"He's been shot in the face with a bolt, Sergeant. Looks like the girl has the crossbow on her lap."

"We can explain," Esea volunteered.

"I'm sure you can," replied the serjent dryly.

"Y-y, yes we can. You s-s-see—" Tellig was interrupted.

"I'll explain, Tellig," Esea said, putting a hand on Tellig's shoulder. "You see, Sergeant, this girl was one of our master's prospective paramours. As you know, it is illegal for the Dao'Tai to be with other races, so she was hidden in his tower house. She got out of her cell and into the street. We gave her chase, and when our master got her, he started to beat her. He was then going to finish her off, and she shot him." Esea was matter-of-fact about his statement.

The serjent sat quietly upon his horse for a moment before he made his reply.

"So, you are telling me that this half-dead girl killed the Dao'Tai sub-captain?"

"Y-y-yes," said Tellig as he nodded his head vigorously.

The serjent laughed. "No, here is what happened; you brought her here and then went back to get your master. You told him she got out. Then the three of you supposedly tracked her here to this dark alley where you shot him and planned on making it appear as if she did it. If she hadn't screamed you would have gotten away with it, too."

"But we told you the truth!" cried Esea as the slavers took hold of him and Tellig.

"I know you did, but that truth would be of little profit to us. You will live in what we choose to be the truth. Take them all to the arena."

The two men, Esea and Tellig, didn't cry out as they were led to a wagon outside the alley. They must know as well as she did that those who resisted were simply beaten. They were put into the back of the caged wagon, along with the barely conscious Jahllia. A few minutes later the jostling of the wagon sparked a sharp pain, bringing Jahllia back to her senses. She had fallen unconscious about the time the slavers had shoved her in the wagon, and she found herself again looking through the bars of a cage. The wagon smelled of the wet straw that lay piled on the floor.

"Hey, l-l-look Esea, she's m-m-moving!" Jahllia turned her head to see two men sitting toward the front of the wagon.

"Where are we?" asked Jahllia slowly. Esea, gave her answer.

"We are in a cage on the back of a wagon, on our way to the arena to be fed to some horrid beast tomorrow, I would guess."

Jahllia smiled. "Then it is not as bad as I thought," she said. The wagon rolled through the muddy streets in the early night, slowly making its way toward the arena as she drifted away into a pain-induced daze.

23

The Darkest Light

S avor the heady passions of youth and the mirth of dance and song for these are the sacraments of Paldrii's twins. Take heed, therefore, not to tarry over-long in their company lest they impart a portion of their doom upon thee.
Essays of the Divine.

Jahllia again found herself waking within a holding cell. There was just enough light to cast shadows from the bars of her room. The smothering scent of mold and excrement hung thick in the air. Each breath seemed to stick in her dry throat as she rubbed her eyes and slowly sat up. Her hearing was the first of her senses to clear. Sorrowful, anguished moans drifted through the stifling air around her. Several minutes passed, and at last her sight slowly came back to its normal acuity. Jahllia saw now that she was in one of many cells. They seemed to go on as far as could be seen in the poor light that fell from a lamp outside her barred compartment. The lamp was hanging from the ceiling of a narrow hall that separated the two rows of cells.

Down this hall Jahllia could see a second light getting closer. She lay back onto the damp straw that covered the floor and partially shut her eyes. Soon the sound of footsteps began to draw near as a large man in poorly fashioned armor came walking down the hall, oil lamp in hand. He peered into the cells on either side of the hall as he passed by. The guard came to a stop in front of the cell next to Jahllia's and held his lamp close to shed more light within. The darkness retreated before the light, and out of the corner of her eye she saw a small figure in the straw on the floor.

Only a thin web of iron bars separated one chamber from the next, so there was little to block her view. The woman on the floor stood up, and her long hair fell nearly to her waist. The light shone brightly on her tattered white clothing. The guard looked her over for a few moments and muttered something to himself. He then turned and walked back down the hall, leaving the two women alone in the dark.

Jahllia again sat up and looked to where the woman in white had been standing. Her eyes were blurry, possibly from the poor light, possibly from her waning life. She wasn't sure. So she gently pulled herself through the filthy straw to look closer. Taking hold of a cold iron bar she pulled herself up and leaned up against the stone wall at the back of her cell. Jahllia still could not yet see clearly into the other chamber, but she looked on and waited for her eyes to adjust. A soft voice suddenly whispered very close to her head from the adjoining cell, startling her.

"Shush, it's alright, don't worry. I won't hurt you."

"Who are you?" Jahllia asked, breathing fast out of surprise.

"I'm Lirah," the stranger said. Her words were so soft that Jahllia had a tough time understanding them. She felt a warm hand reach through the bars and touch her on the shoulder.

"I'm glad you're awake, I was worried you were..." Lirah's hand pulled away from Jahllia with a jerk as she took a sharp breath.

"You are hurt! Hurt so badly." Her voice was louder this time.

"Yes, I don't know...how much longer I will be here," agreed Jahllia. "But how...did you know?" Her words were short and choppy, as each one took greater and greater effort to form.

"Don't you worry about the how. I'll see that you are just fine." There was a determination in Lirah's voice that Jahllia didn't understand.

"Can you lie down close to the bars? I will see what I can do."

Too spent and cold to argue, Jahllia nodded and slumped down onto the floor. Lirah's slim hands passed easily through the bars and held Jahllia's icy hand between them.

"Jahllia...my name...is Jahllia," she said slowly, remembering she had not yet introduced herself. Her voice was now very weak.

Lirah smiled and squeezed her hand gently. "What a pretty name! You will be fine, Jahllia. No matter what you see, hold still."

Jahllia said nothing, only gave Lirah's hands a faint squeeze. Lirah placed Jahllia's hand at her side, then went to work surveying her wounds. She held her hands over the girl, and Jahllia opened her eyes to see a brilliant blue light filling the dungeon. She felt warm inside, and the pain started to dissipate. The light started to change color, from sparkling sapphire to rich ruby, and it began to flicker. It was beautiful. Jahllia felt no panic, though she thought she should be frightened by what clearly was some type of magic. She lifted her head up just enough to see Lirah had her hand over Jahllia's heart. Blinding light was flowing from Lirah into Jahllia's chest. She looked to her healer's face and saw a terrible expression of pain upon it.

Sweat started to drip from Lirah's face, and her breathing became short and labored. Jahllia watched, mesmerized, as Lirah's hand moved from the wounds at her side, found each wound, and paused over it, allowing the light from her hands to enter her body. Each time Lirah moved to a new wound Jahllia could no longer feel the hurt from wherever Lirah had just moved on from.

Suddenly a large tide of warmth washed over Jahllia that drove all the pain away. She again looked up to Lirah. The light was dimmer now and starting to fade. Jahllia could see a few drops of blood fall toward the floor from the corners of Lirah's tightly shut eyes. She thought she must be delirious. As the drops struck the stone of the floor, the light from Lirah's hands flickered and went out. Lirah let out a gasp, then fell forward, leaning onto the bars and breathing heavily. Jahllia tried to speak but no words came out. She felt relaxed and warm, like she might simply melt away into perfect bliss. Their cells were dim again, yet Jahllia could see much better now. She fought off her doziness long enough for her eyes to meet Lirah's.

"You are the first person I've helped that has stayed awake," said Lirah, still short of breath.

Jahllia smiled and again tried to speak. "Thank...Thank...you..." Sleep was overpowering her, and within a few moments her mind was adrift in a sea of comforting dreams.

Lirah was glad to see Jahllia resting, but knew she would need further aid. The earth here was so dead that Lirah could hardly pull any strength from it. Jahllia was so close to death that she could not fully heal her without her healer's bag or more strength from Miljah. Lirah turned and leaned her back against the stone wall of her cell. She now realized that something warm was running down her face. She wiped it away and held her hand toward the light from the lantern. It was clearly blood.

"That can't be good," she said to herself. Lirah took up her tattered skirt and wiped her face as clean as she could. She reached out to try to draw from the earth around her, but there was almost nothing there. She could feel Jahllia and many others in the cells, but the earth under her was dry; it was like trying to get a drink from an empty water skin. She could sense there had been power there, but for some reason it was now gone. Lirah closed her eyes and focused on taking in what little traces of healing strength that she could. It was slow, but she could feel the smallest essence of the familiar power flowing into her. She kept her eyes shut and focused, using a form of meditation Gaileng had taught her to open her awareness. This helped her take in as much life force as she could. It would be sluggish, but she was fairly certain given enough time she could restore herself even in this awful place.

The minutes passed, though not nearly enough when the sound of footsteps started to approach from down the hall. Lamplight soon filled the surrounding cells as four large, armed men approached Lirah's holding cell. From their bright hair and eyes, she guessed them to be from Taivadees. The priests had told her of these people. They formed the cavalry of the Subjugate armies and were fine mariners. They once formed much of the allied navies of the Threefold Defense. When Anoth fell, however, they swiftly sought peace and allegiance to the Subjugate. Now many of their war bands and chiefdoms thrived on the slave trade, traveling wide on the seas and land searching for exotic thralls. She did not think their coming bode well for her.

They now stood at the door of her cell, silently looking in at her. Lirah said nothing, only glaring back at them. Without a word they opened the door to her cell and motioned for her to come. Lirah stood and slowly walked to the men, who then took hold of her, one on each arm. They picked her up in this way and started to quickly walk down the hall. It was terribly uncomfortable and Lirah struggled not to cry out. The two men bearing the lamps led the way, while the other two held Lirah up by the arms so her feet could barely touch the floor as they packed her along. She strained her eyes to look into every cell, hoping to see where Orodan or perhaps the other Tundraihn were being kept, but she only saw female prisoners. The men carried her back down the way she had been brought in earlier that night, and soon they passed over to the opposite side of the complex. Lirah saw these cells held only male slaves. The Taidvadeen slavers finally came to a stop in front of a large, iron-bound door. They set Lirah back on her own feet and opened the door.

Rich crimson light flooded the hall as the door swung open. The four men entered the room, with Lirah still held between them. They all stood in the doorway for a moment, letting their eyes acclimate to the bright light. This room's decor was quite lavish. Brightly colored drapes hung on the walls and cushioned benches lined the room, with two rows of large red lamps hanging from the painted ceiling.

The soft, thick furs that covered the floor felt warm under Lirah's cold, damp feet. However, she was only able to savor this for an instant before her guards carried her over to one of several holding cells that stood at each end of the room. The iron door swung open, and the two men tossed her into a cell. But instead of falling onto a cold straw-covered floor as in her last cell, Lirah found herself falling onto a pillow-topped divan. She quickly sat up and turned around just in time to see the door close and the four men leave the room through a second door that stood opposite from where they had first entered the room.

Lirah looked around her new prison, it was similar to the old in bars only. The rest of her surroundings would have been fit for the highest of royal folk. As she looked about, Lirah suddenly felt the hair on the back of her neck stand on end, and she became aware that she was being watched. She turned her full attention to the other cells in the room. One by one, she searched each cell for signs of another person. Each barred chamber was filled with furniture similar to the one Lirah was in, but they all seemed empty until she saw Irem crumpled in the cage in the far corner.

Lirah gasped. Irem was not moving, and she had a new wound to her head. She was breathing well enough, though, and when Lirah reached out her senses she could feel her life force strongly. She felt relieved, though the uneasy feeling of watchful eyes did not pass. Lirah looked again for anyone else but found no one. Shaking her head, she leaned back into the pillows and continued to watch, keeping a close eye on Irem in case her condition changed.

Her repose ended suddenly when one of the pillows fell from a large, midnight-colored ottoman within one of the other holding cells. Lirah's eyes shot to the spot it fell from as she jumped, and she saw what she thought to be two glinting eyes for just an instant.

"Hello?" she called out, jumping to her feet. "I know you're hiding over there, come out. There is no reason to hide from me."

Lirah again saw the flashing eyes peek over the back of the ottoman, and she started in surprise. They were unlike the eyes of anything she had ever seen. They were large and glowed with a soft, blue-gray light in the shadows cast by the top of the cage. These same shadows hid the features of the face, so only the slight glow of the eyes was visible. Lirah continued to watch whoever was behind the ottoman, fists clenched anxiously, never taking her gaze away. Slowly, a hand crept up onto the edge of the ottoman. Lirah could not be sure, but it looked to be the hand of a woman. Yet there was something quite different about it, it was nearly the same color as the dark blue-black of the ottoman's fabric. *It has to be a trick from these lamps*, Lirah thought to herself.

This was soon proved wrong as an arm followed the hand, and a shoulder followed the arm, till a being both beautiful and terrifying stood in sight of Lirah. Her mouth dropped open as she stared in awe, not daring to move or speak for a time. The person in front of her was clearly female, but she was unlike anyone Lirah had ever seen. Her hair was straight and smooth as it hung down to her shoulders in the front, and then cut up at a sharp angle into a tight bun high in the back. Her breathtaking eyes were set deep into her hard, angular face. All parts of her body had the appearance of finely polished stone. Her hair was deep blue, almost black, shifting as she moved. Her skin was also a shade of smooth, blue-black, the light dancing upon it, like the surface of a dark pool. More than anything else, it was her eyes that captivated Lirah. They looked to be bolts of white lightning held within a jet-black shell through which their light emanated. It was these radiant bolts that produced the steady white glow of her eyes.

The lights in the woman's eyes increased, and Lirah suddenly noticed that just below her hairline two small sharp pointed horns protruded from her sable hair, with another set of smaller ones and yet another, each just behind the first in two rows running back from her brow. The woman gave Lirah a savage smile, revealing long double sets of incisors as she took another step toward Lirah. Lirah swallowed hard and wet her lips, shock still holding her tongue fast, and the two stared at each other silently for quite some time.

Lirah knew what she was, or at least what she thought this woman was, and it was not safe. Guardians and warriors of the Dark Realms. The creatures of fable that stole the unwary away in the darkest of forests. Creatures of nightmares—the Xydarii.

Lirah's mind was a blur of fear and apprehension. She swallowed again hard. The Anthosn priests hardly spoke of the Dark Realms, and even less about the Xydarii. What they had said only fueled the fear Lirah choked back in the face of the woman's fierce gaze.

Patient Father, protect me, she thought—trying to grasp the sudden reality of the fearful being that now watched her unblinkingly. More moments passed in silence. The posture of the Xydar woman relaxed, and she spoke softly in a language Lirah could not understand.

Finally, Lirah noticed the light in the woman's eyes started to dim, and soon their glow was barely noticeable, leaving only shimmering black. Lirah let out a long breath as her wits returned to her. *What do you say to a creature of the Dark Realms?* Lirah tried to think of what to do. She could see the woman surveying her thoroughly, which Lirah hoped meant that she was wondering about Lirah, as much as Lirah was about her. Several more silent moments passed, till Lirah finally decided to at least introduce herself, though she was not even sure if this being would understand her.

"Um, it is nice to meet you. My name's Lirah." She offered a small smile, trying to reassure the Xydar woman that she meant no harm.

The striking woman looked much more relaxed now, though she still said nothing. Lirah walked closer to the bars of her room and stood, holding the cold iron in her hands. She could feel something emanating from the Xydar, like a hot draft from a fire. Lirah was startled from her observation by a silky voice.

"You are poorly dressed for one with so much power within you," the woman said, leering a little. "Or perhaps they took you with much force?" she continued.

Lirah was surprised. This outlandish woman clearly knew the tongue of the land. She spoke with a slight, yet pleasant accent, very sultry in tone. Her diction was perfect, as one who had studied much in life.

"Yes, I can speak your simple tongue. It is rather slow, and easy to master. But I suppose a short life span necessitates an easily comprehended language, for time's sake mostly." The woman took another step toward Lirah as she ran a finger along her lower lip, licking her fangs as she gave a wolfish grin. Lirah could feel sweat beading on her brow and realized her hands were aching from clutching the bars so hard. She let go and tried to calm herself.

"Um, yes, I guess so." She hesitantly felt for the life force in the woman and quickly pulled back. It was like touching a hot stove and staring at the midday sun at the same time. Lirah gasped and stumbled back from the bars. The woman laughed with amusement. Lirah cursed to herself.

That was stupid, stupid, stupid! Now she will take my soul for sure. Or at least Lirah was fairly sure that the priests had mentioned the Xydarii hunger for souls and the like.

"You should be more careful when you journey the river; diving in can be dangerous, young one."

"You are so much brighter than the Tundraihn..." Lirah said, half to herself.

"The Tundraihn? So, you have met our lesser cousins. But I am being rude. I am Vishaya Jurdoitav Xydarii, you are free to call me Vishaya. I apologize for hiding from you earlier. I was not sure what to make of you, your aura was so bright. I am also not overly fond of strangers gawking at my mostly naked body." As she said this, Lirah did note that she was quite scantily clad.

"I understand. How did they capture you?" asked Lirah, feeling a little less unnerved. But at her question, Vishaya grew rigid and the light in her eyes flared up brightly again.

"I would prefer not to think over it. Let us say that I was taken from my home by force, in a vulnerable moment." Vishaya's skin seemed to shift colors as she spoke, and the room around her looked darker for an instant. "They will pay for it, I assure you. They will pay for all that I have suffered."

Lirah took a few steps back from her bars out of fear, hands trembling. There was a terrible passion in Vishaya's words, and her eyes were totally white with light. Lirah could feel a pulse of energy slam into her. It felt hot and angry, like a tongue of flame. It touched her mind in the same manner that Miljah's life force had at the falls, but it was quite different. Vishaya appeared to notice Lirah's terror and she suddenly changed tone.

"Do not fear me, Lirah. I will not harm you. I would only put stock in half of what you have probably heard of my kindred." She gave Lirah a pleasant enough smile, though her long white fangs were still unsettling.

"There is much it seems that you have yet to learn about the energies that surround you. I will restrain myself best as I can for now. I can feel your connection to the arcane. It is stronger even than mine in a way. I readily admit that you intrigue me. Where are you from, might I ask?"

"Allinth; it is in the mountains west of here," Lirah said.

"Hmm, I have never heard of this place. Is it near Andohra, or closer to Dashra?"

"Umm...neither really. They are both gone now. I think Andohra used to include us in their borders, but that was a while ago, before I was born." Lirah rambled, trying to recall the old maps from her studies.

"I would hardly call your lifespan a while, my vibrant little orchid." Vishaya laughed again softly to herself, and Lirah could hardly accept the fact that she was talking face-to-face with a Xydarii! And that they laughed and wondered where people were from. This was not what she had been expecting from one of the scariest creatures in all the realms.

"How is it that you have come to be here?" Vishaya asked, still smiling widely.

Lirah thought of how to answer for a moment and wondered if she should tell her the truth. In spite of the fear she still felt, Lirah wanted to trust Vishaya. She felt a connection to her, similar to the one with Ealë, and this surprised her. Carefully, Lirah reached out to feel the essence of Vishaya. It was easy to find, like a raging bonfire on a starless night. Vishaya felt raw, untamed, savage, predatory, even more than the Tundraihn. Yet Lirah also could not feel anything evil under the tumultuous passions that burned within her. There was a vicious dark edge, like shattered black glass, ferocious maybe, but nothing like the creature that was at the falls. Vishaya's cool voice interrupted Lirah.

"You learn quickly, it seems; are you satisfied that I am no foe?"

Lirah flushed a little, realizing her actions had not gone unnoticed. "I didn't mean to offend, I just needed to be sure—" Vishaya cut her off.

"There is no offense. I have been reading you as well, though by way of practice I doubt you noticed." Vishaya smiled coyly again, licking her sharp teeth.

Lirah cleared her mind and allowed the energies around her to flow freely, and there she saw how subtle and precise Vishaya's aura projection was. Lirah now realized she had been feeling it from the moment she entered the room, soft and warm like a favored cloak.

Vishaya's eyes flashed and she laughed softly, "My, you do learn swiftly, little orchid."

"How did you mask yourself so well?" Lirah asked, unable to keep the wonder from showing in her face.

"When we escape from this place, we can discuss the nuances of the arcane. For now, you still have not answered my question. How is it that they captured a magic wielder as yourself?"

"I'm not a magic wielder, not really. But we...I actually volunteered to be here."

Vishaya looked perplexed. "What do you mean, *volunteered?*"

"Well, it is sort of a long story, but to be short, we met a group of Tundraihn who were after their—"

Vishaya cut in, "Their priestess or something of that fashion, correct?" she said flatly.

"Yes. That is what they said. But how did you know that?"

"She was in that cage a few hours ago," Vishaya said, gesturing toward Irem.

Lirah felt her heart jump and her chest squeeze in anxiety and excitement. "What happened to her?"

"They took her in there." Vishaya pointed to the door opposite the one Lirah had entered the room through.

"The other Tundraihn females made an attempt to get out of their cages. A blue-haired one got out and released her apparent comrade, the one that still lies in the cage. Then together they started to open the cage of the third, the one who must have been their priestess."

"That would be Ealë, what happened to her?" Lirah asked worriedly.

"They had the cage open when several guards returned to the room. They fought, the one you called Ealë killed several of the guards before they ran her through with a spear." Vishaya pointed to a large stained spot on the fur-covered floor as she continued.

"The guards continued to fight to subdue the two Tundraihn, and after a few more guards arrived, they succeeded. They took the wounded one away and left that one beaten senseless in her cage."

"Was Ealë still alive when they took her?"

"Yes, it was not all that long ago really, you were brought here perhaps only a short span after the guards had cleaned up the mess."

"I see...I have to get out of here and find Ealë before it is too late!"

At this Vishaya let out a sharp trill of laughter. "Escape is my goal as well; however, if you examine my cage you will find that the guards have augmented the closure."

Lirah looked and saw a thick chain wrapped many times and secured with a large lock holding the door securely shut.

"I suppose we will have to think of something else..."

"So it seems; but your tale—please go on Lirah; it is Lirah, is it not?" Vishaya did not seem overly concerned with the state of the Tundraihn woman as she beckoned Lirah to speak. Lirah did not want to anger Vishaya, but it was hard not to let her mind swim in worry for Ealë, Irem, and Jahllia, the woman she had just met—not to mention how they all would escape. Lirah made herself focus and she continued her tale.

"Right, so we met up with them, the Tundraihn, and we tracked their priestess here. We came up with a plan to get her out by sending a few of us in here to find her. I and four of the Tundraihn warriors pretended to be captives, and our friends sold us. They are waiting outside for our signal that we have found her, then they are going to help us get out."

Vishaya sat down and looked to be thinking over what Lirah had said. From her dark expression Lirah could guess she did not think much of their plan.

"Well then, we need to go get this Tundraihn lady, do we not? I have never been overly fond of them, but they have never given me a personal reason to hate them either."

Lirah smiled earnestly, "So you will help me?" There was a pause, Vishaya's expression was hard to read, and Lirah could not be sure where she was even looking really. Her eyes gave no hint of what they focused on as the dull white light flickered within their slick black surface.

Lirah caught herself wringing her damp hands and she swallowed hard, trying to choke back her building anxiety. Lirah hoped the stories of the Xydarii were an exaggeration. If they were not, then she also knew that Vishaya was as likely to kill and eat her as she was to help her escape from the camp. The fact that Vishaya kept licking her long fangs thoughtfully did not help ease Lirah's worries. But Vishaya felt right somehow. After several more moments of unsettling silence Vishaya wet her lips and spoke.

"Yes, I think that I will *help* you." Her expression grew savage for an instant, silvery lights flaring up in her eyes before relaxing into an almost beatific smile. "By helping you it would seem that my chances of dealing my captors a measure of revenge is greatly increased."

"Thank you, Vishaya." Lirah sat down, and the two of them were both silently thinking for several minutes. Lirah could not fathom why she still felt that she could trust Vishaya, but the feeling persisted despite her unsettling air and appearance.

Lirah at last spoke again. "There is someone else I would like to get out, besides the other Tundraihn, wherever they are."

"Oh, who might that be?" asked Vishaya with an unconcerned tone.

"There is a girl back where I was first being held. She is hurt badly, and I healed her as best I could, but I will need to get her out of here, so I can heal her properly."

"Ah, so that is what I see in you. You are a healer, an empathic healer at that." Vishaya grinned and chortled as she continued.

"I suppose you can't help but ache to save and help every fates-forsaken soul that Brek throws into your path, little orchid." Lirah could not help but feel unsettled by the savage tone in her voice, and the eager, almost predacious way Vishaya was now looking at her. Her eyes flashed again, her ample lips smiling widely, framing her inhumanly sharp teeth. Lirah shivered a little and dropped her gaze to the floor.

"I suppose, and yes I am an empathic healer or something like that. I have to try. I can't just ignore it. I have to try to help."

"Well, you could ignore it, ignore them, but I don't think you will. It is not in your nature to do so. That is why you burn so brightly. Most of my people can see arcane energy within a person. With most it does not reach beyond their physical form, but with you it fills your cage and spills over into the room." Vishaya sounded a bit awestruck as she said this.

"So, you can actually see it, with your eyes? What does it look like, Vishaya?" Lirah held up her hand and looked closely at it. An absent smile darted across Vishaya's face.

"It looks like...a thousand golden tongues of flame floating about as feathers in the autumn wind."

Lirah let slip a childlike giggle at the thought of how she apparently looked to her new friend. Yes, Vishaya was a friend, Lirah could feel it. She stifled her laughter quickly, hoping she had not upset Vishaya. Apparently she hadn't, as Vishaya continued to speak.

"However, we will have more time to talk about our looks after we get out of here. And that will be made quite easy if you can get my amithyles back," Vishaya said, anticipation etched on her face.

"Amithyles? What are those?" asked Lirah.

"They are what one uses to channel arcane energies. Think of them as focusing amplifiers."

"Alright," Lirah said slowly, though she was not sure what a focusing amplifier was.

Vishaya could see her confusion and continued. "Trust me, Lirah, if we can get them, getting out of here should not be too hard. Even if you insist on saving every slave in this place. Truth be told, there is someone else in here I want to get out, also."

"Oh." Lirah tried not to sound too surprised at this. "Who is it?"

Vishaya hesitated for a moment before answering. "Who is not important. It would be best if we can free him, but first we need my amithyles."

"Where are the amithyles at?" Lirah asked.

"I am sure they have them in that room. When I was in there, I think I spotted both of them in a chest by the far wall," Vishaya said.

"I was not in there for very long and never had the chance to grab them. I don't think after the fight I put up that I will be going back in there. You, however, will probably be taken in soon. When you are inside, try to hold your breath, take shallow breaths if you must, there is a mist they use to lessen your will. All you need to do is slip your hand into an amithyle and let your arcane power go. The amithyle should do the rest, just don't point it at yourself. You should be able to feel them if you are close, like you can feel the spark in others."

Lirah started to speak when the door to the room in question burst open. Vishaya darted back behind her ottoman and Lirah shot to her feet. Two large men, some of the same men who had moved Lirah to the cage, entered the room packing another woman, a Tundraihn by her look, though she was smaller than Irem and Ealë.

That has to be her! Lirah felt a thrill of excitement. But how was she going to get her out of here? The woman was motionless and looked to be unconscious as they dragged her to the cell next to Lirah and tossed her in. Lirah only had time to glance at the woman before the same two men opened her cage and took hold of her sharply by the arms. Lirah did not struggle much, fearing to have her senses knocked from her by the large clubs the guards held in their off hands. Lirah looked back to Vishaya as the men took her away. Vishaya leaned out from behind the ottoman, held up her hand, and made the motion of slipping something on it. The oak of the shutting door cut her view off.

24

Into the Den

T ake care in matters of the heart that Varii does not overplay her hand for your sake. For in nothing is she more invested than the ecstasy of passions sated, or the tension of lovers denied.
Essays of the Divine

The sound of Rovik's boots sloshing in the muddy track that passed as a street seemed to send thundering echoes off the wooden buildings and large colorful tents. He knew that no matter how quietly he moved, it would not be quiet enough to settle his nerves. For years, every action had been a careful exercise of delicate maneuvering. The right words said at the right moment. Actions quietly done or openly displayed at the right time. Always in control. Garadale had once told him that this was one of his greatest strengths, and one the ruler of Anoth admired.

That's why he trusted you enough to leave. Rovik's thought caused a surge of self-loathing and regret, but he had no room for such distractions. Not when he was acting so dangerously. He felt out of control more than ever. What was he doing?

Getting yourself killed, most likely. This thought, he knew, was not wrong. The chances were good that he would die. He would be found out completely and put to death as the ultimate traitor. But he felt wholly committed to try, and the feeling gave him strength.

He was making his way carefully down a narrow winding alley toward the center of what was called the Den. The Den consisted of a massive labyrinth of poorly constructed wooden buildings, shanty hovels, various tents, and the occasional large stone tower house. This was the domain of the slavers' guild and the seedy industry that had sprung up to profit from the Subjugate. Officially, the group was known as In-Kind Mercantile, but it was openly marketed as the finest guild of slave traders in all the realms. In-Kind had a network that spanned most of the known world and even the edges of the unknown. For the right price, you could own nearly anything, or more specifically *anyone* of the many peoples and kindreds of Miljah.

Other guilds and groups populated the Den. Ruffled Silks, Brass Tack Merchants, and several large revelry halls operated by the Brothers of Brek, filled in the spaces between In-Kind's holdings. All these groups played host to, and did business with, the Dao'Tai and the many bands of mercenaries and brigands that seemed to gravitate to such a riotous and crude place. The Den could not have been a truer mockery of all that Anoth had striven to create in the realms.

Rovik hated this place. No act was too vile for most who lived and did business here. Even the more reputable merchants who did business in the Den seemed to be tainted by their dealings. It was difficult to deny the thriving markets of the Den, though, and rumors indicated that guilds who would not trade with the Den came upon hard times in the form of mercenary raids and bandit attacks. Rovik had looked into these claims and found them more than valid. Afyreen was not interested in policing what she had called inter-entrepreneurial disputes, and Rovik knew better than to push the issue.

At the heart of the Den, near the river, was In-Kind's primary compound. Commonly known as the slavers' camp or guild, this compound was the stuff of nightmares for wholesome folk. It was also the place where the Subjugate sent castaways and political prisoners. A place for people to disappear. The compound was constructed around a large arena. This structure played host to blood culls, battles to the death between the condemned, slaves, and even wild beasts. Acts of unspeakable despotism and violence served to entertain the Dao'Tai and others who indulged in the carnal excess the Den had to offer.

This night, however, Rovik was not seeking any such excess. Not the lights of the Ruffled Silks, nor the many exotic slaves and goods drew him to the Den. He was there for one purpose—Sificah. Rovik quickened his pace, hoping to get to the slave compound as fast as he could. His station would only garner him a little protection from the guild soldiers, brigands, and thieves that populated most of the Den.

Get in, get out, fast and simple. At least that was his frantic hope. KaTyle might as well have killed him that night in the scurry. A mission into the Den to free a prisoner was as good as a cudgel to the skull, or a knife to the heart—but Rovik had to try. He had to prove to KaTyle that he could be trusted, that the Sunshadow could trust his information. More importantly, however, Rovik needed to prove to himself that he could choose to make a difference for the good. He had to save her.

The narrow alleyway ended abruptly, opening into a small circular courtyard. On the far side, a high wall signaled the outer perimeter of the slavers' compound. His goal. It was early enough in the evening that many people were still making their way to and from the various shops, lust-inns, and guild halls. Rovik pulled his hooded cloak tightly around him and stepped into the crowd. Taivadeans, Dao'Tai, and many from the Thalyphonie Islands streamed around the flat stone auction platform in the center of the courtyard. Rovik had been here several times before to purchase staff for the palace. He liked to think that though they were his slaves they were at least better off under his roof than as the property of the Dao'Tai or doomed to the warships of Thalyphonie and the far-flung isle realms. The Taivadeans, Rovik knew, cared nothing for the ownership of slaves; rather, they served as blades for hire, seeking the hottest fronts for battle. Most of those he now saw were clearly bodyguards and guild soldiers.

Rovik worked his way through the crowd and soon was standing near a large iron door set deep in the high walls of the slavers' compound. A single lantern set in a nook in the wall illuminated the entry way. The door was propped partially open and two large Taivadean guild soldiers leaned in the opening. Armed with spears and shields, the carefully polished scales of their fine armor and their helms sparkled in the lantern light. They stood straight at Rovik's approach, and one raised his hand, signaling Rovik to stop.

"Stay where ye be, there be no more to sell this day." His accent was slight, and he gripped his spear firmly as he spoke, but his face was friendly enough. This was the moment Rovik was worried about. *Brek, tip to my favor.*

"Hail, friends to the Subjugate! I am Rovik, Chancellor of Anoth and trusted advisor to the Aya Dao'Tai. I have business with some of those you currently hold at the pleasure of the Aya Dao'Tai, and I require discreet entrance."

Rovik finished, proud at the calm tone he managed. He held out his passage papers and his signet ring for the guards to see. The Taivadeans looked to each other for a moment, then the one who spoke took the papers from Rovik and examined them. Rovik managed a smile at the other guard as he watched. Taivadeans were not a stupid people. Though many of their ways seemed uncivilized or overly violent, Rovik knew them to be intelligent and cunning. Presently, the guard handed Rovik back the papers and gave him a knowing smile.

"Be about yer way, sire, we won't be marking your passing." The guards pushed the heavy door fully open and gestured for Rovik to enter.

"Thanks to you both, may the night pass in peace, Sons of Taivad." Rovik waved his hands and bowed a little in a gesture of thanks and the guards returned the salute.

Passing quickly between them Rovik entered the compound, wondering at the expression of the guard. After moving into a hallway he stepped behind one of the many columns of the building to allow his eyes to adjust to the dim light. The air was thick and musty, smelling of moldy straw and sweat. Rovik had only actually been inside this building a few times but never in this section. He knew the general layout, and that the prisoners were kept segregated by gender. From what Rovik could piece together, he should be in the female side of the compound.

Rovik's eyes now adjusted to the dim light and he saw that he was standing in a long hallway flanked by two rows of massive stone columns. Light from several skylights and a few lanterns threw long soft shadows into the hall. Staying behind the row of columns, Rovik slowly walked down the hall, looking for anything that might indicate where to find the holding cells.

As Rovik continued deeper into the compound he started passing doorways. Most were open, and the rooms beyond looked to hold enormous amounts of trade goods and simple foodstuffs. Soon Rovik came to an intersection of several hallways. He immediately noticed one hallway curving away in a gentle arch that was lined with recessed barred cells.

Must be this way. Several guards passed him as he walked, but they paid him no heed. At first the cells were empty with the exception of a few piles of straw and poorly made wooden troughs. Cell after cell passed by and soon, they were no longer empty. Women and girls of all ages and realms filled the cells—three, four, five to a cell. Most were nearly if not totally unclothed, lying down sleeping or huddled together for warmth. Many looked to be from realms far from Anoth, though he saw others from the southern realms as well, Mantorahn, Adohr, and even further down the coast. His stomach knotted up knowing that he held no small part of the blame for the state of these women.

Rovik averted his eyes and quickened his step. The cells abruptly gave way to a wide wooden door set deep in the wall, and he left the main hallway to investigate. He hesitated for a moment as his hand touched the metal ring of the door handle. He still had no real plan beyond finding KaTyle's sister. Once he found her then what? Convince the guards to give her to him? Fight to free her? Rovik would have to figure that out once he actually found her. if he could. Days had passed, and she could have already been sold for all he knew. KaTyle was sure that she was still in here, though, so he had to try to find her.

He pulled and the door slowly opened. The room was very dark, but Rovik could see rows of three-high bunk beds. Many were filled with sleeping guards. Other beds were empty. A small fire waned in a hearth on the far side of the lone room. *Not here.* Rovik quickly pushed the door shut and stepped back into the hall of cells. *Great, have to check each one...This is going to get me killed.*

How was he to find her in here? She could be anywhere, in any room or cell. His status in the realm would only go so far to protect him from snooping around the compound. Strictly speaking, the Subjugate allowed In-Kind to police their own issues. They could kill him, take him as a slave, or do whatever they wished for his trespassing. Not to mention what they would do if they knew he was there to liberate a slave.

Rovik wiped away the sweat that was beading up on his brow. The night was yet new, and he had time to search. He continued to walk past the cells, checking each one. He marveled at the trick of Brek's coin that KaTyle's sister would turn out to be none other than Sificah. He had not told KaTyle, but once he learned that she had been taken by the Subjugate and given to In-Kind; he knew he would try to save her regardless of her connection to the Sunshadow or KaTyle. Her face was burned into his mind now, and he searched every sleeping woman and forlorn girl in the cells for it.

Another doorway appeared in the wall, this one with the door partially open. He could hear several men talking inside and a woman's whimpers. He peered carefully into the room. Several men were inside. Some sitting at a small table eating, others gathered around what Rovik could see was a young Adohr woman. He saw enough to be sure Sificah was not there before he quietly passed the room, cursing that he lacked the courage and prowess to punish the vile men inside.

More guards passed by, and again they seemed to take no notice of Rovik. More cells and more doors. None of them held Sificah—barracks, storerooms, and a large kitchen—but no sign of Sificah. He was near the center of the slavers' compound now and nearing the main entrance to the arena itself.

His nerves were wearing thin, and each clanking lock or rattling chain sent his hand flying to the hilt of his sword. He had just relaxed from a guard suddenly stepping out into the hall when a muffled scream slowly drifted down the hall. He froze, hoping that it was not her, but knowing that it was. Somehow, he recognized the cry of agony as Sificah. She was close, but the shape of the hall would make it hard to guess the exact distance and direction. He moved with determination, stopping each time a new scream slammed into his ears.

Rovik hurried now, starting to run as the screams grew closer. He took a small side passage and then another until he was suddenly standing in front of a large wooden door. He was breathing hard, and a cold sweat clung to him, not from exertion but from fear. His hands felt cold and shaky as he opened the door, and before he could talk himself out of it, he stepped into the room.

It was fairly well-lit and large. Tables covered with bottles, knives, and what were clearly tools of torture sat near a wall. A few small cages sat in another corner, and near the center of the room, strapped to a tall frame, was Sificah. Several In-Kind guards stood near her. All of them staring at Rovik, clearly waiting for an explanation. Sificah hung limp on the frame. Blood ran down her chest onto her legs from several deep cuts on her cheeks. Her clothes were tattered and revealed the bruising from several savage beatings on her body.

Rovik had thought of a hundred ways he could talk his way into escaping with her. He could claim he purchased her. He could insist she was requested again by the Aya Dao'Tai. He had worked out several ways to negotiate it. He was good at that.

Before he had time to say a word, however, he found his sword in his hand. His breath felt hot as he set his jaw for the fight that he now found himself in. With no thoughts other than lethal fury, he rushed in. The guards hesitated. Rovik was not sure if the guards knew who he was or if they were simply shocked by the interruption. It did not matter, for Rovik fell on them before they had time to react. His long two-handed sword found the throat of the closest guard so fast that his body hit the floor before the other guards could get their weapons in their hands.

Rovik was fully committed now, and he knew that if they called out or if one of them got out of the room he would be doomed. Sificah would be doomed. The next guard dashed for a spear and the other three drew their swords and took bucklers from their belts. Rovik lunged hard and wide, plunging his sword into the belly of the guard as he ran for his spear. With a splitting jerk he pulled his weapon free and immediately recovered from the lunge to parry a blow from the next closest guard before he buried the bright steel of his blade into the man's leg. Rovik felt the bone snap and the man collapsed. The last guard took a fumbling step backwards into the room toward Sificah. He held a shaking blade to her neck and spoke in a cracked voice.

"You come any closer, she dies, old man."

Rovik stopped where he was. Despite his soft life and the years spent as little more than a talking figurehead for the Subjugate, Rovik had always been a capable swordsman. He looked over the man before him now, young, and untrained. A vile creature and bully really, no warrior, not even a true soldier. He looked to Sificah's violated form.

Rovik slowly inhaled, allowing his mind to become aware of every muscle in his body. He firmed his grip on his sword and locked his eyes on the guard's neck, where it met his chest. His breaths were coming fast and ragged. He was terrified. With a speed born of countless battle drills Rovik stutter-stepped and lunged as far and hard as he could, hoping that age had not robbed him of the distance he would need to stretch to hit his mark, the hollow of the guard's throat.

"If you let me g—" The guard stopped speaking and dropped to the floor. A sharp pain crawled up the inside of Rovik's leg and he knew he had pulled something. He slowly rose to stand near Sificah and he looked down over the man he had just slain. A growing pool of blood rushed out of the wound at his neck. The other guards had bled out also, and the entire room stank of gore.

Suddenly, there was a rush of movement near the entranceway and the door slammed shut. He wheeled around to face the interlopers, only to stop utterly motionless at the sight of what had just entered the room, fear and uncertainty fixing him where he stood.

Dark tears take me!

25

Frantic Escape

When seeking the grace of Brek hasten to recall that he is pleased with any shift in luck, no matter the good or ill of the turning. Count not upon him to act therefore on your behalf, but that of fate itself and praise be when his split is in your favor.
Essays of the Divine.

Lirah turned her head to the room she was now in. It was even more ornately adorned than the cage room had been. Along the tapestry-covered walls were stacked chests and baskets of goods. Gold verts, silver gibs, gems, scrolls—the assemblage of trinkets and treasure was vast. Lirah saw three chests full of orichalcum and electrum hrids, enough to buy everything in Allinth. There was also a large wooden desk covered with papers in one corner of the room, and next to it an enormous bed. Sitting at the desk was a short, thick man dressed in silken robes. Lirah could not help but notice the mass of jewelry he wore. His fingers, wrists, arms, and neck were all adorned with every conceivable form of jewelry. He gave a sordid smile as he stood.

"Ah! So, this is the one they told me of; she is much better looking than they described. You may leave her here." The two guards at Lirah's sides bowed and they, along with two more guards who had been

"

standing near the doorway, left the room, shutting the heavy door behind them.

"Come here, my girl," said the bejeweled man.

Lirah hesitated, looking quickly about for the amithyles. She couldn't see anything, though she thought she could feel something in the room, a tugging sensation. It was subtle, but there. She took a few steps further into the room. The air was thick with perfumes and spices.

"My name is La'vohr. Now don't be shy, come a bit closer." His voice was kind, but Lirah could sense something vile beneath it.

Lirah took a few more steps into the room, still looking for the amithyles. *I don't even know what they look like!* Vishaya's only clue was her hand gesture. From that Lirah guessed they must be something you wear on your hands, but what was it, a bracelet, a ring? Something else entirely? The man was still speaking and Lirah gave him a nervous smile, realizing she was standing still, looking wildly around the room.

Lirah turned her attention to the man, La'vohr, as he manipulated a strange-looking box in the far corner of the room. It looked to be brass, a few rods in width, with many ornate holes in its face and sides. La'vohr took a pitcher from the floor and poured the contents of it into the top of the box. Thick hazy steam billowed out as the fluid poured in.

"There we are! Now my girl, let us talk."

Lirah glowered at him. She did not like the look in his eyes.

"Ah, I see a little fire in you," he chuckled as he sat down on the edge of the bed. The steam was now starting to drift into the room, its thick powerful aroma filled the air about Lirah, and she started to feel strange. Too late she recalled Vishaya's warning.

"Do you know how rare you are, my girl? Do you know how much you are worth? How much your...children will be worth?"

Lirah was starting to feel detached now; the room looked as if it were melting away, and La'vohr's words sounded slow and deep. The bright colors of the tapestries and decorations of the room melted together. Lirah tried to reach out for more strength, but the earth was even more devoid of life here than it had been in the slave cell. The only thing that was firm was the voice of the man La'vohr, who continued to speak. She looked to La'vohr, he was the only solid thing she could see as the room spun into a slippery myriad of colors and light.

"Yes, I could simply sell you, but what would I gain? As little as a few hundred verts? In a fair deal, ten score hrids, surely. But if we were...business partners, we could make a fortune. He was playing with one of the larger rings on his little finger with an absent-minded expression. He paused and looked Lirah in her eyes.

"Even half-Yiillyar children would be worth much."

Lirah found herself staggering toward his voice. All her senses were hazy, as though she were in a waking dream. She could not look away from him. Reality, and the reason for her being there, started to fade as La'vohr kept speaking to her. She took a few faltering steps toward him, trying to remember what that strange dark woman wanted her to do.

*No, that must not be real, none of this is. It's a dream, just a dream...*A comfortable weariness flooded Lirah's mind and all she could think about was lying down and falling into a deep peaceful sleep.

"Together we could do quite well for ourselves, my girl. That Tundraihn would not see the sense in this, she resisted. But she is weak and common compared to you."

Lirah stumbled and fell onto the bed. She now lay next to La'vohr, staring toward the wall—dazed. She could barely hear his voice, though she could still feel its deep resonating tone. All, to her, seemed a warm distant dream, when she suddenly felt a hand upon her shoulder. This called some of her mind back to her, and her thoughts cleared just long enough for a bright red light to catch her eye.

She made herself focus on it and saw it was a large red gem set in silver bands. There was a strange kind of glow coming from the gem, and as Lirah reached her hand toward it, it shimmered the brighter. She realized that it was not the allure of the soft bed she was feeling, but the tugging sensation from this gem, now grown into a pulling warmth that begged her to draw near.

A distant memory came to her, or perhaps a dream, a spirit from the Dark Realms, slipping something on her wrist. *Vishaya! I...have...to put it on...*She leaned up off the bed a little to reach out and took hold of the gem. It was hot to the touch, and the pain drove the stupor from her mind.

Reality came rushing back to her, and Lirah could now feel La'vohr's hands upon her. She violently thrust him away, keeping her hand on the gem, and delivered a stout fist to his face, sending him onto his back. He cried out in shock as Lirah rolled to the floor. She placed her hand into the silver bands that surrounded the red gem. As she did, a roaring stream of molten flame shot from the gem and blasted a hole through the bed's canopy and the roof of the building.

Lirah quickly took her hand out of the bands, shaking and gasping for air. Horrible stabbing pains were running up her arm. It felt as though all her insides were on fire. Yet, there was also a strange satisfaction and almost a desire for more. Smoke started to fill the room from the burning cloth and timber. The damage to the roof was extensive, and La'vohr lay pinned under a beam that had fallen from the ceiling. Lirah stood up, looked back to the chest from where she had taken the amithyle and saw another. This one held a sparkling blue gem in silver bands. Lirah carefully picked it up, though it did not burn as the red one had. It felt different, but just as powerful. She did not have time to wonder over this as the fire started to spread.

She flung open the door just in time to meet two guards. One grabbed her by the throat and pinned her to the wall, as the second ran to where La'vohr lay. Lirah dropped the red amithyle and struggled to breathe. She pounded on the face of her attacker, and in response he slammed her into the wall with a crack. Lirah hung, barely aware for a moment, till she saw Vishaya jump up from her hiding place and rush to the bars of her cell. Lirah could hardly breathe as the guard started to crush her neck, and she was losing consciousness. With all the strength she had left she managed to toss the blue amithyle toward Vishaya's cage. It fell short on the fur-covered floor. Reaching as far as she could through the bars, Vishaya just managed to catch it with her fingertips.

Lirah was still struggling for air as a fist-sized ball of what looked like blue lightning struck the guard who held her in the side of his head, rendering him motionless instantly. Lirah landed in a coughing heap on top of him, wheezing for air. Two more blue orbs shot past her and blasted into the chest of a guard that had just walked through the door next to her.

"The red amithyle," Vishaya said in a desperate, craving tone. "Quickly, give it to me!" Lirah found it next to the dead guards. She picked it up and again the burning pain rushed up her arm. Still coughing she made her way to Vishaya's cage and handed her the red amithyle. She smiled as she slipped her dark hand into the silver bands and looked to Lirah.

"By the blood of my mother, that is better! Thank you. Now let us make our way out of here." Vishaya spoke with a ruthless tone and gave a most vicious smile. She took the loops of chains that held her cage shut in her hands and the red amithyle started to glow brightly. The chains were soon red and glowing themselves. Lirah stepped back as molten iron started dripping from the chains and bars alike. Soon the entire wad of melted chains and lock fell splashing at Vishaya's feet. Flames jumped up from the molten metal, and Vishaya threw open the cage door and walked through the fire, stepping directly in a puddle of still molten steel as unharmed and unconcerned as one would walk through a mud puddle. Her eyes surged with light and she was smiling savagely.

She stepped past Lirah, over the two guards on the floor, and looked into the room where La'vohr was still lying. She held up both her hands, and two streams, one of flame and one that looked like a bolt of lightning, surged from the gems and into the room. Lirah shielded her eyes from the intense light that lasted for several moments. Vishaya lowered her hands, and the streams ceased. She turned to Lirah, an expression of complete satisfaction on her face, her eyes gleamed even brighter and she was panting as she spoke.

"He will never touch another person again." Her expression suddenly changed to puzzlement as she turned back to look into the room.

"Do you have a battle falcon, Lirah?" she asked.

"Mirris!" Lirah exclaimed, and she ran up to the doorway next to Vishaya.

The room was mostly ash and smoldering timbers now; only a black, burned patch remained where La'vohr had been a few moments ago. Perched on the edge of the hole in the roof was indeed Mirris. She saw Lirah in the doorway, gave her a nod, then flew off into the dark sky.

"I take it that is the bird you referred to earlier?" Vishaya asked. Her voice was once again calm and pleasant.

"Yes, she will let my friends know we are on our way out so they can meet us," Lirah said as she left the doorway and headed to a nearby cage.

"Excellent. Let the Tundraihn out, I am going to find something more decent to put on. One of the guards should have keys for the locks."

Lirah found the keys and hurried to open the cages. Irem's cage was first.

"Wake up, we have to go!" Lirah shook her until she awoke; she tried to be gentle, but they were in a hurry. Lirah placed her hands on either side of Irem's head and pushed a little strength into her. Irem slowly opened her eyes and sat up.

"Sister, what happened...? Syrnii's veil! Behind you!" Lirah spun around as Irem scrambled to her feet pointing a trembling hand at Vishaya, who was hurriedly digging through a pile of cloth in a corner of the room.

"She is our friend. I think your priestess is in that cage, but we have to go."

"No, she is Xydar, a Dark Tear! They are dangerous, they are from Tir'Luthryel. She will kill us just to please Drashtaa and Achylle," Irem whispered.

Lirah looked for a moment at Vishaya. "No, she will not kill us. I am sure she is on our side, no matter what tales we have heard."

Irem shook her head and muttered something under her breath.

"Come on, there is no time." Lirah pulled Irem with her and they quickly approached the cell with the Tundraihn priestess. Lira opened the cell, but the woman remained still, motionless. Lirah touched her forehead; it was cold and damp. Lirah quickly tried the same gentle push of energy she had used on Irem to awaken her, but something resisted the healing. Vishaya, now wrapped in a shred of a drape, looked in.

"Is this her?" asked Lirah

"Yes, this is the Eolai'Mahtair," Irem replied curtly as she eyed Vishaya with mistrust.

"Looks like she wilted," Vishaya chided.

"Sister, is she alive?" Irem asked. Lirah felt for her life force and found it, but there was something shrouding it, like a thick fog.

"Yes," Lirah said. "But I am not sure what is wrong with her, I..." Lirah could not put to words what she was sensing.

"Can you help her, Otheäil?" asked Irem

"I don't know. I can try, but we must get her out of here first," Lirah said, her voice soft as regret, eyes lingering on the lifeless calm of the Tundriahn priestess' face.

"Very well; let us carry her out," Vishaya replied impatiently.

Irem and Lirah slid their arms beneath the priestess and lifted her carefully. Together they made for the door. Lirah peered into the corridor; it was dark and empty. As they stepped into the hall, she turned to the left, but Vishaya moved to the right.

"Right—we go right, little orchid," Vishaya said firmly, her eyes gleaming in the dim light.

"But Jahllia is to the left," Lirah protested, her voice low but urgent.

"We can't carry every hapless slave from this place," Vishaya said slowly, as one might speak to a confused child. "There should be help to the right—including the male Tundraihn. If we are to save this Jahllia too, we might need more able bodies."

"Jahllia?" Irem queried.

Yes. I helped her when I was first placed in a cell. She is just off to the left," Lirah said quickly. "I can't leave her here. But you're right, Vishaya, we will need more help to get her out. Let's go." There was no time for argument. They hurried off to the right, Lirah and Irem following Vishaya closely. The corridor was eerily still as they moved.

"We will go back for Jahllia, won't we, Vishaya?" Lirah asked as they rushed along.

"Oh, my little orchid, if you insist," Vishaya said with a thin smile. "We can run about all night if you wish to—more chances for me to murder every single slaver in this place."

Lirah couldn't tell if Vishaya was joking but she did feel the scorching pulse of her feral aura sweep through the hall like a wave of living flame.

They continued as fast as they could up the hall to the right. It curved around toward the east in a semicircle. Soon they were passing barred cells like the ones Lirah was first in, but these were filled with male captives. They were moving along at a good pace till a shout halted them.

"Irem, raji luta koi?"

Lirah recognized the voice of Orodan. They turned back down the hall, and there in a cell together were Orodan and Shytov.

"Miss Lirah, your name will be sung of in great honor," Orodan was smiling. "You found the Eolai'Mahtair." Lirah opened their cells with the guard's keys, and Orodan and Shytov took the Tundraihn priestess into their arms.

"Mirris was just at our window. Kaileth means for us to escape out the back toward the river; let us go," Orodan said as he started to move. A crystal blue light shot down the hall as Vishaya fired into a group of guards running at them from the north end.

"Xydarii!" exclaimed Shytov, who had been startled by Vishaya. Lirah jumped between the Tundraihn and Vishaya, her hands raised, face pleading.

"She is with us, no matter what you might think!" Orodan and Shytov both regarded Vishaya with expressions of misgiving.

"No time for this, Tundraihn, we must leave, now!" Vishaya said with a commanding tone.

"Indeed," agreed Orodan, and they all took off running back down the hall.

Lirah soon saw that Vishaya was not with them. She stopped and turned to look behind for her. She could see flashes of red and blue light from down the hall, and she ran toward them.

"Miss Lirah, where do you go?" Orodan called back after her.

"To help Vishaya. Go, get your priestess out of here; we will catch up. The way out is not far ahead of you, you can't miss it."

Orodan did not argue as he and the others continued to run down the hall.

She soon caught up to Vishaya, who was walking over several fallen slaver guards. She whirled around at the sound of Lirah's footsteps. Seeing Lirah, she lowered her weapons and spoke.

"Ah, you came to help. I am glad. He is not much further."

They both continued to run down the hall, and soon light from an open door ahead entered their view. The silhouettes of three men appeared in the doorway, and Vishaya let fly a burst of blue light and red fire from her amithyles. The men fell without a cry, and the two women entered the room. Tables and weapon racks lined the walls, and in the center stood a tall cage. Vishaya had been quite a shock for Lirah, and she was still not even sure what she was, but what Lirah saw in this cage was no less spectacular.

The priests of Anthos had told her stories when she was little of winged beings who, from time to time, would come to earth to aid wounded or stranded travelers in the wilderness. She had always assumed that they were either myths, or creatures of the heavens. But there in a circle of iron bars stood a creature of legends. He was taller than most men, and from his back great, gray-feathered wings loomed over his stout shoulders. He was clad in a tight-fitting black cuirass with a gold tunic underneath. His gold hair was pulled back, making his broad face easy to see in the light cast from the lanterns hanging in the room. His frame was lean, and a smile crossed his face as he saw the two women enter the room.

"I am very pleased to see you, dark one, and you have a new friend as well," he said in a soft voice.

"I never thought I would hear one of your kind say that," Vishaya snapped back. Lirah was still standing in the doorway, looking at the man in the cage. If it was fair to call him just a man.

He is so beautiful...and strange. There was something about this face that seemed off. It was sharp and angular with a fierce beauty, but that was not it. It was his eyes. They looked larger than a human's, more like those of a bird of prey.

"Lirah, the keys." Vishaya was holding out her hand.

"Oh, sorry," Lirah apologized, embarrassed by her gawking. She tossed the keys to Vishaya, who then opened the door to the cage.

He stepped out into the room and spread out his wings, which stretched from one side of the room to the other. He was truly an amazing being to behold, and there was an unearthly aura around him. Lirah could feel his life force without hardly trying too.

"Let us be off," he said. Vishaya nodded and the two of them ran through the door. On the way out, Lirah grabbed a spear from a rack next to the door and raced after them.

Cell after cell flew by in the darkness as they ran. Lirah could not help but feel sadness for all the people they must be running past, veiled in the darkness. Lirah was thankful she could not see their faces; it would only make the pain of leaving them greater.

"Olyn. I am Olyn. Thank you for helping to free me." Despite their fast pace, Olyn spoke easily.

"I am glad I could help," Lirah panted. "But all I did was carry the keys."

Olyn laughed pleasantly as they ran. They were soon passing the door where Vishaya and Lirah had been held. Lirah caught sight of several armed guards within it. Shouts and sounds of men running echoed down the hall after Lirah and the others.

"I think they saw us," Lirah warned.

"I doubt they saw me, but those wings would be hard to miss."

Olyn said nothing in response to Vishaya's remark, he only ran faster. A few moments more and light from another open door became visible ahead.

"That is our way to the female side," Lirah called ahead to the others.

"Right, the woman?" asked Vishaya.

"Woman?" asked Olyn.

"Yes, she is dying," Lirah stated. "I have to get her out of here."

"What about the men chasing us?" questioned Olyn.

"You two can go on, but I have to get her, Olyn. I just do." They must have heard the determination in her voice since they didn't leave her, and they all three paused at the doorway, the sound of their pursuers drawing near.

"They are easy enough to kill, and it feels— nice to do so. Go get her, we will hold here," Vishaya said.

Lirah stood, looking surprised for a moment, then said quietly, "Thank you."

"Just hurry, we don't want to get his feathers plucked." Vishaya gestured to Olyn and handed the keys back to Lirah. She then stepped into the shadowy doorway.

Lirah turned and ran on into the dark hall. Sounds of fighting soon started to drift down the hall after her. A long howl echoed through the hallways from a far-off distance.

"Riidak, they are in position..." Lirah muttered, remembering the signal.

It did not take very long to reach the cell where the girl in the blue dress was lying. Lirah quickly opened the door and entered the holding cell. Jahllia was lying motionless in the filthy straw on the stone floor, right where she had been when the guards had taken Lirah away. She knelt at her side and gently touched her shoulder. She felt very warm, almost hot to the touch. Lirah felt her forehead; it was wet with perspiration and very hot. As Lirah had feared, Jahllia had a fever. She took Jahllia's hand and gently squeezed it. Jahllia's eyes opened slightly, and Lirah spoke to her softly.

"We are getting out of here. Do you think you can stand?"

Jahllia nodded her head and started to struggle to her feet. Lirah stood and helped Jahllia up. Taking her under the arm, and using her spear to steady each step, Lirah was able to help Jahllia walk. Back into the hall they moved, as fast as Jahllia could go. The hall was dark and thankfully silent as they passed through it. On and on they went in the darkness, and it seemed to Lirah that the hallway had lengthened. It certainly took a lot longer at this pace than it had on the way in. Still, they went on, and Lirah was starting to wonder if they had missed the doorway out. But then a dim, flickering light fell upon the floor and wall ahead of them. Lirah and Jahllia slowed their pace and cautiously drew near the light. Lirah could see the open door ahead. It was on fire in a few places, as were a few of the ceiling beams, and upon the floor lay over a dozen fallen men. Lirah and Jahllia quietly made their way through the dead men and came near the door.

"They must have moved on," Lirah whispered as she looked into the empty doorway.

"We did no such thing." Vishaya's words startled Lirah and she almost dropped Jahllia. "You didn't think we would stand in plain sight, did you?" Lirah could hear Vishaya smiling, even though all she could see were her softly glowing eyes.

"I suppose not," Lirah smiled back. As they stood there, Jahllia slipped from consciousness and her legs gave way. Lirah was barely able to hold her up.

"Olyn, pick that girl up and let us leave."

Olyn did not move and said nothing to Vishaya's command. Vishaya looked to him and her eyes flashed brightly in the darkness as she spoke.

"Now, Olyn!" This time Olyn obeyed, and he took Jahllia's limp body into his arms. He lifted her with ease.

"This way," Vishaya said, and they all followed her.

They moved with great speed through the narrow corridors, passing door after door on either side. Olyn did not seem slowed in the least by carrying Jahllia. Lirah's bare feet were cold and painfully numb from the chill stone floor, and her lungs burned. *How much longer can I keep this up?* Soon fresh sounds of men in pursuit echoed up the corridor behind them and Lirah found the strength to keep running. Ahead Vishaya quickened her pace. Lirah looked behind and saw the lamplight was steadily getting closer to them. Suddenly, Vishaya darted into an open door, followed closely by Olyn. Lirah hurried after them. Once inside, Vishaya shut and barred the door. Panting for breath, Lirah pressed her ear to the door and listened. Their chasers ran by the room they were now in and continued down the hall. Lirah sighed in relief and turned to her fellows.

"I think they passed us—" she stopped mid-sentence as she saw that they were not alone.

At the far end of what was obviously a torture room stood a man with a bloodstained sword in hand. At his feet lay several men in a widening pool of blood. Next to them was a woman strapped onto a frame of sorts. The man with the sword looked stunned and unsure of what to do. He wore a neat mustache, and his silver-gray hair was closely cut and well-groomed. From his dress and appearance, it was plain he was a noble of some sort.

Vishaya was first to speak as she raised one of her hands and pointed an amithyle at him.

"If you make any attempt to give us away, you will die, human." Crimson light began to fill the room as the amithyle started to glow. The man backed away and lowered his blade. Lirah stood next to the door and Olyn, who spoke next.

"Do not harm him, sable one, he seems frightened beyond posing a threat."

Vishaya was breathing heavily and the light of the amithyle pulsed with each breath. "Who are you and why are you here?" she demanded.

"I...I am Rovik, and I will not harm you, I swear it." He was shaking as he spoke.

"Drop your sword or die this moment!" hissed Vishaya. He instantly did so, and Lirah came up behind Vishaya and spoke softly to her. He didn't look like the slavers, nor was he Taivadean.

"We don't have time for him, we need to find Ralenn and get out of here."

Vishaya's hard posture softened slightly.

"You could get her out of here," the man Rovik said, half to himself. "I...I have information I could trade for your assistance."

"What are you talking about?" Lirah asked. "And why should we trust you?"

"If you will get this woman out of here," he pointed to the frame where she hung, "I will tell you all you wish," he said breathlessly.

"Who is she?" asked Lirah.

"She is...she is innocent," he said. There was a sincerity in his voice that Lirah wanted to trust.

"Alright. I will get her out of here," said Lirah. Vishaya shot her a withering glance but said nothing.

"Thank you...You must warn Paladin Valskar that the Subjugate is marching on Lea'Angleneth and Syrah. The Aya Dao'Tai intends to let the Ikthii consume the people of Thenill. Mantorah must prepare. If I can, I will divert the bulk of the army to Syrah in order to give Lea'Angleneth a chance, but you must warn them."

"Why are you telling us this? Aren't you a part of the Subjugate somehow?" Lirah gave him the fiercest look she could muster. Rovik hung his head and took a deep breath.

"It is a chance...a chance to spare innocents, a chance to do something right."

Vishaya scoffed, licking her teeth as she spoke. "I still say we kill him. He wears the colors of our enemies."

"I have just murdered a Subjugate inquisitor and several others to save a servant. I have no reason to lie to you, and I am more able a friend where I am than if I were to be killed or flee my post. Kill me or not, but please take this woman with you, and take this." He took a ring from his thumb and a small leather bag. The bag was full of papers and had blood on it. He handed it to Lirah.

"What is it?" asked Lirah.

"The bag is Sificah's. The paladin will know what this ring is."

"We will get this to him, but you have to do something to prove your words." Lirah thought fast. "Free every prisoner you pass on your way out of this place, and then you will set fire to the gates."

"What?" Rovik shouted.

Vishaya's eyes narrowed and Lirah was sure she was growling quietly at him. Rovik paled as Vishaya's growl became louder, like a frost lion readying for a fight, her eyes glowing brightly.

"You can't be serious," he hissed, lowering his voice.

Vishaya raised both amithyles as she spoke, her voice still seething with an animalistic snarl. "You will swear to do this, or you will die here and now. Only after I've threshed your very soul!"

Rovik stumbled back away from her. "I swear it, I swear it," he said quickly.

Vishaya snapped her teeth at him and lowered her hands. "That is better," she said, almost sweetly.

"Now that you are finished, may we leave?" prodded Olyn, who was still holding Jahllia.

Lirah stepped forward and tossed the cell keys to Rovik. He caught them and started toward the door. Vishaya and Olyn stepped aside to let him pass, and Rovik looked at them both, trembling with fear, then at the girl in Olyn's arms. He seemed to recognize her but said nothing. Rovik opened the door and looked into the hallway for a moment before turning to speak.

"I never meant for things to get this bad..." With that he turned and ran toward the cells.

Lirah was not sure what he had meant by that, but there was no time to ponder it. She hurried to the woman tied to the frame and loosed her bonds. Her limp form fell into Lirah's arms. She was much taller than Lirah and was not easy to carry.

"Alright, let us finally leave this place," Vishaya said as she turned to the open door.

Lirah was unable to carry the woman for long, soon being forced to drag her as a last resort. They were once again running down the hallway. Lirah, however, was quickly falling behind. Olyn looked back and saw this. He stopped and waited for Lirah to catch up.

"How many unconscious maids must I bear from this place?" He smiled charmingly as he said this and took the woman from Lirah with his free arm, placing her on his shoulder with ease. With a person now on each shoulder, Olyn continued running at about the same pace as before.

Lirah and Olyn soon caught up to Vishaya, who was standing against the wall next to a large arched doorway. She signaled them to remain silent, then moved her dark hand and pointed into the doorway. Lirah carefully looked around the corner in the direction Vishaya was now pointing. There was a short hall that opened up onto a large platform; beyond this platform lay the arena. Lirah looked in awe at the massive circular structure of stone and wood. It had to be more than a bow's shot to the highest seats. Here and there partitioned boxes formed what must have been seats for dignitaries. There was an arched doorway set in the lower walls at each cardinal direction. Through the doorway opposite Lirah she could see the pale light of the early morning as it danced upon the slow-flowing river. This was the way out, though even running as fast as she could, the long distance across the arena would not be swiftly traveled. Still, they were so close to escape.

Lirah's feeling of relief was cut short as she saw the reason for Vishaya's hesitation. There were moving shadows on the platform, in the seats, and near the river; there were many men walking here and there, just beyond the doorway. There had to be more than two dozen searching the arena and riverbank, and they were all armed and armored like the guards at the camp's main gates. Lirah looked at all the open ground and enemies that barred their escape, then turned back to Vishaya.

"Now what?" Lirah whispered, trying to choke back panic that was seeping into her voice.

Vishaya's eyes burst into light and she smiled eagerly as she spoke. "We will kill them all! We fight our way free, little orchid."

Before Lirah could say anything Vishaya darted around the corner and down the hallway toward the In-Kind guards. Lirah looked back to Olyn, he gave a nod, and Lirah followed after Vishaya. She found Vishaya's dark form almost impossible to see in the dim light of predawn. Lirah looked past the guards to the river and could not see any boats or signs of where Orodan and the others had gone, nor had they found Ealë. All she could do at this point, however, was pray to every Aashahl that might care and quietly move down the hall toward the platform, following Vishaya. They were getting awfully close to the guards when suddenly the darkness was rent as Vishaya let fly bolts of fire and lightning into the crowd of unsuspecting guards.

Lirah ran as fast as she could up to where Vishaya was now crouching behind a large pillar. The men who had not been killed in the initial attack were hiding behind similar items and firing occasional arrows toward Vishaya and Lirah's position. Vishaya was breathing hard, trying to catch her breath after the exertion of her attack. It was beginning to be clear to Lirah that Vishaya's magic worked similarly to her healing in that it took a toll on her. As painful as it might have been, Vishaya seemed to like it as a wide smile clung to her lips and her chest surged with exhilaration with each gasping breath.

The slaver guards took advantage of this break in fire and moved into a position that blocked any direct path off the platform and into the arena. Escape was now impossible without direct confrontation. Lirah saw Olyn hiding in the shadows at the mouth of the hall and pointed him out to Vishaya, who then stood and sent a stream of flame into the darkness around the pillars the guards were hiding behind. Olyn saw this and ran with great speed toward Lirah and Vishaya. He soon was also crouched behind a nearby pillar.

"This is not looking too well," he said calmly as arrows and bolts again started to streak past them, snapping off the stonework of the pillars and hallway. Vishaya had an intense look upon her face as she spoke

"Here is how we will proceed—I will attack them from the front, you two shall run for the door into the arena. I will kill the men in your path, then cause the others to hide. Don't stop until you reach the river. I shall catch up with you there." Light was now surging from Vishaya's eyes like lightning in a boiling thunderstorm.

"No, Vishaya! That is too—"

Before Lirah could finish, Vishaya jumped out from the left side of the pillar and sent a hailstorm of blue energy orbs crashing into and around the guards. With her other hand she fired a stream of flames at the guards blocking the arena doorway, moving her hand back and forth to effectively form a wall of flame. Lirah ran as hard as she could toward the gap Vishaya had just blasted in the line of guards, followed close behind by Olyn. Lirah looked back and saw Vishaya was starting to follow them, though she was still firing the amithyles at the last few guards in the hall.

Lirah ran on past the last pillar and into the arena. As she ran, she realized it was bigger than it had looked from the hallway; the river seemed far away. *Too late to go back now, just have to run...Aseairpeth make me fly...*

She and Olyn had not gone far when Vishaya caught up to them. Lirah could see a little dark blood running from her nose and the corners of her eyes. *She is pushing too hard*, Lirah thought, or was she? Lirah remembered how bright her life force was, how powerful, and hoped maybe she was not in any danger. Lirah looked back to her again. Tears ran into the trails of blood, leaving sparkling ruby streams across her dark face. *Or maybe she just doesn't care how much it hurts her?*

Lirah looked up into the seats of the arena and saw more guards running to catch up to them. Thankfully, the seats slowed them down. A few more frantic moments of running and they reached the middle of the arena where all four arched doorways faced each other. Vishaya was now in the lead. Through these doorways scores of guards, mostly Taivadean, better equipped than any Lirah had seen yet, came pouring to the arena.

Dannitar save us! Lirah prayed as any hope of escape seemed to evaporate.

Vishaya came to an abrupt halt, and Lirah almost ran into her. Within moments they were surrounded by a ring of guards. They kept their distance, choosing to stay in easy bow shot, but no closer. A short man with bright blue and gold lamellar armor stepped forward and cleared his throat to speak. Vishaya looked to Olyn with an expression filled with both terror and exultation.

"You best leave, and take them all," she said through clenched teeth, digging her bare feet into the earth of the arena. Before Lirah could do anything Olyn came near.

"Grab my waist and hold on for your life."

He had barely said this when an unfathomably terrible shriek filled the arena. Lirah had just wrapped her arms around Olyn as he jumped into the air, his massive wings propelling them all in a high arch toward the river. Lirah looked down just in time to see bolts of red lightning surging out of Vishaya in all directions. Wherever they hit a guard they seemed to wither then burst into ash and black vapors. The ground around her smoked and she continued to scream as though she was being torn apart one fiber at a time.

"I can't actually fly with this much weight so get ready." Olyn's words drew Lirah's attention back to the fact that she was hundreds of feet in the air. A few arrows whistled by, but nearly all the guards in the arena were dealing with Vishaya. As Olyn's soaring arch reached its apex Lirah could see Orodan and his band hiding on the far side of the river. Three figures were just now pulling up in a boat to the arena side.

Lirah looked back to Vishaya just before the arena walls blocked her view. She was still standing and slowly making her way to the river. A steady stream of arrows and bolts flew at her, but she seemed to be blocking them with radiating pulses from the blue amithyle.

Lirah looked down. The riverbank was rushing up to her at a horrible pace. Olyn was straining to slow their fall with his wings, but the weight was too much even for his strength.

"Try to hit the water and grab her."

Before Lirah could reply she saw Jahllia fall, and she dove after her. The water was cold, but immediately Lirah felt the life force in it and it made the pain of the fall slip away. She kicked hard and found the surface, quickly looking around for Jahllia, but she saw that Kaileth and Jayle were already pulling her from the water. She had landed not too far from the riverbank. Olyn was in the air and still held Sificah.

"Lirah!" Ralenn exclaimed as he rushed into the water toward her.

"I am fine, I'm alright, but we have to help Vishaya!"

Ralenn looked perplexed by this, and even more so as Lirah rushed back toward the arena, Ralenn running after her. Lirah was swiftly at the high arched doors to the arena. She leaned around the corner and saw that Vishaya was nearing the door. There were no more guards on the ground with her, only dozens of ash piles, half-burned bones, and smoking armor. The arena seats, however, had filled with scores of archers. They seemed determined to stop her escape. Arrows and bolts flew in angry clouds at her to no avail as she simply slammed them all aside with the pulses from the blue amithyle. With the red she sent jets of scarlet fire into the guards who dared get too close. It was taking a toll, however. Her steps were slow and staggering, dark blood dripping from her upheld arms onto the red earth of the arena floor.

"Ralenn, do something!" Lirah begged.

"There are too many, far too many for us, Lirah," Ralenn said mournfully.

Lirah looked back to Vishaya. She was close now, only a few dozen more staggering steps. Something glinting in the morning sun drew Lirah's attention on the far side of the arena.

"Ralenn, what is that?"

"It's a ballista."

No sooner had he answered but the weapon fired. A black steel shaft sped through the air toward Vishaya. She raised her hand and sent a blue shimmering pulse toward this new attack. As the ballista arrow hit the pulse a sound like shattering glass echoed off the arena walls, followed by a panicked cry of pain.

Vishaya fell, the black steel arrow piercing her chest. She struggled to rise as another arrow tore into her thigh, then another into her side. Lirah screamed and Ralenn grabbed her, pulling her back from the doorway as arrows began to fly through it. Vishaya shrieked again, even louder than before, yet this was a deep undulating cry of fury and rage, not pain. As Ralenn pulled Lirah back toward the river she could see the arrows in Vishaya's leg pop out of the wound with a spurt of red flame and sparks, and soon the arrows in her side followed suit. Two more arrows struck her in the chest and shoulder, and two more arrows were driven back out of her body in a fountain of sparks and embers as she struggled to her feet to keep moving. Lirah's breath caught at the sight, it was a fury-soaked echo of when she had pushed the dagger out of her own chest during the fight with the Gr-ishkah at the He'Aril falls.

A band of Tundraihn warriors rushed by as Ralenn and Lirah reached the riverbank again. The Tundraihn started firing bows and launching spears with their bronze spearthrowers into the arena, try-ing to drive off the host of slaver guards. Their spearthrowers easily penetrated the armor of the In-Kind guards, breaking up their ad-vance. Jayle ran up next to Lirah, and as Vishaya took the last faltering step back and through the doorway he caught her.

With the Tundraihn protecting the rear, Jayle ran for the boats with Vishaya in his arms. Lirah was already in the boat, along with Jahllia and Ralenn. Kaileth waited on the shore.

"Quickly, we have already stayed too long," he said as Jayle sloshed into the water.

He was covered with thick dark blood, as was Vishaya. Two bolts were still in her lower chest and hip. Sparks and red flames flickered out around these two wounds and the bolts slowly were being pushed back out of her body. Her tattered clothing was soaked in her own blood and her hair was matted with it. The large glittering black arrow was still lodged in her chest, its sharp barbed blades sticking out her sleek shoulder in the back. Wide-eyed, Jayle placed her in the bottom of the long, low boat and watched for a moment as the bolt in her hip fell free of her body with no visible wound to be seen. Shaking his head, he clambered over the side and into the boat himself.

"Humph, I am getting too old for boating," he said as he struggled to heft the weight of himself and all his armor. Kaileth only smiled widely and pushed the boat into the river, jumping into it with a smooth single motion. Jayle shot him a wry grin and they both set to speeding the boat downstream.

Orodan and the other Tundraihn were already waiting in other boats on the far shore, and once they all were moving downstream the Tundraihn near the arena ran with great speed and dove into the wa-ter. The guards followed after them and kept firing their bows hoping for a lucky hit. They were quickly out of reach, though. Just before the arena was out of sight a surging mob of figures burst from the gate, and the guards were swallowed up in their ranks. Smoke poured into the morning sky and Lirah smiled a little to herself.

I guess Rovik kept his promise.

The rhythm of the oars and the pull of the river soon carried the slaver compound from sight. Lirah watched as the last of the Tundraihn rose from the dark waters and hauled themselves into the boats. A profound tranquility settled over them, replacing the chaos and terror of the escape. The sudden contrast left Lirah unsteady. She closed her eyes, trying to anchor herself in the moment. A soft breeze moved over her damp skin, raising goosebumps.

"We did it... but only just," she whispered, her smile hovering somewhere between tears and laughter. She looked down and saw the bottom of their boat slick with dark ruby vitae. Vishaya sat propped against the gunwale, her hands pressed to her side where the black-fletched shaft jutted from her ribs. Thick, pitch like blood oozed between her fingers—slow and heavy.

"Hold on," Lirah whispered, her throat tight. She wondered why this arrow was not expelled in the same manner as the others had been.

Vishaya's breath came quick and shallow. She kept her hands on the wound, grim determination in every trembling motion. Lirah leaned closer; the arrow was long—more javelin than dart—its shaft of hard black metal ridged with cruel barbs that climbed a third of its length. Even to touch it felt wrong, as though the thing drank light and warmth alike.

"This arrow...It was made to kill beings connected to the arcane...it's avertyyn. You wouldn't be...able to break it, and the wound it still sits in...will resist your healing...be careful." It was growing difficult for Vishaya to speak, and Lirah could hardly hear her. Vishaya's skin was burning cold beneath her touch, her eyes already beginning to dim.

"Be still," Lirah said, forcing calm into her tone. "You will be all right. I'll see to it."

Vishaya gave a faint, wry smile. "You sound so sure, little orchid."

Vishaya drew a careful breath, the sound thin as silk.

"It does not feel like I will be alright—but...but I trust you, Lirah, I trust..." She kept her hands at her side, eyes half-closed against the pain as her voice faded away.

Lirah slid her hands under Vishaya's upon the arrow wound.

Dannitar guide me.

With the supplication still in her mind, Lirah closed her eyes and focused upon the damage. The dark metal drank every trace of her power the moment she tried to summon it. It was as though the arrow itself had been forged to consume life. Lirah felt herself being drained by it, the moments stretching out into icy pain and darkness. She pushed harder, pouring more of herself into the effort.

Lirah could feel the lethal arrow feeding on Vishaya's life force. Instinctively Lirah tried to envelop the arrow in her healing aura so she could pull it free. As blue light surged out from Lirah's hands the innate resistance of the barbed arrow reacted with a stabbing jolt of razor edged pain. Lirah and Vishaya convulsed in agonized shock.

"I can't pull it free," Lirah gasped.

"Then don't," Vishaya wheezed. "Just stop... the bleeding..."

"I'll try again." Lirah closed her eyes, willing warmth into her hands. A pale light began to bloom around her fingers, shuddering as it met the black shaft. The barbs drank it in, flickering dull red for an instant before dying again. Sparks shot from the arrow. The ancient spells fighting to keep Lirah at bay. She pushed harder, opening more of herself to the effort, giving her own life force to staunch the arrows hunger. The power within the ancient weapon was not passive. It was an implement of aggression. A sudden blast of ripping energy pulsed through Lirah and she fell back in the boat with a cry of pain.

"Oh no, Please, no" she panted, "no, no, no."

Vishaya's breath hitched, her eyes dark, she slumped in the bottom of the boat. Her now limp hands sliding from her wounded side.

"Lirah, are you alright?" Ralenn asked with concern

"No! I am not— I mean yes. Oh, my head," Lirah clamped her hand to the sides of her aching skull taking a few measured breaths.

"I don't know if I can save her!" Panic crept into the words as they tumbled from her.

"Lirah, use caution. Xydarii are not the same as other kindreds," Kaileth advised.

"Their wells of life force are many thousands of times greater than a man's."

Lirah nodded puffing long controlled breaths through pursed lips. Kail was right, she felt the strength of Vishaya when they were in the cages. If she had actually made the full healing connection Vishaya would probably inadvertently drain Lirah to death in an instant. That black arrow might have just saved her from a lethal mistake.

"I'm not enough to do this..." Lirah looked to Vishaya's still form then to Ralenn. His expression was an odd blend of worry and confusion.

"Lirah— the river." He rasped, as though the words were not fully his own. In a flash of realization and memory, Lirah knew what must be done. She quickly replaced her hands upon Vishaya's wound and closed her eyes. Lirah forced more of her strength into the wound, ignoring the cold that crept up her own arms. She felt the pulse of Vishaya's life faltering beneath her palms, the beat of her heart weakening.

"Stay with me," Lirah pled.

Vishaya's eyes fluttered open, only the faintest spark left in them. "I will... I trust you."

The words came like a sigh, carried away by the river wind. Lirah bowed her head and let the light grow, azure and steady, spilling over her hands as the darkness of the arrow began to drink it in. Yet this time Lirah opened herself to the world around them and found what she needed—the river. She let the life force of the river pour into her, channeling it into Vishaya. Careful to keep her own essence guarded, the powerful healing strength of the river surged through her, overwhelming the arrow's ability to resist. Moments past and Lirah could feel Vishaya's wound shrinking, the bleeding ebbing then finally stopping.

Lirah removed her hands to see the skin mended around the arrow shaft, as if it had always been a part of Vishaya's side. Vishaya slowly opened her eyes and looked up at Lirah. There was only the slightest hint of light within them, but it was not waning anymore.

"There...that should help till I can properly heal it all the way." Cold sweat clung to Lirah's shivering body. She was physically and emotionally exhausted.

"I am sorry I can't take it out yet. I think I need to rest."

"It doesn't... hurt as much now. You did... enough little orchid. Thank you."

Lirah smiled and looked up at Ralenn at the front of the boat. She was glad he was safe, and she felt even better having him close again; she always worried about him.

"Th-thank you for the reminder." She managed as her teeth started chattering. Ralenn smiled a little sheepishly and leaned as far as he could to hand her his cloak.

"Get some rest Lirah, you have done enough for today."
Lirah slid down into the boat and closed her weary eyes. The cloak was warm and smelled like Ralenn and the pine forests of their home. She felt her pulse slow, and her body relax as she breathed it in. The steady sound of the paddles dipping in and out of the river gently lulled Lirah into a sleepy haze and she worked her way into a comfortable position next to Vishaya so they could share the cloak. Vishaya's dark chest slowly rose and fell with her breaths and Lirah felt that at least for the time being, she was out of danger.

I never imagined I would be doing anything like this...But I am so happy to be helping. It felt good to make a difference, to tip Brek's coin in the favor of life. After all the terrible things that had happened the last few days, this at least was good. Lirah could make a difference. She smiled to herself hoping that Gaileng would be proud of her.

26

Slow Waters

Mighty lords and humble serfs both shall note and take heed of the edicts of Anthos. For the Patient Father is over all houses, spheres, and orders and will in his own time see the scales of his justice in balance.
Essays of the Divine

Jayle's hands finally started to feel warm again as the morning sun washed over their line of slow-moving boats. His mind drifted back to the last time he was quietly paddling a boat. His brothers alongside, and his father at the rudder cutting through the breakers near the Manteillis inlet, many hundreds of skain from where he now sat.

"Paddle hard, boys, and we'll make it," he said with a confidence that seemed it could never fail.

He remembered the spray of the warm water, the sound of the oars in the locks and his brothers pulling and breathing in time. They always made it through the breakers with Har'ayle De'Vinor at the rudder, and this time was no exception. They had caught all the soar pike that their longboat could hold that day for his eldest brother's wedding feast.

If Jayle had to have picked a favorite day, that might have been it. The wedding feast, his brothers all around, the warmth of Rah'Thar that year, it was all so perfect and happy then. No Dao'Tai, no wars, and Kei'Ta. Her green dress, how she felt in his arms as they danced, the warm pressure of her lips on his. That was the night they first met, and a night he would never forget. It was all changed now, lost to the hard savageness of the world. Yet the memories still held onto a warmth that time and sorrow could not fully dispel. They had shared too many perfect moments together. Moments that burned bright enough to chase a lifetime of shadows away.

That had been thirty years ago, and the paths Jayle had fought his life through swam in the darkest times his people had known for hundreds of generations. His heart yearned for the simpler days, the gentler times with his brothers and the passion of Kei'Ta's love. But the land of the dead keeps its own and Felairtarh lets none escape her grasp.

Two of Jayle's brothers were dead now and his father along with them. One brother lost to drakes, his father in battle with the Dao'Tai along with Hrett, his youngest brother. What would his father say now of Jayle, the errant son alone on another fool's errand?

He'd say, *you were a Brek-struck fool*, and he would be right...Jayle laughed a little to himself and pulled a bit harder on the paddle in his hand. She would be proud, though; *dance in life's darkness, leave each moment fully lived.* Jayle smiled a little brighter at the memory of her words and let himself drift for a time in pleasant recollections. The river was smooth, the air sweet, and for the first time in years his body had no complaints. Fully realizing this, he marveled at how rested he had felt after only a few hours' sleep in that swampy grove of trees. Even now after many hours of hurried actions he felt as though he were in his thirtieth year again. No aching knee or stiff shoulder complaining of too many years bearing a shield. Jayle shook his head at this as he watched the water swirl about the moving boat. A sudden unexplainable rejuvenation was hardly noteworthy when compared to the other events of the last few days, and the new members of their party.

For several hours they slowly drove their boats downstream to the southwest. It was late enough into the morning for the light to have reached where Lirah and the dark-skinned woman now lay sleeping on the bottom of the fishing skiff. The boat was long enough that Kaileth, Ralenn, and the others could fit with room to move about. With a shallow draft and wide stable bottom the boats had been well suited for the hasty rescue and flight down the river.

Jayle sat in the stern of the boat where he had found it difficult to look away from the strange woman near his feet. He had at first thought her color was a trick of his old eyes and the poor light of the pre-dawn. Now, however, in full light, it was clear that she was not like any woman he had ever seen before. Jayle had witnessed many strange things in his lifetime, creatures, and situations many would think a lie, were he to share the tale. He had faced what had to have been a real Shedim in the forest southeast of Mantorah, and more than once dealt with drakes, even a kythugdon. But nothing like this, nothing like the power this avertyyn-skinned woman had displayed in the arena. Even as she rested fitfully, she seemed more like an ebony frost lion in her mannerisms and expression than a wounded person. A being with an acute predatory instinct and the reflexes and strength to render most merely prey. It struck Jayle as wrong to see her so still, making it obvious that she was truly gravely wounded.

Lirah slowly opened her eyes and sat up a little. It was hard to miss her expression of complete bewilderment as she stared at the battle falcon perched on the side of the boat. Jayle knew that she had seen the bird before, Mirris was its name if his memory served, but presently the girl stared at the falcon as though she had seen Arontarh himself standing there.

"Miss Lirah, are you well?" he asked softly, trying not to disturb others who were sleeping. She did not reply. Her mouth moved to speak but no words came out.

"Miss Lirah? What is it?" he asked again.

She blinked hard and rubbed her eyes. Mirris cocked her head at Lirah and chirped softly then flew off into the morning sky. No one was what they seemed in this troop, Lirah most of all perhaps. Her display of magic at the falls was like nothing Jayle could remember learning about, much like the dark lady, he realized.

"Was I snoring much?" Lirah responded finally, a little abashed.

"Oh, no, miss. You just seemed a bit shocked by your feathered comrade. Are you feeling alright? You have had a rather extraordinary fourthmoon, to say the least."

Lirah looked out toward the small glittering speck that marked Mirris' overwatch. She pursed her lips for a few moments before responding.

"I'm feeling alright, I was dreaming. Guess it took a bit before I woke all the way up."

Jayle laughed warmly. "When you reach my age, you can find yourself dreaming of the past at almost any time." The mysterious woman jerked a little in her sleep, pulling Jayle's attention back to her. Lirah placed a hand on her head, between rows of little horns, and closed her eyes. Jayle squinted, only now noticing the obsidian shimmer of the horns against the blue-black of her hair. Somehow, they suited the lines of her form.

"She is sleeping still."

"What is her name?" he asked, curious.

"Vishaya...I can't remember the other parts, Vishaya something Xydarii."

"So, that is what they look like..." he said with sudden realization.

Jayle could see that she was breathing very slowly, and her cobalt-sable face was starting to take a paler shade. Lirah placed her hand around the arrow shaft and closed her eyes. Her face tightened into an expression that Jayle would know on any face, deathly pain.

"We have to hurry, she is not going to make it much longer." Lirah's voice was filled with concern as she spoke.

"So, I guess the legends about them are not true?" asked Jayle.

"Or she just needed us to escape, and once healed she will do with us as she pleases," interjected Ralenn, who was now awake and watching closely. Kaileth too was now paying close heed to the conversation at the aft of the boat. Jayle could hear his paddle slow with the distraction.

"Yes, she is a Xydar, but no, she is not going to sacrifice you to fallen Aashahl," Lirah said matter-of-factly.

"How can you be so sure, Lirah? Maybe once she is healed, she will—" Ralenn started. He didn't get far before being interrupted.

"No, she won't! She almost died getting all of us out of there. She didn't have to help us. Once she had her weapons, she could have just left us all in there and blasted her own way out."

"Fine, maybe she did help, but come on Lirah, she is a dark otheäil. You are the one who told me about them, they are not like us, they—"

"Whatever she is, lad," Jayle interrupted, "She nearly killed herself making sure not one guard could make it past her to hinder our escape. Where I come from, we call that an ally. I could care less what color she is, who her people are, or how many eyes and horns she might have. She saved your friend here, and possibly us all back there." Jayle tried to explain this gently to the lad; he understood Ralenn's apprehension.

"They were created by Ach'Juln to serve his needs in the War of Dominance. We don't really know what they have been up to since then. And that was eons ago," Kaileth interjected.

"To that point, whatever they have been up to it has been low-key enough that they practically passed into the obscurity of legend," Jayle added.

"Right! Maybe the tales of them hauling the damned back to Ach'Juln to be consumed in agonizing torment is just a tale to scare children," Lirah said happily.

"Or maybe it is the truth. I mean look at her, did you see what she did back there? How is that not the powers of a fallen Aashahl?" Ralenn still sounded upset.

"When she wakes up why don't you ask her if the stories are true? I am sure that would be an interesting discussion. One I would love to hear. The chance to learn from a true denizen of the Tir'Luthryel is singular. Better still is the chance to find an ally in her. The fact that she was a prisoner of the Aya's ilk is a good sign." Kaileth's calm demeanor seemed to settle Ralenn some.

Jayle tried to help allay his fears also: "A sword is just as sharp in the hand of a friend or a foe. If these Xydarii were created as a tool, how are they any different from a sword? It's the wielder's nature that matters more than that of the blade. She seems to have chosen to strike for us so far; I say we give her a chance to prove herself further." Jayle knew the risk of letting such a clearly dangerous being in their midst, wounded or not. But he would be watchful, and it already seemed that Vishaya was more a friend than a foe.

"That is what I think," Lirah said, wetting her lips. "There is something bigger than just the High Sun Realms in the Aya's plans. The Tundraihn priestess, Olyn, and Vishaya—they are all from strange faraway lands that most don't even think really exist."

"True," Jayle mused. "Sending her servants thousands of skain to take prisoners from the peoples of myth, this speaks of broad machinations, but to what end? Did she say anything to you when you were in there?" he asked.

"No, not really. We were preoccupied with escape, and to be honest I was frightened by her myself, at first. I wasn't thinking about getting information. After we got out there was too much running and fighting to talk really. But I know she is not on the Aya Dao'Tai's side, we can trust her. I can't explain it, but she feels..." Lirah paused. "She feels...good. I mean, she *is* wild, and definitely not human, but she isn't evil. When we were at the falls, I could feel the reaper, like its soul, or maybe its lack of a soul? I don't know. But what I am sure of is that she doesn't have that taint, the *darkness* that the reaper had. The Grishkii also had an evil feeling to them, not like the reaper, but it was there. She might be savage and dangerous as a frost lion, but she is not evil. I don't think we really know anything about her people, not enough to just condemn her because her eyes glow and she has rows of horns and such. I think we can trust her..."

Lirah trailed off and her face flushed.

"Well said indeed, Miss," Jayle nodded. "Whatever is going on in the far south could be the key to the Subjugate's defeat for all we know. Especially if there are armies of beings like Vish..."

"Vishaya" Lirah said, smiling again.

"Yes, especially if there are armies of beings like Vishaya that might help us," he smiled back.

"Lirah, if you trust her, then so do I," Ralenn said after a long pause. He smiled, looking much more relaxed now.

"As Uran De'Vinor said, I think her actions speak for themselves, Miss Lirah. She helped get you out, she helped get the others out, and she almost died trying to hold off the guards. That is not something an evil creature would do, at least none that I have ever heard of." Kaileth spoke with surety, and they all let the subject go for the time.

"Whatever else she is, she is about the most beautiful and terrifying creature I've ever seen." Jayle cursed to himself for letting his thoughts slip out, but Lirah laughed a little and looked over to Vishaya.

"She is a bit terrifying, isn't she?"

"The blood and dark magic don't help, but I think we are right to trust her." Jayle added

"Will you be able to heal her?" Ralenn asked after another long silence.

"Yes, I just need to get the arrow out somehow. Might need some tools or something, though. She said it was avertyyn," Lirah answered as she checked the wound.

"We had better make with some haste then," Kaileth said, pulling hard on his paddle. Jayle redoubled his efforts as well and soon the wooden craft sped across the smooth surface of the water. Lirah found another oar and worked to hurry their journey. On they rowed, and again Jayle could not help but recall that favorite day in a different longboat, so long ago. He might not be with his brothers, but it felt good to be pulling as one once more.

Three hours later their goal was in sight, a small village at the southeastern bank. The boats of Orodan's men had already reached the shore, and Lirah could see Ealë being carried up into a wagon at the water's edge.

"They found her!" Lirah said cheerfully.

"She was slowly swimming downstream as we approached with the boats. I guess the slavers threw her into the river thinking she was dead," explained Jayle.

"But she wasn't?"

"No, not quite. The Tundraihn healer took her into his boat and it looks like she is still living," added Kaileth. Lirah smiled widely as she thanked every Aashahl she could think of.

Their boat drew up to shore and was caught by a few of the Tundraihn who had been waiting there in the shallow waters. They quickly helped Lirah from the boat as Ralenn and Kaileth carefully picked up Vishaya and took her ashore, followed by Jahllia. Lirah watched as they then took them to the same large wagon Ealë had been placed in

"Miss Lirah, your healer's kit, clothing, and weapons are already in the wagon," said Kaileth. "We have to get moving, so you will have to tend to the wounded in there."

"That will be fine. Where will you and Ralenn be?" asked Lirah

"We will be on our horses following the wagon." Lirah looked around and did not see any horses save the teams that drew the wagon. "They will be here shortly, with Riidak, and Mirris," Kaileth said, seeing her puzzlement.

Lirah smiled and then got up into the wagon. As she did so, she remembered the leather bag that Rovik had given Vishaya. She took it from the wounded woman and leaned back out of the wagon as it started to roll away from the river, the Tundraihn following close behind.

"Kaileth!" Lirah yelled. "A man named Rovik gave this to us, said he wanted to get it to a Paladin in Syrah." She tossed the bag to him.

"Truly, Rovik, the Chancellor to the Aya?" asked Kaileth as he caught the bag.

"That was his name, yes, not sure about a chancellor though. He was older and a bit strange...it seemed important. He said he was sorry for something. That he didn't mean for this to happen," Lirah shrugged as the wagon took off.

She turned into the wagon. Within the large interior Lirah found Vishaya, Jahllia, Sificah, Ealë, and the Tundraihn priestess. Evidently Olyn had already been there, leaving Sificah behind. All of them appeared to be in need of some form of help.

"Well, I guess I know what I will be doing today." Lirah found her healer's kit and set to work.

27

Syrah

A nd what of they that venerate not the Aashahl and seek to make their way by their own strength alone? Woe be it unto them, for mortal hopes are as wax to the flame in the absence of harmony with the divine.
Essays of the Divine

Devick regained consciousness like a ship slipping from the fog. Gradually becoming aware of the soft bed he was laying in. The fabric was smooth, a tight weave made on a large sturdy loom. He moved his hands slowly across it, letting the sensation fill his mind, giving him something to focus on. With each deep breath and steady heartbeat, the urge to drift back into sleep threatened to overtake him.

Devick forced his eyes open and found a rough white plaster ceiling above him. The space was quiet, with only the gentlest splashes of light upon the dips and edges of the ceiling's white surface. *A castle, I am in a stone fortress.* The thought sparked his mind into sharper focus and all the possible fortresses with proper white plaster walls started to roll through his mind.

Sitting up, he examined the room. It was large, stone walled, and circular in shape with a large balcony. Tall tapestries depicting familiar events told him he was in friendly hands. Devick swung his legs out from under the linen sheets onto the cool floor. His body was stiff and sore, and he wondered what had happened to him and how long he had been in this place. Devick paused for a moment upon the edge of the bed to let his mind clear. Slowly, the memories of the attack on the camp, the rescue of Lady Re'alis, and the event of his healing came drifting back to his mind.

"The girl," Devick said aloud. "The girl healed me."

He felt for his injuries and found them to be gone. The tissues within his body that had been so severely damaged were now whole, and not a mark could be seen without. Amidst his wonder, Devick realized he had no idea what had happened to Re'alis or his men after the fight at the falls. Clearly it went well enough, as he seemed safe. But safely where?

A soft breeze flowed through the open balcony door, tossing the drapes about in gentle waves. Devick took in the fragrant breeze deeply as he started to walk to the balcony. *Warm earth, tall grass, and something else.* His mind worked to place the deeper undertones upon the air as he approached the arched threshold of the balcony. He parted the fluttering cloth and stepped out to a panoramic view of the land. Devick was standing on a stone lip that ran around the exterior of the tower his room was set within. Leaning out onto the smooth rampart, he looked out across the green woods and hills that surrounded him. They looked peaceful and calm in the amber light of the setting sun. Again, a soft, sweet-smelling surge of air pulsed up from the lush realm below.

"The river."

Devick smiled and closed his eyes, letting the flow of air wash over him and carry his mind far off, to simpler times and happier situations. After a few minutes of this respite, he looked directly below his feet to see the fortress the tower was a part of. It sat in a u-shaped bend in a broad, slow-running river. This alone told Devick where he was—the fortress of Syrah.

Syrah had been an independent city-state for many hundreds of generations. During the first Mantorahn expansions, the armies of

Mantorah found Syrah amid a decade-old siege. Recognizing the besiegers as a foe they had fought before, the Camarilla Daradar, the council of all the High Lords of Mantorah took action and broke the siege. Thereafter, Syrah joined an alliance that over the years grew until she was all but part of Mantorah, though she still held her own nobility, system of governance, and rulers. Technically, Syrah was still an independent city-state, though she served Mantorah as a vassal. Devick and the High Lord Rahdans before him had always treated her with profound respect and little interference. Syrah was still very much her own, though the fortress-city now served as the northernmost stronghold of Mantorahn influence. This made it the pinnacle of defensive engineering, both in its ancient foundations and newest additions.

The fortress was built so that the Aril River flowed at the base of its walls around all but a narrow strip of land. The hard, slick stone walls ran directly into the inner bank of the river itself, leaving no ledge or foothold of earth at the wall's base. Thus, landing a boat on the fortress side of the river was impossible, as there was no ground to stand upon. The narrow space of land that led into the fortress had been walled and gated off. The outermost wall angled back toward the keep, giving archers from either side of the gate full view of the ground below. The first gate was set in the high outer wall at the meeting point of the two angled walls. Behind this lay a large yard full of houses and buildings, as well as a partition wall set to block the direct path to the second gate. The second gate had been placed at the far west side of the inner walls. The buildings and partitioned walls made it necessary for a person to weave back and forth around these obstacles in order to reach the second gate. This exposed an advancing foe to attack from every side for a much longer time. The yard beyond the second wall was constructed in similar fashion, including a large partition of stone blocking a direct path into the citadel.

The base of the citadel walls was smooth and sloped to deflect enemy missiles. At every corner and edge of the inner and outer walls of the citadel, high towers had been built, affording a commanding view of all the land about the fortress. Devick was standing on the northwest tower of the inner citadel. To the east the massive keep tower rose high above him. The keep was made of four ascending levels, two angular and two round. They were built one on top of the other, alternating angled then round, each reducing in size until at last a single spire rose a hundred feet above the bulwarks below it. The base of the keep was level with the top of the outer wall and visible for a great distance away from the fortress. The sweeping layered angles created fields of supporting fire from every bastion.

After surveying these familiar surroundings, Devick returned to his room, hoping to find more than his scant present attire to put on. On the far side of the room, next to the bed, stood a tall chiffonier. Devick investigated and found his clothing had been washed, mended, and laid within it. His tabard had also been neatly folded and laid on top of the chiffonier. He took it and held it up, letting the tabard fall open. He could see where it had been torn and slashed in the fight at the camp. A steady hand had carefully repaired it, but the scars remained. A reminder of how close to death he had been.

"That was very nearly my end," he mused quietly to himself. How many times had he faced battle and the death that came with it, yet this was the closest he had come to such a death? No, not the closest; he had been mortally wounded. Such a death had found him, it had struck him down and left him to perish.

Only by her power did I escape death then, only thanks to the girl and her... He paused in this line of thinking, searching for the word to fit.

"Magics?" He let the word hang in the air, letting them shape the memories he had of what happened, the burning light, the sharp warmth that filled him for an instant at the falls before oblivion took him into unconsciousness. Devick grew up on tales of arcane powers and magic spells; curses from dark sorcerers, charms of Shedim in deep forests and weapons that burned with the power of the Aashahl. Devick was familiar with dark powers especially. All in Mantorah had heard of the ikthii and their despoiling powers. But what the girl wielded was no cheap trick or dark spell. It was pure, powerful and had the strength to dismiss the grasp of Felairtarh herself, even when by all rights Devick's wounds placed him clearly in her realm.

Devick did know that the kings of Anoth had powerful healers in their court. Beings not truly human that could heal all manner of wound and sickness. They were thought all slain when the city fell, but perhaps not all? He ran his thumb over a line of stitching holding a savage rent in the tabard together.

"I will not squander this second chance at life I have been given," he promised. "I will live twice as fiercely in the face of my foes."

He set the tabard down, and after washing his face and hands in a stone basin he stood next to his bed and donned his fresh clothing. Fully dressed and feeling refreshed, he went back to the balcony.

His mind felt much clearer now as he again rested upon the stones of the fortress. Soon Devick was thinking of Re'alis once more, seeing her in the tent that night, the fight at the falls, the plans they were making. He had known her since childhood, their paths crossing and parting through the long-troubled years that followed. If the Aya Dao'Tai had not come, and events had been different, they might have been betrothed. That would have made his mother incredibly happy and continued the tradition of his house to keep blood ties with the realm of the high lakes.

His mother was from Lea'Angleneth. Once the Aya Dao'Tai came and disbanded Camarilla Daradar, all ruling duties fell to the High Lord Rahdan of Mantorah. Devick's father was the last Lord Rahdan voted into the position before the Camarilla was disbanded and so the office became hereditary, landing squarely on Devick's young shoulders after his father was slain.

While his father yet lived Devick spent every campaign season at his side facing the traditional foes of Mantorah. If it was not the Srellites, then it was an Adohr incursion from the east or drakes foraging into the north. Devick's father, Lord Caidyrn, always seemed to have

need of his young son. From the planning and logistics of war, to leading upon the field of battle, Caidyrn had Devick at his side, carefully
teaching his son all he could. After each winter as the season changed
to spring, or Arah'Ashli in the old tongue; the ice and snow turned
to flowers and green grass. Devick's mother, Lady Photiin, made sure
they traveled to visit Angleneth. They would stay for a halfmoon or
even a full month or two.

As time passed, Re'alis and Devick grew very fond of each other.
A formal match may have been announced once Devick turned seven-
teen. However, the year before that could happen Re'alis' father died,
though many believed he was assassinated by the Aya Dao'Tai. Devick's mother died also, along with her unborn child. After that Lord
Caidryn basically lived at the front, wherever the fighting was thickest. A few more years passed, and he was killed in battle with the
Adohr and Dao'Tai armies, leaving Devick to rule in his stead. From
that time on, defending the sovereignty of Mantorah consumed him.
Soon after, Anoth fell, and then he saw Re'alis only at the councils of
the Aya Dao'Tai.

"One more thing the Subjugate has taken from me." Soft footsteps
from behind brought Devick back from reflection. He looked back to
the entrance of the tower and saw the hands of Lady Re'alis gently
part the drapes as she walked out to the balcony. She smiled warmly,
coming up close to Devick, and leaned on the stone bulwark with him.
They both stood still, feeling the warmth of the breeze and sunlight
splash around them. Devick could not help but notice how beautiful
she looked in the evening light. He again found himself thinking of
what might have been. Re'alis took his arm and softly rested her head
on his shoulder.

"Devick, I..." Re'alis struggled to find words as her face blushed
a little. "I can't truly say how glad I am that you have recovered...I
thought you were lost to us all."

Devick smiled, surprised at how warm her comment made him
feel. Or perhaps it was her closeness. "It is a work of the Aashahl to be

sure, and our new friends." They stood for a long time without words. The moment stretched, the feelings building in them both, becoming a near tangible aura between them. Devick's panic at losing Re'alis to the Grishkii, her anguish at Devick's near death, the bewildering relief of his healing, and the events at the falls still felt very raw and overwhelming to them both.

"Devick, what do you think our fate will be?" she asked at length, her voice slowed with strong emotions.

"When you say our fate, do you mean our lands, or you and me, milady?" Re'alis looked up. She was smiling, yet Devick saw a few tears fall from her bright eyes.

"Both. All of it, I suppose," she replied, gesturing to the lands about the fortress before placing her hand upon his for a moment.

Devick smiled and gently wiped the tears from her cheeks, not fully sure why they fell but glad that she felt safe enough with him to show such vulnerability.

"I would think the attempt on both our lives is a prelude to war. I would also think we can expect a Dao'Tai army to march on our lands, but we will withstand them." He sounded confident as he spoke, and hoped his words were true. "As for us...I...I stand by what we spoke in your tent, milady." He wanted to say more, to tell her what he really was feeling, but something held him back.

Dark tears take me, I am acting as nervous as a youth!

Re'alis seemed to guess his thought and they shared a smile.

"Together then, the unknown is not as dark a prospect. We will lead our people through this," she said, smiling.

"I can't help but feel like we have a chance to change things, maybe even to stop the Aya Dao'Tai, though my mind tells me it is a fool's hope." Devick searched her eyes, wondering what she was feeling.

"Fool's hope though it may be, I feel it too." She again let her head rest on his shoulder. They were silent once more, each enjoying the warmth of the setting sun and the closeness they shared.

At length, Devick spoke. "Where are our friends to whom we owe my life?"

"You will not care much for the answer," Re'alis almost winced. "They went with the Tundraihn to the city of slavers to find the Tundraihn priestess."

Devick was astounded. "And I thought we were set to a fool's course. Paldrii go with them, it seems they thrive from helping the lost and desperate."

"So, it would seem," she agreed. "But I see the will of the Aashahl in their doings. They seemed to appear where they are most needed, with the ability to tip the coin away from Drashtaa's curse."

"I hope you are right. They will certainly need all the protection the heavens can muster! I wish there had been more time to speak with them."

"It all happened so fast, and I must admit that I was mostly concerned with your well-being. Devick, I...I am not sure how I would have faced the oncoming storms without you with me. Without you as an ally."

"You would have done marvelously, milady. However, I am incredibly pleased to be here, alive, with you." He smiled warmly at her.

"Devick, Re'alis will do," she chided.

"Yes, my lady." He smirked.

Re'alis laughed a little as she leaned closer to him. He knew their sudden familiarity would raise more than an eyebrow or two in court, but here, now, having her close was all he really wanted. All the feelings and emotions that had started to grow between them in their youth suddenly began to burst back to the surface as though no time had passed. In the times to come who Devick cared for would be a small matter compared with the calamities of war with the Subjugate.

They stood close a few moments longer, enjoying the nearness of each other while letting the last shadows of fear and horror from the fight at the falls shed away. The air was warm and the landscape surrounding the fortress and river were verdant and filled with the promise of a lush season. Devick's thoughts slowly turned to the farms of his home country, the good harvests such a season would bring. Only if he could keep the war from ravaging his home. Re'alis stirred presently, alerting to something.

"Devick, do you see that?" she asked, pointing toward a glimmer in the sky.

"I do. And it appears to be heading this way."

They could now hear the shouts of men upon the walls below as they saw it also and prepared to shoot down what they thought to be an enemy spy. Devick and Re'alis looked at each other at the same moment, realizing what it must be.

"We need to halt the men from firing," Devick said hurriedly.

Re'alis nodded and they both rushed from the balcony, through the room, and down the spiraling stairs. They came to a door that led out to a parapet below the room they were just in, and Devick flung the door open, causing the guards to turn about in surprise. They had been training the large repeating crossbow upon the approaching form in the sky.

"Hold that bow, men," said Devick sharply. "Hold your fire. We believe that to be an ally."

The Syrahn guards hesitated. "Lord, the paladin commands that any unlooked-for creature be brought down."

"Trust me, that is no foe; be it on my head should I be wrong, but do not loose on it."

The guards made no motion to shoot the bow, but they also did not leave their posts near it.

"Lord, it approaches from the northwest," said one of the archers anxiously.

"That it does, but we have friends that could be approaching from that direction also. Stay your weapon for a little longer, let us see what it is."

The soldiers, Re'alis, and Devick watched as the form slowly became recognizable as a large falcon wearing silver armor. Re'alis drew close and he offered her his arm, which she took,

"I am certain that's Kaileth's falcon," Re'alis said excitedly.

"'Tis too rare a bird to be mistaken," Devick agreed.

The soldiers relaxed and made no motions to fire on the oncoming bird.

The falcon circled above the walls of the fortress a few times before landing on the stones directly in front of Devick and Re'alis. The great falcon bowed her head before the lord and lady and then stood very still. In her talons she held a leather bag. Mirris looked closely at Lord Devick, then released the pouch and took several steps back before taking again to the sky. All watched as she flew back along the same route she had approached from earlier.

Devick quickly stooped to grab the bag from the ground and open it. Within he found several folded pieces of parchment and a few maps. Devick took a small piece of paper from the bag and read the concise note written upon it. He read it again before speaking.

"We have preparations to make, Re'alis." He turned and led her back into the tower, leaving the soldiers at their post.

They were winding down the stairs when Re'alis spoke, her words echoing down the stone stairway. "What is it, Devick? What was written on that note?" She sounded worried.

"I did not want to say anything in front of the men," he said somberly. "The Aya Dao'Tai is marching on us."

"You mean Syrah?" asked Re'alis.

"Yes, but Lea'Angleneth and Thenill as well."

"Dark tears take me, Devick," she swore faintly, a twinge of panic in her voice. "Lea'Angleneth is not ready for war, not so soon."

Devick stopped and took her trembling hands as he spoke. "Re'alis, we will protect your people, together. I swear it." She smiled and Devick could see her efforts to stifle her emotions.

"Truly, we can save your people," he said again. She nodded her head and an expression of resolute determination settled on her pleasant features.

"We will, then, Aashahl surround, we will do it," she said, her voice calm and firm.

They continued down the stairs, passing a few more doors until they reached a hallway that led them to a large chamber filled with bookcases. In the center of the room a crystal chandelier hung under a round skylight. Under this chandelier sat a long table and chairs, and in one of the chairs sat Gairrle. He shot to his feet at the approach of his lord and smiled widely.

"Lord Devick, it is good to see you are finally with us again!"

"How long have I been unaware?" asked Devick, realizing he still did not know.

"It has been five days since the fight at the falls," answered Re'alis. "We spent four in travel and the fifth here."

Devick nodded thoughtfully, then addressed Gairrle. "Captain, gather the marshal, his captains, and the paladin."

"As you bid, Lord Devick." Gairrle turned and quickly left the room.

Devick emptied the contents of the pouch onto the table and he and Re'alis began to examine them. The first thing that drew Devick's attention was a large map. It depicted the land from Fist Bay to Issa in the north, and from the Western Sea to the Gates of the East. Upon the map movements and avenues of attack had been clearly marked.

"Devick, this is addressed to you." Re'alis handed him an envelope marked with the Sunshadow's sigil. He opened it and began to read.

"Lord Rahdan, I write in haste as I fear my treachery is known. From the maps I have enclosed, I trust you will be able to decipher the Aya Dao'Tai's plan of assault. I copied them from her council room. They have a reaper with them, possibly more than one. Her plans are wide beyond the High Sun Realms. Her agents are active in the Dark Realms and within your own lands. Trust few and expect the worst.

Hope fires the Heart." Devick paused taking in the hastily scrawled letter and the final line. A line from a poem often used for ciphers or pass phrases by the Sunshadow.

"I wonder who penned this."

Re'alis handed him a second piece of parchment. "This one is from Kaileth." Devick read the letter several times before handing it back to her.

"It seems that Lirah encountered Rovik in the slavers camp, and that he plans to help us in a way, by diverting the bulk of the Aya Dao'Tai's army here rather than to Lea'Angleneth."

"What should we do, Devick? We need to warn Lea'Angleneth, but do we trust him? I cannot help but think how he must have played a part in sending a desecrator to kill me," Re'alis said wryly.

"Yes, it is hard to believe that *now* he would have a change of heart." Devick sat down and started to go over the remainder of the maps and papers on the table. "These maps are from the Sunshadow agent in the Dao'Tai palace, and *them* I trust, unless the ruse is that well-planned. Perhaps all the years of seeing his own people trodden underfoot has finally turned Rovik back to a truer course?"

"The letter mentions a ring," Re'alis said as she finished reading.

Devick searched the bag and found it. Re'alis stood behind his chair, looking over his shoulder. "That is the ring Rovik wore," she observed, eyeing it shrewdly.

"Yes, it is the signet ring of the chancellor of Ell'Anoth," added Devick. "He would not part with this easily. I think we have to believe, at least in part, that he will divert some of the Subjugate army away from Lea'Angleneth." Devick looked over the other papers from the bag for a while. They were detailed and certainly could be put to good use. At last, he leaned back and let out a long sigh.

"If what these maps and charts show is true, then Rovik's plan is the best way to give Lea'Angleneth a chance. But it leaves little hope for Syrah."

"Is it as bad as I think it is?" she asked.

Devick sighed again and gave answer. "Syrah can hold out against the Aya Dao'Tai's army for quite some time, years if they are smart and a little lucky. I think it could even hold long enough to buy time for Mantorah to prepare for the reapers. However, Syrah cannot *repel* the assault, they would have to be relieved if they are to escape destruction. But these walls can buy precious time."

"So, it is either Syrah or Lea'Angleneth?" Re'alis asked, and the sorrow in her voice was easy to hear.

Devick gave a slow nod. "Yes, it would seem that is the case, but do not despair, Syrah is always ready for war. It will hold out better than any other keep. We will have to see what the marshal thinks should be done. I fear we have little choice in this, however. The Subjugate has made the first move, and it is a good one," he finished bitterly.

"Devick, I think there is much of the Aya Dao'Tai's plans we still don't understand." Re'alis spoke carefully as she took a seat next to Devick. "She seems to have been busy far to the south, and there are all the raids in the mountains. These letters reaffirm as much."

"I agree, and I think we need to speak with Kaileth and his friends when we can; they are caught up in this somehow," Devick said thoughtfully.

"And there is the involvement of the Tundraihn," added Re'alis, "plus the desecrator asked many questions about the Tears of the Aashahl. I think the Aya is seeking them too."

"There are too many pieces moving here. I wonder why the Aya Dao'Tai would go through so much trouble to capture one of the Tundriahn."

"To start other wars? Set a new enemy against us to the south. There are many possibilities." Neither was certain of what all this could mean, but both Re'alis and Devick shared a feeling of foreboding at the thought of Subjugate agents active within the Dark Realms.

Gairrle soon returned, bringing with him Paladin Valskar, Marshal Penetrah, and several other captains, the captains of the garrison. Valskar was an exceptionally large man, thick-limbed and built for battle. To Devick he always seemed more a living avatar of the imposing fortress city than just another warrior. His character was like rough-cut stone, yet he was swift to laughter all the same. Devick had never seen him unarmored and today was no different. A tight woven hauberk splinted with bronze across the shoulders and spine served the paladin this day. Devick took the Anothn style of armor as a good omen for the day.

Penetrah was a man no less fit for war than Valskar. He was of medium build, keen eyed and shaped by a youth in the saddle, riding the edges of civilization. Penetrah was from a well-known family in Mantorah and had earned the rank of marshal within the frontier armies at a young age. He was generally soft-spoken and introspective in council, swift and decisive in battle. Devick had trusted in him to handle the difficult diplomatic and strategic posting on the northernmost edge of Mantorahn influence and he had not disappointed. He and his contingent of cavalry kept watch over the border lands between the Subjugate, Syrah and Mantorah.

Devick bid them all to sit as he passed the maps, charts, and papers from the satchel Mirris had delivered, allowing each person there to gain a full understanding of the contents. It was easy to see the apprehension and alarm in the faces of the men as they looked at the maps and read the battle plans of the Dao'Tai; all were clearly concerned, save the paladin.

"And we are sure of the validity of this information, my lord?" Penetrah asked after some time of looking over the papers. Devick could tell his mind was working fast, playing out tactical possibilities and military options.

"I am. It is certainly as accurate as possible given the nature of a mobilization of forces at this scale," Devick answered soberly.

"What information I have from the Sunshadow seems to corroborate the plans as well. The Aya has made her opening move, though it has been blunted somewhat thanks to an unlooked-for ally."

Valskar let out a blustery scoff. He was battle hardened in every aspect of the term and spoke with a coarse, almost hoarse voice, permanently rendered so by years of bellowing orders over the din of battles.

"It is hard to believe that, after all he has done, Rovik would turn back to his old loyalties on a whim," Valskar said, and Devick nodded.

"Years serving the Aya Dao'Tai as a puppet must have been galling, even for such a coward. Whatever else is at work here, we don't have time to puzzle out Rovick's exact motivations," Devick replied.

"The validity of these troop movements will be easy enough to prove. No power the Subjugate wields can hide the march of a host. We should send scouts at once to verify the muster," Re'alis suggested, her voice steady—Devick wondered how often she held similar councils in the delicate spires of her home.

"A sound course, my lady. Ivkellore—see that it is done." Valskar pointed to one of his men. Ivkellore raised a clenched fist to his chest in a crisp salute and left the room.

They turned then to the particulars of the Subjugate's battle plans. One by one the men at the table spoke, asking questions and offering replies. By the time the papers had been read and the arguments aired, the sun had long set; lamps were brought in, their light falling in soft golden bands across the maps and the faces gathered round. The gathered knights, warriors, and shire reeves each represented the populated lands that surrounded Syrah. They knew the ensuing conflict would see Dao'Tai foraging parties in every quarter, so they took careful heed of how best to prepare. For a long moment, the council sat like stone, the lamplight carving them into dark silhouettes.

Devick finally cleared his throat. "It seems all here understand what we face and what choices lie before us."

"Aye," Valskar said with a dark chuckle. "We can be struck on the helm and the unarmored groin—or else twice as hard on the helm with but a light touch below the belt."

"I hope you were not referring to Lea'Angleneth as the groin," Re'alis quipped, trying to lift the grim mood.

"You know I meant no offense, my lady," Valskar said, his grin softening. "But speak plain—Rovik's betrayal runs deep. He sided with the Dao'Tai at the most critical moment all those years ago and he has been a faithful servant of our foe up until now. Trusting a missive by his hand is a tall order indeed. I've fought beside yer' father, my lord Devick, and beside those of yer' noble house, my lady. All my life I have served my city and the good people of this realm. I have clashed steel with these selfsame enemies we now face; So I do not offer my words idly." He paused, looking to Devick before continuing.

"We trust your counsel, Valskar," Devick answered soberly.

"Aye, then I say Rovik's plan is our best option. Let their bulk come to us. If not the helm, Syrah can be the shield that takes the blow—she is made for siege, and she will thrive in the contest she was built for. With their main force marching into our strength, we will bleed them while sparing Lea'Angleneth from a death blow. Siege is the Dao'Tai's weakest point; they have never succeeded, and Ell'Anoth was no precedent."

"We could send cataphracts and battle wagons to help our allies of the high lakes," added Marshal Penetrah. "Those of us gathered here have seen enough battles to know that Syrah can hold out long enough to buy time for support to get to Lea'Angleneth, to assemble the rest of the army, and warn the frontier."

"To be sure, and all those wagons and horses locked up inside the walls during a siege would be of little use. Better they make war where their blades are keenest." Valskar smiled, clearly already thinking over the struggle to come.

"A most generous offer, and one I cannot refuse in this desperate hour," Re'alis replied.

"Lord Devick, if I may?" interjected Gairrle. Devick signaled him to continue. "I do not like the thought of Syrah being set upon like this, but that *is* what it is built for; it is a fortress made for siege. It can hold back our enemies for a good span. That means resources stuck here rather than attacking farmsteads and unwalled villages. We can get all those not fit to fight, the women and children, to safety, and the rest can hold as long as possible."

"You are correct, lad," said Valskar. "Anyone who wishes to take our city will pay greatly in time and blood. It would seem that we have a chance to help two realms with our stand here. I can't think of a greater cause to fight for." All seated at the table nodded in agreement with Valskar's words.

"I see no reason to prolong the decision, then," Re'alis gently prompted. "We have no time."

"Of course. Do any here object to the proposed plan of holding against the Subjugate army here at Syrah?" asked Devick.

"Nay, lord, we stand here," the paladin said, planting his wide fist hard on the table.

"Very well then, let us turn to our plan of defense. Marshal Penetrah, take your forces and head with all haste to Lea'Angleneth."

Penetrah stood and gave a bow. "Lord, if I may I would like to prepare to depart now."

Devick smiled at his immediate response. They were close to the same age, yet Penetrah's swift exuberance always made him seem younger. "You may go make ready, but before you depart come and speak with me once more."

"Yes, Lord Rahdan," Penetrah said, then quickly left the room. Devick then turned to the paladin. "Valskar, Syrah is your home, they are your people, and you were defending her long before I was Radahn of Mantorah. I would not take command of your fortress from you."

The elder soldier smiled. "That is well. Thank you, lord. I would have made you arm wrestle me for it and neither of us needs that embarrassment." He laughed heartily at his own joke and more than a few others, Re'alis and Devick included, could not keep from smiling and laughing a little also.

"I will have the men in the best array as may be. We will not make it easy for our foes. We've been spoiling to fight those Dao'Tai for years, and now we don't even have to leave home to do it. We'll hold out, longer than you dare hope, I think." Devick nodded, pleased with Valskar's confidence.

"Captain Gairrle, you must ride to Mantorah and raise the alarm. Be sure to warn them of the imminent attack from sea. Go, prepare, and come speak with me before you leave as well, take those you feel you need with you." Gairrle bowed and left the room quickly. "My lady," Devick now turned to the topic he dreaded most. "What are your intentions?"

Re'alis had clearly been prepared to answer this question. "My place during this time of crisis is with my people," she said slowly, avoiding looking directly at Devick. Devick did not like the thought of letting Re'alis out of his sight. He had prepared to make the case for her to seek asylum in Mantorah, but this argument melted away when he looked at the fiery determination in her eyes and the steadfast tone of her voice. He swallowed hard as he answered.

"You are right. I will see that Marshal Penetrah gets you there safely, Lady Re'alis." He bowed his head in deference to her decision. "I believe he means to leave quickly, so you had best hasten to prepare yourself to depart."

Re'alis stood, and Devick thought he could see the gravity of the situation settle on her shoulders. Was this as difficult for her as it was for him?

"By your leave, my lord," she said softly. Her eyes met Devick's, and he could almost hear the unspoken words in the sunburst-jade of her eyes; a plea for another way, a less harrowing course to follow. She lingered an instant longer before slowly leaving the room by the same door Gairrle and Penetrah had left through earlier.

"You men know what to do at this point, raise the garrison and start an evacuation for those who cannot fight, send messengers to all the surrounding villages and farmsteads. Then return for more orders," Valskar finished, and the rest of the men at the table followed after Re'alis.

Devick leaned onto the table for support as he continued his conversation with Valskar. "Will you need me and my men?"

Valskar chuckled and said, "You gave yer word to see the lady home, is this not so? I even heard that you almost died trying to protect her."

Devick lowered his head, smiling at how Valskar saw right through him, then looked back to the man as he spoke. "Yes, I did, but I would not abandon you to defend alone."

"Well, if you be thinkin' you will get out of keeping yer word to the lady so you can have a piece of my glorious battle to come, then you be thinkin' wrong," Valskar spoke with mock sternness, but his voice grew softer as he continued.

"Go with her my, lord. There is little you can do here, and those horse riders of Penetrah's will need all the help they can get if the Ikthii are truly marching that way."

Devick reached across the table and clasped hands with his old friend. "I always was an easy read for you, Valskar. Make me a promise, though, you hold as long as you can, but when the fortress falls, get out—you and all who can. We will need you at the Red Gates and in the fights to come."

"You speak as though the Aya Dao'Tai is already within our walls picking out her new bedchambers!" Valskar said with a chuckle in his voice.

"We can't afford to lose men like you, not now."

"If it comes to that, I promise I will see yer command obeyed." Still smiling, Valskar stood, as did Devick.

"I will have my men report in the yard in three hours. Will that give you time to ready your men?" asked Valskar.

"Yes, that will be plenty of time."

"Good, then you best be off to comfort your lady, young Devick," Valskar winked at him conspiratorially.

Devick raised a questioning eyebrow, as if he was not sure what Valskar meant.

"Do not be tryin' to hide how you feel for her from me, lad. You have cared for her since you first met as lad and lass. I be sure that you were thinkin' me and yer parents couldn't tell, but we knew. It is right that you two be with each other. After all, it was what yer parents wanted. But after you are done in at the high lakes, best hurry back to Mantorah. It won't due to let the camarilla of lords stew for too long on their own. Not with the threat of war marching south."

Devick let out a slow breath as he looked Valskar in the eyes. "Wisdom as always, my good friend. And wisdom that I will heed. Mantorah *will* come to break the siege—hold the walls."

"We will, now go! Get yer men ready."

Devick smiled, clasped Valskar's hand once more, and obeyed. He left through the same door as the others and from there descended another flight of spiraling stairs. He was directed by a passing servant to the room of Re'alis, in a lower level of the tower. He found it and Ercoln standing watch.

"She is within, lord."

Devick nodded and knocked upon the door, but there was no answer. Slowly he opened the door and looked into the small room. Warm light from a small fireplace in the southern wall was the only source of illumination.

"Lady Re'alis?" he called. There was no answer.

Devick began to cross the dark room when the sound of soft weeping caught his ear from an adjoining room. He approached the doorway, looking for the source, and saw a trembling figure next to one of the pillars that stood in two rows within the room. Devick silently drew near until he could see who it was.

"Re'alis?" he said softly. She abruptly stopped her crying and looked up, wiping her face. "If we are to leave, we should be getting ready."

"I apologize for my unseemly state," Re'alis said quickly, still trying to clear the tears from her cheeks. "I just feel overwhelmed, what with getting captured and almost killed, then being rescued, then thinking you would die, and now this and you'll be trapped here and..." She trailed off and looked at him, "If *we* are to leave?"

"Yes, we." Devick gently wiped one last tear from her cheek and smiled.

She smiled in return and even laughed a little in relief. "But what of Syrah and Mantorah?"

"Syrah has had her own army and rulers since before Mantorah even knew there was an Aril River. There is little I could do here. Gairrle will make sure Mantorah is warned, and the army gathered, so that just leaves you. I swore to see you safe so long as our paths were the same."

"And are they yet the same?" There was a warm, hopeful tone in Re'alis' voice.

"That they are, my lady. And thus, they will be so long as you wish it." He gently took her hand and kissed it.

"Well, enough of these tears then," Re'alis said briskly. "We are off to battle and the start of a war."

Devick set his mouth in a grim line as he nodded. "Yes, we are, very much so. And it is a war I do not know if we can win."

"Do you remember what I told you in the tent, the night I was taken?"

"We spoke of many things, my lady."

"When you spoke of fighting the Aya Dao'Tai together, I said I would have it no other way. I meant that with all my heart, Devick." She looked at him with such openness, he felt that he could drown all reason, sorrow, and fear, leaving only an oblivion of bliss within their warm depths.

"All, of, my, heart." She said more emphatically,

"I feel the same way," he said, meaning it completely. Still holding her hand, he drew her into an embrace. They held each other quietly for a few moments. Re'alis closed her eyes and let her head rest on Devick's warm chest.

At last, he spoke. "Let us go with haste to Lea'Angleneth."

Valskar leaned back in his chair, holding a map of Syrah up to the lamplight. The flickering light played upon the surface of the map, making it appear as if it was aflame. Noting this he laughed out loud.

"Some might say that is not a good omen," he said to himself as he set the map aside. He rose to his feet and started off at a fast pace. All the while talking to himself. "Hmm, if that battle plan is correct, then...but how do they intend to cross the river there?" Downstairs, and through corridors he went, mumbling to himself softly. Within a few minutes he was standing in the armory. The paladin stopped and looked out into the large room—lamp and candle shed a golden light upon the racks of armor and weapons.

"There is enough here to arm twice as many men as I have," said Valskar regretfully. The room was filling with soldiers, hurrying to prepare their arms for war. Valskar stood contemplating all that must be done as he watched their proceedings. *It is going to be a long night*, he thought.

The muffled toll of the tower bells started to echo down the stone halls and into the room where Valskar was standing. He watched, and soon more men began to pour into the armory. Sword and helm, spear and shield, bow and arrow—all were being quickly issued to the lines of soldiers entering the hall. Valskar looked at all their faces as they passed him. Most looked so young, so very unaware of what lay in store for them. Yet, each had a look of determination in their eyes—a look of quiet strength to overcome. Valskar knew that at this same moment these men's families were being loaded into wagons to head for the Mantorahn frontier. He watched a little longer, then retired to don his own armor. These men would not fight alone, he'd save as many as he could. Syrah's contingent of professional soldiers was large, and these brave men here would swell their ranks, giving the fortress a garrison many times larger than a city of its size would normally have. Yet Valskar knew all too well that there was a lethal balance between the number of defenders and the stores of food, water, and medicines.

If not carefully managed his strength in numbers could turn into the fortress's undoing.

Meanwhile Penetrah and his cataphracts rushed to fit their arms and armor to both man and mount.

"Swiftly, men!" he ordered, tightening the cinch of his saddle. "We are to meet Lord Devick and the paladin in the yard in half a bell." His lancers did their best to comply, working with their pages and squires to pack the heavier armor for travel and equip their lighter mounts for the hurried journey.

It was taking longer than Penetrah wanted to make ready. They had already taken an hour to gather and even longer to put their armor on. Penetrah prided himself as one of the finest cavalrymen Mantorah had to offer. His family line had held the charge of Marshal of the East for five generations, and his father had fallen defending the refugees from Ell'Anoth. This was his chance to pay the Subjugate army back for the slaughter of that day, and he would not start this chance to make his family proud with any delays.

He placed his boot into the stirrup and swung up into the saddle. His men followed suit, and they all rode out of the massive stables and into the yard. The pale moonlight made the walls and towers of the fortress look as if they had been frosted with winter snow. Penetrah could see Devick and his men at the far east gate to the citadel. Valskar was also there, ready for battle in his glittering maille and plate. As Penetrah crossed the yard, he could see men on the walls and ramparts making all manner of preparations—baskets of stones, barrels of oil, arrows, and other missiles were being hoisted into the towers and onto the walls. Penetrah and his men rode up in close formation and dismounted in unison. Devick, Re'alis, Valskar, and Gairrle came up and greeted him.

"I take it we all understand our parts in this?" asked Devick solemnly. All nodded in one accord.

"The fortress will be as ready as it can be, Lord Devick," said Valskar.

"I am ready to ride for the frontier," Gairrle responded.

"And we are prepared to ride with you to Lea'Angleneth," Penetrah added resolutely.

Such loyalty touched Devick, it gave warmth and a measure of hope to his heart.

"Very good, no matter what happens, if any of you do not receive word in one month's time, gather what forces you can to the Aril Watch. If it has fallen, then regroup in the Fist Hills." All made signs that they understood.

"I thank you all for your actions to ease the blow upon my home," Lady Re'alis said earnestly. "I promise you all, we will ever be your strongest allies in the struggle to come."

"My Lady Re'alis, we are honored to assist you," stated Penetrah.

"As I fought with yer father, I too shall fight for his brave and beautiful daughter." Valskar smiled at Re'alis as he spoke. "After all, I still owe him for more than a few lost wagers on my part."

"Valskar, should the Tundraihn and Kaileth arrive, please see that they are welcomed and fully apprised of the situation. Though, I think they may be more aware of what is going on than us here," said Devick. "And give them my thanks for my life."

"It shall be done. Now you had best be off. Many ten skain lay between you and the isle on the lake, and our foe has a few days lead on you."

Devick smiled and took Valskar by the hand. "As always, your counsel will be heeded, my friend. Arontarh shield you."

"And sharpen your blade, my lord," Valskar responded formally.

The groups bid each other farewell. Valskar returned to the citadel and the preparations to be made there. Gairrle mounted his horse and saluted Lord Devick and Lady Re'alis; he and half a dozen men then rode out of the fortress, swiftly making their way southward. Lord Devick helped Re'alis into her saddle, then he and Penetrah both mounted their horses.

Though it was drawing late into the night, the fortress was busy with the movements of men and equipment. Defensive weapons made by the crafty engineers of Lea'Angleneth were being placed upon the walls. Women and children were preparing to leave the fort, and supplies were already streaming into the holds of Syrah from the surrounding countryside.

Devick looked up into the clear night sky. The stars were shining brightly, and the moon was now high in their midst. He looked to where Re'alis sat on her horse. She was clad in brilliant white armor; a type and fashion only produced in her homeland. The smooth surface of the steel reflected the starlight into a thousand sparkling rays. The light threw a soft ethereal glow upon the perfect lines and graceful curves of her face, and he paused to take her in. Re'alis smiled brightly, catching Devick as the moment stretched and they drew strength from one another. How he wished they might have more time to just be. Yet this was the challenge of their time and he realized how fortunate he felt to be facing it with her strength at his side.

He turned to the marshal. His line of chargers pranced eagerly, feeling the excitement in the air. They were some of the finest lancers and breydfar destriers in all of Mantorah's service, and they would need every ounce of speed and nerve before the month was up.

"Penetrah, lead your men out, and we shall follow."

"As you command, lord," answered Penetrah.

Penetrah leaned forward in his saddle and his horse sped on to lead the cavalry out of the yard and down the street. Devick, Re'alis, and their men followed after the cataphracts and wagons. There were a few wagons that carried the armor and supplies for Penetrah's cataphracts, and behind these were the battle wagons—large, armored wagons made to hold archers and heavy infantry. They were drawn by six of the largest breydfar Devick had ever seen and mounted on top and at the back was a giant, repeating crossbow. Such advanced weaponry was the work of engineers who had fled to Mantorah from Lea'Angleneth to hide from the eyes of the Subjugate. Ten of these battle wagons, along with their crews, were now going to the land of their creators' nativity.

Penetrah spurred his horse and he and his men rode out. Devick led his men and the wagons slowly through the gates, close behind Penetrah. Valskar's men were already busy placing caltrops and spikes in front of the walls and towers. Devick turned his gaze toward the mountains to the east. The landscape was held in calm silence by the cool light that drifted down from the stars and moon above. The stillness felt brittle, like an impossibly thin sheet of ice, simply waiting for the movement that would shatter it into jagged shards. Re'alis brought her horse up alongside Devick, who turned to look to her. Their eyes met, and he took comfort once again from her gaze.

"I am with you," she said. Devick thought he had never heard more perfect words. He smiled and saluted with his hand held to this heart. They guided their horses down the narrow causeway and past the final set of watchtowers, then on, toward the mountains and Lea'Angleneth that lay beyond.

28

Avertyyn and Blood

A ch'Juln the Fallen and Fair yet is active upon Miljah. Do not pay heed to those who deny his malice. Take note of the histories of Miljah and be wary of his enticements and the folly of his service. For did he not even deceive and abuse his own kin?
Essays of the Divine

Blood was running everywhere, and Lirah's hands shook with fear as she struggled to stop it. The black metal of the arrow resisted her every attempt to remove it or to stop the bleeding. The initial healing had somehow reversed sometime during the night, and it was the warm flow of Vishaya's blood that woke Lirah from her fitful rest in the wagon. Ealë and the other wounded had been tended to some time ago, and Lirah had needed to take a brief rest to regain her strength. Ealë had taken a great deal of effort to heal. Tyllidus had done well to clean and close the wound. However, there was still injury inside Ealë that he had not been able to heal. After her, Jahllia still had a great need for help as well. At the time Vishaya seemed to be resting easily and in little immediate danger, so Lirah focused on the others.

She was cursing herself now as she fought to stop the torrent of blood from the wound. She had used all the herbs she had for staunching bleeding from her healer's bag and was starting to feel frantic. Vishaya's eyes were open, but there was no light in them, they looked like jet-black stones. With a prayer on her lips Lirah tried several more times to use her empathic powers to heal the wound, but each time the arrow resisted and caused more damage to Vishaya and terrible pain to Lirah. The light from the early morning sun illuminated the scene and Lirah could now see that Vishaya was turning a pale blue color. Her breathing was also starting to falter. A thought suddenly came to Lirah.

"Jayle!" Lirah clambered to the driver's seat of the wagon; her voice cracked in desperation. "Jayle, you have to stop the wagon, please. Vishaya is dying. I have to get her on the ground, now!"

Jayle sat for an instant, looking a bit stunned by her bloody frantic appearance. He then stopped the wagon and jumped from his seat. Together he and Lirah took Vishaya from the back of the wagon and placed her amongst the ferns and soft mossy earth of the forest floor they were now in. Orodan, Kaileth, Ralenn, and the others were some ways ahead of the wagon, and so Jayle and Lirah were alone outside the wagon in the growing light of the morning.

Vishaya's skin was starting to turn an ashy gray now, and Lirah thought her eyes looked even more stone-like in the sun. She looked beyond help, yet Lirah could still feel her life force, though it was very faint. Lirah knelt near her and felt for the deep power of Miljah. She could feel it pulsing around her in the dew-covered earth. It was strong here. She was about to start trying to heal the wound again when a sound of rushing wings and Olyn's voice came from above.

"I would not try that just yet." She opened her eyes and saw Olyn standing nearby. He looked stern, but not overly concerned as he continued.

"That arrow will kill her if you cannot get it out. I think you will need help."

"Then please help me!" Lirah begged.

Olyn seemed to be weighing the choice for a moment. Lirah's eyes searched his face, there was a hesitance in his expression, a hint of animosity even. It was gone nearly as soon as Lirah had noticed it, and she could not begin to fathom what it meant.

"Mantorahn, we will need your aid as well," Olyn said at last.

Jayle nodded as he spoke. "Tell me what to do, then."

"Miss Lirah, we will have to drive that arrow out of her, this will kill her unless you can heal the damage as fast as we cause it. The difficulty in that will be the arrow resisting your efforts bitterly. It will cause you great pain and could even drive you into madness or death. I think we only have one chance at this, so do your best if you wish to save her."

Lirah scowled slightly at the cold pragmatism and dire truth of Olyn's words, but she had no better plan. Lirah placed her hands on Vishaya. She was cold, and her skin felt hard and smooth, like polished rock. Lirah did not have time to wonder much at this.

"I have to try...I am ready, Olyn," she said, and she gritted her teeth as she connected to the life force of the forest around her.

"Very well. Your belt, Mantorahn." Olyn reached toward Jayle who took off his broad knight's belt. It was made of thick leather and was more than half a hand's span wide. With Vishaya still lying partially on her side Olyn took the long belt and wrapped the end of the arrow shaft where it protruded from her shoulder. He then sat down, took hold of the belt-wrapped arrow, and placed his feet on Vishaya's back.

"When I start to pull, pound this arrow through her with your sword pommel. Take care not to slip or that arrow will lay you open. When you start to heal, we will start to drive the arrow out. Do not stop until it is free, or she will die."

Lirah did not open her eyes, she only nodded and steeled herself. She reached out with her mind, pulling as hard as she knew how on the life force around her as she placed her hands near the wound in Vishaya's chest and forced her awareness into the wound. Hot red sparks spouted from the arrow shaft and burned into her skin, breathtaking pain rushing into her body. Lirah let out a violent shriek, Olyn pulled, and Jayle started slamming his sword pommel into the back of the arrow. It resisted, and with each impact of Jayle's sword Lirah could feel the arrow's barbs cutting at Vishaya mercilessly. It also seemed to be sending little jolts of burning energy into her, causing terrible damage. Her senses swam, and without realizing it Lirah stopped breathing. It took all of her will and mental focus to push through the pain and force the healing.

Lirah could feel Vishaya fading away, and she fought against it desperately, summoning all the strength she had within herself as well as all she could pull from the earth around her. Jayle was now striking the arrow with the pommel of his sword and all his strength; it was starting to give.

"Brek's piss, it's like driving a spike into stone!" Jayle exclaimed amidst his efforts. Each blow drove the arrow a little bit at a time through Vishaya's shoulder and out the back where Olyn pulled with all his strength. Blood started to seep from Olyn's hands as the razor-like barbs of the arrow worked their way through Jayle's belt.

The metallic sound of Jayle's sword striking the arrow was soon the only sense of the outside world Lirah could feel as she was swallowed up by pain and the effort to heal the wound in Vishaya. The barbs of the arrow caused such terrible damage as they moved, and the metal itself continued to burn and fight back against Lirah's efforts.

Somehow Lirah remained coherent enough to feel a crack forming in Vishaya's back. Like a crack in a stone statue, it suddenly appeared, running from the arrow wound up toward her neck. A few more small cracks ran away from the wound in her chest. Lirah now realized that the reason Vishaya had felt like stone earlier was that she was somehow turning into it! Or something very near to that. She had no idea if it was some spell from the arrow or a process of death for one of her kind. Regardless, she struggled to heal the cracks along with the damage from the arrow. Lirah could feel her strength waning; her mind was on the verge of being overwhelmed by agony, panic, and fear. She started to waiver, nearly collapsing, as the last few inches of the barbed portion of the arrow emerged from Vishaya's back. With a sudden jerk, Olyn fell backward with the bloody arrow in his pierced hands.

Lirah held out a few moments longer and could suddenly feel the rush of power from the earth as its healing force surged through her trembling body. Her cold skin warmed under Lirah's hands as the power of Miljah coursed through Lirah into Vishaya's wounds. Lirah opened her eyes, but all she could see was blinding white light. Everything was warm and numb. It was so strong Lirah lost all sense of her own form and all she knew for an instant was the limitless energy of Miljah. The roots of the innumerable trees of the forest, the beating of birds' wings in the warm air, each drop of dew as it fell from leaf to mossy earth.

Lirah suddenly became aware of a woman's form in the dazzling forces that surged around her. She was somehow made of something whiter than the infinite white glow of the world of energy Lirah now found herself in. As she smiled Lirah became aware of other shapes in the light. In the same way her eyes adjusted to see in the dark they now seemed to adjust to the light. Sparkling trees, bright ever-blossoming flowers, indescribable beauty, depth of color, and dazzling radiance surrounded her, forming a version of the forest beyond anything Lirah could have put to words. Lirah turned her focus back to the woman. She was still smiling, and a feeling of belonging that Lirah had never known washed over her.

"Seek your kin." The voice filled Lirah's awareness completely, though the woman's mouth never changed from her beatific expression.

Before Lirah could try to form any thought in response her awareness slammed back into her aching body. The shift was too abrupt and painful for her senses and Lirah slumped over onto the ground. Darkness overtook everything for a time.

As Lirah slowly regained her senses, she saw Jayle watching her intently. He smiled as she stirred, and Lirah realized she was back in the wagon wrapped in a cloak sitting at the very front, near the driver's seat. Ealë was sitting next to Jayle, and the wagon was again slowly moving. Near Lirah was Vishaya. She was back to her normal color and looked to be resting peacefully now. Lirah could see her chest, and there was only the slightest mark where the arrow had been.

"How are you feeling?" Jayle asked as he turned back to drive the wagon.

Lirah rubbed her eyes and sat up. She felt spent and groggy. "I feel well enough—" A large yawn interrupted her, and Jayle chuckled.

"Deem you might need a bit more rest, Miss. That was something you did back there. That blasted arrow had some power to it. I've never seen its like. Sharper than a razor. Cut Olyn's hands right through my belt."

"Where is he now, Jayle, is he hurt badly?"

"Not so badly, he said it will heal on his own." Jayle replied

"He took the arrow and is flying ahead now," Ealë said as she made her way slowly from the wagon seat to sit next to Lirah. She placed her warm hand on her shoulder and Lirah realized that she was a bit chilled.

"To tell the truth, Miss, Olyn seemed a bit upset by the arrow, though he didn't say why," Jayle added over his shoulder.

"That arrow was avertyyn, wasn't it?" Lirah asked.

"Yes sister, it was." Ealë spoke softly now as she placed another cloak over Lirah. She started to ask another question, but Ealë silenced her with a softly placed finger to Lirah's lips.

"Rest for now. Let me tend to you and we can talk later, when the dark one awakes, I think."

Lirah nodded and Ealë handed her a leather bottle and she drank. The honey-laced water refreshed Lirah's dry throat. She took a few more long drafts from the bottle before leaning back against the wagon. Ealë smiled and leaned back as well and they both simply relaxed for a while, letting the wagon gently rock them.

The portion of the wagon where they now sat was mostly obscured from the back by a thick waxed canvas curtain that ran across the inside of the wagon. The wagon itself was very large and could have held many more people inside comfortably. Lirah took the time to carefully examine her surroundings now. A few knives hung from pegs in the wagon side, piles of furs filled one corner, and the floor of the wagon was covered with many furs as well. They were soft and thick, but Lirah could not tell for sure what kind of animal they had come from. The wood of the wagon was richly carved, as were the wooden spars that supported the leather and canvas roof.

Lirah suddenly realized that Vishaya was awake and looking at her intently. She had a strange look on her face, and Lirah was not sure what to make of it. Her dark features expressed both awe and just a hint of fear perhaps. The expression disappeared as Lirah made eye contact with her, and Vishaya took on her normal calm demeanor.

"Thank you, little orch...Thank you, Lirah. I can only guess what it took to save me; thank you." She sounded tired, but her voice was strong.

"I am just happy I was able to do it. You were not exaggerating about that nasty arrow. Who made such an awful thing?"

Suddenly Olyn landed on the seat next to Jayle with a rush of wind, giving the knight a start.

"I do wish you would call out below before you swoop in. If only so I can make room for your landing," Jayle said flatly as he pushed Olyn's wing from in front of his face. Olyn only nodded and folded his wings in close. Vishaya's eyes darted to Olyn for a moment then back to Lirah.

"Yes, tell her who made this." Olyn raised the black barbed arrow in his hand and tapped it against the wagon frame. Vishaya swallowed hard and sat up straight.

"That *arrow* was made by my people, though how it found its way into the slavers' camp I do not know."

"I should have let it kill you, if not for the irony alone then in retribution of those it was made to slay." Olyn's voice carried such anger, and such a *weight* of meaning that, though Lirah didn't understand it, she instinctively pulled back from him. She could see his shoulders shaking a little. Jayle was now watching him closely, and Ealë assumed a defensive posture.

"Olyn, that arrow is from a war long ended." Vishaya's voice was soft and sincere. "If we are to stop such a thing from happening again, we must let the past go."

Olyn did not say anything; he just kept turning the arrow in the sunlight, letting the black surface reflect the golden light.

"Olyn, I am sorry that you have known such loss. I lost many as well. None of what we did was even our choice." Lirah could feel Vishaya's aura grow, and it felt as if she was reaching out to Olyn.

"I will keep *this*. I may need it, I suppose." Olyn's voice was hard as he spoke, and without another word he took off and flew out of sight.

"What was that all about? Or do I even want to know?" asked Jayle. Vishaya let out a long sigh and slumped back against a pile of soft furs.

"It is about a war fought so long ago I doubt he was alive for it. Once we warred with the Jendayi, with all the Pali'andeo—with everything that was not us or under Ach'Juln's domination. It was an awful thing, bitter and costly. I was very young then, too young to fight in it at first, but I served in..." Vishaya's voice faltered, and she looked pained. It took her a moment before she continued, and Lirah could only guess at what memory could cause her to hurt after so much time.

"I served in other ways. In service to Drashtaa and Ach'Juln. That arrow and many like it were only part of the arsenal we created, an arsenal we needed to fight the Atha'Tarrii, the Shedim, the Kythugdon, the Tundraihn, so many others. The weapons of entropic magic to fight and dominate any our master chose. Our host became unstoppable. The Jendayi were strong then and led by powerful *beings*, but our master wanted victory..." Vishaya's voice trailed off, growing soft and distant. "I think that is all I will tell you of this for now." Lirah and the others sat quietly for a moment. Lirah recognized a few of the names Vishaya mentioned, and all of them were from the oldest myths and legends collected in the books in the Anthosn temple. At last Jayle spoke.

"Fair enough, Mistress. We will be some time together in the forest. Let's hope Olyn lets the past stay in the past. We've got enough troubles as it is without old wars starting up anew."

Jayle quickened the pace of the wagon a bit as the sun drew higher. In the stillness that now filled the wagon Lirah turned over the events since leaving Allinth in her mind. She was certain now that the Subjugate was trying to stir things up in the far south. This could only be part of a much larger plan. She could not help but feel a sickening dread at the names Vishaya had mentioned. Ach'Juln, and Drashtaa. Drashtaa Lirah knew from a very old book in the temple called *The Sojourn of Feldorell*. It was a lengthy translation of a journal rendered into a tale of Feldorell and his adventures in the world when it was yet new.

Together with his love, Inyltray, they faced monsters, and magical beings that Lirah now saw to be Vishaya's people. Inyltray clearly was of the same race as Olyn, and Feldorell yet another being of myth. Within the pages of this book Feldorell came across the followers of Drashtaa, murderous people whose only goal seemed to be the most savage of debasements. Toward the end of the book Feldorell and Inyltray set out to find the Tears of the Aashahl to help defeat a cabal of Drashtaa's followers only to be captured by them in the Dark Realms.

The book was one of Lirah's favorites, full of romantic moments, desperate fights, and wondrous lands, but it had been some time since she last read it. She did recall that Drashtaa was one of the Aashahl themselves and of no small power. If that was true, she could only guess at Vishaya's dark past. That and the potential for the Subjugate to cause all matter of new horrors by reigniting past conflicts.

She thought on this and of the events for the last few days as the hours passed and the wagon rolled along. Soon Lirah could hear the voices of Ralenn and Kaileth as their horses drew near to the wagon. She smiled and took comfort from knowing they were close. She didn't know what would become of them all in the things that were to come; would their story end in tragedy like Feldorell's? She felt so uncertain, but she felt that with them by her side she might just have the strength to face whatever their story would be.

29

To Subjugate

They who would be the servants of the aashahl must take heed of all the creeds and ethos of their patron, order, and house. One cannot grasp and raise the near end of the branch save the other is lifted also.
Essays of the Divine.

Chancellor Rovik had been riding near the head of the Subjugate Army's baggage train for three days past a halfmoon now. He was grateful to be out of Ell'Anoth and away from the chance that his involvement in the slavers' camp fiasco might be discovered. Still, it was unsettling how easily he was able to justify his involvement in the actual campaign. Afyreen seemed surprised by his interest in going with the army. At least as surprised as she ever seemed. He had accompanied or overseen many smaller forays closer to the old borders of Anoth. Such as the raid on Allinth. To make his choice to go seem more genuine, he explained how he was best suited to facilitate the full cooperation of the Grishkii in the new campaign. Additionally, he had argued that his intimate knowledge of Syrah would be critical in taking the city. The Dao'Tai army was massive but their ability to take strongholds efficiently had proved to be poor in the initial invasion of the High Sun Realms. In the years past deliberate efforts had been put into improving this weakness and Rovik had been instrumental in these efforts. Additionally, he had also placed greater emphasis on gathering intelligence and operations founded in guile. Despite all this, they had never secured so much as a map of Syrah's streets nor conducted an actual siege since the efforts to take Ell'Anoth. The Dao'Tai were so novice in the art of siege warfare and the Ty'kahls readily supported Rovik's desire to go with them.

Rovik also knew that if Afyreen did suspect his treachery, it would be better for her politically to have him killed while out on campaign, rather than murdered in the city. The people of Anoth had been peaceful under his chancellorship, and he knew that Afyreen understood his part in this peace. Killing Rovik in an obvious manner could cause open rebellion in Anoth. His death while on campaign for the Subjugate, however, could be the death knell for Anothn resistance; or at the very least the death of the last trappings of royal rule.

The joint Subjugate army had made good time at first, but once they entered the Mantorahn frontier the Ty'kahls started sending out raiding parties to plunder the villages and farmsteads they passed by, adding fresh slaves and stolen goods to their stores. The chance for more raiding along the southern road had made it easier to convince the Ty'kahls to follow his new plan to divert the bulk of the army toward Syrah. Along the road he had continued to talk of Syrah's strength, finally convincing them to only send a single Tar'Thyrt, still numbering near eight thousand men, to attack Lea'Angleneth. The remaining three Ty'kahls' men, over ninety thousand strong, would see to Syrah's destruction.

Due to the slowness of the Dao'Tai heavy infantry, most of the raiding was left to the swift horsemen and chariots of the Taivadeans. They had sent eleven verreen of chariots and six gishvreen of their best cavalry to aid in the war effort, together with squires, young men and the veterans guarding the baggage train, which made a total force of around five thousand. The Taivadean vanguard would surge far ahead to attack and loot any place of value, then wait for the lumbering Dao'Tai army to catch up. Their speed of travel was further hampered by the many slow siege engines. Such machines were foreign to the Dao'Tai way of warfare and were the result of forced labor and enslaved arcanists from Lea'Angleneth and the old army of Anoth. Dozens of engines now followed the army, pulled by teams of oxen and scores of slaves.

Rovik didn't mind the slow march, he was hopeful that each day they spent on their way south would buy Syrah and the other realms now under threat more time to prepare. Days crept by and Rovik found himself more and more withdrawn from the Ty'kahls and other Dao'Tai leadership as they went. The main road would only support a portion of the army and so the Ty'kahls were forced to split into separate commands. Taking smaller roads with some battalions using barges upon the rivers to travel south. This added more time to their journey as the army had to reunite and reorganize at the final approach to Syrah. During this entire process harassing troops of Mantorahn cavalry supported by local militias attacked isolated foraging groups and stragglers. The countryside was hostile and at night the camps were held under close watch, weary of raids by the small groups of resistance fighters.

Rovick still felt a thrill at the spectacle of grand armies on campaign despite it all. He paused on a rise to take in the moment presently before him. The setting sun cast long shadows from the trees and hills around the seemingly endless line of marching men. He knew from the land around them now that they were almost in sight of Syrah. He hurried his mount and caught up to where the commanding Ty'kahl was walking. He leaned forward in his saddle as he rode up a sharp rise in the grassy earth. As he reached the crest of the hill his eyes locked far across the plain on the two watchtowers that guarded the causeway to the gates of Syrah. The towers were closer to small fortresses in their own right and seemed to threaten even at this distance. Rovik signaled his guard to halt behind the hilly ridge line, then motioned for Ty'kahl Acotas to join him. Acotas walked up next to Rovik; the large man stood almost as tall as Rovik on his horse.

"There it is, Acotas. As you can see, we will certainly need the extra men."

Acotas was quiet for a long moment, only moving his fingers as though he were trying to count something. At last the soldier scoffed and cleared his throat.

"This fastness is not so grand. I could destroy this place with half the men we have brought, Chancellor! The excess can rest and strike the Red Gates fresh. We are well prepared for these high walls and towers. These southerners have yet to face us in open battle. They will find no salvation from our blades. Their strength of arms will fail and the prayers to their weak Aashahl will go unheeded. We will show them what true prowess is."

"Perhaps," Rovik nodded, conciliatory. "However, you have never faced them before either, it is unwise to underestimate a foe. The men of Syrah are no easy mark, nor is their stronghold."

"As you have said these many days, Chancellor. Let us hope you prove your worth here in their undoing. They were not a force to halt our first invasion. I doubt their strength has waxed since then. The battle will be the telling of it. I will see to the array of the camp." With that Acotas left Rovik alone atop the hill.

Rovik watched him go, cursing himself for being so openly critical of the Dao'Tai's ability to destroy Syrah. Over the last few years Rovik had found Acotas to be the most level-headed of the Dao'Tai's Ty'kahls. Most of the others would not speak the common tongue and were known for killing and even eating their slaves for the slightest missteps. Those same rumors stated that most, if not all, Dao'Tai had a liking for the flesh of men, so he wasn't so sure he believed that.

Acotas by contrast had never demonstrated any of these barbaric tendencies. This was part of the reason Rovik feared Syrah, and Mantorah for that matter, had little chance of victory. Where other Ty'kahls would simply send masses of heavy infantry to assault in wave after wave, Acotas would take a much more strategic approach. Seeking to understand his foe then exploit his weaknesses rather than simply bash his way in. This calm, calculating demeanor made him a formidable foe. It had been Acotas who personally developed the slave camp that made the siege weapons. After he had carefully studied the initial Dao'Tai invasion, along with records of battles in the High Sun Realms, he independently concluded that siege warfare was the single great weak point in Dao'Tai tactics. He was almost killed by his peers for suggesting their way of war could have a flaw, but Afyreen intervened and placed Acotas in the highest office of the army. For the last several years he saw to the capture of certain arcanists and skilled craftsmen to create machines of war for the Subjugate. Great bolt throwers, digging machines, rams, and catapults were just a few of the engines his slaves created. Rovik had not missed the eagerness in Acotas' expression: at last it was time to put the Ty'kahl's weapons and tactics to use. Acotas had not forgotten the scorn from his peers for his forward thinking. Thus the destruction of Syrah was the chance for his personal vindication as much as it was a chance for a Subjugate victory. Acotas' host of weapons were crude by many measures. Lacking certain refinements. However, they also were large and powerful. Rovik was sure they lacked the accuracy and speed of fire that many of the engines of Lea'Angleneth and Mantorah had. Yet, like the Dao'Tai, their sheer number and brutality of force was overpowering.

Rovik rode from off the ridge line and down into the quickly growing camp. The baggage train had started to pull in and array itself into orderly rows while the Dao'Tai soldiers placed their two-man pack sticks down and began to gather to set up their large tents. The Dao'Tai's refusal to use horses was still a mystery to him. The bulk of the Subjugate instead carried most of their equipment on studded poles. These poles would be carried by two soldiers and with them, they would pack all their personal equipment and enough food and water for several days. They still favored this method over a true baggage train for transporting their arms, armor, and supplies.

For this campaign they had taken a large number of wagons. Many of them empty for the spoils of war, but many others full of food and stores for the sieges that Acotas had prepared his forces for. The Taivadeans set their camp apart from the Dao'Tai as they always did. As did all the non-Dao'Tai members of the Subjugate army. It was in this area of the camp that Rovik also spent his evening. He had left Ell'Anoth with a small personal guard comprised of a few of the palace guard, some of his servants and stable hands, and three others he had personally hired. Or at least that was the cover story for KaTyle and his two associates. A few days before the army had set out, they had appeared in Rovik's private chambers unannounced and explained to him that they would be going with him. Rovik was glad of their presence. KaTyle was no friend, but he was a man of his word and no murderer. Rovik also knew that KaTyle would not jeopardize his cover, not when it afforded him free movement inside the Dao'Tai camp.

By the time Rovik found KaTyle, their tents had been set near a rise in the ground close to the river. A small stand of trees offered a bit of separation from the Taivadeans and the soft grassy earth promised a good night's sleep.

KaTyle approached and stopped Rovik while they were yet some distance from the others of his camp.

"So, we are here, Syrah is yon?" KaTyle spoke softly as he gestured in the direction of the fortress city.

"Yes, the causeway and watchtowers are just beyond the ridge and hills. Acotas plans to begin the assault at first light."

"Best if we don't sleep much, then, I can't imagine the Syrahns letting us camp on their porch in peace. If they raid the camp we hide in the river, no heroics. I'm not interested in spilling their blood, nor do I intend to let them spill yours, for now at least. We hear fighting we all go in the water. Clear enough?"

"Clear enough."

"Good, on to other matters then. Have you spoke with the Taivadean scouts yet?"

Rovik usually had by this time of the day, but they had not yet reported to Acotas, he suddenly realized. "No, I haven't," he said, still thinking on the matter. "I haven't even seen them today, now that I think of it."

"You will want to hear from them what they have to say. They have been back for some time, just past highsun." KaTyle smiled as he spoke and Rovik wondered at the light in his eye.

"What do they report? Why have they hidden within their host?"

"Let us say that the Grishkii will not be joining us for the siege, least not in any large numbers it seems." KaTyle smiled again even wider and deliberately turned and strode off toward the Taivadean camp. Rovik stood a little longer in the failing light running through all the possible scenarios that would lead the Taivadean scouts to fail to report, and the Grishkii to not answer the call to battle.

"I'll show you to them," KaTyle said over his shoulder. Rovik quickened his pace following after him. The two worked their way through the camp of the Taivadeans. They were a proud, warlike people who did not much care for the Dao'Tai, but they also saw no wisdom in fighting against them. They served more or less on their own terms, as scouts and raiding bands, bringing tales of battle and the spoils of war to their far away northern homes.

The band that was with the Subjugate army was led by a young Kyrg named Dreannon Ordjua. Rovik knew this was his first large campaign, and his band's first time in the southern realms. It was common for Taivadeans to seek battle in foreign lands as a way to legitimize their rule through deeds of arms and riches from the battles. Rovik also knew that should this turn into a string of sieges the Taivadeans would lose interest quickly in what they saw as a gloryless form of warfare. Their absence in a protracted war with Mantorah could be a critical factor.

KaTyle led Rovik to a group of small colorful tents circled around a campfire where the Taivadeans were cooking their supper. The soldiers sitting near the fire fell into silence as Rovik and KaTyle approached. The sun was all but set now, leaving the smell of roasting field hens to drift in the cool darkness. They held their faces in hard expressions and unless Rovik was very wrong, they were worried about something, something they were trying to hide.

"You know who he is?" KaTyle finally said.

"Yes, he is the Old King's man." An older Taivadean spoke, his short beard silver from age.

"I am. And whatever news you bring give it to me and I will bear its weight to the Dao'Tai." Rovik said, hoping that he guessed rightly the cause of their hesitation to report.

"This campaign was not what we were promised. Villages and farms, we are sent to attack. Hardly an armed man or warrior among them. There is no field of glory here. There has been no attack on the north lands by Mantorah, has there?" Rovik found this intriguing, clearly the Taivadeans had been told at least one falsehood if not more regarding the cause of this campaign.

"No, there is no attack upon the north by Mantorah, the Subjugate is attacking them, and it will be a war of attrition, a war of sieges, and a slaughter of the innocent, to be sure. However, the spoils will be great." Rovik wanted to see just how far these soldier's disenfranchisement went, hoping to learn if there was a chance for their defection. He knew that the Taivadeans would have no reservations about meeting nearly any army in open battle, but raiding defenseless farmsteads and laying sieges were both things they found no glory in.

"There may yet be some chance for you and your lord to fight the battle you seek. In the meantime, please, trust me with the news of your scouts and I will bear the tidings to the Dao'Tai."

The Taivadeans looked to KaTyle who gave them a reassuring expression. Then the gray-bearded Taivadean gestured for them to sit. The soldier reached out to the field hens and started to carve the birds onto several wooden plates, passing the plates down the line of his fellow soldiers. In turn, KaTyle handed Rovik his own plate. Roasted field hen, kran, yurbs and seed bread filled the plate. Once everyone around the campfire had a plate of food, they held their plates high and lowered their heads. The Taivadean with the silver beard spoke in a reverent tone.

"Arontarh give us strength, give us yet a day of glory in battle. Bok keep open your halls for those fallen and lost. Paldrii see us all safe into their care."

He finished and the Taivadeans lowered their plates and started eating. Rovik and KaTyle did likewise, and they all quietly ate for several moments. Rovick knew that the provisions would only get worse the longer the war went on, so he allowed himself to enjoy this rich fare. A large jug started to be passed around and Rovik found it to contain a tart new wine. They continued eating and drinking and in time the Taivadeans started sharing tales. They spoke of heroes from their legends, brave mariners and dauntless warriors facing creatures of dark myth in lands swallowed by the seas. They spoke of beautiful and brave maidens who left their homes to defend their lands. They shared personal tales of prowess and comedic follies of their youths. Rovik listened, content to be included, to listen to a people so full of life. At length, the silver-bearded Taivadean spoke.

"My name is Rvej Urlon. I have served House Orjua my entire life, Dreannon's father and now him. I remember the Old King in Anoth and the realms that hailed him as liege lord. I saw their prowess firsthand fighting the Dao'Tai in the Freeholdn as a youth. I saw their courage fighting in Vagath'Oth. Even the mighty Dao'Tai feared some of they who fought for the Old King." He paused, clearly thinking back over the memories he referenced, searching for proper names.

"The Anothn Sh'tars and Allitorii. Yes, those were they."

Rovik, too, was recalling the time that Rvej was referencing. It was strange to hear Garadale called the *Old King*. To Rovik, the name still evoked not age but power — that unyielding presence which had once bound the High Sun realms in harmony. He could see him now in his mind's eye: Garadale of Anoth, robed in the regal splendor of his station, eyes like tempered steel beneath the crown of the Morning Star.

He had been the beating heart of Anoth — its law, its mercy, and its wrath. Under his rule the High Sun realms flourished in a golden balance. The roads were safe, the borders strong, and even the quarrels of the Taivadean tribes had found some measure of peace beneath his standard. His was an age when the kings and kindreds still sought counsel from the shrines of the Aashahl, when faith and crown worked in concert rather than in fear.

Garadale was the final link in that long and storied chain of Anothn kings whose wisdom had brought such prosperity. With his loss, the light of that lineage winked out. What followed could not have been more different; the age of the Subjugate.

Garadale's reign was not without its shadows. He was a man of unbending will, and many said that his peace was built on obedience as much as on justice. Yet even his critics could not deny the majesty of his vision. A world ordered and whole, unmarred by the divisions that would later tear it apart. The divisions that the Aya Dao'Tai relied on to maintain her control.

Rovik realized that there were still many among the Taivadeans who remembered him. A large number of their host would have been youths or young men in those years, growing up under the unifying banners of Anoth and the wisdom of Garadale's decrees. They would remember the cadence of his voice when he spoke to the armies, the way his presence seemed to silence even the restless winds of the plains. To them he was not the Old King, but *the* King — the last to lead the High Sun Realms beneath a single crown. Afyreen was right to fear the consequences of a surviving heir to the Anothn throne. An heir to Garadale's throne.

"Today, I was sent to scout far into the steppes of the Vagath'Oth, past the Aril toward what once was part of Andohra. I found the first slaughter field at a ford across the Trixx, Grishkii, slain by the hundreds. Piled in three great heaps. I followed the path of the ones who fought them and found two more battlefields the same. I went further into the mountains till I beheld what looked like an old Andohrase keep. It was then that I saw them, tall as a spear with eyes filled with starlight. I left that place with speed. I know what I saw though. Tyraneth, they were. More than a few too. The Grishkii should have found another road to follow."

The circle of men went still at the mention of the Tyraneth. They were true beings of myth in the minds of most people. Giant warriors who came from the far mountains to fight with the Andohrase and Anoth. Rovik knew they were real. He had seen them in battle, and though they were not true giants, they were far beyond the strength and size of any man, Dao'Tai included. At the first Battle of the West Way their vanguard had broken through the center of the Dao'Tai, killing several Ikthii and both the Ty'kahls. In the end, their small number was not enough to turn the tide of the war, yet the Dao'Tai did fear them, and after the war they hunted them relentlessly. Afyreen publicly displayed heads of their slain and announced them slaughtered to the last.

Clearly, if Rvej was speaking the truth then they had survived in numbers large enough to slaughter Grishkii en masse. This brought a significant unknown factor to the battle plans of the Dao'Tai. A factor that Acotas would not ignore. That is, if he knew about it. Rovik's mind began to turn with all the many ways he would use this revelation, the many options and their possible outcomes branched out before him in swiftly diverging tracks of thought until his mind settled on the one that he knew he must take. The clarity that took hold of his mind was startling, yet also filled him with a hot confidence. Rovick knew what he must choose.

"Rvej, could you find that place again?"

A sudden thundering shook the ground around them all and several of the Taivadeans shot to their feet looking to the northeast. Swift dark shapes rushed down the far hills into the Dao'Tai camp. The sounds of slaughter and death sprang up in the night air. KaTyle nodded to himself, clearly unsurprised. — The camp was under attack.

30

Sides are Set

O*liar stands alone as the warden of time. Seek ye not to bend her power to your mortal cause. Drawing her attentions can only serve to shorten the span of your days.*
Essays of the Divine

"There are two of them on top of the hill. The taller one is Dao'Tai, without a doubt. They look important from their dress." The Syrahn watchman spoke softly, as if the men he watched through his spyglass could hear him.

"Go, send word back to Syrah—the Subjugate army is here. I'd guess their army is camped just there beyond the ridge."

Without another word the watchman handed his spyglass to his serjent and rushed from the tower. The twisting, narrow stairs could not pass under his feet fast enough. Midway down the tower his frantic descent was interrupted by a fellow soldier stepping from a doorway.

"Frethid, what is it?"

"They're here! The Dao'Tai army is here."

"Good! Waiting so long to get bashed has been such a ware."

"You might feel that way, but not all of us have seen battle before, Grager." Frethid frowned with worry.

Grager nodded and stepped back into the doorway, allowing Frethid to pass. A few more turns of the spiral staircase and he was out of the tower and upon his horse. Spurring the horse on, he worked to fight off a rising panic. *They've had days to make it to safety. Will I ever see them again?* Frethid's thoughts were reeling with worry over his wife and their new child. They had left Syrah with the general evacuation, but would any safe haven last long with the Subjugate army on the march? The Red Gates of Mantorah had never been breached, but they had also never faced a host like the one the Dao'Tai would surely bring to bear.

Frethid rode hard toward Syrah's gates. He had lived in the fortress city his entire life and knew her walls and alleys well. Looking at the imposing ramparts and dauntless towers, his worry lessened some. If any citadel could hold off the Subjugate it would be Syrah. No garrison in the realms was more disciplined, and no fortress better stocked and manned. They could hold out for months at least, a year if they could keep the outer gates, more if the causeway towers held.

Frethid smiled, thinking of the time his family would have to get to safety, and the time that Mantorah would have to fully marshal their armies. They would come in force to break the siege, and the splendor of their host would be a marvel to behold. Soon the hooves of Frethid's mount clattered on the cobblestones of the gate yard. Slowing only a little he wound his way around the defensive inner walls and through several more gatehouses before the inner stables were in sight. To his surprise, Paladin Valskar was waiting for him expectantly near the stable gates. Frethid brought his horse to a halt and he swiftly dismounted and bowed respectfully to Valskar.

"My Paladin Defender, we have spotted two foes. What appears to be a Dao'Tai general and an emissary of the Subjugate. He wore her colors, sire. The serjent of the tower believes the Subjugate army to be camped on the far side of the northern ridge near the river."

"A keen eye to spot two so far away, well done. Return and tell yer serjent to prepare to defend his tower and keep the watch wary through the night. I will send you more men. Set an easy watch, rest, and eat heartily. It's bound to be a hard week of it."

"Yes Paladin," Frethid answered as he got back onto his horse. He rode back toward the watchtower in haste, glad that more men would be sent. He felt more confident having seen the determination and calm in the paladin's face. More men steadily streamed out onto the walls. The news that the Subjugate army had arrived must have been guessed. All eyes peered north, trying to spy some hint at the size of the army set against them. Frethid rode on, and soon he was back at the watchtowers. He found Sergeant Dannis and many others waiting for him in the guardhouse.

"What orders, Frethid?"

"More men will be sent to bolster our numbers. We are to set an easy watch and rest and eat heartily. The paladin suspects we will have a rough time of it out here. He wants us prepared to defend our tower and keep a keen watch, Sergeant."

Dannis smiled grimly, "Then our duty is clear. Take the horse below and while you are down there, fill this from the cistern, and bring up a few arrow sheaves." Dannis handed him a few empty canteens. Frethid got from his horse and led it through a narrow doorway and down a sharp sloping walkway into the under levels of the tower. The Syrahn causeway towers were in truth a keep and would have constituted the sole defensive structures in most towns and cities, being closer to a small castle than a pair of towers. A few lanterns threw what light they could to guide him. Now deep under the surface the walkway opened up into many chambers. Frethid took his horse to the chamber that served as a small stable. Six horses total could be housed here, though currently only his mount and two others were present.

He left his horse in a stall to eat and drink, leaving it saddled for the time being, just in case. From the stable he quickly made his way to the cistern room where a steady stream of clear, cool water trickled through a long stone aqueduct and into a vast holding vault. The water flowed from a spring inside Syrah itself. Huge stone blocks could be dropped to seal the aqueduct should a tower fall to the enemy. So long as the towers' garrison fought on, their supply of water would be secure. Frethid stooped to fill the canteens. He could hear the steady whistling chug of the pumps that sent water up into the tower. The hand pump pulled the water up into more storage vaults higher in the tower. These water vaults could be used to put out fires, refresh the defenders, or charge the steam vents. The cistern was nearly full and plenty of water was flowing into it to keep up with the pumps.

From the cistern room, Frethid hurried through the manifold chamber. A space filled with a boiler and complex network of copper pipes and tubes. This was a closely guarded secret of the Syrahn defenses. He moved on swiftly, entering the storeroom next. He passed many rooms stacked full of food and supplies till he came to a room that was nearly filled with tall barrels. On the far wall of this room a dozen cloth sacks leaned against the wall—sheaves of arrows. The barrels in this room were filled with more sacks, each sack holding two dozen arrows within. Even more were already staged in the upper levels of the tower now.

Frethid started shouldering the bags' carrying straps in quick succession. *Shiebrok, relentless defender, guide each of these to its mark. Keep our aim swift and true. See us through this fight, ever dauntless shield.*

* * *

Valskar stood for a few moments thinking, as he watched the rider return to the causeway tower. The towers would see some of the worst of the fighting. Only a small tunnel connected the causeway forts to the main keep. The tunnel could be sealed and would have to be if it looked like one of the causeway towers would fall. If this happened, once the enemy surged past the causeway defenses there would be no way to relieve the garrisons trapped in there. He shook his head, dismissing the thought and focusing on the next move—attack.

"If they dare camp at my gates overnight, they shall not sleep in peace." Valskar turned and made his way through the fortress toward the stables. He saw many of his men on and about the walls, and he spoke words of encouragement to them as he passed. Soon he was standing in the largest part of the stables where he was met by Serjent Taban. The serjent was a stout man with a close-cut dark beard and dark eyes. He numbered among the professional garrison of Syrah.

"Paladin, all is set in order as you directed. We are ready to sally forth at your command."

"Very good, lad, very good. After the sun is fully set bring your troops and wagons to the yard and wait there for the order."

"Yes, sire!" said the serjent.

Valskar grinned at the thought of what he had planned for that night. He was never one to choose a defensive fight, in ironic contrast of his title of Paladin Defender. He took his time, slowly making his way through the stable, inspecting the men and their weapons and mounts. They beamed with pride as their leader showed his approbation at their polished armor and sleek strong horses. Valskar knew many of their names, *most* of their names, he realized. They all seemed like his own sons and grandsons to him now. Or at least, he felt the pride a father or grandfather feels at seeing the fine man their sons have grown to be. These men were the children of Syrah and they were truly the finest they could be. Trained and drilled to the best of the Paladin's ability. He prayed it would be enough. Their proving was now at hand.

After inspecting every soldier in the stable he left to return to the bulwarks over the main gates. He moved deliberately, passing his eyes slowly over the stones of the streets and towers, and the faces of his men. He knew that this might be the final hour of peace his city would see, and so he wished for it to linger, to make a hard mark in his memory.

The sun had set by the time he reached his lofty vantage point over the main gate. The soft glow of campfires gently rose over the tops of the hills to the north. Valskar hoped Lord Devick was making good time on his flight to Lea'Angleneth. Syrah could hold out for a good span, but the number of fires in the distance told of a truly vast host.

Like a starry night sky, the fires sprung to life until the entire northern horizon was aglow. Valskar rubbed his eyes, taking in a long slow breath. He looked down river to the bow lights of the last grain barges making their way to the fortress from the south.

"We'll hold out for some time yet."

31

Swiftly to Battle

Many are the orders and houses that take note of valor in battle and prowess upon the field of war. Be sure, therefore, whose favor you seek when setting your hands to battle and take care of their rites that you may prosper.
Essays of the Divine

Serjent Taban's heart was pounding so loudly he wondered if the men at his side could hear it. They had been moving as quietly as possible for the battle wagons and chariots. It had taken the first half of the night to get into position, atop a low hill to the north of the Dao'Tai armies. It was the sight of the Dao'Tai that made Taban's heart race. It looked as if Syrah were an isle in a sea of tents and men. Serjent Taban and the Syrah vanguard of cavalry and chariots had been sent with all the rest of the Mantorahn battle wagons that had not gone with Lord Devick. All together the host was not small, being many hundreds of skilled men-at-arms.

These wagons were the newest designs to come from the Anglenethn sages living in exile. Larger and better armored than the ones that had gone with Lord Devick, these wagons carried two repeating crossbows, one at the rear and one at the front over the driver's bench. Ten heavy infantrymen could ride inside with all their equipment. Armor plates protected the wheels, front, flanks, and rear of the wagon, and blades were affixed wherever possible to cut the enemy down. Eight armored horses pulled each wagon, with mounted archers riding on the last and second pairs to aid in their defense. Before the teams of horses an armored prow set on iron wheels connected to the wagon by an iron-clad beam. This prow served as an angled ram, crushing and clearing a way through nearly any obstacle or line of infantry. It also protected the horses from practically any harm. These wagons were ideal for shock attacks across the open glades that dotted the frontiers on the mainland that surrounded the Mantorah peninsula.

The Mantorahn foot soldiers that usually rode in these wagons had remained at Syrah, along with all Syrahn heavy infantry and auxiliaries. This host of Mantorahn soldiers normally patrolled the long eastern frontier and the Mantorahn highway, a well-maintained road that ran from the Red Gates to the gates of Syrah. Tonight, they fought in the wagons, allowing more of the Syrahn soldiers to stay in the fortress where they knew the defenses best.

Serjent Taban had been born in Lad'Vinor in Mantorah, but from age seven when he was squired to a Syrahn Uran, the fortress city had been his home. All that barred him from the title of Uran and knighthood were his vigil and oaths. He had been eligible to challenge the vigil for nearly four years now, but something held him back. Regardless, he was treated as a knight by nearly all of the people of Syrah, including the paladin. So it was that he found himself leading the Mantorahn forces this night.

Serjent Taban and his host were to assault the camp of the Dao'Tai in a sweeping charge north to south; they had to cut through the Dao'Tai and damage their siege weapons at all costs. Paladin Valskar knew it would be risky, but they had to destroy as many siege engines as possible. Serjent Taban also knew that Syrah could be defended with a relatively small garrison, and every man that fell tonight was one less mouth to feed during the siege. Not that the paladin was heartless, but there was just no point in stalling this attack.

Taban sat in the arbalester's seat of the lead wagon; he lowered the visor of his helm and signaled for the host to begin the attack by sliding a plate of colored glass over the rear facing lens of a spark stone lantern affixed to the cupula. The Syrahn defenders started down the hill slowly at first. However, once the wagons reached the level ground below, the drivers let the horses run, and the battle wagons sped toward the center of the Dao'Tai encampment. A few hundred yards from the camp Taban signaled the cavalry and chariots again, with the lantern in his hand this time, and they veered toward the river and charged into the rows of siege engines that stood there, destroying everything that could be in haste. Each chariot had racks with dozens of clay jars upon them. The jars were filled with a sticky combustible paste. The crews of the chariots frantically threw these jars as they got in amongst the siege engines, smashing them upon the timber of the machines. Torches and lit oil lamps where thrown also, igniting the fire paste.

Taban continued on toward the main Dao'Tai camp, opting to avoid the Taivadeans and focus on the larger force. By now the great rumble of wagons and horse hooves had woken all within the camp. Bladed chains were stretched between each wagon, cutting down the Dao'Tai pickets and then the soldiers as they ran out of their tents in various levels of dress and alertness. Taban began to crank the firing windlass of his crossbow, and the double-bowed weapon sent bolt after bolt flying into the enemy.

The attack had begun well, the camp had been taken by complete surprise. The Dao'Tai had set their watch upon the river and south side of their camp. With the rest of their armies controlling everything north to Kali'Kern they had only set light pickets on the north side of their camp, and now the battle wagons of Mantorah were driving through the heart of the Dao'Tai camp, leaving death in their tracks. Serjent Taban and the other men in the wagons found no shortage of targets for their bows as startled soldiers ran before them. Several times the Dao'Tai formed barricades in the path of the wagons, attempting to stop them. Yet each time they tried this they were met with defeat, for the teams of braydfar horses drove the angled prow of the battle wagons through the lines of men, shields, and wood.

The southern edge of the Dao'Tai camp was soon in sight and Taban quickly glanced toward the river to see how the attack upon the siege engines was proceeding. Silhouetted against the flames of the burning siege engines he could see the Syrahn cavalry and chariots. It appeared that they had destroyed most if not all of the engines and were now heading back to Syrah with all speed, felling the few who made attempts to stop them.

The shock and surprise of the attack was waning, and as Taban's wagon cleared the camp arrows and other projectile weapons began to strike the wagon around him. He swung his crossbow to the north, continuing to fire into the enemy. By now the Subjugate charioteers had mounted and were giving chase to the battle wagons. As fast as Mantorahn horses might be, they had little hope of outrunning these chariots back to the fortress. As they started to catch up to Taban and his wagons, the serjent started to fire at the drivers of the chariots. However, after five or six shots more, the repeating crossbow had exhausted its supply of bolts, and there were still many chariots on their heels. Taban swung the crossbow back to the front of the wagon and took his short bow from its holster. The enemies were close enough that he could see the faces of the Taivadean charioteers with just the light of the moon and stars.

Taban heard his rear arbalester cry out in pain as a spear cast from an enemy charioteer passed out of view at the back of the wagon. Taban's arrows answered in kind as he felled two more Taivadeans. There were now four chariots behind nearly every one of Taban's wagons. Taban ducked into the wagon's interior. The light from the single red-lensed spark stone illuminated the body of the dead arbalester hanging in the rear crossbow turret. Taban placed a firm hand on the shoulder of one of the two drivers and spoke loudly so he could be heard over the clamor of their flight.

"Drop 'em all and signal the others."

The driver nodded and with both hands took hold of one on the many levers that surrounded him in his seat and pulled it back. There was a mechanical thudding sound and the wagon instantly rose on its suspension. As the driver released the lever the same mechanical sound came from under the rear of the wagon. Taban smiled and quickly peered out his crossbow turret and looked behind them. The wagons were close to the two watchtowers that lay before the gates of Syrah. Taban strained his eyes and could just make out the sea of large iron caltrops that his wagons had just dropped from mechanical doors in their bellies. Those thick twisted pieces of metal were their last trick. A green spark stone lantern shone near each wagon's driver, the signal to drop the caltrops.

The chariots of the Subjugate did not see the Mantorahn wagons drop the caltrops into their path, and they rode straight into them. For the few horses that avoided these iron obstacles, the wood wheels and frames of the chariots did not. The iron caltrops fulfilled their purpose as they felled horses and shattered spokes, sending men and debris flying into the air as the chariots broke apart into splinters, and impaling those that fell on them. In mere moments, a host of chariots, their horses, and men lay in a jumbled heap across the field before the two watchtowers. A surging cheer from his men could just be heard over the rumbling of their war machines.

Taban saw there were still over a thousand or so enemy cavalry and a few dozen chariots pursuing them. He ducked back into the wagon and made his way down to the rear crossbow turret. The bow looked to still be in working order, so he pulled the dead arbalester from his seat and grabbed a full box of crossbow bolts.

At a signal from their leading knights, the Syrahn chariots and horsemen wheeled outward from the fore of the column, dividing into two wings that swept left and right in great arcs to encircle the foe. Their mancuver brought them swiftly about, closing upon the rear of the disrupted escadrons of Taivadean chariots.

Seeing the moment, Taban raised his arm in command. His driver reined the wagon to an abrupt halt, and all the battle wagons of Mantorah followed in perfect order, forming a braced wall of iron and oak. Then, with a thunder of splintering wood and the cries of beasts, the few Taivadean chariots that had survived the caltrops crashed headlong into the angled rears of the Mantorahn line.

The impact was violent but brief. The Mantorahn wagons had been set with their wheels chocked and teams braced. The wagon's rear armor plates were reinforced by heavy crossbeams, forming an improvised angular bastion. The enemy chariots shattered against them, horses screaming as the spearheads and pikes of the wagon crews struck out through the view ports and arrow slots. Men were thrown from the wreckage to lay broken and torn upon fractured spoke and shattered spear.

Even as the first line of chariots broke, the Syrahn wings completed their encirclement of the Taivadeans. With cavalry lances leveled and chariot crews hurling their javelins in deadly arcs, the Syrahn wings struck the Taivadean flanks with lethal precision, driving them inward toward the waiting Mantorahn wall of battle wagons. The ground churned to mud beneath the hooves, slick with blood and torn harness.

Taban's arbalesters loosed volleys from the wagon's repeating crossbows, their bolts plunging into the mass of trapped enemy charioteers. The air filled with the hiss and hum of bowstrings and the dull thuds of impact. Those Taivadeans who leapt clear of the ruined war chariots found themselves caught between lances and hooves, their lines collapsing in panic. Unable to maneuver clear of the chaotic throng, the Taivadean chariots were trapped.

Within minutes, the field was a ruin of splintered wheels, overturned chariots, and dying horses and men. The Mantorahn and Syrahn formations held their ground, disciplined and silent save for the sound of reloading bows and the creak of leather harness. Without command the slaughter ceased, no foe still standing, the Taivadean vanguard was broken—its charge spent against the dual might of Syrah and Mantorah battle prowess.

Taban took several grounding breaths taking in the scene. He knew the Dao'Tai infantry would be pursuing them shortly, so he gave the order, and his companies rode swiftly back into their city's gates.

Taban sighed in relief as his wagon rolled into the yard of the fortress. They had dealt a worthy blow to the Dao'Tai forces. In one night, they had effectively destroyed the Taivadean chariots, giving the civilians who had fled Syrah a hope of reaching Mantorah, and they had destroyed or damaged most of their siege equipment, making Syrah that much harder to take.

Serjent Taban climbed from the rear crossbow and opened the side door of the wagon. He quickly surveyed the host surrounding him. The empty saddles were easy to spot, as were the squires and stable hands dragging the dead out of the arrow-riddled wagons. To his joy, however, the losses were not as bad as he had feared. Several score riders and charioteers lost, along with another half score or so from the wagon crews. None of the wagons had been lost, though many would need repair. The losses on the Dao'Tai side had been much heavier and, most importantly, the siege engines were damaged or destroyed. The gambit had paid off. He found his smile of satisfaction difficult to suppress as Paladin Valskar approached him.

"Well done, lad, well done! They won't sleep much now, nor will they get those chariots back." The paladin sounded pleased as he spoke.

Taban saluted his commander. "Sire, all that was planned has been executed. Their siege engines are ablaze, their chariots destroyed, and their men have taken many losses." Taban could not help but smile now as he gave his report. Paladin Valskar placed his hand upon Taban's shoulder and took him aside from the troopers.

"Serjent, make sure your men savor this victory. I fear it will be one of the few we taste in this fight. Now see that they get some rest. Come morning those Dao'Tai will come knocking on the door."

Taban nodded in understanding and turned to his troopers. Some, mostly the younger men, were filled with the spirit of victory, swapping their perspective of the battle one with another. The more seasoned soldiers, however, were somber and still. After seeing the numbers of the Dao'Tai outside their walls, they fully understood the gravity of the situation they were in. Taban was somewhat betwixt these two groups of soldiers. Their raid had been a sweeping success, worthy of some moment of pride. He knew they had slain many foes this night, but he also recalled the vast legions he saw, the legions that remained un-slain, and the legions that would come with the sun.

Taban walked to a watering trough and drew a bucket of water. He then washed out the blood from the rear crossbow turret of his wagon and sat on the bucket, watching the red water dripping off the steel and wood of the wagon in the light of the lanterns and braziers. The drops fell one after the other into a quickly forming red pool under the wagon.

*What was his name...? Halls take me—what was it? He was from Or'Drel, he was newly betrothed...but his name...*Taban struggled to remember. The arbalester had been a newer soldier, they had only spoken a few times in the last month or so. He continued to think on it as he removed his sallet and fully lowered his bevor. *I guess we are just nameless drops into Felairtarh's bloody sea when death comes for us...Hysdle! That was it. Hysdle of Or'Drel...*

He let his helm drop to the earth and he rested his head in his hands, letting out a long deep breath. He had been in many skirmishes in his life, but the enemy that still awaited them was numberless and beyond any simple band of Srellites or Adohr battalions. They were the Dao'Tai. The ruin of Anoth. They destroyed the flower of the High Sun Realms in its prime.

"Can't think like that..." his words were barely an audible whisper.

His mind returned to all the details of the battle, focusing on the camp. Its array was not normal. The Dao'Tai always built a defensive wall of wooden stakes and barbed chains with a ditch around their camp, no matter when or where they made it. Yet none of this was done. He could remember seeing the piles of chains near the supply wagons. Unused on the earth. They also left the siege engines outside the main host under a relatively small guard. Someone had ordered that done, but who? Who would either seriously blunder like that, or deliberately leave them exposed to attack?

"No, that was no blunder. It surely was deliberate."

32

From Shadows to Flames

*P**ray for those who are abandoned by their wits and heed not the lore of this realm. They who are ignorant to the past will suffer its cyclical blade. Seek ye the wisdom of your forbears and build upon their works.*
Essays of the Divine.

The brake blocks creaked as the wagon suddenly halted. Lirah could hardly wait to get out and stretch her legs. Olyn had not returned, and no one seemed to want to address this fact. Lirah quietly asked Kaileth about it, and he had suggested to her that he had returned to his people. She hoped that was the case. Lirah had spent most of the last eight days in the back of the wagon as they wound their way through the labyrinth of the forest. Several times the unlikely group had pushed on through the night. This caused no small exchange of words. Orodan did not want to stop at all, but Jayle argued that the horses at least would need rest or the Tundraihn would be pulling the wagon in their stead. Orodan conceded this point thanks in part to Ralenn and Kaileth's insistence that a careful pace was in the best interest of the wounded. The best interest of their ill priestess. Kaileth had also suggested that the Tundraihn start a rotation of scouts ahead of the wagon. Having this task seemed to help focus the growing restlessness that the slow pace of the journey caused in the Tundraihn.

Two days ago, these scouts ran into a flock of nurth'ikkil; giant predatory birds. They do not fly but rather can run at great speed. According to Kaileth, such creatures would never be this far north. In the fight the Tundraihn scouts had killed one and driven the others away. That night they had eaten the creature and Lirah was both surprised at how large they actually were, longer than the wagon, and also at how good they tasted roast with a few herbs. This little encounter had also given her two injured Tundraihn to tend to.

Having so many wounded under her care in the wagon had made Lirah feel like she was running a mobile infirmary. She was steadily feeling more ill, and part of her wondered if it was because she had been using the new healing abilities so much. Or maybe it was from eating the nurth'ikkil. She felt drained and achy, but it was mental fatigue as much as anything.

Parting the cloth at the back of the wagon, Lirah looked outside to see they were in a very lush part of the forest. The air was wet and thick with the scent of damp earth and greenery. Beams of sunlight filtered softly through the leaves of the trees above, casting a green tint upon the narrow track they followed. Lirah could hear Kaileth's voice speaking softly toward the front of the wagon. As she strained to listen Tyllidus startled her, stepping into view from around the side of the wagon.

"Good morning, Miss Lirah," he said warmly.

Lirah half smiled back and climbed down out of the wagon onto the soft forest floor. Tyllidus had been paying a lot of attention to Lirah since the escape from the slavers' camp and even more after she healed the scouts injured by the giant bird. She was pretty sure that he had not been assigned to protect her or the wagon as he was not a warrior. He had helped a little the first day with the healing, though he refused to help Vishaya and just ignored Sificah and Jahllia.

Since Lirah healed the scouts, he had always been close by, but she hadn't minded his presence all that much. He shared small, warm smiles with her whenever she emerged from the wagon to stretch her legs or get some fresh air. He was much easier to talk to than the other male Tundraihn and he was a healer. So when they did talk she asked many questions about the art. This morning, though, Lirah was a little irked at seeing him so close to the wagon so early. She was starting to suspect now that his interest in her was more than friendly healer to healer politeness.

"How long have you been outside the wagon?" asked Lirah warily.

A brief hard to read expression flashed over his face for less than an instant.

"Not long, perhaps a few minutes." Lirah knew that he was lying. While the wagon was still moving, she had been getting dressed and even in the dim light of the dawn she could see the silhouette of an unarmored person at the back of the wagon. It had to have been him. Kaileth and Ralenn were scouting ahead on their horses and everyone else wore some kind of visible armor.

"Are you certain it was only a few minutes?" Riidak now came trotting up to Lirah's side. He stopped, glared at Tyllidus, and gave a low growl. Tyllidus chuckled a little, and allowed a smile to linger longer than any she had observed prior. Lirah was surprised as she had not heard any kind of merry sound out of the male Tundraihn so far. Jayle had even tried several nights to get a grin, giggle, or laugh out of them with no success.

"I see that there is no deceiving you, Miss Lirah. I watched for as long as there was something worth watching. In truth, I have been watching the wagon most of the night," he added quite seriously. Lirah was scowling before he finished speaking.

"I can watch out for myself well enough, thank you. Next time speak the truth first; we are allies are we not?"

He gave a low bow to her and smiled. "Allies indeed. Forgive me." She quickly turned before her scowl fully turned to a blushing grin of embarrassment. The thought that a man from such an exotic people would find Lirah worth watching mortified and flattered her in equal measure. She always felt she was too boyish to be truly attractive. Tyllidus was fun to tease and talk to, but it was clear that he was not a human. No boy from Allinth would just watch you dress and tell you about it as though he was confessing to seeing the sun rise.

"Miss Lirah, if I have offended you by my acts I would know. It is different between males and females among our people than it seems to be among yours."

From what Lirah experienced at the falls she understood a little about what he meant. The Tundraihn ideas about romance, nudity, and privacy were clearly different and had Lirah not understood this she might have been a little more upset.

"Such as? Give me an example. How are they different?" She was interested in the topic as it was the first point of discussion she had with Ealë. Tyllidus spoke common Anoth well and did not see Lirah as a religious figure, so he was easier to talk to.

"Well, it is normal for the female to take the male she wants."

"Yes, Ealë told me that much. But she didn't explain anything else." Lirah kept a perturbed tone in her voice, back still to him, arms crossed.

"That is because she is female, that is she is felarra...wild or unbroken might be the best words in your tongue. All the females are." Tyllidus seemed eager to talk this morning so Lirah continued to ask questions, turning back to face him.

"And what does that mean? Felarra? They were nice to me. But they called me something..." She tried to recall the exact words.

"Otheäil? They thought you were sent from Syrnii, didn't they?" he said flatly.

"Yes, that was it, otheäil. Why did they call me that?"

"They are all first-born children of Miljah. There is no akah in them at all. The pure offspring from Syrnii." Lirah looked confused, so he continued, though hesitantly.

"We are not one people as you might say, but two people of the same tree. When mated a female Tundraihn only can have a male child. Female children are born from Srynii's well. And that is all I will speak of that here. Consider it an honor they see you as an avatar of their maker." His expression showed that he thought he said too much already. Lirah touched his arm in appreciation as she spoke. His arm was warm, almost hot to touch under her hand.

"Thank you for telling me, I will keep it to myself," she promised. He bowed to her in response.

"Is there anything else you would know, Miss Lirah?" She thought about his question for a moment then asked the first question that popped into her mind.

"So, what does a male Tundraihn do when he sees a female he wants?"

"He makes sure the female knows he wants her through subtle observation and friendly interactions." His face was expressionless, but his eyes smiled as he spoke. Lirah blushed hard. She popped out the corner of her lower lip and blew an errant strand of hair out of her face.

By all the aashahl, this is not what I need...

She had suspected what his reply would be, but this did nothing to prevent her cheeks from flushing at the simplest turn of a phrase or longing look. She was sure it was getting worse, too. Even Ralenn could make her blush now without even trying.

"So it seems," she said quickly regaining the playful tone in her voice.

"As I now recall Miss Lirah, Master Kaileth tä Allitorii wished to speak with you when you awoke." A hint of a smile now curved the corner of his lips.

"Ah, you now recall it. Thank you for letting me know." Lirah matched his expression and started toward Kaileth. After a few steps she turned and looked over her shoulder at Tyllidus. He was standing near the back of the wagon, watching her with his normal calm expression.

"Thanks for the conversation," she said. He bowed in response, and she continued to walk to where Kaileth was.

Under a truly ancient and massive tree, Lirah saw Kaileth, Jayle, Ralenn, Orodan, and a few of the other Tundraihn warriors standing in a circle, speaking in serious tones. From the look upon their faces, Lirah knew something bad was going on. She slowed her pace hoping to catch some of their conversation before they inevitably changed the subject. She was not sure if they thought she could not handle the seriousness of their situation or if they wanted to spare her more stress in addition to being burdened with the wounded. Ralenn would tell her everything if she asked, but she did not want to need to ask.

Ralenn heard her approach and smiled warmly at her; she smiled back, picking up her pace again. When Ralenn looked at her she felt safe, as if nothing in the world could harm her as long as she kept looking into his brilliant eyes. She felt her cheeks warm and giggled a little to herself. Jayle was speaking as she slid up close to Ralenn.

"If Lord Devick is still in Syrah it may now be impossible to reach him. If the armies of the Dao'Tai have already fully laid siege to the fortress, our path will be blocked."

Kaileth spoke up. "Yes, however, he will be of little use to Mantorah trapped there; if we can I would like to help him get to your armies, Uran De'Vinor. The threat of the Subjugate is no longer just a problem in the northern lands. The fact that your Eolai'Mahtairi was taken proves that. Orodan, we can no longer afford to stand disarrayed in this fight."

Orodan stood silently, considering Kaileth's words. Ralenn looked at the Tundraihn commander, then to Kaileth, then to Jayle. They both looked deep in thought. It was clear that Orodan simply wanted to get back to his lands without any pause. His second sight flared. Sudden concern for the Eolai'Mahtair and how they were to get her home swept over him. Knowledge flooded his mind; he saw an exotic forest, a stone temple, a fountain of brilliant light. There was a ceremony then people, no, Tundraihn, females, came walking out of a plume of sparkling water and dazzling light. He suddenly understood why their priestess was so important. She was the key to their people's perpetuation, like a queen bee; the Eolai'Mahtairi had to lead the ceremony that brought new females into Miljah. The current Eolai'Mahtair was preparing to pass her duties on to her daughter, but they were running out of time. Ralenn realized that Orodan was staring directly at him intently.

"Master Ralenn did you have something to add?" Ralenn looked at Kaileth.

"You were mumbling something," he said with a quizzical smile.

"I think I understand your concerns, but friends keep us safe and speed us on our way, surely you see that by now. The Dactyls helped you catch up to the Srellites and we helped rescue the Eolai'Mahtairi. What good is a swift journey if you simply run into the Dao'Tai army?"

Ralenn was still unsure what to make of this newfound ability. It was as though he could reach out and see the thoughts of others, even feel their emotions a little. It had first happened back at the falls, and again just before they went into the slavers' camp. This time, however, the images were noticeably clear, and he was able to remember more. Wanting to assess his control a bit more, he turned to Kaileth. Jayle was explaining how Mantorah could help make sure Orodan made it home as Ralenn entered Kaileth's thoughts.

He was calm, impossibly calm. His mind felt old and massive. Focusing on a single thought was like staring into a cavernous library and trying to spot a single book. Eventually he took hold of a powerful underlying flow of thoughts. The Tears of the Aashahl. Kaileth was determined to find them and destroy the Subjugate. Ralenn looked for other strong flows of thought and felt one, concern and love for himself and Lirah. This flow of thought clashed with many others and Ralenn could feel the conflict in this. Then without realizing it Ralenn sunk deeper into Kaileth's thoughts and there she was, Epri. She was like a river of sorrow that all the other thoughts and emotions floated in.

"Ralenn." A soft voice called and the images in his mind shook like an earthquake.

"Ralenn." Again, the voice and again the shaking. He realized it was Lirah speaking. He opened his eyes and she had pulled him some distance from the others and was holding his face in her hands.

"Ralenn, what is wrong?" She looked worried and he could see Kaileth looking over his shoulder at them both—he looked concerned too.

"What is it? I am fine, Lirah. I am fine," he said with a confused expression.

"You started sobbing uncontrollably, like out of the blue with no warning you just burst into tears." She dropped her hand and laughed.

"You should have seen Jayle's face!"

Ralenn blushed and put his face in his hands. His face was wet from tears and his cheeks hot and flushed. He would need to practice in private somehow.

"You need the hem of my cloak, boy?" Jayle called over a good-natured laugh in his voice. Lirah turned with a snap and glare that silenced the knight of Mantorah.

"So, what was that all about then?" Lirah asked turning back to Ralenn. She had her hands on her hips and was making the same needy expression she had made when she was begging him to tell her where he was going that day nearly a month ago at the temple. She amazed him. Everything in their world had changed since then. Lirah herself had found out that she was not even a human and that she had more power than any healer either of them had ever heard of. Yet there she stood, still Lirah in all the ways that mattered to him. Ralenn shook his head and realized he was tearing up again, though this time he knew why.

"Lirah, I am so glad you followed me up that mountain..." he said, laughing at himself and wiping his eyes. Lirah's softened with concern, she drew near and wrapped her arms around him, pulling him close. He let out a deep breath, letting his strong arms find the curves of her shoulders and waist.

"I am glad too, Ralenn, more than you can know I think." They both closed their eyes and just stood there for a moment. The physical closeness to each other was comforting, calming, and exciting at the same time. Ralenn realized that what he was feeling for her was more than the comforting embrace of a good friend. Rather than fleeing this revelation he let it quicken his pulse. He felt her chest pressed close to his, her breath coming a little faster as he held her yet closer. She looked up, a warm promise somewhere in the depths of her honey hazel eyes. A sudden sharp pain blasted into Ralenn's shin as Lirah gave him a little kick.

"Can't breathe, mister forge arms!" she said with a playful giggle. Lirah took his hand and spoke cheerfully.

"Come on, let's see if we can find out what is going on, and this time cry quietly if you must." She gave his hand a hard squeeze and led him back to Kaileth and the others. Neither of them noticed Tyllidus as he watched from the back of the wagon. A hard edge marking the lines of the Tundraihn's face.

Jayle was speaking when Lirah and Ralenn returned.

"Orodan, Kaileth, if I may?" They nodded for him to continue.

"Orodan, the best for your...Eolai'Mahtair is a swift course south, if we can join once more with Lord Devick, we will be all the safer with the company of his retinue. The land will be changed, armies of our enemy are on the move and who knows what other evils have come forth to ally with the Dao'Tai war efforts." Orodan silently considered as Jayle continued.

"If we make best speed to Syrah we can take rest and refit in a place of strength. We might be able to gain word of the Dao'Tai's march and from there you will be well provisioned for the rest of your journey home." Jayle rested his large hands on the edge of his lowered gorget.

"The chances are good that a simple retrace of your journey here will run you directly into the war bands of the Subjugate."

Kaileth was smiling to himself as Jayle finished, and the Tundraihn began to speak amongst themselves in their native tongue.

Lirah elbowed Ralenn in the side to get his attention.

"That makes sense to me," she whispered.

Orodan turned from his people and looked expectantly to Kaileth.

"For my part I too think that if we can at least gain some word of the lands about at Syrah we might avoid much trouble. They will surely be well informed of the lands as far out as their patrols run, which I understand to be some many skains in all directions from the fortress city." Jayle grinned a little like a proud parent.

"That is true in no small degree. Syrah keeps a broad swath of the lands free and clear of danger, as do all the peoples and realms that fall under the protection of Mantorah and her allies. I assure you, Master Orodan, that you and your warriors would be welcome guests in the halls of the paladin. There could also be stores of the apothecaries that will aid Miss Lirah's efforts to care for your priestess."

"If the nobility we have seen from your lord and kin run true, I see that this all must be," Orodan said in his typical hard tones. Lirah's thoughts began to wonder as they spoke. A sudden sickening pang of revulsion and pain gripped her. It felt as though she had been slowly punched in the abdomen, but from the inside. Instinctively she turned and looked to the northwest, as though she might see the source of the awful sensation. She saw nothing but endless dark forest. Ralenn turned to look with her, a question in his eyes. Before he could speak Orodan did.

"Lirah, what say you? Will your charges benefit from the walls and herbs of this place?" Surprised by his sudden question, Lirah took a moment to answer, her thoughts having to push back the feelings of illness. Ralenn placed a reassuring hand upon her shoulder and the gesture help dispel some of the discomfort, grounding Lirah back in the moment. Kaileth saw this small exchange and gave Ralenn a questioning look, his eyebrow raised over a concerned frown.

"Yes, I think they all will do better outside the wagon with fresh food and warm beds, lord. What supplies I had for healing are nearly spent. I too am becoming...fatigued and I fear my ability to keep the ague at bay from your priestess is diminished as a result."

At this Orodan's already stern face somehow looked even harder.

"What manner of affliction do you combat with in her?"

"I find no major physical injury on her, lord. She had some scrapes and bruises, but few among us do not." Lirah pursed her lips, unsure how to explain what she felt when her powers connected with the wounded Tundraihn.

"I do feel some sort of terrible anguish within her. "It...it feels like her mind has been hurt maybe, or soul...I don't really know, I just feel something is horribly injured, but not a wound of the flesh. I will keep trying to bring her around, but I think she will have to do a lot of healing in her own mind. A warm and safe bed won't hurt that, I should think." She gave Orodan an apologetic look, and he nodded in return. Lirah hurried on, speaking more toward Jayle and Kaileth now.

"Jahllia and Sificah have been in and out of consciousness for the last few days, but they are getting better. I suspect tha—"

"And the dark one? How is she?" interrupted Kyleeal, who stood next to Orodan.

"Oh, uh, she is doing very well. Her wounds are healed, but she is very tired. I don't think she was eating enough in the slavers' camp, she seemed weaker than normal. Well, weaker than a normal person who has been shot with arrows...It was like she was trying to pour from a glass that was half empty to start, if that makes since. Anyhow, she has been eating more though, and is getting back her strength." Lirah knew she was on the verge of rambling, but the intensity of Orodan's manner made her incredibly nervous.

"We are all in your debt, Lirah güi'shea. As adept as Tyllidus is, his skills are feeble compared to yours." Orodan made a gesture, arms squared, hands pressed back-to-back, fingers toward the sky, bowing over his hands. As he did this all the Tundraihn nearby did the same. Lirah knew this was something significant to them and so she bowed low in return, unsure of what else to do. Kaileth spoke as the Tundraihn finished their salute.

"We should be to the end of this forest by no more than a fourth-moon. From there we can make Syrah in a short day's travel." Everyone looked satisfied by this course of action.

. "Then let us prepare and make haste." Orodan pronounced. He and the Tundraihn gave gentle bows to all, and then returned to where their warriors were resting and eating breakfast. Jayle gave Kaileth a relieved expression.

"Very serious lot, eh." Jayle gave Kaileth a brotherly clap on the shoulder as he went to see to his tack and steed, leaving Kaileth, Ralenn and Lirah alone.

Lirah smiled at Ealë, who smiled back at her from under a large tree. She was the first to be fully recovered. Apparently Tyllidus had gotten to her quickly after she was cast into the river for dead. Despite Orodan's comments, Tyllidus was a powerful healer, and his work had ensured that Lirah had Ealë back on her feet in mere hours. Ralenn and Lirah lingered near Kaileth. This had been the first time the three managed to be alone since the night at the slaver camp. Lirah jumped first at the opportunity.

"Kaileth, I have a lot of questions, and you'd better answer them," she eyed him seriously. "First off, what is a Yiillyar, and a Dycle...Dracty or whatever; and why would my babies be worth a fortune? And why did the slavers bother to keep Vishaya if she was so dangerous? And the Tundraihn priestess, why is she so important to the Tundraihn, I mean besides the obvious priestess-ish part? And what is Vishaya exactly, and the man with the wings? Actually, I haven't seen him for days; where is he? Also, where are we and what does güi'shea mean?" Lirah placed her hands on her hips and waited for Kaileth to answer.

Kaileth smiled, almost letting out a small chuckle at her barrage of questions. He then walked over to a fallen tree and sat down, motioning Lirah and Ralenn to follow. With Riidak at their feet, the three sat together and Kaileth began to speak.

"Well, Miss Lirah, It is clear that I have not been paying you enough attention the last few days. I will answer what questions I can..." He took a deep breath, as though he was preparing to swim under water for some time.

"A Yiillyar is a race of Pali'andeo. They have the ability to create life energy and to draw on the life force in Miljah."

"Why did they call me that?" She asked, though she already knew what his reply would be.

"Because I, as did Gaileng, have always suspected you are Yiillyarii, at least half, but after all this, I am sure you are pure blood. Thus your half-Yiillyar children would have some of your abilities and so they would be highly valued thralls, as would any children born to Vishaya or any Pali'andeo the slavers get their hands on."

"That is horrible!" burst Ralenn.

"Yes, they are horrible men," Kaileth stated bluntly. Kaileth's words somehow finally made her suspicions about her ancestry real.

"So I am not human at all." Her tone had turned more serious and she started to fidget with the torn edge of her skirt.

Kaileth smiled and caught her eye.

"Yes, and thank Shayar, Dannitar, Anthos, and all the aashahl that you are who you are, Miss Lirah. We all would be dead many times over if you were a simple human girl from a small village in the mountains."

Her smile had brightened a little and she grew less tense. Ralenn narrowed his eyes and pushed Kaileth's shoulder playfully.

"Guess I am the only boring human here, Allitorii, whatever they call you."

"Technically you are Anothn and they are not as the other kindreds of men. You are also not boring, Ralenn; your outbursts of uncontrolled sobbing are very entertaining." Lirah smirked and tried to hold in an outburst of laughter, but failed and soon all three shared a long overdue turn of cheerfulness. After a few more moments Kaileth returned to his calm demeanor and spoke.

"Now as to your other questions: A Dactyl is a near-mythical race of beings who live in the depths of Miljah, or at least I have always thought they were a myth; apparently, they are not. From what you have told us, the slavers put you in the same room as all the other Pali'andeo. Vishaya, the Tundraihn heiress, and yourself, were all prime breeding stock as far as those men were concerned."

"Yeah, I figured that part out," Lirah said in disgust.

"Vishaya is of the Xydarii. They live far to the south of here in the Dark Realms. They are a very..." He paused, clearly searching for the correct words, "passionate, sensual people; it flavors their war-like tendencies. They are the most powerful arcane mages I have ever heard of. They use a type of entropic magic and because of this and their ancient servitude to Ach'Juln they are hated by many of the other Pali'andeo. They are also one of only two races that are known to be able to work avertyyn. Because of this and their magic their army is reputed to be unstoppable. Could be that is why the Subjugate never tried to go south, for the fear of them. Or it could be the arcane doldrums..." Kaileth's focus drifted like he was searching for the answers on a page of runes. After a moment he continued.

"I do not know Vishaya, but I would assume she was someone of importance to her people. Olyn, the winged man as you called him, seemed to think that he was taken in order to restart the war between his people, the Jendayi, and the Xydarii. He is scouting ahead and we can talk to him more when he returns. Though I do not think he will stay with us much longer."

Kaileth took a long breath, closing his eyes tightly for a moment, centering himself. Ralenn and Lirah stood silently trying to sort through the names, places, and incredible statements Kaileth had just spouted as if they were perfectly ordinary things known by all. At length Ralenn spoke.

"Speaking of flying; Mirris, what do you think is taking her so long, Kail?"

"I am not sure, but I trust Mirris is just being careful, I sent her to deliver Sificah's bag to Lord Devick." Lirah nodded in understanding.

"It seems we know many pieces of the Aya's plans, we just need to get them all in the same place and figure out what she is trying to do," offered Ralenn.

Kaileth knew Ralenn was right. The sudden attacks upon Syrah, Thenill, and Lea'Angleneth; the raids to the south; the taking of Olyn, Vishaya, and the Tundraihn priestess; and the destruction of Allinth; these things could not be mere coincidence. Kaileth's line of thought was broken as Orodan and his men finished their meal and began to make ready to depart.

"We had best be off, the more distance we have between us and the slaver camp the better," Kaileth said wearily as he stood and stretched a little.

Ralenn and Lirah followed suit, and the three stood still together, looking at the beauty of their surroundings. The dense forest stretched on in all directions, vibrant and green. Beams of sun fell through the gaps in the sylvan ceiling, scattering golden pools upon the forest floor. The trees looked old, yet still full of life and determination.

"Come on, Lirah, I will help you into the wagon," Ralenn said, taking her hand.

"Wait, what about güi'shea?" Lirah asked.

He smiled knowingly, "It means friend to the fates in Tundraihn." With a wink Kaileth turned and made to prepare to ride.

"Did he just wink?" Ralenn asked conspiratorially.

"He most certainly did, not sure I have ever seen him do that." Lirah laughed a little, trying to focus on the way Ralenn and Kaileth made her feel so safe. The awful feeling that had struck her before was dim now and if she worked at it she could almost feel happy and normal again. Ralenn by her side. Her hand safely in his. They walked congenially toward the wagon, finding comfort in the nearness of the other. Tyllidus watched them approach from where he had been waiting near the wagons for the duration of the ad hoc council.

"Best pack your things, master healer, your company is readying their march." Ralenn said in a friendly tone as he passed the Tundraihn.

"We are all going toward Syrah." Lirah added.

Tyllidus' features set like etched glass as they passed, and he quickly turned his back to them and stalked away. Lirah and Ralenn shared a quizzical look but shrugged the awkwardness of the moment away.

At the back of the wagon Ralenn lifted Lirah by her waist and gently set her in.

"It looks like what you said about us men always needing to be healed has come back to haunt you, Lirah," Ralenn looked into the wagon as he spoke.

"Nothing but female patients now!" She laughed and took a seat in the wagon next to where Vishaya was sleeping.

"So it seems indeed."

"Is there anything you need, Lirah? I am not sure when we'll stop again."

"No, thank you. I think I am as set as I can be." Lirah smiled and gave his hand a firm squeeze. Then Ralenn inclined his head to her and returned to his horse.

Lirah leaned back and looked at Vishaya's sleeping form. She had been Lirah's only conscious company during the wagon journey since they started out this day. They had talked about many things, mostly about Lirah: where she was from, how she grew up, and what Allinth had been like. At first it was hard to talk about her home and the devastation she had been trying to forget. Vishaya proved to be very easy to talk to, listening with total attention. After a while Lirah felt like those she spoke of lived on through her words in some way, and it helped her feel less hollowed out by their loss. Vishaya said it was better to celebrate the lost and fallen openly than to bury them in unshed tears in our hearts. Vishaya's manner was like that, all intensity and fierceness, then suddenly soft and tender.

Lirah took a small skin of water and a pouch from the corner of the wagon. She took a drink of it and almost choked. It tasted like old leather and tallow, but she forced it down. The food in the pouch was not much better: very old, very stale bread and some sort of dry fruit. The fruit at least was not too bad; it was just old and a little tough. Ralenn had given Lirah most of what they had left from Allinth, but she had fed the better pieces to the others in the wagon. She wished there were more nurth'ikkil left. That giant strange bird was perfect ambrosia compared to the food that remained. The provisions they had were what had been gathered in the abandoned village where the Tundraihn found the boats and the wagon.

As the wagon began to roll along again Lirah leaned back against the frame and closed her eyes. Jahllia had needed so much attention and care that Lirah had gotten very little sleep the past few nights. With her eyes closed she could see the ceiling of her room back in the temple. Everything was so simple then, so comfortable and safe. She wished there was some way to go back to that place in time. However, she knew that while she may have been safe, she might have never found out who she really was.

Now that Lirah knew, she had a link to her past that could help her learn more about where she came from, something she had always longed to know. More than this, she was really helping people, using everything Gaileng and the other priests had spent so much time teaching her and more. Her ability to call upon the life force of Miljah was something out of ancient story.

"Apla's grace, if Gaileng could see me now..." Lirah smiled and hoped that wherever Gaileng was, he was proud of what she was doing. The motion of the wagon was smooth and rhythmic as it rolled along the soft soil of the forest. Lirah checked on those in her care and upon finding them all resting as well, she allowed herself to yawn, letting the wagon slowly rock her into a peaceful sleep. The remainder of the day passed swiftly, the warm forest air making rest easy to find within the lumbering wagon.

The troop moved as swiftly as the land would allow and after two more uneventful days of solemn travel and soft conversations within the wagon, Ralenn and Kaileth stood with their mounts resting at the edge of the forest letting the deep shadows hide their forms. Before them lay the open hills that announced the approach to Syrah. Some hours behind them the wagon and others were slowly catching up. The night was clear, and the stars above glittered cheerfully over the mortals below. Kaileth found himself holding his breath as he watched the spectacle of battle wagons crash into the camp of the Dao'Tai below. Fires sprung up near the river as men and horses screamed out the discordant harmonies of war.

Long suppressed memories of years spent fighting the same foe scratched at the edges of his mind. A part of him yearned to charge down and vent all the sorrows from his life in the fury of total war. To be lost in the oblivion of each desperate moment. Fighting to steal one more breath, one more thrust of the blade, one more foe to fall. Ralenn moved slightly beside him, the links of his dark maille making the smallest metallic sound. Kaileth pursed his lips and let out a slow breath through his nose. His duty still seemed clear enough, but how to fulfill it had drastically shifted from simply living a small life with Epri and a foundling prince. Watching the chaos below, he suddenly was not at all certain of what the next step should be.

"Kaileth, what do we do now?" The question was full of terrible awe. Before them hundreds fought to wound an army of many thousands. More men and steel than Ralenn had ever imagined could exist in the world. He swallowed hard and looked at Kaileth. Darkness seemed to fill the features of the man Ralenn loved as a father, draping Kaileth with a frightening hardness.

"Kail?" he voiced a little louder. The moment drew on as a palpable fury seeped out of Kaileth like ink in clear water. Ralenn could feel it creeping into his own humors, his heart and breathing quickening, as though he were readying for a fight. Instinctively he reached out and touched Kaileth on the shoulder. The sudden sharp crack of emotions and images felt hot as a forge fire as his fingers brushed the curve of Kaileth's armored pauldron. Ralenn sucked in a sharp uncomfortable breath and stumbled back, his second sight receding. This broke the daze that had settled over Kaileth and he caught Ralenn by the wrist, once more the man Ralenn recognized.

"Are you well? I...I was lost in memory, I fear."

Ralenn steadied himself and took a moment to slow his breathing before making a reply.

"I am, I am getting more accustomed to...whatever fighting the sphinx awoke in me..." He looked at Kaileth with concern and was thankful the darkness hid most of his expression.

"That is well. I am certain we will need all your abilities before this is finished. Even still the Fates push us along. Behold Syrah. We arrive to witness the movements of armies in the opening gambit. This is beyond Brek's chance, but I do not yet see the hand that guides us."

"Kail, what do we do now? Truly, what are we supposed to do about that?" Ralenn gestured hopelessly at the battle that was taking shape. In the distance the lights and towers of Syrah itself were visible. Between them and the fortress city was a tumult of death.

Kaileth slowly shook his head, clearly uncertain himself.

"When faced by the impossible, one must seek the authors of wisdom." Kaileth closed his eyes and centered his thoughts, slowly sinking to his knees. In a crisp surge of movement, he drew and planted his sword in the earth before him, bowing his head to the hilt with one hand on each quillon. Ralenn knew Kaileth was very spiritual, keeping with most of the rites of his sect of the Allitorii. He had seen him pray like this a few times in private, especially after Epri died.

Ralenn took a few steps back and drew up their horses, not sure how long this might take. He wondered if he should pray too but was uncertain what aashahl would even care to listen to him. Kaileth had taught him about the aashahl and the merits of prayer and worship, but he had never forced any faith or religion upon him. Long moments passed in the night. The battle below was changing shape, a great deal of swift movement in the dark, men, chariots, and those massive clattering battle wagons roamed the landscape and were soon charging back toward the walls of Syrah.

Jayle slid out of the forest shadows, coming to a stop near Ralenn. He stood motionless for a time before whispering.

"What is he doing?" Even at a whisper the incredulity in his voice was clear.

"He seeks the guidance of Shayar."

"I see, let us hope he is on better terms with the Aashahl than most men are." Ralenn faced the knight of Mantorahn squarely.

"I promise you this, Kaileth is not most men in near every way there is." His reply held more venom than he meant to loose on Jayle.

"I meant no offense, young master, truly. We are lucky to have him with us, make no mistake. Without him, yourself and dear Miss Lirah, my liege lord would be dead and there would be no force to unify the foes of the Subjugate. So, if he needs to pray by all the aashahl let him. Forgive my crass manner, a soldier's life leaves many deep seated and bitter disappointments."

Ralenn meant to lash back once more but felt his bitterness retreat as an aura of sorrows wafted from Jayle. Jayle was a good man in his heart, a good man despite his own views of himself. Ralenn could feel it.

"Well said, Uran De'Vinor. We are also fortunate to have you with us in this travail." Ralenn moved to stand next to Jayle, the view of the battle still before them both. The struggle seemed to be in the final stages. Nearly all the battle wagons were nearing or within the shadows of the fortress towers.

"Looks like Syrah will not be a haven for us after all. Dark tears take them all," Jayle swore.

"We will find another path, of that, I am sure." Ralenn smiled as he spoke filled with a calm assurance that somehow, they would work out the best next step in this audacious tide of fate they were so fully caught up in. He glanced to where Kaileth yet mediated.

He will find us another path, of that I am truly sure.

33

Something to Fight For

*A karii's eyes are bright for those who persist in the face of great trial.
Patience, deliberate action, and relentless creativity will bring you her
favor in all your works. Yet beware her children, for they make war everlast-
ing upon all her pronounced foes.*
Essays of the Divine

The sun had long since sunk beyond the mountains to the west, and a few stars softly lit the sky by the time Devick had a moment to himself. He was in the upper rooms in the tower of Castle Angleneth for most of the day, watching to the north for sight of the armies of the Dao'Tai. His eyes searched the land before him, seeking some sign of the approaching foe, but instead only found himself remembering days spent in his youth upon the Isle and in the lands there about. He found it easy to recall the feelings he had for Re'alis, easier still to let his heart drift in that direction once more.

The flight from Syrah to Lea'Angleneth had been a blur of long days and nights in the saddle. Though fully healed from his wounds, keeping pace with the hardy frontier companies of Marshal Penetrah proved no small feat. They had made swift progress. Devick suspected it might have been some record for skain traveled in so short a time.

Perhaps in happier days to come the lay of Penetrah's Dash to the High Lakes would become a favorite song in the bards' set lists.

Presently Devick's eye followed the dark water of the lake, past the end of the Isle of Angleneth to a lone isle near the northernmost inlet into Lake Akarr. There, rising like a twisting and swirling horn of metallic white ivory, rose the arcanists' tower, the center of learning in Lea'Angleneth and the home of the largest library known in the western realms. The slick hard surface of the tower glowed with a soft light, reflecting and amplifying the light of the stars through some property of its singular exterior. Devick wondered if the tower would survive what was coming, and if the tower's keepers and defenders would fare better than the rest of them.

The tower, properly known as Kali'Anglen, boasted a military order of warriors of no small repute. They and their non-martial brethren swore an oath to gather, keep, and protect the world's knowledge within a grand library. Re'alis had tried in vain to get them to join their forces with her own at the castle, but they had refused, stating their oath bound them to stay with their library. They did, however, send all who wished to go from the ranks of their unsworn students, some two hundred in all, many well-armed and armored.

The white tower was now fully reflected in the dark waters of the lake, emulating the heraldry of the land almost perfectly. Kali'Anglen was accessible only by boat, and Devick wondered if the Dao'Tai would even bother attacking the tower that first night, or if they would choose a siege to drive the Kali'Anglens out of their sacred tower of learning.

Re'alis had sent the youths least prepared for battle to Frost Haven, and the rest to bolster her reserve near the southern end of the realm. The general muster was only a few days old, and Re'alis had hoped that Castle Angleneth could hold out long enough for her main army to gather and march north to break the siege. Of course, Devick had no success trying to convince her to go south, so her most trusted military advisors and general went in her stead.

Devick felt his whole body tense as he thought about the impending battle, so he tried to unwind by wandering further into memories of the past. Specifically, memories of Re'alis and the moments of that past they shared. He couldn't help but smile and relax some. Devick began to drift into sleep when the door to his back swung open and Re'alis entered. He almost fell out of his chair, which caused the lady to laugh a little.

"Easy, my lord, it would not do for you to fall so early in this conflict." She walked to him and he took her by the hand and stood. They both looked out over the castle, city, and lake below them.

"Angleneth is so beautiful in the starlight," Re'alis said. "I used to come here as a child and dream of the things I would do when I was older and a leader of this land—this was never one of them." She looked back at Devick, who had been watching her. "My lord?"

"I could not help but notice—" he began to say.

"Notice what?" she interjected, apparently fearing he had discovered some great flaw in the defenses. She began searching the perimeter as if she expected to find a section of weak wall.

"I could not help but take note of how beautiful this realm's lady looks in the starlight as well," he smiled, "nor do I overlook how prudently her realm is marshaled and ordered." Re'alis felt relieved and laughed, she then leaned over and kissed him gently upon the cheek. They had hardly been apart since they left Syrah. Devick smiled again. "It is sad that the first time I have been here in my adult life had to be like this. I remember loving this place with all its clever machines, amazing buildings, and beautiful gardens."

"You are here now, in our hour of need, and that counts for something."

They both were motionless for a time, looking out over the isle and surrounding lake. The realm known as Lea'Angleneth filled the Lake Akarr valley and consisted of many small towns and villages settled next to the numerous mountain lakes. Castle Angleneth and its city were the biggest of these settlements and had been built upon a large island that sat in the middle of Lake Akarr. The capital of Angleneth consisted of a wondrous city where each home had fresh running water, and even the simplest structures were crafted with great care and adornment. The mechanical products of the isle were famed throughout the High Sun Realms, and in its past days had made Lea'Angleneth the wealthiest and most splendid realm of them all. Clocks, water pumps, scientific instruments, music boxes, armor, evergleam steel, and machines of war (like the giant repeating crossbows that the Mantorahns were so fond of)—the best of these wonders came from the tower of Kali'Anglen.

The army of Lea'Angleneth was small, but her soldiers were equipped with these technical advantages, some of the finest and most advanced weaponry in the realms. They had finely layered steel blades, and light, fully articulated harnesses of armor that could turn nearly any blow from a blade or a bolt from the best of crossbows. Devick hoped this, and the disjointed layout of the land, would be enough of an edge to hold their attackers at bay.

Re'alis was running through the same tactical estimation in her mind as well. A short distance from the city was Castle Angleneth. It acted as the gate for the bridge that led from the isle to the shore. Any who wished to enter the island on land must pass through the castle's gates. It was built by the Mantorahn as a gift for the aid they had received from Lea'Angleneth during the war with the Adohr. The castle had all the defensive properties one would expect, with the addition of Lea'Angleneth ingenuity. Every aspect had been designed with defense in mind, from the angles on the towers to the shape and spacing of the murder holes. These defenses were now as prepared as possible for the imminent attack.

Marshal Penetrah and Aireathyn had arrived a day before Devick and Re'alis to start the preparations in Lea'Angleneth. Once Re'alis arrived, she ordered an evacuation of all who could not fight to the fortress at Frost Haven. A day ago, her spies reported that the approaching enemy had passed most other villages and towns by, only destroying those in their direct path to Angleneth. Re'alis had sent word to all she could to gather to Frost Haven to prepare for a last defense there. With the rest of the army gathering in the south, all that was left to do was wait and watch.

"Devick, do you really think we can hold out here?" Re'alis asked softly.

"Yes, I do. This castle is strong, and your soldiers are determined. I think we will hold out well enough." His confident tone brightened her mood a little and she breathed out a long sigh.

Devick returned to his chair now and she followed, taking a seat near his. It was getting late, and soon they both were dozing in and out of a light sleep. The stillness of the evening lulled them both into a hazy fog. After the hectic days they'd had preparing for battle the sudden calm was overwhelming. Re'alis shook herself awake, then yawned and stretched, looking out again over the lake and isle. She should probably be concerned with appearances, falling asleep alone in a room with a man, but she didn't care. Devick was not just some man, and the court could say what they want, not that any of them were around to gossip at the eve of battle. There was too much to worry about without adding courtly propriety on top of that. She watched him drift into sleep, studying the strong lines of his face, the gentle curves of his lips. The motion of his chest as he slowly took in breath. She suddenly caught herself wondering what it might be like to lose herself in a kiss, to let everything slip away for a moment and just be in his full embrace.

Startling herself as this line of thinking progressed further she returned her attentions to the view outside the tower. Though she couldn't keep her thoughts from lingering upon him. These simple open moments could be her last such, and the thought caused a panicky tightness in her chest. A sudden light caught her attention and she sat up sharply, waking Devick, who had just fallen asleep.

"Look there!" She pointed to a building far past the eastern end of the bridge. She rose and walked closer to the window, and Devick followed. Flames started to rise from the timber of the structures.

"They are here." Re'alis covered her face for an instant, then she felt Devick's comforting hand on her shoulder, and she turned and met his gaze.

"We can hold this keep, my lady," he said reassuringly.

"I am glad you are here, Devick. This would be much harder to face alone."

"You would have done well enough, though I would have preferred you to go south."

"No, my place is here with my soldiers, where the fighting is. Let's go," she smiled, and started to lead him by the hand toward the door.

"Re'alis." His deep voice caused a trilling warmth to roll through her. He had never before called her by just her name without great coaxing. She stopped and turned to face him. The two looked at each other for a long moment, till at last Devick took her into his arms and there, in the soft moonlight, kissed her, with a delicate intensity that hinted at the depth of his passion. All the cares of the world fell away, and for a brief time the heavy mantles of being leaders faded. They were simply a man and woman falling in love. A battle horn of the castle watch screamed out into the night, shattering the stillness of their shared bliss.

"The fight awaits us," Re'alis sighed deeply. Devick looked down into her eyes and she kissed him tenderly on his lips once again. "We had best not keep them waiting," she said regretfully.

The two of them left the tower and started down the long stairs. Within a few minutes they had reached the castle gatehouse that overlooked the bridge. On the far side they could see Dao'Tai soldiers setting fires in the buildings built near the lake shore.

She turned to Devick. "I need to get ready. I'll meet you near the gatehouse."

Devick nodded in understanding, and she hurried into the castle. Her armor was laid out and soon with the assistance of several of her ladies in waiting she was clad in the finest evergleam armor that her people could produce. She had spent many hours within this second skin of glimmering metal, but never had she donned it for a battle as this was sure to be. Only the small skirmishes about her realm's borders or for parades and practice had seen her wear her full panoply until this moment. She steadied her breathing and placed the flats of her hands tight together, raising them to touch the crown of her head, in prayer. A hush fell over the others in the arming chamber as Re'alis' whispered words flittered from between her trembling lips.

"Dannitar, merciful sister, hear my plea. Spare my people from destruction. Bear your mercy upon us. Sheibrok, relentless defender, shield this fastness with your strength. Paldrii, merciful shepherd, keep those who fall and may Arontarh, master of battles, give us victory over our foes. Patient Father, be with us." Finishing, she gave each of her ladies in waiting a confident look and smile. "We will withstand this." They gave small bows in return but said nothing, clearly unnerved by the impending struggle. Seeing this Re'alis spoke again.

"Go, see that you are prepared to treat the wounded with the others in the hospitalliary, and may Dannitar's healing grace guide your hands." As they filed from the chamber Re'alis took up her weapons, grabbed her helm, and quickly made her way toward the gatehouse. Devick was waiting there, looking out over the gathering foe. He smiled at her approach and beckoned her to his side. They both stood silently surveying the distant shapes that made up the Subjugate forces on the far shore.

Soon Ercoln came running up the stairs to the wall and addressed Re'alis.

"My lady, the remainder of the isle seems to be secure. From what we can tell, their entire force is massing to cross the bridge."

"Understood. Ready all defensive engines and wait for a command to fire."

"Yes, my lady." Ercoln shared a brief expression of solidarity with Devick as he hastened to his duty. He and Aireathyn had both been elevated within their order after surviving the action against the Ikthii. Nearly the entire Alabaster Guard were within the castle with a dozen never far from Re'alis now that she was on the walls of the castle. Re'alis placed her light silver helm on her head and looked grimly at the approaching foe. There appeared to be siege weapons being assembled on the far shore, and Re'alis called for her gunners and arbalesters to target them. She raised her spear into the air and lowered it quickly. An archer upon the wall fired a single flaming arrow down the bridge. All eyes could see it as it flew and fell a few hundred feet short of the Dao'Tai line. Hideous laughter roared from the eastern shore, but their mirth was short-lived as flames started to lick up from the stones of the bridge. As light from the flames began to illuminate the lines of the enemy, every defensive weapon upon the walls of the castle fired upon the Dao'Tai siege engine crews. Archers, ballista, repeating crossbow, and the cyclone catapults all fired. The most devastating were the cyclone catapults.

These pinnacles of engineering fired at a rate that the best archer could hardly match. Four rotating offset arms picked up large clay pots from a track, then at the apex of the arm's rotation the pots would fling free into the air. Each pot was filled with an explosive mixture of oils and minerals, a closely guarded secret of the artificers of Angleneth. These pots would explode into unquenchable flames on impact, sending fire and shards of the pot flying into the target. Even the pot itself was lethal. Shards of glass and iron balls were packed into the inner wall of the pots. These would be cast as shrapnel into anything within the blast area, causing death and harm on all sides.

To power this machine, two men cranked sets of pedals with their legs. A maze of gears, flywheels, and pulleys magnified this force and caused the four sets of catapult arms to be loaded and fired in rapid succession, sending a storm of explosive pots into the air. The flash from the plumes of flame lit up the night's sky and caused the men in the castle to cheer at the sight. The pots continued to rain down on the Dao'Tai siege crews, and soon all the eastern shore of the lake was ablaze with fire. The Dao'Tai retreated out of range, leaving their smashed siege engines to burn.

After a few moments, Re'alis signaled for the firing to stop. She did not want all their ammunition to be expelled in the first minutes of the fight. Even though they had only fired for a small time, they could tell through the billowing smoke that the siege weapons had been destroyed. All within the castle watched and waited, for it was now their attackers' move. No one could be sure what would come next, but they were determined to be ready. For over an hour the Dao'Tai did nothing more than watch the castle from just out of the range of the defensive engines.

Devick hated this waiting game, though he knew well that such a battle could easily develop into months of long siege. Nonetheless, it made the space between his shoulder blades itch, as if at any time the enemy would suddenly appear and stab him there. He looked to Re'alis and spoke softly. "They are waiting for something. I can feel it."

Devick had sent a part of his riders to patrol the rest of the island, and it was in this moment that the clear calls of a Mantorahn trumpet broke the silence of the lull in the fighting. All listened as a rider approached, yelling in excitement.

"Lord, they are on the island! Thousands! And they are coming this way! They floated a bridge down the river and are pouring onto the isle from the north end."

Devick turned to Re'alis. "My lady, that bridge must be destroyed, and fast." If the bridge was not destroyed the entire Dao'Tai army could cross and surround the castle on a wide front. From there sapping the walls would be an easy enough task.

"Devick, I...you are right. See it done, then, Lord of Mantorah." He started down the stairs, but she caught him by the hand.

"Come back to me, Devick," she ordered.

"I will, my lady." Devick stole a last glance with her, then turned and ran down the stairs and to his horse. He painfully pushed Re'alis from his mind—he could not be distracted in this task. As he ran, he called Penetrah and his men to him.

"Penetrah, load three cyclone pots in the last battle wagon!" Devick yelled.

The marshal quickly saw it done and within minutes he and six hundred of Mantorah's best were riding fast to the northern end of the isle. The thundering of their horses' hooves echoed across the quiet land as they made their way from the castle gates. The battle wagons were not as fast as the horses, and they followed to the rear. Their destination was just over an hour's hard ride away. Half an hour into the ride, Devick and Penetrah slowed their pace, not wanting to lose the element of surprise. They halted to form a plan and let the horses rest. Spotting a grove of trees, Devick led his force into its shelter, and they dismounted.

"Marshal, I have an idea," whispered Devick. "If you and the battle wagons can distract the horde that has already crossed the bridge, I and a few of your best will set fire to the bridge itself."

"We can do that, my lord, but not for long."

"We will move with haste, Marshal. Retreat to the castle before you are overwhelmed, no matter our fates."

"Yes, my lord."

With that, Penetrah stood up to issue the orders to his men and sent some to report to Devick. Devick returned to his horse and signaled the men with him to ride out. From the trees they rode due east.

***

Marshal Penetrah took the lead of his cataphracts, and they took up places within the woods, waiting for their enemies to draw near. The mass of men and weapons slowly marched along in the starlight. Though they appeared to be in a normal array for Dao'Tai soldiers, Penetrah felt there was something amiss. A strange sense of doom began to permeate his consciousness. Almost like a tangible mist wringing courage from the heart. He was barely able to push this aside as the marching army drew closer and closer to the trees. He squinted to clear his vision and saw that the men approaching wore the markings of houses from Thenill, and a sizable portion of them were women and older children. They were within a few hundred yards now, and it became clear to Penetrah what they were dealing with. The feeling of despair, the strange way that the host before him moved, it all meant one thing; a carrion reaper was at work. Penetrah quietly sent this word through his men. The host was marching along in a course parallel to the woods. There was a word for people taken by the Ikthii and made to walk after their death; dzum. Penetrah softly said a word of prayer for the poor souls.

In sudden perfect unison, the dzum all stopped and turned their heads to look into the trees where the Mantorahns now lay in wait. Penetrah knew the reaper had sensed them, and he set his lance in preparation to charge. A sudden and terrible shriek sounded from the center of the host, and like a surging wave of the ocean, the entire mass of people rushed toward the tree line.

"Forward and let them fall!" screamed Penetrah as he led the charge of his men, cutting into the mass ranks of the dzum army.

The fight in the woods was not going well. The initial charge cut deep into the ranks of the dzum, trampling many as the braydfar horses reveled in what they were bred for. However, they now were bogged down in an unending mass of bodies. Penetrah dealt death on either side with his keen sword, his lance long-since lost in the corpses of his foe. For everyone he slew, two more took its place. A large dzum that had once been a soldier of Thenill struck Penetrah's shield so hard that he was knocked from his horse. He rose at once, one rein in hand, and turned his mount, signaling him to kick as he turned. Fighting frantically, he was able to keep from being overwhelmed for a moment. His horse fought just as hard, fueled by fear and a fierce protection of his master till he was swarmed and dragged to the ground. It looked like Penetrah was doomed to a similar fate when a thick hail of large crossbow bolts came bursting through the ranks of dzum, and three battle wagons smashed their way to where he was fighting.

"Marshal, get on!" yelled the arbalester at the rear of the wagon. He cursed, looking back at his now slain horse. Arrow and bolt kept the hordes at bay, and Penetrah quickly climbed into the wagon. It took off with great speed, crushing all who stood in their path. All the while, the metallic chugging of the crossbows of the wagon announced the falling of many foes. Each bolt would strike and pass through three, sometimes even four lightly-armored men, and most of these dzum wore little or no armor at all. The wagon cleared the lines of the dzum and joined the other circling wagons in firing into the host. Penetrah signaled for his cataphracts to draw their bows and do the same. The heavy cavalry withdrew from the melee, and soon all the Mantorahn soldiers were circling the host of their enemies, sending a hail of destruction into their ranks.

***

The pounding of their hooves sounded like distant thunder to Devick. He knew they had to hurry. Marshal Penetrah would only be able to hold for a short time before their path back to the castle would be cut off. A few more skain saw Devick and his men within sight of the bridge. It was impressive, stretching from shore to shore, woven almost entirely from hewn, rough-cut timber. Along its flat surface came a stream of figures crossing in the darkness. Once upon the island they were set into ranks, then in large groups they set out marching for the castle. Devick could now see that Penetrah had a steady flow of marching soldiers heading toward him. He halted his men, and they took the three pots from the wagons. Holding each pot between two horses, the cavalry formed a wedge around the ones bearing the pots and set out toward the bridge.

Devick signaled a change of pace to his men and they rode quietly as they could along the sandy shore. They were within a good bow's shot from the bridge now and Devick found it hard to believe they had not been seen yet. The soldiers crossing the bridge seemed oblivious to all that surrounded them, and Devick was going to use that to its full advantage. Now that he was closer, he could see three ranks of infantry forming a defensive semicircle around the mouth of the bridge. He and his warriors would have to push through them to get to the bridge.

He took a deep breath and drew his longsword from the sheath. Holding it in front of him, Devick could see his reflection in the cold steel. For a few seconds he looked into his own eyes, trying to banish his worries about what would happen should he fail in all that was to come. Still looking into the blade, he saw his men behind him, all were looking to him, all were confident in their lord. No matter what, Devick would never betray that trust.

He adjusted his arm in the straps of his large shield and spurred his horse on, and the Mantorahn charged the lines of their foe. The ranks of figures still acted as though they were unaware of the charging cavalry, making no moves to prepare for the approaching horsemen. Devick reached the light of their lanterns and torches and saw that most of the people in front of him were not soldiers, but villagers. Their faces were plain and lifeless, their eyes dark and dead.

"They are dzum! They have been taken!" he yelled, knowing that his men would hesitate to run down youth, women, and untrained men—weapons or not in their dead hands.

The dzum stood motionless before the thundering cavalry. With a slight shift in his weight, Devick signaled his horse to lower her head as she began slashing through the ranks of the dzum with her bladed shaffron. Devick's sword swiftly felled foe after foe as he led his men in a smashing wave through the ranks of dzum. On the other side where the bridge met the island only a few dozen Dao'Tai stood in their path.

A hail of stones and arrows soon met Devick's charge. Their resilient Mantorahn armor and shields defeated most of these darts, however, and the Dao'Tai did not get a second shot, for the cavalry was upon them. They stood their ground but fell quickly to the Mantorahn onslaught. Not even the fine Dao'Tai armor could withstand a direct well-aimed lance strike.

Devick formed a perimeter across the bridge with his men while the explosive pots were placed on the timbers. From the far side of the bridge Devick could hear men running toward them, and he looked about quickly for the source. To the front, the surviving dzum now seemed aware of them and were forming up to make a charge of their own. Fortunately, it took only seconds to place the pots and light the tar and sulfur-covered ropes that acted as fuses.

The dzum and Dao'Tai were now arrayed and marching toward the bridge, their ranks bristling with long pikes. A direct charge would cost him most of his men. Worse still, more foes were marching down from the far end of the bridge — they were surrounded. The fuses on the explosive pots burned low, hissing dangerously close to detonation. His men were beginning to shift uneasily in their saddles.

"My lord?" Harrc called out.

Devick's mind raced. He would not throw the lives of his men away in a doomed charge, nor let them fall into the hands of the Ikthii. Yet if they lingered another moment, the bridge would erupt beneath them. He looked to the edge of the bridge, then to the burning fuses, and finally to the dark water below. It looked deep enough.

The dzum were closing fast, and now the Dao'Tai ranks were charging as well, their spears leveled for the kill. Devick made his choice. He leaned forward and whispered into his horse's ear.

"Don't let me down now, Mina."

The mare tossed her head, as if understanding.

"Follow me!" Devick shouted, and urged her on. Mina bounded forward, her hooves striking splinters from the timber as she galloped straight for the edge. Without hesitation, she leapt — and horse and rider vanished into the lake below.

The Mantorahn troops followed Devick with little hesitation, horse, and rider alike, over the edge of the bridge. The heavily armored horses and men falling into the lake sent water splashing high into the air, creating sparkling plumes in the starlight. Mina hit the sandy lake bed hard, causing Devick's helm to crash into the crinet on the back of her powerful neck, splitting his lip and cheek. *Should have locked my visor...*he cursed to himself.

The dzum and Dao'Tai army was upon the bridge and began to launch arrows and spears at the struggling men and horses in the lake. Devick was trying to clear the blood from his face when the pots detonated. Wood, bodies, and flames were all cast high into the night sky. The hail of arrows stopped, and flaming dzum and Dao'Tai ran from the fire that was now consuming the shattered bridge. Mina had carried Devick back to the shore, and he looked to his men. Most had made it to the sandy shore as well. However, he noticed a few horses left riderless in the lake. He looked for Harrc and soon spotted him scrambling to get back on his horse in the shallow water.

Devick spit the blood from his mouth and called to his men.

"To your saddles, and ride for the castle as fast as you can!" His men obeyed and began to ride off toward the castle, sticking close to the eastern shore as they went. As the last of his troopers departed, Devick and his guard turned and rode to find Penetrah.

Penetrah could feel his temper rising as the army of the reaper continued to advance, in spite of taking heavy losses from the cataphracts' assaults. It was clear there was little he could do to stop them. He could only make them pay for their advance with grievous casualties. Despite the ferocious defense, the dzum did not seem to be concerned with Penetrah's attacks. It was this more than anything that frustrated him to no end, he did *not* like being ignored. He tried to take comfort in the fact that his men had taken only a few casualties. As the wagon he rode made another pass around the dzum, Penetrah looked to the north and saw a second mass of Dao'Tai coming closer.

"Perhaps *they* will give us heed!" he yelled to the driver of the wagon. Penetrah signaled his forces to form around him, leaving six wagons to harass the dzum army. He then took a spear from the wagon's complement of weapons. "Sound the attack," he shouted to his signal officer, who then blew a short burst of notes from his trumpet, sending the lines of the cataphracts surging toward their new foe. The Dao'Tai ranks tightened, and their long pikes fell into place, dense as a thicket of briars before them.

As Penetrah's wagon rushed toward the pikes he looked to the east to see flames of the burning bridge come into view, as did over four thousand dzum and Dao'Tai. Just then, Penetrah saw Lord Devick and his guard cutting across the field in the moonlight. He rode in a sweeping arc between Penetrah's cataphracts and the Dao'Tai infantry. Devick was cutting them off so their men could break toward the castle, and Penetrah turned his charge to follow him. Once united, Lord Devick, Penetrah, and the rest of the cataphracts and battle wagons made with all haste toward Castle Angleneth.

34

Valor of the High Lakes

To the kindreds of Man, it is left to seek patronage of the Aashahl as they will. For the other branches of mortal and immortal alike upon the face of Miljah; they shall seek first the approbation of the master of their house and order. And thence the approval of sundry tother powers.
Essays of the Divine

Re'alis could see the flames were dying down on the eastern shore of Lake Akarr. Devick had been gone for several hours now, and she was starting to worry over him. She continued to watch the enemy's lines closely, and they were moving around too much for her comfort. As she watched, the front ranks across the bridge parted, and a closely ranked testudo began to march through onto the bridge. The shields of the Dao'Tai were made specifically to interlock in this formation, virtually nothing could penetrate the defense.

"Sweep them from our bridge!" cried Re'alis.

The defensive artillery of the castle again launched a full assault against the shielded column of men across the bridge. Stones, bolts, and the cyclone pots found their marks, and soon smoke and flames covered the bridge, totally obscuring the Dao'Tai from the view of the defenders. Once again, her men cheered at the sight of the firepower of their weapons. Re'alis, however, remained silent, watching with dread as the smoke and flames cleared. The Angleneth defenders could hardly believe their eyes; through the fire and smoke the Dao'Tai came slowly marching toward the castle. They were not unscathed. Flames and bolts covered the top and front of their formation, and stones still sat in the dents they created in the steel shields. From the many new and unmarked shields in the lines it was apparent that many dozen had fallen. Yet, each that was slain had been quickly replaced. Neither fire nor crossbow bolts, which began to fly into them again, seemed to impede the Dao'Tai progress. Their tall angular shields were high as an average man and thick enough stop the bolts.

"Hold fire! Save your quarrels for vulnerable marks," Re'alis yelled.

The word was passed, and her men complied. The defenders watched helplessly as the Dao'Tai slowly made their way across the bridge and up to the gates. Once under the walls of the castle the front of the formation opened, and a battering ram could be seen. The moment the shields parted to let the ram through a barrage of stones and missiles flew at the front of the Dao'Tai line. The carnage was staggering, and dozens soon turned into hundreds of Dao'Tai slain by the war engines of Angleneth.

Lethal moments passed as the back of the Dao'Tai formation began to spread out as they set up large metal and wood pavises on the narrow strip of ground before the castle walls. Scores fell to the missiles of the defenders, but scores more took their place in the ranks. From their new defenses, the Dao'Tai began to return fire with their heavy crossbows. Soldiers upon both sides began to fall now, from arrow and bolt, though only a few auxiliaries were vulnerable to the Dao'Tai fire. There had not been enough time to install the hoardings upon the castle's walls, so the defenders were left with only the stone bulwarks for cover from the Dao'Tai assault.

Fortunately, these were well laid and the fine steel placards, high bevors, and broad-brimmed chapel-de-fers that armored most of the Angleneth guard would turn all but the heaviest bolt. At this point, large barges could be seen crossing the lake, each full of men. The cyclone catapults began to fire upon them, scoring several direct hits. As the flames spread over the barges, the soldiers jumped into the lake, only to perish by water instead.

While she watched the battle, several quarrels shot past Re'alis, one snapping off of her finely crafted armor. She stumbled back, only to trip over the body of her equerry. A quarrel had just clipped the edge of his bevor, shattering the dart into several lethal pieces as it smashed into his face. Aireathyn helped Re'alis regain her feet while she tried to keep the image of her herald's broken face from her mind. She straightened her helmet and pulled her bevor lame all the way up until it locked in place just below her eyes.

"My lady? Are you harmed?" Aireathyn asked.

"Nay, though I suspect few will last this night unscathed. See that the Alabaster Guard shelters from this fire. You are to be the reserve, only to join the battle at the critical point with me." He nodded in understanding and saw to his fellows.

Presently a strange booming noise sounded over the calamity of combat, and dozens of iron hooks suddenly flew over the ramparts and wall. Re'alis ran over and looked down to see Dao'Tai soldiers climbing up from their barges on nets of thick rope. She and those by her started to cut the nets from the walls, but their blades had slow effect on the cords, taking many blows to sever. She looked closer and saw that many strands of wire had been twisted into this rope. Needing to buy time for the ropes to be cut, Re'alis climbed up onto the top of the wall, so as to stand above one of the nets. With her long spear in hand, she found the gaps in the Dao'Tai armor, felling many as they climbed.

Dao'Tai soldiers had already made it onto the walls in several places, and the Angleneth defenders had engaged them in close combat. Many of these Dao'Tai wielded cruel pole axes, clearly made to counter the excellent make of Angleneth's armor. With these armor-piercing weapons they savagely drove the defenders back long enough for more Dao'Tai to climb over the wall. These attackers must have been picked especially for their large size, for few could withstand their blows.

Despite this withering onslaught the Angleneth defenders were managing to hold the southeast corner of the ramparts. All the while, the battering ram could be heard as it struck the gates. A thought suddenly came to Re'alis, and she looked to the tower to the north. The cyclone catapult there had stopped firing; the crew slain by enemy arbalesters. Near where she stood was a large store of round stones. These stones would be placed into shallow tracks cut into the wall that led from the central stone pile to several murder holes strategically placed in the walls and over the gates. This system allowed the defenders to drop missiles on their attackers from a central store and behind the safety of the walls.

"You men," she said to several soldiers who were loading round stones into these tracks. "I will take your place. Get to the catapult and bring as many pots down here as you can."

"Yes, my lady!" was their unanimous reply. The four of them ran up into the tower and Re'alis and her guard continued to roll stones into the track. The men soon returned with several large pots from the tower.

"Quick, open them and dump it onto the nets."

They understood and pushed through the defenders over to the edge of the wall, pouring the contents of the pots onto the nets and the Dao'Tai trying to climb up them. Re'alis took a lamp from the wall and leaned out over the rampart, throwing the lamp hard at the first Dao'Tai helmet that she saw. The ceramic shattered and she jumped back. Flames and the screams of men surged up into the air as the liquid from the pots detonated. Re'alis smiled triumphantly as her men cheered.

Her victory was short-lived, however. The fighting on the south and east walls was not going as well, as exhaustion set in on the defenders. The men on the eastern face of the wall overlooking the gates had been overwhelmed, and Dao'Tai troops were now running freely down the wall toward Re'alis and the men with her.

She lowered her spear and took a deep breath. She knew that every inch of the wall they took would cost lives to retake. The advance must halt. She had to act. This was the critical moment, she was sure.

What would Devick do...

The memory of his mounted charge into the glade at the falls dashed through her mind. The look of determination that had been upon his face. She set her jaw, the muscles of her body alive in anticipation of sudden movement. A trill of hot anticipation bloomed for an instance in the center of her chest. Taking in a measured breath, Re'alis carefully took in the details of the scene, and in the stillness of her mind she saw what was to be done.

"Aireathyn, now is the time!"

With a cry she charged the oncoming Dao'Tai, her Alabaster Guard close at her sides. As she reached the top of the curve in the wall over the gate, she lodged the spike on the bottom of her spear into a crack in the stone. Jumping as hard as she could while using her spear for support, she launched herself at the enemy, striking a Dao'Tai serjent with both feet in the chest. He went tumbling down, taking several of his men with him, opening their ranks and stopping their charge. Before they could stand the halberds of the Alabaster Guard fell upon them, and their keen back spikes quickly found gaps in the enemy's dark armor.

Re'alis got back to her feet, praising Brek's split that her foolhardy move worked at all, and continued to fight alongside her men. The Dao'Tai armor was so thick that only an extraordinarily strong blow could penetrate it. It also covered nearly all of their body, leaving only a few weak points at the neck, underarms, and sides. Re'alis fought furiously, as did the rest of her defenders, and many Dao'Tai fell at the end of her spear.

Time dragged on, each minute of deadly combat seeming an age. Presently a large Dao'Tai made his way toward Re'alis. From the bright yellow and white paint on his helm she knew him to be a captain. Aireathyn's halberd haft suddenly dropped over the Dao'Tai's neck from behind in a perfectly executed ambush. As he placed his leg for the hip throw that should follow, the Dao'Tai captain planted his feet and grabbed Aireathyn's wrist, pulling him bodily over his shoulder. The Dao'Tai captain used the head of his pole hammer to hook into the armpit of Aireathyn's white enameled armor, then he threw him like a child's toy into the stones of the bulwarks. Aireathyn crashed hard into the unyielding surface and did not stir.

The Dao'Tai captain then rushed her, swinging at her waist with his weapon. She rolled under the attack and, swinging her spear by its end, delivered a powerful strike to the side of his helm. Her blade glanced off the slick black steel and she hurried back to her feet. She lunged with all her strength and rammed her spear through his armored leg. He growled in pain as she pulled her weapon free.

The Dao'Tai captain took a swift wide step and caught her spear, pulling her toward him violently. She stumbled forward as he swung his pole hammer with one hand into the side of her bevor. The blow was so severe the rivets sheared through, and the smashed piece of armor was sent clattering into the wall. Re'alis tumbled hard onto the stones of the parapet, losing her grip on her spear as she fell. Her eyes swam from the impact as the warrior caught her up by the neck and lifted her into the air. Her guards rushed to her aid and a savage melee ensued as more Dao'Tai piled into the fray. White armor cracked and ran with hot red blood as their brutal pole axes took a toll on the Alabaster guard. The Dao'Tai captain held Re'alis out over the inner edge of the parapet. The next level of the castle's defense lay far below her.

She struggled to remove his large, armored hands from her throat. Were it not for the remnant of her evergleam gorget, she was sure he would have crushed the life from her the instant he took hold. She pulled hard again to free herself, but his thick fingers would not move. With her vision starting to blur, she realized he was smiling at her. She raged internally, wishing she had a weapon, but her spear had fallen to the lower level of the inner wall. Yet her saber still hung at her side.

One of her guards managed to get through the other Dao'Tai and struck the Dao'Tai captain hard from behind. The blow was well placed, the halberd biting through the gap between pauldron and cuirass. The Dao'Tai snarled in pain, almost dropping Re'alis. He quickly turned to face the Alabaster guard while still holding Re'alis out over the wall. She drew her blade as the Dao'Tai cracked the helm of her guard with a single arching blow from the pole hammer sending him clattering to the ground. As he turned his smiling face back to her, she drove her keen saber straight through his smile and out the back of his skull. He collapsed instantly, and Re'alis fell also. As the stones of the lower level came rushing at her, she closed her eyes and held her breath.

35

The Walls of Castle Angleneth

P raise be to Layr and the stars she cast for the delight of Anthos. For be it in her grasp to guide the sojourner and the mariner safe to hearth and harbor.

Essays of the Divine

Devick and Penetrah raced down the final skain back to the castle. A smoky haze and blasts of fiery light turned the silhouettes of the combatants, towers, and walls into a disheartening shadow puppetry display of the hells. Even over the noise of their horses and wagons, Devick could hear the terrible sounds of battle from within the castle, and he hoped the west walls were still held by the defenders. As if in answer to his concern, the Angleneth soldiers quickly opened the western gates, allowing the Mantorahn cavalry to enter. The outer gates immediately shut behind them as the last of their host clattered in under the teeth of the inner portcullis. They rode their horses through the castle's inner yard till the eastern gates were in sight. Cracked and splintered, the timbers of the gates were about to give way to the battering ram.

The inner yard was a scene of violent death with bodies, both Dao'Tai and Anglenethn scattered about where they had fallen from the heights of the walls and parapets above. Devick quickly looked for the silvery white of Re'alis' armor but did not find it among those doing battle upon the walls or those who had fallen in death. Hundreds of Dao'Tai had been slain, yet the ram pounded on, relentlessly sounding its doom. All of the Anglenethn soldiery were upon the two levels of the walls, fighting to hold the Dao'Tai back. A wide crack opened up in the last few timbers of the eastern gate as Devick and his men brought their panting chargers to a stop, forming a line. A final thudding blow burst the timbers apart, scattering splinters and broken iron banding across the stones of the inner yard. A few stalwart pages ran between the Mantorahn cavalry from one of the war wagons, handing out new lances for what Devick was sure would be his final charge.

The moment slowed, the dull thwacking of axes signaling the final moments before the shattered gate would no longer stem the tide of foes. Devick's hand closed on the lance offered him and he looked down just for an instant at the youth as he passed the weapon to its wielder. He looked up, matching Devick's eye and smiled. His young confidence was so unmarred by the current situation that Devick himself could not help but return the expression.

"Arontarh is with us, sir!" the youth proclaimed and Devick felt no doubt this was true.

The smile was still well installed upon his face as he raised his lance high into the starry sky in a last salute to all. As the light caught the steel tip of the weapon he found Re'alis in his thoughts, a hope that no matter the next few moments she would survive the day.

"Valor and Death!" The resounding battle cry of his men pulled him back as they also raised their lances in a salute defying the horror and madness that is battle. Without further warning the broken timbers of the gate fell aside and a flood of Dao'Tai soldiers pushed past and into the castle. Before Devick could sound the attack and without a word, Penetrah took the reins of the wagon he was on and charged toward the gates. Devick's line parted for the wagon to pass, but with a nod and a little confusion, Devick saw the move, and knowing Penetrah for no fool, trusted his gambit and signaled his line to stand fast instead.

Penetrah called back to the arbalesters at the back of the wagon, "Jump! Now!"

They did so, along with the soldiers inside the wagon. The Dao'Tai were passing through the gates as swiftly as the opening would allow, two and three at a time, to form into the start of a defensive wedge. Penetrah drove his wagon directly toward the shattered gates with all the speed the breydfar could muster. When the horses drawing the wagon were a spear's cast from the lines of the Dao'Tai, Penetrah threw the left brake of the wagon and pulled as hard as he could on the reins in the same direction. The team of horses cut sharply to the left. The wagon was thrown, tumbling violently toward the gates, crushing all in its path until it came crashing to a stop against the remains of the gate, effectively blocking the way.

The surviving Dao'Tai did not have their pikes and spears with them through the gate, and the cataphracts saw this. Devick and the Mantorahn cavalry charged at the ranks of these Dao'Tai with full force. The clash of men, steel, and horse was terrible. Swords and lances found their marks, and men fell on both sides, more so on the part of the Dao'Tai. The cacophony of the onslaught echoed terrifically from the high walls of the inner yard, drowning out the sounds of the larger battle without. Though they outnumbered Devick's forces, they were no match for the breydfar the Mantorahn rode. These horses were trained as much for battle as the men who rode them. The men and horses alike were in their element now as hooves crushed and shattered armor and bones with each strike. Soon all the Dao'Tai had been slain in the yard with minimal loss to Devick's men. Devick came up to Penetrah, who had been thrown clear from the wagon, and was now lying on his back upon the ground, wiggling his hands and feet.

"That was quite the maneuver, Penetrah," Devick said as he jumped from his saddle.

"It seemed like the thing to do at the moment," Penetrah smiled.

"Are you hurt?" Devick asked.

"Just stiff, armor took most of the fall. I will be fine. We had better get up to the walls. The inner portcullis has not been dropped and that most likely means the eastern gatehouse is overrun."

Devick looked up. The Alabaster Guard had been driven almost all the way down to the second level and Re'alis was still nowhere to be seen among them.

"Penetrah, place the wagons so that all can fire into the eastern gates. I'll take the rest of the men and push up toward the gatehouse."

"Understood, my lord."

Devick, the heavy infantry from the battle wagons, and most of the dismounted cataphracts now ran up the flights of stone stairs toward the fighting upon the walls. Dead Dao'Tai and Angleneth guards lay scattered on the steps, their blood making the stones slick. As Devick reached the fighting upon the walls, cries from the north and west sides of the castle announced the approach of the dzum army. Once again, the cyclone catapults began to fling their explosive shots, this time into the masses of dzum soldiers. Their ranks neither scattered, nor fled—they simply continued to march toward the castle. Those who were not destroyed by the blast of the exploding pots would continue to march, enflamed till at last the fire consumed them and they fell to be trampled underfoot by their fellow dzum. The Angleneth soldiers continued to fire upon them as they drew near to the castle walls. Soon archers and arbalesters began to engage the approaching hordes as well. Between the defensive engines and the missiles from the defenders, the dzum began to fall by the hundreds.

Devick continued to fight his way further up the stairs; he again tried to spot Re'alis in the din before him, but it was chaos. The castle was surrounded on all sides, and all defenders were engaged with the enemy. In all of Devick's life he had never been in combat so fierce. On every hand he faced attack, and his sword had a constant fresh coat of the enemy's blood upon it. In spite of having gained the high ground, the Dao'Tai began to give way before the Mantorahn attack. Seeing their allies advance, the Angleneth Guard pushed forward from the northwest parts of the wall and pressed hard into the Dao'Tai flank. The attacking soldiers were now hemmed in on both sides.

The arbalesters from the battle wagons had piled the slain Dao'Tai so high within the mess of the eastern gate that it was almost totally blocked. Anyone who drew near to clear the way was quickly cut down. However, the dzum forces were now battering upon the western gates with a second ram. They carried no shields and so the stone and arrows of the defenders took a heavy toll upon them.

On the eastern wall, Devick linked up with a block of Alabaster Guard fighting in good close order, but their advance came to a halt when the Dao'Tai managed to reform their shield wall. The Mantorahn and Angleneth defenders could not break their line, and a deadly stalemate ensued. Devick and his troopers tried to fight their way into a gap between the southern wall and the shields. The Mantorahn heavy infantry charged, deflecting their pikes, and locked shields against shields in an effort to push them back. A line of Alabaster Guard rushed in, their halberds striking from over the top of the Mantorahn shield wall. For an instant, it seemed to be working, but then Devick, along with most of his men, found themselves being cast into the air by a sudden surge forward from the Dao'Tai shield wall. Landing in a heap, one of the Mantorahn soldiers shouted in frustration.

"Aashahl above! We've got to blast a hole in their line!"

Devick knew the soldier was right; they needed help from above, and he now had the perfect thing in mind. Devick turned to the serjent who was leading the heavy infantry upon the wall after the death of their serjent.

"Vladrun, upon my command, fall back. But hold here until I return." The veteran soldier understood and gave the word to his men upon the walls. Devick then ran to the closest tower along the southern wall. As he approached, he could see dzum with ladders and ropes outside the walls. He ran up the tower to the catapult that was placed upon its top.

"My lord, what—" the crewman was incredibly surprised to see the Mantorahn lord there, in the midst of the fight. Devick did not give him time to finish his sentence.

"Do you see that formation of Dao'Tai upon the wall?"

"Yes, my lord, but we can't fire so close to our own men."

"You will, or this castle will fall. When I turn and point my blade at you, fire into them no matter how close we are." The catapult's crew was clearly uneasy about firing over their allies, but Devick's tone and manner made it clear he was not to be disobeyed.

"Yes, my lord, we will. How many shots? We only have eight left."

"If you can give me one, we can take the walls back." Devick hoped his word would be true.

"As you command, my lord," was his reply, and Devick hurried to get back to his men. As he turned to enter the stairs, lights to the far east caught his eye. *Just what we need,* he thought. *More foes.*

He had no time to gawk, so down the stairs he ran. Again, worry for Re'alis flooded his mind; he still had not seen her. Could she have been wounded and taken into the keep? Had she fallen from the walls into the lake? None of her guard seemed to know where she was, stating that most of them had been placed into a reserve before Aireathyn called them to the walls. Devick couldn't find him either. Devick found himself putting these cares aside with difficulty as he left the tower and returned to his men. The Angleneth soldiers upon the eastern wall were about to break before the Dao'Tai, and his men were not doing much better. Vladrun was now wounded and the sixteen men under his command looked to all bear a wound or broken armor.

"Sheibrok, I beg you make this work," whispered Devick.

"What, sir?" asked Vladrun. Realizing he had spoken aloud, Devick gave the order.

"Pull back now!" As he spoke, he raised his sword high into the air and pointed to the southern tower.

The whirl of the cyclone catapult grew louder, then an explosive pot flew from the catapult and struck the shield wall directly in its center. The massive blast sent Devick and his men crashing to the ground. Steel shot flew and liquid flame splashed upon the stone and the armor of the men. Several of the Mantorahn soldiers were burnt, their comrades rushing to help smother the alchemists' fire. However, it was worth the risk, for almost all the Dao'Tai within their shield wall were either killed or blown off the walls. With nothing for the flames to burn on the cold stone ramparts, they soon went out, leaving only charred corpses and hot armor behind. Devick and the rest of the defenders seized this opportunity and closed the gap, slaying any survivors and clearing the eastern wall and gatehouse just in time to drop the inner portcullis. The Dao'Tai upon the causeway pulled back in poor order from the eastern gates and it was clear to Devick that they had won a brief respite at least upon that side of the castle.

Leaning on his sword Devick took this pause in the fight to search for Re'alis. He looked over the eastern wall to the bridge and lake shore and found to his great surprise that there were few Dao'Tai to be seen there. However, the lights to the east were close now, and he feared they were gathering for a second attack. He started searching through the vast numbers of slain men upon the walls and stairs. With each body that was not hers he grew more relieved, yet more frantic to find her. Re'alis' guard soon joined him in the search. He quickly picked out a bright piece of armor among the dark detritus upon the upper parapet. Devick hurried to it and found it to be the upper lame of a bevor, the rivets sheared but the ivory etched evergleam steel largely unmarred and unmistakable as belonging to Re'alis' harness. His focus now upon the area around him, his warrior's mind told the story. Slain royal Alabaster Guard in large numbers along with equally large numbers of assault Dao'Tai infantry and sappers.

She made a stand right here, but then what? Devick called to the men near him, and they too joined in the search. They quickly found Aireathyn. He was alive but clearly injured. Devick knew he would have been closest to Re'alis in the fighting. His heart started beating with the swift pace of panic, so he paused for a moment to compose himself. He could hear the thudding of the ram still upon the western gate and knew he only had moments before battle would demand him. Closing his eyes, he took in a long slow breath, picturing in his mind the pillars and fountains of his childhood home, the sound of the water, the salt breeze from the sea. Centered in this the prayer slipped from his lips unbidden, carrying his hope toward heaven. *Mistress Everhope, hear my plea, see my heart returned to me, guide my sight I beg of thee...*He stood, staring down from the upper wall to the second level trying to sort himself back into the war leader his men needed rather than just the man who needed Re'alis. His eyes slowly settled on something bright amongst the heaps of shadowed and dead Dao'Tai. Below him, the moonlight shone upon a slender white vambrace lying in the midst of the fallen. Devick recognized it at once and ran down the stairs in frenzied haste.

As he reached it, he knelt and picked up the piece of armor. It was not too damaged, but the straps were broken. The dead were piled high on this part of the castle, so he began to dig through the slain. As he pulled a Dao'Tai from off the top of another he saw the shaft of Re'alis' spear. While pulling and throwing the dead aside, Devick's emotions were again causing a knot to form in his throat, and he moved with greater haste, the sting of panic biting at his mind. Members of Re'alis' guard joined in the efforts, heaving the encumbering bodies of the huge Dao'Tai warriors aside. Finally, near the bottom of this pile of death, he saw the top of her silver helm and her long, braided hair. All of her white armor, as well as her face and hair, was now covered in blood, whether hers or another's was hard to tell.

"Paldrii, stay your hand!" Devick cried out in a sharp burst of relief and anguish at seeing her in such a state. He quickly cleared the debris of bodies from her and tried to survey her wounds. Her armor was whole, only dented in a few places, yet there was so much blood that Devick collapsed to his knees at her side. His heart was pounding, his mind racing so fast that he could not think at all. He felt as though he had failed her. Slowly he drew her into his arms. Ercoln and the Alabaster Guard silently encircled them both, their countenances dark at their apparent failure.

Nothing could hold back his silent tears. Devick took her hand and held it in his own. The sounds of battle were lost to him as he felt his heart crushing in upon itself. His despair threatened to consume him when a sudden movement brought his senses back into focus. Again, he felt it, and opened his eyes to look down at Re'alis' still form. He felt it again, and saw it was her hand moving. Her fingers interlocked with his and squeezed tightly as her eyes slowly opened, and she managed a fragile smile.

"Did you enjoy your night ride?" she said softly. Devick wiped away his tears and laughed in relief. His heart sang within his chest; he *loved* this woman!

"I've had better," he managed through spluttering emotions. Re'alis' smile strengthened, and she tenderly touched his face. Devick held her close and praised all the Aashahl within his heart for sparing her.

"Devick, what happened to the Dao'Tai, where are they?" she asked.

"We returned just in time to drive them off the walls and from the eastern gate. Lights have now appeared by the eastern mountains, and they pulled back," he said. Re'alis smiled and looked relieved.

"They remembered, Devick; the Ovanec remembered!" Devick gave her a puzzled look, and she smiled and even laughed a little.

"Ovanec..." Devick started but a clamor in the courtyard drew their attention quickly. Penetrah was forming men into ranks before the western gates.

"The dzum beset us now from the west, however." Devick glared as though he could see through the walls and into the ranks of foes beyond.

"Devick, go, your men need their lord. Send me to the keep with my guard." He looked into her eyes then back to the gate. "Our soldiers need you. I will be fine." Her words were slow and deliberately spoken and he knew it was what must be. She smiled again, the delicate features of her face pale with pain, yet firmly set with fierce determination. With some effort she reached and took up his sword from where Devick had set it, placing it in his hand.

"Go, High Rahdan of Mantorah, and defend my keep." She reached to hold his face for a moment as she spoke. Her hand was cold but its steady touch still comforting.

"So be it, my lady." Her smile reached her eyes this time and pulled his visor down until it locked in place.

"Devick, no matter what, if you see great horned giants, do not hurt them!"

Devick nodded his head as if he understood, but he was utterly dumbfounded at her statement. How much of the fall had her helm taken? There was no time to check. Devick carefully set Re'alis into the arms of Ercoln and the Alabaster Guard. He then stood and looked at her, she was still smiling up at him. She mouthed the word *go* to him with her pale lips and Devick obeyed, turning back to the stairs. Seeing her spear at his feet he took it and his shield, then hurried to the courtyard.

On the hard ground of the yard the Mantorahn and Angleneth defenders gathered before the western gates, watching with great anxiety. Devick made his way through the lines of men in the yard, taking time to buoy the warriors up and bolster their spirits. He knew they had never seen a foe such as the dzum before. War was never a pleasant thing and fighting what had once been innocents made it all the worse. Devick was now up to the front of the lines where Penetrah was setting his men in their positions. He smiled as he saw Devick approaching.

"Lord, it would seem they have given up on their ladders. It could have been because we kept throwing them off the walls as fast as they could throw them up," he grinned. "The gate is a different story, though. It won't hold much longer. We have run out of things to drop on them, and it doesn't seem to matter how many we kill, they keep coming." Penetrah looked around. "Where is the lady of the keep?"

Devick looked back to the eastern walls. He could see the soldiers had carefully placed Re'alis onto a litter. They then took her into the nearby keep.

"She is being taken inside."

"Is she..." Penetrah looked hesitant to finish his question.

"She will recover, Marshal," said Devick determinedly.

"Well then, I guess we are in charge now. All the lady's captains fell on the walls. We are out of bolts for the wagons, so I had the men drive them into the eastern gates. The western gates, though..." Penetrah trailed off as unsettling screams and snarls of the dzum echoed in the courtyard from without the gates. He looked up to the walls. The defenders above were casting their last stones and arrows into the horde as fast as they could. However, he knew with each dzum that fell it seemed three more took its place. The dzum had carried a half-burned beam from the bridge and were now using it to batter the gates of the castle. Devick guessed the best way to defeat this army was to slay the reaper that had raised it, but that would not be easy; they did not even know where the carrion reaper was. Thus far, the iron and wood of the gates were holding together, but only just. Splinters and cracks throughout the gates' surface grew more severe with each insult.

"Lord Devick, what happened to the assault upon the eastern gates?" asked Penetrah.

"They pulled back from the walls. There is a considerable number of lights in the distance, and I fear they may be regrouping. This silenced Penetrah, as Devick continued. "I set a watch, so we will have warning should they return. For now, we must focus on the western gates."

"Very good, sire," replied Penetrah.

The men atop the western walls began to yell and signal frantically to the catapult towers to fire at something. Their words were hard to discern over the tumult of the dzum. Several flaming pots streaked over the wall and into the night. Devick ran to the base of the wall and called to one of the men operating the catapult. He turned and looked down to Devick.

"What approaches?" shouted Devick

"Lord, it looks to be three death hounds, and someone is riding on one," replied the soldier.

"Why are the catapults not loosing?" asked Devick.

"They are out of pots, sire." More shouting and yelling from the defenders atop the wall ended this exchange and Devick ran back to Penetrah and his men.

"Death hounds, three of them," Devick said as he came near Penetrah, who only shook his head in response. Devick had heard of ranilacs, great beasts of the north known commonly as death hounds. He had never seen one, though, let alone fought one.

Flames and screams suddenly came from the western wall, and several burning men fell from its height. More flames began to shoot through the cracks that the dzum had made in the gates. The men round Devick and Penetrah shuddered at this sight, not knowing what was to come. Devick sought to find something great to say at this moment, yet he found none. His actions would have to suffice to give his men courage. A few more bursts of flame shot through the gates, which were now on fire. All fell eerily silent for a moment, even the dzum made no sounds, as if all around were taking a deep breath. Then a horrible, gurgling howl sounded from beyond the gates, sending a chill down Devick's spine. The soldiers around him began to shift uneasily, so he called to them.

"Tight together now, men! Hold together! There is no foe we can't fell together!" His voice sounded confident and sure; despite the fear he felt within.

No sooner had he finished speaking than a terrific crash against the gates shook the entire structure. Something large was striking them from without. Most of the men atop the wall had been driven away, or killed by the flames, so now there was no one to defend the approach to the western gates. Soldiers from the eastern walls were running to help their comrades to the west. Again, the western gates were struck, sending wood and debris flying. They would not withstand another blow.

The men lowered their spears and prepared to receive the enemy. Flame again flowed through the shattered gates, and then they were struck a third time, sending burning wood and cracked iron flying into the ranks of men. Billowing smoke surged from the gateway, and for a moment nothing could be seen. Then a terrible creature came bursting through the remnants. It stood looking this way and that, as if not sure what to make of the ranks of men, shields, and spears. The stars and moon still shone brightly through the smoke and haze of battle, and Devick finally got a good look at the beast.

It was large, well over eight feet to its shoulder, and its hide shimmered in the moonlight as though it were made from metal scales. Over its spine, belly, throat, and the front of its limbs thick overlapping bony plates formed a natural armor, leaving only narrow strips on its flank unprotected. At the end of each thick limb, it had large, disturbingly finger-like appendages with long claws on the tip of each. A long, whipping tale stretched out behind the beast, doubling its overall length. The head of this monster was particularly frightening. It was like a hound, long and angled, but without visible flesh, bony growth covered nearly all of it. At the end of the snout a sharp bony spike sat in front of rows of glinting teeth within the jaw. Over each deep-set eye a large, knurled horn curled down and around. The fierce creature seemed bred for war in every way a beast could be.

Walking forward on all fours, it seemed to be looking for someone in particular in the mass of armored defenders. Devick did not give it time to finish its search. He called to archers upon the wall to fire and a cloud of arrows filled the moonlit courtyard. However, as Devick had feared, most of the darts glanced off the bone armor, with only a few finding marks in the vulnerable sides. The ranilac bellowed in pain and sent a cloud of mist into the air that then ignited into flames.

The next mist blast was directed toward the wall of men. The soldiers ducked behind their shields, and were mostly untouched by the flames, but the hound then charged into their ranks. The front ranks held firm and raised their spears to keep the beast from bounding into the rear. At this point a second hound entered the yard, followed by waves of dzum. They came running in great multitudes, shrieking, and brandishing their arms. The archers of Angleneth directed their fire into the dzum while the Mantorahn warriors in the courtyard contended with the death hounds.

The two hounds charged the Mantorahn line together, this time directly toward Devick. He lowered Re'alis' spear and braced himself. The ranilacs lowered their heads and rammed their way through the spears and into the shields of the men. Devick's shield was bashed into by the hound, and he and those close by him were sent sprawling to the ground. The hounds were now in the midst of the Mantorahn infantry, crushing men with their claws and even picking some up to be thrown into the walls.

The shouts and screams of his soldiers filled Devick with rage as he regained his feet. Penetrah was nowhere to be seen, so Devick took charge of the men around, ordering them to circle around the two beasts and aim for their sides. They attempted to do so, but the chaotic melee with the dzum made it impossible. The entire courtyard was a confused mix of men, beasts, and possessed dead. The heads of arrows glinted in the moonlight as the Angleneth archers tried to thin the ranks of dzum. All this time the death hounds roved the yard, killing most in their path. Not even the well-fashioned plates of Mantorahn armor could withstand the crushing power of the ranilac's jaw, and few could withstand the heat of their flames. Still, the Angleneth and their Mantorahn allies fought on as best they could. Presently a block of Alabaster Guard emerged from the keep and formed a stable line that men started running to join, staying the outright slaughter for a time.

Devick soon found himself surrounded by dzum. These had been soldiers of Thenill, and so they were a potentially dangerous threat should the reaper focus on them out of the horde. Devick drove at them with all his might; knocking two to the ground with his shield, he quickly slew them both before they could rise. No sooner had he done this, though, when another three came at him from behind. Putting all his skill of sword to use, he parried and dodged their every attack, returning death blows for any mistake made in their form. Their leather and maille were not enough to turn the Mantorahn blade, and they soon fell before it.

As their bodies fell to the ground, Devick heard a great howl from behind and turned to find a death hound no more than ten feet from where he stood. The beast was rending Mantorahn and dzum alike with its claws but seemed unaware of Devick standing next to its hind quarters. Devick took a spear from the ground and ran at the beast, driving the tip, blade, and several feet of the shaft deep into the side of the beast where he hoped the heart would be. The hound let out an earth-splitting howl and wheeled about to face its attacker. Before Devick could get clear, it caught him face up in its jaws and began to crush him around the waist.

Moving quickly, Devick drew his sword clear of the monster's teeth and thrust it into the ranilac's eye up to the hilt. The keen steel of the blade glistened with the beast's blood as it burst out the opposite side of its skull. The monster made no sound, only fell dead. As the head struck the ground the force of the fall punched several teeth through Devick's armor and into his back and shoulder. His breath escaped him with the pain of it. He was now effectively pinned within the mouth of the dead death hound. Mustering his strength, Devick managed to push the jaws of the hound open and roll out, letting out a cry as the teeth pulled from the wounds they had made.

He lay still, catching his breath as he looked toward the gates. At the base of the wall by the western gates he spotted Penetrah slumped against the wall, motionless. Devick recovered his sword and shield. He winced in pain as he moved, the wounds in his back and shoulder burning. He began to cut his way through the dzum toward Penetrah in a pain-fueled assault. He quickly broke through them and knelt at Penetrah's side as the battle surged around him. The marshal had been severely burned, and his chest plate had been crushed; blood and pink froth ran from a large hole in the silver steel where his bevor met his cuirass. Devick knew he was beyond help.

Penetrah struggled to stand as he saw his lord approach, but Devick placed his hand upon his shoulder, halting his effort. They looked at each other and exchanged a moment only those bound by the brotherhood of battle could understand. Devick took Penetrah by the wrist and the marshal gripped Devick's tightly as he spoke.

"Lord...my family. Give my love to them...And do not let the reaper take me." The words came with significant effort from his broken body.

"I will tell them, and I will not let you fall to the reaper, Marshal of Mantorah."

Penetrah spoke again, much weaker this time. "Valor *in* Death."

"Courage and blood, my friend."

Penetrah smiled at Devick's words. His grip upon the wrist of Devick loosened, and Devick watched as the life drifted from his loyal friend's eyes. He continued to look into the marshal's eyes until he slowly shut them.

He stood up and turned back to face the battle. He took a step away when an eerie feeling suddenly swept over him, and Devick looked back to Penetrah's body once more. His eyes were open again, and a twisted smile curled his lips. His eyes were black as ink, and his skin pale as new snow. Devick quickly stabbed his sword into the unarmored throat, severing the spine of what had once been his friend. Penetrah's body squirmed for an instant, then his eyes again returned to their natural state as his body went limp.

His reanimation let Devick know the carrion reaper was approaching. Other freshly slain men began to rise, and Devick found himself surrounded by those he once commanded. Their eyes were now black and lifeless, and their skin pale and sickly in appearance, like Penetrah's. They wasted no time attacking the man who in life had been their lord and, slowed by his wounds, Devick was hard-pressed to defend against their onslaught.

By this point the second death hound had finally been slain, thanks to a valiant effort by the Mantorahns. They had no time to celebrate, however, as they saw their fallen comrades rising against the Angleneth upon the walls and in the yard. A proper battle line had been established in the courtyard around the Alabaster center and they moved forward to attack the fresh dzum.

Devick was fighting in the mouth of the western gates. As he struck down a dzum whom he recognized as the shield lead from the eastern wall, he assessed the battle. Men and dzum were mixed in melee everywhere. The lines had broken, and they were horribly outnumbered. The little hope they had held for a victory was quickly vanishing from sight. Devick heard the sounds of something bashing into the eastern gates and was certain their fate was sealed. With the Dao'Tai to the east and the dzum and carrion reaper to the west, all hope was gone. With each defender that fell, the dzum had another warrior in their ranks, and the carrion reaper had more knowledge gleaned from the fragmented memories of the taken. By now the reaper had taken enough of the defenders to know they were losing hope, and so all the dzum wore the same horrible smile upon their pale, dead faces as did their unseen master.

The wagon barricade blocking the eastern gates suddenly exploded, as if the fist of Anthos had punched it away—dust, splintered wood, and wagon parts flew into the courtyard. Devick looked to the eastern gates, waiting to see the Dao'Tai marching upon them. However, instead of hundreds of closely ranked armored soldiers he saw dozens of huge forms walk through the gateway in the dim light. They entered the courtyard and the moonlight revealed them. They stood half as high as the gate, some fourteen feet or more in height. The moon reflected on their black horns and red light shone in their eyes. Their heads and faces were long but looked human, with large eyes set near to where their tight curling horns grew. They were armed with long spiked halberds and great war hammers.

*The horned giants...*Devick marveled as he recalled the words of Re'alis and began to shout to his men to stay their weapons from them. The first giant to enter the yard spoke, and his deep voice filled the castle, drowning out all other sounds.

"We are Ovanec. We are here to fill our debt." The Ovanec then began to slay the dzum in vast numbers. The defenders of the castle gave a great shout at seeing such powerful beings come to their aid, and all engaged their foes with renewed vigor.

Devick also took courage at their newfound friends and struck with redoubled fury. Soon the tides of the battle were turning. The numbers of dzum began to dwindle and the Mantorahn, Angleneth, and Ovanec forces were able to maintain a defensive line in the yard as well as upon the walls. However, Devick was still by the western gates, apart from his men and unable to fight his way through the dzum. As he struggled to defend himself, the sound of claws tearing through burnt wood came to his ears. He turned his head to the gate and saw another death hound with a black armored figure sitting upon its back. A sudden withering feeling of horror and despair started to overwhelm him, and Devick fell to his knees before the beast and rider.

Images of Re'alis being tortured and slain flooded his mind. A black shard of malice piercing her breast, driving the light out of her. Visions of Mantorah burning and her people being slaughtered ripped at his soul. Devick strove to drive these things from his mind, trying to remember that Re'alis lived, and slowly he began to open his eyes just in time to see the head of the death hound rushing toward him. He flew through the air as the ranilac struck him, crashing hard into the dzum that surrounded him. Devick tried to clear the stars from his eyes as he looked about him for a weapon. His sword and shield were gone, dropped as the death hound rammed him. The Ovanec were occupied fighting dzum upon the walls, and Devick's men could not get through the ranks of the dzum before them, it was just Devick and the Ikthii.

The carrion reaper started to make a sound as if it were trying to laugh, and again cruel images flooded Devick's mind. He tried to find something to push them out with, a thought or feeling more powerful than his fears. Before he could find one, though, the death hound again bashed into him with its horns, and again Devick was knocked into the air. This time the attack upon his mind did not lessen, and Devick landed upon the ground crippled with both physical and mental pains. He opened his eyes just enough to see the ranilac rushing toward him, this time with its mouth gaping open to grab and crush Devick where he lay.

Devick closed his eyes to the oncoming ranilac, and the image of Re'alis being tortured at the Ikthii's hand filled his mind. But this time he focused on her face and the love he had for her, rather than the fear of losing her. He remembered that she had said she loved him before being taken into the castle, and his heart filled with warmth. The attack on his mind was driven out as Devick thought of his love for, and hope of a future with, Re'alis.

What had seemed like an eternity of pain and despair had only been an instant, the death hound was not yet upon him. He looked around himself and saw Re'alis' spear down by his legs. He quickly rolled out of the path of the charging ranilac and sprang back to his feet, his lady's spear in hand. Again, the Ikthii atop the death hound tried to invade Devick's thoughts, but the shield of Re'alis' love turned the reaper back, and Devick smiled.

A huge spear suddenly flew over the mass of dzum and struck the ranilac in the narrow strip of its unprotected flank, driving the beast to the ground. Devick looked to the giant who had thrown it, and the great creature nodded his head to him. Devick raised his spear in salute, and then ran to slay the carrion reaper before it could recover. The death hound was still writhing upon the ground, but the reaper was nowhere to be seen. Devick searched the now dead ranilac, and saw no sign of the reaper, only the moon reflecting in a large pool of the beast's blood.

As he searched, Devick was suddenly hit from behind with a blast of black smoke and red flames that crashed into him. Steam burned his neck as his sweat-soaked aketon instantly lost all moisture from the scorching heat of the blast. The shot partially deflected off the hard Mantorahn armor and he spun around to see the Ikthii disappear into a swirling cloud of soot-like smoke by the western gates.

Devick snatched up a shield and charged the Ikthii just as a second larger blast of lethal smoke and flames shot at him. It moved too fast to avoid so he ducked behind the shield and ran harder. The heat was withering as the blast broke upon the shield. The center boss of the shield was instantly white hot. Tongues of vicious flame flared and lapped over the edges of the shield, rendering it into ash along with the hems of Devick's surcoat as he ran. Several spots of his armor were glowing red and he gasped for air in the suffocating heat wave; yet he ran on, undaunted by the pain and power of the Ikthii's attack.

Seeing that the attack had failed, the reaper snarled and fired again, striking Devick in the arm. This shot glanced off the pauldron and penetrated the rings of Devick's maille voider; it left the armor white and sparkling as the edges melted, but it did not slow his advance.

Devick summoned all his might to dash the last few rods into the black smoke. He felt the semi-molten shield boss connect with the Ikthii and he drove it into the creature with the full force of a desperate man. Devick fully committed to the blow, and he and the Ikthii both tumbled out of the smoke cloud in a jumble of burning garb and smoldering wounds. The Ikthii's face was a shattered mess of melted armor splatter and sparking red flames. Devick's body screamed from dozens of searing burns, but he had no time to give in to the pain.

The Ikthii cleared its only good eye and let a streak of smoking flame loose from its outstretched hand. Devick dashed and rolled away, but not fast enough. The bolt clipped his side, burning away his armor and aketon, along with more than a little flesh. He screamed in fury and pain, leaping to his feet and casting Re'alis' spear with all his might, aiming for the reaper's chest. The spear went high and instead severed the Ikthii's head clean just as a second blast shot from its upraised hands. Devick took this blast squarely in both shoulders, burning through his pauldrons, spaulders, and most of his destroyed aketon, sending him hurtling backward in a violent flip. Before he landed upon the ground, the dzum fell also—like so many fish cast upon the shore.

Devick lay dazed for a time, the unsettling sounds of the dzum falling upon the cobblestones surrounding him. He sat up slowly, trying to keep the hot metal from touching his exposed skin. He looked to the Ikthii, watching the strange twisting smoke as it emptied from the crumbling shell of what had been its body. The smoke moved as though it was somehow in agony, writhing into the air. Devick watched the final groups of the dzum about the castle walls falling, released back into death, crumpling to the ground. Once more they were the murdered people of Thenill and the fallen defenders of the Castle Angleneth, dropping where they stood. The horrible dark powers of the carrion reaper's animus dissipating.

Devick slowly rose and picked up Re'alis' spear, leaning on it as he looked up at the sky. A distant thundering drew his eyes west, though he could not see its source. The night was a beautiful one. The moon was bright, and the air was clear and cool with a gentle breeze driving off the last of the Ikthii's smoke. Still looking to the west, Devick thought of Paladin Valskar and Syrah, for the same moon watched over them as well. He hoped its light would see them through the darkness.

Devick slowly walked back to the burning, shattered gates. His numb body started to regain feeling and the sudden pain from his many burns and wounds flooded his senses. He stumbled on unsure feet, using the spear as an anchor for his shaking legs. He forced himself to breathe slowly, in and out, collecting his thoughts as he mastered the pain. He opened his stinging eyes and took a few stronger steps forward, pausing in the gateway to survey the battle-marred courtyard of the castle.

The dead and dying were scattered about as if some ancient Aashahl had simply cast handfuls of men from the sky to fall upon the stones. Many of the host that had defended Angleneth had fallen, and many more now lay close to death. The surviving warriors of Mantorah and Angleneth had already begun the dismal task of clearing the walls and yard of the dead and gathering the wounded.

Devick took his helmet from his head and looked for Penetrah's body. He found it still lying next to the western wall. He knelt upon the ground next to his friend and placed his hand on Penetrah's shoulder. Slowly, he removed the marshal's plumed helm and gently took a silver chain from around his neck. Devick held it aloft in the moonlight to see the ring that hung upon the chain. Three glittering rubies set in a band of gold danced in the light from above.

"This is now yours to bear, Penetar." Devick tried to think of what he would say to Penetrah's wife, his eldest son Penetar, and the other children when a shadow fell over him. He palmed the chain and ring and turned to meet a giant face-to-face. A moist blast of air struck Devick in the face as the Ovanec breathed out through its large nostrils, preparing to speak.

"I am Ruork, son of Ruork, son of Ruork, son of Ruorka, seeker of the star. We are the wards of the east, the Ovanec. Are you the child of Jovis the Knower and Wise, King of Knowers' Tower?" Ruork's voice thundered throughout the castle, causing all to stop and turn toward him.

Devick was at a loss for words, he had never seen anything like the being that knelt before him now. Their armor and weapons were simple but effective, and their size alone would make them hard to match in a fight, yet it was clear that they were no foes. He wondered at their reference to a king. The last man to be called king in Lea'Angleneth was Re'alis' grandfather King Jovis. Devick struggled to regain his composure and speak.

"No...No, I am not. I am Lord Devick of Mantorah. For what reason do you seek audience?"

Devick swallowed hard as Ruork stood up and looked down at him. One swift kick from Ruork would end it all, and Devick knew that he had neither the speed nor strength to survive if this encounter went afoul. Still, he did not want to expose Re'alis to the uncertainty that Ruork and his kin presented.

"We are here to fulfill a debt, long owed but never forgotten. You need not fear us." As Ruork said this, the remainder of his company ducked under the catwalk that divided the courtyard and gathered around him. Devick was now mostly surrounded by their huge forms, and his men began to move forward to support him. However, he signaled them to stand down and back away, wishing for no accidental confrontation. He addressed Ruork again.

"I thank you and your people for coming to our aid. Were it not for your arrival, we would have fallen to the Dao'Tai. As for the one you wish to see, her name is Lady Re'alis Ta'Angleneth. She is wounded and within the keep of this castle." Ruork's long face showed great concern at Devick's words. "She will recover," Devick reassured him. "Her wounds are not too great, I think." Ruork nodded in understanding and stood still for a moment; he appeared to be thinking something over.

"Very well, Lord Devick, child of Mantorah. We go to make sure our foes are scattered. Tomorrow, when the sun has started its climb, it is then that we will speak with the child of King Jovis the Knower and Wise. You should seek aid yourself—you smell like meat that is over-cooked long."

"I will, and we will seek you out as soon as she is risen," said Devick, still amazed at this conversation he was having. Ruork smiled an odd smile, as though it had been over-practiced, and bowed. He and his company then left the castle, half through the eastern gates and half through the western. Devick let out a deep sigh of relief, and all of the men who had watched the exchange with the Ovanec were now staring at him.

"They are going to drive the Dao'Tai from the area," Devick said loud enough for most to hear.

The soldiers continued to go about their tasks of refitting the castle and clearing the fallen. Normally, Devick would have worked at this alongside his men, but his wounds could be ignored no longer. He entered the cellar that was serving as an overflow for the keep's overwhelmed healers' hall. The wounded and maimed were packed in tightly, yet Devick knew that their losses had been light, lighter than he had expected. Most of the ones he saw as he passed would recover in time.

Devick lowered himself onto an empty quarrel barrel, the ache in his limbs catching up with him at last. He waited in silence for one of the chyrurgeons to tend his wounds, though his thoughts were far from the chaos around him. His mind drifted back through each heartbeat of the battle — every shout, every clash of steel, every moment when death had seemed certain.

He had fought in countless skirmishes before, in raids, ambushes, and full campaigns across the realms. Yet none of them had prepared him for the fury of the dzum or the sheer, relentless power of the

Dao'Tai. Even the robust Rahmith plate amor most of his men wore had been only just enough to stave off death. The blows of the Dao'Tai hammers had crushed through lesser armor and bone alike, leaving men broken within their shells of gleaming metal. Their strength had been beyond reckoning — unnatural, almost divine. Yet, Devick's men and their Anglenethn allies had held. They had driven the enemy back, if only for a time. For the first time in many dark months, Devick felt a flicker of something he had not dared to name: *hope.* Could this war still be won? After all the carnage of this first battle in Lea'Angleneth, Devick realized that he genuinely believed the war was winnable, if they could pay the price victory would demand.

"Sire, this will be painful, are you ready?" The yeoman's soft voice startled Devick from his thoughts. He had not even noticed her as she started to tend to his wounds and remove his damaged armor. She was pointing to the areas where the metal had melted into his aketon and skin.

"I am, just pull it off."

She gave a reassuring smile and motioned for a young boy serving as a litter bearer to help her. With the buckles undone they both pulled the melted and cracked breastplate free of Devick's body. It *did* hurt, and he suddenly felt more than a few new cuts and seeping wounds open as the melted steel pulled free from his body. The yeoman and the litter boy continued to remove the damaged armor, and with the tattered and burned aketon removed they started to treat the wounds themselves.

To distract himself, Devick took note of the skill that the yeoman possessed as they carefully cleared and treated each wound with swift confident movements. She applied specially treated bandages that smelled of honey and herbs and soon she stood back, examining her efforts.

"I think that is the best I can do for now m'lord. These will need to be changed on the morrow. If you come back down to the healers' hall, we will see to it. Fur now, m'lord, you should be getting some rest and plenty of dark ale and water to drink."

Her voice betrayed her youthful age, not more than sixteen, he was sure. Her black hair and the soft lines of her pale freckled face spoke of the far northern realms as her home. Devick's wonder at her skill must have been clear to see.

"My father taught me, m'lord," she said, correctly guessing at his unasked question.

"He should be truly proud, then. What is your name, good healer? That my thanks might be properly addressed." At this she blushed more than a little.

"My name is Breahslle, m'lord, Breahslle Ta'Crywmhred."

"We are a long way south from Crywmhred. How is it that you have come to serve as a healer here?" Devick asked.

"My father taught me all he knew, and it was his wish that I continue my learning here at the college of healers' craft. Once I knew the battle was to come, I sought a place here to help."

Devick smiled and stood on firmer legs. "I am in your debt, Mistress Breahslle Ta'Crywmhred. Will you help me put what is left of my armor back on?" She bowed politely and soon the battered armor was once again in place.

Devick took her hand and bowed to her. She curtsied in return but was not able to reply through her broad blushing smile. Feeling less raw and pain stricken, Devick made his way further into the keep. Worrying over Re'alis steadily consumed him as he sought to find where they had laid her. Within the keep's spark stone-lit corridors the cries of the wounded echoed. Devick went from room to room but found Re'alis in none of them. At length he happened upon one of the few Anglenethn nurses who were attending the wounded. When asked, she directed him to the upper rooms of the tower where Devick had been earlier that same evening. He hurried as fast as his wounds and weary legs could carry him, up the stairs and toward the room where Re'alis was. Before the door two Alabaster Guards stood leaning heavily upon their tall silvery halberds. They looked spent, one clearly wounded with hasty bandages covering a crack in his upper cuisse.

"Lord," they said in salutation.

"I wish to see your lady. Any word of Aireathyn?" Devick asked.

They seemed to brighten at Devick's concern for their newly appointed captain.

"Yay, sir, he is awake and will recover so the chyrurgeon says."

"The Fates are with him, so it seems." Devick smiled at them as he passed.

He opened the door and stood gazing into the room for a moment, half afraid to enter for fear of learning of her demise. A yeoman stood near the bed in the corner of the room, upon which lay the Lady Re'alis. Moonlight from a window fell upon her, softly casting a blue aura about her as if she were frozen in a dream. Devick took a few steps into the room but stopped when his eyes saw her bloody armor next to the bed.

Seeing his distress at this sight, the yeomen spoke. "My lord, little of the blood is the lady's. Do not fear."

"Mistress Everkind, be praised," whispered Devick. "How badly is she injured then?"

"The fall battered her hard, potentially some small fractures to a few ribs, cut her head open a bit, but nothing life-threatening, my lord. She will be stiff and in no small measure of pain, but she will mend well enough."

Devick quietly walked to the side of Re'alis' bed and sat in a chair that had been placed there. "Yeoman, you may see to the others. I will stay the night with her." The yeoman bowed to Devick and left the room. All was quiet now, still in the soft glow of the night sky, the lord at the side of the lady, watching over her through the night.

36

Visions, Respite, and the Mark

Leshay'ar weeps drops of coarse wisdom won traveling the harrowing path. Of her it is said the truth of sorrow is known in its purity. The bitterness begets clarity. She holds the gate to the path of the Tears albeit Paldrii who knows the key.
Essays of the Divine

The cold metal of the quillons anchored his thoughts, pulling his awareness within. Pinching his eyes tightly shut, Kaileth pressed his forehead against the hilt of his sword, the tension hovering on the edge of real pain. His senses sharped. He could hear Jayle exchanging soft words with Ralenn a few paces away, Riidak panting contently at their side. He could smell their horses and hear creak of their tack as they breathed. They all still stood upon the ridge overlooking the besieged fortress of Syrah, the dark night cloaking them in shadow. Lirah, Orodan, and the others were still some distance behind them in the forest.

Kaileth pushed the cold metal a little harder, centering his awareness on the sensation. Slowly, the voices started to sound distant, as though he was descending into the depths of a cool dark sea. Kaileth seized upon this plunging sensation, letting himself indulge in a sudden flood of memories. Days spent under a warm sun with the brothers and sisters of his mistthray, a band of youths sired by the same father amongst an Allitorii harem. All having been born at about the same time, this band of warriors was raised as a cohesive fighting unit from birth. Kaileth's mistthray was originally trained for war upon the seas, to serve as the guard of the Anothn royal family aboard their fleet of swift warships.

Of all the aspects of such a life, Kaileth had most enjoyed swimming and diving in the depths of the sea. At that time, he felt a very real spiritual connection to the experience. Far below the surface where one must master the demands of the body through the strength of the mind. Kaileth remembered feeling so grounded in himself, in his place in the world, in knowing what he was meant to do with the years of his life. A being of one purpose, body, mind, and soul in harmony. Life was beautifully simpler then, clarity of identity serving as a wellspring of strength.

Kaileth let his mind dwell fully in this time, feeling the dark coolness of the water, letting the sensation of the chill metal of the sword help slip his senses completely into the memory. He opened his eyes to the past, finding the dimly lit Annetarrow reef just below him. Smiling, Kaileth saw his sister Kail'ar floating near him. Mesmerizing light from the far distant sun softly floated in amorphous patches over the taut muscles and feminine lines of her swimming form. She smiled back at him, beckoning for him to follow her deeper toward the coral below. Kaileth felt as though he had just reached this depth, being yet free of the burning lust for air. Deftly turning, he kicked his legs in a well-practiced stroke, gliding down after Kail'ar. The cool water slipped around him swiftly, the pressure upon his body starting to build.

Kail'ar had been the stronger swimmer, seemingly built to glide through the water no different from the schools of multi-color fish that they so often watched from a safe distance. By now Kail'ar was near the reef, Kaileth trailing after her. The first surges of air hunger stabbed out as he swam, his body craving a fast return to the surface. Kaileth held his self-mastery, knowing he could stay below the water for some time yet. Long enough to reach the reef and then hurriedly kick for the surface. He knew Kail'ar could stay at this depth longer and still outpace him back to the surface. A fact that she took no small pleasure in reminding him of, from time to time.

Kaileth remembered this day from his past so clearly, and so despite being fully immersed in the memory, he was not startled when the ereckii eel flashed through the water like a bolt of lightning through a stormy sky, leaving Kail'ar spinning in a growing murky red haze. She had just reached the minarets and spectacular arches of the reef, when the eel burst from a tunnel formed by the coral, catching her across her abdomen and flank with its dagger-sharp dorsal ridge fins. An eruption of precious air escaped her tumbling body, the silvery orbs rushing skyward.

Kaileth pulled hard against the water, using every ounce of his might to speed to her. Kail'ar was yet a spear's cast below, the crimson cloud of her life blood continuing to blossom. She tried to kick toward the surface, but Kaileth was sure that the eel had struck her so hard that all the air was driven from her lungs. Panic threatened to drown Kaileth as sure as the water was about to drown his sister. He just could not move fast enough. Seizing control over his inner fear, he focused on the form of the stroke, reaching, pulling, kicking hard, riding out the glide through the uncaring depths.

The water seemed to mock him now, shifting from a cool welcoming companion to a spiteful foe, ensuring his strength counted for nothing within its embrace. He saw Kail'ar start to sink back through the cloud of her own blood in the water, the last few silvery bubbles of air slipping out of her lips and capering up and away as though nothing at all was amiss. His eyes fixed on Kail'ar's beautiful, broken form slowly turning in a macabre last dance of serenity. Kaileth willed more speed to reach her, fearing once there he would not have the strength or air left within him to pull her to the surface. In the memory, Kaileth finally reached Kail'ar, wrapping his arm around her waist, pulling her limp form in close as he started to fight toward the surface. Already blackness was creeping into the edges of his sight, the vague light from the sun an impossible distance away. Kaileth swam as hard as he could, desperately hoping against all that he could get them both to safety. He had prayed for deliverance, begged the aashahl to grant him strength and mercy. This prayer formed once more within him. The intensity of Kaileth's dire need for rescue connecting the two points in time and space into one. His yearning for aid resonating between past and present.

The cruel water sapping the last of Kaileth's strength, he held her close, locked in a final embrace that seemed certain to be their last moment. Thoughts now came in a messy jumble, his control over mind and body slipping away to the soft stillness of this watery tomb. He suddenly felt a strong shift in the currents around them. It seemed an age of struggle to will his eyes to open even as his body drew nearer to the precipice of death. Out of his addled state he fought to force his eyes and mind to work in harmony. Something was in the water just in front of him. Pleading with all the aashahl in heart, he managed to blink hard, clearing his vision and bringing clarity of sight just for an instant. An upside-down face realized out of the dark waters, barely an arm's length from his own. The face was at once feminine and seductive, yet savagely predatory. He remembered the thick confusion that distracted him from the dread of sinking.

Now, Kaileth knew full well what the being was, an ilysh. The ilysh slowly spun in the water to match the position of Kaileth and Kail'ar. Dim light sparkled upon the scales of her tail and the dark greens and blues of her gossamer fins and iridescent skin. Kaileth could see himself reflected in the being's enormous, pupilless, golden eyes. Slowly the ilysh moved her slender arm toward Kail'ar, gently holding her face with a long-webbed hand, examining this interloper into her realm of waters. Kaileth found it impossible to look away from her eyes now. Soul-aching echoes of an alluringly haunting song started to fill his mind, all thoughts of leaving the waters smothered in the golden promises behind the ilysh's eyes.

Warmth entered his body and washed away the furnace of need for air, sunlight, or anything other than being near this denizen of the deeps. Kaileth tried to remember why he was there, he knew he had been in desperate need of help, but help with what? The ilysh's other hand was suddenly upon Kaileth's face, the long digits and sheer webbing cupping him from jawline to crown. How had it got there? Kaileth did not see her move, but it was again getting hard to see. The memory was so tangible now, Kaileth could only guess at what reality was, Ralenn and Jayle's presence lost completely to this sudden consuming remembrance.

Kaileth felt once more, for just a fleeting moment, the mind of the ilysh, her intensity fierce and sharp. A sudden jolting spasm shuddered through him in reaction to this connection and the death from drowning that would be delayed no longer. The ilysh maiden tilted her head in curiosity, her lips thinning, brows furrowing for an instant until her expression opened wide in apparent understanding. Grabbing his head sharply with both hands the ilysh pressed her open mouth upon Kaileth's. This sudden contact again returned some focus to Kaileth's fading mind in time for him to feel the rush of air being forced into his body by her.

Several deep breaths passed between the two, the ilysh's impossibly powerful lungs pushing air into and out of Kaileth's nearly dead form. With each cycle Kaileth felt his mind grow clearer, he recalled where he was and that he was in fact remembering. With his eyes now open and his mind clear he could again fully hear the impossibly perfect singing in his mind. The ilysh still had her mouth over his, her eyes closed tightly as she pushed air into him, her body coming close against his, her tail and flowing fins drifting around them both in an ethereal mantle. Her full lips were impossibly warm, but had a firm, slightly rough texture that spoke of her robust nature, a necessity for life in the seas. He could also just feel her inhumanly sharp teeth, veiled just behind her delicate life-sustaining kiss.

With the regained clarity Kail'ar's plight again was at the forefront of his mind. Seemingly sensing this, the ilysh's eyes shot open, her body going rigid. With no hesitation she snatched up Kail'ar and started to force air into her as she had just done with Kaileth. After several long moments, the ilysh released Kail'ar and looked to Kaileth. Her expression was one of absolute sorrow and pain, her enlarged eyes capable of projecting emotions as the sun casts out its light.

With a swift motion she unclasped what Kaileth had thought at first to be billowing fins from around her narrow waist. Once free of her body the blue-green diaphanous fabric proved to be a skirt of intricate fashion. She wrapped Kail'ar in the skirt, tightly binding her up. The fabric of the garment changed colors into a bright warm yellow that intensified until it looked like a glowing hot iron. Kail'ar's form started to convulse within the garment, violently shaking several times. The ilysh watched and waited, her song singing calm and peace into Kaileth's mind.

Abruptly, all the light from the garment faded, leaving it back to its original blue-green color. The ilysh seemed content with whatever magics she had employed and turned to offer her long delicate hand to Kaileth. Reaching to take it the ilysh darted forward catching his wrist, then, taking Kail'ar in her other arm, her long flowing tail whipped into motion, propelling them all with great speed toward the surface. Kaileth's ears popped sharply as they rose with dizzying speed.

They made the surface in what seemed an instant, Kail'ar taking an explosive shuddering breath as they breached the water. The roar of the surf was impossibly loud after the muffled silence of the deep. White foam and crashing waves filling the senses with sharp contrasts, the tang of the sea air, cold mist in the warm sunlight, burning lungs finding purchase on exquisite breaths. The abrupt shift was disorienting; all the senses filled to capacity. Acting now on instinct Kaileth struggled to get Kail'ar upon a nearby rock the low tide had exposed.

As he swam, he tried to look back to the sea seeking the ilysh, but there was no sign of her. Sudden and profound feelings of loss and heartbreak filled him with such force that he nearly turned to dive once more into the depths of the sea after the golden-eyed nereid. The absurdity of this urge to return to what would mean death finally helped Kaileth to master himself and push on toward the nearing rock, helping Kail'ar along.

Once Kail'ar was upon the rock, breathing deeply, he remembered her wounds and hurried to unwrap the ilysh's garment from her. The delicate fabric shed water like the slates of a roof, holding no dampness at all. As it fell away Kaileth searched for the wounds from the eel. Kail'ar sat up, resting on her elbows watching Kaileth in awe. There was no sign of any wound, nothing at all but Kail'ar's perfect skin. Kaileth had laughed despite himself, the feeling of relief so complete that he could imagine no greater sensation at that time. Kail'ar coughed a little, wiping water from her face with a broad smile as well. She was safe and whole. Kaileth looked back to the water, hoping for at least a glimpse of the ilysh that had saved them both. He knew few would believe his story even with the ilysh skirt as proof. Yet, if Kail'ar saw her too, at least she would believe.

He searched the rocks, and at last he spotted her golden eyes flashing from the shadowed side of a great jagged stone. He pointed for Kail'ar to see also, but Kaileth knew she would not. Now they were out of the water, Kaileth's attachment to reality was stronger. He knew that once Kail'ar had fully sat up, the ilysh would be gone. Kaileth clung to the dissipating memory wanting to revisit one last glimpse of the beautiful being, and there she was in his mind again. Her unblinking burning eyes radiant with emotions; peering at him, singing to him, from the shade of the rock she sheltered under. His recollection faltered, only the cold metal of his sword held his focus in the moment now. He wanted to stay in the memory longer, just to feel the wonder once more. He renewed the pressure of the sword hilt, and it helped. The memory lingered; she slowly swam closer to Kaileth. He started; this was not how it had been. In the past, Kaileth reached to turn Kail'ar to see but the ilysh had not been there.

Suddenly the memory was fully turned into something else. Kaileth was alone upon a black rock, the waters surrounding him. The ilysh rose waist high from the deep before him, water flowing from her sleek form in glittering sheets. Kaileth could feel her song once more, but it no longer felt like a memory. Her eyes filled with sadness, as did her song, and Kaileth fought to keep the sorrow from drowning out all other thoughts in his mind. His psyche abruptly submerged in the aching death and loss his long life had thrust upon him. The horror of countless battle fields, the fall of Anoth, the death of his kin, of Kail'ar, Epri dead in the storm, Allinth burned...A stream of horror and sadness played out, the ilysh singing his life's story into a lament of bitterest stinging melancholy. Sinking to his knees, Kaileth wept openly, not seeing any use in denying the pain and loss of his past. She swam near, taking his face in her hands, and once more he felt the heat of her lips as she kissed his brow. Black inky tears trailed from her golden eyes as she released him, drifting apart once more. Kaileth marveled at this vision and the empathy of this being. Somehow, she understood the wounds Kaileth kept from the world, and she sorrowed for him, for his sake. The warmth of her understanding permeated her song and Kaileth's mind filled with an ethereal choir.

The ilysh lingered, watching. The surf grew in its savagery, the first heralds of an approaching storm. The white frothy waves lashed out at the stubborn strength of the black stone and the shifting persistence of the sands. A crawling peel of thunder reverberated from somewhere just over the horizon. This moment felt more real than any Kaileth had ever experienced. He was at a loss as to the passing of time or the reality he had just been in with Ralenn and Jayle. The sky rushed overhead, the storm building far too fast to be natural, yet somehow also slower than any tempest Kaileth had ever seen. Through the flittering tumult around him the ilysh remained, just within arm's reach. She was awaiting something, some moment or sign from Miljah herself.

Kaileth wanted to speak, to ask, but to utter such crudity as spoken words in whatever place this had become felt like a sacrilege. And so, he remained locked in her sorrowfully seductive gaze.

The waves crashed harder now, the tempest was upon them. The wind driving the sea mist into a persistent haze that encompassed them both. Kaileth presently realized he was standing chest-deep in the water, slowly moving toward the ilysh. The intoxicatingly fatal pull of her song was yet there, calling him to the peace of a death in the deep.

She was suddenly right before him, both hands upon his chest in a gesture of intimacy and to slow his progress into the water. Captivated by her song he drank in her form, his eyes unblinking in their survey. Her long streaming hair shimmered between shades of darkest blues and greens, shifting in hue as she slowly undulated with the rhythm of the sea. Streamlets of water trickled down from this dark tumble, flowing around and between the curves of her chest, continuing across her spectral skin and down her sylphic torso. Her song was swelling now and Kaileth fought its pulling undercurrents, holding his breath, wishing for a moment of clarity in the storm.

No sooner had he wished this, but the clouds split overhead with another peal of thunder, releasing a misty fall of soft rain. The sea calmed into a glassy mirror and the ilysh visibly relaxed, releasing what Kaileth now realized had been anxiety born of fear for his well-being. Now in the water with her he again felt the mysterious connection with her that he had shared so many years ago and he wanted nothing more than to join her under the silvery waves.

You are not fated for this release, fair one...yours is to toil yet longer upon the soil of Miljah. I would that you be mine throughout all the times and places, but I am commanded to deny myself in this.

The words formed in his mind, slipping in and around his own thoughts like water flowing around the pebbles of a riverbed. She slowly moved a hand from his chest to his face, brushing a loose strand of hair gently behind Kaileth's ear.

I would, that you might be free from your sorrow, dear one. Be this in the stead thereof a gift, a token of my yearning, a promise of our future, a boon from my Mistress of Sorrows. For you are known to her.

With this she took her other hand from his chest and, with her long sharp fingernail, lifted an inky-black tear drop from her glistening freckled cheek. Using her blade-like nail and tear like a quill and ink, she deftly made three runes. One over Kaileth's heart and one under each eye, running down the sides of his face toward his jawline. Her touch was hot like a brand, but she held him in her unbreakable gaze and Kaileth had no will to move, or wince from her touch. Once done, she darted forward, holding his face in her hands to plant what was clearly a stolen kiss. This was a fundamental act of fierce passion. Kaileth found himself buried in the emotions of her mind and he was swiftly reminded of how much she was a being of magic and nature rather than a mortal woman. Her passions were as treacherous as they were alluring. Her lips searched his, hungrily drinking him in, as if he held for her the breath of life. The moment lengthened and Kaileth could hardly keep his mind his own. Her touch was at once coarse and soft, like the sands of a warm beach. Her arms circled about him, and he could not resist the power of her arcane glamour, returning both the kiss and the embrace.

Her breathing started to come faster, her lips staying parted, urging a deeper kiss. As the moment grew in ardent intensity, Kaileth felt the warmth of his own blood dribble from the edge of his mouth where her razor-like teeth had nicked him. She did not seem to notice but the small sliver of pain helped shock Kaileth out of her spell just enough to gently press her face from his. Still streaked with the black marks of her tears, her face had an entirely new expression upon it and Kaileth knew that regardless of her words to the contrary she wanted nothing more than to keep him as her own.

This thought was immediately followed by a final boom of thunder, so much louder than the prior two that the ilysh clapped her hands over the sides of her head. Kaileth too instinctively covered his ears as they both startled. The ilysh turned sharply to look over her shoulder to the sea as a child might when caught in the honey pot. With a sudden flash of motion, she planted one more desperate kiss upon a stunned Kaileth before dashing back into the waters. Her departure sent a sudden slap of water into Kaileth's eyes, and when he blinked them clear he was once more upon the hill near Jayle and Ralenn.

"Kaileth?" Jayle was kneeling before him, Ralenn standing just over his shoulder. Kaileth found himself sitting upon his backside, his sword in a white-knuckled grip, panting. The war hound circled the three men softly whimpering, unsettled by the episode and Kaileth's state.

"Kail?" Ralenn knelt closer, "What happened? You're bleeding."

Reflexively, Kaileth's hand shot to his face, pushing away a strand of soaking wet hair. His lips felt rough, as though he had vigorously rubbed sand against them. He quickly found the source of the blood, a small clean cut on his bottom lip.

Right where she had...

Jayle again interrupted his thought.

"Kaileth, we heard three distinct peals of thunder, they emanated from..." He hesitated, shooting a quick look to Ralenn.

"Well, it seemed they came from you before you fell as you are now, bleeding, soot-smudged, and soaked." Again, Jayle paused, swiftly wiping a gloved hand through the water upon the earth near Kaileth and bringing it to his lips.

"Soaked in sea water." Jayle could not mistake the scent and taste of the sea. Shaking his head in disbelief he stood.

"Ralenn says you venerate the aashahl ardently, and truly I know you are not of the kins of man, but you are no Shedim either. What is afoot?"

Kaileth looked up at them both, first Jayle, then Ralenn. He worked to clear his mind of the intoxication of the ilysh's embrace. It lingered, permeating his body and mind. This made him realize he had experienced no fitful delusion but something else quite entirely. He could still taste her upon his mouth, a warm nectar that made shaking her pull all the harder. Kaileth held up an outstretched hand and Jayle quickly clasped his around Kaileth's wrist. Ralenn took Kaileth's other arm and together they helped him stand.

"Thank you," he managed, still finding his breath coming short. Kaileth wiped the blood from his mouth. Calming his breathing he reached for his water flask and rinsed his mouth several times before speaking. Jayle and Ralenn watched, giving him time to collect himself. Kaileth found his cheeks and chest were yet hot to the touch and the dark lines of the runes were very visible and real.

"I did not expect that," he finally said giving them both a tight resigned smile.

"What was *that*, exactly Kail?" Ralenn asked, clearly worried.

"I hesitate to name it, not before I have time to sort it all out. Sufficeth to say, I sought a meditative state, a chance to see clearly and know what I should do or even could do. And I did receive an answer, or at least a response to my questing thoughts." Jayle nodded, content to take Kaileth's words at face value. Ralenn, however, still seemed anxious. As Kaileth spoke a clear course of action materialized within his mind, like items slowly washing ashore, and he realized he could see a path forward. A clear next step.

"Come, I know where we are to go next; let us gather the others."

A flash of smiling golden eyes crossed his thoughts, pleased with his confidence.

Curious, I do not recall her actually smiling at all.

37

Within the Knower's Tower

Diverse and ancient are the seed of the fallen stars. In the wake of their passions kindreds both noble and base came to be. There are those who pass as mortal man and others who walk only the shadowed paths on the edge of dreams. From the deeps of the sea to the clouds of the sky. They each wend their way down the paths fate has laid for them.
Essays of the Divine.

She was standing in a green field, the warm sunlight gently brushing her cheeks. The cool grass felt moist from the morning dew under her bare feet. Re'alis looked around and could only see green fields and trees when suddenly there was a very tall youth before her. His hair and eyes were dark, and he smiled warmly.

"Our people are safe, my lady. But you must seek them soon." His voice softly echoed around her, though his mouth never changed from his gentle smile. His expression was the same as one might have after completing an honest and long day of work. Weary, yet deeply satisfied.

"You will have to lead them, take them to a safe place for a time." She began to walk toward the youth when she heard another voice calling her. It was distant and hard to hear.

"My lady?" The voice was muffled. She looked around her lush surroundings for another person but saw no one. Again, the voice called to her, and her eyes began to blur.

"My lady, can you hear me?" It sounded closer this time, the young man and the green landscape were suddenly gone. Only the warmth of the sun remained. Her hand reflexively moved to her chest, an odd twinge hitching her breath for just the slightest instant.

"Re'alis, please, I need you to wake up." Hearing her name this time, Re'alis opened her eyes and began to become aware of her true surroundings. The first thing she recognized was the concerned eyes of Devick. He looked pale and exhausted as he knelt next to her bed, the warm morning sunlight falling upon his face and shoulders. "Re'alis, can you hear me?" Devick asked again.

This time Re'alis was able to answer. "Did we defeat them? Oh, Devick, my head is pounding."

Devick smiled and sat up, laughing out of sheer relief. "Oh, my lady, your spirit is unconquerable!" She smiled as he took hold of her hand. "Yes, we held the castle and the foe is gone, but we did not do it alone."

Re'alis' eyes flew to Devick's in shock. "They came, didn't they? They *are* real. The Ovanec came!" She let a cheerful laugh slip out, but the pain it immediately caused made her wince. "Oh, I hurt everywhere...I guess I did fall a long way, didn't I?" she asked.

"Yes," Devick answered gravely. "Were it not for your armor I fear it would have been your end."

"Well, it will take a lot more than an army of Dao'Tai and a fall from a tower to end me," she said, giving his hand a good squeeze. "But what about the Ovanec?" she asked.

"They came and drove the Dao'Tai from the bridge, and they helped defeat the dzum and the carrion reaper. They left last night to clear the isle of our remaining foes."

"They left already?" Re'alis asked, disappointed.

"They returned this morning, insisting to speak with the child of King Jovis the Wise," informed Devick.

"The Wise? I suppose that is what they would call him," she said to herself distractedly.

"What do you mean? Where did these Ovanec come from, and how do they know your grandfather?" Devick seemed so intrigued she guessed he couldn't help himself from asking a barrage of questions.

Re'alis didn't mind and smiled as Devick took a seat on the bed, close at her side. "Well, it is a tale my grandfather would tell me as a little girl. I was not sure it was real, but he always swore it was. A short time after he was made king over our realm, he and a few of his men were riding the eastern border of our land, by the Shellidack Mountains. They came upon the Gates of the East and decided to explore them. Grandfather said that while they were doing so, giant beasts with the horns of bulls and bodies of men captured them."

"Yes, they are giant," Devick nodded appreciatively.

"That is how my grandfather described them. Do not call them giants, though. They will take offense. Giants are their larger cousins, but they do not like one another, or so grandfather said. When he first found them, they were going to eat him, but he told them that if they would let him and his men go, he would teach them many grand things. The Ovanec were savage and crude, so the simplest of things were amazing to them. My grandfather told me many stories of how he taught them to read and write, chart the stars, and work with metal and stone. He told us that he went back several times after they had let him go to teach them more. He told me that if Lea'Angleneth was ever attacked and her castle lit a fire by night, the Ovanec swore to come to our aid in return for the knowledge he gave them. That must be why they call him 'the Wise.'" Re'alis continued, remembering the story fondly as she told it. "Grandfather said that Heeth sent the Ovanec to guard the Gates of the East. However, they had been left there so long that they had forgotten civility."

"Well, my lady, they seem to remember what your grandfather did for them, and now they wish to speak with you."

Re'alis slowly sat up in her bed. It was excruciating work, but she had no time to be an invalid, though she did wish Devick didn't have to see her like this. He rose and helped her to sit at the edge of the bed.

"My lady, are you sure you are able to—"

Re'alis stopped him. "Devick, I will not lie in bed while our allies wait for me." She spoke with authority, a familiar tone to her here in her own home, but she smiled warmly at him to temper it.

Sitting up in the warm beams of sunlight from the window, Re'alis could see the many bandages and burns upon Devick's body and armor. She reached out and placed her hand upon the steel of his chest plate, slowly feeling the punctured metal.

"Devick, you have been shot?" she asked, stunned by the amount of damage she saw to his armor.

"No, my lady, only chewed upon. They are shallow wounds, I promise. I am fine."

Re'alis gave him a skeptical look and said, "Chewed upon? You look more like you were spitted and roasted. We don't have Miss Lirah with us right now, and if you go off and die, I swear by Paldrii's veil, I'll find you and make you sorry." As she spoke, she grabbed his gorget strap and pulled him toward her to make her point, which she contemplated making with a kiss. Instead, at the last moment she pushed him back, not hard, but firmly and scowled at him.

"Why is it that you have sat here all night, or at least what was left of last night, when you needed the rest more than I?"

"Well, I…"

"Well, nothing, you should see how pained you look right now!" she scolded.

"After the battle they stopped hurting as much…A yeoman saw to me; all I could think about was—"

"Yes, I know, but Devick, please! For my sake, take better care of yourself. I need you."

"I will, Re'alis...I will," he said gently.

She smiled triumphantly at his use of her name instead of a formal title, and when she spoke again it was kindlier. She was truly beyond relieved that he was, more or less, whole. Re'alis didn't want to let her thoughts linger too long on how much she had come to need Devick, and how much she feared losing him.

"Devick, where are the Ovanec at now?"

"They are without the western gates, sitting in the shade," he answered.

"Very well, please send in my yeoman and I will meet you there. *After* you have had your wounds freshly dressed," she ordered firmly.

Devick bowed to Re'alis, making her laugh as much as her wounds allowed at his persistent chivalry. He then slowly left the room, and she sighed, missing him almost instantly. Though she was upset he had not taken care of himself that night, she thrilled like a foolish young girl to think how much he cared for *her*. She reluctantly pushed those thoughts from her mind. She had work to do.

Devick met the yeoman just outside the door. She blushed when she saw him, and Devick surmised she had been watching, or at least listening to, his exchange with Re'alis. Unlike Mantorah, in Lea'Angleneth it was not uncommon to find women in many roles in the main army or castle garrison. He smiled and held the door open for her to enter Re'alis' room. Devick then staggered down the stairs and into the keep.

The castle was much quieter now, the smooth stone corridors no longer echoed with the sounds of battle and the cries of the dying. He found Breahslle asleep in the healer's hall and did not have the heart to wake her, or the others who were resting from the frantic night. The wounds from the hound's teeth had started to bleed a little again, so Devick took a seat on a stool and removed his chest plate, sitting alone in the light from an arrow sloop. Without the castle walls he could hear birds cheerfully singing at the start of this new day. He smiled at how little they heeded the struggles of men while he bandaged his wounds as best he could. They were not overly deep, but they would need careful tending to close properly. He replaced his armor and made his tired body stand and begin to walk toward the doors that led out of the keep.

Once in the courtyard his eyes met with the bright morning sun shining over the eastern gate. There were so few soldiers still on their feet, both Anglenethn and Mantorahn. Near a third of their force had been killed or wounded in the battle. In the daylight he could see the full extent of the enemy's losses, and it astounded him. The dead Dao'Tai lay in great heaps on either side of the bridge. The men of Angleneth were still busy clearing their bodies from the bridge and eastern shore of the lake. To the west, a substantial portion of the population of Thenill had fallen as dzum, all still lay where they had dropped. Devick walked over to one of their number. It had once been a young woman; she had been fair in complexion. Her neck had a single hole in its side. Aside from that, no other mark could be seen upon her.

"She must have fallen when the carrion reaper died, sire," Harrc's voice was distant and soft. He had a long cut across his face and a bad burn up one arm. His breastplate had several holes punched in it and was covered in blood.

"Harrc, how badly are you wounded?"

"Don't worry, sire, this armor doesn't fit me quite proper, and there was room for me and that pole hammer's beak in here. Sure confused the Dao'Tai that was hitting me though," he said, smiling a little, not looking away from the dead girl.

He had been stationed near the stairs to a cyclone tower, and it appeared that he held his post. It looked like he had been staring at the dead girl for some time. She was not much younger than he, Devick guessed. "She is so still now, sire, so still and yet also beautiful..." His voice faltered and Devick placed a reassuring hand on his shoulder.

"War is the most damaging parade of tragedy one can go through, Harrc. It's alright to feel the horror in it, and to let it out." Devick kept looking out over the thousands and thousands of dzum until he felt Harrc's shoulders shaking, and he looked to see silent tears flowing in great streams. The two stood for some time, the lord, and his squire before the fields of dead. Eventually, the tears ran out and Harrc looked up at Devick.

"Milord, how do you go on after this?"

Devick thought for a moment but quickly knew how *he* went on. "You focus on what you protect, not what you lose. The life of a warrior is that of service in the defense of others. We face this so those we love, those at home, do not have to. Think of the chivalric oaths. They are not just words, they are our protection from this, from the evil that is war. They defend against the madness that such horrors might drive us into." He spoke with a confidence born from experience and gave Harrc's shoulder a squeeze.

"Go, get your wounds cleaned. I will yet need my courageous squire before this adventure reaches its end. Harrc nodded and smiled a little at Devick before limping back to the castle.

Devick continued to look over the dead dzum until he found what he was looking for. In a bunch of dead Thenill eagle guards he found Baron Chalid. He had many wounds, and his hauberk was badly rent, but the bloodstains were days old. Yet, he did not have any small puncture to his neck. *He must have died defending Thenill.*

"At least you gave them what fight you could when they came for your city."

"What was that, milord?" asked a nearby soldier. Devick had not realized he spoke out loud.

"How many have this same wound in their necks?" asked Devick as he pointed to a dzum peasant with the small puncture to the side of the neck.

"Near all the villagers and nobles, sire, only a few of the soldiers, though. What do you think it means?"

"All these dzum were once people of Thenill. The Ikthii must have some method of killing masses without damaging their bodies beyond this mark..."

"Bad omens, sire, to be sure..." The soldier looked down at the dzum with increased anxiety.

Devick's mind was full of dark thoughts as he left the soldier to his task. He shrugged them off as he walked toward the western gates, choosing to focus on the upcoming meeting. Devick met Re'alis in the courtyard. She was again in her armor, and in the daylight Devick could plainly see the damage to it from her fall. The left pauldron had been crushed out of shape, and a deep furrow had been knocked into the side of her chest plate. Even her helm had a crack running up the side. The blood and dirt had been washed from it, though. She was dressed for battle, and bore the marks of having already fought one, but she seemed almost more beautiful to Devick this morning than she ever had in her finest gown.

"The holes add character, my lord," she said with a grin. "Did you see to your wounds?" she added with a raised eyebrow.

"Yes, my lady, I did. Are you sure you will be alright moving around so soon?" he asked in turn.

"Of course," she said brusquely. "This is my land and the castle of my people, and I will be the one to thank our unlooked-for allies." She sighed and admitted more quietly, "The armor actually makes my side feel better," she patted the side of her breastplate. Devick bowed in surrender, and she held out her arm for escort. The two of them started walking past the smoldering remains of the gates and out of the western side of the castle. Aireathyn and a band of the Alabaster Guard followed, each looking as worn from battle as their lady. Devick smiled brightly at Aireathyn, who returned the expression and saluted the lord of Mantorah.

They all slowed as they came into view of the Ovanec. Their size and appearance still being novel. Under the shadow of the walls sat over a dozen Ovanec warriors. They all rose when they saw the group coming. Devick recognized Ruork as he stepped to the front of his warriors. The large Ovanec took a knee and spoke.

"I am Ruork, son of Ruork, son of Ruork, son of Ruorka, seeker of the star. Are you the child of King Jovis the Wise?"

Re'alis, steady as ever, did not even blink at the incredible sight of a giant before her. She bowed as well as her injuries allowed and answered, "Noble guardian, I am Lady Re'alis, daughter of Lord Jovis the Second, and granddaughter of King Jovis the Wise." Re'alis looked like a child's doll before Ruork as he stood and smiled.

"Then we are yours to command. For thus we swore to your line. Should the fires of war touch the castle of the Knower's Tower then we should come to her aid till her foes are forever driven past the mountain of Vagath'Oth. So we swore, and so we will do, child of the Knower." Ruork's voice and posture filled with pride as he spoke this oath with a near-religious fervor. His words had the same effect upon his fellows as they stood at attention.

"Ruork, son of Ruork, I thank you for your willingness to honor oaths given in the past. I welcome your aid with all my heart," she said, looking with kindness up at Ruork's large brown eyes. "But I must warn you that this battle was just a small skirmish when compared with the war to come. I feel that your oath has been fulfilled by your aid here; there is no need for your people to enter our lengthy struggle."

"Grurmff, we will pick the time and choosing of the oath's fulfillment, Re'alis, daughter of Jovis, son of Jovis the Wise. For it is our right. What then is thy bidding?" asked Ruork insistently.

Re'alis looked to Devick, and he drew near to her and gave her what he hoped was a *"Don't anger them"* expression. Re'alis nodded subtly and continued.

"Then we must set out for Frost Haven to reunite with the people of my realm," she said with authority. Ruork bowed very low again, sending a rush of air into the bunch of small figures at his feet. He boomed as he spoke.

"Then there we shall go too."

38

Fog and Whispers

In the time of the Old Wars where lands and people perished in arcane flame, the Tears of the Aashahl were at last united against the enemies of all creation. Upon the victory their power was sundered as pettiness entered the hearts of many. Be it to us a warning of the frailty of victory and the threat of unchecked humors indulged.
Essays of the Divine.

Kaileth had led them to the barge as if he had left it there himself. After his odd fugue state and collapse earlier that night, Ralenn and Jayle were only partially surprised by finding the barge. Each assuming that this was only the latest token of the greater powers taking an interest in Kaileth and the events that they all were now apart of. Kaileth smiled, kneeling to pet Riidak. The hound made a small sad sound, looking to the sky. Kaileth was starting to worry over Mirris' absence as well. He had hoped she would be awaiting them near the fortress city. He still trusted, though, that she would find them. Falcons as she, are not easily foiled when it comes to returning to their masters.

The company moved quickly down a sloping hillside through the sparse trees that grew thicker and mixed with dense canes nearer to the riverbank. A frantic hush hung heavily over them all knowing that discovery now would be disastrous. The night air was warm and comfortable, hinting at the change in the season. Gentle sporadic breezes carried the smell of smoke and the sounds of distant battle as it set dangling bunches of bright red olieas flowers softly bouncing on their vines.

The river barge had been abandoned in great haste. Wooded crates, tall amphorae, and large bushel baskets sat in neat stacks upon the upper deck. The heavy timbered vessel was long and slender, sitting low in the water. In a much happier time, someone had taken the care to carefully paint the trim and side decking with bright green and yellow ivy patterns, just visible in the poor light. Fires raged upstream on the banks of the river and the distant echo of slaughter drifted across the land. Kyleeal stopped the wagon near a stone and timbered storehouse a good spear's cast from the river. Quickly Ralenn, Kaileth, Ealë and several others silently moved forward to scout the barge and building for trouble.

"Wait here," Kyleel whispered into the back of the wagon as he and Jayle joined the swift reconnoiter. Sificah moved toward the front of the wagon to peer out as the armed members of the party darted through the shadows searching for hidden foes. She had not spoken much since she regained her wits some six days ago. Lirah felt her silence was due to a mental trauma more than anything physical at this point. She had been reliable help with Jahllia, who had been feverish for the better part of the journey. Jahllia had only truly started to mend some during the last few days. Tyllidus had tended to the Eolai'Mahtair the entire time and seemed put out over something that he did not expound upon when asked.

Presently Ealë returned.

"Come, sister, we have space within for these."

Lirah, Sificah, Tyllidus, Ealë, and two other Tundraihn warriors helped the Eolai'Mahtair, Vishaya and Jahllia from the wagon and into a series of small passenger berths within the barge. The rest of the

Tundraihn kept a close watch on the thick vegetation that surrounded the small storehouse that set near the jetty. Jayle and Kyleeal returned presently from searching the building to exchange quick words with Orodan and Kaileth.

"Looks like everyone left in a hurry." Kyleeal nodded silently as Jayle spoke in a practiced soft whisper.

"Some signs of a fight inside but it's hard to tell for sure. From the upper level we could see the green plains before the fortress more clearly. The Subjugate's siege forces are recovering from a sallied assault from Syrah, but they still command all the approaches to the gate. I fear that even if we make good a path to the walls, we would be slain by shot and arrow before we had the chance to make ourselves known as friends."

Orodan looked slowly to Kyleeal for confirmation.

"All is as Sir De'Vinor has spoken. To approach the fortress is death."

All stood quietly for a moment thinking over this revelation.

Lirah ensured that Vishaya was well settled along with Jahllia and the others before coming to join Ralenn and the growing circle around Jayle, Orodan and Kaileth, and Riidak at her side. It had taken insistent persuasion to get Orodan to agree to journey to Syrah in the first place. All that effort now seemed like a waste. The tense silence stretched, making Lirah grow uncomfortable.

"Your Eolai'...Mahtairi is settled into her room and a few of your warriors are standing watch."

Lirah cringed inwardly at her near fumbling of the Tundraihn priestess' tittle. Despite her efforts to practice pronouncing it in her mind she still found all the sounds difficult to string together. Orodan moved to fully face her and so she went on.

"I am sure I can tend to her needs. This river is...it is full of the life force of Miljah, more than enough for me to bend to healing our injured companions."

Kaileth smiled proudly as she spoke, reassuring confidence in her quiet words. Orodan held her in his stern gaze for some long moments more and Ralenn could feel his drive to keep the Eolai'Mahtair safe filling his thoughts.

"May it be as you say then," he finally replied.

"If it makes a difference to any here, this barge has some sort of artifice to drive it in the water. It looks undamaged. We could slip past this battlefield and seek aid further south if just a little luck drifts our way," Ralenn offered.

At this Jayle took immediate interest.

"An artifice, you say, show me."

Without further discussion all followed Ralenn and Jayle to the rear of the barge where an arch-roofed structure housed a bewildering assortment of gears, flywheels, spokes, and chains.

At the rearmost section of this space stood a brass-worked windlass. Jayle nearly clapped his hands in excitement and Kaileth placed a calming arm upon his shoulders.

"This can move the barge?" Lirah asked, wonder struck by the apparatus.

"Oh, it can move the barge, Miss Lirah, like nothing you have seen, I suspect," Jayle replied, already examining the components with an expert eye. Orodan slowly entered the space, running his hands over the intricate metallic surface of the closest cogs and sprockets. His stance spoke of mistrust, yet his eyes were alight with sharp curiosity.

"I take it you know how to make this move the vessel?" Kaileth whispered, amusement written upon his face.

"Yes, I can put this to function. Our fortune in finding this is beyond..." Jayle's words faltered, the threat of a chuckle, or perhaps something rawer, halting his voice for a moment.

"Well, it is as if it was left solely for our use. In perfect working order as though..." Jayle smiled abruptly, changing the topic.

"This windlass will twist up spring coils in the belly of this vessel. These coils will then spin the clockwork auger drives in the bottom of the hull. And we will slip through the water, silently and sure as the very ilysh themselves."

Kaileth nodded in accord, certain that this was all according to some Aashahl's plan.

"I will ensure we are well aboard swiftly," Orodan said, turning to go. "Daylight will not be our ally here."

"Very true, let us get to work then." Jayle nodded to the windlass.

"We will need a few braces of strong legs to wind that, younger legs than mine if you can spare them." Jayle spoke quickly as Orodan left.

The tall warrior simply nodded in reply. From their first meeting to now, the Tundraihn commander had softened little. Swinging from moments of brooding contemplation to bursts of discussion where his distrust of the broader world and those who called it home were thinly veiled. At this point it was clear to all the non-Tundraihn members of their band that his one and only focus was getting his people's heir apparent home in the swiftest, most discreet, and safest means possible.

Ralenn could sense how out of his sphere of familiarity he was. It was difficult for him to accept guidance from Jayle and Kaileth. It was a humbling realization for Orodan that he knew so little of Miljah beyond his forested home. Though he had come to trust Kaileth, Lirah, and even Jayle, Orodan still held the others, Ralenn included, at some distance. As for Vishaya, she was still looked upon with open hostility by all the Tundraihn apart from Ealë and the few who she nearly died to save. All these thoughts flew through Ralenn's mind as Orodan left them to prepare the barge for travel. Within a short span, Kyleeal and half a dozen Tundraihn warriors entered the artifice room and Jayle set them to work on the windlass while he started manipulating a series of levers and chain-drive pulley blocks.

"Ralenn, come here and take good care to note what I do. It won't be wise for only one of us to know how this works." As Jayle spoke Ralenn realized Kaileth had slipped out as the Tundraihn warriors came in.

"You see this. This is the coil lock. It locks the drive coils, so they do not spin freely while being wound. Always throw that first to this marker if you are having to wind them fresh." Ralenn took particular care as Jayle continued to explain the operation of the barge drive. The room became a whirr of motion and sound as all the carefully crafted clockwork began to clunk, turning and spinning in a virtual symphony of variable sounds, whirrs of rotation and semi-musical clanking.

"I'll leave you to it, then!" Lirah called out with a wave as she left, Riidak trailing after her. She hurried up toward the front of the barge where she spotted Kaileth. He had just finished coiling several large ropes that had been mooring the barge to the jetty. Lirah had not spoken with him much while approaching this place, and she had no idea why he was smudged with sooty black stuff. It almost looked like it had been writing, tok runes perhaps? Maybe it was to help him hide in the night shadows? She had known him her entire life, but he was still a mystery in so many ways and did things that no one in Allinth could understand; so often, in fact, that no one asked what he was about anymore, not that he ever offered anything beyond the vaguest of explanations in reply. Lirah did not expect this would be any different.

"Are the wounded and frail well stored, Miss Lirah?" He softly spoke without turning to look at her. Lirah smiled at another of his otherly habits.

"Stored?" She couldn't help but smirk at this. "Yes, they are settled in. I'll go stay with them when we set out, just needed a bit more starlight and fresh air first."

Kaileth turned to face her with an expression that was an echo of how Gaileng looked when Lirah had made him proud. To see him wear it caught her off guard and the sharp stab of sorrow was breathtakingly keen within her. Her breath caught and she found she could not speak for a long moment, dropping her gaze to the dancing starlight upon the dark water. Kaileth's strong hands found her shoulders and he turned her to face him.

"The grief is yet keen; time will dull it some, but the sting will always be there." His eyes shifted to the distant stars. She could see him looking from star to star, marking the constellations with his ageless eyes. Lirah could remember nights in the Anthosn temple with Detan and Itheil, Fodir sometimes too would join her and Gaileng to mark the motions of the heavens. There were some among the orders of Anthos who believed the path of fate was woven in the movements of the stars. Gaileng had always insisted that she had been brought to him under the very best of stars, Illy'Trai, Anthos' first and ever-faithful friend. If she was honest, Lirah was not sure she believed all of the stories of Anthos and the beginning of Miljah but she hoped they were true. Presently Kaileth returned his gaze to her.

"Our love for the lost would be a paltry thing were it so easily dispersed. Truest love is indelible, marking the soul, in one manner or another." He let out a long, controlled breath. So full of melancholy tension Lirah found hot tears gathering at the edges of her large eyes.

"Be gentle with yourself in this, Miss Lirah. Seek time to let the sorrow be felt. Make space for moments to let the pain bleed away." He spoke tenderly, the weight of his own griefs pulling at each word. He seemed to speak in answer to her own troubled thoughts. Bringing clarity to the miasma of her emotions and sorrows. She felt silly at getting caught off guard, betrayed even, by her own emotions.

Riidak pressed his warm flanks against her legs in a comforting manner. Lirah reminded herself that it really had not been that long since the horrors at Allinth. All that death, home and loved ones gone in a moment. No chance to say goodbye or tell them what they had meant to them. No chance to tell Gaileng how much she loved him. Once more Kaileth looked to the sky and his voice betrayed him just for an instant as he continued, the gravity of his own aching heart becoming acute.

"Epri loved the stars, especially this time of the year when the Casts of Layr are so easy to see." Lirah followed his lead, her eyes easily finding the broad band of stars. There were so many points of light, packed tightly together, forming a shimmering river dividing the black of the night sky in half. Within the river of white radiance dozens of larger stars glittered and shone like emeralds, rubies, and sapphires from a great drake's horde. The starlight suddenly dazzled in her eyes, splitting repeatedly into fragments of color and light.

"Oh Kail, I'm sorry. I'll be fine." Lirah wiped her eyes as they flooded with tears. "All the years you silently must have sorrowed over..." She couldn't say her name. A wave of grief flowed through her, threatening a true sobbing outburst for both their sakes. She fought to cage it all up, to keep it just at the back of her mind.

"Over Epri? Yes, but often not so silently have I mourned her. I had my private spaces for grieving. You will find your way forward too. In time, you will learn to live with the wounds. Somehow, though the pain never fully leaves, the mending of the heartbreak makes us stronger. Our hearts pull closer to the loved ones we still have, and we are faster to see the hand of the aashahl who care to lend us their aid."

He gave her shoulders a firm squeeze, but Lirah darted in for an embrace. She knew Kaileth was not one for such gestures, but it felt like they both needed it. He relented and held her as a father might hold his distraught daughter in a moment of tenderness.

"Anthos sees your good deeds, Miss Lirah. All the aashahl do. I do not think your abilities would be blooming as they are if the great powers of this world did not approve of your path. Take heart in that."

"By all the holy heavens we would be so lost in all this without you, Kail. Thank you."

"You are ever welcome, Miss Lirah." Breaking the embrace, he held her at arm's length for a moment. "But do not underestimate yourself. You and Ralenn faced the mountain and sphinx without me.

At the falls you took bold actions once more and again in the arena of the Subjugate. Trust in your courageous loving heart Lirah."

Kaileth finished setting his jaw firm with a nod as to say there was no more to be said on the matter. He then gave a small bow, politely low as one might to a true lady, and Lirah could not keep a delicate giggle from slipping out as she wiped the last of her tears. Kaileth rose with a hint of a smile and made a shooing motion with his hands.

"Best be below before your returning mirth gets us discovered."

Lirah smiled truly now, feeling reinforced by Kaileth's words.

"Aashahl bless you Kail." She turned and hurried to those in her care leaving Kaileth and Riidak upon the upper deck.

Not long after Jayle and Ralenn had the drives running and the barge slipped into the dark courses of the river. All held to their assumed stations watching the banks of the river in pensive silence. Even with the bows and spears of the Tundraihn it would be an ill exchange should they be found out by the massive Subjugate army that now stood poised to raze Syrah. Just as threatening was the prospect of the Syrahn defenders mistaking them as foes and raining shot and stone from their high walls. Each member of the company prayed in their own way for a swift flight south. The barge moved with extraordinarily little commotion. Jayle manned the helm with Kaileth and Orodan near the bow watching the course ahead. Small groups of Orodan's warriors had stationed themselves around the barge, silently watching the dark outlines of the riverbank slip by. Ralenn kept near Jayle putting the operation of the barge's clockwork drive to memory. He had found Jayle was an adept teacher and Ralenn was confident he could now put the barge into motion himself should the need arise.

The fortress rose swiftly from the darkness, its bulwarks swallowing the stars as they climbed into the night. Colonnades of amber light spilled across the lower walls, cast by the great bronze lanterns hung beneath the hording. Their glow wavered on the river's surface like molten gold, breaking and reforming with the current. This illumination spread over most of the river's width, leaving no hope of the barge passing unnoticed. Before much thought could be bent toward what to do, Orodan spoke.

"Look." Though Kaileth was close to him, he almost missed his whisper. Orodan gestured to the side of the river opposite the walls. Kaileth followed his arm and looked hard into the dark shadows of the reeds and trees near the riverbank. He held his breath and listened to the night, the soft lap of water upon the barge, the distant sounds of battle in the fields before the fortress. Riidak became suddenly still, a low growl building in his throat.

Then the unmistakable clamor of heavily armed men drifted over the calm water. Kaileth focused and there in the starlight glinted hundreds of helmets and broad pauldrons. The enemy was already upon the riverbank preparing some assault upon the walls. Any hope of signaling Syrah of their identity or slipping past unmolested was now well gone. More likely the barge and those within would suffer a crossfire with both the Subjugate and the Syrahns believing the craft was in the employ of their foe.

All upon the upper deck soon comprehended the peril that awaited them spurring motion as the Tundraihn gathered to be ready to defend the barge near the prow. Jayle too darted forward leaving Ralenn to mind the helm, he quickly joined Kaileth and Orodan near the prow.

"No tidy way through this, eh?" Jayle said softly. Orodan nodded his agreement but said nothing. Instead, he watched Kaileth who had become very still. Kaileth seemed to be speaking under his breath, his eyes closed. Before any could interrupt, Kaileth's eyes popped open, and he turned to Jayle.

"Keep us in the middle of the river with best speed. We will be well enough off when the moment comes." Jayle tilted his head, clearly not convinced it would be easy as all that.

"As you say then, I'll push the cogs to the limit." Jayle said. The veteran soldier knew this was no time to debate and argue. Kaileth seemed completely certain in his words. He had not led them astray thus far and Jayle had seen enough in his years of service to Mantorah to know the manner of one whose thread is upon the loom of the aashahl.

Ahead the stone of the walls looked almost black contrasted with the golden lamplight. No lip or edge of footing was present on the wall side of the river, only hard unyielding stone. The barge was close enough now to see the defenders moving within the hoardings. Occasionally a shuttered arrow loop would spill a splash of light into the night as the sentries watched the river for the foe. Only moments separated the barge and its passengers from discovery now. Jayle quickly returned to the helm preparing his mind for the fight he was sure to come. Ralenn guessed at what was amiss, but asked to be sure.

"We are in for a fight?" He asked Jayle.

"Looks like it. Throw those two leavers and get a few backs to help crank up the coils, we need all the speed we can get."

The barge kept its course and started to gain speed. As Ralenn returned with a few Tundraihn to help on the cranks he caught sight of the movements on the far riverbank. A prayer to the aashahl started to form on his lips. He had just started to work the bronze and oak of the windless crank when the softest sound came from the cabin's rear door.

Jayle and Ralenn both nearly cried out in alarm as a figure wrapped in a dark blanket was suddenly present behind them in the helm cabin. A smile danced across Vishaya's soft glowing eyes as they relaxed upon recognizing her. Even the Tundraihn had startled at her sudden entrance, their hands fast upon their daggers. She seemed smaller now than when she had been in the fighting at the arena. She clutched the blanket around her bare shoulders, her naked feet falling soft upon the deck. Jayle was surprised to feel warmth bloom on his cheeks at the sight of her on her feet and recovered some. He started to speak but she closed the distance to him in a moment, placing a slender finger upon his lips, delicately silencing the knight of Mantorah.

"Do you feel that?" She hissed, barely audible. Jayle and Ralenn quickly shared a mutually confused expression as she continued, dropping her hand and looking out at the river before them.

"They have sent her to our aid, for his sake. But she will require blood in payment. I do not think he understands…" She finished with a half-muffled chuckle of disbelief. The temperature plummeted and with the last spoken words from Vishaya's full lips, her breath was starkly visible to all. Before Jayle or Ralenn could ask what she meant or what was happening, thick rolling fog swallowed the barge and the riverbanks appearing from nowhere in an instance. She smiled viciously, an expression that was now only visible due to the growing illumination from her own fiercely luminous eyes.

"Keep the tiller true good man of Mantorah, no matter what." Absolute authority filled her voice now as she left them.

"She seems to be on the mend." Jayle finally said, swallowing hard.

"I am just glad she is on our side." Ralenn replied as he returned to the windlass.

Out on the main deck Vishaya found the railing amidships and steadied herself facing the far bank from Syrah. The thick fog totally concealed the barge and the river up and downstream from them for half a skain. The Tundraihn murmured to each other in their own tongue, drawing away from her, unsettled by the Xydar and the fog. The light from the wall lanterns was only just visible high above them upon the upper surface of the fog. Vishaya glanced for a moment to the prow, her otherworldly eyes finding Kaileth in the gloom. She frowned in concern, seeing more than she expected. Setting her jaw, she faced the far riverbank.

The barge was almost clear of the point of most danger now; the auger drives swiftly pulling it through the water. Cries of alarm went up from the walls at the sudden unnatural fog and the moment filled with tangible energy. Vishaya closed her eyes, keenly aware of this force of animus, eager to release it. Sibilant voices arose in the fog. Orodan turned, bright steel suddenly in his hand. A heartbeat later his warriors were poised for battle, the menacing whispers filling his ears. Kaileth spun, looking for the source of the sounds and saw Vishaya. He started in her direction, but too late.

She pulled in an icy breath through her nose, filling her lungs with the frigid air and the energies of the moment, with the savage promises of the speakers in the fog. She raised a single arm, parting the blanket she wore as her sole raiment. The amithyle glittered with its own light, blood red in the morass surrounding the barge. Vishaya screamed and the night burned away from around her. Kaileth dashed toward her, as did Orodan, all turned to the sound of her cry with alarm. Riidak barked like a thunderclap as the fog seemed to convulse in climatic satisfaction as the crimson fire crossed the distance to the far riverbank in an instant, exploding into flames. Vishaya greedily sucked in each breath now, reveling in the sensation as she burned the riverbank clear of vegetation and the host of Subjugate soldiers who had been lurking there.

No more than a few moments later, Kaileth was at her side as she collapsed upon the barge's side rail exhausted and trembling. The alarm upon the wall was in earnest now as the Syrahn defenders could clearly see the enemy upon the far bank. Arrows quickly began filling the air and those not burned alive by the Xydar fell away from the river, driven off by the defenders of Syrah. More than a few arrows struck the rear of the barge despite the fog that hung over the river waters before they were well and safe past Syrah. Her breathing still ragged Vishaya finally looked up to Kaileth.

"That was certainly unexpected. Though I think we once again owe you a debt." He said sincerely. She wiped the thick bloody tears from her eyes trying to stand. Her trembling legs faltered and once more Kaileth took her full weight into his arms.

"Did you, did you not hear her?" She said between shuddering gasps. "You are marked for all to see know..." Her eyes lost focus for a moment and Kaileth stood to carry her below. There was a troubling amount of blood on the deck where Vishaya had been standing, more still upon her hands and face. She held one hand aloft, seeming to examine it for an instant before licking the blood from several of her own fingers.

"A toll of blood for the mistress of night song." Her voice was weak, delirious even, as Jayle ran to where they were. He caught up the edge of the blanket where it had fallen open, exposing her bare form beneath. He shared a troubled look with Kaileth as he took her from him.

"I'll take her, you best ensure we make a clear break south." Jayle's demeanor brooked no protest and so he soon disappeared below. Ralenn could only see part of what had transpired and though he desperately wanted to know what was happening, steering the barge was clearly the priority.

Kaileth stood thinking for a moment. Vishaya's words were troubling. Orodan approached, his nose crinkled at the smell of Vishaya's dark blood on the deck at his feet.

"She is dangerous Master Allitorii. They are not as we; they are creatures of another order entire." Orodan raised a hand and the three Tundraihn warriors with him put up their readied weapons and dispersed.

"You are not wrong, yet we were drawn together in a manner I cannot easily dismiss as chance. I see the aashahl working in our odd little company. That is to say nothing of the fact, that once more her destructive fury laid our common foes low. For now, any who oppose the Subjugate must suffer as allies. Though I feel there is more good in her than one might think. Vicious and hot, but pure and unrestrained."

"I pray to my mistress that you are right." Orodan spoke his peace and moved back to his station at the prow leaving Kaileth to his thoughts, the sounds of the skirmish drifting into the dark behind them.

It will take us all to gather the tears and end the Subjugate.

The barge moved at a determinedly swift pace, south into the darkness of the warm night. Hardly a half skain was between them and the fortress city when the fog broke up as swiftly and suddenly as it had appeared. Kaileth could hear several Tundraihn muttering what must have been prayers of gratitude. Their language was elegant, soft, and lilting like water over smooth pebbles. One word stood out however, one Kaileth recognized, Nique'Shay.

Epilogue

Afyreen felt her ire rise as she stared at the array of maps and reports upon the table before her. How could so many aspects of her plans have unraveled? How could her spies, seers, and the Ikthii not foreseen the disaster in Lea'Angleneth, the stalemate at Syrah, and the Taivadean rebellion? She sighed, a long hissing breath passing slowly through her pursed lips.

*So much for swift and easy...*She picked out a small weather-worn scrap of paper and read the message that was hurriedly scrawled there.

"Army routed. Falling back to Thenill. Rahdan Devick Tolkol, Re'alis Ta' Angleneth confirmed to command their hosts in person. Will shadow their march and report.

~ Idrin"

A predator's smile slowly crept into Afyreen's features. It seemed that Devick and Re'alis were very much alive. Perhaps, there was a chance she could deal with them herself. A personal indulgence she knew, but it was a pleasing thought. The larger aspects of the war took priority of course. Her forces had only just begun their march south and more reinforcements were due from the east in another fourth-moon. Once they were refitted from their long march they could head for the Red Gates and bring Mantorah to its ruin. In the meantime, she would have to make do with the armies that she had presently.

She knew that Ach'Juln and Drashtaa would not care over the loss of Dao'Tai lives. Nor did they care overly much over any timelines. However, they would care about failure to deliver promised results. Above this, they cared about the Tears of the Aashahl. The news that there was a survivor from the Anothn royal line changed a great many things. This survivor could turn the tide of the war against Afyreen, undo all she was, or they could propel her to new heights of power.

Enough power to shake off the yoke of any would be masters. Whatever the case, Ach'Juln and his ilk did not need to know of this. Better to let the Tears, and the only being who could gather them, stay in the forgotten shadows as long as possible. Long enough for her to bend events to her will once more.

She stood and walked to stand before the massive stain glass window of the upper audience chamber in the old Anothn palace. The red and golden light highlighted the angles of her cheeks, slender neck, and delicate collar bones in such a way that she looked like a being of living fire. She let her delicate fingers trace the metal lines between the sections of colored glass. They were cold and smooth under the skin of her fingertips. She closed her eyes and let her mind drift into distant memories. Her hands tracing the lines on another large stained-glass window. Those lines of metal had been hot. Warmed by the primal fires of her mother's domain far to the south. She could still remember every detail, the old wars, the raw thrill of battle on a divine scale, the sting of betrayal and defeat. To be spurned by her maker.

She laughed a little at herself as she realized the only thing she truly missed from that time, was the freedom of the open sky and the power she felt, born a loft by her wings. She opened her eyes and marked the far too large shadow that fell away from her. With the power of the Tears in her control, nothing was outside the realm of possibility.

Afyreen turned from the window and strode back to the table to prepare a dispatch to Idrin. She would have what was by rights hers. She would have satisfaction. She would bend the fates to her will. She smiled and set the quill to a fresh vellum.

Appendix

Adohr: Nomadic people that live south of Mantorah. Frequently launch raids into the north. Seen as primitive by most in the High Sun Realms due to stark religious differences in their view of the Aashahl.

Ailc East Star: A single bright start that appears due east in the northern realms no matter the season. Used for navigation and in religious architecture.

Akar: Term for the people of Akarii. They live exclusively in the hidden realm of Akaroche. The Akar River north of Kali'Kern also bears this name.

Akaroche: A great hidden realm in the far north, hidden in a labyrinth of slot canyons and plateaus. Akaroche has all but faded into myth for most people in the High Sun Realms.

Akarr Valley: The wide fertile river valley that surrounds Lake Akarr. Populated by the people of Lea'Angleneth with Thenill more or less denoting the far northern edge of the area.

Alabaster Guard: Name of the personal guard to Lady Re'alis. Sometimes called the Angleneth Guard. Their armor is made from the finest evergleam steel decorated with pearlescent enamel and bronze. Aireathyn and Ercoln are two of their number noted for surviving a battle with an Ikthii lead Grishkii ambush.

Alliix Islands, Isle of Alliix: Isle chain across the western seas. Home of the Allitorii and Shayar the Aashahl. There are thousands of islands, many are large with lush jungles and pleasant climates.

Allitor, Allitorii: Kindred from the Alliix Isles. A large contingent of the Allitorii served as the Royal Guard of Anoth up until the sack of Ell'Anoth. A martial society with large family units formed of multiple females who select and share a male in order to sire cohorts of children in large numbers. The Allitorii are the scions of Shayar and her first and only mortal lover. Among certain circles their status as Andeo kindred is hotly debated.

Alpa's Crown: A northern constellation. Useful as a navigational reference and important in many religions for its symbology. Many cults time rituals around this constellation's movement.

Andeo Kindreds, Andeo: Term for kindreds of magical beings who are the offspring of the Aashahl or other beings of arcane power. Often collectively referred to as simply "andeo". Andeo can be of mortal and immortal lineage or of two immortal beings. The term is considered derogatory among many groups of such beings especially those who are entirely the immortal kin of powerful Aashahl.

Andohra: An alliance of linguistic and culturally similar people. Loosely organized into a confederation of villages and fortress cites in the Vagath'Oth mountains bordering the old realm Vagath'Oth proper to the north, Syrah to the west, Lea' Angleneth to the east. Running from Mount Anthos in the south, north through the mountains to about the west road into Lea'Angleneth. The Andohrase elect a chief to represent them as a realm when dealing with outside powers. Their warriors are famous for high quality archers and spear-men. Andohra was once part of the realm of Vagath'Oth but fought a successful war of secession. Andohra resisted the Subjugate invasion fiercely and suffered greatly during the ensuing conflict. Towards the end of the war with the subjugate the Aya'Dao'Tai leveraged the darkest of her powers to curse the realm of Andohra, leaving it uninhabitable, a place of nightmare and shadows rumors of dark entities.

Angleneth Castle: Principal castle in Lea'Angleneth, build to defend the causeway that connects the island of Angleneth to the mainland.

Angleneth: Principal city of Lea'Angleneth. Home to the preponderance of the realm's people Angleneth is built upon an extensive island in Lake Akarr.

Anica: Last Queen of Anoth. Killed when the Subjugate sacked the capitol of Ell'Anoth.

Anoth: Once powerful realm that controlled the central region of the High Sun Realms. Anoth was the center for culture, learning, art, military, and diplomatic power. Anoth was also a hub of novel banking systems that empowered extensive trade with the island realms of the sea. Anoth was principally a city state with many smaller villages, boarder fortresses, and towns spread through the expanse of territory she controlled directly. Anoth operated an extensive diplomatic core with emissaries in most major cities of allied realms. The capitol city of Anoth was Ell'Anoth.

Anthosn Order: A widespread monastic order dedicated to the creeds and philosophies accredited to Anthos and his chosen prophets. This order is organized into a common structure across Miljah; Acolytes, Priest wardens, Priest Knowers, and Defenders of the Alter. These ranks have more to do with wisdom gifted from Anthos than years in the order. Some ranks are more pragmatic and are given to members who perform a specific role or trade within the order. Priest wardens for example are often prior members of military orders and armies of the various realms.

Apothatrist: A highly trained herbalist and medicinal sage. Able to use very simple incantations to augment their repertoire of herbal compound-based medicines. Typically employed by the powerful or working in public houses of healing, Apothatrists can deal with most common illnesses and injuries. Their remedies are primarily practical skills and quality medicinal potions and compounds. They eschew the term healer, as healers rely almost entirely on the power of the arcane for their craft. True healers are practically unheard of in most realms.

Arah'Ashli: High Spring. Third month of the year

Arah'Brav: Ending of spring. The fourth month of the year.

Arah'Donar: Mid spring. The second month of the year

Arah'Far: Start of Spring. First month of the year.

Aril River: Large river that starts in the Vaga'Thoth mountains and runs mostly south parallel to the Anvil Mountains down and through the Tundraihn forest towards the Dark Realms. Used as a waterway for commerce where it passes through the verdant plains near Syrah towards the Red Gates of Mantorah.

Aril Watch: Mantorahn river fortress on their northeastern frontier.

Atha'Tarrii: Immortal kindred of beings that exist just outside of the mortal plane. They are beyond elusive and otherworldly. Many believe they are older than the Aashahl and of an entirely different form of power and magic.

Attriphair: Fierce warrior servants of the Aashahl. Exalted humans in appearance. They cannot reproduce nor do they share all the same emotions as mortals. Normally entirely focused on their charge from the Aashahl they serve.

Avertyyn: A black metal used in armor and weapons. Made from crystalline secretions in active lava tubes. Only arcane power can heat the metal to its melting point. The Xydar, Dactyls, and Akar are the only known kindreds to readily work the metal. It is obsidian black in color and sheen, both durable and flexible when worked with skill. Next to unbreakable it is said avertyyn can never lose an edge. Once formed into a shape it resists magic forces exerted upon it with a violent reaction.

Baldrees vail: Large city state within the Freeholdn.

Bonds of Blade: Warrior's guild common in many cities. They offer protective services, facility guards, personal guards, bounty collection, and similar things.

Brass Tack Merchants Guild: Powerful and extensive trade guild. This guild has outposts on the western continents and several isles of the sea. No outsider knows the exact size of their wide network, but they seem able to source any item given enough time and coin.

Brek's purse: South by southeast constellation.

Breydfar: A breed of large swift war horse native to Mantorah. Often used for both battle and patrol. The breed does well in both roles and is prized for this ability.

Brie nuts: Large hard-shell nut about the size of a child's fist.

Brittle cake: Like baklava. A popular pastry in many realms.

Brothers of Brek: Hospitality Hall guild that is well established in most large cites. They operate inns, gambling houses, and in some locations, bordellos.

Caidryn: Devick's father. Killed fighting Adohr during the Subjugate's invasion.

Dactyls: Beyond reclusive species of beings. They dwell exclusively within the deep parts of the largest mountain ranges. Responsible for many tunnels used by the surface folk to traverse under impassible mountains. The Dactyls are generally regarded as benevolent though mischievous if disturbed or provoked. Some claim that they will take certain mortals as pupils occasionally sharing their great skill in artifice and inventions.

Dao'Tai: Mortal kin of unknown origin. Generally, very large and muscled seeming bread for war. They shun the use of horses and favor heavy infantry in battle. Their females and children are kept in isolation from other mortal kin, and little is known about their culture and habits. They do use slaves of every sort and their officers are known to enjoy the company of non Dao'Tai consorts. They seem to worship the Aya Dao'Tai Afyreen despite her clearly being a different kindred all together.

Durnori: Freeholdn word for sovereign defender or servant of the people. Title given to person elected by all the Freeholdn to rule as a high king or queen.

Dyne: Freeholdn word for a duchess.

Dyvost Canyon: Narrow canyon south of Ell'Anoth. It played host to a disastrous battle during the invasion of the Subjugate. The forests near the canyon bear the same name.

Ean Oich' the hawk: Navigational constellation in the west by southwest.

Ect'ar pass: Strategic Mountain passes through the Vaga'Thoth.

Eed bread: Bread made from oats, dark wheat, and verdm berries.

Ell'Anoth: Ell'Anoth is the most populous city in the High Sun Realms. Being the capitol of Anoth, Ell'Anoth was the principal target of the Subjugate invasions and now plays host to their occupational government and military camps. Ell'Anoth is situated on the north Kray'Bahn plateau, in the bend of the Vryl'Bahn river. At its prime Ell'Anoth was marvelous, sprawling metropolises with entire districts dedicated to trade, the arts, colleges of learning, and all manner of the best civilized peoples have to offer.

Epi'tharo: Equine creature with a singular horn. Very rare and usually associated with either great or terrible events. Imbued with arcane powers. Seen in either the deepest forests or the shifting sands of the southern deserts. Known to roam the Arcane doldrums and it is said their powers of healing are not sapped by those cursed lands.

Erah'Juil: End of summer-start of fall. The eighth month.

Erah'Kaldor: Middling summer. The sixth month.

Erah'Nor: High summer. The seventh month.

Erah'Tadir: Start of summer. The fifth month.

Evergleam: Lea'Angleneth white steel. Multi Layered white steel that is resistant to rust. Regarded as the finest steel commonly known. Used for weapons and armor. Can be polished to a white mother of pearl sheen. Extremely expensive and difficult to make. Not in widespread use even in Lea'Angleneth.

Everguard: Military order dedicated to Sheibrok. They maintain numerous monastery citadels, primarily on well-traveled roads, near remote bridges, and in a few cities. They are known for declaring crusades against what they deem as threats to the balance of Justice and

Mercy. They follow the directive of their Exalted Sibyl. They often work in concert with other militant monastic orders. The Everguard has been openly suppressed by the subjugate with many of their installations being seized.

Far'thonnin's Ford: Norther most ford of the Aril river. Named after a fablette hero, the ford was well maintained and guarded under the golden age of Anoth. The fortifications commanding the ford remain ungarrisoned by the Subjugate.

Forked Blades: A cult of Felairtarh. Outlawed in most realms. Very secretive in their practices.

Freeholdn: A term for a norther realm composed of many cities, villages, and fortresses. Populated by a people unified by language and culture they are at once fiercely independent but unified in their ideals and the concept of a shared Freeholdn identity. The land is composed largely of numerous rivers, lakes, rolling forested hills and mountains. Bordered by Lea'Angleneth to the south, Thenill and Vaga'Thoth to the southwest, Dashra to the west and Taivadees to the northwest. Due north is the mysterious realm of Akaroche.

Grishkah, Grishkii: Intelligent humanoid beasts. They travel in large clan packs and are predominantly nomadic and predatory in their way of life. In appearance they generally possess an enlarged jackal or hyena shaped head with a fur-covered, humanoid body and powerful elongated back legs. Their front legs end in hand-like paws with short, hooked claws. Typically, they are larger and stronger than most men and able to outpace a good horse.

High Crown: Mid summers festival in most High Sun Realms. Typically lasts about a week and is centered on the longest days of the summer. Heavily suppressed under the Subjugate.

High Sun Realms: Term for kingdoms and realms north of Mantorah. Name taken from the position of the sun in the sky and the long mild summers. Anoth served as the unifying heart of these realms and was position in the geographical center of the region.

Har'ayle De'Vinor: Leader of house De'Vinor, a powerful family within the military structure of Mantorah. Focal point of the family is Fortress De'Vinor, one of the most substantial Mantorahn fortresses. Jayle De'Vinor's father.

He'Aril Falls: A secluded broad fall of the Aril river. Still high in the Vaga'Thoth, it had played host to numerous spiritual rituals by the larger cults of Dannitar and other lesser Aashahl of the natural world.

Illy'Trai: A northern constellation that always points to magnetic north. Also is the name of an ancient character of folk lore. Illy'Trai is said to have been a dear friend to Anthos. These tales are not clear as to the nature of Illy'Trai, be her an Aashahl, mortal kin or something else entire. Nevertheless, the Anthosn orders teach a rich doctrine using her as an example of true and earnest friendship and loyalty.

Ilysh, Ilyshn: Andeo kin. Beings of primal magic and uncanny powers. Known by sea faring people for their beauty and lethal habits of trying to keep mortals as playthings. They are beings of legend and are often the subject of folk song and sea shanties. Most people do not believe they are real. Several powerful black inks that are sold abroad are said to be Ilyshn tears, though most are probably counterfeits.

In Kind Mercantile: A very old guild predominantly active in the slave trade. Once a powerful guild in Mantorah until their civil war and the assimilation of the old Mantorahn slave casts into the broader citizenry. In Kind was all but defunct for hundreds of years, operating in the shadows dealing in the worst kinds of human chattel and slavery. Under the Subjugate they have been given a station of preeminence among the guilds of commerce and are powerful in their own right as that of a proper realm. They operate massive slave farms on the southern plateau near Anoth where the food and material support for Dao'Tai armies are made. They also operate a lucrative blood sport arena and open slave markets.

Jendayi: Andeo kindred. Elegant winged humanoids who are lithe graceful men and women with very large, feathered wings that allow them to fly no different from great birds of prey. They live in the tops of the desert mountains and plateaus of the far southern lands near the arcane doldrums and Tir'Luthryel. After the death of their Pali'andeo patriarch, they lost most of their intrinsic magic abilities.

Jovis Ta'Angleneth: Last king of Lea'Angleneth under the Subjugate occupation. Known for his wisdom in judgment and his love of exploration in his youth when he spent part of every year exploring. In particular, he explored the east of the Shellidack mountings. He is famous for leading the furthest mapping expedition past the gates of the east.

Juir: The War Hound constellation used for navigation. North by northwest in all seasons in the north.

Kali'Anglen: Fortress tower in Lea'Angleneth. Home to several renowned artificers' houses. Also, home to a grand library.

Karah'Nuith: Every eight years has sixteen extra days of winter. These extra 16 days are known as the Karah'Nuith. This event is universally observed as a sacred time of renewal and thanksgiving. Pageants and festivals of all kinds are undertaken. During this time, a celestial body called Karah appears in the sky. Tides are more powerful at this time, and the days are slightly brighter and the nights less dark.

King Tyrallen III: Led Anothn refugees to the High Sun Realms after the final catastrophe in the old Anthon homelands. He and his people found the land in cultural darkness, divided with internal wars many of which are discovered to have been orchestrated by the Ikthii and their master. He dedicated his entire reign to forging alliances, striving to end the wars, and driving out the Ikthii and their supporters. Tyrallen found and united the Tears of the Aashahl to finally free the land. As peace was restored under his leadership and the formidable battle prowess of the Anothn army, the realms granted him the territory that would become the realm of Anoth to the people of Tyralenn. Ell'Anoth was also founded by him during this era.

Kray'Bahn Plate: An expansive elevated plateau cut in half by the Vryl'Bahn river system. The northern plateau is the location of Ell'Anoth and is a verdant plain of gently rolling hills, artesian springs, and lush old growth forests. The City of Ell'Anoth is built where the river bends to the west making the precipitous cliffs of the plateaus edge part of the city defense.

Kythugdon: Powerful magical bird. Notable for its jet-black top feathers and fiery crimson flight feathers and long tail. They are unfathomably rare to the point of being mythical. Living mostly in the south it is said they cannot die but are perpetually reborn from the ashes of their fiery demise.

Lake Akarr: Large alpine lake that forms the central heart of Lea'Angleneth serving as a critical source of food and easy transportation from one side of the valley to the other.

Last watch: Sacred day for most realms held in the last days of the year. Fasting and praying is typically observed. pyre alters are used to offer appropriate sacrifices to the Aashahl. The culmination of these events is centered around a solar eclipse that spans from high sun to night fall. The devotees spend this time in fervent worship and thanksgiving for life as they hold the vigil of the Last Watch until the sun rises anew on the first day of spring. Zealots see this as a new sun rising for the next year.

Lea'Angleneth: Realm of the high lakes. A verdant and remote alpine realm of wondrous beauty and civilization. The center of advanced sciences, metallurgy, and artifice in the High Sun Realms. The sparse mountain passes and marshy north lands have kept this realm free of major war and isolated for generations allowing arts and learning to flourish alongside a robust trade in finished goods.

Leshey'ar's spite: A common curse phrase used in most realms. Also, a lethal poison popular in the southern realms. The poison is completely lethal, but it takes nearly a month to kill. It causes a slow onset hemorrhagic fever after weeks of debilitating abdominal cramping.

Mantorah: Powerful and ancient realm based on the Mantor peninsula. Mantorah maintains a massive professional army due in part to the robust economy and trade surplus it enjoys with the realms of the seas. Mantorah's powerful families operate organized large-scale production of many finished goods allowing the realm to enjoy total self-sufficiency in all sectors. They have a knack for taking the refined machinery from Lea'Anglineth and putting it into practical use. Mantorah was only able to be contained by the Subjugate during the first Subjugate war and never was fully occupied or forced to disarm after the war.

Mantorahn Red Gates: Enormous defensive structures that block off the land bridge into Mantorah from the mainland. A series of walls, moats, earth works and fortresses. Name comes from the dark red stone that the largest of the walls is made from. Due to the size of the garrison the Red Gates is also a significant population center.

Miljah: Name of the planet that all life is formed on to include the literal and figurative spirit of the planet. Also used to describe the soil under foot. Some believe Miljah is a member of the Aashahl who gave her body to Anthos from which to form the planet. There are cults who worship Miljah in this manner.

Mistthray: Allitorii term for a band of youths sired by the same father amongst an Allitorii harem. The principal unit of Allitorii society allowing large numbers of deliberately batched children. Women of the harem counsel select what males serve as sire based upon the needed attributes within the society such as warriors, artisans, sailors etc. The children of the mistthray are raised together in close familial clans to imbue them with fierce sibling loyalty and unity. A high matron keeps careful records of the lineage of each child in order to keep the blood lines strong.

Nique'Tarri: Accidental creation of Nique'shay. The Nique'Tarri are those who have survived prolonged physical affection of Nique'Shay herself. The term is also used to refer to the cults of worshipers who form around these individuals. These mortals who share intimacy with Nique'shay typically do not survive, the few who do are fundamentally changed. They can no longer withstand the sunlight, nor can they satisfy their hunger and thirst by simple food and drink. These true Nique'Tarri do not age and cannot be killed by normal means. Through close physical contact they infect others with this power for short amounts of time. This they use to control their cults. True Nique'tarri are dangerous and predatory in the extreme.

Ovanec: A kindred of giant humanoids who live in the eastern boarders of the Shellidack mountains, primarily near the gates of the east. Most of their tribes are dangerous and savage. At least one tribe of Ovanec, however, have developed an honor-based culture after capturing Jovis, the last king of Lea'Angleneth. While in captivity he swiftly learned their language and shared many of the simpler points of civilization with these Ovanec. Ovanec are believed by many to be the children of Heeth and so kindred of the Andeo. They are in form typically twice the height of a man. Strong in body with long equine or bovine faces and curling horns that mostly sweep down from their brows to protect the sides of their heads.

Photiin: Devick's mother. Born to a noble house of Mantorah, Photiin's male relatives are the next heirs apparent. Her line is considered the more noble and her marriage to Devick's father was controversial. The Tolkol line was seen as an expendable military lineage, and her line is seen as a core of Mantorahn blood and nobility.

Pyre alter: Primal summoning gate for elemental powers. Ancient religious artifacts used for sacrifice, burning of the dead, and even ritual summoning efforts for the Aashahl and their servants. Many are unsettled by the esoteric nature of pyre alters and choose to bury their dead or build wooded pyres. For the most faithful however the pyre alter is the only acceptable way to send the remains of the departed to the next world. Rudimentary functions of these alters are accessible to most trained in the ways of the Aashahl and their worship. The deeper and more powerful functions like summoning or teleportation are only known to a few.

Ranilac, Death hounds: Monstrous four-legged creatures. Located in the far north, it is armored with bony scales and features a horned, bone-plated head and beak. Able to spray a combustible mist into the air to then be ignited with a static charge from the monster's beak. A favored mount of the Ikthii in open battle. A fearsome fusion of a drake and a massive war hound, it wields a whip-like armored tail and can effortlessly tear through armored men and horses alike. Mercifully difficult to train and typically only powerful Ikthii employ them as steads and servants.

Ruffled Silks: Largest hospitality guild in Miljah, operating a network of inns, bordellos, and smaller taverns. Generally viewed in a favorable light with a long-standing reputation for fairness, cleanliness and generosity to staff and patrons. Bitter rivals of In Kind Mercantile.

Ryvadale I: Anothn king who was warned in vision and saved his people by leading them north to escape destruction. This occurred in the old world of the western lands.

Sable Maille: Avertyyn maille shirts and plates woven into an armored hauberk. A solid placard covers the chest with larger plates over the neck, spine, and back. Finely woven four in one maille weave covers the limbs with six and one weave over the more vital areas of the torso. This armor was used by the Allitorii and substantial portion of the army of Anoth. Nearly all the maille was seized by the Subjugate when they invaded and crushed the Anoth army. The Anothn sable maille and most of the old armies' arms and armor is held in the vaults under the Kali'Tirlan fortress.

Serjent Valorous: Rank in the Mantorahn army. Typically, low born soldiery who has demonstrated prowess in battle. Able to command up to 60 men and horse, though 20 per serjent is also common for both mounted and serjents a foot.

Shedim: A class of powerful and individually unique lesser Aashahl and other magical being. They are other worldly and often dangerous. Most are truly inhuman in their thoughts and ethics. They are the subjects of many stories where unwitting mortals fall prey to their uncanny charms or malfeasance. The Shedim take many forms and names and include the powerful Devas. They typically assume the role of an avatar of a very specific sphere such as a central grove of trees, a stream, a herd or type of animal etc.

Shellidack Mountains: Massive range of north-south running mountings that form a natural barrier between the High Sun Realms and the eastern lands. They are poorly mapped and mostly unexplored.

Shudayi: Semi-magical creatures who prey upon other beings for food or torturous entertainment. A winged humanoid with avian fathers and the talons of a bird of prey. Only possess the female sex.

Sorrow Wood: A large, soft, ethereal white wooded willow tree that flourishes in Syrnii's domain. It is valued for its medicinal and aesthetic properties. Sorrow Wood is difficult to harvest as the Tundraihn fiercely defend it. The leaves of the tree can be boiled to create an alleviating tea, but the leaves themselves are lethally toxic to consume raw. This tree is empathic, and projects is pain into those who harm it.

Spark stone: Crystalline stone of varied color. Blue and off white are most common, but colors vary from red to yellow. When struck with an iron striker, the stone starts to "burn" with a bright heat less light. A stone the size of an apple will burn for over a month of nights. Once a stone is fully burned it becomes very brittle but remains the same size. These spent stones are easily turned into a fine iridescent powder. Spent spark stone is unused in many other compounds. Cosmetics are one of the most popular uses for spark stone.

Srellite: Reptilian humanoids who primarily inhabit cave systems. They are tribal and savage in the extreme. Hostile to almost all surface kin. Srellites live mostly near the larger mountains and to the south of Mantorah.

Storm Gryphon: Powerful magical creatures who inhabit the heights of the tallest mountains. They can alter the weather to suit their needs causing terrific and destructive thunderstorms. They are known to keep mortal slaves to tend their flocks and ire's. They are very territorial and so only the greatest of mountain ranges play host to one or perhaps two drifts of gryphons.

Subjugate War: Lengthy war of invasion waged by the Subjugate on the Anothn alliance of the High Sun Realms. War was typified by large set piece battles with lengthy periods of maneuvers by both armies for the best positions to attack. After years of steady set back the Anothn alliance fragmented, Ell'Anoth the Anothn capital was besieged and eventually sacked. This was the last major action of the war.

Sulf-char: Magical healing powder made from sulfur, charcoal, desiccated spark stone, juthood mushroom, karran tree pollen, dried blood, and Deeduif Oyster venom. Exact recipes vary by region and kindred.

Sunshadow: Anothn resistance underground born out of surviving portions of the Anothn army. Coordinates closely with Mantorah though it fiercely defends its operational independence.

Syrah: Powerful semi-independent city state on the north-eastern frontiers of Mantorah. Possesses a unique culture and vernacular despite being well assimilated as noble brother kindred in arms with Mantorah. A military state ruled by the most veteran knight of Syrah called the Paladin.

Taivadees: Powerful warrior people who populate a realm north of Anoth, northwest of Dashra and west of the Freeholdn. They are a people highly skilled in horsemanship and assault via their long shallow draft river ships. They often face internal strife between familial clans. They presently have many warriors in service to the Subjugate as a calvary force.

Taiw'Tai: Principal Dao'Tai military city. Built on the plateau south of Ell'Anoth. Host to vast slave farms and military support infrastructure. Also, home to the civilian population of Dao'Tai.

Thalyphonie: Maritime realm of the Thalyphonie Islands. Consisting of the populations of several thousand islands and several massive "city ships". They are the preeminent force on the oceans. Highly militant culture they also are driven to explore the seas and possess the most complete maps of Miljah in existence.

The Tears of the Aashahl: Commonly believed to be a collection of ancient magic objects given to the denizens of Miljah to use in times of great need. Used by King Tyrallen III of Anoth to liberate and unite the High Sun Realms, leading them into a golden era of peace.

Tundraihn: Andeo kindred and the grand-children or children of Syrnii, depending on who you talk to. They are a fierce and secretive people. It is believed they share a powerful connection to all living things of Miljah. They defend their forest home with great military prowess. Their females are very much apart from the males in many ways and seem feral to most outsiders. The Tundraihn actively avoid contact with all others and violently defend their homeland.

Tyraneth: Ancient mythical warriors from the fastness of the deep mountains. Rumored to be giants able to withstand even the magical attacks of monsters of legend. It is rumored that they used to treat with the court of Andorah in the realm's golden age. Many claim to have seen them active during the invasion of the Subjugate.

Vagath'Oth Sundering: Referring to the division of greater Vagath'Oth as a political state into three independent realms of Vagath'Oth, Andorah and Dashra. The war was swift and only saw a few true battles. It was characterized by maneuver in the difficult mountain terrain.

Vagath'Oth, The Vagath'Oth: Both a realm and a massive chain of mountains running north and south dividing the High Sun Realms about in half. The realm of Vagath'Oth once encompassed the entire mountain range until Dashra and Andorah fought a joint war for independence splitting the realm along ethnic and cultural lines.

Xydar: Andeo kindred and the children of Xydrii. Their realms are in the far south in Uthiir'Xyda, The Nightfall Forests, and Smolder Woods. Exotic in appearance and savagely fierce in war, they are a kindred apart from most, beings of darkest folk songs in the north. Many people raise their children to fear the Xydar. Stories of Xydar taking wicked children in the night are a common theme. They are in fact master of the arcane powers and in working avertyyn into weapons and armor.

Ydril River: Large tributary of the Aril River. Joining the Aril just north of the Rividall plains. Aril Watch is built near the joining of these two rivers to give it command of both the water ways and the principal.

Yiillyar: A kindred of Pali'andeo imbued with a powerful connection to the spirit of Miljah. Able to heal almost any wound given the right circumstances. They once operated several houses of healing in the High Sun Realms. During the Subjugate invasion these refuges were sought out with particular aggression. The Ikthii in particular saw that the Yiillyar were hunted to virtual extinction. Some few mixed blood Yiillyar yet live in slave service to the wealthy, though their powers of healing are a paltry shadow when compared to pure blood Yiillyar. A precious few true Yiillyar live as fugitives and hermits in the most remote corners of the realms. Some believe they are the literal children of Dannitar.

Of The Aashahl

The Aashalh were created by Anthos, the name given to the creator of the world and the orchestrator of the systems and beings who populate it. There are hundreds of Aashalh. They are separated into groups based upon their innate power and spheres of influence. The first born of the Aashalh are the most powerful of their kin. They created all living things in Miljah except the mortal kindreds. They also shaped the elements into land, sea, and all aspects of the world. Anthos directed them to do so as it pleased them allowing their natural proclivities for certain creative aspects to focus their efforts. However, Anthos was selective with whom he gave the power to create sentient life to.

The variety in all life upon Miljah is the results of the character, preferences, and passions of the Aashalh who created it. The Aashalh continue to manage and tend to their creations in their own ways. Some are very involved and live among their stewardship. Others are distant and content to simply observe and answer the occasional prayers.

Many Aashalh took more of an interest in the elements, emotional powers, and primal forces, life, death etc. These Aashalh draw their power from anything that is associated with their sphere of interest. Some Aashalh overlap in their spheres of interest, dominions and influence. This is most prevalent in the Aashalh who deal with elements, primal forces and creatures in nature.

Still others are actively working to lead or drive their creations in a certain direction. Others watch and test their stewardship, blessing and elevating those who pass the tests and trials sent their way. Lesser Aashalh nearly always take the shape of their creations when on Miljah. For example, a lesser Aashalh who created and oversees stags would appear as a large perfect stag. Such Aashahl still retain the ability to change into their proper form but are frequently loath to do so. The true name of an Aashahl will compel this change however.

An exception to this are the Aashalh who created true sentient life. In these instances, the children of these Aashalh take their features and appearance from the Aashalh who created them. Many of the first Aashalh took lovers from among the kindreds of Miljah at the cost of their place among the divine. Without the blessing of Anthos, these forbidden liaisons created many new kindreds of people. These Aashahl sired Pali'andeo always share major traits with their Aashahl parents.

Anthos took pity on the Aashahl who took mortal lovers and raised kindreds unto themselves. He offered them two choices; renounce most of their divine essence and live with their creations or forsake the mortal planes of Miljah and retain all their powers. Arch'Juln and others thought this was far too merciful and secretly began to undermine and subvert the will of Anthos upon Miljah. Arch'Juln and his allies were eventually discovered and expelled from the realms of the Aashahl. Unfortunately, events were already in motion that led to centuries of bloodshed among the Pali'andeo kindreds of Miljah.

In this aftermath, Anthos created binding rules that governed the Aashahl's interactions with their creations and the spheres of dominion. The Aashahl gain or lose power from the strength or lack of strength of their creations. The Aashahl's essence is bound to their dominions and the stronger the created the stronger the creator. The opposite is also true. Some of the lesser Aashalh depend entirely on the worship of their creations and acolytes as they used all their own power to create their progeny. Essentially, they divided their own essence to give life to their children. Without the devotion, faith, and worship from their children they would dwindle, but so would their children. The Dactyl are an example of this, as are many of the elemental creatures and beings.

For example, a group of Elm Spriggan could have their Aashalh living with them as their leader and another group of Hemlock Spriggan could have their Aashalh living with them as their leader. These groups would essentially share a life force and connection. This connection is sometimes so strong that the separate beings are literally connected on a mental level, and able to share thoughts, feelings and so forth. This is especially true for creatures in the primal sphere and the spheres of nature, the forests, jungles and so forth, what we would call plant based sentient life.

Prominent Aashahl among the High Sun Realms

Arch'Juln: A greater Aashahl. One of the first born after the breath of Miljah. Actively undermined Anthos' plans by seducing and corrupting Xydrii and her children. Worked to keep the children of the greater Aashahl at war with each other.

Akarii: A fallen Aashahl and primal mistress of creation and reformation of elements. - Triplet sister of Xydrii and Shayar Mistress of creation and endurance. Loves her people and seeing their works multiply. Stubborn but slow to anger or any reactions. Patience and deliberate actions make her course.

Alpa: A greater Aashahl. The Seeker, Wanderer's shield. Of the first born after the first breath of Miljah. Protecter of the wanderer, seeker of the lost. Often offers people opportunities to help her avatars in need. Is keen to repay kindness on the less fortunate. Keen to aid the lost traveler and the road weary. The remote and isolated tribes of men venerate her most often. Most cities have small monastic orders dedicated to the poor and road weary in her name.

Anthos: Known as The Patient Father in the High Sun Realms and the Mistress Eternal in the south. In reality Anthos is two beings intertwined into a perfect harmony of will and thought. They created their children, The Aashahl in several generations, each successive generation being an order of magnitude lesser than the one prior forming a hierarchy. Each generation is counted as siblings to each other and in the eyes of Anthos. Some believe that Miljah is the female portion of Anthos and that she gave her form and essence to give life to the planet that now bears her name.

Arontarh: Lord of war master of battle - Believes that only the strongest deserve to live and that life is for testing prowess. Loves a good laugh and a good fight. An Aashahl of the 3rd order of power. He is particularly venerated by the Taivadeans.

Aseairpeth: Swift Sister, Lady on high - Mistress of birds of prey, the air, and the hunt. Lover of the chase, a thrill seeker and an excitable being with a hot temper. An Aashahl of the second order of power, she serves as a foster mother to the Jendayi. She is rumored to indulge in mortal trystes when the mood takes her.

Bok: Queen of the Dark waters Lady Blue sea - She is an Aashahl of the third order of power. Worshiped extensively by the Taivadeans. She is believed to aid those upon the Oceans.

Brek: Father of fate, Split of the Coin, Lord of the Winds - He is an endless prankster who enjoys the twists and turns of life and the unexpected. Also, the hand of fate and karma. An Aashahl of the second order.

Dannitar: Mistress Evernew, Mistress of Renewal, Mistress of Mercy, Merciful Sister, Sister of Seasons - Known by many names and among the most venerated of the Aashahl. Master of the seasons, nature, renewal, rebirth, and healing. An ally of all who love the earth and serve the balance of nature. Kindhearted and quick to sorrow for the pain she sees in the mortal realms. With Anthos' blessing she created her children the Yiillyar to ease the suffering she saw. An Aashahl of the second order of power.

Drashtaa: Master of Murder and defilement. An ally to Ach'Juln. Petty selfish and blood thirsty to a fault. He delights in exploiting the weak, defiling the pure and murdering to gain power. Most of his followers can be marked by their blood sacrifice rites and the violations of innocents and the weak. Aashahl of the fourth order of power he is venerated by the Srellites and Ikthii among others.

Felairtarh: Mistress of Slaughter, Death's Daughter, Scythe of the Fates - Neither good nor evil, she revels in the struggle of battle for its own sake. Prowess and might in the slaughter of foes draws her attentions. Many cults worship her in the hopes they will be empowered by her and spared from death. Dark covens of arcane sorcerers often sacrifice sentient beings in her name hopping for a boon. She is an Aashalh of the third order of power.

Fiivan: Son of the fast waters. Master of rivers and lakes - A literal son of Frothvar, Fiivan is master of the swift running mountain rivers and streams. It is said he can be seen at times walking the shores of alpine lakes, skipping stones upon the mirrored surface. He is good-natured, though a known trickster, often taking a little fun at unsuspecting mortal kin's expense. He is an Aashahl of the fifth order of power.

Frothvar: Father of the High Forests, Gryphon Lord, Icy Father, Lord of the Alpine Forests and mountain tops - He cares little for most mortals, only concerning himself with those who live in his Alpine realms. Known to directly intervene when interlopers disrupt the way of things under his sight. Though a bit arrogant and condescending, he is not cruel or unjust but more a reflection of the harsh nature of the Alpine forests and high mountains. He is an Aashahl of the second order of power.

Heeth: Master of Works, Hammer and Thong - Heeth delights in shaping elemental things into works and tools. Many wondrous natural caverns, statues of other Aashahl and architectural marvels are attributed to Heeth. He is venerated by craftsmen and those who live by the works of their hands. He is an Aashahl of the fifth order and patron of the Ovanec.

Jillii: Everhope, Kindeye, Lady Kindeye, Mistress Everkind - Kind, gentle and tenderhearted she is the mistress of the small, vulnerable and keeper of hope. The daughter of Dannitar; like her mother she seeks to aid all she can, especially the outcast, forsaken and hopeless. She is particularly venerated by mortal kindreds of men. She has several widespread houses of healing and refuges in her name. Most orphanages are operated in her name. She is an Aashahl of the third order of power.

Leshay'ar: Sister of Strife, Mistress of Strife, Suffering Sister, Wailing Loss, Hard Master - Dour and stern yet quick to aid those who seek her. She sees the pain in life as the only way to progress. Many believe that the painful struggles of life are her gifts to help purify and strengthen the soul. Others believe she stands to aid those caught by the bitterness of a hard mortal life. Venerated by the Adohr and some pods of ilysh. She is an Aashahl of the third order of power.

Nique'shay: Mistress of Night, dance, song, and passions - Truly mercurial in character, she is wild and free. Fast to love and fast to forget. She is the embodiment of lust, jubilation, and ecstasy personifying the climatic release of complete carnal satisfaction even unto death and complete oblivion. She often takes mortal lovers, never to be heard from again. Enjoys temping mortals with her beauty. She frequents dark and secretive corners of civilization and the deep darkness of ancient forests and glens. Nique'shay is known to dance for nights on end, often cursing those who have wronged her to dance with her until they perish from the exertions. She is liberal with gifts to mortals, but there is always a price to be paid. A debt to be called for at her leisure. She is the daughter of Paldrii and Arch'Juln by way of his deception and assault upon Paldrii. She is the mother of the true Nique'tarri. She tries to aid those who find themselves cast into dark and frightening paths. She is known to answer the desperate and fragile when the strong pray upon them. Many venerate her in myriad manners asking for her to watch over them in their shadowed paths. She is an Aashahl of the fourth order of power.

Paldrii: Mistress of the Lost, Merciful Shepherd, Guardian of the Dead. Keeper of Souls - She guides the dead to the afterlife they merit. Calm and fair, she is the judge of souls and can connect to any being and feel their true nature letting the reality of their life serve as witness to the quality of their soul. Mother of Nique'shay and Dar'Nique'tar, she was consort to Arch'Juln before his fall was openly known and he took her unwillingly to sire the twins. Men venerate Paldrii hoping for mercy in death and nearly all placate her for aid in the face of danger and lethal threat. Numerous orders claim her as their patron, including a few military orders and monastic cults. She is an Aashalh of the third order of power.

Shayar: Mother of the Allitorii, Matron of War, The Relentless Spear - Warlike and savage to a degree, she is also very calculated at times and clings to self-imposed rules to control her powerful emotions. Sometimes lover of Arontarh and the elder triplet sister to Xydrii and Akarii. Her children, the Allitorii, take their name from Allitor, Shayar's original mortal lover. She is an Aashahl of the third order of power.

Sheibrok: Relentless Defender, Dauntless Shield, Just Hammer, Swift Justice, Master of Justice, Arbiter of Retribution - An absolute rule keeper and avenger of the wronged. Strives to keep the scales balanced. His ethos and mantras are venerated by many who serve as shire reeves, agents of the law and so forth. He is an Aashahl of the third order of power.

Syrnii: Mother of the Tundraihn, Mistress of Forests - Somewhat aloof and detached from many of the cares of her siblings. She places nearly all her attention on her many daughters including the female Tundraihn. She is also venerated by the Yiillyar who are powerfully connected to her. An Aashahl of the third order of power.

Utarb: Deep Father, Gem Caster - Slow and deliberate, fast to forgive quick to trust. Utarb avoids others as he has learned the hard way that his trusting nature can be exploited. Father of the Dactyl. Aashalh of the third order of power.

Varii: Lady Lost Heart, Haven's Maiden, Mistress Ever-yurn, Lady of Love, Passion's Touch - Deep thinking Varii is slow to anger, but her moods dominate her awareness to the point of complete exclusion to anything else. She loves the thrill of romance and the ecstasy of love and passions between mortals and Aashahl alike. She often seeks to play match maker and finds joy in star crossed lovers finding a way to unite. She is the mother of the Shedim in their myriad forms. She is difficult to predict and incomprehensibly powerful. Only her focus in the small interactions of love keep her from dominating the higher orders of power in Miljah. Many see her existence as theoretical. An Aashahl of the second order or power.

Xydrii: Dark Matron, Shadow's Wroth, Mistress of Smoke and Flame - Mistress of primal forces, destruction and arcane powers of war. A being of powerful passions tempered by years of heartbreaking suffering. Mother to the Xydar. She is the betrayed lover of Arch'Juln. Discarded by him after he took what he needed from her powers. Few in the north know of her in real detail. Of the few who do have knowledge, they do not willingly speak of her or her children. Xydrii is an Aashahl of the third order of power.

Central High Sun Realms

Arden Emil was shaped in the desert winds of Southern Utah, where red stone cliffs rise like the towers of sleeping giants and the Henry Mountains brood on the endless horizon. In such a land, stories do not feel created so much as remembered. His life has carried him far from those quiet canyons—through old world bazaars where lantern light sways over spice-laden stalls, across dune seas where caravans drift like dark ships, past ancient fortresses older than scripture, and along mist-wreathed highlands where stone circles watch the passersby. He has shared fires with nomads, spoken in rooms where many flags hang, and walked roads where history lingers like a ghost at one's shoulder.

A craftsman at heart, Arden has worn the weight of real armor, known the balance of honest steel, and learned the old ways with his own hands. His writing draws from these lived truths: the sting of sand on the wind, the rhythm of marching feet, the cold understanding of danger, and the fierce beauty of wilderness. These experiences lend his worlds a rare authenticity. His battles feel weathered by sun and blood, his characters shaped by mountains and memory, and his realms alive with the gravity of a place that might truly exist—somewhere just beyond the edge of the map.

At the center of this creative synergy is Arden's dauntless faith in Jesus Christ, the Son of God, and Redeemer of Mankind. May all truth and beauty forever point the hearts of men heavenward to the throne of the Most High.

GLORIA IN EXCELSIS DEO

Luke: 2:14